# Sword and Veil

Book One of the Everstone Series

A J Chase

CnC Publishing

# Contents

Part Three: The Escape

# Prologue

A s consciousness threatened to slip from her grasp, the stifling confines of the dungeon warping her sense of reality, Evalynn drew each breath with quiet defiance. Refusing to give in to the growing despair, every gasp demanded what little strength she had left. Her chains bit into her wrists as she hung with arms raised, shoulders aching while fresh blood trailed from the raw wounds.

Another blow to the stomach. Eva gagged, iron coating her tongue.

"Your boldness must know no bounds for you to think you could invade the Citadel and leave unscathed." Her torturer's voice was deep, matching his hardened, middle-aged appearance—made all the more menacing by his black leather armor and the network of scars etched across his face.

"Save the speech," Eva said between gasps. "I just walked right in. Turns out the great spire has lax security."

Eva's vision blurred as another punch found its mark, her head recoiling at the force. The chains rattled, biting her wrists as a new layer of crimson dripped to the stony floor.

*Breathe*

Stubborn strength rose from within, and she willed herself to endure—refused to betray her secrets. She focused her mind beyond her cell, outside the cold stone walls, away from the prison's suffocating darkness.

A hand grabbed her jaw, wrenching her head upwards, her torturer now inches from her face.

"Tell me why you're here," the man drawled, a promise of pain in his tone.

Eva breathed in and spit in his face.

Her torturer closed his eyes, wiping the blood and saliva away with his free hand. He shifted his grip on her left arm, driving his elbow down onto it and unleashing a sickening crack. Pain tore through her chest, her vision filling with stars at the fresh fracture.

A gut-wrenching cry drowned out her scream.

"Help!" a male voice shouted.

She squeezed her eyes shut again, clenching her jaw as tears formed at the sound of his voice.

"He's going to die because of you," her torturer said, his breath hot in her ear. "It's your fault."

"Evalynn! Help me!"

Mar swallowed her disgust, watching the heir of Sylvara sleep. The thought of depending on a lesser being turned her stomach, but Mar had little choice. Gevir not only tied her hands, he had dug his own grave and asked her to bury him in it.

She hovered unseen, her ethereal form flickering, half visible, near the white drapes of his medical bed. His chamber was still, the ward quiet. Blue light of the mage stones glinted off the sweat along his brow.

He stirred with a grimace, then stilled.

The memory was lost to her—the sensation of rest. After so long, she couldn't even fathom what it felt like anymore. Watching mortals sleep had become a fascination, studying them in the cradle of their dreams.

But this one—this one made her pause.

Not because of what he was, but because of what he offered.

His presence at the Citadel was no accident. Threads had been pulled. Names whispered. Gevir would call it fate—the fool.

She did not believe in fate.

Destiny was for the broken. The weak.

Mar believed in power. In will. In forging the future with blood and fire. And if that future now depended on a boy, battling the nightmares in his own mind, unaware of the war around him, then so be it.

Even now, the armies of Adiel bled themselves dry across distant valleys for reasons they claimed were noble, seemingly unaware of their own mortality. The Farron Gap alone devoured dozens of warriors each day, yet their two nations continued the onslaught, leaving so few left to fight.

Mar reached out, her essence curling toward him like smoke, pressing against the air above his sleeping form. Over his chest, she felt it—a flicker of something buried deep.

It resisted her touch—recoiled with slumbering power.

*Interesting*

"You don't even know what you are," she murmured, her voice no more than a thought on the wind.

She lingered for a moment longer, before drawing back into the Veil, her form dissipating like fog before the sun.

Let Gevir dither in his caution, pretend he still held the leash. The time was nearing. And when this boy—Elijah Danon—finally awoke, he would be the key to destruction.

One step closer to opening the door.

# Part One: The Beginning

CnC Publishing

# Chapter One

Leaving home for war was easier than living with the ghosts of what his family used to be, or so Eli thought, as he closed the door to his younger sister's room, wondering if he would ever see her again.

He descended the wooden steps in the early morning, treading softly to avoid waking the tenants upstairs. Turning the family home into an inn was a costly decision, one brought about by desperation. With just the three of them, himself, his father, and his younger sister, Harper, their entire existence revolved around running the business. He reached the bottom of the steps, expecting to see his father, but the main room was empty and quiet.

The ground floor of the inn held several quaint rounded tables, as well as a bar to the right of the stairs, where Eli's father spent most of his time. Eli walked over to a stool and sat, placing his leather satchel on the counter. The windows were open to the cool morning air, helping him wake up with the scent of wet fields.

He rubbed his eyes, strained from the late night. The inn had grown busier as the war raged on, with more people vacating their homes, either to escape the carnage or because they no longer had a home to return to.

Footsteps sounded from the cellar stairs to his right. His father appeared in the doorway in the corner, carrying a small crate filled with new bottles of firewater. His father had a kind face and soft eyes. His thick mustache covered his upper lip, accompanied by a full layer of stubble, all turning gray. One of the hardest things Eli ever experienced was watching his father, a pillar of strength and wisdom, steadily fade with time.

His father didn't speak as he shuffled over to the bar, set the crate on the counter, and began restocking the empty spaces. Staring at the dark bottles of alcohol, Eli opened his mouth to say something, anything, to bridge the growing gap between them, but couldn't find the right words. The tension had reached the breaking point a month earlier, ending in a shouting match about why he should stay, work at the inn, and remain far away from the horrors of war. He regretted the cruel things he accused his father of, but in the end neither of them conceded. He respected his father and knew he was proud of Eli's bravery and desire to serve their people.

But his father didn't understand Eli was suffocating in his own home—ever since Mom died. Twelve years was a long time for resentment to fester, for animosity to grow like a cancer. Today was the first day of his freedom, the first step to becoming a Guardian, to achieving a long-felt dream. And the closer this day drew, the more he felt relief in his soul. He would come back, he promised Harper and his father both. He was doing this for them, as much as for himself.

"Dad—"

Eli woke with a start, sitting up quickly, glancing about the room. He was in a bed, the white sheets damp from his sweat. A white curtain surrounded him, suspended from the ceiling. A small stone on the wall glowed blue with magic, dimly lighting the narrow space.

It was a medical ward.

A young woman swung open the curtain. Her brown hair and dark yellow eyes appeared welcoming with a smile on her face. She wore a gray tunic with a red scarf, which Eli recognized as a healer's uniform.

"You're awake. Excellent. I'm Nazzat. How are you feeling?" she asked as she walked to the edge of the bed, reading a piece of parchment which lay on the bedside table.

Eli didn't respond, uneasy, not knowing how he ended up in a medical ward. He strained to remember, but the answer eluded him. He jumped as her hand touched his bare shoulder.

"Sir Danon? Do you know where you are?"

"A medical ward," he rasped.

"That's right. You're inside the Citadel, in Eldan City. You received your first Thought Wave Analysis yesterday."

He stared blankly, her smile pleasant and comforting.

"I don't . . ."

"It's all right. Slight memory loss is very normal. The analysis isn't perfect, though the magic is improving, and the Council believes the side effects are worth it."

"Right. Why did I get it again?" he asked, failing to veil his confusion.

"It's standard procedure for all recruits of the Citadel Guardian program to undergo Thought Wave Analysis. It's the first step in your training, to help your inner magic." She spoke nonchalantly, clearly satisfied he was in no medical danger.

She glanced at the piece of parchment once more before looking back at him, staring for a moment at his black hair and orange eyes.

"The side effects should wear off with time." She encouraged. "For now, here is a new uniform for you to put on." She placed a folded brown tunic and leathers onto the bed.

"You are to report to the recruitment desk and await the Leadership in the Sparring Hall as soon as possible. It's out this door, down the hall to the right. You can't miss it." She smiled and turned to leave before he could ask any clarifying questions.

*The Citadel. My training*

Excitement washed over him, tempered with trepidation.

*I made it in. I'm going to be a Guardian*

Eli looked around for a moment but could see nothing beyond the curtain, though faint snoring sounded from somewhere in the ward. Acutely aware he was wearing nothing but his undergarment, he dressed, surprised the uniform fit perfectly.

The brown tunic was comfortable and ended just below the waist. The same-colored pants fit well and didn't drag on the floor with excess material. The leathers provided modest protection over the shoulders, chest, and thighs, as well as some leather bracers.

As he dressed, Eli caught sight of a black tattoo on his left wrist. It was crooked and poorly executed, but the distinct shape of a star was evident, identical to the one Harper carried on her right ankle. A gentle smile formed as the memory flashed in his mind—the laughter they shared months before as they stayed up all night deciding what marking to get before he left, something that reminded them of home and family. He still had to thank his friend Kael for loaning him the money.

After donning his armor, he noticed a small piece of glass hanging on the wall behind the bed and stared into its reflection.

His face was masculine with a sharp jawline. His ears were pointed, the tips following his shaggy hairline. Muscles bulged underneath his clothing, reflecting an active lifestyle or lucky bloodline. He looked well fed and well rested. He looked like a warrior.

There were no greater threats on the battlefield than Guardians, and he was going to become one. Bring change for his people—and for Harper. He had never heard of a Thought Wave Analysis and was anxious for the amnesia to fade. But whatever it was, he would do anything asked of him to achieve this goal.

Attempting to shake off the unease, he strolled out of his curtained space to the entrance of the medical ward. A smattering of other patients occupied the beds which lined the walls, and he wondered how many were also Guardian recruits.

A gasp escaped his mouth as he stepped into the massive walkway, which circled the base of the Citadel, as tall as it was wide. Long intricate tapestries adorned the inner walls, reaching toward the floor from the ceiling a hundred feet above, between the etchings in the stone. A thick crowd of people shared the walkway, accompanied by the gentle roar of conversation. Many of them wore military leathers like Eli's, yet others bore gray tunics with red scarfs or white robes, even colors of foreign countries.

"The Primarchs built it hundreds of years ago. No one remembers how they did it," Nazzat said, standing next to Eli as he stared slack-jawed. He glanced at her. "Don't worry, you're not the first one to stare when they get to see the Citadel for the first time."

*The great spire. The pride of the Zentari empire*

"I'm sorry," he responded with a slight smile. "I'm still a bit groggy."

"Of course. It's completely normal. The Primarchs were the first Zentari to colonize the area and build what would later become the great city of Eldan. No one is quite sure of the original purpose of the Citadel, but it has always been a haven for our people. And now, it's a training ground for our greatest warriors. Congratulations on being chosen."

"Yeah," he responded uneasily.

Despite the nagging amnesia, there was one thing Eli knew with certainty: it was a distinguished honor to be selected for Guardian training. The continued influx of recruits was the reason the walls of Eldan City remained against the ongoing war with the Aniyans.

And he made it. One step closer to his dream.

"The recruitment center is down that way," Nazzat said, pointing toward his left. "Just keep walking until you see the Operatives standing in the walkway. He'll show you where to go, but you should get going." She offered one last smile before turning back into the medical ward. Eli obeyed, entering the sea of Zentari officials.

The walkway was busy, but not overcrowded. No one paid him any mind, everyone appearing determined and resolute, a thousand tasks needing completion. It shouldn't surprise him, knowing the Citadel was a place of war, yet, despite the sense of importance the space commanded, a heaviness lingered.

On one hand, Eli was immensely proud of his people's accomplishments, demonstrating great ingenuity with the creation and management of such a structure. He'd spoken with numerous Zentari warriors at their inn, who kept him updated on his people's war efforts—how the Zentari held their own against the Aniyans, despite being fiercely outnumbered. He envied the warriors' opportunities to bring change and take up arms for their nation.

Yet, as he stood in the great spire—filled with excitement—there was a sorrow present, knowing the only reason the program existed was because of generations of violence. This should have been a building of celebration and art, displaying his people's culture, but it was nothing more than a testament to how far their people would go to protect—and kill.

It didn't take long before Eli spotted a tall man, standing with a stiff posture and a stern gaze. He wore similar armor to Eli's, though it was brown and black. The Operative caught his approach and nodded.

"Medical ward?" he asked pointedly. Eli nodded. "This way." He turned and walked toward a nearby door, which bore words etched into the stone.

*Ulam Krav*

Eli was led down a narrow hallway and into an enormous rectangular room. The ceiling was as tall as the walkway, with windows aligned along one wall, permitting natural light into the space. The air buzzed with excitement, young men and women, all wearing the same uniform, which Eli presumed were all Citadel recruits. Glancing around, he guessed at least a hundred were present.

Murmurs and whispers hissed, each of them shifting nervously.

*Obviously I'm not the only clueless one here*

Eli thanked the guard for his help and moved aimlessly into the crowd, searching for anything to anchor himself—a familiar face, a familiar sight, something that his hazy brain could recognize. Yet he spotted nothing. He wondered if he would even recognize something known if he saw it.

At either end of the room were large iron doors covered with odd markings, matching those etched into a stone circle in the center of the floor.

Eli meandered to it, watching the recruits keep a healthy distance from its edges, unsure of its significance—if any. He squatted down and touched the inscriptions. Something about the symbols struck a chord—the answer lingering under the surface, just out of reach.

*Bleeding rot, this memory fog is infuriating*

Eli was shocked from his thoughts as a loud crash sounded toward the far end of the room. Silence fell and Eli stood, seeing one of the metal doors close. The recruits froze, listening to the steady beat of a single pair of boots hitting the stone floor.

A woman strode with confidence to the center of the room, her white cape trailing behind as the sea of recruits parted. Her gray hair was tightly held in a bun, aided partially by her eye patch. Scars adorned her face and arms, with many more surely hidden underneath her thick white armor, which boasted plates of metal that clanked with her movements.

Her black eye explored the crowd with piercing confidence. The room remained silent as she examined the recruits, turning to look at each of them individually.

"Recruits!" she shouted with unyielding authority. "I am Commander Talia Voss. Welcome to the Citadel."

Murmurs rumbled at the sound of her name. Commander Voss was a legend. Little was known about her, other than her unmatched prowess in battle and that the Zentari military became deathly efficient once she gained control.

"You have all entered our great spire hoping to become revered Guardians. It is an honor to serve our people as a warrior, and even more so, as a wielder of magic. Your country thanks you for volunteering to serve, but this is only the beginning of what will no doubt be the hardest three months of your life. Your training starts today."

She paused, allowing her words to hang in the air.

"Let me be clear, many of you will not survive this training. We cannot hold the front with weak-minded warriors, our people cannot lean on the strength of brittle comrades. Throughout this program, you will be tested to your absolute limit and even further still. You will either graduate as a Guardian, having brought forth your inner magic, or you will not leave at all. Are there any questions?"

No one dared speak—the room held its breath as the Commander waited, her presence suffocating.

"Good!" she shouted. "There is no room to question the will of the Citadel or the Zentari Council. If at any point you act on your own, question your orders, or openly defy your leaders, it is considered treason and punishable by immediate execution. You would do well to remember that."

Another pause. "Captain Renard will explain what is next to come."

On cue, a man of average height with graying brown hair entered the room and marched up to the Commander. Moving with great authority, his gray armor followed each contour of his muscular form. Yet, when Eli's eyes met Captain Renard's, he did not see the same darkness he saw in Voss.

Renard gave the Commander a curt nod, clicking his boots together before surveying the hundred wide-eyed recruits.

"Ladies and gentlemen, or should I say, boys and girls. Because that's what you are: children. You know nothing. You are infants on a battlefield—nothing but a burden." Renard spoke with eloquence and conviction. And as much as it humiliated Eli, the man was right.

He had never seen battle, nor taken a life. Death had been a looming companion since childhood, but he had never been the messenger. Granted, he could handle a drunken brawl, but nothing akin to a real battle.

"With that in mind, I'm sure all of you share the same dream of becoming a Guardian, to have your name written on the scrolls as a wielder of magic. This program is the only way that can happen.

"Yet I need not remind you that dreaming for something isn't enough. The gift of The Ethereal is common in our people, but having the strength to draw it out—command it—is a rare thing indeed. To accomplish that task, be prepared to surrender everything you are, everything you have, because it *will* be demanded of you. If you wanted an easier road, you should've volunteered to become a healer."

Renard waited a moment, before continuing.

"Right now, many of you may be feeling disoriented after the Thought Wave Analysis. That's normal. You should feel the effects lessen over the next few days. There will be only two WAVEs, the first of which you've just experienced. The second is performed at the midpoint of the program. The Thought Wave Analysis helps bring forth any inner magic you carry. More will be explained as you progress."

*Good to know the amnesia is temporary. At this rate, I wouldn't remember the training if I tried*

"Think that means they know our secrets?"

Eli glanced up at the grinning recruit to his left. He stood at least six inches above Eli, with hazel eyes and hair. His smile spread wide, a conspiratorial glint in his eye.

Eli stared at the stranger, silently reflecting on his comment. Who knew how far the scan went, or what secrets were no longer safe.

"I don't know," Eli muttered.

"As the Commander explained, this program has a singular purpose: to train Guardians. In truth, there are only three ways out of this program. First, you graduate and are honored by your peers and revered by all Zentari people as a hero. Second, based on your attitude or actions, you are dishonorably discharged and expelled from the Citadel permanently, cursed to live the remainder of your cowardly life in shame having fallen short when called upon. Or lastly, you die.

You should be warned, option two is rarely ever seen. If you have a problem with that, I don't want to hear it."

Eli couldn't recall hearing such gruesome details about the program, let alone reports of death. He searched his memory, but his head was clouded—a thick fog obscuring his thoughts. He could remember wanting to join the military, but very little else. All he knew was the infamy of the Guardians—titans on the battlefield. Thousands of Aniyans had been slain at their hands, their very presence casting fear into their enemies. If anyone wielded the power to end the war, to bring this conflict to a close, it was the warriors of the ethereal.

He would give anything—gave everything—to come here and become the most powerful Guardian in Adiel. But the thought of dying here, and leaving Harper alone—

*Maybe it's just for show. A way to scare us in the beginning*

Eli turned to the smiling recruit on his left.

"Hey, what's your name?"

The man leaned toward him and whispered, "Arlo Miller. Yours?"

"Elijah Danon. Do you remember hearing about deaths in the program?"

"No. But then again I've been fuzzy all morning," Arlo said, keeping his attention on the Captain.

"Same. I don't even remember how I ended up in the medical ward."

"You were in the medical ward?" Arlo snickered.

"Yeah. You weren't?"

"Nah man, I woke up in a bunkroom with a bunch of other recruits. I don't remember climbing into bed, but I remember going in to get the analysis done. You must have had a bad reaction."

"Doesn't it unnerve you to lose some of your memory?"

"Ha, some days I don't remember breakfast," Arlo replied, his smirk returning. "Listen, jokes aside, I wouldn't worry about it. And honestly, I don't remember hearing anything about this being a death camp. Renard's probably just trying to rattle us."

Arlo gave him a gentle slap on the back. Eli shifted his weight, not sharing his new friend's confidence.

Renard continued. "If you have questions, you direct them to me. Commander Voss has graced us with her presence today, as she may do at times of her choosing. You do not speak directly to her. You are grunts. Nobodies. The bottom of the proverbial food chain. Is this in any way unclear?"

"No, Captain Renard sir!"

The combined voices reverberated in Eli's chest, but he didn't speak.

"Lastly, you are not in the military yet. You hold no ranking or authority. As I said, this program's purpose is singularly focused. After graduation, you will be trained in the routines and regulations of our military, from mission briefings to morning formation. Since these have no bearing on using magic, they are not part of this program, ensuring you have the highest chance of success."

After a pause, Voss spoke, nodding to Renard. "I take my leave Captain."

The Captain turned to face the Commander, clicking his boots together, arms at his sides. "Vor' Irath, Commander!"

"Captain," Voss replied. She scanned the room once more. "Vor' Irath, recruits!"

"Vor' Irath!" The room echoed, and this time Eli joined the chant, his heart beating faster as adrenaline filled his blood.

The words they shouted were familiar, yet foreign on his tongue. It was Primarch script, the language of the original Zentari people.

*Until Victory*

As the Commander left, Eli's resolve hardened. If Renard spoke the truth, then there was nothing that would stop Eli from graduating. He would never forgive himself if he left home—left Harper—only to die here. He would return home a warrior, a hero—a Guardian.

Renard turned his attention back to the recruits. Doors throughout the room opened, as more ranking officers entered.

"The room we are in is called the Sparring Hall. Much of your physical training will happen here. Right now, there are Operatives and Captains stationed around for your first training exercise. They are here to evaluate and assess you."

Eli watched the officers standing against the far walls, all of them wearing full leather armor. Each carried a distinct weapon: swords, long knives, pikes, war hammers, axes, and some he couldn't identify. Men and women alike shared a uniform appearance, with armor color indicating rank: black and brown for Operatives and gray for the higher rank of Captain.

While Eli admittedly felt unmoored in his new environment, he shared the expression that shone through each of their eyes—determination, resolve, and grit. A tide of will rose deep in his soul, a desire to serve his people—to aid and protect—to carry the mantle of battle in the hopes the next generation would be spared that burden.

At the swell of pride, a memory unlocked. His thoughts drifted to home, picturing the small farm where his family lived growing up, feeling the warm breeze of summer and the rough texture of the firewood as he worked alongside his father.

Yet the cherished memories were tainted by a longing for the simpler days before—

"All right! Listen up! Everyone find a partner!" Renard shouted. "For your first exercise, you will fight in pairs. Two against two. Hand-to-hand combat only. The round ends when both team members are incapacitated, dead, or tap out. This circle is the combat zone. You are to remain inside until the match is over. Are there any questions?"

The crowd of recruits gave no response.

"I said, *are there any questions*!" Renard shouted.

"No! Captain Renard, sir!"

"Good. You have exactly two minutes to find a partner. Names will be called at random to battle another duo."

Speaking, shouting, and the shuffle of boots on stone escalated to a roar of activity. Eli was already standing at the circle's perimeter, and before he could ask, Arlo slapped a hand on his shoulder.

"Shall we dance?" he said with that same smirk.

This time, Eli returned the smile.

# Chapter Two

Crouched in the shadowed underbrush, Eva's hooded form blended with the dark, her stark white hair veiled as moonlight cast over the grassy plains. The silver light illuminated the darkness enough to navigate, but not reveal her as she stalked her enemy. Inside the cover of the trees, the thick canopy overhead made it nearly impossible to navigate at night—for anyone else.

The terrain of Northeastern Adiel was etched into her memory, after being sent on countless scouting and assassination missions. It was why she was chosen for this particular task and why she had gained notoriety, at least among her kin. Joining the military at the minimum age of fourteen, while also demonstrating unmatched stealth and physical prowess, drew both positive and negative attention during her eight years in the Legion.

She never wanted it. It was only her inner defiance, and pride she supposed, that prevented her from pretending to be less skilled, falling into the comfortable haze of mediocrity. To spite her further, fate had granted her thick, snow-colored hair, despite most of her kin being born blonde. She had the blue eyes of her mother, but the white hair made her stand out—serving as a constant reminder to everyone around her that she was different.

Eva took a deep breath, shunning her wandering thoughts as she monitored the three Zentari scouts sitting around their fire in hushed conversation. They stopped to rest for the night, setting their meager supplies aside to share a meal on the edges of the Midbar Desert, a few miles west of the Yaqar outpost where Eva was stationed. Aniyan intelligence caught wind of the scouting party as they were crossing the desert, and Eva was sent to dispatch them as soon as possible.

Information was as precious as rubies, and a scouting party gathering intelligence was an unacceptable risk. Stolen secrets, weaknesses of Legion outposts, or leaked plans of attack—all of them resulted in dead Aniyans. When she was told to take a comrade along for the mission, Eva slipped out before one could be chosen, violating a direct order. She might pay for that one later, but for now she didn't care. It was faster and easier on her own.

Eva had shadowed the Zentari scouts for two days, delicately balancing the need to stay close enough to overhear against the risk of being detected. Despite her efforts, it eventually became clear—they either knew nothing useful or were careful to speak so quietly even Eva couldn't hear.

One female and two males, one of whom was twice Eva's size, boasting forearms as wide as her thighs. He would need to be the first target.

They each wore the standard brown and black leather armor of the Zentari Operative. To her relief, none of them were Guardians. She thanked the Heavens when she confirmed they were only scouts, knowing they weren't likely to be the Citadel's best fighters. The Zentari were selective about who they assigned to specific missions, and scouts were typically deemed unfit for open combat.

*It's time*

She absentmindedly touched each of the six daggers sewn into her black leather armor. She would need to deal with them tonight, before they returned South, back to Heika.

"Oi, Nyx," the larger scout said, addressing the female seated across the fire who was sharpening her long knives in silence. His bald head emphasized his thick beard. "What was the Captain wanting to talk to you about before we left?" He pulled his rucksack over and reached inside, sifting through the contents.

"Why do you care, Bjorn?" Nyx replied, disdain evident in her voice. It reminded Eva of why she liked to work alone. Nyx kept her emerald eyes on her blades as she spoke, a strand of black hair falling from her tight bun.

"I care because we're on the same mission. If you know something that involves the mission, then that involves me." Bjorn pulled a strip of dried meat from his sack and began tearing apart the flesh.

"Instead of feeding your stomach you should mind your tongue. The privileged information you're so curious about is above your rank."

*Finally*

Bjorn's eyes narrowed. "How about I beat your face in?"

Nyx's attention lifted from her blades—the threat of a challenge in her stare.

Bjorn smiled before speaking. "Maybe I'll just kill you and take your seat as mission leader? You already turned down a promotion, so I'll command the next assignment, and get all the information I want."

Nyx opened her mouth to respond, when the third scout spoke.

"Enough. Both of you. We're tired and have spent days behind enemy lines. Do not allow your exhaustion to stain your honor," he said, staring at the flames.

Both other scouts were quiet, giving no rebuttal.

"Apologies, Operative Nyx. I spoke out of turn," Bjorn begrudgingly said, bowing his head.

"Accepted." Nyx took a deep breath. "You are not as misinformed as you think, and our orders have not changed. What I was told dealt with finding something specific, but I was only given a vague description of an object. I heard it was a request directly from the Council."

Both other scouts stiffened in surprise.

"The Council?" the third scout asked. "Why make that request to a simple team of Operatives? On a scouting mission no less."

"I do not know, Attow. When I asked for clarification, I was strictly reminded of the punishment for questioning Leadership."

She glanced at Attow and Bjorn with raised eyebrows, suggesting they would do well to remember that fact themselves.

Bjorn said, "I do not question the will of the Council. Yet, I much dislike being kept in the dark."

The others seemed to agree, but did nothing more than nod. Attow stood and walked quietly away from the fire.

"Oi, if you're going to drop a load don't do it here." Attow stopped, glaring at Bjorn. "Go in the woods will ya'? The last thing I want to do is be kept up all night by the smell of your *Gut'pa*."

Eva didn't understand much of the Primarch script used by the Zentari, but that needed no translation.

Attow grumbled as he strolled away from the fire into the woods. Eva held her breath to silence her presence. She had remained downwind, knowing the senses of the Zentari were superior to Aniyans. As the scout entered the long grass, she positioned herself out of view and used the noise of his travel to stay close.

Nyx finished sharpening her blades, wiping them clean and placing them into the sheaths on either hip. She brushed a strand of her black hair behind her pointed ear, a stark contrast to her light skin tone. She looked up from the flames, scanning the tree line again, well aware they were on enemy land. But rotting Hells she was tired.

She could feel her senses dull as the days pressed on, worsened by the heaviness of her recent failure. Her shoulders slumped at Bjorn's mention of her promotion opportunity. He didn't understand the gravity of the comment.

"Bjorn," she murmured, glancing behind him to where Attow disappeared. "I found—"

Nyx stopped, staring at her comrade in shock. His eyes were wide as his mouth went slack. His body leaned forward slowly and fell into the firepit, a knife firmly embedded in the back of his neck.

Nyx leaped to her feet, long knives instantly in her hands.

"Attow! *Loch'Et!* We are under attack!" she shouted, ready to fight, facing the tree line. She avoided the light of the fire, willing her eyes to see past the heavy darkness.

"He's not coming," Eva said, stepping out from behind a broad tree, not twenty paces away.

"Cretin scum! What have you done?" Nyx shouted with fury, knuckles white as she grasped her blades.

"I have questions for you," Eva replied, keeping her voice calm. She may have given up the element of surprise, but she wasn't outnumbered any longer. Nyx eyed the bloody daggers in Eva's hands, ready to strike.

"As if I would betray my secrets," Nyx spat, holding her ground as Eva stepped cautiously out of the tree line. Nyx watched her movements with calculated interest, her green eyes glinting in the firelight.

Eva spoke with authority. "What is the object you were told to search for?" she asked, hoping to sound more diplomatic than she felt.

"What is it to you, Aniyan?" Nyx growled.

Eva lowered her hood, never turning away from her enemy. "My name is Evalynn."

Nyx scoffed. "Are we to become friends then? Sit around the fire and sing songs. You just killed two of my comrades in cold blood."

"I took action by the orders of my superiors. The same thing you would have done had the roles been reversed. Don't preach to me, Shell. I've seen what your people do to our prisoners."

Eva waited for her enemy to offer a rebuttal—none came.

"I propose a deal," Eva continued. "You give me the information I seek and you walk away tonight. No more bloodshed."

"And if I refuse?"

"Then you join your comrades after I force you to talk."

"If you think you can torture answers out of me then you do not know your adversary."

"Listen, Nyx." Eva spoke as softly as she could. Nyx's eyes narrowed, upset by the use of her given name. "We can both walk away."

"By giving you the information you want? Unlike you Aniyan, I would never betray my people."

"I am offering for you to live another day. A wise warrior knows when to retreat."

"*Chol'pach!* Save your self-righteous speak for someone who cares. You will never stop being my enemy!" Nyx raised her long knives. Eva prepared herself, that pang of sorrow deepening.

"I hope, for your sake, that's not true," Eva said.

Nyx lunged, attacking. Eva brought her knives up and deflected the blade, but the force behind the assault pushed her back.

Nyx was fast and strong, but Eva had not earned her reputation on a whim. She spun low, kicking Nyx's feet from under her. Nyx gasped as she landed on the ground with a thud, the air choked from her lungs. She sliced Eva's right shin before rolling away, narrowly avoiding Eva's blade as it found purchase in the dirt.

Nyx sprang to her feet in an instant. Eva, still crouched, hurled one dagger while yanking the other from the ground. Nyx deflected the first swiftly, but she missed the second—Eva's blade sunk deep into her left thigh.

Nyx cried out as her knee buckled. Eva was back on her feet, new daggers in each hand.

"Surrender," Eva said, breathing heavily. Nyx yanked the blade from her leg and tossed it aside.

"Never!" Nyx rushed in, aiming to tackle her. Eva sidestepped, slashing Nyx's back as she stumbled past. With a cry of agony, Nyx fell to the ground.

"Just tell me what I need to know," Eva demanded once more. She approached Nyx, who lay facedown in the dirt, panting.

"*Vor'Irath*," Nyx whispered with a heavy breath. She spun viciously in a final attack, but it was too late. The battle was over, even before Nyx's body dropped limply to the ground.

The stillness of the night resumed. Eva caught her breath in the cool air and closed her eyes. After the adrenaline wore off, the tunnel vision faded, the pounding heart settled, all that was left was silence—and death.

A foul stench wafted her direction, and she quickly found Bjorn's corpse smoldering against the embers of the fire. She averted her gaze, retrieving her blades and resheathing each in its proper place.

Eva never joined the Legion to fight, but her natural abilities made her the perfect warrior. Yet, the Legion had become a refuge for those seeking vengeance, breeding more hatred and disdain for their enemy, channeling their people's rage into something darker—a blind malice for the Zentari race. But when she lay eyes on the bodies of her enemy, something stirred in her heart, and she couldn't reconcile the inner tension that grew stronger each day.

Having grown up witnessing darkness and cruelty at the hands of her father, she now felt a desperate growing need to be a part of the solution, not another Swordsman blindly obeying orders. Eva wanted to trust her leaders, to believe their intentions were just, but the longer she fought the harder it became to ignore the unease twisting in her gut. Her trust had begun to shatter after witnessing too much suffering, too many decisions that felt less like strategy and more like betrayal.

Eva spent time methodically searching each scout, seeking a piece of parchment, a scroll, anything with information to bring back. While searching Nyx, she found an object tucked into a hidden pouch, sewn into her pants near the small of her back. It sent vibrations into her hand through the cloth as she unwrapped it, finding a small black stone. The opaque ebony rock shimmered against the moonlight, polished surfaces joined by sharp edges.

It was warm on her skin. The vibrations grew, sweeping up her arm as she held it—transfixed. It became hotter, burning her fingers. She tried to let go, but her hand was paralyzed.

The stone began to glow, turning from the inky black into a bright white. Hot, searing pain shot into her skull. She closed her eyes in a silent scream, the agony now flowing throughout her in cascading waves.

She writhed on the ground, the burning in her head giving way to a high-pitched shriek, which grew louder each moment. Everything in her pleaded for the torment to end as her senses were overwhelmed. Yet, with ringing in her ears, the burning sensation ceased, leaving a tingling in her limbs. It gave way to a sense of energy, a rush of power, something inside her ready to explode forth—

It stopped.

Eva opened her eyes, still lying in the grass. Her hand felt the memory of the burn, but there was no mark. In fact, her skin appeared perfect—untouched.

She sat up. The stone was gone, the ragged cloth gently tossed by the wind on the grass.

*What in the Nine Hells*

She stood, wiping her sweaty palms as she scanned the area, feeling the faintest reach of another panic attack. Rubbing her face, she took a deep breath, wishing Nyx had agreed to give her answers—especially now.

Anxious to leave and put this behind her, she quickly gathered the leftover food from the scout's packs, and as much medicine and weapons as she could carry.

Before she set out, she made sure to leave some food and water for when Nyx woke.

# Chapter Three

M aelyn Mercer and Laranna Nightingale! Into the battle circle with your partners!" Captain Renard announced.

Filtering out of the crowd, Maelyn, Laranna, and two others stepped up to the Captain.

"Each of you announce your names so we can record them for later review," Renard ordered. Both Maelyn and Laranna had chosen male partners. All of them stood rigid, ready and determined. If they were nervous, they didn't show it.

"Maelyn Mercer! Captain Renard, sir!" Maelyn reported. The shortest of the four, her skin was a few shades darker than the others. By how she carried herself, Eli assumed she had some military in the family. Maelyn's partner stood a head taller than her, with striking red hair and a lean build.

"Finn Adler, Captain Renard, sir!" Judging by how less confident Finn appeared, Eli wondered how he and Maelyn partnered.

"Just 'sir' is fine for now. Let's keep things moving." Renard grumbled, scribbling a mark on the parchment. He turned to the next pair expectantly.

"Laranna Nightingale, sir!" Laranna shouted, standing with a more relaxed posture, her auburn hair brushing her shoulders.

"Sol Richter, sir!" Sol's intimidating voice rumbled through the room in a guttural tone. A beast of a man, dwarfing every other recruit in the room. His hair was cut into a mohawk, which flashed a jagged scar running along the left side of his scalp. His black hair matched the thick beard around his rugged jaw.

"All right," Renard said. "You heard the rules. The fight starts and stops on our command."

As Renard marched to the edge of the circle, the surrounding recruits gave him a wide berth. Maelyn, Finn, Laranna, and Sol stood on opposite ends—the room now silent and dripping with anticipation. The recruits closest to the circle moved in for the best places to view the match.

"Begin!"

Sol charged, rushing in like a bull, throwing a punch for Finn's head. Finn, smaller and nimbler, dodged the blow and threw a jab in response, hitting Sol across the right side of his face. Despite the attack finding purchase, Sol was unfazed. He replied with a wide sweep of his arm, catching Finn on his right side, shoving him toward the inner part of the circle.

Maelyn used the battle between Sol and Finn as an opening and ran to Laranna. Losing her relaxed posture, Laranna met her half-way. Maelyn expertly dodged Laranna's right jab, responding with a punch to Laranna's ribs.

Eli was impressed, and already nervous about his own skill. He felt bad for Finn, whose swiftness meant little against Sol's hulking frame. Their bout ended abruptly when Sol delivered a merciless uppercut, knocking Finn out cold. Laranna and Maelyn were far better matched. Eli traced their movements, analyzing their techniques, which were clean and practiced. Both Maelyn and Laranna seemed to have previous combat practice. Eli wondered how many others in the room had been trained, and how far behind that set him. Maelyn was eventually bested, the match called by Captain Renard. She was near helpless to take on both Sol and Laranna together.

All three conscious recruits were dismissed into the crowd, while Finn was carried out by healers.

Eli furrowed his brow.

*Interesting*

He turned to Arlo, speaking in a whisper, "Hey."

"Yeah?" Arlo leaned toward him, but kept his eyes on Laranna.

"We need to work together. I think that's why we're fighting in pairs."

"Makes sense. You afraid to lose one on one?" he asked, flashing what Eli now recognized as a signature grin.

"Not a chance," Eli said, returning the smile despite his unease. There was something about Arlo's nonchalance which proved infectious. Add to that, Eli had never backed down from a challenge.

"Roth Wilder and Esme Vogel!" Renard bellowed.

Four more recruits entered the circle. "Roth Wilder, sir!" Roth was muscular, but stood below average height.

"Kian Keller, sir!" Kian was tall but lanky.

"Esme Vogel, sir!" Esme was more masculine than Kian, standing as tall as him and twice his weight.

"Shira Weiss, sir!"

*Shira*

Eli's vision faded at the edges, and the room seemed to go silent as he was transfixed by the fourth recruit.

Shira's ebony hair carried such depth it shimmered with hints of blue, starkly contrasted to her sharp indigo eyes, which shone like moons over a dark sea. The tips of her pointed ears peaked out of her hair as it cascaded past her shoulders in waves of silky black. She stood at Eli's height, carrying a lean and athletic frame, toned with years of discipline, but never losing her natural feminine curves.

Not only was she the most beautiful woman Eli had ever seen, but the intensity of her expression made him pause. She carried herself with confidence and determination, and Eli had to admit, her expression was intimidating.

He didn't hear anything after she spoke and paid no mind to the other recruits' fight—only her. She moved with grace and precision, each step, each attack calculated and intentional. It was evident she not only was trained, she had experience.

After the match ended, Shira strode out of the circle as one of the victors—and her gaze met his. Her cerulean eyes pierced his soul, filled with intensity—a sense of will and resolve. His breath caught, and he meant to look away, but was hypnotized. He caught the slightest narrowing of her eyes, but she made no other expression, as she filtered back into the crowd and disappeared.

Despite Eli's festering anxiety, the hours began to drag by. The majority of the fights were unremarkable, resulting in black eyes and bruises. A few suffered broken bones and were quickly rushed to the medical ward, while many others were knocked unconscious by far superior opponents.

To no surprise, none of the recruits tapped out, not even the one trapped in a choke hold. Eli sensed the tension in the room, the need to prove themselves as worthy of being brought into the program. No one wanted to be the first one to quit, not with the Operatives and Captains supervising.

"Elijah Danon and Orion Wilder!"

Eli tensed, adrenaline shooting in his veins.

Arlo nudged him playfully. "Show time," he whispered.

As they took their places in the ring, Eli scanned the crowd, while Arlo's gaze was fixed on Renard. Two male recruits soon emerged to join them.

"Orion Wilder, sir!"

Eli glanced at his opponents, before returning to attention.

"Rowan Thorne, sir!"

A bead of sweat drip down Eli's forehead onto his nose.

*Stay calm. Keep your head*

"Arlo Miller, sir!" Arlo shouted, his playful demeanor absent.

Finally, Renard looked at Eli expectantly.

"Elijah Danon, sir!"

Renard nodded, and the four of them took their positions. Eli wished there was time to go over a strategy with Arlo, but he was pretty sure being unprepared was the point of this exercise.

Eli thought his heart was about to burst as he turned and faced his opponents. This was it, the first step to greatness. He had no way of knowing how skilled his opponents were, but by the Nine Realms he wouldn't be the first to tap out.

"Begin!"

Rowan charged in first while Orion hung back, waiting for an opening. Rowan aimed a kick at Arlo's left side, but Arlo caught his leg, absorbing the blow. Seizing the moment, Eli threw a hard punch to Rowan's face, sending him crashing to the ground.

Eli winced as pain flared through his right hand, but before he could react, a fist slammed into his ribs. The air was knocked from his lungs, doubling him over, as Orion struck his stomach again.

Arlo grabbed Orion around the waist, lifting and slamming him down. Orion struggled but couldn't land a solid hit, blinded by Arlo's rapid punches to the face. Orion tried to push Arlo off but was overpowered by sheer size and strength.

Eli gasped as his breath returned and saw Rowan staggering upright, lunging toward Arlo. Eli tackled Rowan's legs, sending him down again. Rowan kicked wildly, and the sole of his boot struck Eli's nose. Eli's vision filled with stars as Rowan scrambled free.

Arlo stood, his fists bloodied, as Orion lay defeated, having tapped out from the onslaught. Before Rowan could fully rise, Arlo grabbed his armor and smashed his forehead into his. A sickening crack echoed, and Rowan collapsed, eyes glazed.

Eli, still on the ground, tasted blood and winced at the sharp pain in his face. Arlo extended a hand, and Eli took it, stunned by his partner's raw skill.

"Where did you learn to fight like that?" Eli asked, feeling his nose to ensure it wasn't broken, before wiping the blood from his face. His right hand throbbed. He'd never hit someone so hard.

"The underground pays well for decent fights," Arlo replied with a wink.

Eli raised his eyebrows. "You have a troubled past, or just like risking your life on a bet?"

Arlo shrugged. "It's entertaining, and a quick way to make money."

"It's also highly illegal," Eli whispered.

"Only if you're caught," Arlo teased, elbowing him.

Both men smiled, standing bloodied and exhausted—but victorious. They glanced at their downed opponents. Rowan was unconscious, a pair of healers coming to carry him off, while Orion writhed on the floor, his left eye swollen shut.

Renard mumbled an order to a nearby Operative who nodded curtly, walking toward Orion and lifted him onto his feet. He pulled a knife from his side and plunged it into Orion's chest. Gasps echoed.

Orion inhaled sharply before falling to the ground—dead.

# Chapter Four

The stars burned bright in the night sky as Eva reached the top of the dune, overlooking the valley where the Yaqar outpost lay hidden. While the journey back could have been made in less than a day on horseback, Eva hadn't been allowed the luxury. Tired, hungry, and sore, she shuffled down the gentle slope toward what had been her home for the past eighteen months.

Yaqar was nestled in a valley between the Midbar Desert and the Modi'in Plains. Its location was ideal for warning the Aniyan capital, Ashdod, of any incoming enemy invasions.

When Eva neared Yaqar's perimeter, she held up the hand signal to the nearest sentry, who returned the gesture as she passed through the Southern gate. Housing at most one hundred and fifty warriors, the outpost was modest compared to others, with sleeper tents on the outskirts and important supplies kept safe further inside. The center was reserved for the most vital resources and the Lieutenant's tent.

Eva navigated between the structures by memory, spending most of her mental effort in keeping her eyelids open. She took the shortest route to her bed, desperate to collapse into the arms of sleep.

Her military cot, cushioned only with hay, was insufferably uncomfortable. However, on nights like this, when her body screamed from exhaustion, there was no greater respite. Protocol demanded she report to the Outpost Lieutenant, Benton Drax, and debrief upon returning, but she didn't care. By all rights, he didn't know she'd returned, and there was nothing to report.

Well, almost nothing. The thought of explaining what happened with that stone made her stomach turn, the memory still sending a shiver down her spine.

As much as she wanted to shun the thoughts and forget what happened, she had a feeling it wasn't something she could simply disregard.

Before she could reach her restful oasis, a hand grabbed her arm and yanked her between two adjacent tents.

"Hey—"

She stopped short upon seeing his smiling face. Like a receding tide, her exhaustion eased as she embraced Lucas, his warmth surrounding her. His familiar scent of pine needles and wood fires carried her to a place of calm and safety—of home.

It'd been too long. All it took was a fleeting gesture for him to dissolve the stress she carried while he was away. He held her close, pulling her to him, his very presence bringing peace.

After a long moment, he loosened his hold and met her gaze. His gentle smile—his stupid, crooked, perfectly white smile—filled her vision and warmed her heart. She couldn't help ensuring he was all right, scanning his features—his sandy hair and eyes like a calm, still water.

"Sorry I'm late," he said.

"Late?" she whispered loudly, smacking him on the chest. He stumbled backwards with a grin. "You were supposed to be gone for a week, how did that turn into six?"

"We got rerouted before we even reached the mountains. A courier met us part way and delivered new orders to divert to the gulf."

"The gulf? Why?"

"I'm afraid that's above your rank, Swordsman," he said, feigning seriousness.

"Oh, shut up, *Chief*," she snarked, yanking the gray ribbon tied to the hilt of his sword that signified his rank. It was only one promotion above Swordsman, but he still outranked her.

"Seriously though, we were told the orders came directly from Chosen Lieutenant Cooper. When I asked why the sudden change, I got the standard 'those are your orders.'"

Eva didn't push the issue, having received more than a few lectures from Drax, and Lucas, about keeping her nose clean.

It wasn't just her curiosity, it was that it involved Lucas, having grown so protective of him since he was promoted. She understood it meant more responsibility and that he would now be leading squads on missions—be privy to information he couldn't share because he now outranked her.

It never mattered that she was denied promotions in the past—until now. All she could hope for was that he'd soon be promoted again from Chief to Lieutenant and be swimming in logistics the rest of the war. Sure it would be boring, but he would be safe and stay in the same place.

"How long are you here for?" she asked.

"Three days."

Relief washed over her, grateful to have more time. Lucas had been her best friend since childhood, and even after all these years, she felt hollow whenever they spent any time apart.

"Any news of Matthias?" she asked, knowing his brother's disappearance was still raw.

It had only been a month, but anything could have happened. And knowing your other ten siblings were safe did little to lessen the dread and grief.

"No. Nothing," Lucas said, his attention drifting a thousand miles away.

"I know he's alive," she comforted. "And I know we'll find him."

Missing persons weren't unheard of in war time, by any stretch, but their conflict with the Zentari had been present for generations. More than four hundred years. Eva couldn't help the feeling that something was shifting among the shadows of their war.

Lucas sighed, and she longed to ease the burden, in the same way he had for her so many times. They shared a lifetime of laughs and tears—griefs and dreams—yet there was nothing she could do in the moment.

"You look terrible," he said, snapping back to the present, looking her up and down.

"Gee, thanks," she said, knowing he wasn't ready to talk about it. Still, seeing him tonight rested an ache in her soul, and by the Nine, she could sleep for a week.

"Go debrief and get some rest. I'll see you in the morning. We've got three days together and I don't want you to ruin them by being cranky. I know you need your beauty sleep."

Eva sighed as her shoulders slumped. "I'm going to bed first. I'll talk to Drax tomorrow."

"Lieutenant Drax," he scolded. "Conduct like that is why you keep losing out on a promotion."

Eva rolled her eyes. "You know *exactly* why I've never been promoted."

"I'm saying that despite your father's influence, breaking the rules will eventually catch up to you and get you into serious trouble. Yes, maybe he's the reason you're still a Swordsman, but he is also the reason you get away with pulling crap like that."

"So what, they're afraid of him, but not beating me over the head? And Drax is the worst of—"

"Lieutenant Drax," Lucas interrupted, "is your superior officer. Look, I know you don't care about being promoted, but if you end up on trial for crimes against the Legion, there's nothing I can do to help you."

"I haven't committed any crimes."

Lucas's eyebrows raised. "No? Then what's this about you leaving without a comrade?"

Eva pursed her lips. "Drax knows I'm better on my own."

"And *Lieutenant* Drax keeps an extremely accurate account of your behavior. Trust me, I've seen it. He's just waiting for the right time to send you up the river, and you're making it too easy for him."

Eva huffed, but Lucas held his ground—glaring. She sighed, too exhausted to argue any longer.

Besides, he was right.

"Go talk to Drax, then get some rest," he said, rubbing her shoulder. "I'll be here in the morning."

*Fine*

Eva took a breath before she moved aside the leather flap that opened Drax's tent. Technically it was the *Outbuilding used by the leading Lieutenant for manage-*

*ment and oversight of all local Legion proceedings*, but really it was just an oversized hovel.

"Swordsman Evalynn Katz returning for debrief, Lieutenant," she announced, standing at attention.

"Rest, Swordsman. I know it's physically painful for you to follow formality," Drax said dryly.

Eva's posture relaxed. The Lieutenant waited, sitting at his wooden desk. Fatigue was evident in his eyes, and his face betrayed his age, with most of his long hair turning gray. Drax still possessed the same sternness and fortitude he claimed as a youth, contrary to most Aniyan military leaders, who became more lenient with time.

"What's the report, Swordsman Katz?" he asked, shuffling papers around.

Eva bit her tongue. No one called her by her last name—except Drax—who did it purposefully, knowing how much she hated it.

"I intercepted the Zentari scouts four days after departing Yaqar. Three scouts in total, two males and one female. Lightly armored, no horses or dire boars. No sign of reinforcements. I monitored them for two days before determining the best time for engagement. All three threats were neutralized. No correspondence could be found on their person or equipment."

She waited for his response as he absentmindedly stroked his beard.

"Excellent. So no pertinent information was gathered? No findings worthy of note?"

She paused, questioning whether to tell him what happened with the stone. But it was too late—he caught her hesitation.

"There was mention of an object," she said abruptly.

"An object?" he asked, eyes narrowing.

"Yes. The scout leader mentioned receiving specific orders to search for an object of interest for the Zentari Council, and that the orders came directly from the Council itself. They did not mention any further specifics."

"Straight from the Council?" he mused, his attention drifting across his tent. "If they gave the order directly, then these—what did they say they were?"

"I don't know," she answered. "It was only a mention of a small object, perhaps multiple."

Drax nodded in thought, his tongue running over his teeth as he mumbled. "But if the Council is interested, it means something serious. You may have stumbled upon something . . ."

The Lieutenant's voice trailed as his eyes twitched. He stiffened in his seat. Eva studied his expression carefully.

*He knows what they are*

"Very well, thank you Swordsman Katz. You are dismissed for recovery." He turned his attention back to his notes.

"If I may, Lieutenant Drax, what is our status? Have there been any changes at the front?"

She knew Drax would interpret her boldness as defiance but didn't care. She hated feeling useless and out of the loop, as if they were only waiting around and not actually helping their people.

"We have not received any new orders for advancement. The retreat of both Aniyan and Zentari forces from all fronts has not been overturned, and the Farron Gap remains quiet. At this point, most of our attention is focused on sniffing out the trap."

Her brow furrowed. "The trap?"

Drax gave her a mocking grin. "Surely you don't believe the great Zentari military would just stop fighting—that the almighty Council would pull back pressure on our resources for no reason. I believe they are gathering for a greater push somewhere, some weak point they've discovered that we aren't aware of. General Malachi agrees."

Eva bit her lip, unsure of how to ask her question subtly. "Does Ashdod know anything about the objects the Zentari are looking for?"

Drax's expression grew foul—his jaw clenching. "That, *Katz*, is above your lowly rank," he said. "Do not forget yourself. Again."

*Yeah yeah*

He continued. "You are asking about matters that don't concern you. The Legion will investigate your discovery as it sees fit. And the Leadership is under no obligation to keep you informed."

Eva nodded, fighting the urge to roll her eyes.

"Furthermore, do not think I forgot about your blatant dereliction of orders to take another warrior with you on this mission. I already filed a formal report to Chosen Lieutenant Cooper regarding your behavior and have assigned you to night watch tomorrow."

Eva breathed out a sigh of relief. She was getting off easy. Night watch was a nuisance, and Cooper might choose a harsher punishment, but for now it was a slap on the wrist.

Not wanting to risk further wrath, knowing simply standing in Drax's tent aggravated him, she bowed and turned to leave.

"I'm not done," he spat. She turned back, biting down on her frustration. "I saw your hesitation earlier."

Eva swallowed.

"Were you planning to tell me about the objects, or skulk around like the rat you are gathering information behind my back?"

She masked her anger, waiting for him to finish—but he expected a response.

She said dryly, "I provided all known information required of me as the—"

"Boar spit. I'm not going to argue with you again, Katz, I'm too exhausted. Were it anyone else I wouldn't question the accuracy of the report, but with you—"

He paused, his eyes darkening as he pointed a finger at her. "This war has taken a turn into a cesspool of spies and deceit, and I've had enough of it. I expect all Legion warriors under my command to focus on their duties and keep their gossip—and questions—to themselves. Now get out."

She bowed and left, before throwing the slew of insults on her tongue.

*Yeah. Sure*

# Chapter Five

E li couldn't tear his eyes from where Orion's body had laid not a moment earlier, the healers carrying the corpse away, droplets of blood trailing behind them.

*What in the rotting Hells was that*

It seemed Renard's claims of the program were true—direly true. It didn't matter what Eli had or hadn't heard, the Leadership just executed one of them.

*For tapping out*

Eli glanced at Arlo, whose mouth was slack, his cheerful demeanor evaporated.

The next pair of recruits was called, but the atmosphere in the room shifted, now carrying death's presence like a poisonous smog. And as Eli demanded his mind focus, return to the present, he noticed the fighting was more reserved—the recruits were holding their punches.

"Very well! That concludes the initiation exercise. These drills were designed to help us evaluate who among you stands out, and how to adjust your training as necessary."

Renard handed off his parchment as the other Captains and Operatives began leaving.

Eli swallowed, fear seeding in his chest. This was only an exercise—*an evaluation*—the first one of the program, and it already cost someone their life.

"The Leadership will discuss your performances today and where you best fit in the coming events," Renard touted. "Starting tomorrow, each day will begin with lectures on various topics, needed information for you to grasp your role in our military and how it functions. The afternoons are for sparring and weapons practice. During those times, a proctor will occasionally declare a match official. Only in those matches are the rules of engagement applied."

*Otherwise we'd all be dead in a week*

As much as Eli understood their reasoning, he couldn't agree with their methods. Limiting the formality of sparring practice only served to prevent every bout ending with an unconscious or dead recruit—since tapping out was unacceptable.

*What have I gotten myself into*

"The rest of the night is your own. Those of you who need medical attention should seek it. Follow the signs to the medical ward. For the rest of you, I recommend finding your bunkrooms. Beds are not assigned, but quarters are separated by gender. If you are found violating this rule, that is a punishable offense. Fraternization of any kind is not tolerated. Your luggage has been delivered to the entrance of the barracks on the main floor."

Renard pointed to the ground.

"There are six levels of the Citadel, but you are only permitted up to level three. Don't ask about the upper levels. They don't concern you. If you have any questions, you can ask me now, otherwise there will be an Operative in the barracks available at all times to enforce the rules and be a resource if needed."

Eli glanced around the room. The only person who didn't appear exhausted, defeated, or scared was the hulking man: Sol Richter. Eli caught himself scanning the crowd for a glimpse of dark hair and indigo eyes. He couldn't help trying to get another look at Shira—something about her took his breath away.

Renard continued, "Lastly, as I'm sure many of you are wondering, there will be no contact between you and your families during your training. We require your complete attention, and if you are to survive and excel, distraction is your greatest enemy. We will keep your families updated on your progress, and you will be able to reunite with your loved ones after the program is complete. Dismissed!"

With Renard's dismissal, ninety-nine recruits filed out of the Sparring Hall. Some limped, many nursed bloodied faces, but all carried the weight of their new reality—become a Guardian or die.

Once their belongings were stashed near their bunks, Eli and Arlo sat in the common area provided between the male and female bunkrooms, the air in the tight sleeping quarters having become rancid after the fights. The barracks was divided into three levels, with the uppermost one for Lieutenants and Operatives stationed at the Citadel. There were four bunkrooms available to the recruits, each housing about two dozen beds.

As they lounged, Eli waited expectantly to see Shira, but she was nowhere to be found. He recognized Maelyn and Laranna from the fights sitting at nearby tables. Laranna still appeared upset by the match, glancing daggers at her opponent. Surprisingly, so did Maelyn, who did well in her match against Laranna, and lost only after Sol intervened. Evidently, neither was happy with that result.

Anxious to gain any advantage in the program, he spoke to the two women. "Hey. You guys fight as fierce as Unger Cats."

They both looked up, before glancing at each other.

"And you fight as well as a drunken dog," Laranna snarked, though her smile was friendly. Maelyn said nothing.

Arlo jumped up and sat at Laranna's table, giving Eli the distinct impression he was quite the charmer.

"Hey, we won our match didn't we?" Arlo said smoothly.

"Barely!" Laranna countered with a grin. "You beat those guys like you were fighting at the local tavern!"

"Laranna, right?" Eli asked.

"Lara, please. *No one* calls me Laranna."

Maelyn remained silent, picking at a knot on the wooden table. Eli took notice and addressed her directly.

"And you're Maelyn, right?"

She looked up and nodded.

Eli said, "You seem like you've had military training. You have Guardians in the family?"

Maelyn watched him for a moment with calculated assessment. Arlo and Lara kept quiet, anticipating her answer.

Guardians for parents would be a tremendous edge. Not only for the insider knowledge of what to expect in the Citadel, but having Guardians as personal instructors. Eli couldn't help but imagine all the advantages Maelyn may have.

"Yes," she said curtly.

Lara's eyes grew wide, taking in her dark hair and tanned skin.

"Wait." She held up a finger, staring at Maelyn. "You're High Captain Mercer's daughter!"

Eli's ears perked. Memory loss aside, even he could remember the legends of Zentari's great Guardian Nathaniel Mercer. Famous for defeating an entire battalion of Aniyan warriors with no more than his magic and his Warhammer, the High Captain had turned the tide in many battles.

The group paused, the room quieted.

"Seriously?" Arlo asked, eyebrows raised. "Is it true?"

Maelyn exhaled, throwing her head toward the ceiling.

"Ha! I knew it!" Lara beamed.

"By the Nine!" Arlo said. "Mercer's daughter."

"I was hoping it would take a little longer than a few hours for someone to notice," Maelyn said, her nostrils flaring.

"Why would you keep that a secret?" Lara asked, leaning her chair back precariously.

"Because she didn't want the attention," Eli answered. Maelyn's eyes caught his.

"Something like that," she said. "Why, you a military kid too?"

"Oh no!" He laughed. "Just observant. I'm only the son of an innkeeper."

"Ah, high class!" Arlo teased.

"Says the illegal underground fighter!" Eli retorted.

"Hey, that was more of a hobby."

"So that's where you learned that sloppy right hook," Lara said. "What, they didn't teach you how to really fight in the underground?"

"Listen," Arlo said, pointing at Lara. "It's an old habit. If the fight is over too soon, everyone makes less money."

Eli interjected, "Do you actually make a lot of money doing that?"

"A bit. It's more than what you get for the simple work you can find near the city."

"It's just extremely dangerous," Lara said.

"And despicable," Maelyn added.

Arlo raised his hands. "I never admitted to anything."

Eli and Lara laughed. Eli said, "Actually, you just did."

"Speaking of which!" Arlo said abruptly, standing. "I want to check this place out. Who's with me?"

Eli and Lara stood and followed as Arlo walked to the stairs, but Maelyn remained in her seat.

Eli turned around. "You coming?"

"No," Maelyn said curtly.

"Come on," Lara touted, hands on her hips. "You're not salty about the fight are you?"

Maelyn's eyes narrowed.

Arlo added. "Well, I can see how she would be. If Sol hadn't intervened when he did—"

"Watch it, pretty boy," Maelyn barked.

"That's all right," Lara said. "It's humiliating being around someone who—"

Maelyn stood and strolled up to them with a blank look. Lara grinned and descended the stairs to the first floor.

All four of them spent some time exploring. They meandered along the walkway, making a complete circle around the first level of the Citadel. Connected to the walkway, they noticed a library, the mess hall, the medical ward, and of course the barracks.

Eli looked for Nazzat as they passed the medical ward, but didn't see her. They decided to invade the mess hall, hoping some food was available for a late-night snack, as none of them felt tired enough to sleep, despite the sun having set.

The dining hall was one spacious room, boasting a long buffet, stocked even at the late hour with fruit and pastries. The far wall was lined with windows, open to the dark plain behind the Citadel.

The four of them sat together at a wooden table in the corner, having the space to themselves.

"Okay, can we talk about this?" Lara asked in a whisper, leaning forward as she sat next to Arlo, "What in the Nine Hells happened with Orion?"

No one answered at first, the question hanging in the air.

"He tapped out," Eli said softly, picking at a hangnail. "He quit."

"That wasn't a punishment for quitting, that was an execution," Maelyn said, with a glare Eli knew wasn't directed at him, but the absurdity of the circumstance.

"Look, it's just a guess," Eli rebutted, "but clearly that was the message they wanted to convey. No one else was harmed, even when the Leadership called the match. Orion was the only one to tap out. But you're the one who's supposed to have insider information. Did your father ever say anything about Leadership killing the recruits themselves?"

Maelyn shifted in her seat, straightening her shoulders. "No, he didn't. He and I didn't exactly talk."

"Didn't?" Arlo asked.

"Don't," she corrected.

"But he had to have said something," Lara added. "What did he say when you applied?"

"Nothing really. He simply nodded at me and said, 'make it count,'" Maelyn responded, remaining stoic.

Eli sighed. "Well, if it makes you feel any better, my father wasn't exactly packing my bags when I told him I wanted to join."

"Look, we all knew signing up meant a grueling program," Arlo said. "Why are we surprised the Citadel isn't going easy?"

It was a beat before Eli answered.

"Because we didn't think our own military would hand out executions."

Maelyn added, "Or that the teachers would be killing the students."

"Or that we'd be putting our lives at risk before we even saw battle," Lara responded.

"Okay okay," Arlo said. "Fine. I'm just trying to help."

"Look," Eli said, "there's nothing we can do about it now. Renard already said we can't back out, and I don't think any of us want to. That being said, I think the best way to survive this thing is to stick together. Help each other along the way."

At that, Maelyn stood. "Yeah. No offense, but you guys have fun with your little alliance. I gave you a chance, but I didn't come here to make friends. I'm getting some sleep before tomorrow," she said, starting the walk back to the barracks.

"Don't worry." Arlo smirked. "I'll look out for you guys."

Eli raised his eyebrows in jest, leaning back with his arms crossed. "That so?"

"I feel better already," Lara teased, rolling her eyes with a grin.

Eli couldn't help but smile, grateful to have found friends.

Eli loaded half a dozen grogs of ale onto a tray for the travelers in the corner. Ample weaponry, hardened gazes, and cloaks wreaking of horses meant they were likely military. Messy to clean up after, but they tipped well and didn't start any fights.

It was a busy night. Of course, during harvest, most nights were busy. The Star-Light Inn was a convenient stop along the main road for merchants carrying crops, shepherds herding through the villages, and military guards inspecting wares for contraband. It was good business, but meant long days for innkeepers and brothels in the area. And as the night wore on, the chatter in the inn had grown from modest dinner conversations to an increasingly inebriated roar.

Eli stared at a few of the customers, admiring their sense of adventure, their ability to leave everything they've known and run toward their goal, thinking little of the consequences. He returned to the bar as his father poured another two mugs from the hefty barrel.

"Is room four still available?" Eli asked, wiping the spilled ale off the bar. "The two at the back changed their minds about staying tonight."

"No one has claimed it, so they can have it," his father said, sliding mugs across the bar to Eli. "But remind them of the rules. Additional parties still pay in full but sleep on the floor."

"Right," Eli responded, grabbing the two fresh mugs.

As he rushed them to the waiting table, the door to the inn slammed open. Everyone in the room stopped, staring at the menacing figure in the doorway.

"Where is he?" the figure shouted in a guttural inhuman tone.

Eli stood frozen, heart racing, glancing at his father. The figure stormed into the space, a black cloak covering his head. Eli couldn't make out his features, apart from burning yellow eyes.

The stranger scoured the space, as his father stepped up to him.

"You need to leave," his father ordered.

The stranger towered over Eli's father, not saying a word. A deep tribal fear ebbed from Eli's stomach. The stranger drew a blade faster than Eli's eyes could follow and slit his father's throat. Eli screamed, lunging forward, but an arm wrapped around his neck before he could take a step. Held back by someone Eli couldn't see, the stranger marched toward Eli with pounding steps.

"You can't run away from what you did!" the figure screamed.

Eli thrashed to get free, desperate to get to his father, and keep them away from Harper. He caught the glint of silver metal in the candlelight, before a searing pain ignited in his stomach—

Eli jolted awake, sitting up so abruptly his head hit the top bunk. Arlo stirred above him but made no sound other than gentle snoring. Eli winced as he grabbed his forehead, checking for blood, but his hand was only moist with sweat. His heart thundered in his chest—his muscles restless.

Taking a deep breath, he calmed himself from the nightmare, sitting on the edge of his bed. The mage stones cast enough light for him to see around the bunkroom, which was quiet, apart from the gentle snoring—and his own ragged breathing.

He sighed, willing the adrenaline to leave his system.

*Bleeding rot, what a nightmare*

Grounding himself in the stillness, he cast his thoughts to Harper and home, thinking of fond memories to banish the dark images of the dream. He wondered how they were doing, if his father was handling the inn on his own, or if it was finally slowing down as summer ended. He knew his father could manage the inn, but he relied so much on Eli doing the manual labor and menial tasks, his father would no doubt have to hire some hands.

Harper's face filled his mind, her long flowing hair shimmering like sunlight, her eyes the color of a cool winter's sky. He could see her laying on her bed, her pointed ears twitching as she poured over her schoolwork, humming that infernal song she always sang. It drove him crazy hearing it all the time, and he endlessly pestered her to stop. But it now warmed his heart as the tune resurfaced.

He wondered if she was still struggling with mathematics, recalling how many hours he spent repeating the same lessons again and again. No doubt their father would step in and take over teaching her, as much as time allowed. But a quiet heartache formed as Eli pictured Harper's gentle smile, her crooked front baby teeth finally coming loose. She was so excited, praying to the Heavens her adult teeth were straighter.

As he closed his eyes, he could feel the warmth of her head on his lap as she slept, which she often did while he read into the night. It saddened him, but it was something she did less often as she grew older. He cherished those hours, staying up reading whatever books his father could provide, while brushing Harper's hair as she snored softly. He clung to her memory like an anchor—a lifeline among his inner storm of uncertainty. The death of Orion rattled his resolve, fearing his decision to leave would cost Harper the only friend she had.

Harper followed Eli around everywhere he went, his little shadow, wanting to know his every thought and opinion. Her view of the world bent at his whim, and she emulated everything he said and did, trying to become a mirror image of her brother whom she worshiped.

Yet, though Harper was the reason he longed to return home, she was also the reason he'd left. He loved her fiercely—more than anything in the world—but there was a part of him, one he rarely acknowledged, that had grown bitter. Bitter that the moment their mother died, Harper's needs swallowed everything else, including Eli's childhood. His father had tried, but the grief left him hollow, and Eli stepped in to fill the void.

He'd read to her each night, braided her hair when she cried for their mother, cooked what meals he could manage. She had become his whole world. But a boy isn't meant to be a father.

Eli leaned back against the wall, and a memory surfaced of Harper curled in his lap. She was begging for him to read *The Ashen Fox* for the hundredth time, her little voice insistent and bright.

*Wait*

*Was that the name of the book*

He chased the memory, but the image blurred. The title slipped through his fingers like smoke. He saw the book in her hands, his sister's innocent smile, but the words on the cover blurred.

Eli frowned, now uncertain. The memory faded the harder he reached for it. Rubbing his eyes, he took a deep breath. It was likely his own exhaustion, or the WAVEs, but something in him didn't feel right.

He stood and walked out of the bunkroom into the barracks hallway, closing the door silently. The lighting was equally dim, but the air was much cooler on his bare chest. The quiet of the Citadel brought a steadiness to his turbulent thoughts. He embraced the serenity of the stillness, until the sound of footsteps from the stairway broke the silence.

He carefully leaned against the wall in the corner, standing engulfed in shadow. A figure appeared at the top of the steps. The feminine outline crept with slow and deliberate movements, careful to avoid drawing attention. He found it odd for a recruit to be sneaking around, but perhaps there was a curfew he didn't know about, or she was using the washroom.

But she didn't act casual—rather the opposite. The woman shuffled toward the female bunkroom, her fingers brushing the doorknob before she froze. Her head snapped in his direction, eyes wide. He wasn't sure if she could see him, but her icy gaze cut through the shadows, piercing him clean through.

Eli held his breath, keeping his body rigid. If she hadn't spotted him, surely she could hear his heart thundering in his chest. Agonizing seconds passed before she quietly stepped into the bunkroom, the door closing with barely a whisper. The reality of his nightmare was washed away by a seeding curiosity. He waited a few minutes before returning to bed, Shira's face lingering in his mind.

# Chapter Six

Eva's feet moved of their own accord, ushered forward by an unforgiving and irresistible pull. The room lay silent and bare, cloaked in rock and shadow, two figures standing to her right. Neither of them was familiar, one notably younger than the other. They stood before a massive door, its stone surface etched with intricate symbols stretching its full height. Ancient words of a forgotten tongue spiraled within an ornate circle, every line and curve meticulously woven into the design.

By the command of their very presence, the door opened, grinding against the floor, dust falling as it awakened from its long slumber. The room beyond was occupied only by an enormous orb of black rock levitating in the center, above a stony platform.

She watched the two figures step forward, transfixed by its presence, drawn to the deep hum which echoed in her chest—

"Hey, Eva!" Maya said, waving her hand in front of her friend's face. "Nine Hells girl, where did you go?"

"What?" Eva asked, dazed a bit as she focused on Maya's dark eyes.

"You spaced out," Lucas said, sitting down next to Eva on the wooden bench, mouth already stuffed with bread. "Kinda creepy."

The gentle roar of the mess tent rushed back to Eva's ears. She took a bite of her now lukewarm food.

"But really, you all right? You seem out of it," Maya said.

Eva smiled weakly, rubbing her eyes. "Yeah, I'm just tired. I let my mind wander."

"Anything good?" Lucas asked, taking another bite.

Eva gave him a sour glare, knowing she'd told him about her vivid dreams growing up and how she was sensitive about them. Lucas just smiled.

"Hey," Maya said. "I got more dye from the last shipment of supplies. It's not too late to change your mind."

Eva shook her head, wrinkling her nose. Maya had offered to dye Eva's hair a few times, as she had done with her own. Maya's hair was now a deep magenta, contrasting her natural blonde.

"That stuff can't be good for you," Lucas said with a grimace. "You know it's for leather, right? And not actually for human use."

Maya rolled her eyes. "Do I look like I care? What else is there to do around here?"

"You mean other than saving the country?" Lucas touted playfully.

Eva huffed. "As if."

Lucas turned to her. "What? The white-haired devil feel in a slump?

"No," Eva said. "I just don't feel like we're making any difference."

"Oh no, we are," Maya said, leaning forward. "Sam said the Legion found a renegade group of Zentari hiding out near the Western base of the Ha'Negev mountains. They found a cabin stained with blood and near fifty Aniyan corpses in a shallow grave."

Eva's mouth gaped. "Civilians?"

Maya nodded gravely. "And worse."

"Rotting Shells," Lucas breathed. "Send them all to the block."

*What kind of people could do that to children*

Maya said, "They think most were just innocent bystanders, but some were obviously Legion."

"How many Zentari were involved?" Eva asked.

"About six," Maya answered. "They were kidnapping unsuspecting travelers along the main road, gagging them and dragging them to whatever torture awaited in that cabin."

"As if we needed more reasons to keep fighting," Lucas said, finishing his coffee.

"I wish Ashdod would set up their own version of that cabin just for them," Maya muttered.

Eva didn't speak, unable to find the right words for such an atrocity.

The three of them returned their meal trays and headed to the meadow outside the gates for a midmorning rest. Winter was well on the way and Eva wanted to absorb as much sunlight and warmth as she could before the temperatures plummeted.

None of them having any immediate duties, they found a sunny place to sit.

"Hey Lucas," Eva asked, watching the sun climb over the tree line as it warmed the morning air.

"Yeah?" he responded, squinting at the horizon.

"What do you know about the objects the Zentari are searching for? What are they?"

She didn't feign innocence. Though she knew Lucas would likely scold her for asking about privileged information—*again*—she couldn't help herself. The memory of what happened with the stone haunted her, and Drax provided nothing useful.

Maya spoke before Lucas could answer. "Eva, stop it."

"What?" Eva asked.

"Forcing Lucas into this position."

"I need to know," Eva argued.

"It's not your place to ask."

"So what," Eva spat. "If I'm expected to fight, I'm allowed to ask questions."

"It doesn't matter—" Maya's words were cut short as Lucas raised his hand. He glanced around to ensure they were far enough from prying eyes and itching ears.

"I'm not sure." He started, speaking softly. "I overheard Chosen Lieutenant Cooper mention something about ancient relics a few months back when I was passing through the Duran Wall. There was an intel report of the Zentari searching for these small stones. Our spies say the orders were given to everyone, regardless of rank. Every Zentari in the field was told to keep their eyes open."

Eva's thoughts wandered back to the black stone, the searing pain and tingling sense of power. She couldn't make sense of it, or why the Zentari wanted them.

Lucas continued, "The further I dug the more the intel became conjecture. Rumors of specialized task forces to capture Legion warriors who may have information, double agents in our ranks, even hearsay about some voodoo science sacrificing people. All I can say is the Zentari are losing their minds over this."

Maya glared, shifting uncomfortably.

"Come on Maya," Eva said, "you're not a tiny bit curious?"

"I am. I'm not pretending like I haven't heard the rumors," she answered. "But I know when to keep things to myself."

Eva sighed and rolled her eyes, ushering for Lucas to continue.

"We're not really sure why they're so fixated on them," he said. "To be honest I'm curious myself. The real question is why. What would be so important that they would focus so much effort on it? It's a rumor, but some think it's why they originally ordered a retreat from the front."

Eva paused. "Drax said he and the General think the Zentari are planning a strike. Focusing their efforts on a weakness, taking the resources from the front to make it happen."

Lucas nodded. "I wouldn't put it past them. Everyone is happy the fighting has ceased, but it's only brought a lingering sense of dread, waiting for the other ax to fall."

Eva stared into the open field, watching the wind brush against the tall grass. She absentmindedly rubbed her fingers where the stone seared her hand.

"What if it makes them stronger?" she asked.

Maya froze, clearly invested in the conversation, even if she refused to speak. Lucas gave Eva a knowing look.

"That's what the higher ups are worried about," he said. "It's the only reason I can think of that they would stop pressing the front—"

"Wait," Maya interjected. "What do you mean?"

Eva raised her eyebrows.

"Fine. Shut up. I'm already an accomplice just standing here," Maya said. "Just answer the rotting question."

Lucas said, "No one knows this, but we were losing ground. The Zentari were overpowering our forces, having diverted more Guardians to the front. That's why everyone is so tense. They were winning, essentially, yet they're the ones that retreated."

Maya's gaze drifted. "Where did we learn about the stones in the first place? Did we discover them first?" Maya asked.

Lucas hesitated, fiddling with a strand of grass in his hands.

"Look, what I'm about to tell you stays here," he said reluctantly.

"Of course," Maya assured.

"Just spit it out." Eva pushed.

"About two months ago there was a unit of ten Legion stationed at the Northernmost crest of the Gulf. While there, they intercepted a civilian group of travelers, men, women, and children. Some were Aniyan, but some were Zentari. Immediately suspicious, the unit started searching the caravan."

"You can't search civilians without cause," Maya protested.

"Anymore being Zentari is enough," Eva muttered.

"While they were searching, one of the Zentari travelers started challenging the Legion. Things got violent. Then bloody."

Eva's shoulders dipped, knowing where the story was going.

"While they were erasing the evidence of what happened, they came across a satchel with these odd black stones. Each was small and polished, like nothing we've ever seen before. The Legion didn't think much of them, and it sounds like they were more concerned about the incident itself. But, during transport one of the stones fell into a ravine. It shattered on a boulder causing an eruption of blue flame."

The three were still, the hissing of the trees the only sound around them.

"That's why you were redirected to the Gulf," Eva said.

Lucas nodded. "We were called in to cover for the unit while everything was being sorted out."

"You mean while they buried the bodies," Maya murmured. He didn't correct her. Eva knew Lucas wrestled with standing for what was right when doing so breached protocol.

"Anyway," he continued, "the moment Ashdod was notified, General Malachi immediately took control. As in, he *personally* oversaw the transfer and management of these things. And each of us was given strict orders to remain silent, under punishment of execution."

"Execution?" Maya asked, astonished.

"Yeah," Lucas said. "The General knows something and isn't shy about using death threats to keep things secret. Rumor has it that nearly two dozen Legion at The Capitol have lost their commission over this. He clearly doesn't want word getting out, but that's only caused a stir. The only common thread I've found is something called Archancy, but Hells knows what it is."

"Guys, I have to tell you something." Eva started, her eyes dancing around, hands fidgeting with a piece of grass she plucked from the field. She took a deep breath, knowing these were the two people she trusted most in the world, although that didn't mean much when you only have two friends. Maya and Lucas waited.

"I found a stone," Eva blurted.

Their eyes widened.

"Where?" Maya asked.

"On my mission to intercept those scouts. One of them had a stone on her."

"Where is it?" Lucas asked, his face gravely serious.

"It's gone," she replied, shrugging. "I didn't know what it was. The leading scout had mentioned those objects, and I found it hidden in a pocket searching one of them. But when I touched it . . ."

Her voice trailed.

"What?" Maya asked impatiently.

"I don't know, something happened," Eva said.

"You don't know?" Lucas asked.

"Are you okay?" Maya added.

"Yeah, I think so. I don't know how to explain it. I remember a vibration from it, sensing like it was full of energy of some kind. But when I picked it up, it burned by hand. I tried to let go, but my hand was paralyzed. The burning pain worsened, and a screeching ringing sounded in my head."

"What in the Nine Hells," Maya whispered.

"But it didn't last long. The pain went away and I felt a tingling, but it was euphoric. It was the strangest sensation. I went from experiencing pure agony to feeling a rush of strength, like I could leap over a mountain. And then it stopped."

"That's it?" Maya asked in astonishment.

Eva nodded. "When I opened my eyes the stone was gone."

"Gone?" Lucas asked.

"I don't know. It just disappeared." Eva waited for their response.

"Did you say anything to Drax?" he asked, concerned.

A pang of guilt struck her. "No, I didn't."

"Good," he said. Eva gave a quizzical look. "All I know is that the Legion is taking these stones extremely seriously. If you had told Drax you'd probably be half-way to Ashdod for rot knows what reasons."

Maya's brow furrowed. "Are you applauding her for breaking the rules?"

"No, but I am saying that you should keep this quiet. Clearly these things are dangerous, and our leaders are considering them an immediate threat to the war. I'm saying you should drop this and forget anything ever happened."

Maya didn't respond. Eva stared at Lucas, wishing she could read his mind, but decided not to press the issue. Despite the frustration that built when he denied her information, she knew that he would never put her in harm's way. If he said to steer clear, she would do so.

Or at least try.

Eva's watch started only two hours ago, but she already felt the inevitable boredom and exhaustion taking hold. She stood at the Southern entrance to the outpost, cleaning her nails with her dagger. Crickets sounded through the field, jumping in the still air, which was slowly taking on the crispness of the night.

She heard Lucas's footsteps before he spoke.

"Do you remember when we were kids, and we used to hide in the woods?" he said fondly.

Eva smiled. "We'd wait to see how long it'd take before your mother told my father and we had the entire Northern Legion looking for us."

Lucas laughed, soft and infectious. His presence cut through the heaviness around them like a hot blade, dissolving the darkness like a roaring fire.

Eva's smile widened. "How about the time we put burr berries in the outpost porridge?" she asked.

"And counted how many times each troop went to the washroom." Lucas added.

"And then that Lieutenant who ran out half-naked!" she said. He burst into a belly laugh.

"Lieutenant Barker," he answered, still laughing at the absurdity of their childish games. "We used to call him 'Barky' the way he sounded like a yapping puppy when he gave orders."

Eva's laugh echoed across the camp. She threw her head back, getting lost in the simple joy of being with her best friend once again. The world fell away and opened into a field of cherished memories. Lucas would always be her anchor in the storm—her candle in the window. She knew that he still felt the same. And even though time had a way of eroding bonds, of weakening connections that were once as strong as steel, theirs was different.

Tales of their childhood antics passed between them well through the night. Her exhaustion seemed distant as they recounted particularly perilous adventures involving stealing her father's horse. Eva was surprised how quickly the sun rose over the horizon, having lost track of time. She leaned on Lucas's shoulder, ever grateful for his friendship. The time he spent with her, keeping her awake, made Drax's punishment an enjoyable experience.

They spoke of dreams and longings, of plans they both knew were nothing more than sandcastles before a storm—but they built them anyway. Each word and thought was a fragile tower, each new idea as stable as dry sand. And though fate cast its winds against the shore, they dared to believe that some things, however fleeting, could leave traces even when swept away.

Eva woke, sitting up with sleep in her eyes. It took a moment before she realized that she was not in her tent. She rubbed her face, feeling much too comfortable to be in her own bed.

*Oh. Right*

Eva and Lucas had spent the entire night shift together, and once morning came, she followed him to his tent like a lost puppy. He offered his bed, knowing it was far more comfortable than her own. She was eternally grateful, with the full force of night watch weighing her down. He said he was off to listen to the morning report anyway.

His tent was spacious compared to hers, adorned with all the needs of a battle leader. She reluctantly crawled out of bed, cursing Legion policy. All Aniyan military members were required to be always battle ready—even while sleeping.

She stepped out of the tent, squinting at the sun, which was higher than she expected. She lazily shuffled through the bustling outpost to her own tent to grab a fresh tunic and undergarments, before heading to the latrine to wash up. Once as refreshed as possible, she adorned her black armor once again and headed for the mess tent. It was long after breakfast, but the outpost cook, Bereeth, always looked out for her, hiding away some snacks in case she missed a meal. Drax loved to assign last minute tasks which cut into mealtime, and Bereeth took notice when Eva kept asking if there was any food left.

As she entered the mess tent she saw Bereeth cleaning the dishes and straightening up before the next meal. She took notice of Eva and smiled.

A stout woman, Bereeth wore no armor, only a simple light brown tunic with a cloth apron. Her hair was tied up in a bun, though many strands refused to remain constrained. Her face was gentle, which contrasted the level of backbone the woman had. When Drax harassed her about her lack of armor, she scolded him like a child. Eva could barely hold back her laugh, and Drax—surprisingly—never brought it up again.

"Well girl, you slept in pretty late. Night watch?" she asked, drying the next plate from the wash bin.

Eva nodded with a drawn-out yawn, placing her hands on the wooden counter. She stared at Bereeth with the pleading eyes of a child.

Bereeth returned the look with a warm smile. "There's some bread and dried meat in a sack on the back table."

"That's why you're the best," Eva responded, heading to the back of the tent.

Bereeth gave a wry grin. The two bantered for a time while Eva ate to her stomach's content. Bereeth was full of old stories, tales of truth and legend, which Eva could listen to for hours. As soon as one ended, Eva was begging for another. And despite Bereeth's protesting, she always gave in and started a new tail. Eva was envious, hoping to have beautiful stories to tell her daughter someday.

After eating, she thanked Bereeth again before leaving. She started back toward her tent, but stopped, and headed to Lucas's tent instead. As she threw open the entrance flap, Lucas looked up from his desk.

"Come in, I guess," he said with a grin. She rolled her eyes and walked over to lie on his bed. Lucas returned to his work. It wasn't long before the full stomach and comfortable mattress lulled Eva to sleep.

"Chief! Permission to enter, sir!" a voice shouted from outside.

"Granted," Lucas said.

A young Swordsman threw open the tent with a rush, stopping inside and standing at attention.

"Rest, Swordsman Keinen," Lucas said, his commanding demeanor taking over. "Report."

The warrior started to speak but stopped short as Eva sat up, surprised to see a woman in the Chief's bed. The Swordsman stared at Eva for a moment—mouth agape. Eva's cheeks burned. Fraternizing among unequal ranks was strictly forbidden. While most in the camp knew she and Lucas were old friends, she hated to give Drax a reason to spite her further.

*Hopefully Keinen is discreet*

"Hey, Keinen!" Lucas said, snapping his fingers. The young man's eyes shot to him.

"Sir, you are needed by Lieutenant Drax. He says it's urgent."

"Send word. I'm on my way."

Keinen bowed and left. The warmth in Lucas's face receded as he turned to her. Something was wrong.

# Chapter Seven

R ecruits, welcome to your first lecture."

A man paced along the stage of the auditorium, his hands clasped behind his back as his white robes dragged softly across the small stage. His bald head accentuated his pointed ears, with his well-kept white beard framing his face.

"My name is Keeper Thaddeus Darby. I am tasked with providing you with all the needed lecture material for the Guardian program."

The Lecture Hall was massive, with stadium seating facing a quaint stage, posters and tapestries on the back wall. Darby's voice echoed as he spoke loudly enough for everyone to hear.

"Welcome to the Citadel Lecture Hall. For the next three months, you will attend daily lectures over various topics, including history, weapons, combat, and magic."

Eli felt the tension in the room rise, every recruit sitting on the edge of their seat. They were all eager to hear Darby's explanation of magic, knowing its secrets were closely guarded.

"Magic is inherent in all Zentari and is the very thing that grants us dominance on the battlefield against the Aniyans. Yet, it is a dormant thing, hidden deep within, and is not spread equally among our people. Though we all possess some level of magic, not everyone is capable of bringing forth enough to wield it in battle."

Eli swallowed, praying to the Heavens he was one of the special few.

"This program is specifically designed to draw out your inner magic. The physical training, which you will experience this afternoon outside in the Practice

Field, and the use of the Thought Wave Analysis, all increase the likelihood of your success in drawing out what magic you possess."

The stiffness in Eli's muscles lessened a touch.

"The Thought Wave Analysis is called WAVE for short, and is a precious secret for our people. It has granted us twice the number of Guardians we were able to train in the past, so you can agree the lingering side effects are very much worth it. That being said, before you ask, we will not go into detail about how the procedure is performed. The process is under the direct supervision of the Council, and they demand absolute secrecy."

Eli was painfully curious, but knew better than to openly defy the Council. Grunts and sighs sounded from the class, but Darby's stoic expression indicated the matter was closed.

"Before we begin, you should all pay close attention to the program timeline provided. This program lasts approximately twelve weeks, at which point you graduate to our general military training for an additional three months."

Darby pointed to the extensive parchment behind him, which covered a fair amount of the wall. It detailed the current date and the future dates for named events in the program. Eli followed on the parchment handed to him as he entered earlier, which mirrored the same timeline.

"First thing of note, you have one remaining WAVE, which will take place in six weeks. Each of you already received the first WAVE before the program started. This is done in the beginning to ensure the limited time we have is utilized to the greatest extent. The second WAVE, as you can see, takes place around the midpoint of the program itself. Those of you who suffer a poor reaction will be granted ample time to recover as needed, so rest assured."

*That's good to know. But how many others had the reaction I did*

"Second, there are two endurance challenges that await you. The first, which will take place tomorrow, is The Proving. Once squads of four members are chosen, you will proceed to the Southern cliffs and work as a team to complete the assigned task. This challenge will test your teamwork and push you to your physical limits. Keep this in mind: the success of one means the success of all."

A quiet hiss of murmurs spread.

"The second challenge, known as The Crucible, is scheduled two days after the second WAVE. This challenge takes place on Mount Asir to the north and carries greater risk than The Proving. With this challenge, you will need to weigh the cost of failing your mission against the safety and well-being of your comrades. I will warn you, that even if you survive the challenge, failing the objective is met with dire consequences."

A rock settled in Eli's stomach, thinking of what awaited him.

"Thirdly, the Rune Blade Ceremony. This sacred tradition is granted only to those who survive the program to that point and is scheduled in nine weeks. This ceremony takes place on the third level of the Citadel and utilizes the Rune Forge where you will manifest your unique Rune Blades. This, recruits, is the pinnacle of success for this program. Should you manifest a Rune Blade, you will forever seal your name in the scrolls as a warrior of The Ethereal. This is how you achieve the title of Guardian."

Eli could sense the excitement that rippled through the room, with everyone energized by the idea. And he felt the same rush, but Eli caught Darby's wary look.

"However, you will notice, there is one final event which is scheduled immediately following the Rune Blade Ceremony. I will not speak of The Reaping at this time, so as not to distract you from your coming tasks. All I will say is this: give everything you have to finding your magic and succeeding at the tasks we place before you. Do whatever is required to find your inner magic, for only those who fail at the Rune Forge undergo The Reaping. And I assure you, you do not wish to be a participant."

Another rustling of murmurs spread among the recruits. Eli absentmindedly touched his left wrist, grounding himself to why he was here, and why he would succeed. He shunned the speculative thoughts and nerves about what awaited him, hardening his resolve.

Darby continued, "Before we begin today's lecture on the history of the war, does anyone have questions about the program schedule?"

A hand shot up to Eli's right. A female recruit asked her question before Darby could nod for her to speak.

"How do we know if our magic is manifesting? Are there signs we should look for?"

"An excellent question," Darby praised. "You will feel a sense of strength, of energy none of you have experienced. Your physical skills, and senses, will all heighten on their own. There is no other way to explain it, but rest assured, you will know when your inner magic awakens."

Another hand rose to the back of the room. A male voice spoke. "Is it possible to manifest a Rune Blade during training or in the challenges?"

"No," Darby said. "Utilizing the Rune Forge during the Rune Blade Ceremony is the only way this can be achieved."

Another hand rose. "Can Guardians use their magic without a Rune Blade?"

Darby sighed. "I understand that you all are excited to learn about your magic, but we are getting ahead of ourselves, and we have only limited time for today's lecture. The short answer to your question is no. But we will discuss this more in detail later on."

The room groaned with disappointment.

Darby began pacing. "Today, we will briefly explain the history of the war and who it is that we face as an enemy."

Most of the recruits carried pieces of parchment or scrolls to scribe notes and comments. However, this wasn't a class for scholars—this was a war college. Many of the students stared into space with disinterest, lost to the fact that an apt warrior keeps their mind honed alongside their body.

Eli kept his attention on Darby, soaking in all the information he could.

"Who here is familiar with our Heika outpost, to the South of the Midbar Desert?"

At least half the room raised their hands, Eli included. It was the most critical, and most vulnerable, of their outposts being the furthest from the safety of the Citadel.

"Excellent. Recently a group of scouts was sent North to investigate the Legion's movements near their outpost they call Yaqar. Three scouts were sent, but were ambushed before they could return. An unknown number of Aniyan warriors killed two of the three, leaving the third marred, beaten, and for dead. This Operative bravely crawled her way back to safety, with little to no supplies or comrades. What can we learn from this?"

Three hands rose quickly. Eli had his own thoughts, but waited to hear the others first. Darby nodded to a female recruit.

"The information about the scouting party was leaked, sir."

*Not necessarily*

"It is possible," Darby said. "But keep in mind, they may simply have been spotted."

Another recruit spoke, "We can presume at least ten Legion warriors were involved in the ambush."

Darby shrugged. "We are confident it must have been a few, given our superiority on the battlefield. One properly trained Zentari Operative is worth at least five Legion warriors, while Guardians such as yourselves are worth a hundred or more. But that is only speculation and yields no useful information. I am looking for something deeper. A more menacing truth behind the event."

Silence settled in the room. Eli raised his hand. "Sir, why did they leave one of our own alive?"

"Precisely," Darby said. "Can anyone answer that question?"

Maelyn raised her hand. "Sir, the Aniyans allowed their hatred to affect their mission. Instead of eliminating the enemy, they chose to inflict a torturous end."

"Exactly," Darby said, pointing to Maelyn. "Recruits, we face a malicious adversary. Why would the Legion leave an enemy alive, who could easily report back critical information to the Citadel? Track their attackers to a hidden safehouse? Ambush the attackers at a later time? The answer is simple. They relish any opportunity to inflict pain and suffering on our people. Do not be fooled. They fight for domination of the land of Adiel, with hatred in their hearts. We fight for survival."

The room was quiet, Darby's words hanging in the air like a humid fog.

"The Aniyan and Zentari war began hundreds of years ago," Darby said. "I will not bore you with the entire history, nor the minutia that we keepers are sworn to protect. Here is what you need to know: we cannot recall an era when our two peoples experienced true peace, always living with a grave tension under the oppression of our northern neighbors. According to the oral history we Keepers preserve, our conflict began with our people's attempted extermination."

Eli's brow furrowed.

*I don't remember hearing that*

"Nearly five hundred years in the past, when our people first arrived in this country, we were labeled as enemies of the Aniyan kingdom. Because of our differences, and the innate magic of the Primarchs, our ancestors were hunted without mercy. Slaughtered without reason. The Primarchs were the most powerful magic wielders in history, but Aniyans vastly outnumbered them. In an effort to survive, the Primarchs retreated to this section of the Adielan territory and erected the Citadel, a fortress to shelter them from the North. To our record, we have had the Millennial conflict ever since."

Eli sat still, absorbing the information. The only sound in the room was the scratch of ink pens on parchment. The origin of their people was something obscured with time, with neighboring countries appearing more like Aniyans than Zentari. But Eli wasn't surprised the hatred he'd seen growing up reached that far back.

Most of the violence was isolated to the battlefield—leaders orchestrating death between two groups of disposable soldiers. Yet there were extremists who would act on their own. Fighting in the shadows, they held a deep-seated hatred for their enemy, or determined the nation's leaders weren't making change fast enough.

Eli heard gruesome stories over the years, travelers from both the South and the North speaking of atrocities beyond that of a battlefield. Whispers of bodies hung in the trees or burning in the streets, entire families disappearing leaving only blood in the home. He at first thought the stories were exaggerated—nothing more than fantastical tales to stir up discourse and spur the war effort. But over time, the rumors and stories kept coming—horror after horror—each one bloodier than the last. The last one he was told, before deciding to leave home for the Citadel, was a father who'd returned home to his young daughter and wife—left to bleed to death, nailed to the side of their home.

"Though initially outnumbered, our people held against the first wave of the Aniyan Legion. Our innate magic, coupled with superior weapons, was more than enough to defend our home. With the natural boundaries of the sea to the South and East, and the mountains to the North, we were given perfect ground for defending our people. Perhaps that is why the Primarchs chose this cliffside to erect our spire."

A hand raised from across the room. A young woman spoke.

"Why couldn't the Primarchs win the war, if the Aniyans don't possess magic?"

*My thought exactly*

Darby stopped, eyeing the girl closely. "What is it you are implying, recruit?"

She shifted in her seat. "I just mean, if the Primarchs were the strongest magic wielders of our time, could they not have easily overpowered the Aniyans? If the Guardians of today are any indication."

Darby remained planted. The air shifted, growing tense. "It is by the sacrifice and blood of our ancestors that you sit in that seat, recruit. If you are able to draw out your magic, perhaps you would like to test your mettle against a hundred thousand trained Legion warriors to prove your claim and fault of our forebears."

The girl stammered, but decided to not respond. Eli's eyes narrowed.

*Why the scolding? It's a fair question*

Darby stopped pacing and turned to face the recruits, waiting for further questions before he spoke. A hand raised behind Eli. "What can you tell us about the sympathizers over in Sheket?"

"Ah, yes. For those of you unaware, there is a small colony to the far west in a village called Sheket, which is a name from the old language meaning "silence". These people are Aniyan sympathizers and have chosen to abstain from the war efforts, making an exodus from Eldan altogether. They chose silence in a time when one should be shouting over the injustice of their people."

"Could it be that they are simply tired of the war?" Eli asked, chastising himself for speaking out of turn. Darby stiffened as his attention veered to the interruption. Eli swallowed, but held the Keeper's stare.

"What is your point, recruit?"

Eli took a breath, feeling all eyes on him. A gnawing sensation in his gut erupted that he couldn't explain. "My father owns an inn that has seen and housed many travelers coming from throughout Adiel. I've spoken with those from Sheket and near the Farron Gap. Some I've met speak with accents and languages from other regions. There are many people who have grown tired of the fighting. It's not that they are choosing a side, but are rather refusing to offer more bloodshed."

"Well," Darby drawled, "then perhaps we should all just walk off the cliffs into the Great Sea and be done with it."

Eli's brow furrowed. "Sir?"

"How convenient it is to be able to choose to step aside and allow an entire society to fight on their own!"

The room fell silent, and Eli's heart pounded, but he pressed further. "But there are even Zentari people, like those in Sheket, that feel there should be more talks of peace. Surely they—"

"If you are here to convince anyone that standing our ground in this war is *not* the answer, then you have made a grave mistake in coming to the Citadel, recruit."

A stark warning rang in Darby's voice. But Eli persisted, something in his chest pushing him, his voice growing louder. "I understand, but it's been centuries, surely there is more to—"

"Enough!" Darby shouted, throwing his hands out, face flushed. "You will remember your place! Or do you question the judgment of the Council?"

Eli swallowed, glancing around at the sea of eyes watching him.

"I expect an answer, recruit!" Darby took a step toward him.

"No, sir," Eli muttered.

Darby spoke to the entire room, but kept his eyes pinned on Eli. "I expect each of you to uphold respect for our Leaders, and most certainly the Council. Inquiring about the current status is one thing, but questioning whether there is a better solution than what they have declared will not be tolerated."

Eli's gaze fell, his cheeks burning as the room remained silent. It felt like an eternity before the lecture resumed. He did everything physically possible to sink into his seat and vanish, the remainder of the lesson passing in a blur as his thoughts raged on. It wasn't that he questioned the Council, but an unease lingered within. Something in the back of his mind bothered him, like a pebble in his shoe—something he couldn't remember. The memory of his life before the Citadel felt clear, but as he searched for the answer in his psyche, anything critical he'd forgotten, he came up empty-handed.

Once the students were dismissed for lunch, Arlo stood and nudged Eli. "Let's go, man! I'm starving."

Eli remained in his seat, still timid from his scolding. "I'll meet you down there."

Arlo glanced at Darby, who was speaking with another recruit. "Don't push it, man."

"What do you mean, push it?" Eli asked. "All I did was ask a question."

"Apparently the wrong one."

"How can you ask the wrong question?" Eli stood, clenching his jaw. He was more upset than he'd care to admit.

"It doesn't matter. Just drop it."

"What, are we not allowed to ask questions? Aren't we supposed to learn?"

"We are, but you didn't ask a question, you argued with the Keeper. And we're here to learn how to fight with magic, not debate politics."

Eli sighed. "Yeah, you're right."

All the recruits shuffled to the lunchroom, bantering about the morning's lecture. But despite Eli's best efforts, he couldn't let go of the argument with Darby. He had questions about why the war had gone on so long—why there wasn't more being done to talk about peace. There were more rumors he'd heard, like one about the Citadel sabotaging a meeting, an offer to discuss peace, the Legion set up. People whispered that the Legion offered a talk of peace in earnest and were met with a bloodbath. Eli came here to fight for his people—his family—and he was loyal to his Nation. But that didn't mean he couldn't help find a diplomatic solution, or for the sake of the Nine Hells, ask a rotting question.

After lunch, the recruits were ushered out into a vast grassy plain behind the Citadel. It was beautiful in the afternoon light, the vast green expanse setting the stage for the breathtaking view of the Southern cliffs. The grass was trimmed short and extended all the way to the cliffside. Eli marveled at the Great Sea, shining a deep blue on the horizon to the South.

As the recruits crested the hill leading to the Practice Field, Eli noted a tall woman waiting for them. Clad in gray armor, she bore an engraved and bejeweled battle ax slung across her back. It was the most ornate weapon Eli had ever seen. Her black hair was only partially restrained, the rest falling gracefully to her shoulders.

"Recruits!" she shouted as they all gathered around. "My name is Captain Liora Evergreen. Welcome to the Practice Field!"

Her voice carried a steady confidence, complementing her commanding presence.

"This field is where the Proving and The Crucible will start, as well as be the location for weapons training. This field and those mountains," she said, pointing North toward the Ha'Negev Mountains, "is where you will be pushed to your limit. Your bodies broken, your wills tested. Keeper Darby will tell you Guardians are made in the Lecture Hall. I'm here to tell you that the battlefield is where true Guardians stand out."

A few smiles were shared.

"Today, we return to the basics of sparring. Many of you demonstrated adequate skill in your first exercise yesterday. However, we want to ensure we equal the playing field as much as possible."

*Thank the Heavens*

"These afternoon sessions will start with hand-to-hand combat, to minimize injuries, before progressing to training with weapons. How well you learn your fundamentals will greatly determine your rate of success. Believe me when I tell you, train as if your life depends on it."

Eli shifted, uncomfortable being reminded yet again that his life was at stake.

"For the last time, find a partner. Tomorrow you will choose your squadmates to practice with and follow the rest of the program." Evergreen smiled. "And try to relax. Today is about practicing the basics, not taking out your classmates."

Arlo elbowed Eli. "Good news for you, you could use some basics."

"Says the guy who's stuck with me as a partner," Eli rebutted with a grin. "Thanks for volunteering." Arlo laughed, but Eli felt the weight of Arlo's words. He did need to get better. And at the moment, Eli felt miles behind most of the recruits.

The afternoon was spent in the hot sun, throwing each other around. Captain Evergreen was eloquent and an excellent instructor. Eli was grateful for her oversight, soaking up any information he could get. By the end of practice, exhausted and aching from head to foot, Eli followed the mass of recruits to the mess hall once they were dismissed. Evergreen said their day was complete and they had the evening to themselves.

Eli waited in line for his food, the simple act of standing bringing its own challenge, while his stomach refused to stop rumbling. He prayed his body would acclimate quickly to the demands of the program. To his delight, supper was two bananas, roasted pork, and buttered bread, the very smell of which sent a wave of elation through him. Eli, Arlo, and Lara sat at the same table they found that first night, all of them diving into their meals among the clamor of the mess hall. Arlo had invited Maelyn to sit with them, but she declined. Evidently her comment about not coming here to make friends was spoken in earnest.

"Okay! It's official!" Arlo announced. "Evergreen's my favorite!"

Lara smiled. "Have we met all our instructors?"

"Yeah," Arlo said with his mouth full. "I overheard that Captains Renard and Evergreen are assigned specifically to oversee our program. Apart from Operatives who help with proctoring challenges, I think they and Darby are our faculty."

Eli said, "Good to know there aren't dozens of Captains ready to torture us." He winced as he massaged the knots forming in his neck and shoulders, rubbing them between bites of food. Arlo pointed to Eli with his spoon, leaning toward Lara.

"As you can see, while the Danon family is known for spotless rooms and luxurious suits, they are far from comfortable on the battlefield, developing muscle aches after only a short afternoon of combat training."

Eli glared at him, but Arlo winked.

"Lara," Eli said, "my sparring partner is a sadistic brute. Any ideas for a new one?"

"Sorry, I already got one," she said, chewing her fruit.

"Who is it?" Eli asked.

"Please don't say Sol," Arlo said.

"Or Soren," Eli added.

"Oh, don't even get me started," she said, looking over her shoulder. "Sol is a complete *Rai-pat*. When Evergreen told us to partner up, I grabbed the first person I could find. Some guy named Mernan. Nice guy, but said exactly two words to me the entire afternoon."

Arlo gasped in jest. "The horror."

Lara smiled, rolling her eyes. "Hey, speaking of which," she said, "do we get to choose which squad we're in?"

Arlo shrugged. "No idea."

Eli said, "I don't know why we wouldn't be able to, seeing as we were able to choose our own partners. I'd assume it's part of the strategy."

"To choose the right comrades?" Lara asked.

Eli nodded and gave a wry grin to Arlo. "You going to abandon me to Sol's team?"

Arlo laughed. "Fear not, brother."

Once they finished their food, Eli stood and turned in early, hoping for a better night of sleep. Arlo and Lara said goodnight, but remained at their table talking. Eli entered his bunkroom, still rubbing his neck, ready to lapse into a coma. But as he stepped up to his bunk, he froze.

His things had been moved—his blanket tossed around, his trunk opened and rifled through. He scanned his belongings, but everything was there. Nothing was taken. Scanning the bunkroom, he didn't see anyone loitering around, or anything that seemed out of place. And Arlo's things were untouched.

*Who would—*

*Shira*

She was sneaking around last night. She must have seen him in the corner, and—

*What? Rifled through my things as a warning? What was she doing last night anyway?*

Eli collected and reorganized his belongings, which was only a single outfit he wore to the Citadel and the clothing they had provided him. He didn't bring anything of value to be taken. As he laid in bed and night fell, he found himself wide awake, tossing and turning.

*What was she looking for? Was it even her*

*Why was she out last night? Maybe she just used the washroom, but then why act like an assassin*

Curiosity getting the best of him, he got out of bed with a huff and dressed, donning his tunic but leaving his armor. He crept out of the bunkroom amid the snoring and closed the door gently. There was no way of knowing if Shira would be out again tonight, or where she went. But he had questions, and if she went through his things, then he had every right to approach her about it.

As he paused in the common room, he saw nothing. Heard nothing. He walked over to the stairwell and peered down. Again, *nothing*. He was sure his previous nightmare awakened him about this time of night.

Eli descended the stairs onto the main level. The Operative on guard noticed him but returned to reading a book. Eli quickly checked the open space before entering the walkway. And there, across the distance, amid the dim light of the night, he saw a feminine figure with black hair.

He strode after her. Despite the scattered groups of individuals wandering about, the Citadel was unnervingly silent. They spoke in hushed tones, voices muffled as though afraid to disturb the quiet, while others patrolled in silence—eyes vigilant—carrying an unspoken tension. The walkway seemed colossal when vacant of its steady river of personnel. Eli's footsteps reverberated off the walls, making each uncomfortably loud, as if the tower itself was highlighting his presence. He hugged the inside wall, catching sight of Shira as she scurried further ahead, glancing around. He ducked behind a decorative clay jar as she peered behind, heart thumping.

*What is she doing*

He chanced a look around the corner, only to see the looming door to the library close with a slight creak. He jogged over to the extensive library, pausing at the threshold to listen. Nothing. He opened the door, a grating high-pitched squeak accompanying the movement. He grimaced.

*Why the library*

Eli stepped into the vast expanse of the Citadel library. While the mage stones provided some blue light, the massive space was mostly enshrined in darkness. A table near the entrance held dozens of candles, lanterns, and matches. Leather bound books and scrolls filled countless shelves, all organized and in their proper place. There were tables set up in various locations for reading, as well as small nooks, utilizing every possible space to hold more literature.

As Eli scanned the room, meandering through the maze of shelves, he was in awe of the overwhelming number of books. But upon closer inspection, there were layers of dust on the shelves—as if they hadn't been disturbed in years.

*I assumed the Keepers tended to this place*

He picked up one of the dusty tomes.

*History of Zentari Literature*

Eli would have given anything to have this collection at his fingertips growing up. He imagined reading the tomes, mastering the knowledge within, spending his days devouring information. He could feel the leather bindings under his fingers, smell the parchment and ink—

"Looking for a bedtime story?"

Eli jumped at the voice behind him. Shira stood between the bookshelves, arms crossed. His heart raced at her presence—and her scowl. He swallowed. "I could ask you the same thing."

"It's not your concern what I do with my time." Her voice was stern—threatening. But he held his ground.

"It is my business when you go through my things," he said, replacing the book on the shelf. He was guessing, and maybe it was only an excuse to find her. But nevertheless, her behavior piqued his interest.

"I know nothing about that," she quipped, lifting her chin. "And the next time you follow me, I won't give you a warning." She turned and strode away.

"Hey, wait," he called, but she disappeared into the maze of shelves.

# Chapter Eight

W hat does he want?" Eva asked, panic rising in her chest. It wasn't that Drax had sent for Lucas—it was the look on Lucas's face. She had seen it before, and the memory beckoned a slumbering terror.

"I don't know," he said, organizing some papers as he stood to leave. Eva caught the twitch in his lips—the aversion of his gaze.

"You're lying," she snapped, sitting up to lace her boots.

"For rot's sake, you don't know everything."

"Like Hells, I can tell when you're lying. What's going on?"

"Well, you're wrong this time," he muttered, striding out of the tent.

"I'm coming with you," Eva said, still leaning over and tying her boots.

"Just stay here Marie," he scolded. "I'll be back."

She finished and scrambled out, tying up her hair as she marched after him. Falling behind as Lucas jogged to the Lieutenant, she was halfway to Drax's tent when Maya came up behind her.

"Hey, girl!" Maya said. "I was just looking for you. I checked your tent, but you weren't there."

"Sorry. I'll explain later," Eva said, walking faster.

Maya followed. "What's wrong?"

"Nothing."

"Oh, please."

"It's nothing. Lucas was just called to Drax's tent."

Maya's brow wrinkled. "For what?"

"I don't know!" Eva barked, stifling her anxiety. She couldn't wait for him to be promoted. Or kicked out of the Legion. She caught Lucas entering Drax's tent, and grunted as she remained outside.

"It's probably nothing," Maya encouraged. Eva remained silent. "Look, I'll be right back."

Eva sighed as Maya jogged off. It was agonizing to wait, and Eva nearly wore holes in her boots as she paced. The Lieutenant's guard kept giving her stern glares, but she returned them with her own. She wanted desperately to eavesdrop, to figure out whatever Lucas was hiding, but knew she would be caught. Maya walked up to her after half an hour, returning from her errand. "Anything yet?"

"No," Eva said.

"What's got you so riled up?" Maya asked. "He talks to Drax all the time."

Eva's mind wandered to the last time she saw that apathy in Lucas's eyes, ten years ago—

*Eva's heart pounded. Lucas had never been invited to see her father. He was barely tolerated in their home. When she was told Lucas was ushered inside, that her father asked for him specifically, her heart leaped into her throat. Not even Glorana knew what was going on.*

*She waited, wringing her hands outside her father's study. She tried to listen at the door, but the thick wood prevented any audible voices from getting through.*

*She shouldn't have snuck out again. What if this was her next punishment? What if her father took away the only thing she cherished?*

*After an eternity of waiting, the door opened momentarily, and Lucas slid through. Without meeting her gaze, he walked past her to the front door.*

*"Lucas, what's wrong?" She pleaded. His eyes remained glued to the floor. "Lucas, talk to me!"*

*"It's fine, Marie. I'll see you later."*

*"What did my father say?"*

*"Nothing," he spat.*

*"What did he want?"*

*"Nothing!" he said. "Just leave me alone."*

*"Wait! I'm sorry!" she pleaded, his sudden apathy throwing blades into her heart. "Did I do something?" She grabbed his arm, but he yanked it free.*

*"Stop!" he said. His eyes finally met hers, and held a sternness, a cold distance—and a deep turmoil within. "Not everything is about you. I said leave me alone."*

*He turned and stormed out without another word. She stood, frozen, a cold dreadful terror gripping her chest. Lucas left. Her best friend. Her only friend. Gone. Tears wet her face as she sprinted to her father's office, pounding on the door.*

*"What did you do?" she screamed. "You can't do this! You can't take him—"*

*The office door was thrown open, and her father filled the doorway.*

She couldn't remember what happened after that. All she recalled was waking up the next morning with a limp that lasted a month. Eva and Maya turned in unison as Lucas emerged from the tent. A pit formed in her stomach as her eyes met his.

*Bleeding Hells*

Lucas stiffened as he noticed them waiting. "Back to your tents, both of you. That's an order." He walked around them, pushing Eva aside as she stepped in front of him.

Maya said, "Yes, Chief Miller."

But Eva chased after him, grabbing his arm. "Hey!"

"You're out of line, Swordsman! Return to your bunk as ordered!" Lucas stood his ground, but his gaze shifted to Drax's tent behind her.

*Drax is listening*

She didn't hide her defiance, but she got the sense this was a fight she would not win. "As you say, Chief," she whispered, every ounce of anger evident in her voice.

She shoulder-checked him as she left—blood boiling—marching for her tent. He'd rarely ever raised his voice to her, only when he was truly rattled. And she knew his intentions, trusted he was probably protecting her, as he had ten years ago. But to Hells with his intentions. She didn't need his rotting protection, and it wasn't fair for him to hide it from her.

Eva was quickly back in her tent, pacing like a rabid animal.

*What in the Hells could it be*

She grunted as she slammed her fists down on her cot, throwing her blanket on the ground. The sharp and creeping reach of panic gripped her mind, and she pushed against it—another battle within herself. One she had fought countless times. As if by her father's design, she felt as though she were constantly balancing a tightrope over a dark expanse, praying not to fall. Though she hadn't seen her father since she left, his reach, his influence, was still deeply embedded in her psyche.

Maya stepped into her tent and Eva spun around.

"I thought he ordered you to your bunk," Eva snipped.

Maya shrugged. "I guess I'm learning from the best." She strolled over and picked up Eva's blanket. "And he ordered me to follow you." Eva scoffed, running her hands through her hair. She took a deep breath and began whispering.

"Day thirty, Winter's Touch." She closed her eyes as she grounded herself. "Day eleven, Harvest's Moon. Day four, Midsummer's Eve. Day nineteen, Autumn's Sigh."

"Day twenty-two." Maya finished. "Spring's Promise." Eva turned around, staring at Maya sitting on her cot. "I've heard you recite them enough times. What are they?"

Maya patted the cot. Eva took a deep breath, sitting with a slump.

"They're my most peaceful memories," Eva admitted, picking at her nails. "My ninth birthday. The day I met Lucas. The day I escaped and joined the Legion. The day I first felt safe from my father. And the day I vowed to survive."

"There are only five?" Maya asked in astonishment, but shifted the subject given Eva's seriousness. "Look, Eva, you don't even know what it is. Just wait and let him tell you."

"You don't get it!" Eva said, regret clinging to the heels of her outburst. She held her head in her hands, the rebellious strands of white hair flowing down in gentle waves from her loose bun.

"Is this just another panic attack?" Maya asked. "Or do you know what he and Drax spoke about?"

"I don't know," Eva mumbled into her hands, wrangling her thoughts.

*Calm down*

"Girl, take a breath. Lucas is the best warrior I know, other than you. Besides, you're assuming it's something bad. He probably got reprimanded for telling you more privileged information or you sleeping in his tent, which was *stupid* by the way. Hells knows Drax has it out for you."

Eva lifted her head, remembering Keinen.

*Rotting sell out*

"Yeah, probably," she breathed. Heavens help her if she got him in trouble. Lucas already warned her that her actions would eventually catch up to her, but she never thought he would be the one punished.

*Stop assuming things*

She stood, trying to nurse the insatiable desire to keep moving.

"Would you sit down?" Maya scolded. "I know you'd rather punch or stab something, but I'm fresh out of practice dummies, so for Hell's sake, just take a minute."

Eva gave her a glare but complied again with an exaggerated sigh.

"Lucas gets shipped out all the time," Maya said. "Hells, he gets orders every few hours. What happened that makes this so different?"

"His eyes," Eva whispered. Maya furrowed her brow. Eva clarified once she saw her confusion. "My father hated me befriending someone of another social class. So, he waited until I broke the rules and decided to punish me by forbidding Lucas to come see me. My father invited him to the house, and I never found out what he threatened him with, but Lucas left with that same look in his eyes. I didn't see him for six months."

"Well, that's harsh, but you were kids."

"No, Maya, you don't get it, you had siblings. You grew up always having someone, but Lucas is the only person I've ever had that's been mine—that's been there for me. He never failed to visit, to get me a birthday gift, even if he made it with his own hands. My father would have the maid lock me in the house, or my room if there were guests, for days on end. You don't understand that level of isolation. I still wake up with panic attacks having to sleep in this cramped tent, even after eight years."

"Woah," Maya said. "I knew you had those attacks, and I knew your dad was cruel but—days?"

Eva nodded. "And he's done worse than that." Eva folded the memories of that time away, tucking them back into the recesses of her mind.

Maya placed a hand on her shoulder. "Eva. Do not tell me he—"

"It's fine Maya," Eva said. "Please don't make me say it." Eva felt her emotions numb and fade at the edges—refusing to face the haunting memories.

Maya's eyes widened, grasping the gravity of her father's sin. "Couldn't your mom protect you? You never talk about her."

"She died," Eva muttered.

Maya flinched. "Eva, you never told me that. I'm so sorry."

Eva shrugged. "I never knew her. Nothing to talk about."

Maya bit her lip. "Why would your father do that to you?"

Eva was still, having asked herself that question countless times. "I don't know."

"Okay, fine," Maya said. "So, Lucas means the world to you, and your father deserves to burn at the stake a hundred times over. But this is war, Eva. Lucas is going to have to leave at some point."

"I know. It doesn't mean I have to like it."

It was a moment before Maya spoke, and Eva was ever grateful for her friend's ability to lift her spirits.

"Honestly, the way you talk about being friends but then hug each other like that, I'd swear you were getting married next week," Maya said, raising her eyebrows.

Eva grinned. "There was a time, when we were younger, that I would've said yes. But something changed."

"What? Joining the Legion? You did volunteer at what, fourteen?"

"Yeah, the day after my birthday. But no, it wasn't that."

"What then?"

Eva's brow knitted, searching for the right explanation. "I . . . had a dream," she mumbled. Maya burst out laughing. Eva didn't join, but smiled at the sound, her cheeks burning.

Maya cupped her hands over her mouth. "I'm sorry. Sorry. Go on."

"I'm not going to tell you if you're just going to laugh!"

"No no, I won't. I won't!" Maya assured, clamping down on her giggling, sucking in her lips.

"I dreamt about someone else, okay? The dreams happened on and off for years, and were so real and vivid, the feelings were so strong, I just never saw Lucas the same."

"Rotting Hells, that's a bloody good dream," Maya said with a breathy laugh.

Eva's attention drifted. "It never felt like a dream. More like a promise. Like I'd finally found the other half of my soul, not just a hand to hold. He's everything I'm not, everything I want to be, seeing all of me without asking me to change. He doesn't shelter me, but stands alongside, ready to fight."

Eva looked at Maya, who still held a playful grin.

"You dumped your childhood guy for a dream!"

"Oh, shut up!" Eva said, unable to help the smile pulling at her mouth despite her face burning. "And he was never *my* guy!"

"It gives a new meaning to 'man of your dreams'!" Maya was now uncontrollably laughing, tears welling in her eyes. Eva sat on her bed with a smirk, her cheeks rosy, waiting for her friend to stop. Maya wiped her eyes, her laughter gently abating.

"Well, don't stop now," Maya said. "Please regale me with how Sir Dreamy looked."

Eva glared at her. "Not on your life."

"You know he loves you, right?" Maya said finally. "You're not that out of touch, I hope."

The weight of her words fell on Eva's shoulders. "Yeah, I know."

"I don't get it, Lucas is literally perfect. He's got a perfect face, a gorgeous smile, a well-established career, and a great sense of humor. Any girl should fawn over his attention."

Eva twitched at her words, her eyes narrowing at her friend.

"See! And you're immediately jealous!" Maya shouted, pointing her finger.

Eva huffed. "He's my best friend, I'm allowed to be jealous over who's interested in him."

"Trust me, the way he looks at you, you're all he sees," Maya said. "Why don't you give it a shot?"

"Other than the fact that he's my superior officer?"

"Don't give me that boar spit, you've never cared about breaking the rules."

Eva scoffed, fiddling with her hands. "I tried, okay?"

Maya wrinkled her brow. "When?"

"A few years ago."

"Like, you dated or tried something more intimate?" Maya asked, a devious grin on her face. Eva glared.

"No, like I tried to see us together. I thought about it, imagined our future, was intentional about writing letters and spending more time with him. I almost kissed him. But whatever, it didn't work."

"You act like you failed a mission."

Eva sighed, fixing her disheveled hair. "And your point is?" she asked.

"I'm saying don't give up," Maya encouraged. "You can't force love, but come on girl, what else do you want? That guy in your dreams might be perfect, but he doesn't exist."

"Yeah. Maybe," she said.

"What did you feel when you guys kissed?"

Eva's cheeks burned. "We never did!"

"Come on! You're telling me in all the years you've been friends—"

"No," Eva said sternly. "I've never—" She caught herself—too late.

"Wait." Maya paused, narrowing her eyes again with a grin. "Have you never kissed anyone?" Eva folded her arms, trying to think of a sarcastic response—but the moment passed. "Bleed the rotting Hells, the infamous white-haired devil has never kissed a boy," she whispered with a smile.

"Be quiet or I'll kick you out!" Eva spat as Maya giggled again. "Tell me your story then! Let's hear it!"

"Well, now that you ask, I do have someone in mind. I didn't dream him into reality, but he seems nice. He's way out in Mar'Hek right now. I haven't seen him in two months."

"You wench, you've been holding out on me," Eva said playfully, whacking Maya's shoulder. "What's his name?"

"Brok."

"Brok?" Eva wrinkled her nose.

"Oh, be quiet. Don't even, *Lady Dream*."

As the evening dragged on, Eva was increasingly grateful for her friend and the company they shared. With each moment that passed, Eva's fear lessened. After Maya left for the night, with the sun nearly disappeared under the horizon, Eva lit her lantern and laid down. She drifted in and out of a fitful sleep. Every insignificant sound broke her slumber, from rustling outside her tent to distant voices bantering about useless things.

Unsure of the time, and unable to fall back asleep, she strapped on her boots and stepped outside. Apart from the steady footsteps of the patrols, the outpost was otherwise quiet. Most lanterns had been extinguished, the only light coming from a quaint fire set at the center of camp. A few warriors stood around swapping stories, though Eva didn't care to join. She walked out of Yaqar, giving the sentry a signal she would return soon. She strolled up the hill to the North, standing at the crest, gazing into the clearing to the Northeast.

With a deep breath, she listened to the hushed turbulence of the gentle breeze, and the long grass' reply as it swayed with its movement. Spending a moment outside was always a way to remind herself of the greater whole. To hear and feel so many different things—living things—helped to ground her to the world. It reminded her that no matter what else was going on, the rest of Adiel continued to move and grow—promising a future.

Her concentration was broken as footsteps approached behind her.

"Doing some late-night brooding?" Lucas asked. He stepped up next to her, grazing her shoulder. She kept facing on the shadows.

"Helps to clear my head."

"If I didn't know you better, I'd say you were going for the mysterious warrior girl thing," he teased, watching her for a response.

"Just tell me, Lucas," she muttered. "Please."

He sighed. "I just got done speaking with Drax about it. When I got the orders, I was still trying to process the entire thing. I didn't want to say anything until I had said my peace, hoping it would change the plan."

*No apology*

"And?"

"After you and Maya left, I sorted through a plan, a counter argument. I went back and talked to Drax. Tried to convince him . . ." His voice trailed. "Long story short, I didn't. You know how well Drax listens to his subordinates."

"And what did Drax decide?" Eva turned to him, the rock in her gut returning once she saw the fear in his face.

"I'm leading a raid. We're striking Heika." Eva's heart stopped. "We leave tonight," he whispered, the seriousness of the moment deepening the creases in his face.

*Heika. The outpost to the South*

*It's a fortress*

"How many are you bringing?" she asked.

He hesitated. "Thirty-five warriors."

"That's suicide! That isn't even close to enough!"

"Drax doesn't think so," Lucas said, holding his hand up. "If we bring too many the garrison may be spotted, and we lose the element of surprise."

Eva balled her fists. "Why?" she asked, pushing against her returning panic. "Why now?"

"I can't tell you all the—"

"Spare me the lecture and just tell me!"

His jaw clenched, but she wouldn't yield this time.

"I'm not supposed—"

"For Hell's sake, Lucas, do you care about me or not?" It was an unfair question—manipulative. But she saw the answer in his softening gaze.

"Because of the withdrawal of Zentari Warriors along the front Drax thinks it's better to strike first than to wait for them to show their hand. Scouts say Zentari warriors were pulled from Heika for something, Guardians included. The outpost went from a hundred Operatives plus Guardians, to a fraction of that. It seems the last thing the Zentari expect right now is an attack. Drax volunteered me to lead a targeted, unplanned strike against the outpost and pitched the idea all the way to Ashdod. It was approved."

Her thoughts reeled as she clenched her fists.

"Who's assigned to go with you?" His silence was answer enough. "I'm coming," she said, turning to leave.

Lucas grabbed her arm and pulled her back. "You're not on the mission!"

"I'll come anyway!" she shouted, pulling from his grip.

"Then Drax will have what he needs to arrest you and charge you with dereliction," Lucas argued. "Evalynn, there is nothing you can do."

"I don't care!"

"You'll get me reprimanded!" he said, which was enough to make her stop. "I already asked to bring you along, as our best warrior, and he refused. He threatened to strip me of my rank if I told you."

She stood, grinding her teeth and shifting her weight. The air felt thin as she breathed against her panic.

*I was right*

"If he wants to annihilate Heika then he should march over there and do it himself!"

Lucas sighed. "You know as well as I do the price of joining the Legion."

*Then this is my fault*

Eva wanted to give into the hopelessness, the despair pulling at her, beckoning to drag her down into that darkness below. Her protective instincts for Lucas ran deeper than her own sense of self-preservation. She clamped her eyes shut for a moment, refusing to yield to her emotions.

"He can't," she insisted.

"He can," Lucas said. "He's the Lieutenant. We're warriors, Marie. We follow orders."

"Refuse to go," she argued with a stern look.

"I can't," he scoffed.

"You can! You tell him—"

"It was an *order*, Evalynn!" he yelled. "Regardless of how you feel, I will not break my vows as a Legion warrior. I'm already breaking direct orders by telling you, do *not* ask me to violate any more."

Eva accepted the jab, reluctantly. She stared at him—her best friend—and did everything to force her panic back into the pit she created for it so many years ago. She prayed to the Heavens that fate would not claim the greatest friend she was ever granted.

Lucas stood motionless, waiting.

"Why do I get the feeling this is the end?" she whispered.

His posture fell at the impossible question. "I don't know."

"Come back," she demanded.

"You know I can't promise that." A wrenching fear surged through her as she watched his eyes water.

"Yes. You can," she pressed.

He stepped closer, gently grabbing her hand. "Marie."

"Say it."

His eyes flickered between hers. "All I can promise you is that as long as I draw breath, I will find you."

Within an hour, Eva watched Lucas ride out of Yaqar with his unit. She didn't wait a moment longer, heading straight for Drax's tent, seizing the opportunity now that Lucas couldn't stop her. Standing at the entrance, she spoke as calmly as she could.

"Permission to enter, Lieutenant Drax, sir?"

"Granted, Swordsman."

Drax was seated behind his wooden desk, working into the late hours of the night. He kept his eyes on his scrolls, scribbling notes, as she stepped up and stood at attention.

"Sir, I request to be assigned under Chief Lucas Miller for his current mission to Heika."

Drax stopped and sighed.

"Of course he told you." He set down his quill, the lack of sleep and toll of his position evident in every line on his tanned face. "I'm too tired to reprimand you for the intrusion into privileged information, Swordsman Katz. Request denied. Besides, I believe the Chief in question has already left."

Eva bit down hard to keep her defiance at bay—withhold the objections on her tongue—as her eyes danced with his.

"Why?" she asked, quickly adding, "Sir?"

Drax scoffed.

"In all my years serving in the Aniyan Legion I have never met another Swordsman as talented, yet as unruly as you, Evalynn Katz. You know *exactly* why I am refusing that request. Dismissed."

She stayed, her jaw clenching.

"But—"

"*Dismissed*!" he shouted, erupting from his chair.

She didn't move.

"Oh, I am finished dealing with you, girl." His voice was a low, threatening growl. "Swordsman Katz, you are hereby assigned to patrol duty at Manoach. You are not to interfere with this assignment, nor speak of it to anyone, or you *will* be tried for insurrection and treason. And if I hear that you've stepped *one* foot out of line, I promise you, I don't care who your father is, I will personally strip you of your rank and place in the Legion. *Is. That. Clear?*"

Her heart rate spiked, remaining planted. She should leave and take the assignment. If Drax arrested her now, then even if Lucas came back—

The alarm bell sounded, its deep bellow vibrating in her chest. Their eyes widened, and Eva straightened.

Yaqar was under attack.

# Chapter Nine

E li caught a glance of Shira as the recruits gathered in the Sparring Hall to start the day's events, but she disappeared into the crowd. He assumed her threat was hollow, but he had to admit, he couldn't stop thinking about her.

"All right! Listen up!" Renard announced. "There are two items on the agenda for today. First, you will be choosing your squadmates in groups of four. The decision of who is in your squad is up to you, and I would strongly recommend choosing wisely. These will be your partners for the remainder of the program."

A wave of murmurs spread through the room, before growing silent as Captain Renard addressed them. Arlo elbowed Eli with a grin.

"Second, you will undergo the Proving today, the first challenge, which takes place just outside on the Southern Cliffs. Whether you succeed depends on your teamwork and your physical resilience. Choose your squadmates with intention. The Crucible is only six weeks away and will be a greater challenge than what you face today. Even your success at the Rune Forge may depend on the comrades you choose to walk beside."

"During the Proving today and all future events, you will be closely monitored and judged by your faculty and peers. Your successes and failures, areas in which you shine as a recruit, as well as any glaring weaknesses, will have a great effect on your continued service in the military, *after* graduation."

The room stirred.

"Additionally, throughout your training here in the Citadel, each of you will be evaluated for a position of coveted squad leader. Because only one leader is needed per squad, that means only ten of you have that distinguished privilege. If you want to stand out as one of the best, be mindful that we are watching. Who is chosen as squad leader is up to your faculty and not open for discussion. These positions will be chosen before the Crucible, so you have until then to impress us."

A thrill of excitement overcame Eli.

*Just another reason to give this everything*

He was more than willing to lead and stepping up to the challenge was why he came here in the first place.

"Is anything unclear?" Renard asked, giving the recruits a moment.

No responses.

"Here's how squad selection works. We start with one recruit naming another. The chosen recruit can accept and join the squad, then pick the next person, or challenge the choice. If challenged, the original recruit can either accept the challenge or choose someone else. If a challenge occurs, a match is held, and the winner decides if the chosen recruit joins."

Renard opened his scroll. "The first name is: Soren Mitchell!"

The room shifted toward the first recruit. Eli recalled Soren sparring on their first day. The man demonstrated exceptional skill, but also satisfaction in making his opponents bleed. Something about him made the hair on Eli's neck raise, reminding him of—

"Sol Richter!" Soren yelled.

*Speaking of which*

Sol's voice boomed near the back wall. "Accepted! Kairah Richter!"

*Interesting. I wonder if there are any other siblings here*

"Accepted! Arlo Miller!"

Eli glanced at his new friend. Arlo shook his head, his expression making it clear—*not on their life.*

"Challenge!" Arlo responded.

A beat.

"Fjord Orin!"

Eli exhaled in relief. As the name selection continued, Arlo was called out three other times—his challenges never met. Evidently his skills were not unnoticed, given Eli barely contributed to their first bout. Renard called out the first name of the next squad.

"Laranna Nightingale!"

Her response came before the echoes of Renard's voice faded.

"Arlo Miller!"

He smiled and winked at Eli.

"Accepted! Elijah Danon!"

"Accepted!" Eli shouted. "Shira Weiss!" His heart thundered, having spoken the words before considering the implications. Arlo gave him a quizzical look, probably assuming he would choose Maelyn.

"Challenge!" A voice rang out.

"Challenge!" Eli responded, palms growing sweaty. He smiled, despite knowing he was likely about to be horribly injured. Shira stalked her way to Captain Renard, and Eli was unable to remove his nervous grin as her piercing gaze locked into his.

Arlo whispered in his ear. "You're dead, man."

Renard directed them to a practice mat away from the main group. Eli and Shira faced each other while the others resumed the selection process. The Operative acting as proctor spoke with indifference.

"You know the rules by now. Unconscious, tap out, or dead—go."

Eli's heart pounded as he wiped his sweaty palms on his pants. Shira's expression was difficult to read, but the slight furrow in her brow and the rigid set of her jaw made it clear—she was far from pleased he chose her. Eli tried to relax, shaking his hands before bringing them up in fists, stepping on the balls of his feet as they circled each other.

"Why don't you want to join our squad?" he asked.

"This isn't a game," she hissed, arms relaxed at her sides.

"I agree." Eli lunged forward with a right hook. Shira dodged the blow with ease, grabbing his arm and throwing him down with his own momentum. Eli landed face first but scrambled to his feet. "But that's not why I selected you."

Her eyes narrowed. "You don't even know me."

Eli threw a series of punches, unrefined and sloppy. Moves that would lay out a drunken man but meant very little to someone familiar with fighting. The only advantages he possessed were his size and Shira's curiosity—his ability to keep her distracted from killing him.

He spoke between grunts. "None of us know each other. That's the point."

"What's the point?" she asked, landing a jab to his ribs. He leaped back out of her reach.

"Everything about this program is a test. We're expected to choose squad-mates to help us survive, told it could make all the difference, when none of us know each other."

He threw another punch, but she stepped behind him, grabbing his arm behind his back. "Then why me? What do you want?"

He grimaced as pain shot up his arm. He tried to relax his muscles to prevent his shoulder from dislocating.

"To survive this program. To live beyond Guardian training." He grunted through clenched teeth. Shira wrenched his arm tighter. Eli groaned as she kicked the back of his leg, bringing him down on one knee.

"That's not enough. There's more to this program than simply surviving it."

"I know," he pressed, twisting and swinging his leg around to catch her off balance. She released his arm, jumping back. "Why are you here? Why did you sign up?"

He held back, catching his breath. His left arm throbbed, but he brushed off the pain. Her response came with a feigned jab and a knee to his stomach. An elbow to the center of his back pushed him forward onto his chest, face down on the mat. Pain shot up his left arm again, radiating into his shoulder and neck.

"You clearly know how to fight," he said, grimacing. "And I saw you out late the last few nights. You seem to be looking for something." He couldn't see her reaction, but the increased pressure on his arm told him she heard him.

"Maybe we can help each other." He grunted. His vision was turning black. "I won't survive without someone to teach me how to fight, and I could help you—" He couldn't speak through the pain any longer, and he couldn't tap. He was going to black out, before the pain in his arm ceased. Eli gasped, rolling onto his back, cradling his tingling limb. Shira stood above him, the intensity in her eyes still present, but he saw the results of his efforts—curiosity.

She stepped back as he stood, guarding his aching shoulder. He didn't bother continuing the fight—she won. But he never expected to best her. He only wanted her attention, in the same way she ensnared his own from the moment he saw her. And now that he stood under her gaze, he found himself desperate to know the swirling thoughts behind her piercing indigo eyes.

He was still awaiting a response when she spun, knocking him out with a kick to the head.

Eli woke to the sight of the medical ward ceiling, his head pounding as light filled his vision. He sat up, the pain in his head flaring, his vision spinning. Closing his eyes, he waited for the world to level. Sitting on the edge of the bed, overriding his body's protests, he noticed he was still dressed in his brown and black leathers.

*Wonder if I missed the Proving*

Eli stood on shaking muscles, gripping the bed frame as a rush of dizziness came over him. He pulled back the curtain of his medical bay to find the ward empty—and quiet. He headed for the door, shifting unsteadily between steps.

"Sir Danon!" Nazzat exclaimed, rushing to him, her red silk scarf flowing behind her. She held his shoulders and assessed him. He smiled at her welcoming face.

"I'm all right," he assured. "Just a bit dizzy."

"Be silent. Follow my finger," she said, moving it in front of his face. She stared intently into his eyes, covering one then the other with her hand.

"Squeeze my fingers," she instructed, placing two fingers in both of his hands. He complied.

"Are you nauseous?"

"No."

"Feeling faint?"

"A little."

"Trouble seeing?"

"I'm all right," he said, grinning. She stepped back, apparently satisfied.

"I do wish they'd find ways to train recruits without sending all of you to my infirmary or the grave."

"It's the only way to become a Guardian," he said, though he agreed.

"Surely there's a less violent way to bring forth inner magic."

"Apparently none that they've found."

*Or none that proved useful in war time*

"Besides," he continued, "magic isn't enough. Guardians need combat training as well if we're to win this war."

"I know," she said, her face falling. He wondered how many wounded or dead recruits she treated over the years. Before he could ask, Arlo came barreling through the door.

"Hey man!" Arlo said with a smile, breathing heavily. "You're awake! And just in time! We need you for the Proving!"

Nazzat's eyes grew wide.

"Most certainly not!" she protested, lifting her chin. Eli smiled and placed a hand on her shoulder.

"I'll be fine. I'm feeling better. And I know just who to see if I get into trouble."

Nazzat opened her mouth to speak, but stomped off in disapproval.

"Okay, now that we have mom's permission, let's go!" Arlo said.

Eli squinted as they stepped onto the practice field and into the sunlight, the brightness reigniting the ache in his skull. The recruits were gathered near the cliff's edge, most facing the ocean below. Arlo led Eli to where Lara waited.

"You didn't miss much," Arlo said, a spring in his step. "Renard brought us to the cliffs after we finished squadding up. Evergreen's judging the Proving though. I know you took a blow to the head, but we need four people for this."

"What's the challenge?" Eli asked, trying to keep up with Arlo's long stride, struggling to keep his balance against the lightheadedness.

"It's a team exercise," Arlo responded. "The squad is chained together, and we scale the cliff down to the water and back."

Eli's heart sputtered. "We're chained together?"

"With belts. It's just a climbing exercise. Oh, and there are three buckets linked to the chain, between us. We have to fill the buckets with water and return them at least half full. Otherwise, we start again."

Eli stopped. Arlo walked a few feet before he noticed.

"Start again?" Eli asked. "From the top of the cliff?"

"Yeah, that's what Evergreen said." Arlo nodded, appearing far too relaxed.

"Arlo, do you know how high the Cliffs of Longing are?"

Arlo thought for a moment and shrugged. "I didn't get a good look."

Eli's eyes darkened. "Get a look."

Pushing past the crowd of recruits, Eli and Arlo tiptoed to the edge. A rush of humid and salty air rode up the cliffside, tousling their hair as they watched the waves beat the rocks below. Jagged stones jutted out from the cliff face, potentially serving as hand holds for the climb, but appeared as sharp as daggers. Eli breathed a sigh of relief. This section of the cliffs wasn't nearly as high as others he'd read about.

"I see what you mean about the height," Arlo mused.

"This is better than I thought," Eli said. "They're over three thousand feet in some places."

"Well, this can't be more than a hundred feet here. Plus, we don't need to reach the bottom. Only get the buckets filled. And we have each other!"

A team of four was already half-way down, creeping closer to the crashing sea.

"How many squads have gone?" Eli asked.

"This is the second," Lara said, coming to stand beside Eli.

"Aeron's squad finished already?" Arlo asked. "How'd they do?"

Lara's face was grim. "They fell."

Eli then noticed how quiet the rest of the recruits were, the heaviness of that first failure settling between them. Four recruits were dead in a matter of moments. Counting Orion, already five of the initial hundred were gone.

*How many of us are going to be left by the end of this thing*

He noticed the pile of extra chains, belts, and buckets nearby—hollowing his stomach.

"Who's going now?" Eli asked, closing his eyes, willing his headache to cease.

"Hard to tell from here," Arlo said, crouching down, squinting at the recruits scaling the cliff.

"Maelyn's in this group," Lara said.

Eli remembered their first night in the dining hall and her refusal of friendship. But if this was the challenge, the last thing Maelyn could do was finish it by herself.

"How do we help?" he asked.

"I don't think we can," Lara said.

"Whoo! Go Maelyn! You can do this!" Arlo shouted. Eli looked at him like he'd lost his mind, among other recruits. Arlo just smiled. "Everyone needs a champion." His signature smirk was plastered on his face as he faced the cliff. "Give it your all, Maelyn!"

To Eli's surprise, another voice joined.

"You got this Rowan!"

It didn't take long for the onshore winds to carry their whoops, hoots and hollers.

Maelyn's forearms burned as she gripped the rock, her fingers bleeding from the sharpened edges of the stones. She was doing well, keeping her breathing steady and her weight on her legs, but one of her *squadmates* was shaking like a newborn Venith.

*Squad*

It was ridiculous. Guardians didn't operate in squads. She could do this by herself—no problem. On her own she would be half-way back to the top by now. Instead, she was tethered to three other strangers, her life literally in their slippery, bloodied hands.

Maelyn glanced up the cliff face. She thought she may have heard voices, but the roar of the waves crashing and wind gusting drowned it out. She and her teammates descended in a horizontal line: Esme to her immediate left, Rowan to her right, and Fenner to her far right. While Maelyn had limited interactions with Esme and Rowan, Fenner was a complete unknown. He was Esme's choice, and Maelyn didn't know why. The guy was scrawny, timid, and seemed barely old enough to be here.

Maelyn would have preferred stronger squadmates, which was why she chose Rowan. But at least she wasn't paired with Elijah. His physical ineptitude was enough to make her dismiss him, but his arrogance and need to ask questions made him thoroughly unlikeable. Arlo could hold his own on the sparring mat, but couldn't go two minutes without cracking a joke. Lara had the skill, but not the discipline.

Esme already demonstrated her physical capabilities, essentially taking out both opponents herself in that first sparring match. And she didn't play around like Arlo did. Esme quickly dispatched them with lethal efficiency. With more brawn than half the male recruits, she could probably scale this cliff with Maelyn on her back. She also bore a striking resemblance to Captain Evergreen.

Rowan's movements were steady, but Maelyn could see the subtle shaking in his arms. Carrying his muscular frame was a disadvantage in this challenge. He already demonstrated a temper, but he wasn't useless. He was aggressive and didn't hesitate to rush in—hesitation kills. Fenner was a lost cause.

*If he pulls us into the ocean I'll drown him myself*

The four continued their steady descent. None of them spoke, waiting to see who stepped up as the leader. Maelyn normally wouldn't hesitate, but she was being judicious. She knew better than to blindly paint a target on her back, especially given death was a very real part of the program. And she'd never admit it, but her hands were weakening—muscles trembling. Clinging to a cliff's edge, chained to three near-strangers, was a test of will as much as strength.

Maelyn placed her foot on a narrow rock—too brittle. It crumbled into the churning sea. She gripped harder, scrambling for a new foothold. Blood-slick hands made the rock slippery. Adrenaline surged as her heart pounded.

*Rotting Hells*

Esme raised her eyebrows in a silent question. Maelyn nodded, insulted she was asking.

*I'm fine. Worry about yourself*

As they neared the roaring sea, Maelyn shouted above the waves, "Everyone! Climb down until the larger waves reach the buckets! We'll wait for them to be filled and then climb back!"

Esme nodded.

Rowan said, "If we climb down farther, they'll fill faster! Less time to get knocked off and fall!"

"Assuming you don't get your rotting Nines sucked out to sea, yeah!" Maelyn argued. Rowan glared but said nothing. The constant spray of ocean water and gusts of wind robbed Maelyn's body heat. The water crashed across the rock with unimaginable force, sending a shudder through the stone. As Maelyn reached for her next foothold, she realized how slippery and smooth the rocks here were.

*How in the Nine do we get close enough*

Movement to her right caught her attention. She turned just in time to see Fenner slip and plummet down to the sea.

# Chapter Ten

Whatever animosity Drax and Eva shared vanished in the moment. They leaped into battle mode, the alarms reverberating through the camp.

"Get to the Southern perimeter!" Drax ordered, drawing his sword from his side. Eva nodded and sprinted out of the tent.

As she bolted across camp, she was thrown into a sea of chaos. Warriors, both Swordsmen and Chiefs alike, ran to their stations with weapons drawn. Heavens help them if Guardians were here. With clashing swords and screams of battle erupting, Eva reached the entrance on the South side of the outpost—Yaqar's most vulnerable point.

Four Zentari Operatives and a Captain were engaged with a dozen Swordsmen at the entrance. Eva wasted no time. She hurled a dagger at the nearest Zentari, striking him near the collarbone. He screamed before her comrades overran him.

She lunged at the next enemy—a male Operative pulling his knife from a fallen Swordsman. She aimed for his neck, but he deflected the strike and slammed his shoulder into her, sending her sprawling. Her dagger flew from her grasp.

Rolling to her feet, she dodged his sword as it struck the dirt. She palmed a smaller blade, flung it, then slashed again. The thrown dagger buried into his shoulder with a grunt, but he blocked her second attack. Yanking the blade free, he swung wide. Eva ducked, his sword slicing the air above her. She pivoted, sweeping his legs. He hit the ground with a grunt, and she pounced, driving her knife toward his chest. He caught her arms, stopping the blade. Eva's muscles strained as they fought for control.

She pressed harder—all of her body weight and adrenaline funneling into her arms. She felt a surge of strength and forced the dagger down inch by inch until it pierced his armor. His breath hitched—eyes wide—as she gave one final push.

The blade sank deep.

No sorrow. She stood, reclaiming her knives. The remaining Zentari lay defeated, but fresh battle cries rang from the other side of camp. A Swordsman dragged a wounded ally toward the medical tent, his screams grating in her ears. She waited alongside the other five surviving Swordsmen. It took everything in her to stay put, standing alongside her brethren—believe in her comrade's strength. Every instinct screamed for her to fight, refusing to remain in place.

*Don't make the same mistake twice. Stay at your post*

The memories of the last raid came to mind as she held herself back. She felt victorious, having rushed from gate to gate, aiding all her comrades and leaving a wake of dead Zentari. Until she was told another three Swordsmen died at her post. Drax wasn't shy about placing those lives on her shoulders, knowing she may have been able to save them.

*But how many more did you save by helping elsewhere*

She closed her eyes, taking a deep breath, demanding silence. But the relentless sounds of war refused to lessen—the clanging of metal, the shouting of warriors, the screams of death. Eva paced, her senses racing into overdrive. She heard the owls in the trees outside camp, smelled the sweat and blood in the air, and swore she could feel the faintest vibrations through the earth each time a body struck the ground.

As she tried to calm herself, a bright flash of blue light came from the west side of camp. She gasped. Yaqar had never been attacked by a Guardian. Just one could chew through their ranks unless everything was thrown at them. The Zentari had knowingly sent the Guardian to the less defended side of camp.

But she could help, drive the Guardian back—protect the outpost. She rushed past her comrades and sprinted for the Western edge of Yaqar.

"Swordsman Katz! Return to your post!" a comrade shouted as she ran between the tents.

She evaded the Swordsmen flowing around her. Chiefs were barking orders, trying to keep order among the chaos and panic. Rounding a corner, Eva dodged a limping Aniyan as he retreated and arrived at the Western opening of camp.

A tall figure, with steel plated armor, swung his ax as he battled a dozen Aniyans. As his weapon flew through the air, a wave of blue magic erupted from the end, like a release of pressurized steam. Eight Legion warriors were thrown backwards as the plume of indigo magic made contact. Screams of anguish sounded as her comrades writhed on the ground—some growing still and lifeless.

*Heavens help us*

Eva plunged into the chaos, seeking a way to engage the Guardian without harming her comrades. It was exceptionally difficult to attack a single enemy with so many allies around. But she saw an opening and jumped in. With unmatched senses, the Guardian anticipated her advance and turned to block. She struck down with both her daggers but met only the hard steel of his ax's handle. He twisted his weapon and swiped at Eva's midsection. She jumped backwards, narrowly missing the slice, a narrow cut now present in the leather covering her chest.

Sparing no quarter, the Guardian used the momentum to swing his ax overhead, coming down over her skull. Eva deflected the blow, stepping to the side. Before she could counterattack, the Guardian threw his ax's handle toward her, and another blast of blue magic erupted from the weapon.

Eva was thrown back with more force than she'd ever experienced, as if a dozen horses gripped her clothing and pulled. She landed fifteen feet away, the air choked from her lungs. In a shock, she realized why her comrades screamed with such agony at the Guardian's magic. Pain cascaded over her like rushing water—agony piercing every nerve ending. Mouth agape in a silent scream, she writhed on the ground against the anguish. Her joints were aflame, her head was about to explode, and her stomach felt gutted. She couldn't think—couldn't breathe.

She clenched her eyes shut, scrambling to focus, to endure. But the pain was too great, crushing her will underfoot as it—

Her eyes shot open. The magical influence left as abruptly as it came, but the damage was done. She stood on shaking legs, her previous strength zapped from her muscles. All Legion warriors were debriefed on the latest intel of known Guardians, detailing the capabilities and power each of them wielded. Needless to say, it was a short list—and nothing like this was ever mentioned.

The Guardian was still on his feet, but his movements were slowing with each attack. Eva could hear his ragged breathing underneath his helmet, grunting with each swing of his ax. The greatest weakness of every Guardian was fatigue—utter exhaustion at the hands of their own magic. With some, it took only a few uses of their inner magic to claim their strength. And if they overextended the use of their ethereal essence, it could claim their very life.

*Just keep fighting. Wear him down*

But bodies littered the ground. Now more than two dozen Legion lay at the Guardian's feet. The other Zentari were already struck down. Now was her chance. Spurred forward as her strength slowly returned, she called upon whatever endurance she had left.

Gritting through the ache in her joints, Eva returned to the fight, more Legion pouring out of Yaqar. She pushed through her fellow comrades, closing in on her enemy. The Guardian grabbed a Swordsman by the head, releasing another blast of magical energy. The Swordsman's head exploded with a shower of red mist.

Amid the fray, she caught an opening in the Guardian's left side as he fended off a Swordsman. She seized the opportunity and rushed in, attacking the Guardian with a flurry of slices from her daggers. Aiming for the weak points between the armor plates, she utilized her speed, cutting through his slower defenses.

The Guardian couldn't keep up, his magic no doubt claiming its price. She could see blood flowing between his armored plates and continued her volley of strikes among his counterattacks.

Suddenly, the Guardian screamed, throwing his shoulders back in a loud cry. A massive wave of blue magic exploded around him, throwing Eva and all twenty of her comrades away from him. Eva landed further back than before, her body retching from the magic's influence again. She didn't think the anguish she suffered earlier could have been worse.

She was wrong.

Thrashing and flailing on the ground, Eva arched her back and grabbed her head. Her body screamed louder than before. Her skin was on fire, as if a thousand red hot irons were pressed against every inch. Amid the torture, she felt a clawing desperation for it to end, for death to claim her.

*No*

She commanded her thoughts and muscles to obey. She felt a rush of strength bellow against the pain as she forced her eyes open. She curled forward, lying on her side. The Guardian was on one knee, bracing his weight on his ax as his chest heaved. None of her comrades recovered—all of them lying still in the dust.

Eva rolled onto her knees, staring at the Guardian. Lungs burning, she grabbed a blade from her right thigh, gritting her teeth against the flame in her joints. Summoning what little strength she yet claimed, she threw the blade with a grunt. Her vision went black as she released the knife. Another wave of searing fire was her punishment as her body screamed.

The blade missed its mark, grazing the side of the Guardian's neck. He reached for the wound as blood leaked from the shallow cut. She stumbled forward, waiting for the magic's influence to lessen as before. It was slow, the Guardian's power stubbornly refusing to withdraw its connection to her nerves, but it began to fade.

She stood, stumbling toward the Guardian, blades ready. He straightened to his full height, gripping his ax at her approach. When she neared, he swiped with his Rune Blade. Eva ducked backwards, the steel missing her by a hair's breadth.

She righted herself and ran her dagger over the soft leather covering his right elbow. The weapon found its mark, cutting between his plates of armor. The Guardian groaned at the wound, swiping his hand backwards at her jaw. She dodged the attack, her speed besting his—but only just. She made another cut to his right armpit, stabbing her blade as deeply as her weakened state could muster.

The pain in her muscles and joints lessened further, but it was only replaced with exhaustion. Eva was fighting as if their bout had lasted days. And it was only the Guardian's own fatigue that prevented him from cutting her down.

Another swing of his axe forced her back. The Guardian removed the blade from his arm and tossed it on the ground. Eva scrambled forward and threw all of her weight into a kick at his chest. The Guardian braced against the attack, shoved only a few feet backwards. He retaliated with another swing of his weapon. Eva tried to dodge again, but the exhaustion was worsening—her movements slowing.

She grunted as the Rune Blade cut across her stomach, biting through the leather and into her skin. In reflex, she tossed the blade in her right hand, holding her stomach. The dagger buried in the flesh of his right thigh, near the hip, above the metal plating. The Guardian groaned, falling to one knee. She rushed him, seizing the chance and deflected his swipe as she approached. But she missed his counterattack, and his ax's handle clubbed the side of her head.

Stars filled her vision as she stumbled sideways. Shaking her head to clear her vision, she palmed her last dagger. The Guardian ripped her blade from his thigh. He braced himself to stand, an indigo mist surrounding his weapon. But before he could react, she ran up and slipped behind him, yanking his head back and burying her blade into his throat.

Gurgles sounded as the Guardian choked on his blood, which poured down the front of his armor. He fell forward in a slump—dead.

As her enemy fell, the lethargy pulling at her body overtook her. She went numb, her muscles refusing to listen to her commands to remain standing. Her head was floating as her eyes rolled back, and she was lost to darkness.

# Chapter Eleven

Maelyn's heart leaped into her throat as Fenner slipped off the cliff, his body now suspended awkwardly by his leather belt. The heavy chain connecting Fenner to Rowan pulled taut, but the segment between Maelyn and Rowan remained slack. Rowan, now supporting Fenner's full weight, gritted his teeth.

"Fenner!" Maelyn shouted. "Pull yourself up before you kill us all!"

Maelyn turned as a hand grasped the strap around her waist. Esme scaled over, bracing Maelyn in case Rowan fell. Fenner was flailing as he dangled, the largest waves engulfing him as the surf hit the cliffs.

"He can't climb back with the waves finding him," Esme said, her voice calm. "We need to pull him above the ocean's reach."

Maelyn glanced at Rowan, who hadn't moved—white knuckles clinging to the rock face. His eyes were closed as his neck veins bulged with the strain.

Maelyn said to Esme, "We need to help Rowan. I don't know how much longer he can hold Fenner."

Esme nodded. "Leave it to me."

Maelyn was impressed, watching Esme climb over her on the cliff, and followed. Their empty buckets scraped against the stone, the wind clubbing the wood against the rock face. Esme reached Rowan and scaled around to his right side, where the chain held Fenner. She ensured she found solid footing before holding the cliff with one hand and grabbing the chain. With a grunt, Esme lifted Fenner's weight off Rowan.

Rowan opened his eyes at the relief of pressure. He glanced down before grasping the chain, working with Esme to pull Fenner out of the waves' reach.

"Fenner!" Maelyn shouted. "Climb, you rotting fool!"

Fenner gasped, spitting ocean water from his mouth. He flailed—panicked. Maelyn yelled. "Climb or we all die!"

Fenner gripped the chain around his waist and pressed his feet against the cliff. He tried to pull himself up but slipped back down as another wave crashed into him, tossing him against the rock.

*Living Hells, what do we do*

She glanced at Esme and Rowan, who both shared Fenner's weight, but weren't able to pull him up themselves. She needed to pull with them but would need to scale below Rowan.

*This is stupid. This is stupid. This is stupid*

Maelyn descended as quickly as she dared, knowing a slip would mean pulling all four of them into the sea. Halfway between Fenner and Rowan, she stopped, the cliffside now treacherously smooth and wet. The highest waves kissed her boots. With adrenaline pumping in her system, she grabbed Fenner's chain and pulled with all her might. Pain erupted as her shoulder popped, but Fenner rose from the water. Her arm screamed, but she continued pulling, now working with Rowan and Esme.

The three of them worked in unison, lifting Fenner from a watery grave. Eventually, Fenner at last held his own body weight, and all three relaxed. With heavy breaths, they shared glances.

Fenner shivered on the cliffside. "I'm s-sorry," he stammered.

"Shut up!" Rowan yelled. "You fall again, I'm letting you drown!"

"I'm sorry," Fenner said, a tremor in his voice.

"Enough!" Maelyn shouted. "We still have to fill the buckets!" She looked at the bucket chained between Fenner and Rowan, water spilling from the rim.

*One down. Two to go*

"Esme! Rowan!" Maelyn said. "Climb lower so the buckets fill!"

Esme nodded, but Rowan argued.

"And who in the Nine made you queen!?"

Esme said something to Rowan, grabbing his armor. Maelyn turned to Fenner. "Climb up and hang on. Your buckets filled, so your job right now is to stay on the rock. Got it?"

Fenner nodded, shaking as he ascended slowly. Whatever Esme said to Rowan worked, since they both climbed down next to Maelyn. They waited, gripping the slip and wet rock, for the remaining two buckets to fill.

"Close enough!" Rowan shouted. "Let's go!"

Maelyn saw the buckets were only half-filled. "No! We wait until they're full!"

"Why?" he yelled. "Evergreen never said they had to be overflowing!"

Esme interjected. "Do you really wish to risk repeating this challenge?"

Rowan spit with a glare but remained where he was. Maelyn checked on Fenner, who still shivered, but remained steady. Eventually, as Maelyn grew numb from exhaustion, their buckets finally overflowed with water.

"They're full!" Maelyn shouted. "Let's go! But take it slow! I refuse to die on the first challenge!"

Rowan cursed under his breath as they began ascending the cliff. Maelyn bit down on her tongue. Antagonizing her *teammate* would not help them climb any faster.

*Rotting pig*

Atop the cliff on the grassy plain, the other recruits were restless. Some still watched the four, silently praying for their success, while others were chatting as if it were any other beautiful day. Eli couldn't understand how some people disregarded others in danger.

Thankfully, his head was feeling better, the dizziness now absent. And with each minute that passed, the throbbing lessened. But as Eli knelt at the cliff's edge, straining his eyes, it only caused his headache to return. Peering down, he saw Maelyn's team ascending.

"Guys! They're climbing back up!" Eli said.

Arlo and Lara rushed to his side, other recruits following suit.

"Let's go guys! Never had a doubt!" Arlo shouted.

Eli rolled his eyes but couldn't help to smile at Arlo's infectious positivity. As Maelyn's hand grasped the top of the cliff, Eli grabbed her wrist and helped her to safety. The four squadmates laid on the grass gasping for breath—shivering, drenched, with blood smeared on their hands and arms. Fenner was soaked to the bone—hypothermia not far behind.

"Excellent!" Evergreen announced, strolling over to the recruits. She stopped and acknowledged each of them. "You all pass and are the first squad to return. Congratulations."

The Captain unbuckled the squad, before pouring out the buckets of water. Maelyn, Esme, Rowan, and Fenner watched in shock as their hard work splashed into the sea below.

Rowan stood, a dark look in his eye. He marched to Fenner, who was still shaking on the ground.

"You rotting fool!" he shouted, grabbing Fenner's shirt, his right hand balled into a fist. "I should drown you myself!"

The crowd murmured as Rowan punched his squadmate. Eli looked to Captain Evergreen, who continued pouring the buckets over the edge, ignoring the interaction.

He stormed over to Rowan. "Hey!" Eli snagged Rowan's arm before he could hit Fenner again.

Rowan yanked free and spun around. "Back off!"

Fenner coughed on the ground as blood poured from his nose.

"He slipped!" Eli argued. "It wasn't his fault!"

"And who are you?" Rowan shouted, face red. "I didn't see you down there! You didn't almost drown because of this gutless worm!"

"You're alive! He fell and you saved him! That's what comrades do!"

Rowan punched Eli in the chin. Eli stumbled to the ground, knowing he couldn't handle Rowan by himself and wondered if he held a grudge against them for getting his partner killed at the start of the program.

Rowan stood over him. "He nearly killed us all! How many times have they told us the weak die here! Voss said you can't rely on a weak comrade, and that's exactly what he is!" Rowan shouted, pointing a finger at Fenner.

Eli stood, spitting the blood from his mouth. Rowan glanced over Eli's shoulder, before returning his attention to Eli, now inches from his face.

"We are all weak!" Eli argued. "Renard said we are *all* infants on a battlefield! We are here to train *because* we're weak."

"Well, if you're so in love with him, you have him as a squadmate. Let him pull you down instead!"

"Enough!" Evergreen shouted. Rowan and Eli both turned to the Captain standing at attention. She faced the rest of the crowd, tossing the last bucket on the grass.

"Rowan. Eli. You are both correct. If you remain weak in this program you will die, but there is a reason we chain you together. War is not won by heroes, it's won by comrades, men and women who rely on each other in combat. If you do not learn that lesson now, you have no business being here."

The crowd settled, and Eli turned, surprised to find Esme behind him. She placed a hand on his shoulder and whispered in his ear.

"Pick your battles, sir Danon. I will handle Rowan."

Eli was silent as she stepped around him to help Fenner, two healers already approaching with a stretcher.

Evergreen shouted, "Sol, Kairah, Soren, and Fjord! Buckle in!"

Waiting for Sol's team, Eli wondered how well they would fair, and how much Sol's size would work against him on the rock face. After some time, they returned appearing unharmed—but missing a squadmate. Their fourth, Fjord, was absent, his chain belt unbuckled and dangling over the cliff.

Evergreen approached, dumping their buckets over the ledge. "What happened to your squadmate?"

Sol shrugged. "He fell."

Evergreen's face was masked as Soren and Kairah snickered. A pit formed in Eli's stomach, and he made a mental note to avoid Sol's squad if at all possible.

Finally, it was Eli's turn. He, Arlo, and Lara stepped up and began buckling themselves in. Eli took a deep breath, calming his racing heart as he picked up the thick leather strap. He was surprised how much chain was present between each belt, at least ten feet. It gave them room to navigate the rock, but that much chain was heavy, ensuring they'd be pulled under if they hit the water. Eli winced, thinking about how heavy the climb back up would be with the buckets of water in addition to the chain.

"Hey, who's our fourth—" Before he finished his question, Shira emerged from the crowd and walked toward the last belt. She stepped up to the empty spot next to him and began buckling in. Eli, speechless, watched her for a moment—grinning.

Before they began their descent, Maelyn approached Eli.

"Be careful at the bottom," she murmured. "The water has eroded the rocks making them smooth at that point. That's how Fenner fell."

Eli, surprised by the warning, nodded in thanks.

She continued, "Test the rocks before bearing your full weight. A number of them are loose."

"Thanks for the warning," he said.

Maelyn, absentmindedly rubbing her injured hands, nodded and walked away.

They began their descent, climbing over the edge in unison. Despite the weathered surface of the rock face, Eli could make out areas that had been used as footholds. His boots were not meant for climbing, though they provided adequate protection from the sharp edges. He winced as his right hand was already sliced open.

"Hey guys, mind your footing!" he shouted. "Some of the rocks aren't as sure as they seem."

Arlo and Lara gave curt nods. Shira said nothing. Lara climbed the slowest, hesitation behind every movement and shallow breath. Fear was etched into every line of her face. Meanwhile, Arlo and Shira moved like restless flames, racing downward with effortless grace, pausing only when forced to wait for Eli or Lara.

They were about halfway down the cliff when Eli and Shira shared a glance.

"So, I have to ask," he said, climbing down to her, but keeping his attention on the rock. "Why did you decide to join our squad?"

"Is this really the time?" she asked, again waiting for him to catch up. Though she sounded frustrated, she waited until he descended to her level.

"Well, I'm curious. And seeing as we might die in a minute, I figured there's no time like the present."

She stared at him with her piercing sapphire eyes. Wondering what she was thinking, Eli held her gaze. Her eyes bounced to the mark on his chin, which throbbed alongside his heart.

"What I accepted was your offer," she said, in a hushed tone, glancing at their squadmates. Lara had stopped climbing, hesitating on a narrow foothold. Arlo was yelling instructions to help her.

"Offer?" he asked.

"You suck at fighting," Shira said. "You act like a blind man swatting a bee." His eyebrows raised, a smile tugging at his lips.

*Not a totally inaccurate description*

"And you really are looking for something," he said, eyes narrowing. She pursed her lips, shifting her body weight on the rock. "That's why you knocked me out, isn't it? So I wouldn't keep talking in front of the Operative."

"It's more that I have questions. I've found something and I need answers."

"What did you find?"

"That doesn't matter!" she argued. "All that matters is our deal. I teach you to fight, you help me answer my questions." She gave him a stern look before descending the rock again.

"All right then," he mumbled.

"You got it, Lara!" Arlo encouraged. "Take your time! There's a good hold just below your left foot!"

Waiting for them to catch up, Eli shouted over the waves, which grew louder as they descended. "Hey Arlo!"

"What?"

"They teach you how to rock climb in the underground?" he asked with a smirk.

"Wrong underground!"

Nearing the bottom, they paused. Arlo and Shira were doing well, but Eli and Lara needed a brief respite. His hands were now slippery from the bleeding, and his forearms burned with a fire he'd never experienced.

"Everyone move closer together! That will get the buckets as low as possible!" Eli shouted over the crashing waves and gusting wind.

"We need to get lower!" Arlo said, scaling toward him.

"I know!" Eli responded. "But we won't have to get as close if the chain is given more length!"

The squad cautiously moved toward each other, slowed by the slick rocks. Shira didn't appear fatigued at all. She was steadfast and confident, showing no signs of weakening. Lara was shaking, and Eli could hear her teeth clattering from some combination of cold, exhaustion, and fear.

As the three came shoulder to shoulder, the chains between them stretched to their fullest, lowering the buckets ever closer to the water—yet not close enough. The ocean teased them with its rhythm, waves rising with promise but falling just short. The crests of the largest swells kissed the bucket's bottom, without surrendering a single drop.

"Move down!" Eli shouted.

The squad descended together, each step less solid than the last. Maelyn's warning came in full reminder as Eli's grasp became increasingly feeble. They remained tightly together, until the buckets found the water's edge. With each wave moving up and down, they could feel the buckets' weight ebb and flow, the sea lifting the weight, before leaving them with more water.

As they waited, a massive wave came crashing up, engulfing all four of them in a torrent of freezing water. Eli gripped the rock with a ferocity that left his arms numb. His mind went blank, waiting to be pulled away from the cliffside. He couldn't breathe, the freezing ocean draining every bit of warmth his body had retained. Water filled his ears, and his dizziness returned.

As the wave receded, the water pulled at him, beckoning it to fall captive to its depths. Eli glanced at his squadmates. Arlo and Shira held fast to the cliff, but Lara was gone. There was nothing but the leather belt that once held her to them, and the crashing white water below.

"Lara!" Arlo shouted.

Shira said nothing, staring at The Great Sea below.

Eli, without thinking, reached down and unbuckled himself, leaping from the rock into the cold, unforgiving sea.

# Chapter Twelve

E va woke to blue skies and wispy clouds sailing above her, catching the orange glow from the sun, which was low on the horizon.

*I must have been out all night*

She reached for her pounding head, finding a soft cotton bandage. She sat up, pain shooting through her skull and down her back. Her comrades had laid her in a row of wounded warriors outside the medical tent, healers scurrying around, tending to the many injuries. White bandages and splints stood out among the sea of black leather and dirt. She searched the nearby bodies for Maya but didn't see her.

Eva attempted to stand but stumbled backwards with a shock of pain. She crawled to the tent and sat against the structure. Giving herself a moment, she listened to the shouting and scraping of boots against the dirt, praising the Heavens the sounds of fighting had ceased. She opened her eyes again and stood, bracing herself against the medical tent, willing the vertigo to pass. She needed to see if Maya was all right. With a few unsteady steps, she watched her comrades, her kin, work with sullen faces.

They won the battle, but at a steep price.

It was a blessing from the Heavens that Guardians were a rare thing among the Zentari. If their enemy commanded only twice the number of magical warriors, Eva couldn't fathom the destruction that would be wrought upon her people. Rounding a corner, she nearly ran into a fellow Swordsman. It took her a moment before she recognized his familiar face.

"Keinen," Eva said.

"Swordsman Katz!" he said in surprise. Eva's ears rang at the sound of his voice.

"Call me Eva, Keinen."

"Yes, b-but—" he stammered. "Lieutenant Drax says—"

She closed her eyes, having no strength to argue.

"It's fine," she said, glancing around. "How many did we lose last night? I was knocked out."

Keinen's face fell. "A lot. At least a third of the camp."

*Bleeding Hells*

"How many Zentari attacked?"

"It was a targeted strike. An ambush. Little more than a dozen or so," Keinen answered. "Including the Guardian."

*They waited for Lucas's detachment to leave before striking*

More than thirty Legion warriors brought to their knees by a dozen Zentari.

*Shining Heavens help us*

"Thank you, Keinen," she said, clasping a hand on his shoulder. "Go help the wounded."

He gave a curt nod before resuming his duties. She watched him jog away, trying to shake the heaviness of their losses. It wasn't long before she fumbled her way to Maya's tent, pulling open the flap.

Empty.

Eva cursed herself for not checking the medical tent first. She wasn't thinking straight. But they lost over thirty comrades, and she prayed desperately that Maya wasn't—

"Eva!"

She spun at the sound of her friend's voice. Maya ran up to her, embracing her with enough force to rattle her aching bones.

"Are you all right?" Maya asked, stepping back and examining Eva's bandage, concern etched into her face.

"I'm all right," Eva said. "Are you?"

"Yeah," Maya replied. "We lost a lot of people."

"We were lucky there were so few of them."

Maya nodded, then said, "Two Zentari were captured, I heard."

"By who?" Something in the back of her mind began to boil.

"East gate. Freyja reported it, saying she and four others bound them. One surrendered, the other was unconscious."

"One surrendered?" Eva asked, astonished. She'd never heard of any Zentari giving up.

"Yeah. He's either a coward or lost all faith they could win."

The burning in Eva's mind worsened. An idea seeded, something dangerously close to treason, but utilized the opportunity at hand.

"They brought them to the pit?" she asked.

Maya hesitated. "Evalynn Katz, don't you dare think about going anywhere near that prison. You're already on thin ice with Drax."

Eva shrugged, feigning innocence. "I'm not!"

"You're lucky, by the way," Maya said. "I saw two guys carrying you from the West gate, which you and I both know isn't your post. Drax is strung tighter than a lute string and saw you by the medical tent. He asked what happened and I told him you were unconscious at the Southern gate. That man would've skinned you alive for disobeying orders, *again*."

Eva rubbed her eyes, speaking in a harsh whisper. "There was a Guardian there! I helped bring him down!"

"It doesn't matter! Not according to the Legion. And you better hope no one from the Southern gate sells you out!"

"I saved you! And the outpost! I did what no one else here could."

"Look, I'm sure you saved lives. And you and I both know you're our best fighter, promotions or not, but you have *got* to start following protocol."

Eva's cheeks burned, as if she were being scolded by her mother—or at least, what she imagined a scolding from her mother would be like. After all, it was Maya's safety that pressed her to leave her post.

Maya embraced her once more. "I'm glad you're okay."

Eva closed her eyes and allowed herself a breath of relief.

"Swordsman Katz!" a voice called. Eva and Maya turned to the male Swordsman jogging to them. "You are to report to Lieutenant Drax immediately."

Eva swallowed, catching Maya's knowing glance.

Eva stood at attention, once again in front of Drax's desk.

"Very well, Swordsman Katz," Drax drawled, rubbing his forehead. "Thankfully it will be a long time before you're standing in front of me again. My orders stand. You are to report to Manoach first thing tomorrow morning and relieve Swordsman Morrigan. You will instruct him to return to Yaqar outpost. Swordsman Lane will accompany you to ensure you don't deviate from your assignment."

*Not Lane*

An honorable man, with unflinching—and blind—loyalty to the Legion. Swordsman Atlar Lane made Lucas look like a deviant. Drax stared, waiting for her to acknowledge his orders.

"As you say, Lieutenant," she said.

"Remember this, girl." His eyes turned dark, holding up his index finger. "*One* step out of line, and you will know the meaning of shame and suffering. Dismissed."

She nodded and turned to leave. But against her better judgment, she stopped after a few steps and spoke over her shoulder.

"Permission to speak freely, Lieutenant."

He looked up from his desk—leery. "Granted."

"I already know shame and suffering." She left, hoping to the brilliant Heavens to never see his face again. Once outside, she spotted Maya leaning against a post.

"Manoach?" Maya asked, stepping into pace with Eva as she marched to her tent.

"Yeah, I was going to tell you. It slipped my mind after the attack."

"When did he decide that?"

"Last night. I asked to go with Lucas and he refused. I argued, furious that he sent Lucas on a suicide mission. And as punishment, he's filing formal charges and assigned me to patrol duty."

"Patrol duty? For all things holy, he knows you're his best fighter. We just got attacked! By a Guardian! The Zentari know we just drained our forces! What is he doing?"

Eva stopped and turned toward her.

"He's getting even. He thinks I'm a spoiled brat that gets whatever I want."

"Well, he's not wrong there," Maya said wryly. Eva scoffed, but grinned.

"You know what I mean," she said, rubbing the bridge of her nose. She stepped closer and lowered her voice. "Listen, I need your help."

Maya's eyes narrowed. "Why do I get the feeling you aren't actually leaving?"

"I am, just . . . not yet," Eva said. Maya exhaled in protest. "I will. I will. I have until tomorrow morning. But do you remember Lucas telling us about those stones?"

"The ones the Zentari Council are looking for? Like the one you found?"

"Yes." Eva kept her voice to a whisper. "We need to know why. Something tells me it's the difference between winning and losing this war."

"What are you talking about?"

"You remember what I said," Eva pressed. "Just touching one of those things nearly killed me, at least it felt like it. And why are the Council so obsessed with them? Have you ever known the almighty Zentari Council to do anything without extreme intention?"

Maya examined her. "Did you learn something?"

"No, but my gut tells me whoever discovers these things first will win the war," Eva said.

"Well, I'm sure your feelings are *spot on*, but I know you," Maya said with a stern glare. "You don't just have feelings, you act. Do not do anything stupid. Okay?"

Eva rolled her eyes.

"Hey, I'm serious," Maya said. "Do you want to be charged with dereliction? To face banishment or execution?"

Eva's gaze shifted, wrestling with the advice of her friend. And the gnawing in her stomach.

"Fine. I'll let it go," Eva lied.

The remainder of the day was spent tending to the wounded and reassigning tasks as needed. Their outpost was no longer in shambles, but between the losses suffered and the warriors sent with Lucas, they were operating in minimal numbers. Drax already sent word for reinforcements, which were due to arrive by morning.

By the time Eva laid in her bunk after dark, she was ready to collapse. She rested for a few hours, drifting in and out of sleep. But the burning idea in her head kept her tired mind from a deep unconsciousness. Despite Maya's protest, if she was to be banished to patrol duty, she might as well bend one more rule before she left.

She sat up, listening to see if the quiet of night had settled. She tiptoed to the entrance of her tent. Silence. Peering outside, she wondered if the restlessness of the camp was overcome by everyone's exhaustion.

There were night watchmen muttering to each other in the center of the outpost, but otherwise everyone had gone to bed. The moon shone in a thin crescent, leaving mostly darkness throughout the camp.

*Perfect*

Donning a cloth mask and hooded cloak, Eva stepped out into the cold night air. She stalked behind tents and along the fenced barrier. Stopping at the north entrance to camp, she paused, listening for the three patrols. She waited, tracking the positions of her comrades as they circled the perimeter. At the perfect moment, Eva darted through the entrance, rushing up the gentle slope. She moved quickly but silently, knowing exactly how to avoid the sight of the hidden sentries.

She reached the tree line and stopped, crouching behind an oak, steadying her breathing. Resting on the Northern hill outside the outpost, near their makeshift prison, she strained her ears. As she listened for other guards, or a warning call of being spotted, the air carried only crickets and the gentle breeze caressing the oak leaves.

*What are you doing*

Eva stalked through the thin brush and tall grass to their prison, spotting the sole female Swordsman keeping watch over the pit. Sneaking around, further into the trees, Eva positioned herself behind her comrade.

As quiet as the night, Eva sprang out. Before the sentry could turn or call out, Eva wrapped an arm around her neck and squeezed. The Swordsman thrashed about, trying to free herself, grasping at Eva's arms. The two fell backwards, Eva wrestling against the guard's kicking. The Swordsman was unable to call out for help before her body went limp.

Eva laid her down carefully and checked her pulse. Breathing a sigh of relief, she grabbed the key off the guard's waist and strode over to the pit. Two Zentari prisoners, one male and one female, sat with their heads down. Eva unlocked the chain, opening the gate over the top, and jumped into the pit. The Zentari looked up, bracing against the wall. To Eva's surprise, they weren't preparing for a fight—they were frightened.

Their faces were dirty, their lips dry and cracked. She doubted they'd been given any water since their capture. Their armor was removed, leaving only the thin fabric of their tunics for warmth against the chill of the night.

"What are your names?" Eva asked, her voice muffled by her mask. The prisoners glanced at each other.

"My name is Xerza." The male spoke, his bald head contrasted by a thick black beard, a long scar across his left eye. "And this is Thalia."

"What are your ranks?"

They gave quizzical looks.

"I am a Captain," Xerza said. "Thalia is an Operative. I speak for us both."

"You will not speak for me, coward!" Thalia spit, spinning to Xerza. Her golden eyes were in stark contrast to her black hair. He growled at Thalia's impunity but did not argue.

"I don't care who speaks, only that you answer my questions," Eva said.

"And why should we give you answers?" Thalia said, eyes flaring. "Do you plan to torture us before our appointed time?"

Eva's eyes narrowed. "No one's going to torture you," she assured.

"Don't bother with lies, Aniyan," Xerza said in a deep voice. "We know far too well the methods of the Legion."

Eva paused.

*Methods*

"What are you talking about?" she asked, keeping her voice level.

"Come here to play the fool?" Thalia mocked with a smile. "I suppose next you'll let us go free, is that it?"

Eva waited, her eyes flickering between them.

"You are acting outside your orders," Xerza accused, crossing his arms. "It's night. I heard a rustling, and you are not the guard that was stationed on watch. Your face is covered, and you speak like an assassin."

Eva watched him scan her features, assessing her intent. "You betray your people," he said.

"I betray no one!" she snapped, remembering to keep her voice low. "I am here because I need information. Whether or not you decide to rot in this cell or go free is up to you."

Thalia scoffed. Xerza kept his attention on Eva. She could see him weighing her words.

"Ask your questions, Aniyan," he said.

"Don't you dare—" Thalia began, but Xerza cut her off, shoving her against the dirt wall, an elbow to her throat.

"Remember your place, Operative. To question authority, your superior officer, is treason. You would be wise to not emphasize rules so much, when you also disobey them yourself." He released his hold, and Thalia held her throat, breathing heavily. Despite the fury in her eyes, she remained silent. Xerza turned back to Eva.

"What—" Eva started.

"Before I answer your questions, Aniyan, what guarantee do we have that you will let us go? That is what you intend, is it not?"

Xerza's posture changed as he spoke. He stood straight, lifting his chin—a challenge.

"You have my word as a Swordsman of the Legion."

"That means very little to us, Aniyan," he retorted.

Eva thought for a moment, then reached up and removed her mask and hood.

"My name is Swordsman Evalynn Katz. I bargain my identity and the risk of dereliction and execution as a traitor." Eva watched as Xerza studied her face, his eyes dancing over her hair. She caught the vaguest sense of respect in his features.

"Then I will answer in truth, with my word as an honorable Zentari."

"And what guarantee do I have?" Eva said. "I trust your people no more than you do mine."

Xerza paused and sighed. "I have no identity or value to wager. But I am older and have lived around the suffering and hatred of my people for many years. Yet I have found darkness on both sides of this war. If there is one thing I've learned, it's that neither of our Nations can move forward until trust is extended."

"You cannot betray—" Thalia began.

"Be silent!" he scolded. "You are too young to realize that evil begets evil. I do not betray my secrets, I extend a hope that one day our peoples may trust each other."

Silence spread between them. Eva wasn't satisfied with his answer, but he wasn't wrong. There was nothing to force his honesty.

"What do you know about the objects the Council is seeking?" Eva asked. She didn't have time for any more banter, not knowing how long before the sentry outside would wake.

Xerza stiffened. "How do you know of the stones?"

"I'm the one asking questions. You will escape with your lives, not information."

He hummed. "They are called Obelisks. I do not know where they come from, nor how they are made. Some believe them to be ancient relics, magical artifacts from years gone. I believe the Council deems them critically important because they contain magic, though I cannot say for certain."

"Is that why the Council is so intent on finding them?"

"I do not know the thoughts of our Council, nor their intentions."

"I find that hard to believe being a Captain."

"Then I do not know what to tell you," he replied calmly. "The Council's intentions are only shared with a few."

She clenched her jaw. "Is it true every Zentari warrior in the field has been given the same orders to watch for the Obelisks?"

"We were given the order, yes. I cannot say whether others were, but I was instructed to watch for them."

Eva thought through the new information, thinking of the most pressing questions. "Where do the Zentari hold Aniyan captives?"

Xerzawrinkled his brow. "I know nothing about Aniyan captives."

"My friend's brother went missing after a raid on his village. If the Zentari are responsible and he were taken prisoner, where would he be held?"

"Most prisoners are brought to the nearest outpost for questioning."

"Where else?" Eva pressed. "Why would the Zentari be interested in civilians at all?"

"Our people do not—"

"Do not lie to me!" she spat, her heart thundering as she ran out of time.

Xerza swallowed, his expression gentle. "On my honor, I know nothing of this."

They stared at each other for a long moment—a battle of wills—of trust as brittle as glass, shattering at the slightest touch.

"All I can offer you are rumors," he continued. "It is dishonorable, and conjecture, but I've heard that some Aniyan prisoners are taken to Eldan City as slaves, tortured for information."

Eva's heart twisted, thinking of Lucas's family being beaten. If they were taking civilians, then what in the Nine Realms were they doing? What fresh evil would she still see in this war?

Eva drew her daggers and approached them. Xerza stilled. Thalia's eyes grew wide, opening her mouth to speak, but stopped as Eva's blades nestled against their throats.

"There are two sentinels on the peaks of the South and Western hills. Stay in the shadows and follow the tree line west. Don't go east. At the ravine, turn South into Midbar and make for Heika."

"We have no supplies to get across Midbar!" Thalia argued, holding still, aware of the blade at her neck. "Heika is a two-day ride! Four days on foot!"

"That is not my problem," Eva responded with cold indifference. Xerza did not move or speak. "If I ever see your faces here again, I will not spare you a second time."

Eva turned and climbed out of the pit, leaving the gate unlocked.

# Chapter Thirteen

The ocean embraced Eli in a cruel, frigid grip, a thousand needles piercing his flesh. The cold crept through him, stealing sensation from his limbs, numbing him to his core. For a breathless instant, he went rigid, his instincts screaming to gasp and draw air. Blind to direction, he reached for the surface, yet the world turned shapeless. The way upward was lost in the endless, suffocating depths.

*Hells what have I done*

His lungs burning, body freezing, and mind racing, Eli's head pierced the surface. The roar of the sea crashed in his ears. He gasped for breath, choking on the saltwater invading his throat.

"Eli!" Arlo shouted from the cliff. "What in the Hells are you doing?"

Eli couldn't respond as the sea threatened to yank him under again. He thrust aside the rising panic.

*Lara. Where is Lara*

He blinked the salt water from his eyes and scanned for Lara. He saw nothing. His stomach lurched as a wave lifted him, throwing him toward the rock face. He reached for the cliff but couldn't gain purchase.

"Do you see her?" he shouted, coughing as water choked his voice.

"No!" Arlo shouted. "You need to get out!"

Eli took a deep breath and dove, pushing off the stone swimming beneath the waves. He forced his eyes to open against the burning of salt water. Beneath him he saw only rocks and blackness, an infinite chasm promising death. He turned under the surface, his lungs crying for air. He searched the torrential depths for any sign of his friend. And there, like a gift from the Heavens, he caught sight of a blurred figure suspended just below the surface above him. He swam with all his might, his hands burning from the saltwater finding his recent wounds.

As he came closer, he prayed it—

*Lara*

He reached her limp body and spun her around, pushing her head above the surface. He gasped, drawing in the air his lungs demanded. He placed his mouth over Lara's and forced air into her lungs, but there was little he could do while tossed in the current. Summoning what little strength he had left, he swam toward the cliffside and grabbed the rock face. He protected Lara's body from scraping against the stone as the waves pressed against them. He clung to the cliff, clamping his eyes shut as he was beaten against the stones.

Before he could call for Arlo and Shira, a hand grabbed the leather armor over his shoulder. He looked up and saw Shira had climbed down to the water's edge. She grabbed his shoulder and pulled hard, while Arlo braced their weight above. Together, Shira and Eli secured Lara with her belt.

Something in Eli relaxed as he felt Lara's thumping heartbeat. She hung, limply like a rag doll chained at the waist. Arlo bore her weight by himself, waiting for Shira and Eli to climb. Shira helped Eli reattach his harness. She grasped his waist as he swayed with a surge of dizziness and exhaustion.

The four of them rearranged their positions, strapping Lara between Shira and Arlo, with Eli on the end.

"That was the stupidest thing I've ever seen someone do!" Shira scolded.

Eli stopped to rest, pleading for his tremors to lessen. "I wasn't about to let her die," he muttered.

"So you throw your life away?" Shira snapped. "You're an idiot!"

He met her gaze—her glare. "If we don't help each other now, then none of this matters."

"Hey!" Arlo shouted from above them. "Everything okay? I can't hold on forever!"

Eli tried to steady his breathing. Shira scaled closer, meeting his eyeline.

"Climb," she ordered. "And don't you dare fall."

Eli wondered whether she spoke for her safety or his. "Or what?" he asked sarcastically. "You care if I fall?"

The intensity in her eyes seemed more like perseverance than contempt. But there was nothing soft in her face as she waited for him to continue.

"Climb," she said.

Each step they made was agony. Not only were they more exhausted, the added weight of their comrade and the now full buckets, all beckoned them into gravity's pull. Eli was trembling so aggressively he was having trouble grabbing the rocks. He shook his throbbing head to clear his double vision.

Wet and bruised and bleeding, the four squadmates made it to the top. Arlo and Shira gently placed Lara's body on the grass, and ensured each bucket was brought up, sparing their contents. Eli collapsed near the edge. His exhaustion finally overpowering him. A figure knelt above him as he lost consciousness.

"Elijah?"

"Yeah, Harp?"

He and his younger sister sat on a fallen log overlooking the creek bed, listening to the sounds of the chirping birds, taking a break from the day's events. It was one of their favorite places, tucked away just behind the inn, but far enough to escape the noise and chaos. A narrow stream of clear, crisp water rippled as it flowed between the towering trees before them.

"Are you really going to leave?" Harper asked, her head hung as she kicked her sandals in the dirt.

Eli had avoided telling her about joining the military, but it was no longer a secret. He knew how to deal with his father. Hells, they had argued for the third night in a row. But Harper was only nine. Since their father was busy running the inn, Eli knew exactly how much she depended on his presence—his consistency in her life. If he left, there was no one else to watch out for her. But despite himself, he didn't know what to say. He couldn't speak the truth—couldn't outright say he needed to run away—that he was being crushed under the weight of their family.

To tell her the truth, would be to tear her heart out.

Eli had done everything he could to give her a normal childhood, one he was never granted. Harper couldn't risk leaving home or going to town anymore, their father essentially died alongside their mother, and it was Eli's fault their mother was gone in the first place. Nothing was as it should be.

But somewhere in the last few years, something in him shattered. He couldn't bear the weight any longer and decided the best thing for Harper, and himself, was to leave and enlist. To become his father was unacceptable, cowering away in the countryside hoping things would change. Eli would do what he could to help end the war.

It was a comforting lie, one that left room for selfishness. And he hated himself for it.

"Elijah?" Harper asked again. Her gentle and sweet voice shocked him from his ragged thoughts.

"Who told you that?" he responded, playing coy.

"I heard you and dad talking the other night."

*Shouting, you mean*

"When? After your bedtime, young lady?"

"Don't change the subject!" she shouted, standing with clenched fists. "You want to leave don't you! You're tired of us and you want your own life! You can't wait to go and never come back!"

Her voice echoed across the trees. Her quiet weeping did not.

"Hey, no, Harp, that's not it at all." He held her in his lap, wrapping his arms around her. Heavens above, seeing her cry shattered his soul.

He took a deep breath. "Remember last week when that man came to the inn and started a fight with dad?"

She hummed in response, wiping her tears.

"He was drunk, angry because his son died fighting in the war."

"I know," Harper whimpered. "Dad tried to talk to him about it."

"Yeah," Eli said, brushing her hair. "Harp, so much of the evil around us only exists because this war hasn't ended. It festers and breeds. It's the reason you can't leave home. I want to help so stuff like that doesn't happen anymore."

She sniffled, leaning into his chest. "So, it's not because you want to leave? You want to help people?"

"Yeah," he said. "I promise it has nothing to do with you and dad." The lie felt bitter on his tongue, and something caved in his chest as it left his mouth.

"Then you have to promise to save someone," she said, looking at him. "At least one person. To make it worth it."

He grinned, holding her chin and wiping her face. "I promise, Harp. And how about this? Let's get something we can share, to keep us connected. Something to have before I leave, just for me and you."

She smiled. "Like a—"

Eli opened his eyes, instantly overwhelmed with the throbbing in his skull. His hands and fingers burned as he lifted them, seeing them wrapped in white bandages. The motion shot pain up into his shoulders and neck. He winced, waiting for the thundering in his head to abate. How much time would he spend here in the medical ward throughout the program? For certain, he wasn't so keen to get out of bed quickly this time.

He heard the gentle rhythmic snoring of another patient as he rested under the warm blankets. With the space so dimly lit, there was no way to know what time it was, or how long he'd been out. It didn't matter.

"You're an idiot."

The now familiar voice sent shockwaves through his skull. Yet despite the pain in his head, he felt a thrill of excitement at her presence, though he didn't feel like turning his head to stare down Shira's glare.

"Speak quietly please," he rasped.

A beat passed.

"Don't tell me what to do," she said, though she indeed lowered her voice. "Did you even think for one second before you jumped after Lara like a frog with a death wish?"

"I told you, I couldn't just—"

"You left us!" she barked. Eli winced. "Forget Lara, you abandoned your squadmates. If you had died, or if we hadn't pulled you out, Arlo and I would've had to complete the challenge on our own! But instead of thinking about that, you leaped into the water like some would-be hero and then expected us to risk our skin to pull you out!"

Eli was silent. He hadn't thought about that, at least in the moment.

"Listen, I don't know you very well," she continued, her voice quiet once more. "But you talk a lot about helping others, which I mostly understand. But if you're going to act like our squad leader, you cannot pull stunts like that."

Cheeks burning, his neck ached as he turned his head to face Shira, who sat in the corner among the dim lighting. "Look, Shira—"

"I'm not done. Lara. You don't know her either. You've been in this program all of a few days and you should have died pulling that stunt."

"What does that have to do with anything?" Curse the ever loving Nine Hells every time he spoke his throat felt like it was filled with gravel and salt.

"You told me you are trying to survive, that you need help to stay alive. But then you go off and leap into death's mouth. So, which is it?"

"Why do you care? You're lecturing me like—"

"Like I'm the one you left for dead on that cliff? You don't know if Arlo and I would have been able to complete the challenge ourselves. And I'm lecturing because I know the consequences of taking rash action. Now answer my question. Why?"

"Could you stand by and watch someone die when you have the power to do something about it?" Eli argued.

"This isn't about me."

"I'm making it about you. You keep asking me why I would risk my life for a near stranger. So I'm asking you: are you so messed up that the idea of risking your life for someone else is unacceptable?"

She pursed her lips. "For my friends, without a thought, for my enemies, never."

"Lara isn't my enemy."

"You don't even know her! Our lives are on the line every day in this program. Hells, Sol just killed his squadmate without consequences, and Orion was killed for tapping out."

"Sol said Fjord slipped."

"Do not tell me you are that naive."

Eli held her stare. He wasn't naive to what Sol, Soren, and Kairah likely did, but hoped it wasn't true. He waited for her to continue.

"Whether or not you'll admit it, this program is do or die. Lara is better on the mat. She could kill you at her leisure. So why save someone that might try and kill you tomorrow in the Sparring Hall?"

"Look, I made a decision—"

"You have a hero complex."

"And you like to interrupt me."

"You like telling others what to do."

"And you like to pass judgment on others' actions."

Shira's eyes narrowed. "You can't fight your way out of a beehive."

"But I can swim." Eli tried his best to display a smug smile, but it did nothing for Shira's scowl. "Thank you. For saving me, I mean."

"I didn't save you," she said, standing and walking in front of his bed. "And I wasn't the one who saved Lara." Shira pulled back the curtain to his left, revealing the patient in the bunk next to his before leaving without a word.

Lara lay unconscious, her breathing shallow and steady, covered in bandages.

*Thank the shining Heavens*

Eli closed his eyes, his pain lessening knowing Lara survived. He pulled back the bandage on his left wrist, revealing the coin-sized star tattoo.

*I did it, Harp. I saved someone*

With that, he fell into a deep dreamless sleep.

# Chapter Fourteen

Eva woke in the early morning, last night's memories rushing back. She should feel guilty for freeing her enemies, betraying her people. But she couldn't. She had to find out everything about Lucas's brother, and where he might be if he was still alive. She had hoped to bring Lucas a sliver of hope, a whisper of news about his lost brother—just as he had so often mended the wounds in her own heart.

But the interaction wasn't completely fruitless.

*The Obelisks*

Something about them didn't add up. She remembered Xerza's words, how they contained some form of magic. But then why would the Zentari, masters of the ethereal and creators of Guardians, need external sources of magic? She wondered if the Legion could use the stones, despite not possessing inner magic themselves. It was the difference in heritage—bloodlines—that determined if someone had their own source of the ethereal within.

An Aniyan could never wield magic like a Guardian. Perhaps the Obelisks would allow that. But if that were true, why did she have such a severe reaction to the one she found with nothing to show for it?

*Too many questions*

Too many questions without enough answers. If only she—

"Swordsman Mona, you are a disgrace!"

Eva shot up at the sound of Drax's voice.

*Rotting Hells*

Guilt swirled in her stomach. She sprang off the bed, lacing her boots and racing out of her tent. She followed Drax's voice to the center of camp, where he stood over a cowering Swordsman. Her nose was bleeding, eyes glistening. And Eva immediately recognized her.

*Because you attacked her last night*

Eva slowly approached the edge of the crowd which surrounded Drax and Mona.

"You are a disgrace to the Legion! Give me one reason why I shouldn't dismiss you right now!"

Drax's face was red, his veins bulging in his neck, spittle flying from his mouth. Eva swallowed the lump in her throat. Even at his worst, she'd never seen Drax this livid.

The Swordsman remained on the ground, wiping the blood from her nose. "Lieutenant, sir—" she pleaded.

"You've jeopardized the safety of everyone here! I'm filing formal charges on your record. And as punishment, you are to be thrown into the pit for two days, after which you will spend the next month with more miserable work than you could imagine."

"Wait!" Eva shouted, regret rushing through her as the words left her mouth. All eyes shifted to her. Drax stopped, his furious gaze drifting to the sound of her voice. The anger in his features grew, and for a moment, Eva felt like he could see everything that happened. She kept her face stoic under his stare.

"What did you say?" he whispered.

Eva lowered her head in respect. "I can bring the prisoners back."

His eyes narrowed. "And how in the bleeding Hells do you know the prisoners escaped?" he asked, his tone seething with disdain. "You had something to do with this, didn't you?"

"No, I didn't. But I know that Swordsman Mona was on guard duty at the cellar last night."

"And how do you know that?" he shouted.

"This camp is small, Lieutenant Drax. It's not hard to keep track of where everyone is."

"Don't—" he began, but stopped himself. Turning back to the cowering Swordsman, he considered her offer. Eva was counting on his pride to sway his decision. Drax's primary focus was his reputation and his military status. Losing two Zentari prisoners under his watch would be inexcusable—an unsightly blemish on an otherwise perfect military record.

He returned his attention back to Eva. "They have half a day's head start."

"I can catch them. You know I can."

His mouth twitched as his eyes searched hers. Curse this constant game of theirs. Despite Manoach being a punishment, she would be thankful to be out from under Drax's control.

"Very well, Swordsman Katz. Do the Legion proud and return the prisoners unharmed."

Eva stood at attention and bowed before striding for her tent.

"Wait!" Drax shouted. Eva stopped—waiting. "Why are you helping Swordsman Mona? What is it to you?"

She turned around to face him before responding, standing at attention. "I have brought upon myself a reputation which reflects poorly on the values of the Legion. I want to remedy that."

"I don't buy that for a second," he quipped. "But Hells knows I'll never get the truth out of you. Least you can do is be useful. Go fetch my prisoners, Katz, and don't come back until you do. And do not think you get to decide to go alone. Swordsman Rollo goes with you."

She sighed. This complicated things—especially Rollo.

He pointed a finger at her. "Oh, and Swordsman, do hurry back. You've got a long journey ahead of you."

Drax sneered at Mona before lumbering back to his command tent. A pleading question formed in Mona's eyes, but Eva didn't have the heart to speak with her and turned to leave.

"Wait!" Mona said, standing and rushing to her as the crowd dispersed. "Why?"

Eva swallowed the knot in her throat at seeing Mona's bruising face. "Because it wasn't your fault."

Eva turned and strode to her tent before Mona could ask anything more. She threw a few days' worth of supplies into her travel satchel. It was one of the only things left of her mother who spent many years wandering the continent, visiting Adiel's neighboring countries to the north, before Eva was born.

Maya quietly entered unannounced, her face covered with disappointment. "Did you do this?"

Eva froze, exhaling. "Maya—"

"Don't you *dare* lie to me."

Eva flinched at her tone. "I needed answers. And I—"

"No!" Maya shouted, before whispering. "You don't get to make excuses. You crossed a line, Eva. People could have gotten hurt."

"But they didn't!" Eva stepped toward her, matching her tone. "And they can't have gotten far."

Maya gave a puzzled look. "You broke them out just to recapture them?"

Eva shrugged. "It was the only way I could think of to get them to give me information. And I learned something, the objects they've been seeking are called Obelisks."

"Great, so you learned what our enemy calls these little stones. Congratulations."

"Shut up, you're not listening!" Eva continued packing her things. "They also said the Zentari have no idea where they come from, or how to make them."

Maya scoffed. "They're playing dumb!"

"I don't think so."

"Eva, you're way out of line!" Maya said. "You fly in the face of authority, you *attack* your own comrade and then let war criminals go! By all rights you should be brought to the block!"

"They are not war criminals! They are warriors who were captured in the line of duty, Hells one *surrendered*. And did you also happen to know the Legion has a renowned reputation for torturing our prisoners?"

"Of course they would say that!" Maya argued, checking the volume in her voice. "Eva, they lied. That's what the Zentari do. They lie, steal, and kill to get what they want, and you trusted them like a fool."

"Yes!" Eva said, spinning to her. "I trusted a Zentari. Is that so impossible to imagine?"

"Of course it is!" Maya argued. "And you're sounding like a sympathizer."

Eva huffed. She turned back to packing, wrestling with her thoughts. She believed Xerza was being honest—saw the truth in his eyes—and that alienated her from her kin. To be a sympathizer was akin to being a traitor.

"You weren't there," Eva muttered. "I believe him."

Maya sighed. "If the Zentari aren't responsible, then who in the Nine Realms is making these magic rocks?"

"I don't know," Eva said, tying her bag shut. "And neither did he. But don't you find it weird the Zentari have no idea how they're created?"

"That doesn't matter, Eva. You let our prisoners go for that?"

"No. I also asked him about Aniyan prisoners. I thought maybe I could find out where they're holding Lucas's brother, if they have him. Or whether Zentari even take Aniyan civilians captive."

"And what did *the enemy* say?" Maya snarked.

"Xerza said it was a rumor, but some are bought and used as slaves in Eldan City."

*Or tortured*

"Oh, good to know his name is *Xerza*. So glad you're friends now."

"Maya, stop it. You're not listening."

"Just tell Drax what—"

"Drax doesn't care," Eva whispered harshly, throwing her pack down on the cot. "You know he's a rotting sack of boar spit who thinks about nothing other than his own ego. I just met a Zentari Captain who spoke to me with more respect than Drax ever has."

Maya took a step back, eyes narrowing. "What are you saying?"

Eva exhaled sharply. "Remember when Drax sent me, Chief Port, and Swordsman Lane on that mission West? To investigate the suspected spy?" Maya nodded. "We met with a civilian informant who had already captured the Zentari spy. We were ordered to exchange information and to bring the prisoner back *for questioning*. Port killed them—both."

Maya gave a puzzled look. "Why?"

"I asked him the same thing. Demanded, actually. He said the orders came directly from Drax. When we got back and debriefed, I asked Drax myself. He said the order was from higher Leadership."

Maya threw her arms out. "So, we got orders to kill a spy and a sympathizer."

"No, Maya," Eva pressed. "Port slaughtered an innocent Aniyan and a defense-less Zentari. That's not what we're supposed to be doing."

"This is war!"

"And that's not an excuse!" Eva snapped. "Don't defend his actions!"

"I'm defending a man acting *under orders!*"

A rock settled in Eva's stomach. "He enjoyed it," Eva breathed. Maya's gaze averted. "Port and Lane laughed about it—*laughed*—on our way back to Yaqar. That's not following orders, Maya, that's relishing the suffering of others."

"What are you saying?"

"I'm saying right and wrong have gotten a whole lot harder to distinguish over the past few years. And doing something just because Leadership says to isn't enough anymore."

Maya crossed her arms, remaining silent.

"Maya, you know me. I need you to trust me," Eva said. "I'm just trying to end this stupid war, and I think these stones might be the answer. I know releasing the prisoners was stupid, but we aren't doing anything here. And in one conversation I got information that may change everything." Eva's heart thundered alongside her turmoil of emotions. Her outlook and Maya's were drastically different, their beliefs contrasted at times, but Eva trusted her friend knew right from wrong.

"You're asking a lot, Katz."

Eva flinched in response to the name. Maya smirked.

"You're such a jerk," Eva said wryly.

"Seriously though," Maya said, her smile gone. "No more games. Please don't make me turn you in. Because I will, the Hells as my witness, if you pull something like that again."

Eva couldn't ignore the unwavering conviction in Maya's tone. Eva loved her friend. But Maya walked the path of the righteous only within the confines of the law, while Eva saw morality as a force beyond rules—a duty of everyone, regardless of circumstance.

Maya turned to leave.

"Thank you," Eva said, "for not turning me in."

Her friend spoke over her shoulder. "Don't thank me. Just fix your mistake."

*It wasn't a mistake*

Eva finished packing her satchel and left Yaqar. She started her search for the escaped Zentari at the pit, checking the ground for footprints or broken twigs. She was an excellent tracker. Sneaking out of the house and avoiding her father's search parties unnoticed gave her plenty of practice at becoming stealthy—skills that served her well in her early military career.

Eva quickly found two sets of footprints headed west.

*At least they listened*

She stood as she heard someone approaching. Swordsman Evan Rollo stood a head above her, with toned muscles complementing his chiseled jawline. His sandy hair was trimmed short, and his eyes were the color of mist. Eva bit down on her frustration having to bring someone along—especially him.

"You ready, Swordsman Katz?" he asked plainly. Judging by his restless shifting and averted gaze, Eva could tell he would enjoy this no more than she would.

"Don't slow me down," she quipped, turning to pursue the newly escaped prisoners.

# Chapter Fifteen

What's that one, daddy?" Eli asked, pointing his young fingers at the next brightest star cluster.

"That's the Drake's Claw," his father responded. "See how it's shaped like a dragon's claw with four fingers?"

Eli stared at the stars for a moment, cocking his head and squinting to make out the constellation's shape. "Oh yeah! I see it! I see it!"

With a broad smile, Eli laid back on the grass next to his father, a gentle breeze on the crisp night air. His cheeks burned from too much sun, after spending all day helping with the chores around the farm.

"What about that one?" Eli asked, pointing at a single, bright ruby star.

"Ah, that one. Good eye, Z. That's the Phoenix Flame cluster. That crimson color symbolizes the Phoenix's sacred flames. Do you remember the story of the Phoenix?"

"Yeah. It's the bird that dies and comes back to life."

"Exactly. The phoenix is a symbol of renewal and rebirth. It reminds us that even when everything seems to be over, when everything comes crashing down, there's always hope. Always a second chance."

Eli stilled, resting his head on his father's broad shoulders. The comforting scent of pine needles and pipe smoke wafted over him.

"Dad?" Eli asked.

"Yeah, pal?"

"What's a Zephiron?" Eli asked, struggling with the pronunciation.

His father giggled. "Finally figured out the riddle of your nickname? It's someone with a sharp mind—wise beyond their years. Just like you."

Eli grinned, beaming with pride at his father's praise.

"Can we do this every night?" Eli asked. He turned to look at his father who was only bones and seared flesh. Eli leaped back in horror as his father's corpse began to move, reaching for him with flesh sloughing off the white of his skeleton. A horrifying rasping breath erupted from the skeleton as its jaws opened.

Eli woke with a start, his body moist with sweat. The air in the crowded bunkroom held a stifling warmth, carrying the musky stench of the men in the confined quarters. He rubbed his eyes.

*Bleeding rot, these nightmares*

He sat up on the edge of his bed, careful to avoid Arlo's bunk, letting his heart rate drop. The room was quiet, apart from the soft snoring of a few. Eli rubbed his neck, trying to work out the stress from his shoulders. The days in the program were beginning to blur together, each one moving faster than the last. It had been only a week since he was in the medical ward after the Proving. His mind was numb from absorbing all the information, while his body ached from forcing it to endure worsening hardship each and every day.

He rubbed the bridge of his nose. Maybe he wasn't cut out for this.

*No*

*Remember why you're here*

But that was the problem—he didn't know why he was here.

Eli traced the black ink on his wrist, the memory of Harper's joy a tether to something real. He smiled, remembering her elation at their shared marking. But as his thoughts drifted to home, the weight he tried to leave behind resurfaced. He had told Harper he came to help others—a half truth. There *was* a deep longing inside him to fight against the evil lingering over their generation. But how could he offer light in the darkness when he could barely see himself? The man he saw in the mirror was a stranger.

Before he could save anyone, he needed to save himself, and he had no idea how to do that. How could he mend something so deeply etched into his own being it had grafted itself as a part of his soul? How could he remove the echoes of his failure—the loss of his mother, the breaking of his family, the weight of promises unkept?

The answers felt distant—an intangible mist, entirely out of his reach.

He took a deep breath and laid back down, willing himself to rest. Perhaps the path forward was not in searching, but in becoming. If he could be a Guardian, if he could stand firm in something outside himself, maybe the rest would follow.

He didn't remember falling asleep, and morning came all too soon.

"Eyes up, recruits!" the night watch Operative yelled. "Five minutes to breakfast!"

Eli twitched. It was the most abrasive way to be woken up he ever experienced. Arlo, chipper as ever, was starting to get on Eli's nerves each morning. Eli couldn't understand how Arlo seemed immune to the constant stress and lack of sleep. Not to mention, it took at least twenty minutes for Eli to wake up most mornings, but Arlo jumped out of bed as if he never fell asleep.

"Morning sunshine!" Arlo said, pulling on his clothing.

"Can you keep the noise to a minimum, please?" Eli muttered, his eyes glazed over, still sitting on his bed. He willed the fog over his mind to leave. Arlo stopped dressing and leaned forward to examine Eli.

"You sick?" he asked, feeling his forehead.

Eli glared, his annoyance growing. "No, I'm just not a mutant like some people," he said, standing to dress.

"Ha, you'll feel better after some food," Arlo said, patting Eli's shoulder.

After a satisfying breakfast, Eli did indeed feel more awake.

"Recruits!" Captain Renard announced, entering the mess hall. "Morning lecture is canceled. You will all report to the Sparring Hall immediately."

Obediently, the recruits followed the Captain. Eli groaned as he saw the mats laid out in an orderly fashion, disappointed he was denied at least a few hours of physical rest sitting in the Lecture Hall.

"Everyone is to complete at least ten practice matches in total!" Renard announced. "Mix up pairings in your squad. Share the load helping the least experienced of you. Stick to your squad and begin when you're ready."

Eli noted four proctors in the corner of the room speaking in hushed tones as he slipped on his leather gloves. The cliff had wreaked havoc on many recruits' hands. Even once the scabs healed, the fresh skin couldn't stand up to their brutal physical training. And Eli wasn't the only one. Over the past week, he watched more recruits using wrappings and joint supports. He assumed such things were originally perceived as weaknesses, but with so many injured recruits, there was nothing to hide any longer.

The room echoed with bodies slamming on the padded mats—grunts and cheers following suit. A quiet buzz of activity rose.

"All right," Eli said, turning to Shira as he stepped on the mat. "Teach me."

"No," she said, arms crossed. "Fight Lara."

He threw his arms out. Lara was finishing wrapping her left shoulder.

"But you said—"

"Shut up, I know what I said," she snipped. Arlo gave a questioning look between the two. "But I need to watch you fight first to see where your form is lacking. Besides, you're still recovering."

Arlo grinned, bearing no injuries from the cliff. Eli held his hands up.

"Okay, fair enough," he said, waiting while Lara hesitantly rolled her left shoulder. Despite her still-recovering injuries, she fell into her comfortable fighting stance.

"Feeling okay?" Eli asked Lara, who had already thanked him profusely.

She nodded. "Yeah. Thank—"

"Stop it," Shira interrupted. "Don't stroke his ego."

Eli rolled his eyes. He took a deep breath and lunged forward, throwing his body weight into a right hook. Lara pushed his fist aside with her left hand, gritting her teeth against the ache in her shoulder. She used Eli's momentum and brought her right knee into his abdomen. Eli stumbled, holding his stomach, a loud yelp escaping his lips.

"Pathetic," Shira commented. "Again."

Eli stood, spinning to Lara, ignoring the heat in his cheeks. Eli kept a close eye on the proctors, still standing in the far corner. He didn't think he could handle a formal match so soon.

Shira crossed her arms, wondering where to even start improving Eli's form. It was abysmal.

"You lose a bet?" Arlo asked, beside her.

Shira glanced at him. "No. He asked for my help."

"You don't have to humiliate him," Arlo said, watching Lara land another blow. "He's getting a lot of grief already. Mostly in the face and stomach."

Shira wasn't surprised he came to Eli's defense. "He asked for my expertise in combat techniques. And my current assessment is he's too confident. He needs a beating so he learns how defenseless he really is." Shira kept her attention on Eli, analyzing his maneuvers. The second bout lasted only moments longer than the first, though Eli managed to stay on his feet.

"Eli's just one of those natural-born leader types," Arlo said. "They take charge, but he's not really that confident. And at least he's admitting his weaknesses."

"Natural-born leader? No. He's controlling. He has a problem being vulnerable and compensates with control."

A shout rang out from across the room. Sol stood with his arms stretched out. "Is there no one here to challenge me?"

Shira rolled her eyes. Arlo huffed.

"Hey," Eli said out of breath, pointing toward Sol. "What happens when a squad loses just a single member?"

Lara answered. "I saw Renard introduce a new recruit to them from another squad that was dissolved. It sounds like the Leadership does their best to always keep four people in each squad if possible, dismantling squads with only one or two members."

Eli nodded, humming in agreement.

Arlo mumbled, "Poor guy got thrown to the wolves."

Shira said nothing. She was curious how the recruits were chosen to join new squads, given the squads were the recruit's choice in the first place. There were so many things about this program that didn't make sense. Nothing like what she was told, or what she expected.

Eli and Lara resumed their bout.

"Anyway," Arlo continued. "Natural or not, he can have squad leader. I don't want it. And I don't see you or Lara gunning for it either."

Shira's ears perked. "Why don't you want it?"

"It's too much to think about. Too much responsibility. As long as I have a full belly and a good fight, I'm happy." He smiled.

Shira's eyes narrowed. "That's entirely too simplistic. You can't possibly be that naive."

"Well, I'm a simple guy," he responded with his signature smirk.

She paused, considering Arlo's statement. "Is your family as simple as you?"

"Assuming that's not an insult, no, they're not. My dad kept a very tight ship at home. Growing up with so many brothers and sisters, you learn to go with the flow."

"What do you mean?"

"Well, between routines and chores, duties and chain of command, living with more than a dozen family of younger siblings you learn to keep the peace and not rock the boat."

Shira watched Lara flip Eli over after he overcommitted an attack. "Were you close with your siblings?"

"Kind of. I was one of the oldest brothers, so I had a lot of responsibility. I was working as much as my old man by fourteen. It was exhausting but we needed the money. What about you?"

"I don't have a family."

Arlo turned to Shira, his smile gone, replaced by concern. "Really? You an orphan too?"

"Yeah, you could say that," she said, pursing her lips. "I don't like talking about it."

Shira was saved from the question as Arlo's shoulders were shoved forward. He and Shira turned to find Kairah Richter pushed him with a glare.

"Arlo. I've been meaning to pay you back for rejecting my invitation to join my squad," Kairah spat, her brown hair sticking to her sweaty face. "Hells knows why you chose this sorry lot."

Arlo swallowed and shifted his weight. "Look, I just don't want to be on the same team as Sol the Barbarian. Or Soren," he said, rubbing the back of his head.

"Sol and Soren are the best fighters here. And that's my brother, you rotting *Gut'pa*. They're the strongest and they take charge."

Shira said, "They also have a personal vendetta to break the neck of every recruit."

Kairah ignored her. "I thought you were going to help me, Arlo," she said, her demeanor changed to something akin to pouting.

"Yeah, sorry . . . I . . ." Arlo's mouth twitched, but his voice trailed. Kairah left in a huff, not sparing him the chance to explain. Arlo blushed, releasing a breath of air. He and Shira turned from where Kairah left to find Eli and Lara staring at them with questioning looks.

"I talked to her the first day here," Arlo explained, palms up. "We chatted a bit. I laid it on thick. Turns out she's crazy and she's Sol's sister. Okay?"

No one replied. Eli shrugged and turned back to Lara, arms in a defensive stance.

Arlo sighed. "So," he said, "what were you saying about your family?"

Shira glanced at him, shifting her weight. "Doesn't matter," she said. "Where'd you learn to fight? Was Eli joking about the underground on the cliff?"

Arlo's eyes narrowed, but he let the question slide. Shira was grateful, tension easing from her shoulders. Her squad was kind, but distance was better. None of them would understand, and no one wanted to hear old ghosts.

"Growing up poor you learn to fight, or everyone walks all over you." Arlo said. "Well, maybe not quite so dramatic, but you get my point. After that, I did in fact fight in the underground. Although, it was technically a black market."

"What's the difference?"

Arlo shrugged. "Semantics and legality."

"And now the military is your next big match?" Shira asked, a smile tugging at her lips.

"You catch on quick."

"I'm observant."

Arlo paused, grinning. "Not observant enough," he murmured.

"Excuse me?" she said, turning to him. Arlo didn't respond, that annoying smirk back on his face. "Well, I can observe this—you feign nonchalance as a coping mechanism. You aren't looking for a fight, you're running."

"Running from what?" he asked, brow furrowed.

Shira shrugged. "Don't know yet. I haven't *observed* enough."

Eli landed with a grunt as his back hit the mat, air stolen from his lungs. He lost. *Again.*

As he rose, his gaze drifted to Arlo and Shira. There was something in the way she looked at Arlo—something soft, unreadable, yet absent of the sharpness she saved for him. A quiet weight settled in his chest—jealousy creeping in like an unwelcome shadow. He swallowed it down, but the taste lingered.

"All right!" Lara announced to the group. "Tag out!" Her labored breathing made the sweat on her neck shimmer in the light of the room. She walked over beside Shira and collapsed on the floor.

Eli bent forward, hands on his knees to rest. He unbuckled the upper part of his armor to cool himself in the increasingly humid space. Shira stepped up and placed her hand on his chest.

"Nope. Back out there," she said, pushing him back onto the mat. A sinking feeling told him a beating was imminent, and Arlo's mocking smile did nothing to ease the certainty. Eli held his hands up, asking for a moment to catch his breath. Shira crossed her arms.

A scream cut through the air, snapping the nearby healers into motion as they rushed to an injured recruit. Eli watched them pass, his gaze shifting to the proctors who had abandoned their corner and now stood watch over various mats. One lingered where the wounded recruit writhed in agony. He exhaled slowly, hoping they wouldn't come his way. If he was placed in a formal match he would undoubtedly lose, and his head couldn't take another hit so soon.

"Come on," Shira ordered.

Eli readied himself, lunging at Shira with a right jab. She pushed the punch aside casually and threw a kick to his right knee. He fell, cradling his injury. Clenching his jaw, he glanced up at his teacher. Shira held no compassion in her expression.

"Stop using the same opening move," she said. "You've done it four times now."

Eli stood weakly. "It's what I'm comfortable with." He gingerly put more weight on his right knee.

"That's the problem, you can't sit in your comfort zone. If you want to grow, get uncomfortable."

He glanced around for the proctors again, terrified of being the next formal match. Thankfully they weren't near. As he turned back, Shira was right in front of him. She punched him, clipping the same spot Rowan found on the cliffside. It hurt like the living Hells, but he remained on his feet.

"Pay attention."

Eli limped his way along the food line, his knee swollen from Shira's aggressive teaching methods. Bleed the Hells his body hurt. He grinned at the irony of finally having Shira's attention, at the cost of his own anguish. Regardless of the pain, Shira was keeping her end of the deal. He'd learned a great deal.

*Now if I can only put it to use*

Eli prayed his injuries would somehow miraculously heal before afternoon practice with Evergreen. A low murmur filled the spacious mess hall, swelling a little more each day. As the recruits grew familiar with one another, the once-hesitant exchanges gave way to effortless conversations, their voices weaving together in a steady, rising hum.

The serving cook scooped some sort of gray food onto his plate. He didn't recognize it, but it smelled delicious. And despite the less than appetizing appearance, he was hungry enough to eat anything. Eli thanked the server with a smile. He noted her warmth and kindness, wondering how long she'd served in the Citadel.

Soon after sitting with his squad and devouring his meal, Maelyn came over and joined them. They all paused, staring in silence.

"What?" Maelyn snarked. "I need a break from my squad. They're just . . ."

"Observant? Harsh?" Arlo asked.

"Violent? Brutal?" Eli added.

"Controlling? Aloof?" Shira chimed.

Lara giggled, pursing her lips to keep from spitting out her water.

"Sure," Maelyn drawled, with a questioning look.

"What's bugging you about your squad?" Lara asked.

"What isn't?" Maelyn said. "I told you last night that Esme is the one keeping Rowan in check. But then all I deal with is Rowan running his mouth, Esme glaring at him, and Fenner constantly apologizing."

Arlo said, "Is Rowan still pissed about losing the first fight in the beginning of the program?"

"No," Maelyn said. "At least, he hasn't mentioned it. He did make a comment about wanting to be more like Sol's team, though."

Arlo gave a grunt of disgust.

"How is practice going?" Lara asked.

"It's all right," Maelyn replied, taking a bite of her food. "Esme is annoyingly good. Rowan is average. But Fenner is awful and won't stop apologizing for everything. He's like a puppy that got dragged out of the gutter. It's pathetic."

Arlo snickered.

"He's just grateful you guys saved him." Lara encouraged.

"Yeah, he owes you a life debt." Arlo added. "Think of all the favors you can ask for now."

Shira kept her eyes on her meal as she spoke. "He's weak and he knows it. He's trying to save his own skin by finding other ways to be useful."

"You sound like Rowan," Eli said to Shira.

She raised her brow. "I sound like a hot-headed, short-minded pig?"

The table quieted. Eli held her sharpening gaze. The pain in his knee pushed his patience to the limit, and regardless, he wanted to see what exactly lay beneath Shira's thick skin.

"Just because he's weak doesn't mean he can't get stronger," Eli said.

"Says the weakest one on our squad," she quipped.

"If I'm the weakest, then I have the greatest opportunity for growth."

"Improvement. Not growth."

"You're saying I'll get stronger on the mat but be no better a person?"

Shira shrugged. "I'm saying we're not here for personal growth. We're here to train for war."

"If the price of your training is the loss of my humanity, then you can keep it."

"Are you implying I have no humanity?"

"I'm saying I haven't heard you say one positive thing since I met you."

Eli searched her eyes, sensing the density of the shield she carried around herself—a protective shell keeping others out. But something underneath drew his attention, pulled at him like gravity.

"How's the knee?" Shira spat, dropping her fork and grabbing her plate. Without another word, she stood and stormed away. Eli returned to his food.

"She's gonna bury you, man," Arlo murmured from across the table.

Eli sighed.

"I'm sorry, did I miss something?" Maelyn asked. "Who's she and why are you mad at each other?"

Eli opened his mouth to respond, but Lara spoke first.

"Shira's our fourth squad member. She's really good, and the best on the mat, but a bit . . . intense."

"Best is a strong word," Arlo teased.

"Well, she's not wrong about Fenner." Maelyn added.

"She might be right," Eli said, "but it's still the wrong way to look at things."

"Have you guys been able to talk to her outside classes?" Lara asked. "Arlo, you guys were chatting by the mat."

Arlo shrugged. "Yeah, but it was just pleasantries. She was more asking about me than anything else, and dodged the questions aimed at herself."

Eli swallowed the jealousy that crept up his throat.

*'She was more asking about me'*

He wondered where Arlo and Shira's conversation had wandered.

*This is stupid*

He shouldn't be jealous and didn't even know why he was. Shira's distaste for him was no secret. At best she tolerated him. But he couldn't help it. While she had thus far been critical and abrasive, he didn't believe that's who she truly was. Something beyond her guarded exterior sparked an interest in his soul. She was exceptionally talented and inquisitive, determined and fierce. And despite his harsh words, she wasn't anything like Rowan.

"Hmm," Maelyn hummed, taking a sip of her water. "Mysterious."

"She seems on edge to me," Lara said. "Like she's under a lot of pressure. I bet she's really hard on herself. Maybe she's afraid of disappointing someone?"

"Maybe," Arlo said. "Or she has standards to live up to outside the program."

"I know what that's like," Maelyn muttered.

"Am I controlling?" Eli blurted. His friends froze, puzzled by the sudden change of topic.

"I mean." Arlo started. "You're not shy about speaking your thoughts or saying what you feel needs to happen."

"But that's not a bad thing," Eli retorted.

"Hey, you asked," Arlo said.

"Don't let it bother you," Lara said. "You're a natural leader. We'll let you know if you start getting bossy."

"Yeah, thanks," Eli said with a sigh. "I'm gonna grab some rest before practice."

Returning his plate, he headed for the bunkroom knowing he never felt he had a problem taking control. Stepping into a role of pseudo-father for your younger sister *and* helping run a family business requires being organized and confident. No one liked being vulnerable, but Eli didn't think his leading came from a place of fear.

In fact, he didn't feel he controlled much of anything in his life. He didn't choose to grow up during a war. He didn't choose to lose his mother, start a family business, or be forced to raise his little sister. Joining the military was the first thing he *was* able to choose. And most people didn't step up when they needed to. In fact—

He stopped as a grunt and a thud sounded from the women's bunkroom—the barracks door slightly ajar. He peeked through and saw Shira toss something onto her bunk angrily, before running her hands through her hair. She paced for a moment, and he swore her eyes were glazed as she slumped onto her bunk, holding her head in her hands.

He thought he heard a sniffle, but that would be a drastic display of emotion for Shira. He scanned the room as best he could, but it was otherwise unoccupied. Guilt tugged at his heart. He reached up to knock and apologize but stayed his hand.

*Why? I make one snarky comment and I'm supposed to make amends? She's rude and abrasive. If she can't take it, she shouldn't dish it out*

Yet, Lara's comment echoed in his mind. Eli knew the weight of others' expectations. And his aching body was only a testament to Shira's commitment to training him. She was keeping her word, upholding her end of the bargain. He reached for the door again, but a whistle blew from the first level.

"All recruits report to the practice field! Five minutes!"

Eli scurried away from the door, down the hall and stairway.

*Heavens help me survive this practice*

# Chapter Sixteen

Following Xerza and Thalia's tracks was easy for Eva, given her natural skills and plentiful practice. She kept Rollo at a brisk pace, hoping to catch up to the Zentari. Their enemy was sleep-deprived, hungry, and thirsty, evident by their slowing pace. Rollo had remained quiet since they entered the woods, which Eva appreciated. Silences never made her uncomfortable, and in truth she could get overstimulated quite easily by loud environments.

Eva and Rollo crested a ridge, the footprints growing closer together.

*They're tiring. Shortening their strides*

Rollo stumbled over a tree stump, hitting the ground with a grunt.

*Heavens help me*

While Rollo was an adept warrior, a rogue he was not. She hoped his noisy presence was worth having capable back up. Vermin scurried across the underbrush as birds sounded in the trees, which starkly contrasted the desert stretching out to her left in a sea of heat and tan hues. She often wondered how two opposite climates could occur so close together.

"So," Rollo said loudly. "Word around camp is you're getting transferred."

"Keep your rotting voice down. Unless you enjoy being ambushed," she scolded.

"Come on, Katz, you're not still mad, are you? It was six months ago, let it go, for Hell's sake."

"Which part would you like me to let go, Rollo? The part where you grabbed my thigh, or the part where I broke your nose?"

"All of it, actually. Look, I didn't mean anything by it, okay?"

"I know you didn't. You were drunk."

"So, what's the problem?"

She spun to him. "Why do you care, Rollo?"

"You can call me Evan."

"No," she quipped. "We're not friends."

He shifted his weight. "I'd like to be."

Eva scoffed. "You told your buddies that I was the one coming onto you, and that I lost my temper when you turned me down."

His mouth fell open. "I must have forgotten that part."

She placed her hands on her hips, reflexively landing on her daggers. "You're lying, Rollo. You do remember. You know how I know?"

He remained silent—his gaze dancing nervously.

"Because you kept retelling the story and emphasizing how *my temper would keep things spicy*."

His face looked panicked. "How do you know that?"

"It's a small camp, Rollo."

"Look, that was just guy talk, we were being stupid. Let's just bury the sword."

*In your chest*

"Well, at least we can agree that you're stupid," she said.

He shrugged. "Come on, I'm trying to make amends."

"Then apologize," she demanded, crossing her arms.

"Okay, I'm sorry," he said, his sincerity somewhat lacking.

"Good. Thank you. Apology not accepted," she snarked, turning back to the trail.

Rollo mumbled something under his breath. He was a pig, who thought far too much of himself. She didn't care to be his friend. Besides, she rarely got along with anyone.

Though she never knew her, the world never ceased to remind Eva she shared her mother's fire. Defiance was her birthright, tempered beneath the iron will of a father who sought to break her, but only seeded further insolence. Yet neither his hand nor his silver tongue could wound Eva more than the quiet truth of her existence—that the price of her birth was her mother's life.

And it was through a childhood spent questioning herself—questioning the value of her own life—that she forged a spirit unwilling to be broken. Guilt and rebellion wove themselves into the fabric of her being, and Eva refused to allow herself to ever be made small again. She had long understood that kindness was a rarity, that most hands reached only for selfish gain, and if you wanted something—even validation of your worth—you had to claim it for yourself. Lucas was the only person she ever deemed worthy of trust. Beyond him, she sought no approval, asked for nothing. Hers was a will forged in solitude, unyielding, and wholly her own.

She stopped, crouching low, and signaled to Rollo to do the same. A noise reverberated between the trees.

*Groaning*

"What?" Rollo whispered.

"There's someone close," she said over her shoulder.

"I don't hear anyone."

Eva stalked forward, examining the tracks. It was too soon. They shouldn't have caught up to them yet. She motioned for Rollo to follow. He drew his sword as she reached for the blades at her sides. They crept through a narrow ravine, climbing to the other side. As they crested the hill, Eva signaled to stop. Her sharp senses and honed skills analyzed the timberland.

Another soft groan, off to the right, ahead of them. She signaled for Rollo to stay put and keep watch. Inching forward, her gentle steps found the open areas between the fallen branches and leaves. Her vision found boots. And legs. Someone was sitting at the base of a tree. She cautiously rounded their position, keeping her distance, until they were completely visible. As the figure came into view, recognition came over her.

*Xerza*

Eva ran to his side, placing her blade to his neck. He didn't move. His eyes cracked open, mouth agape, blood dripping from the corner. His breaths were wet and ragged. He was wounded—mortally. She signaled Rollo to remain in place while she searched for his injury. Xerza was clutching his right leg, over a deep gash to the inner thigh. Blood seeped from the tissue despite the makeshift tourniquet he had applied. His tunic was soaked from more stab wounds in his abdomen. He hadn't been attacked—he'd been mutilated.

*Would Thalia do this to her own comrade*

Eva leaned forward, keeping her face from Rollo's sightline. "Where is Thalia?"

Xerza responded between ragged breaths. "Gone. Attacked. Surprised." His eyes closed again.

Eva sheathed her knives, putting pressure on the wound to his left thigh. He grimaced, clenching his jaw.

"Where?" she asked, catching Rollo striding toward them. She prayed Xerza would be cautious of his words. He mumbled something she couldn't make out. He was fading quickly, growing paler each moment.

Rollo crouched next to her, examining the bleeding enemy, his face devoid of compassion or pity. "Did he say anything?"

"His partner attacked him," she said, keeping her eyes on Xerza.

"No surprise. Rotting Shells don't have any morals."

"Where is your comrade?" she asked, with a sternness that rang hollow in her chest.

Xerza opened his eyes and looked at Eva, ignoring Rollo's presence. "Yaqar," he rasped.

Eva's eyes widened. She spun to Rollo, her hand still on Xerza's wound.

"Run back to camp, *now*! Warn the others that the female prisoner is returning to the outpost!"

"What is one unarmed half-dead Shell going to—"

Eva grabbed his shirt. "Did you forget how many of them it took to wipe out a third of our camp? Go!" she shouted, shoving him backward.

He cursed but obeyed. As he trotted up the hill, Eva turned back to Xerza. She could think of no words for him—no comfort. A strange, foreign sensation ebbed in her gut, akin to guilt. And sorrow.

This was the enemy, the ones she had been raised to hate. A ruthless, vicious, and barbaric Zentari that would take any opportunity to kill her in the most painful way possible. Yet, in this moment, something gripped her heart, the same thing she felt when she spared Nyx. This was not a rageful warrior dying in battle, nor a hateful being cursing Eva's kin. This was a person—a living being—feeling his life slip away.

Eva grappled with her inner emotions as she grabbed his hand. His eyes opened to slits, their dark depths locking onto hers.

"There is nothing I can offer you except a quick death. You won't make it to help in time, and I can do nothing for you here." She swallowed the emotion rising in her chest. "And I don't wish for you to suffer at the hands of my people."

Xerza started to shiver. He gripped her hand harder, yet there was little strength in his grasp. "You . . . gave me a chance . . . to live," he rasped, taking a deep breath. "You showed me . . . honor."

"Xerza, please. Can you tell me any more about the Obelisks? Help me end the bloodshed." Eva held his hand, waiting for his answer. She hoped that Xerza would agree it didn't matter which side won, if everyone was dead.

"I . . . assume . . . the Obelisks are . . . for the Guardians."

Eva had considered that already, but it didn't make sense. The Guardians didn't need magic, they *were* magic.

"Do the Obelisks make the Guardians stronger?"

Xerza nodded weakly. "But how . . . they are made . . . has been lost. I . . . searched . . . but someone . . . has buried . . . the past."

He was fading. Eva knew the question she wanted to ask but didn't want the answer it came with.

"Tell me what the Legion does with prisoners. Do the Aniyans truly torture your people?"

"It . . . is hard to know truth . . . from hatred. But I have seen . . . some who have escaped . . ." He coughed, blood spurting from his mouth, coating his teeth. "Flesh mutilated . . . minds broken . . . children . . ."

Eva hung her head, uncertain of what weighed heavier—the hatred so deeply rooted in her people that they embraced the unspeakable, or the leaders who fed the flames, turning lies into fuel for the rage.

Xerza coughed again. "I am . . . sorry. I . . . know nothing more . . . I offer my thanks and . . . my apologies, Aniyan."

Eva gripped his hand tighter. "Evalynn. My name is Evalynn."

"I . . . thank you, Evalynn," he rasped, closing his eyes. "Please . . ."

She pulled her dagger from its sheath and held it to his chest over his heart.

"You die with honor, Xerza," Eva whispered, plunging the blade into his chest.

As the last flicker of light left his eyes, Eva's heart filled with anger—a bitterness of witnessing honor and integrity within those she had long despised. And grief—pure, unveiled sorrow—for a life she had never known, yet now felt the ache of losing.

The Legion taught her Zentari were ruthless, merciless savages. Yet here she was, watching one die with the same noble character she expected of her kin. Xerza was nothing like the enemy she was trained to hate, and it questioned everything she held to be true. The distrust which had grown in her heart like a seed, reached further. And it asked whether her people were even on the right side of the war.

But Thalia.

*This was her fault*

Thalia attacked her comrade, ended his life for her own selfish reasons. It wasn't the Zentari that were savage and ruthless, it was people like Thalia. And now her hatred was pointed back at the Legion. Eva wouldn't let—

A scream sounded from the forest, back toward Yaqar.

*Rollo*

Eva sprinted up the hill, pulling a blade from her side and racing back along the trail. Yaqar was a day's journey for someone so tired and hungry. How far had Thalia made it? Or had she been hiding, waiting.

*For us to come stumbling into a trap*

Eva cursed her own stupidity, running as fast as her feet could carry her. Rollo wouldn't be a match for Thalia on his own, even if the witch was already weak. Eva willed her body to move faster. She rounded a berm and caught sight of Rollo. He was on the ground, beside the trail, hand on his side. Thalia was standing nearby, his sword in her hands. She looked up at Eva and cursed, sprinting down the path toward Yaqar.

Eva ran to Rollo, inspecting his injury. It was deep. He may yet survive, but he needed a healer, medicine for infection. She glanced at Thalia, who disappeared into the forest. Eva cursed in frustration. She could either save Rollo or catch Thalia.

She reexamined his bleeding side. The blade had been small, but the wound drove deep. A few more inches and it would've run him through.

Rollo gripped her arm as she pulled at his armor.

"Go!" he said, gritting his teeth against the pain. "Stop her, before she sticks anyone else!"

"You won't survive if I leave."

"Just go, Katz! I'm not going to die bleeding out like a wounded animal. Rotting Shell snuck up on me."

Eva cringed at the slur. It was a racial insult invented by the Legion decades before. The Zentari killed with such ruthless precision, without any sign of remorse, they seemed at times like hollow vessels—empty shells created solely for death. And as Xerza's face entered her thoughts, Eva felt guilt tug at her heart, knowing she had used the word herself.

"Just shut up and hold still," she scolded. Pulling a clean cloth from her satchel, she tore Rollo's tunic, revealing the wound. Rollo shouted in pain as Eva packed the injury with as much cloth as would fit, before wrapping the bandage around his torso. It wasn't pretty, but it would buy him time.

He still needed a healer.

*Now*

She helped him stand, searching for thick sticks to use as a walking brace, but she found nothing. Wrapping his arm around her shoulders, they marched toward Yaqar. Rollo grimaced with each step, holding his side as blood seeped between his fingers. His complexion paled with each minute, sweat beading on his brow.

As the hours passed, doubt crawled into Eva's head. If Rollo was bleeding internally, they would never make it in time. At their current rate, they'd have to walk all night before reaching Yaqar.

Rollo spoke with wet breaths. "Please tell me you bled some useful information out of that Rotting Shell by the tree."

"No. I didn't."

"Why? You lose your nerve?"

"He died before I could get anything," she lied.

"Pity. I would've liked to get my hands on him."

Eva bit down on her response. Rollo's callousness toward the loss of life filled her with anger, yet she understood his hatred for the Zentari. She'd grown up on the same stories—witnessed their cruelty firsthand. Hells, she was hunting one now.

But mercy had crept into her heart, one she dared not share. Perhaps Maya or Lucas would understand, but not Rollo. He reveled in war, glorifying the bloodshed over drinks and laughter. Killing had never thrilled Eva, but she knew there was a time and place.

"They're still people, Rollo," she said, grunting as he stumbled and leaned against her.

He scoffed. "You sound like a sympathizer."

"I'm just saying there's no point spitting on someone's grave."

"I'll spit on whoever I want. Keep your bleeding heart to yourself."

"All I'm saying is the world is dark enough. Don't make it worse."

"Don't toss accusations," he said, breathing heavily to maintain the conversation. "You've killed more than I have."

"I don't celebrate my kills," she said. "Or mark them on my belt."

"Oh, spare me. I'm not the only one. For Hell's sake, there's a scoreboard in Port's tent."

Eva kept her eyes on the ground, and her remaining thoughts to herself. She focused on the sturdiness of their steps to quiet the buzzing in her mind. As they marched into the night, Rollo's pallor worsened each time Eva checked. The cool night air worsened his shivering.

"I need to stop," Rollo rasped, eyes glazing over.

She grunted as his feet gave out. Bracing him against a tree, she felt his forehead and covered him with her cloak. His breathing was shallow and quick—eyes closed. She prayed silently that he'd make it as she knelt beside him.

"I'm going to scout ahead for a minute. See how far we have left." She already knew but used the excuse to let him rest.

Rollo nodded. "I'm fine," he slurred. "Just need a minute."

She jogged up the trail, fighting her exhaustion and climbed to the top of a ridge. Barely visible through the darkness of the night, the gentle orange glow from the torches around Yaqar glimmered in the distance. If you didn't know where to look, you'd miss it.

*Not far. Maybe a few hours at this pace*

Eva considered leaving Rollo and continuing by herself. She could make it there in less than an hour if she sprinted, send help back for him. Even warn them of Thalia, if she hadn't attacked already. She returned to Rollo, who sat on the ground—unconscious. There was no heat from his skin against her palm. His shivering had stopped.

*Nine Hells*

"Rollo! Rollo wake up!" she yelled, slapping him.

He struggled to open his eyes, but he didn't move. She had no choice. Either she ran or he died.

She held his pale face in her hands. "I'm getting help. Don't you dare die."

Eva left her pack next to him and sprinted into the night.

# Chapter Seventeen

A ll right! Listen up!" Captain Evergreen shouted, her voice carried by the wind across the vast openness of the practice field, as the recruits lined up in a semi-circle. The relentless heat of the sun cut through the clear sky, offset only by the steady cool breeze from the cliffside. But Eli paid little mind to the warmth of the sun, or the aching in his knee—his concentration was stolen by the pile of weapons behind Evergreen.

Four wooden carts contained a myriad of swords, long knives, axes, spears, war hammers—any tool desired. Judging by their rusted and dulled appearance, neglect and abuse evident at first glance, they were for practice only.

"Today marks another step on your journey to becoming Guardians. Your afternoon training will now encompass the use of battle weapons. Over the past three weeks, you have improved with hand-to-hand techniques. And to your credit, most of you are proficient in unarmed combat."

*Speak for yourself*

"But the Rune Blade Ceremony is not far off. Nine weeks may seem lengthy, but you have a great deal to master in that time. There is no telling what weapon will be manifested from the Rune Forge, what your unique inner magic will bring forth. So today, choose one of these tools based on your intuition. Trust your instincts, and don't be afraid to try a few options. You also never know which weapons will be available or needed in the field, so your familiarity with each is a useful tool."

The recruits hummed, and Eli felt a swell of excitement. They were one step closer to the top—the pinnacle of the Zentari military.

"While expertise in weaponry is a must for any Guardian, your ability to wield your Rune Blade will be augmented by your inner magic. Your Rune Blade is unique to you, an extension of your being. It will feel like a third arm—another limb to exercise and hone. If you are able to master the same type of weapon before you find your magic and summon your Rune Blade, I cannot overstate the combative advantage you will wield."

Eli wasn't familiar with anything akin to a sword, unless you counted proficient use of the empty grog glass.

"Also, those of you doomed to participate in the Reaping, heed my warning: train as if your life depends on it. Without magic, the skills you learn in this field will be your only protection from the grave. Keeper Darby will explain more about Spirit Steel and the Rune Blade ceremony later. For now, come grab a weapon that speaks to you, and we will begin."

Eli stepped up among the chaos and reached for what he perceived as a simple one-handed sword. Its sheath was weathered, with holes formed in the black leather-wrapped wood. Its steel surface was coarse and unpolished, rusted in places, making its edge dull. But a rush filled Eli when he held it—something in him sprang forth in excitement.

Arlo grabbed the largest two-handed sword he could find. The cursed thing was as tall as Eli. Lara hesitantly chose a wooden staff, a thick dowel of metal-reinforced timber rounded on each end. Shira stalked forward and made a more intentional decision. After grabbing a handful of blades, testing their weight before tossing them back, she decided on a pair of long knives.

Sol took a war hammer. Soren seemed even more familiar with weapons than Shira. He picked up a double-bladed axe, smiling as if recalling a memory. Rowan also grabbed an axe. Eli huffed, amused that axes called to those with darkness in their soul. Maelyn found a longsword, handling the weapon with comfort and familiarity. Fenner picked a broadsword, with a thick but short blade, similar to Eli's.

Once each recruit held a weapon of choice, Evergreen readdressed the crowd. "The weapon you chose is yours to practice with until the Rune Blade ceremony. There are all varieties of weapons available within the Blade Room on the second floor, but those are to remain in that room at all times. You may carry the ones you have now as you see fit."

"Unauthorized use of your weapons against other recruits or persons in the Citadel is considered high treason and punishable by immediate execution. Additionally, the rules of sparring are still in effect if a match is declared official. *No weapons.* We don't need recruits cutting off each other's limbs. Are there any questions?"

*Yeah, how in the bleeding Hells do I use this thing*

Eli glanced at Shira, her face betraying none of the heaviness he saw earlier. She was his one edge in this program—the one tether of hope he claimed to keep him out of the grave. He fought the pang of guilt that ebbed in his chest. His infatuation needed to die, reminding himself of her disinterest.

The afternoon crawled forward as each recruit learned how to handle their new weapons with awkward and crude maneuvers. The healers were running around assessing cuts and scrapes until near every recruit bore a white bandage someplace. Based on the presence of additional healers prior to practice starting, this was entirely expected. The thought had crossed Eli's mind more than once, wondering how they healed the more serious injuries so quickly. Some recruits, such as those with broken bones, were often back in practice the next day. Others, in critical condition, like Lara after the Proving, took only a few days to recover. But without fail, they all returned to full health. He assumed magic played a part but wished to see it firsthand.

Eli stood facing Arlo, both of them smiling, feeling more like Guardians today than ever before. The surrounding field overflowed with clanging metal, shouts of effort, and grunts of battle—it was intoxicating. A rush of excitement ran through Eli as he felt the steel in his hands, as if they stood in a real battlefield.

"Don't kill me please?" Eli teased.

Arlo winked and lunged forward with his claymore in an overhead strike, bringing the lengthy blade down in an arc. Eli swung his sword with a sidestep, catching the broadside of Arlo's steel. Eli's weapon cried out at the awkward collision as Arlo's sword stuck into the dirt with a quiet thud.

Eli slammed his shoulder into Arlo's chest, forcing him to stagger back. With a swift motion, Eli swiped his sword toward Arlo, but his friend was faster, bracing against the hilt to block the blow. Using the momentum, Arlo shoved Eli's hands upward, disrupting his grip and delivered a kick that sent Eli stumbling. He lost his balance and fell hard, striking his head on the ground.

"You're supposed to attack with your sword," Eli said, his head pounding as he sat up with a grimace.

Arlo pulled his claymore from the dirt and laid it on his shoulder. "I can use whatever I need to," he said before something behind Eli changed his expression. "I'm gonna go find Maelyn."

He walked off, leaving Eli confused on the grass.

"Get up."

Eli shut his eyes, dropping his head. He picked the wrong day to piss off Shira. All she had to do was gut him and be done with it. Although that was against the rules, he could only imagine the physical damage she could deal with her skillset. He sighed and stood, pushing away his nerves as Shira twirled her long knives, face unreadable.

"Look.," he began, glancing at the other recruits fighting. "I didn't mean—"

"Shut up," she scolded. "Show me what you can do."

Eli scoffed. "Would you just let me—"

"I know what you're trying to do," she said, taking a step closer. Two recruits caught in a heated battle stumbled nearby before retreating. "And I'm saying there's no need for it."

He shifted his weight. Somehow, she was exemplary at being both intriguing and infuriating. Yet here he was, utterly helpless in her presence.

"Why *are* you still helping me?" he asked, turning his sword in his hand. "As I recall, the deal was to help me survive and I help you with your questions. But so far all you've done is beat my face in."

Her eyes darted around, and his curiosity peaked. "What's your point?"

He grinned, amused at ruffling her feathers. "You act like you hate helping me. So why do it?"

"I never said that," she retorted, and Eli tried desperately to grasp the shift in her tone, but living Hells she was good at masking her intent.

"Fine," he said after a moment. "So, when do I help you?"

"Tonight," she muttered, stepping closer to avoid the battling duo behind her. "Now shut up and attack me."

"You going to kill me if I do?"

"I haven't decided yet," she said with a raised eyebrow.

Eli grinned and lunged at her without warning, swinging overhead. He didn't bother holding back, knowing there wasn't a chance in the dark Hells he could harm her. And as expected, Shira deflected his blow with ease and brought one of her long knives to his throat. He froze, scanning her face for any sign of his earlier concerns, despite his rush of excitement at her proximity.

She pulled the blade away, retreating a step. "Don't overcommit. Every attack leaves you vulnerable. Be ready for a counter and think ahead."

Eli rubbed his neck. "Okay," he said, nodding.

"Again," she demanded.

He attacked, this time as a stab to her stomach. The result was the same. She acted bored, her face remaining blank—her gaze wandering. And as they sparred, the desire to impress Shira only grew. Eli threw everything he had into training, but the remainder of practice with her was agony. The afternoon dragged on, and his knee pain became excruciating, his hand was numb from holding his sword, and his muscles were on hot coals.

To his surprise, Shira never harmed him. Yet after hours of practice, he had not landed a single blow. The greatest challenge was holding his focus. Despite his efforts, his control unraveled in her presence. He tried to stifle his attraction to her—respect the boundary she had built—but he felt lost in a flash flood. The momentary frustration he felt at her ire faded so quickly, leaving only questions. He wondered what it was she carried, if there was a hidden burden on her shoulders, invisible to those around her.

After witnessing the quiet distress in the bunkroom, his curiosity became melded with compassion. This program wasn't easy on any of them, and he questioned if the shield she bore was only a mask—an illusion—for the vulnerable woman underneath. And he found himself longing to be the one person allowed in, permitted past that barrier.

As she instructed and taught, Eli's eyes traced her every movement—not merely to study her technique, but with an unspoken admiration. At times, only fleeting moments, their sparring felt less like a battle and more like a dance. A dance where one partner fumbled over his own feet, yet one that carried its own rhythm. And as the sun dipped low on the horizon, the weight of the day's exertion settling upon Eli, his spirit soared. He was another day closer to being a Guardian, to obtaining magic, and winning this war for Harper.

Though he might be crazy—Hells, probably—he swore he could feel the magic inside him waking up. He knelt on the ground, panting like a dog. Sweat soaked the front of his tunic, stifled by the leather armor. Arlo and Maelyn wandered toward them.

Eli teased Arlo, speaking between breaths. "How'd you do with that giant toothpick?"

Arlo smiled. "Fine!" he said, sticking the end of the blade in the dirt. "I think it gets heavier over time. Some kind of magic maybe."

Maelyn laughed. "Is that the same magic that made you slow down?" she asked with a smile before wandering off. "Thanks for the help."

"Hey, where's Lara?" Eli asked.

"She's helping train Fenner," Arlo said. "Maelyn told me she's sick and tired of babying him and wanted to fight someone else for a change."

Eli grunted in response, sheepish at his similarity to Fenner.

Arlo turned to Shira. "So, I have to ask, did he actually land an attack with that thing?"

"No," she said.

"Ah, Hells, I just lost fifty dmei," Arlo said, sitting on the grass, along with many other recruits.

Shira said, "You made a stupid bet. You gamble a lot?"

"That depends." Arlo grinned. "What'd you have in mind?"

Eli rolled his eyes as he laid back, closing them against the blue sky. The afternoon sun beat against his face, but the breeze of the open air felt gentle on his skin.

"Elara Borne and Kairah Richter!"

Eli's eyes shot open. An official match was called. He jumped to his feet, at the protest of his muscles. The recruits gathered toward the base of the Citadel, where a proctor waited.

Eli, Arlo, and Shira jogged over to observe. Kairah and Elara stood apart, already prepared with weapons cast aside. Kairah bore an expression akin to homicide, while Elara panted, her skin glistening with sweat.

"Begin!"

Kairah spared no mercy as she came at Elara with a dark fierceness. She had a clear advantage, appearing well rested, as if she skipped the afternoon's events. Elara, hair sticking to her face, took up a defensive stance, avoiding her opponent's relentless attacks.

Kairah threw a jab, which Elara deflected but missed the counterattack as Kairah slammed her palm into Elara's nose. Her head reeled back, blood flowing from each nostril. Elara blinked twice, holding her arms up in defense, but it was too late. A spinning kick came to the side of her head, Kairah's boot causing a loud crack as it made contact.

Elara stumbled, dazed from the blow and fell to one knee. She gulped down each breath as she swayed, furiously blinking to clear her vision. As Kairah strolled to her opponent, a rock settled in Eli's gut. He glanced at Arlo who shared his grim expression.

Kairah stood before Elara and grabbed her hair, bringing her knee into Elara's forehead. Blood pooled down Elara's face as Kairah repeated the same attack.

Again.

And again.

And again.

*Why isn't the proctor calling the match*

Eli glanced at Shira, but she shook her head. Arlo turned away.

Kairah grabbed the front of Elara's armor as her body went limp. Grasping her opponent's chin, Kairah twisted Elara's neck violently. With a loud snap, Elara's body collapsed onto the grass. Kairah sauntered over to her weapon, picked it up, and waited for the proctor—who nodded. As she returned to the crowd, Kairah looked at Arlo and winked.

"Practice is finished for today!" Evergreen announced. "Everyone report to the mess hall!"

As the recruits filtered into the Citadel, Eli hung to the back of the crowd. He approached Captain Evergreen who stood alone watching the healers carry Elara's body away.

"Captain Evergreen, ma'am?" Eli asked.

"No 'ma'am,'" she said, her attention remaining on the dead recruit. "Despite what Renard says, rules of conversation are rarely enforced, recruit Danon. What is it you need?"

"Captain, with all due respect, why wasn't the match called? Elara didn't stand a chance after that first attack, especially toward the end. And Kairah looked like she hadn't worked all afternoon."

Evergreen sighed. "It is not your place to question what a superior officer should or shouldn't do, recruit," she said, turning to him. "Even if you or I would have called the match, our military's rules are absolute. It is not our place to question the Leadership, and they have extensive reasons for the program they've established."

"But Captain, that wasn't even a match," he said, a budding seed of unease forming in his gut. He *was* questioning the Leadership—again.

"And what happens if a recruit graduates unprepared?" she argued. "What happens if a Guardian is granted a position they are unequipped for and dies in the line of duty while others are depending on them? How many more lives will be lost?"

Eli bit his lip. He hadn't thought about it that way.

Evergreen took a step toward him. "My advice to you, recruit, is to keep your head down and abandon this optimistic outlook of yours. Part of the reason this program contains death is to prepare you to watch your comrades die without faltering in battle. A panicked warrior is a vulnerable warrior. Things will make more sense over time. Until then, do as you're told."

She gave him a small pat on the shoulder before walking away, following the healers inside. Eli was the last one to enter the Citadel.

The mess hall was the usual chaos, though tempered with a heaviness in the air. Eli spotted Maelyn and Fenner sitting with his squad as he approached their table. And to his surprise, the seat next to Shira was open again. He noticed their seats were always together during meals, whether by chance or design. He wouldn't put it past Arlo to arrange such a scheme.

". . . because that's the rules." Maelyn said. "Only the proctor can call the match."

"Why aren't we allowed to tap out?" Lara asked, unrest written on her face.

"Guardians can't quit," Fenner said, his voice meek and high-pitched. He was young—by far the youngest at the table.

"Oh, for the love of the dark Hells!" Shira argued. "In what world are Guardians, or any warriors for that matter, not allowed to retreat? Is it not better sometimes to live and fight another day?"

The group quieted. Eli answered her. "They want to teach us to never give up."

Shira spun to him. "Are you saying that the Leadership values reckless abandon more than the lives of their own people?"

Lara chimed in. "Shira, you're not asking a fair question. No one is saying we aren't valued, but this is how you become the best. There's no other way to do it."

"No," Fenner said. "You mean there isn't any other way to bring out your inner magic."

"Actually," Eli said. "I don't think that's true."

Fenner gave Eli a questioning look.

"We're basing everything on assumptions," Eli said. "We assume Orion was killed because he tapped out, but they never said that."

Lara muttered, "They never even mentioned it."

"Exactly," Eli continued. "All we know for certain is the program has a singular focus, but they never said this was the only way to bring out inner magic."

"Right," Maelyn said. "Darby said they may be able to explore other options outside war time."

Lara chimed in. "He also said this program was carefully designed to train Guardians."

"Evergreen just told me the same thing," Eli said. "She said the reasons for the rules were extensive. Which begs the question, how much of this program is predetermined?"

The group waited for him to elaborate.

"Try again," Arlo mumbled, his mouth full of food.

"I mean think about it. Is death necessary for this? Between Darby and Renard, they've both explained this program is only concerned about bringing forth our inner magic, not even training us for the military. Renard said that comes later. Which means we can assume that they've found multiple ways to find our inner magic and filtered out the other safer but less effective methods. And this program is what's left."

"You mean they took out the rainbows and butterflies?" Arlo teased. "By the fates, I've been had!"

No one laughed.

Maelyn addressed Eli. "So, you're saying death is required to obtain magic?"

"It would seem so," Eli answered. "You don't need the threat of death to learn how to fight, only time and practice. The way I see it, the only reason death is such a significant factor is because it's the best and fastest method to bring out our magic. The program is only three months after all."

Shira's eyes narrowed. "Which leads back to your original idea."

He nodded. "If that's all true, I wonder if some recruits are marked for death from the beginning, just to ensure our success."

"Like Orion?" Maelyn asked.

"Evergreen told me exposing us to death is intentional," Eli continued, "and I wonder how much the threat of death, that desperation, plays a part in drawing out our magic in such a short time."

"Wait," Lara said, glancing among the group. "So that first day, Orion was chosen? Like a bloody sacrifice?"

Eli said, "At this point, I think the first person to tap out would have been chosen. It just happened to be him."

Tension pulled at the group like a bowstring, the idea hanging in the air.

"Then I have a question," Fenner said, the table turning to him. "If you're right, then what in the Nine Realms is the Reaping?"

Lara answered, "Just another gruesome part of this program, probably."

"Maybe," Shira said, "but Fenner's right. Darby specifically said we don't want to be a part of it."

"Why keep it a secret?" Arlo asked, still eating. "Why all the mystery?"

"I don't know," Eli said. "But if the Reaping is the worst part of this program, then to me the real question is what's worse than the threat of death?"

The table quieted again.

"Bleeding Hells," Lara muttered, returning to her food. "Can we talk about something else?"

The rest of the group resumed eating, turning to lighter topics—except Shira. Eli noticed her attention after a moment and was surprised by the weight of her stare. Curiosity flashed in her eyes like a spark catching the wind, and he wondered what caused her thoughts to spur.

But there was something else—something new and unspoken. For a breath, he was weightless under her attention, caught in the quiet moment of her lingering gaze. He froze, praying the flickering of her eyes, the slight parting of her lips, were confirmation of a newfound interest held for him.

"You gonna' kiss or som'in?" Arlo asked, mouth full of his bread roll.

Eli gave him an annoyed look.

"No," Shira said, death in her gaze, "but I'll cut out your Nines if you ask that again."

Arlo held his hands up, still chewing. "Easy now."

They finished their meals and walked back to the barracks, mixed among the crowd. As they neared the barracks, Eli saw Captain Renard leaning on the wall speaking to the Operative assigned to night watch.

"Recruit Danon!" Renard announced.

Eli froze, before standing at attention. His group slowed to a crawl, befuddled looks on their faces. A few other recruits took notice but scurried away. Arlo stepped alongside Eli.

"You're dismissed, recruit Miller," Renard ordered. "All of you."

Arlo nodded, he and the rest briskly retreating into the barracks. Eli's palms became sweaty.

*What did I do*

"Ven'So, Danon. Walk with me, won't you?" Renard asked with a pleasant grin.

"Of course, Captain Renard, sir."

The Captain ushered him along the inner wall of the walkway at a leisure pace, hands clasped behind his back. Renard took in the surroundings, the high walls and ceiling, as if appreciating the decorations and ornaments for the first time.

"It really is a marvel of our time, isn't it?" Renard mused.

"Sir?" Eli asked.

"The Citadel, boy! A marvel of Zentari history."

"Yes sir."

"You seem to be struggling with physical combat, son. Is that correct?"

*Odd question*

"Well, yes sir. I haven't had much experience before coming here."

"And where exactly was that? Your home?" Renard asked, glancing at him.

"I grew up in the country sir. My father owned an inn."

"Along the Darom road in the South, I assume. Is that right? A perfect place to set up for travelers."

Eli opened his mouth to speak, but his mind went blank.

Renard gave a knowing look. "What was the name of the inn?"

"The Starlight Inn, sir."

Renard's mouth curved down in thought. "I don't recall hearing about it. Your father owns it?"

"Yes, sir."

"What's his name?"

"Um . . ." Eli paused. "Sir?"

"Your father, boy. Surely you know your father's name."

Eli furrowed his brow, thinking it his nerves at first, but the answer refused to surface.

Renard stopped and turned toward him, no empathy in his features. "What was that, son?"

Eli stuttered—his mouth went dry

*Rotting Hells*

"You can't remember, can you?" Renard asked, a snide smile on his lips. "What about the nearest town you lived by? Surely you would travel there for supplies living in the country?"

"Um, we just went to the nearest one."

"Oh, of course!" The Captain stepped closer. "And what was the name of the *nearest one?*"

Eli couldn't answer.

"How far did you live from Eldan City?"

Straining against his racing heart, Eli searched for the answer to the simple questions—but there was nothing.

"What about getting here?" Renard pressed. "How did you get to the Citadel to join the program? Surely you didn't just walk here."

Eli's hearing faded to a high-pitched ring. His vision blurred at the edges.

*What's happening*

"You see, son, there are sometimes lasting side effects of the Thought Wave Analysis. I've been told you've been asking concerning questions, causing disruptions during lectures, openly disagreeing with the Leadership, even wandering around late into the night. I told you I was available for questions, for anything you needed, isn't that correct?"

Eli's face burned. He swallowed.

"Well here I am. But before you begin prying into matters that don't concern you, I would advise you to tread very cautiously." Renard glanced at a passing Operative, speaking lower. "I mean, let's be honest, if you can't even remember your father or childhood home, how can you trust anything that mind of yours finds peculiar?"

Eli was reeling. He grasped at threads—anything to anchor himself.

*Harper. I remember Harper. My sister*

*Kael. He was my best friend*

*I can see the Startlight Inn. Our home*

*But dad's name*

*What was dad's name*

A hand clasped his shoulder, shocking him from his thoughts.

"Just some food for thought." Renard slapped Eli's arm as he strolled away, whistling.

But Eli remained in the walkway, his breathing growing ragged.

He couldn't remember.

# Chapter Eighteen

The sun crested the horizon as Eva sprinted through Yaqar's Western gate. Her lungs burned, and she tasted blood. With numb legs, she ran to the nearest warrior, a man she recognized.

"Orro!" she shouted, grabbing him by the shoulders. His eyes widened. "Grab a healer and head West along the trail. Rollo's hurt!"

"What happened?"

"He was stabbed by one of the escaped Zentari."

"How far?" Orro asked.

"An hour at full sprint. Hurry!"

"Right!" Orro said, running to the medical tent. Eva collapsed onto her knees, trying to wrangle her breathing.

*Please, Heavens, let Rollo be okay*

A hand clamped on her shoulder. Orro's partner at the gate knelt beside her. "Do you need a healer?" he asked.

Eva couldn't remember his name. "No. I'm all right."

As much as her body demanded rest, she still needed to warn Drax. Thalia could be anywhere. Muscles trembling, she walked toward the Lieutenant's tent. Drax's head snapped up as she ripped open the front flap.

"Sir, permission to enter," she gasped.

He stood. "Granted."

As she walked in, Drax shuffled around his desk. Before she could speak, he struck her with the back of his hand, sending her stumbling sideways. Her cheek warmed under her palm, the burning radiating into her head. Stars sparkled in her vision as she met Drax's glare.

"Sir."

"Do not speak!" he shouted. "You have failed your mission! And because of that two of our own are dead and three others are injured!"

Eva's heart stopped, her breath stilled. She couldn't tell if Drax's fury was over the loss of life, or simply at her failure. It didn't matter. She deserved this.

*Two are dead*

"I won't bother asking why you let those prisoners go. I've grown tired of your lies," he said, pacing like a rabid animal trapped in a cage. "And for the love of the Nine Realms, the *one* time I agree with you that you could actually handle a situation, *this happens.*"

Eva held her cheek—unmoving. Her white hair fell partially over her face as her breathing slowed.

"Rollo is hurt," she muttered.

"Then you better pray to the Heavens that he is alive because if he isn't, I'll find some way to charge you with his death, as well as the death of your comrades."

Her hand fell to the side, unable to meet his stare.

*Two are dead*

"You're an overconfident, selfish brat who can't obey orders. You have been nothing but a thorn in my side since you were assigned here. The great, untouchable Evalynn Katz, the famous white-haired devil of the Legion, is nothing more than a snot-nosed child!"

Spittle flew from Drax's mouth as he lectured.

"You have a problem with authority because you grew up under a great leader in the Legion army, but here's the truth princess: you're an adult. And as a Swordsman in the military, you must answer for your actions."

He paused, straightening. She knew what was coming before he spoke.

"Poe!" he shouted. A young male warrior stepped into the tent, standing at attention. "Swordsman Evalynn Katz, you are hereby banished from the Yaqar outpost and are to pack and leave for Manoach immediately. Swordsman Poe will ensure you do not delay, and Swordsman Lane will escort you to Manoach, where you will serve under Lieutenant Ollon until your trial. I will be filing formal charges against you to the upper Leadership for the death of your comrades. We will inform you when you are to present to trial at Ashdod."

He leaned closer, lowering his voice. She could see the satisfaction in his face—relishing the moment.

"You better pray I don't find evidence of your guilt. Were it up to me I'd execute you for your crimes this very moment. Hang you from the Northern gate. But because I'm required to present proof of your crimes, you are granted a few more days of freedom. So enjoy it while you can, girl. Now get out of my sight."

Drax returned to his desk as Eva shuffled to Swordsman Poe. He met her shameful glance. From her experience, he was a gentle man, slow to speak but quick to smile. His gaze shifted between her and Drax, his dark eyes like onyx against his tanned skin, a silent order in his expression.

*No funny stuff*

As she stepped to leave, Drax spoke from behind her. "I cannot wait to inform your father how far his daughter has fallen. It's been my curse to have you as a niece. I always knew you were a waste of skin."

*I have no doubt he feels the same*

As Eva stepped into the noise of camp, something Drax mentioned came to mind, something she missed amid the chaos.

Two are dead, three are injured.

*Maya*

She gave Poe a look, before taking off for the medical tent. He followed her without effort, her weakened legs only half as fast as normal. A cloud of dust trailed her as she flung open the tarp. A female healer paid no mind, bent over and tending to the three bodies lying on the beds. There, on the end of the row, Eva recognized the red tinged hair.

Emotion flooded over her as she spun to Poe. "Give me two minutes, please," she begged.

"No delays, Katz."

"For Hell's sake, Poe, I'm asking for one rotting minute."

He sighed, pressing his lips together. "One," he said. She turned to approach Maya, and Poe grabbed her arm. "*One*, Katz."

Eva stepped to Maya's side, taking in her condition with unbearable shame. Maya's head was bandaged, her left arm was in a sling, and a wooden splint braced her left leg. Eva knelt beside the bed, grabbing her friend's hand. Maya's eyes opened at the contact, and Eva's eyes burned.

*Thank the shining Heavens*

"Tell me you killed the other one," Maya rasped.

Anger emanated from her friend, pouring out of her expression and tone. Eva was taken aback, until she realized their recent experiences with the enemy were worlds apart. Eva witnessed the glimmer of honor, while Maya bore the darkness of hatred. Eva couldn't say anything, wondering whether she was a fool to believe a hopeful delusion—that change was possible. And now, seeing the wounds her actions inflicted, Eva took her newfound mercy and tried to bury it.

"Yeah," Eva said. "What happened, Maya? Is the prisoner—"

"Dead? Yeah. I cut off that rotting Shell's head. It took four of us, but we got the job done. Witch ambushed us when we were changing guards. How she got past the sentries, or knew about them, we don't know. It doesn't matter now."

Guilt flushed over Eva like a raging river. "I'm so sorry," she whispered.

"Eva, stop," Maya said, lowering her voice. "You didn't mean for this to happen. I don't know what happened in the pit, or what goes on in that head of yours, but I do know that you'd never willingly endanger anyone."

"I'm just—"

"Stop with the pity party. I'm done trying to argue with you. I'm probably the only one in this camp who knows that under that hard exterior, you're a deep blob of feelings."

Eva swallowed past the lump in her throat. "I'll help take care of you."

"Don't worry about it," Maya said, shaking her head. "I'll be up and out in no time. Besides, you have to run away to Manoach. Just please *try* and keep your nose out of trouble."

Eva forced herself to grin, making the promise to herself as much as to her friend. "Yeah, I will."

She refused to tell Maya about the report to upper Leadership, or her pending trial. Execution, or banishment from the Legion, was very possible. But Maya needed to rest. And the last thing Eva would do is make this about herself.

"Do you need anything?" Eva asked, knowing her minute was up.

"No." A smile cracked at Maya's mouth. "The healer is really good. You go rest. You're exhausted. And you've got a long journey ahead tomorrow."

Eva gave a brief smile and squeezed her hand. As she left her friend in the care of the healer, a shadow coiled around her heart. If this was the price of showing her enemy mercy, then they would receive no more from her. It wasn't the guilt weighing on her shoulders, nor the escort signaling her impending dismissal that drove her to pack. It was the realization that she no longer belonged in this war—that she failed to bring real change to her comrades.

Despite Eva's attempts to rid herself of her father, she did believe his influence was the only reason Drax didn't dismiss or reprimand her already. At least something good came from the wretched man.

She packed up her belongings while Poe waited outside her tent. There wasn't much to collect. Some prized daggers she'd purchased over the years, a necklace Lucas gave her for her eighteenth birthday, and a few mementos of her mother. When she was done, her leather travel bag sat on her cot, staring back at her. It was humbling to know that everything to her name could be carried on her shoulders.

Eva sat on the edge of her bed, exhaling sharply. The weight of her failure, her misjudgment, filled her limbs with iron. Her reckless, would-be heroics weren't just dangerous—they were going to get people killed. And yet, if recent events taught her anything, it was that answers were the only way to end this festering war. She had to keep digging—no matter the cost.

And though it brought bile to her throat, ripped open old wounds long since closed, her father was right. Mercy was a risk, a liability, not a virtue. Especially with heartless foes like Thalia.

She stood, donning her cloak and bag, leaving behind the stifling confines of her residence in Yaqar. Poe said nothing as she strolled past him. They walked in silence to the Northern edge of camp where Swordsman Lane was standing beside two stallions saddled and ready. His long hair was kept in a loose bun, and his eyes shone with an icy indifference. The last time Eva and Alart Lane spoke, it nearly led to blows.

"You got her from here?" Poe asked Lane.

"Yeah," Lane said, nodding. He gave Eva a smug grin as he mounted his stallion.

Eva gave Poe a nod of thanks before mounting her own horse. She and Lane rode out of Yaqar, headed North to Manoach in silence.

It was a two-day journey on horseback to the small town in the North. The sun's warmth shook the humidity from the tall grass as the hours crept by, and Eva prayed for a thick cloud to bring shade from the afternoon sun. It wasn't long before her exhaustion overcame the stress and adrenaline from the day's events, which played over again and again in her mind. Her stomach growled, reminding her she hadn't eaten breakfast.

*Bereeth*

"Oh!" She stopped, head propped up to the sky.

Lane looked to her, riding to her right. "What?"

Eva sighed. "Nothing," she mumbled. She never said goodbye to Bereeth, nor stole something for breakfast, now that she thought about it.

"So, what'd you do this time?" Lane asked, squinting at the sun.

"What does it matter, Alart?" She asked, feeling his eyes on her. He still boiled her blood, even before their mission with Chief Port.

"That's Swordsman Lane to you."

Eva slowly turned his direction. She huffed at his wry grin. "Do I look like I'm in the mood, *Alart?*" she snarked.

He clucked his tongue. "I'd be careful, Katz. You don't want to get on my bad side. There's no one else out here."

Her eyes narrowed. "I'd rip out your Nines and force feed you."

"See, but I could say whatever I want to Drax. Or Lieutenant Ollon. It'd be my word against that of a shamed Swordsman awaiting trial."

Eva clenched her jaw and tried to discourage him with silence.

"Come on, Katz," he pressed. "It's a long ride. Why don't you get it off your chest?"

*Maybe I can kill him and make it look like an accident*

"All right, fine," Lane drawled. "How about I tell you all the rumors I've heard?"

She took a deep breath, counting to a hundred.

*Bleeding Hells, has he always talked this much*

"Bant said Drax finally caught you red handed in something, and now he just needs to wait for formal approval."

Eva remained silent, not the least surprised by how quickly rumors spread across the camp.

"Orro said you came into camp panicked because you got Rollo killed screwing up the mission, and you wanted to make a scene so you didn't look guilty."

She gripped the reins tighter, the leather biting her palms.

"Skeer said someone caught you in Lucas's tent, but I don't buy that. The Chief is too by the book to muddy his record. Or his bed."

*Thanks, Keinen*

Eva shut Lane out, closing her eyes and disconnecting from her environment. The mention of Lucas brought dread rushing back like a tidal wave. There had been no news. And with Eva now banished to the Northernmost post of the Aniyan kingdom, she doubted she would hear anything soon.

She prayed desperately for his safety and stayed her hand from turning her stallion South to Heika. As Lane continued, she thought back to the lifetime of memories they shared, and the first one danced in her mind.

*Eva blew out the single candle buried in the sweet roll Glorana had given her, which marked her seventh birthday. The morning sun cast orange rays into the quiet of her bedroom as she sat alone. She was disappointed but not surprised her Nana could not celebrate with her. All the staff at their home were kept extremely busy, and Glorana was no exception, despite being hired to care for Eva personally. Bringing her a dessert, let alone a lit candle to celebrate her birthday, was more than Evalynn could have hoped for.*

*She had spent most of the night decorating her bedroom as best as she could, setting up her toys and stuffed animals in all manner of places and positions, utilizing the ornate shelves and polished bookcases which sat against each wall. The entire day was planned out, roleplaying her favorite stories and reading her favorite books.*

*"Oh, Teddy!" she said, speaking to her stuffed bear, which sat across the table. "I forgot to tell you! I met a friend yesterday! A real-life friend!"*

*Pulling the candle from the sweet roll, Eva carefully set it aside, ensuring no wax dripped on her favorite yellow dress. She had worn it for three days straight. Glorana said the yellow made her look like a ray of sunshine.*

*With a dull ache, Eva rubbed her left eye. Her evening meal would be fully eaten, and she would take great care to hide the burnt candle, or else risk the same punishment. She was grateful her vision returned, once the swelling receded.*
*"His name is Lucas. I met him in the market with Glorana. He was really nice and didn't mention my hair at all!"*
*She paused, listening to the silent words of her inanimate friend.*
*"I know! I think the Heavens blessed me with a birthday gift too! My first real-life friend. He said his family lives outside The Capitol and has lots of brothers and sisters . . ."*
*Her voice was caught by a wave of grief. Despite her efforts to remain joyous on her birthday, her lip quivered as a gentle sorrow rippled in her heart.*
*"He was really nice, Teddy. He reminded me of Glorana. I wish . . ." She glanced out her window, before clearing her throat. "I'm going to ask Nana if we can go back to the market and find him again. If we sneak out like last time, father said he'd—"*

Eva returned to the present, realizing Lane was now quiet, waiting for her to speak.

"Finished?" she quipped.

"Oh, now you want to talk?" He bit.

*Oh for the love of the Nine Realms*

"Fine!" Eva shouted. "You win! I snuck out of camp and released the prisoners in exchange for information. I let them go for my own gain, only to turn around and hunt them down myself. But one got away and stuck Rollo before beating me back to camp."

Lane rolled his eyes. "Yeah," he muttered. "Sure."

She took a deep breath, watching a dusktail spring from the tree line.

"I don't get it, Katz," Lane said. "Why in the living Hells did you even join the Legion?"

"What does it matter?"

"You preach about being honorable but then bark at every single one of your comrades. You shirk the rules and run around like you own the place without any respect for the Legion, and then say Port and I broke some moral law doing what we were told. You're a talented warrior, but act like you hate fighting. You say you want the war to end but are the first one at the front lines to shed blood. So, which is it? Do you want this or not?"

"I don't bark," she spat. "And it's none of your business why I joined."

"So, what, you get a free ride off your father's reputation? You get a quick thrill of battle, make two friends and that's it?"

"How do you know how many friends I have?"

"All I know is that Lucas and Maya are the only two that defend you in front of everyone else. I know you have only two friends, because there's only two people in Yaqar that tolerate you."

"Whatever."

It wasn't obvious to Eva whether she was socially isolated by choice or by circumstance. She had always been a loner, mostly because her father's ruthless reputation kept others at a distance. She told herself she preferred it that way. Independence was strength, relying on others was weakness. But now, she would give anything to hear Lucas's laugh, be on the receiving end of Maya's sisterly advice. And in truth, she would be lost without them.

So why was it so hard for her to trust anyone?

Her father would have chastised her for depending on others—or even worse, showing compassion for the other side. She had to admit, she wanted to skin Thalia alive for what she did to Maya, yet her heart broke for Xerza's death. She didn't know which side was right, which ideal was greater, and the two emotions warred in her chest.

Eva's mind swirled with questions and uncertainty, a restless storm that only settled when she and Lane reached Manoach that next evening.

# Chapter Nineteen

W hat?" Eli asked Harper with a breathy laugh. "How does your mind get sixteen from that?"

He tapped Harper's forehead gently on the hazy red mark, which glowed brighter as the night dragged on. She truly was hopeless when it came to mathematics despite turning seven last year. It had to be close to midnight, having been dark for some time. Eli had helped her finish every other subject before supper—except this.

"I did it right!" Harper argued, holding up her fingers. "Ten, plus eight, minus four."

Harper's eyes shone bright with an icy stare as she stood her ground. Eli smiled, unable to be mad at her beautiful face. It reminded him of their mother.

"Sorry, Harp," he said, crossing his arms. "Try again."

"Ugh!" She grunted, throwing her head up in frustration. "Why do I need to learn this anyway! I've never seen you use math!"

"As if!" he argued. "Dad and I have to count the day's profits every day. Not to mention currency changes between foreigners."

Harper rolled her eyes. "You've never had to do that."

"No, but," he said, pointing at her, "just in case. He still makes me practice sometimes."

"Can we just be done?" she whined. "I wanna go to bed."

"No, you want me to read to you," he said with raised eyebrows.

Harper stuck out her lower lip—whimpering softly.

"No. Try again."

"Oh." She groaned. "You're heartless."

He laughed, brushing her hair behind her pointed ear, the gentle shimmer of honey rolling off her shoulders.

"All right," he said. "Take ten and add—"

Eli woke up being shaken, a silhouetted figure pressing a hand on his bare chest.

*Shira*

Without a word, he rubbed his eyes and sat on the edge of his bunk. He slipped on his tunic and crept out of the bunkroom. Closing the door with a soft click, he stepped up to Shira who waited for him in the hallway. She wore a slim-fitting black outfit—athletic and comfortable. His cheeks heated.

"Come on," she whispered. "We'll grab a lantern when we get there."

Eli stood still, the conversation with Renard fresh in his thoughts. He didn't remember falling asleep, having returned to his bunk reeling from the truth of his memory loss. He was supposed to help Shira in the library tonight, but he felt entirely too distracted.

"Shira, can we do this tomorrow?" he whispered. If Renard was right, he shouldn't trust his own thoughts, and Shira shouldn't be trusting him.

She turned around. "What? No, you're coming. Now."

"Look, I just don't know how much help I'm going to be," he lied, grappling with the unease now firmly planted in his stomach.

"I don't care. We had a deal. Now are you a man of your word, or not?" she asked, planting her feet.

He flexed his hands.

*Bleeding Hells, I've been trying to get closer to her this entire time, and now here I am making excuses*

"Yes, it's just—" He started, catching himself. As much as he desired to explain, to open up to her, he held himself back. He didn't yet trust her to take his concerns with sincerity. Shira was talented, and incredible in his eyes, but tender was not a word he would use to describe her.

"What?" she asked, brow arched.

"Nothing," he said, stepping around her to the stairs.

"Keeping secrets?" she said, following him.

"I'm not the one with secrets," he argued. "You were the one sneaking out at night."

When they reached the main level, the Operative on duty looked up from his book. He eyed them both for a moment, then returned to his reading.

"Maybe, but at least I'm not hopeless on the mats," Shira said.

"Are you going to tell me what we're looking for now?" he whispered, keeping in stride with her despite the limp in his gait from his still aching knee.

"Just wait."

He took a breath, frustrated with being kept in the dark. If this turned out to be nothing more than crazed curiosity, or needless pursuits, he would find some way to end their deal and take his chances. He had already drawn Renard's attention—in the worst way.

Yet, as much as his gut demanded caution, this was his chance to get closer to Shira, if they didn't kill each other first. She was infuriating, abrasive, and guarded more than a stone wall, but there was something about her that took his breath away. And though it crushed any pride he held, he desperately needed her help. The truth of the matter was, he wouldn't survive without her. Arlo and Lara were taking it easy on him, even though they argued otherwise. Shira did as well, though she liked to hit him more. But eventually, he would face a recruit who exploited his weakness, or face anyone on Sol's team, and meet a swift and painful end.

The door creaked as they entered the library, the sound carrying through the open space and between the scattered bookshelves. Eli wondered what time the Keepers spent monitoring the contents. Given the decrepit and neglected state of the place, none of them bothered to dust the shelves.

Shira stepped to the side and procured one of the lanterns provided, lighting it with a flint in a smooth motion, an indication she'd done this numerous times. She walked straight ahead into the sea of bookshelves, the overwhelming size of the library hitting him once again.

He searched the books and scrolls as they walked, with a longing to take his time and explore. A few of the books had been disturbed, judging by the changes in the dust around them. Most appeared as if they had been untouched for years—even decades.

Eli glanced at a few of the titles as they strode past, trying to assess any level of categorization among the vast media.

*Myths and Legends of the Realms*
*The Celestial Compendium*
*Lore of Forgotten Lands*

The smell of mildew and old parchment hung in the air as he followed Shira to a dead end. At the end of the aisle sat a rounded wooden table, a stack of seven books, and two chairs. Shira walked over, set the lantern on the table, and turned around. She didn't speak—waiting for something.

Eli crossed his arms. Her stillness would have seemed strange to him if Shira weren't such an enigma, always carrying the weight of unspoken thoughts, never allowing her mind to be idle. It was the first time he encountered someone more intuitive than himself, smarter even, and he had to admit, her very presence demanded his attention like nothing he'd ever experienced. Even amid the quiet, he could sense the electricity of her sharp mind, the storm of ideas dancing behind her indigo eyes, and he found himself desperately longing to know those thoughts.

*Burning rot, I'm in trouble*

"Where does our magic come from?" Shira's voice was only a quiet whisper yet carried in the silence of the abandoned space.

"What do you mean?" he asked, stepping closer.

"I mean it doesn't make sense. How did our people develop magic?" she asked. Eli could hear her trepidation. She was asking dangerous questions, and Renard's warning echoed in his mind.

"We've always had—"

"Come on Eli, don't let me down that easily. You know they aren't telling us the entire truth."

His heart skipped at her veiled compliment. "They're lying about our magic?"

"Yes," she said. "Think about it. Where does our magic truly come from?"

He paused, racking his tired brain, but he didn't have an answer. The Zentari always possessed magic, as far back as the books could state. Or rather, as far back as he was *told* the history books stated. He never read them for himself, not having access to a library growing up.

There were differences between Zentari and Aniyans certainly, beyond the ears and the magic. Being such close neighbors, splitting the country down the middle, they shared the same language and many cultural traditions. He never questioned why Aniyans didn't possess magic, other than it wasn't inherent in their blood—their lineage. Something lingered within the Zentari bloodlines that carried the secrets to Ethereal, and Aniyans naturally didn't possess those traits.

"There's something in our blood, our makeup," he responded, his mind waking.

"Yes, agreed. Then why does it need to be teased out of us?"

He rubbed his eyes. "I don't understand what you're getting at," he said. "Every Zentari is born with magic, but it doesn't just manifest on its own. And not all of us have the same level of magic inside, it's why only some can become Guardians."

"No," she said, spinning toward the pile of books. She moved three of them aside and picked up a heavy, old white tome. The leather was faded, yellowing with age, and the cover was torn at the edges. The tome's spine groaned as she opened it toward the middle, using a tattered piece of cloth as a bookmark.

Eli stood over her shoulder, biting his tongue as his face flushed, her scent washing over him.

"Here. Read this." She pointed to a sentence in the middle of a page.

*In the annals of antiquity, it is chronicled that the Zentari, since consummation and made known by youth, have possessed the sacred art of magic, their arcane mastery transcending epochs as it flows through the eons of lineage.*

"It just says Zentari children are born with magic," he mused, scanning the rest of the page.

"No no, you're not getting it."

"I don't understand what you're asking," he said, growing frustrated. "Stop being cryptic."

He stepped back as Shira grabbed another book and shuffled through the pages while she spoke. "How did they know the oldest generations of Zentari had magic at a young age? Unless . . ." She prompted.

"Unless . . ." He paused, his thoughts beginning to grasp what she found so inquisitive. "The very first generations were able to manifest the magic themselves. Without help *and* at a young age."

"Exactly!" she said, spinning to him with a grin. "And if they could express and manifest magic in youth, but now, generations later, we need to perform some form of magical surgery on adults to get our magic to manifest, then . . ."

Her voice trailed as she invited him to finish the sentence, willing him to see the truth. He caught a desperation in her eyes to discern the gravity of what she was saying. His mind spun until the realization hit him, settling like a stone in his stomach.

"We're losing our magic," he whispered.

"Yes. So then . . ."

"The question is why."

"Which brings us back around to what I originally asked: where does our magic come from?"

"Why don't we just ask Keeper Darby, or one of the other scribes? Why all the cloak and—" He stopped. She didn't need to answer, his inquisitive mind finally kicking in. He now understood the fear he saw earlier. "You asked already."

She nodded.

"And they gave you an explanation that didn't make sense."

She nodded.

"And when the questioning eventually found its way down to the core of the problem, you were warned to back away."

She didn't move, but the apprehension in her face said enough.

"Which is?" she asked, in a soft, vulnerable voice.

"Where do our people come from?"

"Eyes up, recruits!"

Eli rubbed the sleep from his face, moving his limbs which felt filled with iron. He and Shira had stayed in the library late into the night, pouring over the texts until he couldn't keep his eyes open. Somehow, even after hours of searching, he was left with more questions than answers.

To no surprise, Arlo leaped out of bed, the wooden floor straining as he landed. A gentle pat rattled Eli's shoulder as he fell still again in sleep's grasp.

"Hey, sleepy sloth!" Arlo teased. "Get up! It's time for sunshine!"

Eli's eyes opened to slits, his friend's smile the least comforting sight early in the morning. "I fear the day I find something that dampens that sunny disposition of yours," he said, peeling the blankets off.

"Fear not, my friend," Arlo said in a low, playful tone, "there is not a being in this universe that can withstand the might of the great sir Arlo Miller."

Eli would have rolled his eyes if he had the energy. It was agonizing and slow, but he managed to dress himself. With his eyelids still heavy, he made it down to mealtime with the squad, though he didn't speak to anyone. His only mission was to survive the day before collapsing on his bunk.

Breakfast at least smelled appetizing, some sort of potatoes and cheese with what he assumed was chicken. He hoped this morning's lecture wasn't canceled like yesterday. He could use the respite from the physical abuse of practice.

"You look like death," Lara said, sitting next to him with her forehead wrinkled. Eli could imagine how unsightly the bags under his eyes must be.

"Thanks. You look great too," he replied, returning to his meal.

"Seriously, are you sleeping okay?" Lara asked, still concerned.

Shira sat down across the table next to Arlo. "He sleepwalks," Shira said, taking a bite of food.

"What?" Arlo asked, feigning offense. "And you never told me?"

"No," Eli said, his annoyance growing. "I don't sleepwalk. I just haven't slept well."

"I slept amazing," Arlo mused, staring out the window.

"I know." Eli grumbled. "And you wake up acting like it's your birthday. Every. Single. Day."

Lara laughed. "Trouble in paradise," she said to Shira who winked in response.

Eli caught Shira's knowing glance but said nothing. The remainder of the day was a blur. In lecture, Darby droned about military strategy and the history of Zentari military ranks—the perfect background noise to lull Eli to sleep. Arlo, who always sat to Eli's right at lectures, elbowed him three times, after Eli started snoring. It was a kind gift of the Heavens that Keeper Darby didn't notice.

During the afternoon, they were back in the sparring room. Four proctors roamed around, declaring official matches at random, each time resulting in one of the recruits being knocked unconscious. Eli wondered if a proctor would ever call a match before it truly ended.

Arlo volunteered to spar with Shira in Eli's place as he sat against the wall. Lara sat down next to him. As tired as he felt, he was quite curious who would win in a match between the two. Arlo boasted a fair size advantage, but Shira demonstrated far more knowledge about fighting. Eli truthfully wasn't sure.

Arlo started with a quick jab, which Shira dodged fluidly. Instead of throwing him forward, as she would have done to Eli, she managed an elbow to his ribs before jumping away.

"Who's going to win?" Lara asked.

Eli fought with everything to keep his eyes open. "My money's on the new recruit," he said. Lara giggled. "Hey, can I ask you something?"

"Sure."

To his amazement, Arlo landed a blow to Shira's shoulder.

"Why are you and Arlo always in a cheerful mood?" he asked. "Don't get me wrong, I don't mind in the least, but given the circumstances, I find it unusual."

"The less you have, the more you learn to appreciate," she said without hesitation.

His eyebrows stitched. "You appreciate being in a death camp?"

A loud thump sounded as Shira threw a jumping kick toward Arlo's head, only for him to block it with his muscular forearms. He grabbed her leg, keeping her suspended. She used the anchor point to kick with her other foot, smacking his face with her boot and breaking his grip.

"No! I appreciate having comrades, having goals," she said, pausing. "I appreciate having a bed."

A pang of guilt hit him. "You didn't have one before?"

"Nope."

"Where did you live before this?" he asked, wondering if she remembered. The question was earnest, but deep down, he hoped she didn't know—that he wasn't the only one with vague memories.

"Everywhere. You can't stay in one place for too long before the city kicks you out."

"Oh. Right," he said softly.

"Stop it!" she said, nudging him in the shoulder.

"What?" he asked with a smile.

"Feeling sorry for me. I hate it. I don't need your pity."

"I wasn't trying to."

"I know you weren't. Just don't treat me different, okay?" she said, brushing her short auburn hair out of her face.

"Okay," he agreed.

At that, their squadmates' bout was finished. Arlo was on the ground, though not unconscious. Shira was still standing but breathing heavier than Eli had seen yet. Another recruit was carried out, this one with his left arm bent awkwardly. Lara tapped in to fight Arlo, and Shira sat down beside Eli, catching her breath.

"I'm surprised he actually landed a few," he said, watching Lara and Arlo start after a moment of rest. It was obvious, after Arlo's bout with Shira, that he was being gentle with Lara. Eli didn't have to wonder why.

"I'm not invincible," Shira said, taking a drink from her water skin.

"Never said you were. Just talented."

She didn't react to the compliment. "Be ready for another late night."

He huffed. "Am I not dead enough? Look," he said, lowering his voice. "I agree with you, they're hiding something. You've got me—I need answers now. But walking around as a zombie won't help me survive."

She turned to him. "You want to learn how to be talented? Be ready for another night."

His exhaustion burned through his patience. "Being talented means nothing if I'm too exhausted to fight."

"Then have fun being well rested and learning on your own."

She held his stare, and he swore he saw the glimmer of amusement. "You enjoy holding this over my head, don't you?"

"Think what you will."

"So, you're saying you'd be perfectly fine leaving me to die on the mats?"

"I'm saying you're not the only one that needs help," she answered, her attention drifting back to their squadmates.

Eli scoffed, but a grin tugged at his mouth. But it was quickly erased as Renard's words echoed in his mind. A thought came to him, and he wondered why it hadn't sooner.

If Renard was right, and because of his memory loss he should be cautious about what he finds peculiar, then perhaps Shira should warrant the same caution. If she also had a poor reaction to the WAVEs, then maybe their questions were seeking nothing more than a ghost of uncertainty—something only in their imagination.

"Hey, I need to ask you something," he whispered. Shira grunted, watching their comrades as she drank.

"When did these questions in your head start?"

She turned to him. "What do you mean?" she asked.

"You and I are the only ones asking about everything behind the scenes. For me, the questions started from my memory loss. Nazzat told me that poor reactions to the WAVEs can cause lingering amnesia about life before training. Did you have a bad reaction to the WAVEs too? You never said."

"No. As far as I know, I've been unaffected. Fuzzy the day of, maybe, but I remember everything before coming here. I would say I just don't trust everything I'm told. And if someone scolds me for asking, it makes me want to know all the more."

"So, it's what? Curiosity?"

"More like defiance," she said with a wry smile. "Look, this goes beyond curiosity. Beyond us. This war has been going on too long, and the Council is hiding something. I've been around this place long enough to smell the deceit. There are too many things left unanswered, and I'm done blindly following the Leadership. And that feeling in your gut you said you had? That something is off? It's the same one as mine."

Something in him relaxed at her words.

"Elijah Danon and Rhoda Sylvan!"

His heart jumped at the sound of his name. An official match. He glanced at Shira with wide eyes, whose jaw clenched. They both stood, Lara and Arlo approaching them.

"You'll be fine," Shira said, her hands fidgeting at her sides. "Select your attacks and be patient."

A male proctor headed their direction, side by side with a female recruit.

"Do we know her?" Arlo asked.

"No," Lara said. "I don't even know what squad she's in."

Eli's panic gave way to a quiet nervousness. There was no getting out of the match, but he was in no condition for a top tier fight. Regardless of how aggressive this girl was, he couldn't hide behind Shira forever. If he was to finish this road, to claim the title of Guardian and claw his way home, he needed to step up and earn it.

He commanded his mind to sharpen, flexing his muscles to coax his body into action. Recruit Sylvan walked up to their mat alongside the proctor. He swallowed, relieved his opponent appeared as nervous as himself. He met her on the mat with the proctor off to the side.

"All right, unconscious, tap out, or dead. Go."

Eli held his arms up, standing on the balls of his feet. He waited for Rhoda to attack, Shira's instructions fresh in his thoughts. Rhoda lunged at him with a spinning kick. Eli jumped back, far enough to dodge the attack, but too far to counter. He stepped forward with a left jab, avoiding his usual habits. Rhoda pushed his fist aside, but not before his knuckles found her left shoulder.

She grunted and threw an elbow to his chin. Iron coated his tongue as his head knocked back.

"Stick to your roots. Nothing fancy," Shira said.

Eli shook his head to clear his dizziness. Rhoda threw another kick, but this one Eli caught, her heel biting his stomach. He used the opening, pulled her forward and brought his elbow to her temple. She reeled from the blow, falling dazed onto her knee.

He waited out of habit.

"Eli, end it!" Shira yelled.

"Enough!" The proctor scolded. "Do not interfere with the match, recruit!"

Eli jumped forward, throwing his knee for Rhoda's head. But she took advantage of his poor form and landed a solid strike to his abdomen.

Eli's lungs screamed to fill with air as Rhoda threw a series of fast punches. He was only able to block some of them, his opponent coming at him with a rising fierceness. He didn't know what to do. There wasn't an opening, and he was getting pummeled. In an act of desperation, he crouched and lunged into her, catching her waist. He pushed all of his body weight into bringing her down, which worked after she stumbled backwards.

Rhoda's head knocked onto the hard ground, missing the mat by an inch. Her body stilled as she blinked—stunned. Eli didn't waste the opportunity twice and pressed his hands into her neck. Her face turned red, grabbing at his wrists, squirming under his weight. A pleading look flushed over her. She let go with her right hand, reaching for the mat to tap out. Eli panicked for her, catching her wrist, pinning her in place as he pressed harder against her neck. She would die otherwise.

As the two struggled against one another, something stirred within Eli, burned like a searing flame awakened from a stray ember. Locking eyes with Rhoda, Eli felt the heat of a rage deep inside. It growled, shifted in its slumbering form. But as his opponent's muscles went lax, Rhoda's gaze drifting into the distance, Eli stiffened.

*What in the Hells*

He didn't leave his hand on her throat a moment longer. Rhoda was unconscious. He stood, turning to the healers as they approached.

"Elijah Danon is the victor. Excellent job recruit," the proctor said, leaving with the healers.

Eli paced on the mat, catching his breath. Fingers running through his hair with shaking hands, he waited for his thundering heart to slow. As Rhoda was carried to the medical ward, he couldn't stop staring at the markings on her neck—the bruises he put there. And with a deep breath, the anger inside him vanished.

# Chapter Twenty

The stallion's hooves clicked against the smooth rocks along the stone road which led into Manoach, slick from the recent rainfall. Eva and Swordsman Lane rode side by side as the day slowly came to a close, the sky turning a burnt orange.

"You ever been here, Katz?" Lane asked.

Eva scanned the varied faces, leery of two Legion warriors entering town on horseback. "No," she said.

"I've seen it in passing," Lane said. "A few other Swordsmen at Yaqar grew up around here. They said the biggest thing is don't talk about the war. People live this far North to escape the conflict and get easily spooked by trespassers. Even the Legion."

"They just want peace, Alart."

"No, they're cowards," he muttered. "Leave the fighting to everyone else and then get mad at the warriors keeping the Zentari off their doorstep."

Log cabins and buildings with straw and stone roofs lined the main road, signs depicting all manner of commerce from inns to taverns to blacksmiths. Eva was surprised by the lack of activity this time of day, though she had little experience with quaint towns.

"Where's the Legion headquarters?" she asked. They stopped in front of a wooden sign which hung by short lengths of chain. It depicted a white horse with a long mane, the calligraphic lettering also in white.

*The Stallion Inn*

"Ask in there," Lane said.

Eva waited. Taking orders from him was more than distasteful. "Didn't they tell you where it was?"

"It's a village, Katz. Just ask so I can go home."

Glancing around, she dismounted and ascended the steps to the inn. The front door groaned against its hinges, revealing a modestly sized dining room. A bar sat to her right with an open area to her left, adorned with tables for games and food. An elderly man sat eating what looked like porridge of some sort, his clothes ragged and stained.

A middle-aged burly woman stood behind the bar polishing some glass dishes. She wore a headband that complemented her deep golden hair. An apron covered most of her dress, which confessed the evidence of a hard day's work. Her stern face and caramel eyes lingered on Eva, drifting up and down as Eva stepped up to her.

"We leave the war outside 'round here," she said, her voice daintier than Eva expected. It carried the slightest Northern accent, from beyond the reaches of Adiel—but it sounded forced.

"I understand," Eva said. "I'm here to exchange patrols. I just need to know where the Legion headquarters is here in town."

A patron descended the stairs and walked between them as he left. Body odor wafted over Eva, leaving a lasting stench in the room. She fought the urge to scrunch her nose.

"Keep followin' the road North. Et's the small cabin on the west side at the edge of town. Can' miss it."

Eva gave a polite smile and glanced over at the older gentleman eating at the table. He had stopped, mid-bite, and was staring at her. His face was unshaved and gaunt—homeless, she assumed, or in a rough spot at least.

"Thank you," Eva said, as she bowed to leave. Following the woman's instructions, she and Lane eventually spotted a quaint cabin which displayed a thick brass sign under the eave.

*Legion*

The cabin had no front porch and no décor or landscaping she could see. Eva and Lane dismounted, and Lane knocked on the door. Footsteps sounded before a handsome, older man answered.

He had short hair, graying at the temples, and light blue eyes, almost gray themselves. His beard, trimmed and well kept, retained a dark blonde hue. His face was soft and friendly, a gentle smile on his lips. He wore a simplistic variation of the typical Legion armor and bore no weapons to Eva's surprise.

"Can I help you?" he asked, looking at them up and down.

"I'm Swordsman Lane," Alart said, standing at attention. "You are Lieutenant Ollon, sir?"

"Oh," the man said, surprised. "Yes. Rest, Swordsman. What's the news?"

Lane relaxed. "Sir, I'm escorting Swordsman Evalynn Katz to be placed under your authority pending her trial for crimes against the Legion."

*Unproven crimes*

Ollon straightened, glancing at Eva.

"Under whose orders?" the Lieutenant asked.

Eva stepped forward, annoyed by Lane speaking for her.

"Sir, I was assigned here as a replacement for patrol. Swordsman Lane and I were both stationed at the Yaqar outpost. I am to relieve Swordsman Morrigan."

The Lieutenant's eyes narrowed. "Yaqar?" he asked.

"Yes, sir," Lane said.

The Lieutenant nodded. "All right, then. Swordsman Lane, you are dismissed. Safe travels."

Alart bowed, giving Eva a knowing glance before returning to the horses. Eva wasn't surprised Drax didn't bother sending word ahead.

"Come on in," the Lieutenant said, stepping aside in the doorway.

The living space held a narrow countertop with a washbasin next to a modest stove, and a table for two set under a square window. A few scattered chairs and a desk sat near the front door. The room was so small Eva felt as though she could touch both walls.

"Have a seat," he said, holding a hand out to one of the chairs at the table. He sat across from her as she set her bag down.

"Thank you, Lieutenant."

"Please, call me Jafeth," he said, warmly. "You're Evalynn?"

"Yes," she responded. "But everyone calls me Eva."

"Pleased to meet you, Eva," he said with a smile. Her nerves calmed in the presence of his kind demeanor.

"So!" he said, propping his feet up on the table. His chair creaked as he leaned back, placing his hands behind his head for support. "What evil scheme did Drax concoct this time?"

Eva gave a surprised look. "Sir?"

Jafeth smiled. "I knew who you were before you came in. I'm sure you're aware your white hair gives you away." Eva fidgeted with her bun. "No, it looks great! I just mean your reputation precedes you."

"I hope in a good way," she said, hating when her first impressions were tainted with assumptions—something she never seemed to get away from.

"Well, that's my point. A well renowned warrior getting assigned patrol duty? The Legion's White-Haired Devil being charged and sent to trial? I'd maybe believe it, if it wasn't Drax filing the report." Despite the subtle accusation, his grin persisted.

Eva smiled. "Does my uncle have a worse reputation than me?"

Jafeth's eyes widened. "He's your uncle? That makes more sense why you don't get along."

Eva was taken aback again. "I'm sorry, Jafeth, but how—"

Jafeth held his hand up. "Lieutenant Benton Drax has garnered quite the reputation among the Legion Leadership. He's not only the most annoying outpost Lieutenant, with near constant letters and requests running back and forth to Ashdod, but he has made it quite clear his disdain for a certain female Swordsman. The fact that you're his niece is hilarious, and it's obvious why he ensures that piece of information remains hidden."

Eva gave a breathy laugh—thankful she hadn't landed in the hands of a fan of her uncle.

"But I suppose I need to ask," Jafeth said, his smile disappearing. "Is it true? This trial?"

Eva swallowed. "I failed a mission and two of our own died. Drax is charging me with their deaths."

Jafeth's eyes narrowed, weighing her words. He huffed. "Bloody Nines, that guy's a piece of work."

Fidgeting with a knot on the wooden table, she changed the subject. "How long have you been here?"

"Almost five years now," he said. "I requested to be stationed here."

"Why?" she asked, surprised someone would wish to be banished here.

"Well." He began, pulling his feet off the table. "The Aniyan military doesn't let you quit whenever you want. So, this was the only way for me to try and have some semblance of a life."

"Living here?" she asked, her forehead wrinkled as she gestured to the cramped space.

He laughed softly. "Nah, I'm only here during the day. I built a cabin outside town."

Her brow raised. "You're handy with nails and a hammer?"

Jafeth shrugged. "I do okay."

"And how is it you haven't been transferred?"

"Well, that's the advantage of being a Lieutenant, there aren't that many people that can give you orders anymore. I always said we needed more ranks to balance the command structure, but now I get the benefits of that system."

"You live here by yourself?"

"No actually, I—"

The front door burst open, revealing a younger man wearing a healer's tunic. "Jafeth!"

Jafeth sat up, his calm demeanor evaporated, replaced by worry. "What?"

"She's pushing!"

Jafeth glanced at Eva, his grin returning. He stood, fingers twitching as he scanned the room. "Okay, um, I have to go. Throw your things on the spare bed. There's some bread in the pantry and just patrol the perimeter at dusk. Find me if you need help!"

Before Eva could ask any questions—like who exactly was giving birth—Jafeth was gone with the stranger. She smiled. It seemed being sentenced to patrol duty wasn't going to be as miserable as she thought.

*So far so good*

After making herself at home, she left for patrol before the sun fully set per Jafeth's instructions. There was a narrow, beaten path which circled the town and marked the outermost borders—so short, she could walk the entire perimeter in less than an hour. She draped her cloak over her shoulders as the air turned cool. The town was quiet, settling in for the night, the windows of each home displaying the light of indoor candles.

Apparently, there wasn't much of a nightlife here. Yet, the stillness welcomed her weary heart, and to her surprise, it was strangely comforting to be away from Yaqar. She missed Maya, but had a good feeling about Jafeth, who had created *quite* the life for himself here. She wondered if she would be able to meet the new little one.

Against her efforts to banish Lucas from her mind, her wandering thoughts returned to him. There was nothing she could do at this point, and dwelling on the situation would only incite more frustration, lead her down a road she must avoid. She prayed for his safety, but she wasn't sure when she would see him again.

She didn't know what would happen with Drax's accusations or with her upcoming trial. Even if she lost her place in the Legion, at least she wouldn't have to deal with petty rules anymore. The problem was, there wasn't anything else she could see herself doing with her time. It didn't matter if she refused to return home, she'd likely end up in prison.

Ironically, she would miss the fighting, and the knowledge that she was working toward a solution for her people. The adrenaline rush of battle was alluring, as much as it had worn her down over the years. She wondered if being stationed here would serve to bring healing, help her sift through the turmoil in her own head. Remaining neck deep in the throes of war provided no time to reflect on herself—her desires and dreams. Maybe there was more this place had to offer than Drax thought.

As she rounded the corner of a building on the edge of town, she didn't notice two civilians before nearly running into them.

"Excuse us," a man said, surprising Eva as she stumbled to avoid running into his young daughter, who seemed not a day over six.

"I'm sorry," Eva said, holding her hands up.

"Don't worry about it," the man said with a nod, a protective hand over his daughter's chest. "What do you say, Veira?"

"Excuse me!" the girl said with a smile.

"Of course," Eva said.

"Come on sweetie, I bet mommy has dinner ready," her father said, smiling politely as they left. Transfixed by the father's gentleness, Eva's attention was locked on them as they walked around her. The young girl turned and waved.

"Bye!" she said, her meek voice slicing through Eva's heart. She waved back, unable to imagine what it would be like to smile while holding her father's hand.

As Eva turned and headed back to the cabin, she strained her mind to recall any pleasant memories of her father—anything worthy of remembering. The closest thing she could think of was during archery practice at eight years old.

*"An excellent shot, Evalynn," Glorana cheered, sweating under the hot sun. "You have improved."*

*Eva took a deep breath, rubbing the fingers of her right hand together, wincing at the blisters that had formed underneath the calluses. Though archery was something she'd been forced to learn for the past two years, it was only recently she focused all her attention on the craft.*

*"I've been sneaking out here at night," she whispered, grabbing another arrow from the barrel.*

*Glorana huffed. "For how long?"*

*Eva shrugged with a wry grin. "For the past three months."*

*"Evalynn Marie, you haven't been in trouble in some time. Don't jeopardize—"*

*"Jeopardize what, Glorana?" Eva's father asked, approaching them, flanked by two of his personal guards. Eva stiffened. But this was a perfect opportunity.*

*"Oh, my Lord," Glorana said. "Nothing. Look at your daughter's skill. She has improved a great deal."*

*Her father stepped up behind her, assessing her archery skills by the half-buried arrows in the hay target—four of which were bullseyes. He hummed, waiting for her next shot.*

*She said nothing as she notched the arrow and reached back, determined to find something to impress him. She hoped his sternness was merely his way of raising her to be strong—determined and skilled—and not a rejection of who she was. And within, slowly fading, was an ache that screamed from the depths of her soul, needing his approval.*

*She released the arrow, which landed square on the target, nicking the shaft of*
*another arrow in the dark center circle. She breathed out and turned to him, but*
*his eyes never met hers.*
*"Well done," he mused.*
*A deep swell of pride rushed through her.*
*Her father added. "If shooting a stationary target were a skill worthy of note."*
*Eva's shoulders fell.*
*"Try again, but close your eyes."*
*Her brow wrinkled.*
*"My Lord," Glorana said. "That could be dangerous."*
*Her father said nothing, only waited. She caved under his crushing presence. Eva did*
*as she was told, notching another arrow. She closed her eyes, picturing the target in*
*her mind. She leaned on her muscle memory, the familiar placement of her hands*
*on the bow, the feel of the bowstring.*
*The arrow flew, but the response of the target was absent. She opened her eyes.*
*Missed.*
*Her father hummed. "Pity," he muttered, before turning to leave.*

Over that next year, Eva dedicated herself to practicing archery on horseback, mastering moving shots—even while standing on the horse. She became so skilled, she eventually *could* hit targets with her eyes closed.

But her father never attended another practice session and never recognized her achievement. The only thing Eva gained from that year was chronic pain in her right shoulder. Their family healer said to give up archery unless she wanted to lose the use of her right arm.

The cabin was still vacant upon her return, though she assumed Jafeth would be gone until morning. Overall, the patrol had been uneventful, other than dealing with two drunks yelling at everyone they passed along the road. Giving one a bloody nose after they harassed her was more than enough to send them both stumbling home.

She unpacked her things in the bed chamber, noting the belongings of who she assumed was Swordsman Morrigan. It struck her as odd for him to be absent, but the privacy was a luxury as she slipped into her nightwear. Being free of Drax meant she could at least sleep comfortably from now on. Lighting the tight space with a single candle, Eva placed it on the dining table. There was a shelf on the back wall about a foot below the ceiling, which held a modest number of books, all varying titles. She scanned them briefly and grabbed one that piqued her interest.

*Tales of Terror and Triumph*

Eva laid on the spare mattress, far more comfortable than her cot at Yaqar. She opened the book of short stories, escaping into fantasy—her refuge since childhood, when reading was her only solace from the prison of her home.

Locked in her room by her father, she had survived only through their vast library and Glorana's kindness. Eva loved tales of noble knights slaying dragons, always imagining herself as the hero rather than the princess. Once, she had seen herself as a damsel in distress, with Lucas as her savior, but now she knew she had saved herself. Lucas was merely a steadying presence, a lifeline, not the knight who carried her away.

And she never felt the need to be swept away—quite the contrary. The man she dreamt of, the one she told Maya about, was another warrior—someone who stood beside her in battle, meeting their enemies shoulder to shoulder. Somehow, he felt as familiar as her own skin, carried a fire deep within him. He stood beside her with a fierce guardianship, yet a gentle hand—refusing to allow her to be anything but her greatest and truest self.

Eva didn't read to the second chapter before sleep overtook her. Her dreams were pleasant and full of wonder, before the thud of the front door opening woke her from sleep. Light poured in the window above her bed. She wasn't sure if there was an early wake-up call, but it didn't matter, as she would've already missed it.

She sat on the edge of her bed with a yawn. As she kneaded her tired muscles, she noticed she forgot to blow out the candle, which was now burnt all the way through.

*Oops*

She wondered if Drax would qualify burning down the Legion cabin as stepping out of line. The trickling of water being poured came from the other room. Half-awake, she stood and pushed open the bedroom door. Jafeth, dressed and bright-eyed, stood by the stove. He placed a kettle on top and was stacking wood inside.

"You know," he said, "technically there's an early morning watch."

Eva leaned against the doorway. "Well since the senior warrior in charge didn't explain my duties before leaving his post, let's call it even."

He looked up at her with a gentle grin. "I always have tea in the morning if you want some."

She smiled, not used to such kindness. "Sure."

# Chapter Twenty-One

M aybe we're asking the wrong questions," Eli said, his wooden chair creaking as he sat back and rubbed his eyes. This was the seventh night over the past two weeks he and Shira had been down in the library scouring for clues to the origins of Zentari magic. And time was slipping away from him. The only positive thing that happened this past week was Soren Mitchell being suspiciously absent.

"Keep reading," Shira pressed from across the table.

But Eli couldn't. The days passed in such a blur, he felt like he was watching someone else live his life—going through the motions of each day disconnected from everything around him. A terrible state to be in when the next Thought Wave Analysis was in two days. He feared the side effects, still unable to recall the memories he'd lost—his hometown, his father's name, and a dozen other facts any normal person would never forget.

Worse than that, the second WAVE was followed quickly by the Crucible, the second challenge, which marked the halfway point through the program. His journey to becoming a Guardian was near half-complete, and he had so little to show for it.

In addition to his fatigue, since that first night, and worsened by his conversation with Renard, an unease seeped into his stomach. Something in the back of his mind was gnawing at the truth—as if he could reach out and touch it—but not bring it to the surface or name it. The truth of his amnesia from the WAVEs wasn't lost on him, but by the Nine it was infuriating.

Shira was more or less herself. And despite the late nights, she was still untouchable on the mats. Her abrasiveness hadn't improved, but Eli felt a slight change when they were deep in the library. She was more vulnerable and open—softer. Maybe it was just his imagination, or more likely, wishful thinking. He cursed himself for being so easily drawn to someone, especially someone who enjoyed hitting him.

"You didn't answer my question," he drawled.

Shira sat across from him, nose stuck in one of the more recent scrolls they had pulled from a top shelf on the other side of the library. The number of books was so enormous it would take them years to sift through all the available literature, let alone read everything. Thankfully, they were given all the peace and quiet they needed with the library remaining abandoned night after night. He had spotted a few Keepers during the daytime in passing, but none after lights out, and never any recruits.

Yet, regardless of the insurmountable challenge, neither of them was willing to quit. Shira moved forward with her own unstoppable determination, and for Eli, he now bore his own quiet reasons. He had yet to tell Shira about his conversation with Renard which plagued his thoughts. Even without Shira here, he didn't think he could let this go any longer.

Shira spoke, her attention remaining on the scroll in her lap. "You didn't ask a question. But I think we're asking the right ones, we're just getting the wrong answers."

Eli yawned. "No, I'm saying let's look at this from another angle," he said. "Was there something present years ago that increased inner magic that isn't present—"

"Here," Shira said. Eli sat up straight, peering at her scroll. "In olden years, when the silver-threaded ley ran thick through the bones of the world, the Zentari stood as wardens of the unseen tide. Bound by birthright to the veils between realms, they wove strands of The Ethereal. Yet, in this amorphous age of soft flesh and wayward kin, the blood thins and the old bonds fray."

"The blood thins," Eli breathed, mulling over the words. "We were right."

"About the magic getting weaker, but not about anything else so far."

"Does it say they found a solution? Or why it happened?"

Shira skimmed the remainder of the text. "Even now, seekers delve into the hidden vaults of their forebears, tracing glyphs long forsaken, whispering secrets of old, unspoken for an epoch. And there, among the relics of our past, stands an artifice, a forging of flesh anew, to purge the lesser strain."

A silence grew between them, the words hanging in the still air of the library.

"They found an answer," Eli said.

"No." Shira shook her head. "They were seeking one."

"When was this? How old is this scroll?"

"It's dated to the forty-fifth year of the tenth era."

*This is the thirteenth era, in the thirty-second year*

"That's nearly three hundred years ago."

"Two hundred eighty-seven."

Eli rubbed his face, pleading for his mind to remain sharp. This was the first step forward in days. "But this proves our point. They've known this was a problem for a long time."

"Yes. And we can assume the WAVEs are the solution, but it doesn't say why it ever became a problem. And we have no way to know how long they've been using the WAVEs."

He sighed. "What else does it say?"

Shira tossed the scroll onto the growing pile on the table. "Nothing. The rest talks about the wisdom of the Council and Zentari government. It doesn't even say how the Council started."

She blinked wearily. The dark circles underneath her eyes grew larger every night—the only indication of her fatigue. It was infuriating to find minute pieces of the truth, yet nothing more.

"What if it is just intermarrying?" Eli asked again.

"Between two nations that hate each other?" she argued.

"Five hundred years is a long time. That's what, sixteen generations?"

"It's too simple," Shira said, "if that's all it was why wouldn't they just say that?"

"Because it undermines their narrative."

"Of hatred?"

"Exactly. Can't fight a war against a people you like."

"How do you even know Aniyans and Zentari are compatible?"

"I don't. But sometimes the simplest answers are the best."

Shira exhaled. "Yeah. Maybe."

After a moment, Eli said, "Look, we need to rest."

"No," Shira argued. "We're getting closer."

"Shira," he said, holding her stern glance. "I want to keep going, but if we keep reading this exhausted we might miss something. We need to step away and let our brains mull through what we've read. If we catch up on some rest, we can come back with fresh minds."

She nodded but remained silent.

As much as Eli would like to bring someone else here to help, he knew they were asking very dangerous questions. Not only did no one else seem to inquire about these things, but if anyone told the wrong person, they could be in serious trouble. The questions they were asking could be construed as treason, or worse, they could be labeled as spies.

It was only yesterday he asked another Keeper, Anaro, in a subtle manner about their questions, and was sternly dismissed yet again. They found a reference detailing the applicable punishments for defying the Council and Zentari Leadership within the military. Needless to say, there wasn't much considered to be off limits—mutilation, torture, or otherwise.

Nausea spread through him, imagining Shira being tortured. Eli never asked anything close to these questions in lecture, yet that was enough to get approached by the Captain. They were treading a dangerous line. Suffice it to say, there was a reason Shira had originally kept this close to the chest. Eli was grateful now that he was wrapped up in it.

They gathered the books they collected and returned them to their respective places, not trusting any leery Keepers. As they crept out of the library into the quiet of the walkway, Eli pushed aside his exhaustion and seized the opportunity.

"So, what did you like to do for fun growing up?" he asked, nodding at a night watchman who raised an eyebrow at them. Eli questioned which of the Operatives told Renard they were out late, or if they all reported to the Captain about the recruits' whereabouts. Despite the stern words of the Captain, it didn't seem to be against the rules.

"What every kid likes to do," she said, wiping her hands of the dust from the books. "I played in the mud, built forts in the creeks, and pretended to storm the castle."

"That sounds like a far too generic response."

"You asked a dumb question, so I gave you a generic answer."

As they strode together, Shira untied her hair, which fell in thick strands of rich black. Eli ripped away his gaze, not wanting to stare.

"Okay then, please regale me with an intelligent question."

She stopped, tying her hair up. "Where did you learn to swim?"

"In the water." He smiled at her glare as they resumed their trek. "I know, I know. When I was younger I went with my father on his trips. He helped a local merchant with trades from the farm, but it meant he was on the road a lot. I made him stop by any lake or river we came across. It was my favorite thing to do growing up."

"I thought your family owned an inn?"

"We do, but only after selling the farm. The inn wasn't built until I was twelve."

"Why sell the farm?"

"It's a long story. But basically we couldn't run the farm with just the three of us."

"You and your dad are close?" she asked.

"Yeah, actually. Well, at least back then. He and I sort of drifted apart over the past few years."

"He disagreed with you joining the Citadel?"

"Yeah, you could say that." He swallowed, his lack of memory feeding his unease. He didn't want to have that conversation right now.

"What happened?" she asked. They entered the lower floor of the barracks and stopped at the foot of the stairs. The vast stillness of the Citadel did nothing to tame his excitement over her attention.

"That's another long story," he muttered, clearing his throat. "Where did you learn to fight so well?"

He was grateful she let the question drop, but she crossed her arms. "There's been war in this country since before I was born. You fight or you die. Try again."

His eyes narrowed a touch. Her response sounded more like an invitation than rejection.

"Okay, are you close with your father?" he asked, catching the slightest flinch.

"No. He died."

Her curt response caught him off-guard as pain flashed in her face.

"I'm sorry," he said softly. He opened his mouth to ask how or when but decided against it. Not knowing how else to respond, Eli changed the subject. "I can't stop thinking about Rhoda."

"Get over it," Shira said, shrugging. "It's going to happen again."

He bit his lip, unsure if he could.

"I saw you move her hand," she said.

Eli averted his gaze, rubbing the back of his neck. He'd crossed a line.

"Stop it," she scolded. "You saved her life."

"No, I didn't." The taste of that strange fury yet lingered. "I took away her choice."

"She panicked. You saved her."

"Then why do I feel guilty?"

She stepped toward him. "Because you have an overhyped sense of responsibility, and that comes with a price."

He huffed. "You speak like you know me."

"You're not hard to figure out," she said, the shadow of a smile on her mouth.

He crossed his arms. "You are," he said, his heart thundering in his chest. "I can't decide if you hate me, tolerate me, or find me as intriguing as I find you. I can't even figure out why you're here."

A part of him relished her uncomfortable shifting, at least until she squared her shoulders. "Stop wasting your time. I didn't come here to make friends."

She moved toward the stairs, but Eli blocked her path. The defiance in her stare was becoming commonplace and didn't rattle him in the moment.

"I gathered that," he said. "So, what did you come here for?"

She didn't answer right away but made no effort to walk around him. Eli caught her fidgeting—a nervous habit. Yet here she was, standing closer than she ever had.

"What does it matter?" she asked.

"Like I said. I can't figure you out."

"Maybe I don't want to be figured out."

"I'd like to know."

"I don't care."

"Okay fine," he said wryly. "I need to know."

She raised her eyebrows. "Can't help yourself?"

"Is it so hard to believe I find you fascinating?" Eli felt his cheeks burn. "Besides, you're the one who took advantage of my curiosity."

"I'm not a puzzle for your amusement."

"No, but you are rather defensive," he said, watching her squirm under his attention. "Come on, Weiss. Why do you fight?"

She took a deep breath as her fists clenched, glancing at the empty desk where the night watch would normally be.

"I fight because arrogant men like you keep showing up to join the military, vowing to be the next hero of change, yet somehow end up only contributing to the hatred. I fight because I'm done hoping someone else will do what's needed. So, excuse me if I come off as defensive, but I have a hard time believing everything people tell me."

"And you're the model of humility, I suppose?"

"I never said that."

"But you're implying that *you* are the one to bring change," he argued. "As I see it, this isn't you having a problem with the next hero, this is a problem with you trusting others. Everything about you screams for everyone else to piss off, which would make sense if you refuse to trust anyone."

"Is that so?" she asked, stepping back.

He watched her guard build under his pressure—unrelenting against his prying.

"Yeah," he said, holding her icy stare. "So you need to decide whether you can trust me."

Her forehead wrinkled. "That your professional opinion?"

"Just an observation," he said with a wry grin. "And a request."

"Your observations are childish," she huffed, before walking around him. "And I don't want your trust."

He sighed, watching her climb the stairs. She didn't turn back. He heard a gentle click of a door he assumed she wished to slam shut.

Eli wondered who destroyed Shira's ability to believe in others, feel safe with anyone, and it stirred a deep, protective aggression within him. He couldn't decide whether to take her at her word and back off or keep pressing—be the one person who cared enough to break down her barriers.

With lethargy seeping into every cell of his body, Eli finally laid down to sleep. Regardless of the lumpy straw mattress, he was unconscious as soon as his head hit the pillow. He was grateful the Heavens blessed him with dreamless sleep, but morning came all too soon.

"You look like death, man," Arlo commented as they both dressed in their leathers. "You getting any sleep?"

A pang of guilt hit Eli, having not told Arlo about the nightly escapades to the library. While he assumed Arlo would be supportive, he didn't want him involved. And Shira seemed drawn to Arlo, which only seeded Eli's misplaced jealousy.

"I've been having nightmares," he answered. It was the truth—at least part of it. What he didn't mention was that ever since he started staying up late reading old manuscripts his nightmares disappeared. Maybe his mind was too exhausted to conjure new horrors each night.

"Really? That sucks," Arlo said, now finished dressing, strapping his claymore over his back. "You want me to talk to the medical ward? I can grab a sleeping tonic for you."

"No, it's fine," Eli answered, a bit too quickly. "It's just stress I'm sure."

"Okay." Arlo's expression showed genuine concern, worsening the pit of guilt in Eli's stomach.

After breakfast, the recruits attended their morning lecture. Darby stood on the auditorium stage beside a brutal-looking man clad in black leather armor and a lengthy black cloak. His face, etched with years of scars, remained emotionless, framed by a thin fabric tied over his hair. His black eyes scanned the crowd with a quiet viciousness—a predatory gaze. Something about him made Eli uncomfortable, as if he could see into your very soul.

Darby said, "Recruits, we have an honored guest today, High Captain Azazel."

At once, the recruits all stood at attention. This was the second in command of the Zentari military. *Orridan Azazel.* The pit in Eli's stomach was justified. The man carried the same presence as Voss, and near the same authority.

"Ven'so, recruits." The High Captain's voice was deep, carrying throughout the auditorium with ease. "I am here today to assist with your lecture, speaking about a field in which I am the leading expert: the nature of psychological warfare."

The High Captain paced, his gloved hands held behind his back. "Who here can tell me the greatest weakness of the Aniyan military?"

Immediately a hand shot up in the front row. Azazel nodded to the male recruit—Tori if Eli remembered.

"They do not possess magic, sir!" Tori answered with confidence.

"Excellent point," Azazel said. "The Aniyans do not possess the inner magic that is innate in Zentari blood. Our gift of the Ethereal not only grants us the power to become Guardians but overall enhances our physical and mental capabilities. What else?"

Eli glanced at Shira who was seated a few rows to his left. Her head was down, focused on her parchment as she scribbled notes. This was a perfect opportunity to ask the question they were both thinking, but also the worst timing with the High Captain present. Another hand raised toward the back of the room—a female recruit.

"The Aniyan military is more lax and less organized than ours, leaving vulnerabilities in their day-to-day routine in the field. And their training and combat education is lacking, sir."

"Valid points recruit, but I'm looking for a specific answer yet to be brought forward."

Azazel waited. The atmosphere thickened under his presence, no one wanting to answer incorrectly. It was a while before the next hand raised, and to Eli's dismay, it was Sol.

"The Aniyans are weak minded. They fight because of their hatred. We fight for survival. Our reasons are stronger, sir."

Azazel eyed Sol for a long moment. "You're Sol Richter."

"Yes, High Captain Azazel, sir!"

Eli rolled his eyes. A simple nod would have sufficed.

"I've heard about you. It seems your reputation suits you. That is exactly the answer I was looking for." The High Captain turned to address the rest of the room. "The Aniyans are vulnerable because their minds are weak, their resolve fragile. I have had the opportunity to interrogate many members of the Legion, and I can say beyond a doubt their mental resolve is nothing short of brittle. Some of you may not be aware, but I am a Guardian."

A handful of gasps and murmurs echoed in the room. Eli wasn't surprised, knowing most of their instructors were Guardians.

"My magic, when manifested, did not present as expected. Through this program, I discovered that I had an exceptionally unique skill set. Using my magic, I am able to invade someone's mind. With proper techniques I can see what they see and hear what they think, I can even make them see and hear what I wish. The weakness in this is the participant has to be weak-minded or willing."

A sense of unease slithered under Eli's skin.

"This gift of mine has made me the foremost authority on interrogations. You can guess how much easier it is to obtain information by simply reading someone's mind. But the subject of my interrogation is able to resist my magic by casting their mind away from the idea or truth that I am pursuing. I am explaining all of this to say that I have yet to find an Aniyan prisoner I am not able to dominate."

A hand raised to Eli's right. "How many prisoners have you interrogated, sir?"

"I've lost count."

Another hand raised. "Is there any mental damage caused by your interrogation, sir?"

"Yes. I've seen everything from emotional instability to hallucinations and delusions."

Another recruit raised their hand, asking the very question Eli was thinking. "Is it often that a Guardian's magic manifests in a noncombative way, sir?"

Azazel didn't answer, handing the question to Keeper Darby.

"It all depends on the environment." Darby began. "We are unsure entirely of why, but we have found over the years that the intensive training of the Citadel program tends to facilitate more combat-oriented manifestations of inner magic. Perhaps, with the proper time and resources, we could experiment with differing settings. Unfortunately, our current political climate does not grant us that luxury."

Murmurs emerged. Two hands shot up this time. Darby nodded to a girl in front of Eli.

"So, it's possible to affect how inner magic manifests?" she asked.

Eli glanced to Shira again, who'd stilled in her chair.

"We believe so, though we are not entirely sure. You must understand, this program was designed around the necessities brought on by the war. As we refined the process of training Guardians, and given the difficulty of bringing forth magic, this program carries the singular goal of creating battle-ready Guardians. By any means necessary. Whether or not we could investigate alternative methods of magic, is not an area we will discuss. You are all here for one purpose. Do not lose sight of that."

The room fell silent, and Eli's palms were sweaty as he raised his hand. "Have you noticed any change in how powerful inner magic presents over time?" He swallowed, as both Darby and Azazel looked at him. Eli swore Shira was drilling him with a stare, though he dared not check.

Darby furrowed his brow. "What do you mean, recruit?"

"I mean." Eli started, choosing his words carefully. "Do we see weaker or stronger manifestations than we did in the past with the refined methods of the program?"

Darby's face betrayed no emotion. "It is because of the dedication and expertise of the Citadel that our Guardians and warriors are more powerful than ever. But this does not detract from the honor our ancestors demonstrated as they unveiled their inner magic out of necessity and desperation. Before the program, many Guardians discovered their magic in the field, amid the chaos of battle."

The keeper glanced at Azazel before continuing. "Do not think I have forgotten your insolence earlier this month, recruit Danon. You would be wise to not step on the toes of those who have carved your future with blood and sweat."

Eli's face burned, waiting for another recruit to take the attention off him. Shira gave him a knowing look.

*Yeah yeah, don't rub it in*

Why they would be so touchy about these questions—he wasn't sure.

*Unless there is some merit to them. No one hides what doesn't matter*

And considering the scroll he and Shira found last night, this was a problem the Council found centuries ago.

Another hand raised. "How greatly do you feel the Thought Wave Analysis has affected how a Guardian's magic manifests?"

Eli's ears perked.

*Shira was right. Why do we need the Thought Wave Analysis now? How long have we needed it? If that was the answer they found, it still doesn't explain the why. And if it only made Guardians stronger, then why not just say that?*

Considering what they'd found so far, the Citadel was certainly guilty of keeping secrets. But that wasn't a crime. Another question popped into his head, but he didn't dare ask in front of the class again.

*But the next WAVE is tomorrow*

Darby said, "We have not noted any difference, only that it expedites the process. But we have already touched on the Thought Wave Analysis previously. If you have a specific question regarding it, you can ask after class is dismissed."

The Keeper turned and nodded at Azazel, giving him back the floor. The remainder of the lecture detailed the importance of psychological warfare, and different variations of how to utilize it in the field. Once class was dismissed, Eli waited in his seat for the room to vacate for lunch.

Arlo stood. "You coming?"

"Yeah, I'll catch up," Eli said, bouncing his knee, still sitting.

Arlo glanced at Keeper Darby, who was speaking with another student. "Don't push it, man."

"I won't," Eli said. Though even if he was, he couldn't help it. And he didn't have a choice. It was more than just curiosity at this point, it had evolved into a compulsive need to uncover the truth. The entire structure of questions and bread crumb answers was beginning to swallow him. Every time he and Shira found some semblance of an answer, it only brought up more questions.

He came here trusting his nation's leaders to train him into a weapon of war, build him into something greater for his people. But now, his trust was being undermined more each day. And if there was anything greater than his own curiosity, it was his refusal to follow a falsehood—to stand by something akin to the evil he'd experienced as a child.

If his leaders were involved in something, *anything*, he couldn't stand by, he would take his chances and leave. And he agreed with Shira—they were hiding something. If the Council was willing to kill some of its own just to ensure a few of them became Guardians, they would be capable of anything.

As the last few recruits left the auditorium, Eli approached Keeper Darby, who was finishing a conversation with another recruit. All contentment in Darby's face vanished at Eli's approach. The Keeper remained silent, waiting for him to speak.

"Keeper Darby, sir," Eli said. "I want to apologize for my earlier questions. I didn't mean to disrespect our ancestors, nor question the incredible feat they accomplished by manifesting magic on their own."

"You have an inquisitive mind, recruit Danon. A rare gift. But be cautious that it does not lead you down the wrong path." Darby's expression remained stoic.

"Sir, if you please, I have one more question. About the Thought Wave Analysis." Darby nodded. Eli glanced over his shoulder, ensuring all other students had left. "I had a poor reaction to the WAVE and was told that can happen in rare cases. But I need to know, apart from memory loss, have you seen any recruits exhibit more serious symptoms?"

"Such as?"

Eli hesitated. "Have you seen some recruits lose touch with reality?"

Eli sat down at their table, taking a bite of the dark meat provided for lunch. His hunger had only grown as the program continued, which he assumed was due to the immense physical exertion he was forced to endure.

"These eggs are amazing," Arlo mused, shoveling the food into his mouth.

"You need to try red wing eggs," Eli said. "They're the best by far."

Lara's brow raised. "I didn't know you liked to cook."

Eli grinned. "No, but my father is an incredible cook. His sausage and red wing eggs was my favorite breakfast growing up. Harper's too."

"That's cute," Lara said. "You and Harper have a lot of the same favorite foods?"

Eli huffed. "The same favorite everything."

"Imitation is the sincerest form of flattery," Arlo said.

"It's overbearing though," Eli admitted.

Arlo shrugged. "I didn't mind, honestly. My younger brother Tanith did the same thing."

"Yeah, but didn't it—" Eli caught himself, unable to speak poorly of Harper. "Never mind."

"Siblings are a blessing, even if they can be much sometimes," Lara said, pushing aside her eggs. "And I hate cooking."

Arlo's fork clanged on his plate as he turned to Lara. "What? You lied to me."

Lara smiled, winking at him as she took a drink. Soren's laugh cut through the mess hall's roar as Sol cracked a joke.

Eli asked, "Hey, where did Soren go?" Arlo and Lara gave puzzled glances. "He was gone. For like four days this week."

Lara shook her head. "I didn't notice."

Shira asked, "You keeping tabs on him?"

"I'm not crazy. No one noticed?" Eli asked. His squadmates shook their heads as Soren laughed again.

"Oh, just marry the guy already," Arlo said under his breath.

Lara giggled, taking another bite of her dark meat. Shira gave a breathy laugh and smiled.

Eli was taken aback, gazing at Shira's actual authentic smile. Heavens above, it was the most beautiful thing he had ever seen. He would've taken notes on how to make it appear again if he wasn't so jealous that it was Arlo who coaxed it out of her. Despite Eli's best efforts over the past few weeks, nothing could get through that thick skin of hers.

*Except Arlo*

Lara said, "I saw them comparing physiques in the mirror last week in the weight room."

Arlo and Shira snickered.

"You did not," Shira said accusingly.

"No, I'm serious!" Lara said in a harsh whisper.

Arlo glanced over his shoulder toward Sol's table across the room, before turning back to Eli. "Hey, you all right?"

Eli shook off his scowl. "Yeah."

"You suck at lying, man," Arlo replied.

Eli sighed. "I'm just nervous about the WAVE tomorrow."

It was the truth—especially now, after what Darby told him.

Arlo spoke, snapping his fingers. "Oh, right, you were in the medical ward that first time."

"You were?" Lara asked with a quizzical look. "After the first WAVE?"

Eli threw Arlo a glare but turned to Lara. "Yeah. Apparently, I had a poor reaction to it."

"That happens?" Lara asked.

"Rarely," Eli answered. "According to Darby."

"Weird," Lara said. "What was it like?"

"I had amnesia for a while. I couldn't even remember how I got to the medical ward."

Eli paused for a moment, contemplating whether he should explain further. The last thing he wanted was to repeat what Renard or Darby told him.

*And yet*

"But there's been a feeling in the back of my mind that I can't shake," Eli said finally, "like I'm missing something."

"Missing?" Arlo asked.

"What do you mean?" Lara asked, leaning forward.

"I don't know," he said quietly. "Haven't you guys felt like something isn't right? Like something is coming?"

"Coming?" Arlo asked. "You talking about the Reaping?"

Arlo's expression made it clear he'd never considered that and found it odd that Eli asked. As Eli waited for an answer, he looked at Shira who was sitting on his left. She was glancing between the three of them and answered once she noticed Eli was waiting for her to speak.

"I think that's the stupidest thing I've ever heard you ask," she blurted out, with a straight face that felt like a slap. "Nothing's coming. You feel that way because of your bad reaction to the WAVEs and your hyper sense of paranoia."

Eli's jaw clenched.

"It's true," Arlo added, picking at something between his teeth. "You are a little paranoid."

"I am not," Eli said, trying to keep his voice low as he defended himself. "And when exactly have I acted paranoid?"

"From the get go!" Shira said with a smirk. "I'm surprised you don't know this already."

Lara chimed in to defend him. "I think what Shira's trying to say is that you just ask some interesting questions."

"Am I not allowed to ask questions?"

"You are," Lara assured. "You just . . . ask unusual ones."

"Don't sugar coat it," Shira said.

Eli said nothing, stifling the frustration that built in his chest. Either something was wrong with his perception of reality, or Shira was shutting the conversation down.

*Maybe both*

Something oily slipped into his stomach, wondering what other parts of his mind had fragmented and what that meant about tomorrow.

"Look, man, don't worry about it," Arlo said. "We all have our quirks."

"Like your ability to underrepresent every problem and carry your nonchalance despite dire situations?" Shira asked, equally accusing.

"Yes!" Arlo answered, pointing a finger at her with a smile. "And I'm proud of it, thank you very much."

"Or like your ability to hurl accusations and judgment?" Eli quipped at Shira. Shira raised her eyebrows.

"Hold on, not to change the subject, but can we go back to Arlo's comment," Lara said. "Has anyone figured out what in the Nine Hells the Reaping is?"

Shira said, "All I was told is that it's scheduled immediately after the Rune Blade Ceremony. Which isn't that far off. Evergreen said the Crucible marks the halfway point through the program, which is scheduled two days after the second WAVE tomorrow."

"Halfway?" Arlo said. "Bleeding Hells, that went fast."

*Speak for yourself*

"I spoke with Maelyn," Lara said. "Since her father was a Guardian, I assumed she'd know more about it. But she said the same thing Darby did: The Reaping is the last place you want to be."

"Who gets assigned to the Reaping?" Shira asked.

"Anyone who fails to manifest a Rune Blade at the Rune Forge," Lara answered.

A heaviness settled over the group. Shira broke the silence. "So, you either get a Rune Blade, or face the worst part of this program."

"That's what I was told," Lara said.

"Speaking of which!" Arlo barked, which was his common way of changing the subject suddenly. "Some good news at least! I heard that after the WAVE tomorrow we get the next few days to ourselves. Since some people have a poor reaction"—he moved his eyes and nodded toward Eli—"they need extra time before restarting training."

The pit in Eli's gut grew wider. He sighed, finished with his half-eaten meal.

"Oh!" Lara sounded excited. "What do we want to do?"

"That, my dear, is the question!" Arlo answered.

To Eli's utter dismay, the remainder of the afternoon was more grueling than he had expected. As they would have the next few days to rest, the recruits were scheduled to work ahead. And after a full afternoon of physical torture, to end the day on a high note, Eli couldn't sleep. Of course, the one night he and Shira decide to actually rest, his own mind refused to allow it.

Between his insomnia, his nightmares, and the late nights in the library, Eli was surviving on a mixture of sheer determination and adrenaline. He remembered reading that after only three days of no sleep someone is considered mentally insane.

*Wonder if I fit that description*

It was possible his sleep deprivation played into his persistent memory loss and apparent paranoia. And if it did, maybe that's what his friends were talking about. He wondered why they didn't share his feelings, and why in the Nine Realms Shira made him seem like the town fool when he asked in earnest. Clearly, she didn't trust him to not out her as a conspirator, which hurt in itself. He supposed she was only making good on her earlier comment of not wanting his trust—or anyone else's.

After staring at the bottom of Arlo's mattress for a few hours, Eli hopped out of bed. He couldn't tell what time it was, and he really didn't care. He donned his tunic, leaving his leather armor behind, but grabbed his practice sword from the end of his bed before leaving the bunkroom.

As he walked down the stairs, he heard a few other recruits chatting in the common area. Finding it odd, he peered around the corner, spying Soren talking to two others, Kairah and another he didn't recognize. They were deep in a discussion, and Soren was sharing his well felt opinions. Eli thought of eavesdropping but decided against risking Soren's wrath. Before they noticed him, he descended the stairs and headed for the Sparring Hall.

The iron door echoed against the stone walls as it latched. He set up some torches for light, pulled his sword from its sheath and set the scabbard aside.

He had been trying desperately to master his swordsmanship. Maybe because he felt so inferior to some of his fellow recruits, or because he wanted to finally land a blow on Shira. He certainly felt ill-equipped compared to his comrades, and he hoped to find a hidden talent to help him stand out—be more than a simple country kid who had dreams of becoming a Guardian.

As he stood in the firelight, a heaviness settled over him. He still couldn't remember his father's name. Who in the Nine Hells forgets their father? But Eli could picture his face, his stained apron he always wore, even hear his voice—but nothing else came to mind. He remembered his sister, Harper, and even his childhood friend Kael. He should've asked Darby more questions about whether the side effects of the WAVEs were permanent.

He shook away the thoughts and held his blade in front of him, imagining a fake enemy. A very slow, easy-to-defeat enemy. He spun his blade, sweeping the air in makeshift strikes, carefully managing his footing and balance. The motions weren't aggressive, but he only felt awkward and clumsy.

Regardless, he continued, tripping a few times, until his body was moist with sweat, his breathing heavy. He dried his hands on his pants knowing his blade could easily slip from his grip. He started another sequence when a voice cut through the silence.

"You'd have to practice all night to make up for how far behind you are."

Eli froze. His heart didn't sputter as it usually did when Shira was around. Call it exhaustion or indifference, he was more agitated by her presence—especially after lunch. He wanted to say he wasn't in the mood, but he decided to ignore her, not gratifying the verbal dig with a response.

*I'm trying, for rot's sake*

He had been in the medical ward more than anyone else, as far as he was aware. Half of those times, she was the reason.

"What? Sprite steal your speech?" she taunted from the corner.

He glanced in her direction but could barely see her silhouette. It was impressive how she snuck in without making noise, but he bit his tongue. Anger boiled in his chest. His heart began racing. He knew it wasn't pointed at her, only their situation—the helplessness that lingered behind each moment. He was sleep deprived, dealing with amnesia, and living with the constant threat of death at his own lack of skill. He used that emotion to spur his movements and throw harder, faster blows.

"You're dropping your left elbow on your backswing. It leaves you open."

Her words distracted him, and he tripped, stumbling forward. Eli threw his sword to the ground with a loud clang, spinning around to her, holding his arms wide.

"What do you want?" he shouted, the volume of his voice carrying the echo around the stone room.

"I'm helping you train," she said. "We made a deal—"

"No, I asked for help!" he yelled, but paused to reign in his anger, reminding himself she didn't know how far his memory loss went. Hells, she didn't know half the turmoil in his mind.

He continued—softly. "I'm sorry that I'm not like you and Arlo and even Lara. I'm sorry that I didn't grow up learning how to defend myself, but I've trained twice as hard as you. And you just told me you don't want a friend, and you don't trust me, so I don't know what you want from me!"

Eli tried to settle his ragged breathing.

"Stop apologizing," Shira said.

He scoffed, smiling and running his hands through his hair. His head was swimming. Silence spread. He didn't know why she was here, if only to antagonize him.

"By the way," he said, clenching his fists, "thanks so much for your support earlier."

"You were going to get us caught."

"No, I wasn't!"

"You can't ask them about what we've found in the library."

"I wasn't going to!"

"Then why did you—"

"Because I'm losing my rotting mind!" he shouted. Something in him collapsed at his own words. "I can't remember my father's name! I can picture our family inn, but I can't remember where we lived! I remember Harper, but I can't remember the last time I saw her before I left! That's not normal and it's driving me crazy! But *apparently*, according to you, and everyone calling themselves my *friends*, I'm paranoid for asking why!"

Breathing heavily, he turned around and paced, rubbing his face—crawling out of his skin. He shouldn't have yelled, shouldn't have focused any of it at Shira. She had been abrasive, yes, guarded, absolutely—but also had not abandoned him. True to her word, she had trained him well.

But he desperately needed something else. Someone close enough to bring validation for the storm in his chest. Somehow saying everything aloud made it all the more real. It gave his amnesia more finality and his concerns more validity. He felt alone and isolated, the only one struggling among a crowd of warriors. Eli recoiled at the thought of dying in the program, that instead of finding himself and returning home a changed man, he had only abandoned his family—abandoned Harper—for nothing more than a selfish fantasy.

"I didn't know that," Shira said softly.

"Then you should've—" he bit but stopped himself. Shira was here. It was the middle of the night. She should be in bed, like everyone else. But she'd come to see what was bothering him.

He hoped, at least.

"You could have asked me, Shira," he said finally.

The tumult of emotions was a storm in his chest. His hands were shaking, his mind spinning. He felt like crying, like punching something, like screaming, like hiding away in a dark corner for the rest of his life.

Footsteps sounded on the stone floor. Shira was wearing very comfortable night clothing, the color of a winter sky. It was made from some material much thinner and softer than the tunics provided to the recruits. Eli remembered hearing of tailors in the North who sold special fabric, boasting it was as smooth as water, as warm as wool, and as strong as iron. Lofty claims, he was sure, with a price tag to match.

Despite himself, he got lost again in her eyes when their gazes locked. The cerulean danced with the dim firelight into a shimmering display, like a frozen lake under a firestorm. Her ebony hair fell below her shoulders in cascades that blended with the darkness around them.

She was beautiful—breathtaking. His focus drifted along her outfit, the way the fabric hugged her body, but he turned his head before he blushed.

"What do you want?" he asked, flustered, and yet enticed by her presence.

"You were upset earlier," she said. "I wanted to know why."

Eli scoffed, "Then you should have asked."

"I didn't have a chance."

"Well, I'm fine," he said, demanding his emotions to calm. "Thanks."

Shira didn't move. "I didn't come here out of curiosity,"

Her tone caught him off guard. That softness he'd seen in the library—the opening in the hardened wall of her defenses—showed itself again. Silence stretched between them, and he squirmed under her compassionate gaze. He took a breath, thinking of a random question, unable to help but fill the emptiness between them.

"Does your family come from money?" he asked.

"Yes," she answered quickly—sincerely.

He fidgeted with the bottom of his tunic. "Then where did you buy those clothes?"

"They were a gift," she said. Eli caught the glimpse of pain in her face. "They were my mother's."

Guilt slapped him.

"Were?"

She nodded, not requiring an answer.

"I, um . . ." He started. "I know what that's like."

He didn't know why he said it, why he was willing to reopen the old wound so easily. His heart screamed that he had even spoken the words, but something about Shira tore through him—drew him in like the warmth of sunshine.

"When?" she whispered, stepping closer.

He watched her carefully but saw no harshness—no judgement. He was right before. She was different when others weren't around. But this—there was nothing deeper in his soul than this.

"When I was young," he whispered. "Ten. Maybe eleven."

"What happened?" she asked gently.

He paused, praying the emotional dam would remain in place.

"Dad was gone getting supplies from a nearby town. Harper was only a few weeks old, so it was only my mother and I tending to the farm. I was in the barn when I heard shouting from the house. I grabbed an ax, saw the front door was kicked in, and heard shouting inside. But after I ran in . . . I can't remember. I blacked out."

He looked down, eyes burning as he nervously wrung his fingers.

"I woke up on the floor. The ax was gone. The men were gone. I don't know who they were, or why they came. But Harper was crying in the other room, untouched. I was covered in blood, and my mother was dead. Mutilated. It was a few days before my father returned, and I couldn't bring myself to move my mother's body or clean up. I didn't know what to do, so I tended to Harper and waited until he got back."

Shira took another step closer. Empathy flowed from her presence for this, the truth that lay in the heart of his family's past—the seed of its collapse.

"I'm sorry, Eli," she breathed, resting her hand on his forearm.

He stood rigid at her touch, stifling the emotion that arrived without permission—those horrific images flashing in his mind once again.

"That's why you fight," Shira said, echoing his question from last night. "Why *you* joined the program."

He nodded. "I won't let my sister live through what I did."

"Eli, there will always be hatred in this world. You can't save everyone."

He felt pathetic when his heart leaped at the sound of his name on her lips—the feeling of her comfort.

"I don't need to," he said. "Only her. Only Harper."

"She means that much to you?"

"More than my own life."

The atmosphere between them warmed. Her indifferent expression was gone, melted into one of empathy, one that had seen the horrors of this world and felt some equal semblance of his pain.

"I'm sorry," he whispered. "I shouldn't have yelled."

"I already told you to stop apologizing," she said, the corner of her lip rising.

"Is this you saying you trust me now?" Eli heard her breathing shudder, but she remained silent as he drank in her appearance. "Why do you fight, Shira?" he asked. "Truly?"

Reaching toward that opening in her defenses felt like approaching a scared animal—or a predator—praying it wouldn't bite your hand.

"Because it helps," she said.

He closed the gap between them, gently touching her hand which brushed his arm. His heart thundered at her presence. She stood still at his approach, allowing him close enough to feel the warmth of her breath.

"Helps with what?" he asked.

An apprehension formed on her face, her eyes dancing between his—and his lips. Time slowed to a crawl as he awaited her answer. But she abruptly stepped back, pulling out of his reach. With a sharp breath, she squared her shoulders.

Eli's brow furrowed, his arms going slack at his sides. "Answer the question, Shira."

She lifted her chin, remaining silent. He waited but was met with only her indifferent stare. He took a step closer, but she moved away—a fierceness in her gaze returning.

Eli's eyes narrowed. "What are you so afraid of?"

The answer flashed in her look of apprehension as she turned to leave. In silence, Shira marched out of the Sparring Hall, leaving Eli in the dim firelight.

# Chapter Twenty-Two

E va sipped the last of her tea in the quiet of the morning, sitting across from Jafeth, when a young warrior barged in the front door. His shoulder-length hair and facial stubble were caked with dirt, and he bore a travel bag slung over his back. She gathered he was returning from a trip of some sort.

Jafeth turned around in his chair to face him. "Gareth!" Jafeth said, standing and slapping his arm. "Welcome back. This is Swordsman Evalynn Katz. Evalynn, this is Swordsman Gareth Morrigan. She's your replacement."

The young man barely glanced at Eva before staring slack-jawed at Jafeth. "S-Seriously?" he stammered. "Where am I being sent? To the front?"

"Yaqar outpost, it sounds like."

"Yaqar. That's on the border of Midbar right?" he asked with wide eyes.

"Yes," Eva said, surprised by his excitement.

"Is there plenty of action there?" he asked.

Eva's brow stitched. "We had a raid not a week ago."

A smile came over his face as he turned and shook Jafeth's hand. "Thank you, sir! I'll pack my things right now!" he said, striding to the bedchamber.

Jafeth sat down at the table once more, refilling his teacup, offering some to Eva. She declined, wondering about Morrigan's enthusiasm. Maya's injuries flashed in her thoughts, and she felt a pang of concern for the young Swordsman.

Gareth returned, a grin still on his face. "Thank you again, Lieutenant Ollon, sir!"

Jafeth nodded. "You're relieved, Swordsman. Make speed to Yaqar, and take care of yourself."

Gareth nodded and quickly left the cabin. Eva spotted the trail of dried mud he tracked through the freshly swept room. She was about to ask for the story, but paused at Jafeth's forlorn face.

"How many did you lose in that last raid?" he asked.

"A third."

Jafeth closed his eyes, dropping his head.

"Is he as naïve as he seems?" she asked.

"More so," he said with a sigh. "I sent him on a survival trip to try and toughen him up, hoping it would put some fear in him, or at least burn away some of that youthful enthusiasm. He took nothing but his supplies and wasn't allowed to come to town for assistance until after one week."

"That explains the mud."

"Yeah," he said with a smile. "He's been here six months and has not stopped talking about a desire to do *actual* military work."

"He wants a fight," Eva said. Jafeth nodded. "He's going to get one down there."

"That's what I'm afraid of. The Legion will have to answer for letting children join the war," he said, staring out the window to his left.

"I joined at fourteen," she said, not knowing why she offered the information.

"Why so young?"

"Escaping home."

He gave a wry look. "Well, considering who your father is, I'm not surprised. Come on!" he said, standing up. "Let's show you the town."

Eva and Jafeth strolled along the main road as he explained the ins and outs of patrol duty. She was growing fonder of the town each moment. It felt too good to be true. Apart from their own presence, you wouldn't even know a war was going on, based on the gentle smiles and kind glances.

"We have two inns, two taverns, one blacksmith, and an apothecary," Jafeth explained. "Most of the people are farmers and local tradesmen. The town primarily lives on travelers wandering through along the Midnah Trade Route, though they never stay long."

As Jafeth spoke, they walked by The Stallion Inn, near the center of town.

"Hey, what's the name of the woman who runs the inn?" Eva asked pointedly.

"Kyan. Lovely lady, makes the best roasted pig you've ever had, guaranteed."

"Jafeth," she said in a hushed tone, "she's Zentari isn't she?"

Jafeth stopped, turning to her with a stern expression. "Yes, she is. Is that a problem?" he asked, crossing his arms.

"No, I mean—" she said.

"Things are different out here. Kyan never hurt a fly. Well, that's not true. But the point stands, she's a model citizen."

"No, you misunderstand." She pulled him aside and moved out of the way of a horse-drawn carriage as it passed. "I've never been in a place with . . ."

*Hells, I can't even say it*

"Sympathizers?" he asked, eyebrows raised.

She breathed out. "Jafeth, you know how it is out there. I've seen the Legion charge Swordsmen as spies. Hells I've heard the stories of us turning on each other for simple acts of kindness. If you even mention the fact that you're soft on the enemy, you take your own life in your hands."

"So, you're willing to despise an entire race of people because you might face some ridicule by your comrades?" he pressed. "Or do you think the Legion is correct? That all Zentari are evil?"

"Jafeth, it's not that simple," she argued. She bit her lip, trying to give a voice to the turmoil she'd faced the entire ride North. "The Legion sees only the worst of the Zentari. And we've been at war for hundreds of years."

"Look." He put his hands on his hips, staring for a moment. "Come with me," he said, pulling her elbow gently.

He walked her down the main road and out of town to the North. This was the direction he had run with that stranger last night. After a short time, they turned onto a narrow path into the surrounding woods.

The Eilat forest extended for miles to the Northwest, far into the neighboring country of Meraan, boasting enormous trees with thick foliage. Eva was plunged under a beautiful canopy of green, the air feeling at least ten degrees cooler, though far more humid. She could smell the moss growing on the roots, her boots slipping off the rocks scattered half-buried in the mud.

Marveling at the timberland, she spotted a beautiful oak cabin, much larger than the Legion's, with smoke billowing from the chimney on the roof. The deck out front held a rocking chair, with a wood pile stacked against the side of the house.

Jafeth stepped up to the front door and opened it, knocking softly.

"Ala? Honey?" he asked, beckoning Eva to follow. She heard some noise from the back of the house, when a beautiful woman stepped out holding a newborn baby.

Jafeth smiled broadly as he walked up to the woman and kissed her. Her short black hair was tucked behind her pointed ears, which twitched as she grinned, returning the affection.

"Evalynn, I would like you to meet Ala, my wife," he said.

Ala smiled, but Eva was stunned. Jafeth was married to a Zentari. He had a *child* with a Zentari.

*No wonder he requested to be stationed this far North. If the Legion found out—*

"Nice to meet you!" Ala said sweetly. "Did you come to meet the baby?"

Eva's mind snapped to the situation and quickly recovered herself. "Yes!" she said. "What's his name? Or her name?"

Jafeth laughed along with Ala.

"It's a boy," Ala said. "We named him Nolan."

Eva stepped forward and opened the swaddled cloth. The baby was asleep, snoring gently. Eva brushed his smooth skin, noting his hair was blonde and his ears were rounded. She glanced at Jafeth with a question in her eyes. She didn't want to be rude, but obviously there was a greater reason to bring her here than to share in the joy of his newborn son.

"Yes," Jafeth said, "to your question, he's half Zentari. My wife is originally from Eldan City. She left to escape the war and corruption. She made for Sheket and was eventually smuggled past the Aniyan outposts to Manoach."

Eva's brow furrowed. "Smuggled?"

"Yes," Ala responded. "There are many Zentari refugees fleeing Eldan and the South. More leave each year. Many through the Namel port, but others head North. In response, the Legion patrols the Farron gap. Mercilessly."

"I didn't know that," Eva said.

"I know," Jafeth said confidently. "That's why I brought you here. Swordsman Katz—"

"Please!" Eva begged. "Don't call me Katz."

His brow knitted. "Fine. Evalynn, I understand why you feel the way you do. I brought you here to at least give you a glimpse of life outside the war."

Ala said, "Obviously we have to be careful about who we tell. For all intents and purposes Jafeth isn't married to the knowledge of the Legion."

"I can imagine," Eva said. "What do you think they would do?"

"Oh, I have no doubt they would find a way to strip my rank or kick me out. Maybe throw me in prison as a spy, or assign me across the country, maybe at the front, just to punish me."

"But that's why Manoach is the perfect place to settle," Ala said. "Most people don't mind here, and there are more than a few refugees hiding away."

Eva nodded. She had no words. This was sudden, and she was more enthralled by the child. The sight of the infant captivated her—half Zentari and half Aniyan. She eagerly studied his features to see which lineage was dominant.

"They're lies," Jafeth said abruptly.

"What?" Eva asked.

"The rumors of stillborn babies. The Legion's claims that Aniyans and Zentari can't procreate because our bloodlines are too different."

"How much have Aniyans and Zentari intermarried?"

Jafeth and Ala glanced at each other, but Jafeth spoke. "No one knows, really. But it seems that appearance wise, you look like one or the other. And since neither side is tolerant, any intermarrying is kept strictly secret."

Eva grinned as little Nolan grasped her finger. "Why doesn't he have the pointed ears of Zentari? Or at least, half-pointed?" she asked.

"We don't know," Jafeth said. "We've been making bets about who the kids will look like. It's hard to say what traits will show up."

Eva bit her lip at her next question. Jafeth raised his eyebrows—giving her permission.

"Will Nolan have magic?" she asked, waiting as they both tensed.

Ala answered this time, "Again, we don't know. And whether or not the kids will want to join the military or become a Guardian is up to them."

"Well," Jafeth said, "not entirely. If any of them look like Zentari, the Legion would never accept them. They'd have to join the Citadel if they wanted to be part of the war. And vice versa."

Eva's mind reeled. She had always assumed that it was only among the Legion—the Aniyan populace directly affected by the war—that the hatred for Zentari lingered. The thought of such prejudice beyond the military, leaching into every part of Adiel, tied her stomach in knots.

"Thank you," she said finally. "I know what this means. What you risk bringing me here."

Jafeth nodded. "I know. But I'm not worried," he said, smiling. "All right, we should go. I just wanted to check in and show off Zaza." He turned and kissed Ala.

"Zaza?" Eva asked with a wry smile.

"That's my fault," Jafeth admitted, laughing to himself. "A compromised nickname."

"He came up with that when I demanded to name Nolan after my father, Xerza," Ala explained.

The ground tilted under Eva at the mention of the name.

*Xerza*

After Jafeth finished pointing out the notable businesses and friendly faces of the town, they returned to the Legion cabin for lunch. Jafeth, to her surprise, was an incredible cook. While they ate quietly, Eva's mind was stuck in that living space with Ala. That name repeated in her thoughts, images flashing in her head.

*It's a coincidence. Leave it*

"You've been quiet," Jafeth said, taking another bite of his bread.

"I'm actually a fairly quiet person," Eva said, staring at her plate.

"I know. I can tell."

The front door opened and closed briefly. Eva turned around, but Jafeth paid no mind. A few letters were thrown onto the rug by the door.

"What are those?" she asked.

"News," he said simply. "I'm a Lieutenant, remember? I get updated on most of the latest intel. Keeps the patrol stations sharp on what to look out for."

Eva turned back around and finished her meal. She was still trying to decide whether to ask the question when the words fell out of her mouth.

"How common is the name Xerza among Zentari?" she asked, feigning nonchalance.

He kept eating. "Somewhat. Why, you know one?"

"Yes," she said. "He um . . ."

Jafeth paused, his attention now on her. "Go ahead."

Eva was surprised—again—by the gentle expression on his face. He was giving her permission to unload the heaviness on her heart, waiting patiently until she was ready.

"I lied to you," she admitted, coming to terms with the consequences of her actions. "I'm here because I released two Zentari prisoners in exchange for information. Their Captain, Xerza, was an honorable man. He was willing to help me, providing information in earnest trade. But his comrade didn't share his nobility. She called him a coward, killing him in cold blood. I held him as he died."

Her eyes burned with unshed tears—a flame of emotion she despised but couldn't quell. She didn't know why that moment had cleaved so deeply. Death was an old friend, and yet this time, it changed something inside her.

"After what Ala said, I didn't know—"

"Evalynn, Xerza died years ago," Jafeth said, "so it's not the same person."

Her eyes jumped to his, some of the heaviness evaporating. He held her stare, without judgement or accusation.

"You gave that man the honor of your presence as he died. Which in my opinion, speaks far more of your character than the fact that you let some prisoners go."

"His partner, Thalia returned to Yaqar and killed two more Swordsmen. That was my fault. They're dead because of me. And one of my only friends was hurt." She pressed a hand to her mouth as grief overwhelmed her, fueled by the weight of her guilt.

Jafeth sighed. "The hatred in Thalia's heart alone caused the death of your comrades," he said. "Remember that you, and you alone, are responsible for your actions. While your act of kindness saved Thalia, a vengeful killer, remember that it also saved Xerza. They were both given the opportunity to respond to your mercy, and their choices are not accountable to you."

Eva had no response, not knowing how to receive his kindness. She wondered why he wasn't angry or questioning her further. After all, her admission was the very thing Drax wanted to hang her for.

"Evalynn, the fact that your soul mourns the loss of your enemy tells me everything I need to know about who you are. It's why I wasn't worried with bringing you to see Nolan. Don't allow this world, or the Legion, to take away that part of you."

She wiped her face, burying her emotions into the quiet corners of her heart. She barely knew this man, yet his presence covered her like a sheltering warmth—an unspoken assurance that she could tell him anything.

She wondered if this was what a father's love should feel like.

After finishing their meal, they left for a midday patrol. Jafeth tossed the letters on the table and turned their conversation to lighter topics. Eva was grateful for this man she'd only just met, her soul feeling more free than it had in years.

"Lieutenant Ollon!"

Shortly into their walk, a stout, plump man with a receding hairline waddled down the stairs to their left along the main road. He was dressed in finer clothing, which didn't match his angered face.

Jafeth took a deep breath, turning around, whispering to Eva. "The city town-head. He's got a knack for being a rotting pain in my Nines." He turned back around. "Headman Tuttle! What's the matter?"

"Your comrade assaulted a citizen last night!" Tuttle exclaimed.

He breathed like a snoring dog. Eva choked down a laugh.

"Oh, I see. What exactly happened?"

"Your new partner broke a man's face and left him bleeding on the ground without provocation!"

"I—" Eva began.

"Hold on, Swordsman Katz," Jafeth said, holding his hand up. "Headman Tuttle, your concerns are noted. But I do not need to inform you that you have no jurisdiction to reprimand members of the Legion."

"Now see here—" Tuttle barked.

"You and I *both* know how these things are handled. I am aware of the situation. Now, your concern has been noted and will be handled by official Legion warriors. Thank you."

Jafeth stood his ground with an intimidating stance. Tuttle huffed but made no retort. He stormed back up his steps to what Eva assumed was the town office. They paused for a moment, before continuing forward on their patrol. Eva waited for Jafeth to ask, but he didn't.

"Did you want to know what happened?" she asked.

"I figured if you laid out the town drunk after he threw a bottle at you, you deserve a reward for not doing more damage."

"Wait, how did you know?"

"This town is small, Evalynn. I got the nightly report from Winno, the lawman in town, before you woke this morning. Bune has a reputation for an overly aggressive relationship with firewater. I've had to help him home a few times before."

"So, I'm allowed to break a few noses?" Eva said with a grin.

Jafeth laughed. "Only if needed, my dear. But be careful. I've worked really hard to change the Legion's reputation around here."

"Does the Legion really have that poor of a reputation?"

"Unfortunately, yes. Too many of us glorify the battlefield and forget what we're fighting for in the first place."

"Xerza told me the Legion is known for their torture," she said heavily. "At least among the Zentari."

Jafeth nodded. "Yeah, Ala told me all about it. I almost abandoned the military over it."

By the late afternoon, they both returned to the Legion cabin to eat supper. Eva was staring at the letters on the table, her curiosity growing. Each one was equally sized, using military standard parchment with official seals. The front displayed the name of the destination, and most were from Ashdod, but some were from different outposts, including Yaqar.

Without thinking, Eva grabbed the envelope from Yaqar and ripped it open.

"You know, that's a punishable offense," Jafeth mumbled as she read the contents, slurping his soup.

*To the Lieutenant stationed at Manoach, the following updates are of highest*
*pertinence.*
*Ashdod remains strong.*
*Duran wall continues development.*
*Four Zentari refugees captured at Mar'Hek.*
*Two Zentari warriors captured near Terakh and sent to Ashdod for interrogation.*
*Strike on Heika failed. High casualties expected. No report of survivors.*
*Reinforcements sent to Yaqar and Mar'Hek.*
*Continue to monitor for Zentari refugees and any possible spies.*
*Long stand the Legion.*

Eva's heart stopped. She jumped from the table and ran out the door.

"Evalynn? What is it?" Jafeth shouted, running after her.

By the time he made it outside, she was already a hundred feet down the road. She slid to a stop at his shouting, finally thinking, and spun around as he jogged to catch up to her.

"I have to go!" she shouted.

"Stop! Slow down!" His hands gently clasped her shoulders. She was hyper-ventilating. Her face was flushed—her heart about to burst. "Evalynn, what's going on?"

"The strike at Heika failed." She managed, gasping for breath, her eyes darting everywhere. "My friend, Lucas, was leading the raid. I can't—I have to go!"

Jafeth sighed as his face fell. "Evalynn, you know as well as I do the casualties of war."

"No! No, I can't!" She clamped her eyes shut, desperately trying to manage her panic. "I can't live without him! I have to go!"

She struggled in his hold, but he gripped her tighter.

"If you leave now, you'll be charged with dereliction and dismissed! Drax will have what he needs for your trial! Your career in the military will be over!"

"I don't care!"

"If you're dismissed you can't help him!"

She stopped, commanding herself to breathe slower. She clenched her fists, grounding herself.

*Day thirty, Winter's Touch. Day eleven, Harvest's Moon*

"Evalynn, I've lost one too many friends of my own," Jafeth said. "I understand what you're going through. It's why I requested to be stationed here so I didn't have to live through it anymore. Now I will help you, but if you go running off into the night and get dismissed, you'll be arrested and held until your trial. If that happens, there's nothing you can do for your friend."

Eva clamped her eyes shut.

*Day four, Midsummer's eve. Day nineteen, Autumn's Sigh. Day twenty-two, Spring's Promise*

As her panic lessened, she was able to weigh Jafeth's warning. He was right—Drax would jump at the chance to charge her with abandoning her post. But this was *Lucas*. Her best friend. He would come for her, if the roles were reversed.

"Come back to the cabin—"

"I have to *go!*"

"I will let you!" Jafeth said, a plea in his eyes. Eva froze—surprised. "But you can't go running in blind and without supplies."

Leaning into the promise of Jafeth's words, she turned with him back to the cabin. She threw open the door and grabbed her bag, collecting all her things. Jafeth quickly wrapped some dried meat and bread into a sack. He filled her water pouch from the barrel in the corner and set it all on the table. While Eva had her attention on packing, she heard him yell from the front.

"Don't leave!" he said, as he jogged outside, headed North out of town.

Eva's chest ached to run—all the way South—but she did as she was told. She trusted Jafeth, even after so little time. He already said he'd let her go.

By the time she finished packing and was placing the food pouch in her bag, Jafeth came back leading a horse, saddled and ready. Eva's mouth hung open. Jafeth tied the horse to a nearby branch and stepped inside.

"This is Beacon," he said, out of breath. "I know, dumb name, but the horse always finds his way home. You get to Heika, find your friend, and come back as soon as you can. Even if you leave Beacon, he'll find his way here. I'll cover for you as long as I can."

Eva was astonished—grateful. Her gaze danced around the room, trying to heed Jafeth's words and think ahead.

"Where would the Zentari keep Lucas if he was captured?"

Jafeth stilled. "Just get to Heika and come back here."

"Where?" she pressed, her lip trembling—imagining the worst.

"Evalynn, do you realize the likelihood—"

"I do! Just shut up and—" She stopped, taking a breath. "Jafeth, please. *Please*, tell me."

Jafeth held her pleading stare. She saw the moment the realization came over him, the gravity of what this truly meant. Either she found Lucas, or she didn't care if she came back at all.

"Evalynn, talent or not, one warrior won't survive—"

"Jafeth," Eva pressed, "I'm going, with or without your help. But I stand a better chance with it."

He sighed. "If your friend isn't held at Heika, then by *all rights* he is dead. And if by some fate of the Heavens he is alive, then he is almost certainly at the Citadel."

Eva's brow wrinkled. "The Citadel?" she muttered. "Wait. Xerza told me some Aniyan prisoners are sold as slaves in Eldan City."

Jafeth nodded. "That's true, but Legion warriors are usually interrogated until . . ." He swallowed. "What rank is Lucas?"

"A Chief."

"And he was leading the strike?"

"Yes."

"Then if he survived, and that is a *major* if, the Citadel is where you'll find him."

Jafeth strode to a drawer and pulled a piece of parchment and a graphite stick—drawing as he spoke.

"Eldan City is surrounded by a wall, guarded by innumerable patrols, with undercover Operatives throughout. It's impenetrable. The Citadel is a tower with six levels and two entrances on the main floor. All guarded."

Eva watched as he drew a crude map of the city, and the great Zentari spire.

"The city was built after the Citadel was erected, and if our spies are correct, you can enter the Citadel directly from the East, avoiding Eldan altogether. You couldn't lead an army that way, but one or two stealthy warriors might make it passed the guards."

He took a moment, finishing the rushed drawing.

"Last I knew, the Leadership's best infiltration plan was to send a small covert team, two or three of our best, bypass the city to the East side and take our chances with the less guarded entrance."

"Okay," she breathed. "Where are the prisoner's held?"

Jafeth stood, tossing the graphite stick on the table. "We don't know. Our best guess is somewhere beneath the tower itself, but Evalynn, this information is months old. We wondered whether or not there's a hidden entrance to be found, but it's anyone's guess. The plan was abandoned—complete suicide."

She grabbed the drawing, memorizing the details—praying they weren't needed. While she folded the parchment and placed it in her pack, Jafeth grabbed her arm.

"Evalynn, even if you get in there, and if by some miracle you avoid every Operative and Captain between you and the dungeon, there's no guarantee he's alive."

She paused, furiously holding onto her composure. "I know."

"And remember, if the Legion come looking for you while you're not here I can't—"

"Tell them I fled," she interjected. "Tell them I left without your knowledge or knocked you out. I don't care what you say but protect Ala and Nolan at all costs."

He sighed, a gentle sorrow forming his features.

"Thank you, Jafeth," she said.

"Don't thank me. Just come back."

There was more behind his words, she could tell. Something like a promise—a feeling akin to painful memories. She would honor his help and return if she could. She knew then—this was what it was like to truly have a father.

Time stilled for a moment. The two of them stood together—kindred souls caught in the relentless tide of war. Somehow coming to Manoach was exactly what she needed, and she prayed she could return.

She slung the travel bag over her shoulder. "I need to ask. Why help me?"

"Because you remind me of myself," he said with a grin, "and I know I can't stop you anyway."

Eva marched out and jumped onto Beacon. "I'll be back as soon as I can," she said, kicking Beacon into a gallop.

With the crisp evening air brushing past her face, Eva's mind became singularly focused. And as she passed through Manoach's front gate, her senses sharpened, her skin tingling with raw determination. The reality of the situation settled in her mind, the panic inside her turning to longing, then pain, then despair.

*It's not fair*

None of this was fair. She would not let this rotting war take what was left of her heart. She prayed, with everything in her soul, that Lucas was alive. And if he wasn't, then nothing in the rotting Nine Hells would keep her from eradicating Heika off the face of Adiel.

And storming the Citadel for him.

As she rode hard into the night, the darkness looming over the edge of that precipice in her heart grew—and she beckoned its call.

# Part Two: The Collide

CnC Publishing

# Chapter Twenty-Three

The heaviness in Eli's heart grew with each article of clothing he packed into his travel bag. He knew what needed to be done—that leaving was an act of desperation—but he wondered if he was truly capable of doing it. His entire life revolved around his father's business—around Harper. It should be unthinkable to leave, to abandon them, whatever the reason.

*That's the problem*

It was too easy to leave and too suffocating to stay. If remaining home meant losing himself, then leaving was the only path to freedom. He would go, to escape yes, but to also rediscover the young man who once found joy in caring for his family, not the one smoldering with resentment for all they had taken.

"Elijah?"

Eli turned to the bedroom door at the sound of Harper's voice. She stood timidly, wearing the pink dress Eli made her summers ago. Her twelve-year-old frame had nearly outgrown it. It was crude, and the color was uneven, yet Harper said it was her favorite dress.

"Yeah, Harp?"

The sight of her warmed his heart, despite the heaviness her presence brought, reminding him what he was leaving behind. She could whisper a wish, and he would carve through the Nine Realms like a storm—relentless and unwavering—until it was hers.

"You're going to hurt people?" she asked, innocent and quiet.

Eli sat on his bed and patted the mattress beside him. Harper walked over and joined him, playing with the fabric of her dress.

"Why do you ask that?" he said, brushing her shimmering hair out of her face.

"That's what warriors do."

Eli sighed. "Harper, it's not that simple."

"Yes, it is."

"When someone gets drunk downstairs and starts a fight, what do Dad and I do?"

Her brow wrinkled. "You kick 'em out."

Eli smiled. "Yeah, but in order to do that, sometimes we have to join the fight. Right? Even if it hurts them."

"But you're not trying to hurt them."

"No, but if we don't stop the fight, they'll hurt other people," he explained. "So, in the end, we're really helping and protecting everyone else in the inn. And our people need all the help they can get."

Her gaze drifted as she thought on his words.

"Harp?" he asked softly.

"I don't like it."

"I know," he breathed.

"Promise you'll come back?" she asked, a tear grazing her cheek.

Eli pulled his sister into his arms, wrapping around her petite frame, but his chest burst with pain. A searing burn that spread through his body, up his neck and into his back.

Eli woke suddenly, heart pounding in unison with the pain in his chest. He was lying in a bed, a dim blue light reflecting on the ceiling. White fabric hung around him, obscuring his view of the rest of the room.

He sat up in a jolt, sending a shock through his head. A ringing sang in his ears as he made fists, trying to shake the tingling in his fingers. With a deep breath he threw off the wool blankets and stood, which made the ground tilt beneath him. His body felt different—foreign.

*Where the bleeding Realms*

Suddenly the white drapes swung open, revealing a man in a gray robe and red scarf.

"You're awake," he said with a polite smile that quickly disappeared. The man lifted his hands in front of him. "Sir Danon, you're all right. You're safe."

Eli's breathing quickened. "Where am I?" he shouted, panic rising uncontrollably. "What's going on?"

Eli spun and grabbed the small wooden table next to the bed. He held it in front of him, grimacing at the pain that pulsed through his body. Two more healers approached behind the first. One seemed familiar, with brown hair and dark yellow eyes.

*I know her*

But Eli couldn't recall her name. She stepped forward, pulling the male healer back.

"Sir Danon. Elijah," she said gently. "You're safe. You're in the medical ward. You've been here before. I helped you. You know me."

She spoke slowly, feeding him easy-to-understand statements. Eli still could not recall her name—but her face. His gaze jumped to the other two healers, who stepped backwards.

"Do you remember me?" the woman asked. "What's my name?"

Eli's attention flickered around the room, desperate for something to anchor him.

"I don't . . ." he said, unable to finish the thought. His skin felt clammy as sweat beaded on his forehead.

"I'm Nazzat. I'm your friend."

"N-Nazzat," Eli murmured.

At the sound of her name, a rush of memories crashed into his mind. Images flashed in his thoughts—the second WAVE, searching the library with Shira, sparring with Arlo and Lara, arguing with Keeper Darby, surviving the Proving, waking in the Citadel to be trained as a Guardian, leaving Harper for the military—everything flowed back into his consciousness.

He stared at Nazzat, still reeling, and slowly lowered the table.

"The . . ." he tried to speak, but couldn't form the words "The WAVE . . ."

"Yes." Nazzat nodded. "The Thought Wave Analysis. You underwent your second treatment last night."

"I'm . . ." He closed his eyes, willing his thoughts to settle. "Bad . . ."

"Yes. You're having a poor response. I just need you to breathe and let go of the table."

Eli allowed her to take the table and hand it to another healer. She grasped his left hand and gently held his shoulder, guiding him to sit on the bedside. He could feel his body relax. The ringing in his ears faded, the pain in his muscles lessening. But the prickling in his hands and feet remained.

Last time all he felt was a hindrance of his thoughts—which was present yet again. But now there was a looming sense of power, a heightening of his senses. The world around him grew more vibrant each moment, as if he were perceiving it through new eyes and ears.

Something happened. Something was different.

He was different.

Shira grimaced, her alcohol-induced migraine throbbing in protest as Arlo slammed his fist on the table. The silverware clanked as their grogs of firewater and ale sloshed over. The tavern was so loud no one paid any mind to Arlo's boisterous act. Men and women both shuffled in the crowded space, around the spilled drinks and trampled food.

Their table was set up in the middle of the chaos, and Shira felt more uncomfortable each minute. But it was the only table available at the busy time of midnight.

"No! See, that's the point!" Arlo hollered over the roar of conversation. "Taquir never knew that Jesper was a spy, so he had no reason to hide the jewel in the first place!"

"Or was it that Taquir and Jesper were actually working together?" Lara added, her cheeks red from the drinks they enjoyed that evening. Despite the awkwardness of the environment, their conversation was enough to pull Shira from the jaws of sleep. She sat rubbing her head, as if she could physically remove her migraine.

"There's no way!" Arlo shouted.

"Oh, as if you were actually there when the book was written?" Maelyn said, sitting unusually close to Arlo.

"I'm just saying I've read the book a hundred times and there is no way that Taquir would work with Jesper. He was a Quixel!"

"Quixet!" Fenner corrected from across the table.

Arlo waved him off. "You know what I mean!"

"Shira!" Maelyn shouted. "Are you alive over there?"

Shira looked up, opening her glazed eyes. "Yeah! I just didn't know I'd be hanging out with a bunch of nerds!"

"We're not nerds!" Arlo rebutted. "We're educated!"

"Don't tell me you've never read The WestFall Mystery," Lara said.

"I remember reading it once years ago when I was a child," Shira said. "Because that's what it is. *For children.*"

"It's the greatest book ever written!" Arlo shouted. "I can't believe you would spit on the finest work of scholarly literature of our era."

"I wouldn't go that far," Maelyn corrected. "It is a children's book."

A glass shattered as a drunk patron lurched sideways, crashing into their table before stumbling off.

"So did you guys have any reactions to the second WAVE?" Shira asked.

Fenner leaned forward, struggling to hear. "What?" he shouted.

Lara repeated the question.

All the recruits shook their heads, except for Arlo.

"This time felt different," he said. "I woke up feeling all tingly, and my head was a bit fuzzy. But otherwise, I'm more, like, aware. Alert. I don't know what word to use."

The others gave befuddled glances, but Shira nodded thoughtfully.

"Has anyone checked on Eli?" Lara asked.

"Last I was told he was still asleep when we left," Arlo answered.

"I hope he's all right," Lara said.

"I hope it makes him better on the mats," Maelyn said with a wry grin. "It's painful to watch him sometimes."

Shira gave a muted grin. There were times when she cringed at his awkwardness, but he was getting better. It was entertaining to say the least, how clumsy he could be at times. Yet she found herself silently cheering him on more as the days passed.

Finally fed up with her migraine, Shira stood from the table. She chugged the rest of her grog and slammed it down. "I'm out. *Vor'Irath,*" she said sarcastically. The group waved goodbye.

Shira shoved her way through the crowd, ready to be free of the stifling confines of the tavern. She was never one for popular sites or large gatherings, but she didn't want to miss the outing. Despite her resolve to avoid friendships, and her attempts to keep everyone at bay, she grew increasingly drawn to them. Hells, she even caught herself smiling on more than a few occasions.

As Shira left the tavern, a bell chimed above the door. The streets were dimly lit with pyres along the gravel road, the city quiet after nightfall. Shira turned and started the thirty-minute walk back to the Citadel, but as she stepped into the street, the bell above the door rang again.

Lara stepped out and hurried toward her with a smile. "Thought you might want some company," she said. "Plus, I'm completely exhausted."

Shira returned the grin. "Yeah, sure."

They walked in silence at first, the gravel crunching under their footsteps. Shira never spent time alone with Lara and wasn't sure what to say. Still, she enjoyed the quiet companionship, feeling her headache lessen as the noise of the tavern faded behind them.

"I'm glad you decided to come out tonight," Lara said finally.

"Yeah. It was fun," Shira admitted.

"Just between us, we were taking bets on whether you'd show up."

"Really?" Shira asked, her brow stitched.

"Well, since Eli is still in the medical ward, he obviously wouldn't be here. So—"

Lara had a comical grin on her face as Shira gave a sharp look.

"That's a stupid bet," Shira quipped.

"But you're not denying it." Lara pointed at her, speaking in a singing voice.

Shira huffed, but a smile tugged at her mouth. Yet, as quickly as it arrived, it vanished, the memory of her last interaction with Eli returning to her mind. She knew what held her back—what prevented her from remaining in the Sparring Hall with him that night.

Shira could see the talent under the surface, see the good man he was and his ability to grow into a strong and true Guardian. It was her own fears that weighed on her thoughts, and the reason she kept him at arm's length. She tried to shake the thoughts from her head, still desperate to remain distant to everyone here, knowing what being here meant. But she had to admit, it was currently a losing battle.

"Shira?" Lara asked, her forehead wrinkled.

"So, I wanted to come hang out," Shira snarked. "Big deal. There's nothing to do in the Citadel for two days straight."

Lara shrugged. "Sure. Uh huh."

"You're one to talk!" Shira teased, shifting the focus from herself. "You follow Arlo around like a puppy."

"Actually, he follows *me* around. And it seems he's caught Maelyn's eye as well."

Shira laughed. "I saw that."

"Yeah, I'm not worried about it. Easy come, easy go. His positivity is nice to be around though. I can see why everyone is drawn to him," Lara said.

Two people were arguing across the street as they stood on the porch of their home—something about relatives in Hof. Shira used the distraction to change the subject.

"How're you feeling after the WAVE?"

"Fine, more tired than usual," Lara admitted.

"You don't feel like anything's changed? Nothing out of the ordinary?"

"No, I don't think so." Lara pressed her lips together at the thought. "Why? Did you have a bad reaction?"

"No, I'm fine. As far as I can tell," Shira said. "I'm just wondering about Eli. Why he seems to be the only one affected."

"Yeah, poor guy. How many others had bad reactions?"

"Not many, from what I heard."

"I wonder why his are so bad. Keeper Darby mentioned that some people have a terrible reaction to the WAVEs but never said why."

"Yeah." Shira wondered how far those poor reactions truly went, or whether Darby would be honest if he was asked. Guilt remained on the heels of Eli's words, when he admitted to how far his memory loss went. She hadn't asked, and learning the truth left a lingering taste of regret. She wanted to help him, if she could.

"Watch, Eli's going to somehow become one of the strongest of us after all this." Lara laughed.

Shira joined, despite herself. "He's getting better," she added. "But yeah, he is still a little hopeless."

"All thanks to your tutelage."

"Ah, but it's painful at times," Shira said with a breathy laugh.

Lara joined. "I agree he's gotten quite a bit better since the start, but he still has a long way to go. And if he doesn't improve, I hate to imagine what would happen if he got paired with Sol or Kairah, or any other recruit looking for blood."

"I know," Shira said, the thought turning bitter. Despite her early hesitation, Elijah's gentleness and keen mind caught her attention. Imagining him harmed, or dead, left a hole in her stomach.

"I can't stop thinking about that first sparring match with Rowan and . . . what was that guy's name?" Lara asked.

"Orion, I think."

"Feels like forever ago."

Despite the tragedy that shocked them all that first day, death had become a constant companion. After six weeks of training, they grew accustomed to wondering whether tomorrow would be their last day. And in a circumstance which brought its own sensation of terror, Shira felt herself beginning to care whether her squadmates made it through the program.

"It's nice to have a break," Lara said, crossing her arms against the cool night air.

"That's for sure. It's been a long six weeks," Shira said, rubbing her face, "and the Crucible is only two days away."

"What do you think it is?" Lara asked.

"I have no idea," Shira mused, "but Evergreen said it's worse than the Proving."

Lara sighed. "Rotting Hells. I wonder how many we'll lose this time."

After the Proving, and the loss of so many early in the program, no one wanted to speak about the challenges—let alone the Reaping. As if pretending it didn't exist would spare them when the time came. Shira's thoughts were interrupted as they passed a couple walking together, holding hands, laughing at some topic of conversation.

"Hey, listen." Shira began, fiddling with her fingers. "Can I ask you a personal question?"

"Only if you answer one back," Lara responded. Shira gave an annoyed look. "Oh, come on, Ms. Mysterious. Tooth for tongue or no deal."

Shira huffed. "Fine. Why did you volunteer? Why are you here?"

"That's your personal question?" Lara asked with a smile. "Okay, well, I grew up an orphan in the city. I've spent my entire life around shaded alleyways, food in the trash, shifty individuals, you name it. It's not only why I joined but how I knew how to carry myself beforehand. If you ask the Leadership, the Aniyans are the reason I'm an orphan. I can't prove that, but this war has affected all of us."

"I figure, the more of them I take out, the fewer orphans there'll be. But if you're looking for an honest answer, then I'd say I joined for a better life. With nothing and no one to my name, I figure fame and glory in battle is better than begging for food. *That* and I made a promise."

Shira nodded. "A promise to who?"

She caught the briefest glimpse of grief in Lara's face. "It's a long story."

Shira took the hint and moved the conversation forward. "Do you think they're as evil as we're told?" she asked quietly. "The Aniyans."

Lara wrinkled her forehead. "What are you saying?"

"I'm not saying anything," she responded defensively. "I'm just asking. I'm well aware of our people's view of the war. And I've been thinking a lot, long before I joined to be a Guardian, and the longer I'm here the more questions I have about what's really happening with the war. What they aren't telling us."

"Not telling us? What, you think the Council is hiding something? You sound like Eli."

Shira's gaze drifted in thought. She didn't know how to word the question or give a voice to the tumult of emotions within her. Everything had become so complicated in such a short time.

"Look." Lara started, once Shira fell silent. "I'm no fool. There are always two sides to a conflict, but we're on this side. If it's them or us, I choose us."

Lara waited for a response, but none came. Shira didn't disagree, nor did she find Lara's reasons flawed—but the answer settled in her stomach like a stone.

"My turn." Lara hummed in thought. "Did you have a special someone before coming here?"

Shira scoffed with a smile.

"Hey! You promised!" Lara said, pointing. "And I figure if I only get one question for the stoic Shira Weiss, then I'm going in deep."

They laughed, and Shira felt her soul lighten. For the first time in her life, it didn't bother her to answer a personal question.

"There's not much to tell," Shira said. "Sure, there's been the steady flow of prospects—"

"Not surprisingly," Lara touted.

"But no, there's no one that owns my heart. There were some guys over the years, but it never turned out the way I thought it would."

"Owns my heart? Is the mighty Shira Weiss actually a hopeless romantic?"

Shira stared at the night sky, gazing among the endless spectacle of stars. Her mind was miles away, and years in the past.

"What happened?" Lara asked.

They stopped, standing among the fluttering light of the pyres. Shira's gaze drifted to her friend. "I don't know. Have you ever had something that, in your head seemed perfect, but in your heart wasn't right?"

Lara thought for a moment. "Yeah."

"I think that's what it came down to. Every time I thought someone was logically perfect, there was something missing. Something I could never explain or quantify but it always ate at my heart until my original feelings were gone."

"So, what you're saying is, you're available?" Lara teased.

Shira rolled her eyes and resumed walking. "If that's how you want to put it."

"That's just how it is! And I know for a fact you've caught a certain pair of orange eyes."

Shira spun to her. "Will you stop?" she asked playfully.

"Come on, do not tell me you don't like him!"

Shira stammered, her mouth agape trying to find the words. "I didn't come here for that!" she said. "We're here to become Guardians! And Eli's nice, but I can't just—"

She paused at Lara's smug grin.

"Oh, you are the worst," Shira growled.

Lara shrugged, a broad smile on her face. "Don't worry. Your secret's safe with me."

Shira huffed but said nothing—still flustered. Their conversation turned to lighter topics the remainder of the walk. Lara expressed a love for painting and a longing to live in an open field, raise animals in a small village, and foster a family of orphans. Shira, in contrast, desired a cozy cabin in the middle of thick woods, hiding away from the rest of the world. Perhaps there was room for a family in that dream.

When they reached the Citadel, Lara headed to the barracks for rest, bidding Shira goodnight. But Shira couldn't stop thinking about Eli. She wanted to know whether he was still unconscious and if he would be all right.

At the medical ward, she approached a short male healer with black hair, seated at a nearby desk scribing notes.

"Excuse me," she said quietly. The healer turned to her. "Is Elijah Danon awake?"

He stood from his desk and approached her, speaking in a hushed tone. "Is he your comrade?" Shira nodded. "He woke up about an hour ago, but he's asleep now. We gave him a tonic to help him relax."

"Is he all right?"

"We believe so. Just another poor reaction to the WAVE, similar to his first. You can see him if you wish, but please don't wake him."

The healer directed her toward a curtained bed to the rear of the ward. She pulled the white fabric aside and stepped to the foot of his bed. Eli slept, peaceful and unguarded. She moved toward him, intending only to ensure his well-being, but she hesitated.

*What are you doing*

Nothing. Only checking on a squadmate.

*A friend*

A kind-hearted and gentle man, as steady as the tide. A friend who met her gaze with a quiet admiration, a warmth and reverence she had never known. There was more behind his eyes—a longing she pretended didn't exist. She ignored it, smothered it, willed it into silence, hoping it would die on its own.

Yet it didn't. It turned inward, tangling itself with her, until it revealed the truth that night in the Sparring Hall, when Eli spoke of his mother. The baring of his soul revealed the reality in her own heart she'd chosen to ignore, and it left her frightened.

She had come to the Guardian program with clarity, resolve—purpose. No entanglements. No distractions. And Eli had become both. He seemed deeply familiar, as if she knew him in another lifetime. And his presence had become a soothing constant each day—one she sought out.

He was a contradiction she could not resolve, a truth which gave her hope and questioned her own integrity. War had shaped him. Loss had touched him. Yet he remained unbroken and untainted, not through ignorance or indifference, but by choice alone. He saw the darkness around him, acknowledged it, and still chose to stand against it.

Not like Arlo who ignored it. Or like her, who ran from it. Only a fool would—

"Miss?" Shira jumped at the voice and turned around. It was the male healer, bringing in a tray of tonics. "Is there something wrong?"

"No," she responded quickly, glancing back at Eli once more. "Thank you."

She gave a polite smile as she walked past the healer and headed to the barracks. She needed to pull herself together and make a decision. Either she denied the truth in her heart, or she crossed an invisible line for which there was no return. But as she laid in bed that night, staring at the ceiling, the reality settled over her with a heavy finality. Whether or not she agreed, the decision was already made.

Eli woke to loud snoring from behind the curtain to his right. He rubbed his eyes in the bright daylight despite feeling quite rested. Sitting up, his body felt refreshed and new—strong and agile. Swinging his legs over the edge of the bed, he stood. It brought the slightest wave of dizziness but faded quickly.

His mind was a different story, a lingering fog looming over his consciousness. Searching for greater holes in his memory, Darby's words echoed yet again.

*"There have been some unfortunate reactions to the Thought Wave Analysis, which we cannot seem to avoid. For unknown reasons, the minds of some recruits cannot*

*handle the forceful manifestation of their inner magic. They lose touch with reality, becoming delusional and crazed—even violent—and are eventually mercifully euthanized."*

He sat back down on the bed, placing his head in his hands. He willed himself to settle and began sorting through his thoughts, setting a foundation.

*My name is Elijah Danon*

*I am twenty-two years old*

*I grew up in the country near . . .*

*I have a father, and my mother died . . . somehow*

*I have a sister . . . Harley . . . no . . . Harper*

*My father is a good cook. He runs a . . . tavern . . . no . . . an inn called . . . called*

*. . .*

He grunted in frustration and stood. It was impossible to remember something he'd forgotten, or to identify whether something he remembered before was now gone.

*Please, shining Heavens, don't let this happen*

As he paced, he saw something on his left wrist. A tattoo of a star. It looked new, within a few months. As his fingers brushed the sensitive area of skin, he tried to recall getting the marking.

But the memory remained locked away.

*Harper*

*It's something to do with Harper*

A surge of fractured memories rushed back. Arguments with his father, tears with his sister, and his own orange eyes staring back at him in the mirror, determined to join the military.

*"Promise you'll come back?"*

*"Yeah, I promise, Harp."*

His clothing was neatly folded on the bedside table. Staring at his armor, Eli hardened his resolve. Nothing would stand between him and graduation or returning home to his sister. Setting his fear aside, he adorned his leather bracers.

*Keep your head steady. Stay focused*

After dressing, he opened the curtain and glanced around the medical ward. Walking to the entrance, a young male healer organized some tonics.

"Excuse me," Eli said. The healer jumped. "Sorry."

The man held his chest for a moment and breathed out. "No, no, I apologize. I didn't hear you approaching."

Eli could see the moment the healer recognized him as a patient.

"Sir Danon, you're up! How do you feel?"

"Fine," Eli said, but paused for thought. Something struck him as he flexed his right hand, that tingling sensation of power still present. Before the healer could respond, Eli marched out toward the Sparring Hall.

He needed to try something.

# Chapter Twenty-Four

As another hour passed reexamining the plan, Lucas gave up trying to convince himself the strike was anything other than suicide. Having gone over the strategy dozens of times, he kept searching for reassurance he knew was nowhere to be found. Flattening the maps, his breath erupted in a brief cloud against the cold desert air. The detachment of thirty-five warriors was now on the South end of the Midbar Desert, primed to strike the Zentari outpost as soon as Lucas gave the order.

But this was dangerous—insanity in its own right. And everything hinged on the accuracy of the latest scouting intelligence, which reported a withdrawal of enemy forces from Heika. The typical number of warriors dwindled from near one hundred to just under two dozen.

*But it doesn't make sense*

Scouts' reports were commonly flawed, or at worst, completely wrong. Hinging the success of this strike on a single report, especially without verification, was rash—even for Drax. Lucas agreed that the Zentari may be hiding something, using the retreat from the front as a smokescreen. And taking out their strongest and most vulnerable outpost would deal a decisive blow to their war efforts. It was known that Heika only received reinforcements and supplies through the mountain pass, and it could be weeks before they received more warriors. But as Lucas glanced around at his comrades, brave men and women fighting for their country, he couldn't remove the stone in his gut. It wasn't his place to question orders, but he could certainly disagree with them.

Their group was camped three miles Northwest of the enemy outpost based on their map markers. They kept the fires low and the horses quiet as the warriors gathered around for the briefing. Lucas cleared his throat, praying for the words to inspire his kin.

"Warriors of the Legion." He started. "You have all sworn oaths to your kin and country. And tonight, you will make good on those vows. I will not lie to you, nor will I lessen the truth. Many of us will not live to see the sunrise."

A few shifted, but most held his gaze with pride—grit.

"Our enemy is very aware this outpost is their most isolated and thus has invested considerable resources to ensure its safety. However, we have on solid authority that nearly three quarters of the warriors normally stationed at Heika have been recalled. We are unsure of the reason but are determined to not lose this advantage. If we take Heika tonight, we will drastically alter the enemy's hold in the North."

A Swordsman raised his hand—Arando. Lucas nodded.

"Chief, how many Zentari does that leave for us to defeat?"

Lucas paused. This was the hard part. "Around two dozen."

Murmurs echoed among the group. Lucas didn't bother quieting them as they were all thinking the same thing.

Arando spoke again. "Can we be sure there are no Guardians?"

Lucas sighed. "Our latest intelligence says there shouldn't be."

More murmurs. They were rightfully upset.

"Sir, with all due respect, why?" a female warrior spoke from the back. Some of the others moved aside to allow a line of sight to Lucas. "This mission is near suicidal. We should wait for reinforcements to be sent to Yaqar and bring another battalion of warriors."

"An excellent plan, Swordsman. And one I already presented to Drax as an alternative. He said this mission was already approved by General Malachi himself, or at least by Chosen Lieutenant Cooper. They feel the chance of taking Heika is worth the risk as we don't know how long before their forces return to full strength."

"Besides," another Swordsman said, "too many warriors lose the element of surprise. Any more than fifty could be spotted too easily."

"Exactly," Lucas agreed.

"Chief, but why not send two smaller cohorts?" another warrior asked. "Yaqar can be defended with half as many that stayed."

"I agree," Lucas replied, "but Drax was concerned about a counterattack. He and I felt that if we were watching Heika and knew about a change in personnel, then the enemy may be doing the same. He's concerned the moment we left, the enemy would strike Yaqar in much the same way."

Lucas retained his commanding demeanor among the silence, allowing them to absorb the stakes. They needed a leader now more than ever. He knew none would flee, but losing hope was a deadlier threat than even the Guardians.

"The plan is simple," Lucas continued. "We approach Heika from the West. The outpost is made of solid stone, with thirty-foot-high walls and sentry towers on each corner."

He pointed to a hand drawn diagram for reference.

"There are two entrances to the outpost, one north and one west. The Western gate is smaller and more vulnerable to attack. We're counting on being able to forcibly lift or destroy the gate to gain entry. Once inside, stay with your partners. Watch each other's backs. I don't have to tell you to avoid confronting more than one of them at a time. Our advantage is the element of surprise here. If we catch enough of them off guard, we should be able to handle most of them before they have a chance to rally."

He met each of their eyes. "Remember: no mercy. You will receive none from them. Any questions?"

A female warrior to the left raised her hand. "Sir, how do we destroy the gate if we can't move it?"

Lucas grinned. "Great question. The Legion has a new trick up their sleeve."

Under the cover of darkness, the Aniyan warriors left the sandy, barren North slope to the far west of the outpost. At the base of the Ha'Negev Mountains, warm desert air greeted the cool breeze descending from the peaks, creating a zone of humidity where plant life could thrive. The lush greenery allowed the Zentari to covertly move warriors and supplies along the mountain's edge, undetected once they cleared the treacherous mountain pass.

Lucas used this same canopy to lead his detachment, creeping through the brush along the narrow dirt road the Zentari used that ran right into Heika. He didn't expect much resistance along the road—the Legion had never attempted anything this aggressive. Moving as quiet as the darkness around them, the Aniyan warriors crept toward their enemy. The archers were on point, tasked with taking out any sentries before an alarm could be sounded.

As they neared the outpost, Lucas motioned for everyone to halt, scattering into the surrounding brush. Two Zentari Operatives emerged up the road, walking casually on patrol.

He drew his knife from his left boot, leaving his sword sheathed. The dagger was faster and less clumsy in an ambush. If he could take out just one of them, the archers could kill the other. But coordination was essential. If either Shell alerted the outpost before they got close, this would become a bloodbath.

The two scouts were speaking idly as they stepped closer to the hidden Legion. Lucas wiped his forehead—heart pounding. This was it. Either the mission went well, or he would fight his last battle. He bore no fear of death, certainly not dying for his country or his kin. But as he tasted the dread of the moment, his thoughts drifted to Eva.

*Evalynn Marie*

Her name still felt like honey on his lips, even after so many years. From the first moment he laid eyes upon her, he felt the universe weave their fates together, binding his life into the fabric of hers. As fate would have it, the childish excuses and stolen moments became answered prayers—a thread connecting him to the woman who became his entire world.

No matter what Eva believed, Lucas knew she was destined for greatness. There was a fire in her spirit, a quiet resolve that could bend the very Heavens. She walked with courage and an unrelenting determination he had never seen in another soul. He cherished every second by her side and pleaded with the Nine Realms for more—even one second more.

She always laughed off his teasing proposals, brushing them aside as nothing more than playful fantasies. To her, he was a brother—a relic of her childhood she kept close—a constant in her life she would always carry with her. But for Lucas, he had never been more certain of anything in his life. His love for her was not a fleeting thing. It was rooted in his bones, in the spaces between his heartbeats, and in the silence of words never spoken.

There were moments he nearly told her—reached for her hand and bared his soul. But he held back, swallowing the words, knowing she was meant for open skies. She had spent her entire life imprisoned in a cage, and he refused to add another lock on the door. So instead, he vowed to be her anchor, her shelter, her unwavering tide. If this night was to be his last, he would love her from the depths of his soul, until the stars themselves burned out.

As the Zentari scouts strolled into view, Lucas prayed silently as he lunged out of the shadows. Both warriors saw the movement and spun in response—fast but also surprised.

He threw himself on the female Operative as the enemies drew their weapons. She fell backwards against his weight, and Lucas drove his dagger to its mark in her chest. Arrows flew above his head as they hit the ground, two embedding into the other scout. Before the Operative could shout for help, two more Legion warriors burst from the shadows, and silently finished the job.

He stood, blood streaking down the front of his black armor. He exhaled slowly as his men gathered around him. As one, they turned toward the outpost and marched on their enemy. Nearing the Western side, the detachment of Legion remained behind the tree line. One of the archers pulled out the arrow bound with the black stone and waited for Lucas's order.

Watching the sentries, he gauged the best moment of attack. There were Operatives on each corner tower and another six patrolling along the perimeter. Voices sounded from within the stone walls.

*Heavens help us*

One sentry marched overtop of the Western gate, and Lucas gave the signal to fire. With skillful accuracy, the arrow struck the peak of the doorway. The moment the black stone cracked upon impact, a storm of blue magic shook the ground, erupting in all directions, demolishing an enormous portion of the wall.

Lucas and his warriors sheltered themselves from the falling debris. A few cursed under their breath as fragments of stone rained upon them. None of them had witnessed anything like this before. Whatever devilry Ashdod was creating with Archancy and these stones was certainly paying off.

Before the dust could settle Lucas stood, raising his sword high.

"To the end!" he shouted. His warriors screamed in unison as they followed him into battle. The enemy had only moments to recover before shouts of fury and clanging steel echoed among the outpost walls. The Legion warriors swarmed the fortress like water crashing upon rock—unrelenting and unforgiving.

Lucas's focus narrowed, his muscles recalling years of training as he fought alongside his men. The battle passed in a blur, each moment gone in a flash—yet stretching out endlessly. Before his very eyes, the Zentari warriors fell upon their swords. There were fewer than the scouts reported, each of them astonished and frozen in surprise at the aggressive maneuver by their adversaries. And with utter determination—the sheer desperation of the moment—the Legion were winning.

*Please, shining Heavens*

It took only minutes, but the air grew thick with dust, bodies lay dead on the ground. He took a slice to his left shoulder, the pain radiating up his neck. He'd lost warriors, but more than half of them remained strong. Lucas fought with a ferocity he had not yet known. Something in his blood spurred him forward, demanding he live beyond the night.

He charged the next Zentari warrior. Blood trickled from a gash above the Operative's left eye as he gripped his ax. Lucas struck first, aiming for his left side with a sharp thrust. The Operative deflected the blow with his ax's handle, countering with a sweeping strike. Lucas barely dodged, and the motion sent him stumbling backward.

Before the Zentari could press his advantage, a Swordsman rushed to his aid.

*Thorn*

The Swordsman surged in with a fierce cry, his sword carving into the enemy's side. The Operative bellowed in pain, and he dropped to his knees. Seizing the moment, Lucas sprang to his feet, and together, they overwhelmed their wounded foe.

As the Operative fell, his ax clattering to the ground, Lucas turned to the courtyard. Dust choked his lungs against ragged breaths. But the battle was nearly over.

They had won.

*Praise the Heavens*

*We did it*

Relief washed over him like the chill of a cool spring. He clasped Thorn on the shoulder with a smile.

"I owe you my life, friend," Lucas said.

"No, brother," Thorn said, matching his triumphant grin. "You led us. We celebrate together."

They moved into the center of the courtyard, taking account of their losses. His remaining warriors, now battle-worn, walked around the bodies as they gathered amid the silence. The first drops of rain landed on Lucas's shoulders, threatening to wash away the pools of blood. Despite the relief of victory, there was no cheering or rejoicing.

They had lost too many.

He turned to Thorn. "Count the dead. Check the wounded. We can't stay—"

"Chief!" a Swordsman shouted, rushing back into the outpost from the Western wall. "Guardians!"

Lucas's eyes widened, his heart stopped. The Legion sprang back into action, gathering together in the center of the courtyard, creating a tight formation, shoulder to shoulder.

The soft clanging of metal armor sounded as three Guardians emerged from behind the toppled stone, flanked by a garrison of Operatives.

Lucas swallowed, staring at the two-handed flail in the lead Guardian's hands. The weapon appeared covered with ice, and a frigid wind swept past him. "Steal yourselves!" he shouted.

Without a word, the Guardian stepped forward and swung his flail wide. A burst of white magic emanated from the weapon, flowing outward toward them. Everything it touched froze instantly.

Lucas turned away from the wave of ice, his back burning fiercely at its touch. Despair overcame him as his body went numb.

*I'm sorry Marie*

His weapon fell to the ground as he dropped to his knees. All sensation left him as his very bones chilled.

*I couldn't keep my promise*

Eva's face was the last thing he pictured, before he was lost to darkness.

# Chapter Twenty-Five

Eli landed on the practice mat, finishing a maneuver he never could perform before. He straightened, catching his heavy breaths as Arlo walked into the Sparring Hall. Sweat glistened on Eli's bare chest after practicing for the past few hours. He never checked where everyone else was, distracted by his own elation.

"Well, you're looking well!" Arlo said with his crooked grin. "Everyone is looking for you."

"Hey," Eli gasped. "Spar with me."

Arlo cocked his head. "Shouldn't you be taking it easy? The healer said you woke up but didn't say anything when you left. Have you been here the whole time?"

Eli grinned. "Look." He stepped up to Arlo and lowered his voice. "My mind is still fuzzy, yes. And probably more than before. I'm trying not to think about it. But physically? I've never felt better. I'm stronger, like there's lightning in my muscles. I just landed the spinning back kick without trying."

Arlo remained silent, but the glimmer in his eyes told Eli he experienced the same surge in power. Arlo removed his upper armor, tossing his tunic aside and stood on the mat. His physique was a step above Eli's, individual abdominal muscles flexing with each movement. The man looked chiseled from a slab of marble. Taller *and* stronger.

"Show off," Eli muttered.

Arlo smiled. "Well, it's gotta be a fair fight."

Without warning, Eli charged, leaping into the air in a spinning kick—one he previously never achieved. Arlo ducked, letting the strike whirl past before driving a sharp jab toward Eli's ribs.

Eli deflected the attack with precision and countered with a solid blow to Arlo's solar plexus. Arlo grunted, but struck back, his elbow catching Eli's cheek.

"Hells, you are better!" Arlo praised.

"I'm not even trying!" Eli taunted, throwing another kick. "Come on Miller! Fight like you mean it!"

The two battled relentlessly, trading blows and dodging counterattacks, their friendly sparring growing into an all-out brawl. Eli felt invincible, weightless yet unmovable, as he sparred with his friend. The world faded at the edges, his focus narrowing on his opponent. Arlo was stronger than him still, but Eli was now faster. He could read Arlo's movements, predict his opponent's actions. And to his great delight, Eli's body actually followed through with his commands—moved from an instinct previously dormant.

Without noticing, Shira, Maelyn, Lara, and Fenner all leaned against the wall nearby, watching the fight. As the bout came to a pause, Eli finally caught sight of their crowd. Arlo was unfazed by the audience, but Eli's cheeks burned. As he and Arlo turned to their friends, Eli felt blood drip from his right eyebrow. He wiped it away as his focus landed on Shira.

But her eyes were locked on Arlo.

Eli bit down on his jealousy, chastising himself for feeling like he had any claim on her affection. He grabbed his tunic from the floor before approaching his friends. He didn't feel like dealing with them quite yet, uneasy about his now worsened memory loss. And he refused to let Shira berate his improvement.

"Not bad guys!" Lara cheered, clapping slowly. "Have you been practicing when we weren't looking?"

Eli remained silent. Arlo answered for them, putting his tunic back on. "I didn't know we had drawn a crowd. How was the performance?"

Maelyn rolled her eyes. "Oh, please."

"The fight looked pretty intense to me," Fenner said. "Do you guys feel stronger after the second WAVE?"

Arlo looked over at Eli but answered for him. "Yeah, actually. It's like our training jumped forward six months."

"You'd still kick his Nines in a fair fight," Shira said to Arlo.

Eli met her glance, his frustration giving way to anger. He remembered how different she was around their friends, but he refused to stand by and take it. He shook his head with a huff, putting his shirt on as he strode to the exit. The group eyed him as he left.

"What's eating him?" Maelyn asked.

"I have an idea," Shira said with a sigh.

"Not sure about that, but all I can say is, he's way better," Arlo said, finally catching his breath.

"Yeah?" Lara asked, eyebrows raised. "High praise from sir Miller?"

"Seriously," Arlo said. "It's like he's a different person."

"He was keeping up with you pretty well," Maelyn added. "It was almost a draw."

"I wouldn't go that far," Arlo mused, pulling a hard drink from his waterskin.

Shira pushed off the wall, slipping quietly toward the exit while her friends continued laughing, oblivious to her departure.

The Blade Room carried an ominous atmosphere as Eli stood under the soft glow of the mage stones, gazing at the numerous polished weapons hung on the walls. Ever since Evergreen mentioned it on the Practice Field, he'd wanted to see it.

The space was open for practice, but the walls were covered—floor to ceiling—with weapons of all kinds. Swords, flails, maces, axes, spears, daggers, hooks, knuckles, and many more he couldn't identify. Each one worn with use, but not nearly to the same degree as their practice weapons provided to them. These weren't neglected, they were honored—battle worn and proven mettle.

As he stood in the silence, he felt the lingering sense of excitement over his physical improvement. He wished he could send Harper a letter, telling her how much stronger he'd become, and how much he missed her.

Shuffling to the wall, he gingerly touched a pristine longsword. Its handle was partially wrapped in black leather, the guard etched with a floral pattern, shining jewels adorning the ends. The blade's fuller was ground through, removing the innermost part of the steel.

The weapon was far lighter in his grasp than he expected, pulling it away from the wall. The electric sensation returned to his muscles as both hands gripped the handle. With wide arcing swings, the blade sang as it cut through the air. In a sweeping motion, Eli spun around, cutting a long slice. He flinched as the blow landed against Shira's long knives with a sharp pitched clang.

Pressing against her blades, he remained frozen. Shira's face was unreadable, as always, but he noticed she was searching his eyes for something. He dropped his sword, relaxing his posture, but his earlier frustration resurfaced.

"What do you want?" he asked as Shira attacked with frightening speed. Eli reflexively deflected the strike to his left shoulder, moving far faster than he did before. His eyes widened. She could've seriously injured him.

"Hey, watch—" Another attack from her off hand knife, this one aiming for his midsection. He dodged left, her blade slicing empty air. Parrying her weapon, he struck at her chest, some inner power fueling his strength. She deflected the blow, the clash of metal ringing sharp—but the impact sent her stumbling.

Eli seized the opening, sparing no quarter, and spun low to sweep out her legs. She hit the ground with a grunt. A thrill shot through him—finally landing a decisive hit. He moved to pin her, driving his knee down, but she rolled clear and sprang back to her feet.

He smirked, the sensation of energy growing within. Not only was he stronger, faster, he was finally giving Shira a challenge. Whatever the WAVE had done to him, he liked it.

Shira remained stoic, gaze locked on him. He charged, striking from the right, his longsword's steel singing as it flew through the air. She met it head-on, steel clashing, sending the vibrations into his arms. The tiniest flicker of sparks shot from Shira's rusted practice blades.

She took the brunt of the attack, barely holding against his newfound strength. But before he could recover, she pressed forward, trapping his sword with one blade, while the other found his throat.

He stopped, wrangling his heavy breathing. Defeated.

*Again*

The slightest grin pulled at Shira's lips. Eli watched her, his frustrations evaporating at her attention. He cursed himself for being so malleable in her hands, so easily overthrown—and yet he couldn't help himself. Didn't *want* to help himself.

Shira lowered her blade as Eli did the same, the close distance between them remaining, less than an arm's length. Eli felt her warm breath on his face as it steadied.

*Living Hells*

Her eyes were brighter somehow, burning through him. Everything about her drew him in, like a moth to flame. He swore his senses were heightened, sharper than before, finding every piece of her presence. She smelled of lavender and honey, her skin glistened softly with sweat. He could hear the gentle drum of her heart, feel the warmth radiating from her body. Her presence felt tangible, so real and close, as if he could reach out and touch her with nothing more than his mind.

"How did you learn so quickly?" she asked softly.

He waited a moment before responding, embarrassingly caught up in her presence. "I don't know. After the WAVE I felt different—stronger. When I woke, I went to the Sparring Hall to test whether or not it was true. And you saw. I guess the WAVE worked this time."

"How's your head?"

His brow raised. "Does it matter?"

"I'm asking you this time."

"It's hard to tell what I can and can't remember. I still feel clouded. Physically I feel great. Amazing even, but something still nags at the back of my mind."

"Have you forgotten anything else?"

"I wouldn't know. I can't remember something if I've forgotten it."

A silence formed between them, and he swam in her gaze, bathed in her attention. Again, as if she were a completely different person, her features held no animosity or harshness. Elation flushed through him as he swore he saw a sparkle of desire in her eyes.

Eli said, "You're standing pretty close for someone who didn't come here to make friends."

A grin tugged at her mouth. "What if I am?"

"I've seen how you look at Arlo."

She scoffed with a breathy laugh. "What?"

"Don't deny it."

Her forehead wrinkled. "You're an idiot."

Eli couldn't help the smirk that formed without permission. "I thought you said you don't want my trust."

"I also said your observations were childish."

"Yet here you are. So, which is it?"

"Which is what?" she asked playfully.

"Do you trust me or not?"

"I said I didn't want it," she whispered. "Not that you didn't have it."

His face was on fire, the sensation of blushing more intense. She sheathed her blades, closing the gap between them until her face was inches from his. He fought the urge to step back, his heart exploding out of his chest.

*Shining Heavens help me*

Shira's gaze flickered between his eyes, his hair, his lips. His breath caught as his mind went blank.

"And I lied," she breathed. Eli's heart leaped, but she turned and walked toward the exit. "Oh, and we're not meeting in the library tonight. In case you forgot, the Crucible is tomorrow. Get your rest."

She left before he could respond. He stood in the middle of the room, stunned—and euphoric.

*Bleeding rot, I really am in trouble*

Eli wrestled to find the right words as he sat at the bar, watching his father restock the bottles of orange firewater. Neither of them spoke—there was nothing else to say. They both made their opinions clear over the past few months, and neither was willing to concede. His father didn't understand, and Eli didn't know how else to explain what he felt.

The bigger problem was Eli couldn't decide if his father's aversion to the military was for his only son's safety, or because Eli helped tremendously with running the inn.

*Maybe both*

Eli picked at a sliver on the wooden counter, hoping his father would say something first. He glanced at his travel bag he'd packed that morning. There wasn't much in it. And in a selfish way, it made him all the more determined to leave.

Guilt had become a constant companion, knowing his mother's death was his fault. And because of that, Eli set aside any desires of his own, trying to make up for his mistake the past twelve years. The shame of his failure lingered behind each morning, hidden in every interaction with his father—who never attempted to alleviate the guilt.

It took years, but Eli began to realize the truth behind his father's indifference, how he must blame him, which made his behavior finally make sense. It was the lingering, ghostly presence of that resentment which spurred Eli to leave, if even for a time.

"Dad." Eli started. "Don't forget to help Harper with her butterfly collection this spring. The Baeltrix hatches around—"

"I know how to care for my own daughter," his father said, his eyes never leaving his work.

"Oh, you do?" Eli spat. "Because it feels like you haven't been present for years."

"You know bloody well why it's been . . ." His father's voice trailed.

Eli didn't care to hear another excuse. Though legitimate, none of them changed the chasm between them, which grew wider each day. The frustration in Eli's chest was tempered with sadness, reminding himself he wouldn't see his father for a long while.

"Dad, we lost her too," he said softly.

His father sighed but didn't speak.

Eli waited, emotion building in his throat. "Will you say something?" Eli snapped.

His father turned around to face him, and Eli was met with milky white eyes, blood dripping from his father's mouth and nose, face contorted in agony. Mouth agape in a silent scream, his father reached out with a deformed hand toward Eli.

"It's all lies!"

Eli shot up from bed, hitting his head on the bottom of Arlo's bunk at the shouting of the other recruit. The bunkroom stirred, everyone awakened by the crazed voice.

"The walls are caving in! I can't tackle the bear!" the recruit shouted.

Eli forgot the pain in his forehead as fear struck him, finally witnessing the dreaded fear of his own fate.

"Lick the wounds! Don't drink the flash!" The recruit stumbled around shouting, holding his head, screaming at the ceiling. At once, the Operative on watch burst into the room.

"What's going on?" he demanded.

The crazed recruit saw the Operative—and lunged.

"You stole my cane!" he shouted. "My wife!"

The attacks were clumsy and awkward, and the Operative easily pinned the recruit down, wrapping an arm around his neck.

"Someone call for Captain Renard!" the Operative ordered. Two recruits leaped out of bed and ran out of the bunkroom. After a short time, they returned with the Captain in tow. Renard marched over to the recruit, examining the situation.

"You stole my cane! My wife!"

Renard whispered something to the Operative holding him down. The crazed recruit was carried out of the barracks and down the hallway.

"Go back to sleep. All of you," Renard said. "You knew the risks coming here. Don't look so surprised."

Eli swore Renard gave him a knowing look as he left. The sound of the door shutting left the room in a crushing silence. No one spoke. And Eli doubted anyone would sleep after that.

"Hey," Arlo whispered from above him, "you good?"

"Yeah."

Though he didn't believe it. Staring into the darkness, Eli wondered how far he was from becoming that man. Darby already made up his mind about him, so maybe it was time to ask someone else the questions in his head—ask how far he was from the edge. After Renard's earlier conversation with Eli, he felt trepidation every time the Captain was around. But maybe Renard had given him more of a warning than an accusation.

Knowing he would find no rest, Eli hopped out of bed. Pulling on his shirt, he left the bunkroom, heading for the stairs and followed the sound of voices in the level below. He took the stairs two at a time. Three other Operatives had joined the effort, all of them now carrying the crazed recruit toward the medical ward as he thrashed about.

Renard was standing just outside the barracks, watching. The Captain glanced at Eli as he cautiously approached, before returning his attention to the crazed recruit.

"What can I do for you, recruit Danon?"

"Sir, I have to ask." Eli started, and Renard hummed. "Are there any warning signs? That one of us will lose our minds?"

"Ah, I see our earlier conversation was not lost on you. Good to know you didn't lose *that* memory. To answer your question, no. At least to my knowledge. But it always happens at least once with each new batch of recruits."

Eli swore to himself he would remain sane, watching the recruit thrash in the Operatives' hold. He worried about Shira, knowing she shared his trepidation with the Leadership, but she hadn't displayed any—

A hand clasped his shoulder. "You should get some rest, recruit, before tomorrow," Renard said.

Eli nodded, turning to leave.

"Oh, and Danon, a fair warning." Eli turned back, brow stitched. "You've been chosen as squad leader. Tomorrow is when you get to prove why."

"Sir? But what you said earlier—"

"What I said was to be cautious about what you find peculiar," the Captain said. "Feeling less than qualified?"

Eli nodded, not knowing what to say. He didn't feel at all up to the task, let alone worthy of the honor. It was something he hoped to achieve but now wondered if it was deserved.

"Son, there's more to a Guardian than brute strength. Are you aware of our Northernmost outpost, Heika?"

Eli nodded. "Yes, sir."

"Well recently, there were rumors and scouting reports that the outpost was being targeted. No one thought they were legitimate except one of our Guardians in the field, who had the idea to set a trap for the enemy. His comrades said it was ludicrous and foolhardy, assumed our adversaries weren't foolish enough to fall for it. But he held his ground and explained his plan. It not only succeeded but granted us a number of strategic opportunities. Captured enemies and a counterstrike against their own outpost."

"My point is," Renard continued, "you have the mind that asks questions and doesn't stop thinking, despite everything. That's why you were chosen."

Eli remained silent.

"See you in the morning, *squad leader*."

At that, Renard followed the Operatives. Eli returned to his bunk, thinking over the Captain's words.

*How the Hells am I supposed to sleep now*

# Chapter Twenty-Six

B y the time Eva rode to the base of the Ha'Negev Mountains, just West of Heika, it was near midnight. The four-day journey from Manoach was grueling, and it was all she could do to not push Beacon past his limit. She would never forgive herself if by her hand Jafeth's horse perished after he'd shown her such kindness.

Though skilled at navigation, Eva had never been to Heika. The winds and sand covered most of the tracks left by the Legion assault, but the subtle signs of a group on horseback were still evident. It was the grace of the Heavens their tracks were yet visible.

She directed Beacon into the lush greenery, leading him straight to the narrow brook at the base of the ridge. Dismounting, she peered along the narrow road for any sentries, relying on the cover of darkness to remain hidden. Beacon nearly tugged the reins from her hands as they crossed the road and reached a gentle flowing stream. She stroked his neck as he drank his fill.

"Take your time, buddy," she said.

Grateful for the crisp water and a moment's rest, there was only one thing on her mind. She refilled her waterskin and led Beacon to a secluded area nearby.

Setting her pack down, she held Beacon's snout. "Thank you for carrying me," she whispered. He nudged her head, as if answering her thanks. "If I don't come back, don't wait. Go home to Jafeth and Ala, okay?"

She turned and gathered her weapons, rechecking her armor and gear. Beacon huffed, nudging her once more gently.

"Hey," she said with a grin, "I'll be all right. Just wait here."

Eva moved away slowly, holding her hand out. Beacon obeyed, remaining untethered in the brush. She stepped into the road, skirting alongside the cover of the bushes amid the starlight, and crept her way toward Heika.

Nearing the outpost, she came across a dark stain in the dirt. It was dried blood. A week old, maybe more. But no bodies lay nearby. Her heart quickened, mind narrowing on the task at hand.

*Find Lucas. Kill anything in the way*

She continued forward until she had a full view of the outpost from the safety of the brush. A sharp breath escaped her lips when she saw the gaping hole in the Western wall.

*What in the Nine Realms*

Panicked thoughts threatened to steal her focus, but she reminded herself there was no way to know whether the damage was caused by the Legion or the Zentari. It was possible a Guardian created it, but if there was one stationed here—

*Stop it*

She scanned the fortress, marking the sentries. Four turrets stood guard, each occupied by a single warrior. Two sentries patrolled the outer perimeter, and another two up top. Based on the positioning of the Operatives, the Southern wall was her best bet, which sat against a sheer ridge. Climbing it wouldn't be easy, but she couldn't simply walk in either.

Focusing her senses, she scanned the horizon one last time before sprinting toward the South wall. With swift and silent steps, she raced across the clearing as the tower sentry turned her focus. Eva wedged between the cold stone wall and the rocky landscape of the rising mountain behind her. She paused, waiting for an intruder signal.

Nothing.

*Yet*

The wall before her was twenty, maybe thirty feet tall. The stones were smooth, but decay had caused them to shift, leaving uneven edges that could provide footholds.

*I can climb this bloody thing, but Heavens help me if I fall*

With the only other option being the front gate, she stepped on the first foothold. A lighter frame was a great advantage with climbing. As a child she practically lived in trees whenever she was allowed outside. Building makeshift tree houses dozens of times with Lucas kept them occupied for days on end. It was a miracle the things didn't collapse under their own weight being so poorly crafted. But each one had been an oasis for them, a place to spread their imaginative wings and fly far away from Adiel.

Only once had she fallen and broken her arm. Her father scolded her mercilessly for being so clumsy, not even remotely upset at her injury or her pain. After her bones healed, he hired a personal trainer to teach her the skills of climbing, and how to land without injury. What was likely meant as a punishment of some sort, turned out to be a great joy.

Halfway up the stone wall, Eva froze at the sounds of voices.

". . . news about the Citadel graduates," a male said. "I heard there was a good lot this time."

"I haven't heard anything," a female responded. "The Citadel spits out new grunts every few months. I wish they would train more Guardians for the field. Then maybe we could put this war behind us."

"Guardian magic ain't common though. I was told a lot of recruits die in that training."

"That's the price of wielding the Ethereal. They can keep it, if you ask me."

"Still, I find it exciting. I was told we hold the upper hand in the war at the moment."

"Yes, but the retreat makes no sense to me. Thanks to the Citadel's training, our new Operatives are lasting longer in the field, and we effectively forced the Legion from the Farron Gap. If we keep finding more Obelisks, we'll win this war in a matter of months. So, why the hesitation from the Council?"

A pause. Eva stifled her heavy breaths, her fingertips burning as she clutched the stone.

"Emra," the male's tone turned quiet. "Don't start speaking out of turn again."

Emra sighed. "Yeah. How's your brother doing?"

"He's all right. Still banged up, but doing better. Aniyan cretin stuck him in the side, but Jhorgin tore his face off."

"Good. That stubbornness of his may actually benefit him this time."

"Speaking of which, any news on the—"

Eva heard a more distant voice speaking but couldn't make out the words.

"Yeah yeah, I'm coming!" the male said. "He's *Rai'pat* that one."

Emra giggled, before footsteps faded into the distance. Every inch Eva climbed higher, her heart beat with more vigor. With steady breaths, and sweat dripping down her face, she strained her ears as she neared the edge. Fingers and toes burning, she held her position and peered over the stone wall.

The nearby Operative, Emra, leaned against the tower's wall, facing away to her left. A narrow path circled the outpost, bordered by a low stone parapet—just high enough to duck behind if the alarm was raised.

*Perfect*

With no sentries nearby, Eva took her chances. With trained silence, she lifted herself over the edge and crept against the parapet. Eyes locked on the unaware Operative, Eva crept toward her. Peering around, she used her speed to grasp the Operative's head, clamping a hand over her mouth. She forced her back, quickly slicing her throat. Laying the body down behind the stone railing, Eva willed the shaking in her hands to lessen.

With another peek over the parapet, Eva counted thirty Zentari. Three more sentries stood on the corner towers, and two walking the wall pausing to speak. The rest stood scattered about the courtyard.

Various wooden sheds littered the area, barrels and boxes stacked around them. A few wooden tables adorned the area, but otherwise she couldn't make out any prisons. No cells or cages. No prisoners. There was a staircase that led from the top of the wall into the courtyard, but it was on the Northern wall—opposite her current position.

She retreated to cover and breathed deep, gritting her teeth. She pictured Thalia's face. Maya's broken body. Lucas bruised and beaten. Her blood began to boil. She was here for one reason, and there were thirty Shells in her way.

Yet her heart ached for them. Thirty enemies, yes, but also thirty lives. Some barely older than she was, no doubt with families and loved ones. Some of them gripped their weapons with stiff, nervous hands of men who had never truly killed before.

Her fingers twitched, recounting each face—each life she'd taken. She'd lost count over the years, but their faces, their screams, never left her mind. Lives stolen. Families shattered.

*What about my life*

*My family*

She thrust aside her compassion—buried it under an iron fist. She thought of Maya, of Lucas.

And she moved.

Crouching below the parapet, Eva followed the path along the Western wall, toward the Northwest sentry tower. Heart beating out of her chest, her eyes remained locked on the male Operative standing watch. He remained facing away, leaning against the stone as he stared into the darkness.

She chanced a glance over the parapet, scanning for any warriors able to spot her from their vantage point. Her instincts flared, but she had no choice.

*I need a distraction*

She palmed one of her throwing daggers. Praying to the Heavens she didn't miss, she threw it at the sentry. It found its mark in his skull. His body was pressed forward from the momentum of the attack, falling limply over the edge. Holding her breath, she waited. His body hit the ground with a thud, louder than she anticipated.

*One down*

". . . you hearing something?" a distant voice called from the courtyard.

She risked another glance over the edge. Two Operatives were walking toward the gaping hole that was the Western gate. They would find the body. She had to move quickly and use the distraction before this place was on high alert.

Summoning her speed, she crept along the pathway toward the staircase on the Northern wall. Ensuring the coast was still clear, she snuck halfway down the stairs before jumping off the side. Landing as gracefully as an Unger cat, Eva scurried into the closest storage shed, yanking open the wooden door.

The inside was a compact room with various supplies and boxes—tools, weapons, food, and even clothing. A female Operative was standing near the back, scribbling a letter, and turned to the noise of Eva entering. With lightning speed,

Eva lunged at the woman, blade ready. The Zentari was too surprised to act. She froze, eyes wide.

Eva placed a hand over her mouth and the blade to her throat. The Operative's eyes searched Eva's, wondering why in the Nine Realms an Aniyan warrior was infiltrating the outpost. Eva took whatever pity she had and burned it. *This was her enemy.*

"Do not move, and you may yet live," Eva whispered. The woman remained still.

Keeping her blade pressed against the Operative's neck, Eva quickly glanced around the shed. Wooden crates lined the walls, filled with weapons, medical supplies, and emergency rations. A steel workbench stood in the corner, unremarkable at first glance. But then she saw it. The tattered strip of gray fabric tied to the end of a sword she instantly recognized.

*Lucas*

She turned back to her enemy, rage building in her chest.

"There was an attack on this outpost recently." Eva growled, digging her blade into the woman's neck. "The leader, a Chief Aniyan, *where is he?*"

Eva couldn't stop the tremor in her hands—the dread in her chest. The Zentari woman began sweating. She shook her head carefully, as to not cut her own throat with Eva's blade.

"Where are prisoners kept?" Eva pressed. "Is there a place here in the outpost?"

Again, the woman simply shook her head.

"I'm going to remove my hand. If you make any noise, you will die. Tell me where Aniyan war prisoners are kept and how many were taken after the raid."

Eva's hand burned as she gripped her blade harder, slowly removing her other from the woman's mouth. The Operative's eyes remained wide, holding a questioning look.

"We don't hold prisoners here," she said, voice trembling. "And you will find none. We left none alive."

Something struck the side of the shed. Eva's head snapped toward the sound. Her captive shouted. *"Ick'To!"*

*Intruder*

The warning cry barely left her lips before Eva's blade cut through her flesh, slicing clean to the spine. With gurgles and sputtering, the woman fell onto the wooden floorboards. A pool of blood formed at her feet, and Eva's panic rose uncontrollably.

*He's gone*

*Lucas is actually dead*

Her head pounded, clenching her teeth, tears falling down her face. She pulled another dagger from her waist as footsteps sounded around the structure.

Fear and despair spread like wildfire—grief fanning the flames. Eva hoped she could find a shred of humanity in her enemy, something akin to what she saw before, something to prove they were more than the wretched beings she had come to know.

She was wrong. Jafeth was wrong. While some might show a semblance of honor, mimic the integrity of her people, the rest were animals—wretched beasts with only darkness in their souls. If they had no problem taking Lucas from her, then she would have no problem taking their lives from them.

Eva spiraled. The grasp of despair clutched around her heart, and a pulsing sensation drummed in her chest. Something beyond her heartbeat was answering her call for wrath—for vengeance. Time slowed. Every second extending outward, as if she could stretch it at will. Each breath lasted a day. Each blink lasted an hour.

Yet she felt disconnected, as if watching herself move and breathe. A tingling sensation ebbed through her limbs, granting her muscles strength, her mind focus.

The door to the shed burst open. Three Shells stood in the doorway, weapons drawn.

Eva wasn't sure what happened next.

The Operatives were helpless as she burst from the structure, cutting flesh and bone with every movement. She was weightless, floating across the landscape, yet bound to the earth as an immovable object. Vision blurred by tears, blood splattered across her face as she cut them down one by one.

Her body was acting on its own, meeting every blade, every attack, and finding every throat. Nothing slipped passed her senses—not the whimpers of fear, nor the stench of death. Every single minute sensation lay caught in her attention.

She didn't need light to see in the darkness—she *was* the darkness. And there was nowhere for her enemy to hide, tearing into them as some turned to flee. There was no pain from their attacks, no blood of hers spilt in battle, because none of them could touch her.

It was euphoric. The dam of her rage unleashed, an eruption of panic, sorrow, and fury. And Eva embraced it. Pushed into it. Death was her name, and vengeance was her voice. She felt free, powerful, invincible. Nothing could stop her.

And as the blood of her enemy dripped down her armor, stained her hands red, Eva felt herself step to the edge of that inner precipice. The darkness beneath her, the evil her father so desperately forced upon her, began to call her name.

But before she lost herself, fell over the edge, the brilliance began to fade. The rage subsided, and her heart slowed.

With shallow and gentle breaths, she blinked as her vision returned. Water poured on her head. It was raining. And she was standing in the middle of the courtyard. Among bodies.

The Zentari. *All of them.*

Dead.

Her hands were coated in crimson—reeked of iron. As the rain soaked her clothing, she could feel the heat leaving her body. The strength she wielded faded, and her limbs began to shake.

She turned around and took a step toward the shed, toward Lucas's sword. But her legs buckled. Her vision was black before she hit the ground.

# Chapter Twenty-Seven

E yes up, recruits!"

Eli was already awake as the rest of the bunkroom stirred in the early morning light. Sleep had eluded him, drifting in and out of unconsciousness as he spent the night thinking on the ramifications of Renard's claim.

*Squad leader*

It was the last thing he felt qualified to be. Arlo was far more sociable, and annoyingly talented at that. Shira was one of the top fighters in the program, and Lara hung with the best, claiming a quiet and relaxed sense of confidence. All Eli had done was demonstrate a lack of talent for physical coordination and an overzealous ability to question authority.

Yet the title was his—whether he liked it or not.

Despite his own unease, a subtle pride budded in his chest for having been chosen. The irony of how much had changed in such a short time wasn't lost on him. He was another step closer to being a Guardian and becoming the change he desired yet felt less like himself than ever before.

Eli stood and began dressing.

Arlo leaped off the bunk. "Morning sunshine!"

"Morning," Eli muttered.

Arlo caught his sullen demeanor. "You all right?"

"Yeah, I just didn't sleep well."

"Another nightmare?"

"No," Eli said. "But thanks for asking."

"Well, I don't know about you, but I feel amazing. Those WAVEs are incredible."

"Me too, actually. Poor sleep or not, physically I still feel great."

They both shared a smile. Eli already noticed his right knee had long stopped hurting, and the aches and pains he endured as constant companions vanished.

*I wonder if that's my magic waking up*

His mind, however, was a different story. Between lost memories and a slew of unanswered questions, Eli felt unbearably stretched. It was infuriating to know something was lost and be entirely helpless as to what that something was. The training he had received up until this point would mean little if it slowly faded with his memories, not to mention the truth he and Shira were digging up. There were still so many unanswered questions.

*What was the answer the Council found for their fading magic? If it was the WAVEs, why was it being kept so secret? Why wouldn't the Leadership just say that? More than that, why was their magic fading in the first place? And what did that mean for their future as a people entrenched in a never-ending conflict?*

The idea of asking Arlo to help in the library presented itself again. Eli felt bad about keeping everything secret, and Arlo had been supportive otherwise.

"Crazy night," Arlo mused, before realizing his blunder. "Well, you know what I mean."

Eli would have laughed if he didn't feel he were only a few days from the same fate. The thought brought its own terror before something else struck him.

*What if Shira's newfound affection was a warning sign*

"Hey," Eli said, "has Shira seemed different to you?"

Arlo wrinkled his forehead, strapping his practice blade to his back. "What do you mean?"

"Does she seem different after the WAVEs? Acting strange? More friendly or not her usual abusive self?"

Arlo thought for a moment. "No, not that I've noticed. Why, what are you worried about?"

"Nothing. I just—"

Eli didn't know if he was ready to confess his memory loss to anyone else yet, or his feelings for Shira.

"Just what?" Arlo asked, pausing with concern.

"Worried after last night, that's all. It's nothing, I'm sure."

Arlo eyed him but shrugged. "There's that paranoia again." Eli scoffed. "And you have an overhyped sense of curiosity, to be honest."

"I do not," Eli argued.

"You've been yelled at by Darby *twice,* man. No one else has even been mildly scolded."

"I'm asking legitimate questions. It's a *Lecture Hall*. Aren't we supposed to be learning?"

"Learning? Yes. Questioning what we're told? No. Questioning the Leadership and getting us reprimanded? Double no."

Eli clenched his jaw, irritated he was expected to take what was fed at face value without the slightest bit of insight. His question of whether to tell Arlo was answered at that moment.

"Yeah, you're right," Eli said.

"Let's go!" Arlo said, slapping Eli's shoulder.

Upon arriving at the mess hall, Eli saw Shira sitting at their table, already eating. Arlo joined the line, but Eli strode to her. His heart sputtered, recalling her confession yesterday.

"Hey," he said, leaning on the table.

"Morning," she said with a wry smile.

"Did you hear what happened last night?"

"Everyone heard it."

Eli bit his lip, afraid to ask the question. But Shira was the only one who knew.

"Do you think—" He started.

"No," she interrupted. "Not a chance."

He held her gaze, trying to claim some of her confidence for himself. "Shira, I still don't remember."

"It doesn't matter. You're fine."

"You don't know that."

"You and I have been talking since this whole thing started. I think I'd realize if you were slipping into insanity."

"Have you felt any different?"

Her gaze dropped for a moment. "No. I feel fine."

"Okay, but if I say something that doesn't make sense, or—"

"I'll tell you," she promised.

He grinned. "You love to interrupt me."

Shira shrugged, giving another wry grin. "I don't hate it," she said. "Go get some food. Sounds like we'll need it today." She jutted her chin toward the line, just as Arlo sat down.

Eli glanced around, now noticing Lara's absence. "Where's Lara?"

Arlo said, "Maybe she had a late night."

"You would know," Shira said accusingly. Eli's brows raised.

Arlo glanced between them. "There were a few of us hanging out! It's not illegal!" he said defensively.

Eli smiled and joined the breakfast line. After his tray was filled, he turned to walk back to his table when Soren appeared in front of him. They collided, and Soren slapped Eli's tray. His food went flying, splattering on the ground.

The room fell silent. Soren's face held only jaded aggression—and a touch of amusement.

"*Zoltharûn vek' morgar un Sylvara*," Soren murmured, stepping into Eli's face. "Watch where you walk, *Rov-An*."

Eli knew better than to antagonize Sol's squadmate, but he wouldn't back down either. He stood, holding Soren's stare. A devilish smile came over Soren's face as the silence stretched. Some returned to their meals, but the tension in the air remained. Shira and Arlo stood but stayed at their table seeing Sol did the same.

"I've been waiting for a chance to meet you officially," Soren said. "It's hard to find a chance."

"We don't have anything to say to each other."

"Oh, but we do," Soren mused. "Like what you and your black-haired bond mate are doing in the library so late at night."

Eli's eyes narrowed.

Soren continued. "Or why you seem to have personal guards as squadmates. You better watch your back on the mats Danon. You never know when your name will be called."

"What are you going to do, Soren? Kill all of your comrades before they can graduate?"

"No no no no, just the ones of my choosing."

"Yours? Or Sol's?"

Soren grinned.

"What do you want, Soren? Surely, you're more than a simple bully with nothing else to do."

"Your little girly professor won't be able to help you in an official match, Danon. Maybe I'll put in a request. See what you're really made of."

"Go ahead," Eli said. "Assuming Sol lets you off your leash."

If it weren't for the heightened senses from the second WAVE, or the newly attained reflexes, Eli wouldn't have seen Soren's fist before it reached his face. Eli ducked under the blow and delivered a solid strike to Soren's abdomen. Soren reeled backwards with an audible gasp.

Half the room stood in astonishment—shouts erupted. Sol was behind Eli in seconds, followed quickly by Arlo and Shira to Eli's left. Eli held out his hand for them not to engage. This was his fight. He could feel Sol's presence next to him, but he waited.

Soren lunged at him again, somehow moving faster than before. Soren grabbed Eli by the waist. Eli bent over, throwing his elbow repeatedly into Soren's back. Soren plunged Eli down on the ground. The wind was knocked from his lungs as Eli hit the cold stone, the back of his head bouncing off of the unforgiving surface. As Soren's fists collided with Eli's face, he felt a strange sensation of strength leaving him. A dark weakness, cold and insidious, crept through his limbs.

But that slumbering rage within stirred. Eli caught Soren's fist and rolled, throwing him off and leaping back to his feet. The room was now in complete chaos. Some left to find the Leadership, others shouted in support. And Eli's senses took everything in. For the first time, he could read his opponent—each kick, each jab, Eli saw it coming.

But Soren was unbelievably fast—faster than Shira. And every contact leeched more strength from Eli's limbs. Whether it was Soren's magic or not didn't matter. The burning fire within Eli awakened and he was holding his own.

He dodged Soren's wide swing and grabbed the front of his armor. With strength previously absent, he pulled Soren forward, slamming his fist into his face. He felt a crack under his knuckles as Soren fell sideways, reeling from the blow. With his squadmate on the ground, Sol stepped in front of Eli.

*Rotting Hells, the man is a mountain*

Soren stood, blood dripping from his cheek. Before the fight escalated further, boots sounded from the entrance to the mess hall.

"Everyone stay where you are!"

The room fell silent, and every recruit froze at Captain Renard's voice. He sauntered up to the group, and Eli swallowed at the sternness in his face.

Glancing between them, Renard's attention settled on Eli and Soren, the only two breathing heavily. Eli's lip was split, and Soren's eyebrow was bleeding.

"Would anyone care to explain this demonstration of despicable, childish behavior?" the Captain asked.

"Ask recruit Danon, Captain," Soren said.

Renard turned Eli. "Did you attack your comrade?"

"Yes sir, but only in self-defense."

"Khar'veth!" Soren shouted.

Renard held his hand up. "If you don't mind, recruit Mitchell, I will determine the truth."

Soren muttered something under his breath Eli didn't understand.

Renard addressed the room. "Who here saw recruit Danon strike Soren Mitchell?"

At once, numerous hands rose in the room. Eli let out a breath of frustration as Soren smiled.

"And who here saw recruit Mitchell strike Elijah Danon?"

Again, multiple hands rose. Soren's grin slowly disappeared.

"Well, since you both seem to enjoy fighting so much," Renard said. Eli saw nothing but a blur as the Captain struck Soren with a kick so hard Eli felt the thud in his own chest. Soren flew fifteen feet across the room, rolling on the ground in a limp heap. This time, Eli's new senses did nothing to stop the back of Renard's hand from finding his face. His neck twisted violently as he flew sideways into a table. The vision in Eli's left eye went black.

This time Eli stayed down, not daring to challenge Renard.

The Captain turned to address the room. "You are all in this program to become Guardians, the most respected members of our military. If you cannot act like it, then you will be forcefully removed from this program or *this life*. So, if anyone wants to fight outside of practice, they fight me. We will not tolerate barbarians in the Citadel."

No one dared breathe.

"You will all face the Crucible today. This second challenge will make the first half of this program seem easy. Some of you will not survive, and all of you will be pushed to your limit. You're about to experience the hardest thing in the program thus far, and if this is an indication of your attitude leading into it, then Heavens help you all."

Renard turned to Sol, stepping in front of the giant. "That includes you, recruit Richter. Do not forget yourself."

Sol's face betrayed his frustration, but he said nothing.

"Excuse me, recruit?" Renard shouted. "I didn't hear your response to a superior officer!"

"Yes sir, Captain Renard." Sol growled.

Renard turned and helped Eli to his feet. "I told you to be careful, Danon," the Captain muttered quietly enough that no one else heard. "Do a better job."

Renard left without another word, his gray cape flowing behind him. The recruits slowly resumed their meals, chatter returning to the room. Once Renard was gone, Sol strolled over to Eli, bending forward as if speaking to a child. Eli held his ground, yet again, but felt his heart rate climb. WAVEs or not, Sol would eat him alive.

"I've been watching you, Danon," Sol said. "The know-it-all with a hero complex. I don't care if you carry around bodyguards"—he glanced over at Arlo and Shira—"and I don't care what some second-rate Captain says. If you touch my squad again, I will end you. Official match or not."

"Try it," Eli spat.

Sol gave a wry grin, and returned to his table, muttering something to Soren. The vision in Eli's left eye slowly returned, though his lower lip still throbbed.

"You all right?" Arlo asked, stepping to him. Eli nodded, quietly grabbing another tray of food and sitting down at their table.

"What the bleeding Hells was that?" Shira asked from his left.

"Sorry," Eli said, his jaw aching as he chewed. "Clearly Soren can't handle snide comments."

"You laid him out though, man," Arlo said with a smile. "And I saw you dodge that punch, that was amazing."

"I've never seen anyone move as fast as Captain Renard," Eli said.

"Yeah, but you just went toe-to-toe with Sol's squad," Arlo said. "That sends a message."

"Except you now have a target on your back," Shira murmured.

"Something tells me it was already there," Eli said, biting into his bread. "So, what do we know about this challenge? The Crucible?"

Shira responded, "That it has an ominous name."

"Everything is ominous around here," Eli said.

"Well," Arlo mused, "I heard we have to fight snow creatures on the mountain."

"What?" Shira scoffed.

Arlo shrugged. "That's what Ado said."

"Ado's an idiot," Shira spat.

"What did Maelyn say?" Eli asked, glancing at their table, noting Fenner was absent.

"Nothing," Arlo said. "She was never told what the challenges entail. Apparently, they change them frequently for this reason."

Eli hummed. After breakfast, the recruits were led to the practice field to start the Crucible, as the challenge would require the remainder of the day. As they all gathered around Captains Renard and Evergreen, Eli continually scanned the crowd for Lara.

"Where in the Nine is she?" Eli asked, leaning toward Shira.

Shira glanced around. "I don't know. She wasn't in her bunk when I got up. I assumed she got in an early morning and went for a workout or something."

A rock formed in Eli's stomach. He turned his attention to the Captains. Evergreen held a satchel filled with red fabric while Renard opened a scroll.

"Recruits!" Evergreen started. "This is it! Today you will face the Crucible, your second physical challenge of the program. This event will take place behind us, upon the snowy face of Mount Asir!"

Eli gazed at the mountain behind the Captains, dwarfed by the surrounding Ha'Negev range.

"This challenge is similar to the Proving. You must work together as a cohesive squad to succeed, but there is a difference. The success of this mission does not require, nor promise, the lives of your comrades."

Murmurs spread through the crowd. Maelyn came up behind Eli and placed a hand on his shoulder.

"Fenner's gone," she whispered.

"So is Lara," Eli said, the pit in his stomach growing. "Where are they?"

"I don't know," Maelyn said, "but they're not the only ones missing."

"Before we explain the challenge," Renard shouted. "Squad leaders have been chosen! The positions were decided for differing reasons, but the Leadership has determined that each of you stands above the rest. The honorary recruits will be called by name and receive a red arm band to mark their achievement and authority. This responsibility should not be taken lightly, and the challenge today will be your first chance to prove we were correct in our choices."

"When your name is called," Evergreen said, "come grab an arm band and a gold medallion."

Renard glanced at his scroll. "Maelyn Mercer!"

Eli watched Maelyn proudly approach the Captains, accepting her armband from Evergreen.

"Cara Marruk!"

The next recruit received the arm band and medallion tentatively. As each new leader was announced, Eli heard soft praises and pats on the back, as well as murmured curses and grumbling. Clearly not everyone was proud of who was chosen as squad leaders.

"Sol Richter!"

The giant moved through the crowd and grabbed his arm band, which barely fit around his forearm. Eli wasn't surprised as much as he was disappointed in the Leadership for choosing him.

"Elijah Danon!"

Eli strode to the Captains.

Evergreen gave a polite smile. "Congratulations recruit."

Eli nodded, grabbing a band from the bag she held out and a medallion from the bottom. He fixed it on his left arm as he walked back to Arlo and Shira. Once the last squad leader was called, Evergreen addressed the crowd again.

"Recruits!" Renard shouted. "You may have noticed that there are some people missing this morning. That is not an oversight. Squad leaders, it is your responsibility to ensure your comrades are cared for and that your squad works cohesively. Their lives are your responsibility now, in the same way each comrade under your command will be in the field. To emphasize this lesson, we have taken one member of each squad captive."

A faint hum of voices sounded.

"These members were chosen because they were seen as the weakest of each squad. They have been abducted and brought to various locations near the peak of Mount Asir. You have exactly forty-eight hours to retrieve your comrades and return them safely to the Citadel. Before you say the captured recruits have it easy, know this: they are facing a challenge all their own. And, even if they succeed, if their squad fails to find them in time, they will die. They are bound, without food or water, as a punishment for falling behind in the ranks."

The murmurs in the crowd grew. Evergreen took over.

"Squad leaders, guide your squad to the location marked on your map of Mt. Asir and return within the time provided. There are resources available for this challenge, and you are in charge of deciding which provisions to take and which to leave. Only a single travel pack is assigned to your group. You are allowed, and it is advised, to bring your practice blades along."

Renard said, "If any of your team does not survive the Crucible, it is you, squad leaders, who will pay the price. The mountain will *absolutely* kill you if you leave unprepared. The thin air, bitter cold, and dangerous creatures that roam the mountainside will be your challenge."

"Most importantly," Evergreen said, "the medallions given to the squad leaders are to be protected *by any means necessary*. The squad leader decides who carries the treasure. If you return without a medallion, the punishment is severe. If you return with *more* than one medallion, your entire squad is rewarded, however many times over. You leave in twenty minutes!"

"Dismissed!" Renard shouted.

"Bleeding Hells, this is gonna be a bloodbath," Arlo said, watching the recruits scramble for their squads and supplies.

"Not necessarily," Eli said, mind churning. "You're punished if you lose your medallion or any of your squad fails to return. Risking that by attacking another squad is dangerous."

"They also didn't say what the reward was," Maelyn added.

"Exactly," Eli agreed. "Since we don't know what the reward or punishments are, we have no way of balancing the two options. The risk of losing your medallion or another squadmate might not even be close to worth it. I would venture that most minimize risk and protect their own, rather than attempt to capture medallions."

Shira said, "That's what Evergreen meant about the success of the mission."

"We don't need everyone to return to keep the medallion safe," Eli finished. "Which clearly is something they want us to remember." Eli gathered his thoughts, constructing a plan amid the chaos. He glanced at Shira and Arlo, who for the first time, was not making light of the situation.

"We will get her back," Eli said. "I promise."

"Good luck," Maelyn said, turning to leave.

As they gathered supplies, Eli considered every angle—every contingency he could predict.

"Arlo, you take the travel bag," Eli said, holding the map of the mountain, gauging their position. He decided to take along a single hunting knife to be used as a defensive weapon, carried by Shira. While they still had their practice weapons, they remained dulled with use, and Eli didn't trust them in a real fight.

"Arlo, leave your sword and take Shira's long knives."

"Why?" Arlo asked, throwing supplies into the travel bag.

Shira answered for Eli, "Because it's huge, heavy, and duller than a rock."

Arlo sighed. "Right."

Shira handed him her long knives and took the much sharper hunting knife. Eli marked Lara's location, West of the mountain peak. A few squads had already begun the trek North, some heading more West or East along the mountain's edge. Eli scanned the map, Shira standing next to him while Arlo finished packing the leather bag.

"Okay." Eli started, analyzing the route. "It's a straight shot to the base of the mountain, maybe half a day at a decent pace. The first priority is finding Lara as soon as possible."

"Agreed," Shira said, tying up her hair and buckling her leather jacket for the cold.

"Second, we need to decide where we'll camp."

"Camp?" Shira objected. "Let's just punch straight through. If we go all the way, resting as needed, we could make it back in just over a day."

"Yes, and risk carrying a wounded, dehydrated Lara on our back down a mountain in the dark. That leaves us too vulnerable."

"The longer we stay up there, the longer we deal with the wild animals and cold," she argued. "And the longer we risk running into Sol's squad."

"But if we are targeted, we want to do it on our own terms. Well rested and prepared, not exhausted and stumbling around in the dark." Eli finished.

"True," Shira agreed, "but something tells me we'll face Sol either way."

It was an impossible balance to strike. Arlo finished strapping the travel bag together and slung it around his shoulders.

"I agree with Shira," Arlo said. "Let's go all the way. Rest as needed."

Eli scanned Arlo's face, noting his seriousness. He'd never seen Arlo so restless. And being a good leader is knowing when you're outvoted.

"Okay," Eli responded, "but we keep a steady pace. If we burn out, we risk everything."

"We should get moving," Shira said. "Most have already left."

"Wait," Eli said, the gears in his mind assessing the different angles to the problem. "What are the odds Sol's squad is going to be content with just one medallion?"

"Likely zero," Shira said, "and considering your recent performance in the mess hall?"

Eli had to think. They had forty-eight hours. It would take at least a day to trek up and retrieve Lara, assuming there were no major barriers. A few hours to rest, and the much faster trek down and back in just over half a day—leaving between six to twelve hours for complications.

"Shira," Eli said, handing her the medallion.

Her eyes met his. "Why not Arlo?"

"You're our best fighter," he said. "Arlo carries the pack, and if Sol's squad attacks, he'll likely target me first."

She pulled the medallion from his hand, a strong determination behind her face. Eli knew nothing in the Nine Realms could pry that gold from her fingertips. She took it and tucked it into a small pocket in her leathers.

"Okay," Eli said. "We go all the way, stopping as needed. But keep a sharp eye out. Something in my gut tells me this challenge is just the excuse Soren needs for a little payback. Let's go."

The three recruits broke into a determined jog, each of their faces set. They had one mission, and they wouldn't stop until their comrade was safe.

This was for Lara.

# Chapter Twenty-Eight

A swell of warmth and power slipped into Eva's being in the presence of the enormous floating orb of black stone. The surface was uneven, but the edges were smoothed with time. And amid the darkness, unmistakable, was the presence within—ancient and immeasurable.

Eva watched the two unfamiliar figures approach the stone hesitantly before vibrant white light erupted through a web of cracks across the orb's surface. Loud crunches echoed in the room before the stone shattered, sharp fragments scattering to the ground.

Eva guarded her face from the explosion while the two figures remained still, not reacting. The room grew silent once again. And there, on the ground among the rubble, was a small glowing white stone. The air shifted, filling with a sense of power—and evil.

A third figure appeared before the first two, malevolent and seething, reaching for the glowing stone. Without reason, panic struck Eva as she lunged forward, reaching for the two figures, urging them to flee—

A huff of hot air blew over Eva's face, and a soft fleshy snout nudged her cheek. She opened her eyes to slits, the light of day blinding her. Squinting, she turned her head at the creature standing over her. It blew another huff of air in her face. Her arm cried out in pain as she reached up. The hair was short and brown.

*Beacon*

"You stayed," she rasped.

Eva's tongue stuck to the roof of her mouth, and her head pounded with each heartbeat. A burning flowed through her abdomen as she sat up. Beacon nuzzled her head as she sat with a grimace.

"I'm okay buddy," she whispered. "Thank you."

Waiting for the dizziness to settle, she wondered how long she had been unconscious. She glanced around, her neck cracking with the movement. There was
a body lying in the dirt, flies buzzing around the corpse—dozens of bodies.

The memory came flooding back.

*Bleeding Hells, what did I do*

Images flashed in her mind—blurred and unclear. She remembered blood and
pain and rage.

Sorrow.

*Euphoria*

The memories brought a wave of fear. Either she blacked out from the emotional, traumatic event, or—

*The stone*

The obelisk she had touched. It had disappeared. She recalled the sensation
it caused, both the pain *and* the feeling of power. Lucas said Aniyans couldn't
use Obelisks, lacking inner magic. But what if it was more complicated than
that? Xerza said the stones were for the Guardians, that they made them stronger
somehow.

*What if we can use them, just not in the same way*

There was no way to know. Regardless of what happened, she was in enemy
territory—weak and alone. Bracing against Beacon, she stood slowly. Her legs felt
like jelly, all the strength in her muscles now faded.

*Lucas*

She turned around and stared at the wooden shed. Holding onto Beacon's
harness, she stumbled to the structure. Shuffling inside, nausea struck her. The
Zentari woman lay dead on the floor, and there, in the barrel along with a number
of other weapons, was Lucas's sword with the gray fabric hanging from the hilt.
She would know it anywhere.

With trembling hands, she pulled it from the barrel. Dried blood stained the
scabbard. She bit down on the welling emotion and fished out a leather strap
to hold the blade. With his sword draped over her back, she quickly scanned
the contents of some of the boxes. Most were medical supplies, others were new
weapons or spare clothing. But among the contents lay the half-written note of
the Zentari woman.

*Tamsin,*

*How I miss you so. Every day in this wretched outpost takes another piece of my soul. Though it pains me to say, I am glad you aren't here. The Captains are the worst kind, and we live under the constant threat of attack. I'm sure you'll hear word of the raid, but rest assured I am all right. We lost some but won and even claimed some prisoners. I never feared for my own life until after we found out*

Eva stared at the words, parchment shaking in her hands, before she crumpled the paper and tossed it aside. Liars. *All of them.* She led Beacon around to the next shack. More boxes and supplies, but this one had some fruit leather and dried meat. She grabbed all that she could carry, filling a cloth bag she stole, and fed some to Beacon.

Though it took some effort, she was eventually able to mount the horse. Without being prompted, Beacon walked out of Heika. Guiding him South, Eva found where she stashed her travel pack. She fastened it firmly to his saddle, too weak to bear it on her own. Sitting atop Beacon again, she pondered where to go. She needed to find a place to rest and recover, not knowing when reinforcements or guard changes would come.

Beacon sauntered up the road as she led him back North, around the outpost. She could make camp Northeast of Heika and likely avoid any unwanted attention.

Riding alongside the plush foliage, the snow-covered peaks gave way to blueish-silver stone, and eventually to evergreen trees. Midbar stretched out to her left, the dunes fluttering from the heat. Eva spotted a narrow cave up the hill, tucked against the base of one of the mountains. It was just large enough for her and Beacon. She didn't dare trek Midbar in her current state.

Gravel crunched under Beacon's hooves, carefully finding purchase on the incline. As she struggled to remain upright, thunder roared overhead. A dark cloud cover slowly invaded the sky, blocking the afternoon sun. Eva hadn't noticed it roll in but felt some drops on her skin. Another storm would be detrimental if she didn't have shelter.

The images of last night flashed in her mind again. She shivered, desperately wishing for a fire. When they reached the cave, she fed Beacon more fruit leather before leaving to collect firewood. The rain picked up by the time she returned bearing sticks and logs. With the flint from her pack, she made a modest fire.

Smoke wafted onto the cave ceiling, billowing from the wet wood. Eva lay by the fire, staring out the mouth of the cave as the droplets fell. Her exhaustion was rivaled only by the sorrow that draped over her heart like a mourning veil. The fragile dam of strength she built to stand against the reality—*that Lucas was gone*—finally shattered beneath the weight of her grief.

She held his sword in her arms as she lay on the cave floor, the crackling fire the only sound above the rumbling thunder and rainfall.

*You should hide the fire, in case someone sees the smoke*

She didn't care. It was over. She made a gamble, and it didn't pay off. Perhaps if she returned to Manoach she could restart—disappear into the folds of by-standers and let the war play out as it will. But she knew in her heart she would only ever be hiding from this moment, living as a hollow husk of the woman she once was. A woman that not only had been granted the power to bring change, but to march forward and see it through.

Closing her eyes, she willed her mind to drift to happier times. She stretched out her thoughts, seeking any comforting memories, but they all revolved around Lucas. At some point, with tears falling down her face, sleep overtook her.

When she woke, the fire had burned to glowing embers. It was night, and the storm had worsened. There were some branches left over from what she had gathered, kept dry by the cover of the cave. Shivering from the cold, she remade the fire and huddled beside it. Beacon stood a few feet away, content in the warmth of the makeshift shelter.

*Okay, that's enough self-pity. What now*

She didn't know. Could she allow herself to return to Manoach, pretending nothing happened? Maybe she should tell the truth, face her trial with whatever honor she still retained.

*What if he isn't dead*

It didn't matter. The letter meant nothing. Even if he was alive, Jafeth said Lucas would likely be taken to the Citadel. Maybe they would hold him at a nearby outpost, like Tekhpal or Hof, but that would be a guess. And if he were dragged to Eldan City, they would torture him without mercy. Xerza said some captives were sold as slaves, but she couldn't run off and search for him blindly behind enemy lines. Even if Lucas was alive, she was a fool to think she could ever get to the Citadel. Going there *was* suicide, and she couldn't rely on whatever happened last night to save her again.

*Who could help you*

She could return to Yaqar and demand Drax give her ideas or tell her what he knows. It was a satisfying thought, to pummel answers out of Drax for as long as needed—and maybe a bit more.

But there were more than a few Legion members at Yaqar that were not only loyal to Drax, but would most certainly intervene. Besides, she had left her post. Drax would have exactly what he needed to dismiss her and lock her up for a dereliction trial if she returned. There was no one in the Aniyan military that cared enough to help a defiant and lowly Swordsman.

*There is one*

No, she wouldn't ask him. She would rather die than beg him for help.

*But would you rather Lucas die than beg him for help*

Rage and anger boiled at the thought of her father's face.

*Curse his rotting, bleeding, wretched soul*

Curse him for forcing her to join the military, for not protecting her, for not saving her mother, for destroying everything Eva ever held dear. When she left, she vowed to never return, at least for herself.

It was morning by the time Eva made her decision. The rain ceased, and the sky filled with the faint blue light of dawn. She gathered her things, strapped Lucas's sword around her back, and re-saddled Beacon. Gently holding his snout, she whispered softly.

"Can you help me with one more thing, buddy?"

He nudged her gently with his snout. She smiled and led Beacon out of the cave. The air was still cool from the night, holding onto the moisture from the storm.

Mounting Beacon, she spurred him to a gallop—heading North. It was a three-day ride to Ashdod.

The sun was high in the sky as Eva left the Zina River behind, and the Duran Wall finally came into view—the newest accomplishment of the Aniyan Empire. General Malachi, leader of the Legion and King of the Aniyan people, ordered the construction of the wall nearly twenty years ago. He felt it would simultaneously display the strength of the Legion, while also defend against any army marching directly to the capital.

Ashdod was the epicenter of the Legion, as well as the primary home of the Aniyan populace. It was where General Malachi and Chosen Lieutenant Cooper coordinated the war effort. Hundreds of carrier hawks flew in and out of the city each day, carrying messages across the country. Malachi all too quickly fell in love with the role as the General of the Aniyan Legion, forsaking his role as king.

It was because of this that the Aniyan people became split. Those who wanted to support their King and aid the war effort were either active in the Legion or helping them in some way. Those that chose inaction and peace, fled to the neighboring towns and cities in the region. Some left the country altogether. Eva had met more and more Aniyans no longer supporting the crown, stating their King was drunk on the attention and support the war granted him.

A rock formed in her stomach as she neared the Duran Wall. The massive structure stood over the landscape like a tidal wave, its iron gate spanning the length of the road. Made entirely of stone and iron, the wall stretched more than fifty feet in the air, and in its current state, would take at least a day's walk to go around.

Archers stood atop, in-between the mounted iron shields, with sentries pacing the length of the wall itself. A few hundred Legion were stationed at the base, near the gate. One met her as she approached.

"State your business," he said, his mustache obscuring his lips. He was a Lieutenant, based on the red fabric on his sword.

"I am to report to Ashdod and see the Leadership on urgent business," Eva said sternly.

"We have not received word of any arrivals from . . . where are you stationed, Chief?"

Eva didn't correct his mistake, forgetting she bore Lucas's sword on her back. "It doesn't matter. My name is Evalynn Katz, now let me pass or explain your refusal to the Leadership."

The Lieutenant's eyes narrowed, before his attention lifted to her white hair, and his demeanor changed. "Yes, yes ma'am," he stammered. He turned, holding his hands around his mouth. "Open the gate!"

With a loud crack, the left door of the gate moved aside. Beacon was restless, but obeyed Eva's command to walk through. It was a short ride before she came upon Ashdod city, its main gate embarrassingly dwarfed by its successor. The Aniyan capital was the greatest in Adiel, apart from Eldan.

Once inside, Eva was thrust into a sea of chaos and commerce. Carriages, horses, salesmen, and endless crowds flooded the area, all rifling about among their varied errands. The noise was insufferable. The air was heavy with both the sweet scent of freshly cooked meat, and the rank odor of too many bodies. Men and women ran around, as if today was their last day on Adiel.

After suffering the constrained proximity of the busy main streets, to her complete and utter dismay, Eva finally reached the steps of The Capitol. The structure was solid stone, with pillars arranged around the perimeter in a show of strength and royalty. Eva always felt it haughty.

The Capitol building stood above the rest of the city that surrounded it. Stores and homes arranged in no particular order, flowing out from it like a wave. She tied Beacon to a post designated for travelers' horses at the bottom of the steps. Leaving Beacon and her belongings felt wrong, but the two guards stationed nearby would hopefully ward off any would-be thieves.

She removed her hood, squinting at the sun. Marching up the steps, she kept Lucas's sword on her back. Her weapons would undoubtedly be taken, but she wouldn't risk losing it by leaving it here.

A dozen more Legion stood at the entrance to The Capitol building, guarding the main door. To her knowledge, it was the only way in and out. But she didn't believe for one moment there weren't at least a few secret passages hidden somewhere. The Lieutenant in charge approached her, hand on his sword.

"Halt. Remove your weapons and state your business," he demanded.

She didn't bother with any pretense this time. These guards had heard all the tricks to get an audience with the King and General.

"My name is Swordsman Evalynn Katz. I'm here to see my father."

# Chapter Twenty-Nine

The nausea in Lara's stomach worsened as the ground tilted beneath her, the dizziness from the tonic yet swirling in her system. Whatever they made her drink when she was taken last night left her entirely disoriented.

At first, she thought herself in trouble, until realizing she wasn't the only one being escorted out. When Captain Renard handed her a glass of blue liquid, her senses screamed for her to flee. But refusing orders was treason—so she complied.

Hands behind her back, abrasive rope bit into her wrists. The air was musty and thick, smelling of dust and mold. The floor was freezing under her seat. Lara opened her eyes, revealing a barren room of stone. Light shone through a narrow slit above her, shining a thin line on the adjacent wall. As her vision adjusted to the darkness, she saw several other recruits, also bound and unconscious. At least twenty.

Lara coughed from the dust scratching her throat, which made her ears ring. Her head was underwater. She attempted to stand, struggling against her bindings. Her legs trembled and buckled beneath her.

"Okay. I'll just rest for a moment," she whispered to herself, gulping air from the simple task. Surveying the room, she noticed Fenner sitting against the wall to her right. His eyes were closed, but he was breathing steadily. Grasping for an idea of what was happening, she recalled what Captain Renard said before she passed out.

*"Your squad will rescue you, only if you are worthy to be saved."*

Her pulse quickened, the reality of their situation settling on her shoulders. She was trapped and had to escape, so Arlo and the others could reach her in time.

"Okay, so where in the bleeding Nine are we?" she whispered.

Lara strained her muscles to stand, this time succeeding. Clenching her jaw, she pulled at her bindings, pain searing as the fibers peeled flesh from her hands. With a final yank, the ropes fell.

She hissed, inspecting her minor injuries. Walking over to Fenner, she knelt and shook him.

"Hey! Fenner!"

Fenner groaned, lifting his head and staring with glazed eyes. Lara reached behind him and worked the ropes loose around his wrists, but he slumped over limply onto another recruit.

"Fenner!" Lara said, grasping his shoulder. But his eyelids remained shut.

She stood and scanned the room, the strength in her muscles returning in stride with her rising concern. Faded symbols and markings covered the stone walls, their meanings lost to time. She stepped forward, her eyes drawn to a smooth slab at the far wall.

"A door," she breathed. Squinting in the darkness, she traced its edges, searching for a handle or latch. Nothing. Just cold, unyielding stone.

She turned and marched to the back of the room where the slit in the stone hugged the ceiling, providing a steady stream of light. It was too high to peer through, and too narrow to allow a hold for her fingers. But she could feel cold air drifting down from the gap.

Fenner stirred, and Lara knelt beside him as he woke.

"Hey, Fenner!" she whispered. "We need to see what's on the other side of this window."

He blinked, opening his eyes and shaking his head. He reached for Lara's shoulder and attempted to stand, wobbling against her support.

"What?" he slurred. "Where are we?"

"I don't know, but if I lift you up can you look through that gap?"

Fenner glanced upward at the slit of light and nodded. He shuffled over to the adjacent wall and Lara knelt, offering her hands as a foothold. Fenner stepped into them and held the wall for support as he grimaced, staring into the bright light.

"What do you see?" she asked, straining to hold his weight.

"White. It's nothing but white and blue sky," he said. "Wait, there's a tree. It has snow on it."

*Snow. We're in the mountains*

Fenner screamed, jumping out of Lara's grasp. She cursed, shaking her hands which ached from the sudden movement.

"What?" she asked, as a figure moved directly in front of the opening, the light in the room dimming momentarily as it passed.

"Something's outside," Fenner breathed.

As she froze and listened for whatever stalked them, a piece of parchment fell from her armor. She stooped and unfolded the old, weathered note. It bore only one hastily scribbled word.

*Leave*

Eli gripped the thick rope stretched across the unnamed river, its slow, punishing crossing creating a silent bottleneck of tense recruits on the far bank. Among them stood Esme, alone and watchful. Eli approached her as he climbed out of the water.

"You the first across?" he asked, wringing out his clothing as best he could, adorning his dry jacket.

Esme nodded, staring at her squadmates across the river. Eli assumed squads would traverse together, but no one wanted to chance more than one person on the old rope. Glancing behind him at the looming peak, dread settled in Eli's stomach. It would be a hard climb, and he noted the dark clouds settling into the sky.

Esme turned to the mountain and spoke quietly. "Sol's team has already passed. I saw them split up before reaching the base."

Eli's brow furrowed. "Setting a trap?"

"Most likely." Esme pursed her lips. "And I fear Rowan may also be a threat."

"Rowan?" Eli asked. "Isn't he with you?"

He turned back, searching across the river, but only saw Maelyn.

"No," she said. "He moved on ahead without us. Be watchful, Danon."

Arlo and Shira joined them quickly, ready to continue their trek. Eli slapped Esme's shoulder.

"Thanks," he said. "Be safe."

She nodded, waiting for Maelyn. Every squad moved in different directions, each seeking the specified location of their captive comrades. The mountain was smaller than most in the Ha'Negev range, but still gave ample space to hide recruits anywhere among its frigid peak.

As Eli, Shira, and Arlo approached the base of the mountain, the ground inclined, the grassy plain blending into a terrain of sharp rocks and gravel.

"Wait," Shira said.

Eli spun to her, and then to the bloodstain on a nearby boulder. The three of them examined the streak of blood dripping down the stone—fresh and shimmering in the daylight. A bloodcurdling scream sounded from far West of their position, up the mountainside. The cries echoed between the thick evergreen trees, preventing isolation of its source.

Eli turned around to Arlo and Shira, only to see Soren stalking up behind them, a dagger in his hand.

"Look out!" Eli shouted, before an arm wrapped around his neck. A spike of adrenaline flashed through him as his airway shut.

If Sol was here, they were dead.

Eli caught his attacker's other wrist mid-swing as a dagger plunged for his chest, stopping it only inches away. Eli's muscles burned as he fought to keep the steel from piercing his heart, calling on every ounce of his strength. Arlo and Shira spun to face Soren just as he lunged for Shira with murderous speed. She tore her hunting knife free and slashed at his neck with a grunt.

"Help Eli!" she shouted, deflecting Soren's axe as it came for her leg.

Arlo didn't hesitate, throwing down the travel bag and charging. Eli, still grappled, shifted his weight and slammed his attacker into the boulder behind with a crunch. The man grunted, his grip faltering. Arlo was there in a second, wrenching the dagger from his hand with brute force.

The arm around Eli's neck slackened, and Eli twisted free. He spun, gasping, in time to see Rowan draw a sword from his hip—face dripping with sweat and fury. Eli unsheathed his broadsword. Arlo was already moving, landing a vicious punch that Rowan barely dodged, before retaliating with a long, shallow slice across Arlo's forearm.

Eli swung his sword overhead, which Rowan parried. But the guard left him open. Arlo threw his right elbow into Rowan's face, sending him stumbling onto the uneven ground. Despite Arlo's injury, Eli turned away to help Shira. Arlo had the upper hand, not even bothering to draw Shira's long knives with Rowan on the ground.

Shira and Soren had each other's blades locked, faces twisted with effort. They clawed for footing, each trying to break the other's stance. Eli sprinted in and slashed Soren across the ribs. The armor dulled the blow, but it opened a line of dark blood, forcing Soren to stumble back—tearing his hands away from Shira's.

Soren's eyes darkened. He clutched his side, blood seeping through his fingers, and glanced back toward Rowan, who now barely held off Arlo's unrelenting fury.

Soren said, "You better hope we don't find your comrade before you do, Danon." Shira lunged for Soren, but the coward sprinted away shouting. "*Klo'Tir! A'areck!*"

Eli grabbed Shira's shoulder and turned back to help Arlo. Rowan was attempting a retreat, and Arlo had finally drawn his weapons, another cut across his left leg. They dashed over to him, but Rowan heard Soren's order to retreat. He spit at Arlo's feet before running around the boulder, following Soren's trail.

Arlo turned around to meet his comrades as they watched their enemies flee.

"Do we go after them?" Arlo asked, catching his breath.

"No," Eli said, glancing around, wondering where in the Hells Sol and Kairah were. "Shira, are you hurt?"

"No. But we need to move," she said, sheathing the hunting knife. "Soren's threat wasn't idle."

"I guess you do have a target on your back," Arlo said. He walked over and opened the travel bag, digging out the medical kit to bandage his cuts.

Eli nodded, an inner panic rising. He had no doubt that was only the first encounter. "Does Soren know where Lara's being held? Could he know?"

"It's possible," Shira said. "If he had a copy of our map."

"Or if ours was switched. Or we were given the wrong one."

"Either way, we need to move," she said, searching the tree line.

Eli shifted his weight. "Why did they split up?" he asked. "Why not attack us all at once?"

Arlo stood. "It doesn't matter," he said, ready to continue. "We lick our wounds and move."

Eli gave a sharp breath, racking his brain for answers. His gaze met Shira's, which held her stoic confidence.

"Let's go," Eli said, continuing their ascent. Thunder bellowed overhead, shaking the ground. Eli's dread worsened as he saw the first snowflakes fall.

Lara stared at the note, repeating the word dozens of times in her head. She handed the note to Fenner, who furrowed his brow as he read it.

"Leave? Here?" he asked.

"That's what leave means, Fenner," she said, folding the parchment. "Do you have a note?"

Fenner patted himself down, checking each individual pocket of his leather armor. He shook his head. Lara began checking each of the still unconscious recruits.

"What are you doing?" Fenner asked accusingly.

"I'm seeing if we can get more information," she said, searching each recruit as they remained slumped against the walls. Nothing.

*No weapons either*

"What did you see outside?" Lara asked.

Fenner swallowed. "Something with teeth," he whispered.

The hair on the back of her neck rose. There were rumors and bedtime stories about vicious creatures in the Ha'Negev Mountains. Yet they were nothing but myths. Regardless, the last thing she wanted to do was find out for certain.

Lara walked to the front of the room, to the door as a few of the recruits began stirring. She skimmed along the edges of the frame but still found nothing to open it. Bracing her hands against the stone, Lara pushed.

Nothing.

"Help me," she told Fenner.

He walked over and pushed on the door with his shoulder. They strained together, pressing all their might against the solid piece of stone. Their boots scraped against the loose pebbles on the floor. As Lara was about to give up, the door shifted the slightest amount. Her elation was made impossible, however, at the sound of a shrieking roar outside in the same moment.

Fenner and Lara spun around toward the narrow window. The sound was terrifying, and unlike anything she had ever heard before. A low, guttural growl rippled through the room, before the light dimmed again—the creature pacing on the other side of the window.

"And you want to go outside?" Fenner accused.

Lara's heart was pounding.

*What do we do*

"Let's just stay here," Fenner said, his fear palpable. "Wait for the others to find us."

Lara didn't blame him. The same fear seeded in her own mind. A few other recruits were waking, groaning as they pulled against their bindings. Lara and Fenner walked over and untied them.

Half of them were complete strangers to her. It was never a priority for her to form attachments—quite the contrary. The closer you were to someone, the harder it was to charm them, to claim their belongings for yourself before you never see them again. You can't survive on the streets without learning how to smooth talk your way into food and shelter. And you were guaranteed to be killed if you weren't the first to betray those that claimed to be your friends.

Lara untied the bindings of a female recruit with dark hair and yellow eyes. She blinked wearily, glancing around.

"What's your name?" Lara asked.

"Jezza," the girl slurred.

"Jezza, I need your help," Lara said, her adrenaline now peaking as she'd made up her mind. "We need to open the door to leave."

"Okay," Jezza said, standing on unsteady legs. She walked with Lara to the door and braced to start pushing again.

"Hey, *hey*!" Fenner shouted. "What are you doing?"

"I'm getting us out of here!" Lara spat, shoving her weight against the door. Jezza gritted her teeth as she helped.

"Stop it!" Fenner yelled. "You're going to let that thing inside!"

Jezza stopped. "What thing?"

Lara breathed deep, unsure of what to say. An uneasy dread had settled in her stomach, something screaming for her to flee this room. The heavy terror engulfed her like a thick wet blanket. Claustrophobia was never her weakness, but despite the creature outside, she would rather face it than remain in here.

"We heard a noise outside," Lara explained calmly, "but between all of us, if we stick together, we'll be just fine."

"*A noise!?*" Fenner shouted. "Try a shrieking roar! There's a beast outside, and you want to let it in!"

Lara's heart thundered. Fenner was becoming aggressive—hysterical. He'd never acted like this. She didn't know if he was only panicking, or if he was sincerely convinced they needed to stay here. But Renard's words echoed in her mind again.

*Only if you are worthy*

How could they be found worthy by cowering in a small room? Surely their side of this challenge, the Crucible, was not to simply shelter inside a dungeon waiting to be rescued.

No, there was something else going on. She didn't know who wrote that note, but she agreed with the consensus. They needed to leave.

Lara grunted as she pressed against the door once more. But Fenner rushed behind her and yanked her away onto the floor.

# Chapter Thirty

A creeping sense of nakedness overcame Eva as the guards took her weapons, leading her into the main lobby of The Capitol. Though much quieter than the city streets, numerous individuals moved about with a display of importance. Politicians, ambassadors, and wealthy heirs, all of which were cut from the same cloth, walking with upturned noses and indifferent expressions.

Though they wore different faces and clothing, inside they were all the same—thieves and liars. A quiet hum hung in the air, and Eva caught the hushed voices behind each doorway. She grew up around these two-faced individuals, and returning felt like climbing into a tar pit. It said a lot about her father to keep these snakes as company.

She was ushered through the lobby and passed another pair of beautifully crafted double doors. The war room, previously the throne room, was now a hulking empty space, holding only a massive ornate table in the center beneath a shimmering chandelier. The vast space was decorated from floor to ceiling with gold accents and polished wood in all matters of intricate designs. Figurines and patterns were etched into each surface, emphasizing the painted portraits along the walls. A staircase and narrow balcony sat to the far left.

It was originally set up to hold a throne in the center for public statements and holding an audience with the king. Now, it had been devoted to under-the-table dealings and endless talk of more creative ways to slaughter the enemy.

A few dignitaries were positioned around the oak table, speaking about every realm of politics. And there, seated at the head, was General Malachi.

His face was middle-aged, bearing weathered skin that hinted at a life of experience, complemented by his now graying hair. Yet, despite the price of time, none of his harshness had been lost, still claiming piercing moonlike eyes able to cut down the strongest man with a single glance. Wearing polished black armor with silver accents, the General retained a considerable intimidating presence.

Malachi held the slightest grin while speaking to an ambassador from what Eva guessed was the Eastern continent, across the sea, judging by the man's dark skin. As the General spotted who exactly the guards brought in, his smile vanished.

The room quieted as Malachi's attention shifted to the uninvited guest.

"Hello father," Eva said, unable to banish the tremor in her hands, nor the turning of her stomach. Despite her ever-growing animosity for her father, he still made her recoil in fear.

The guard to her right stomped his foot on the ground. "You will speak only when spoken to when in the presence of the king!"

Malachi raised his hand. "Rest, Lieutenant Varrok," he said calmly. "You may leave."

Varrok bowed and left without a word. Silence lingered until the ornate doors thundered closed. The air thickened.

"And to what do I owe the pleasure of my daughter's presence after so long?" the King asked, his face exuding confidence, but betraying no emotion. Eva knew better than to begin their dance of defiance and control, one they had performed countless times. It brought bile to her throat, but the truth was she needed him—whether she liked it or not.

"Lucas has gone missing," she said.

"Lucas? Your friend?"

*Wretch*

He knew exactly who Lucas was to Eva. Despite Malachi's attempts to *discourage interactions with the rabble,* he had eventually tolerated Lucas's presence. Still, he never acknowledged the depth of Eva and Lucas's bond.

"I'm here to ask for help," she said, keeping the frustration from her voice.

"Well of course," Malachi said, folding his hands. "I would never deny my own daughter aid."

*Liar*

"But perhaps we should speak in private." He finished, standing from his chair with a nod to the ambassadors.

*Away from prying eyes and listening ears.*

It would harm his own interests if he were seen as merciless to his own child in front of distinguished guests.

"Of course, father," she said, bowing.

The words felt like acid on her tongue, but she knew far better than to antagonize him in front of others. Last time she did that, he locked her in her quarters for a month and banished Lucas from the grounds until she begged for forgiveness. The tips of two of Eva's fingers were still numb from trying to claw her way through the walls. It took the maids weeks to clean all the blood.

Malachi held his arm out to his right, toward the door on the far wall, camouflaged by the intricate floral designs. Their footsteps reverberated relentlessly, and Eva heard gentle whispers from the war table. She stepped into his private office, standing before a massive stone desk which stood in the back of the space. Adorned with all varieties of trinkets and trophies, everything claimed a proper place. The back wall was a bookshelf—various jewels, ceremonial weapons, and treasures displayed alongside aging literature. Eva's gaze danced to another door on the adjacent wall, which she assumed led to a hallway.

Malachi strolled around and sat in his chair, interlocking his fingers. Eva remained standing, if only to quell her insatiable restlessness. The King simply stared, patiently waiting for her to speak. She decided that honesty was her best chance since he'd see through her lies in an instant.

"I need to know where the Zentari bring Aniyan prisoners, and I need help getting there," she said, as diplomatically as she could.

"Oh, is that all?" Malachi asked, raising his eyebrows. "And why exactly would a lowly Swordsman need that kind of information?"

"I'm going to save Lucas."

"Right, your friend, of course. But that begs the other question, how a simple Swordsman would be allowed to take on an assignment of her own choosing? Maybe if you were the Chosen Lieutenant, you wouldn't have this problem."

"It's *your* reputation that's kept any promotions at bay."

Malachi scoffed. "As if you carry a shining and spotless record, daughter. I've read all of Benton's letters."

True. But the denial of her promotions were because Leadership believed Eva didn't deserve them, thinking her nothing more than a privileged royal. Or, because she *had* earned them, but they didn't want to appear to be playing favorites.

"I'm asking you to send me on that mission," she said.

"And where exactly would you like to be sent?"

"To where Lucas is being held. Or wherever the Zentari would keep him."

Malachi crossed his arms. "Speak what you really want, daughter."

Eva took a deep breath. "I need to get to the Citadel. Find Lucas and escape."

"Okay, we're making progress with our honesty. So, let me get this straight." He leaned forward in his chair. "You would like privileged information outside your rank, to abandon your current post and be sent on a mission of *your* choosing, for me to redirect considerable resources to infiltrate our enemy's greatest stronghold, and you would like my blessing to ensure you aren't charged with dereliction? Did I get everything?"

Despite herself, the tiny sliver of hope she cradled coming in here slipped between her fingers. This man was her father. He should want to help her—no pleading, no reluctance. Never again would she give him the pleasure of seeing her beg.

"Yes," she said curtly. "That is exactly correct."

The King hummed, attention wandering, chewing on his inner cheek. "And what would you have me do about your current charges?"

Eva swallowed. "What charges?"

A snide grin formed across his face. "Well for starters, you've failed to address me properly this entire time. You've spoken out of turn, *twice*, and not once have you used my title or shown the respect that is *required* by Legion law. You arrived without summons, which is a blatant misuse of your royalty. All of which are violations I could charge you with at this moment."

He paused, but Eva held her tongue, knowing he wasn't done. He was baiting her to speak out of turn and prove his point.

"Also," he continued, "I've heard reports of suspicious activity at Yaqar from Lieutenant Drax. I know my brother-in-law isn't fond of you, but he reported some fairly compelling evidence of your involvement."

Again, she said nothing. Malachi wasn't seeking an argument—he was drawing out her list of sins. She hoped her silence was not the confession he wanted.

"And lastly," he said, "I am aware of your assignment to patrol duty at Mano-ach. Which means if you're here, you've abandoned your post. By all rights, I should throw you in prison immediately. Did I miss anything?"

At least he didn't mention Jafeth, or the fact that Drax promised an execution if she was caught deserting.

"No," she bit.

"I thought so. Now, I am far more lenient than my brother-in-law. I will not charge my own daughter with dereliction and desertion, nor do I wish to send you to the block. And I wouldn't dream of dismissing you from the Legion. I will however require payment for this favor—well, let's be honest, multiple favors," he said with a smirk.

Eva's forehead wrinkled. "Payment?" she asked, feeling her stomach sink.

There wasn't time for this. If Lucas really was still alive, every minute—every second—could be his last.

"Of course. Surely you understand the gravity of what you're asking. You fly in the face of our laws, flaunt your lack of respect for authority, abuse your position as royalty, and then march in here making demands. I feel that payment, a trade of sorts, is very reasonable."

Her jaw clenched. "What do you want?"

"Oh, my dear daughter, it's not what I want, it's how I can help you." That diplomatic smile came over his face. It made her nauseous. "I will provide you with what you need, and I have some additions to the original agreement."

Her gaze averted, unable to look at him a moment longer. Coming here was a mistake. She should have stormed the Citadel and taken her chances. Malachi could lock her up with a single word, and she didn't doubt his desire to do it either, regardless of what he said. But she couldn't leave, and she couldn't say no. She was trapped.

And he knew it.

"Here's what I propose." He began, looking at his fingernails as if this was idle talk about the weather. "First, we get your rescue plan figured out, then we send the most qualified warrior for the job. And in return, you remain here

in The Capitol full time. You obey orders and uphold the Legion's best interests—*my* best interests. I could use a talented Swordsman here, and you could
learn a great deal. Maybe even earn a promotion *finally*. Hells, I'll even assign
Lucas to the Duran wall to keep him safe. We do that, it's a deal."

Not safe.

*Close*

Close enough to control, but far enough to prevent Eva from seeing Lucas. The
thought of staying here, *with him,* sent a wave of dread through her. She knew
getting her father to help was a long shot in itself, and him asking for something
in return was not surprising, but this—staying here was unthinkable. There was
certainly a reason behind his request, and Eva highly doubted it was for her own
good.

"Oh!" Malachi added, "and you will hereby go as Swordsman Katz only. No
more first name basis nonsense."

Some proverbial salt in the wound.

"With all respect, *father,* you don't use your last name either," she retorted,
trying her best to keep the disdain out of her voice.

"What I do and don't do is none of your concern, *daughter*. Now, I am a
very busy man. Do we have a deal?" His casual mannerisms ceased, a façade like
everything else. Malachi was a statue, eyes boring into hers. She'd have to give him
an answer.

She clenched her fists, frantically forming a backup plan. "I formally request to
be the one to rescue Lucas," she said. "I am a skilled fighter and expert in stealth."

"Denied," he replied curtly. "I will choose the party in question."

"Then I request to remain at my current station of Manoach after the proceedings and once Lucas has been returned."

"Denied. You will remain here, effective immediately." Her father's icy stare
remained. He would not let her dictate any part of the deal. But she couldn't say
no. Malachi would, without hesitation, have her arrested if she tried to leave.

Defeat wrapped its arms around Eva. Her eyes fell to the floor as her shoulders
slumped. "Then I agree with your terms, General Malachi," she said, bowing.

"Excellent!" He stood, that diplomatic smile returned to his face. "I will send
word immediately to Chosen Lieutenant Cooper to begin planning."

Eva refused to meet his gaze—the monster that called himself her father. Malachi walked around his desk, grasped her gently by the shoulders, and kissed her forehead. Fighting every instinct to shove him away, she remained still. A searing burn erupting where his lips touched her forehead.

*I will not rot in this palace as his trophy*

He reached for the door handle, but Eva spoke before he opened it. "General." She started, the wheels turning in her head. "*Father*, I formally request to be a part of the planning team. My skills and insight may prove useful. And if I am to earn that promotion, I should start learning tactics and Leadership as soon as possible."

He eyed her for a moment, but she held only sincerity in her expression. "Granted," he said, the corners of his mouth turning down.

Eva grinned.

*And so the snake ensnared what he thought was a bird*

# Chapter Thirty-One

E li's lungs burned in the frigid wind as he pushed his aching muscles harder with each step. They were only halfway up the mountain, but the snow was already knee deep. The temperature had dropped considerably, and it was only their provided jackets and physical exertion that kept them warm enough to withstand the cold.

Besides, they couldn't stop. Eli knew from the map they were only a few hours from Lara's location, having pushed themselves because of the blizzard. But the snow had slowed their progress considerably. His vision of the mountain peak was entirely eradicated by the snowfall. It wasn't a complete whiteout, but his ability to navigate was becoming increasingly difficult. And that wasn't even the least of their worries.

Another scream sounded to their left—a shriek of horrible pain. The three of them turned that direction but kept moving. Ever since that first scream at the base, dozens more had sounded. Either someone was slaughtering their comrades, or something else was out there on the cold mountain.

"Eli!" Shira shouted over the wind. "We need to stop!"

Eli spun around. Arlo was holding his arms, eyes shut tightly as his body shivered violently. Eli trudged through the snow to him.

Arlo's fingers were partially white. "I c-can't feel them," he stuttered.

*Bleeding Hells*

Another scream sounded. Eli frantically searched for a nearby location to hunker down and warm themselves.

*We need fire*

Maybe they could wait out the storm, or more likely, warm themselves enough to keep going. Eli caught sight of a subtle dip in the steady incline of the mountainside and galloped through the thickening snow. There was a narrow valley where the snow collected in a heaping drift, enough to dig out a makeshift shelter.

"Over here!" he shouted, as Shira and Arlo followed. Eli began fiercely digging through the snow, using his broadsword, and cutting out their own cave of sorts. Shira helped alongside, packing down the snow on the inside.

Once a large enough area was opened, the three of them crawled into the tight space—all of them shivering. Eli grabbed the travel bag from Arlo and dug out the flint and sticks they collected along the ascent. It wasn't much, but it was enough for a brief fire.

Having practiced the skill numerous times on the farm, he quickly ignited the brittle sticks. Among the various books he'd read growing up, he recalled that a fire inside a snow fort will reinforce the ceiling and was curious about testing the theory. Eli rubbed his hands together before guiding Arlo's fingers toward the flames. Arlo was still shaking severely, lying on his side with his eyes shut, as if not looking at the snow would bring back his body's warmth.

"Here," Eli said, draping their only blanket over Arlo.

"I was never one for the cold," Arlo said, his voice jumping as he spoke.

"Me either," Shira said, wrapping her arms around herself.

Eli smiled as he said, "I stayed out in the snow so long as a kid I got frostnip on all of my toes. Felt like I was standing on coals for a week."

"Sounds good," Arlo teased. "You go grab Lara, and we'll stay here with the fire."

"That how you learned to build a snow fort so quickly?" Shira asked.

"Yeah, actually," Eli said. "I remember the few times it snowed at our farm. My mother had to practically drag me back inside before I froze to death."

Between the gentle flames and their own body heat, their cave warmed considerably. Eli fed the fire as needed, rationing the meager amount of sticks available. But the storm wasn't letting up. They couldn't stay here long, yet they had no choice at the moment.

"I wonder how the others are doing," Eli mused, watching the worsening blizzard. He glanced at Arlo, whose shivering had lessened, but his eyes were still clamped shut. Shira hugged herself as her teeth clattered.

Eli shifted closer to her, his movements slow, almost hesitant. He wasn't sure if she'd welcome the contact, so he kept his hands to himself, letting the space between them narrow until their shoulders nearly touched. The fire crackled softly in front of them, casting warm, flickering light across her face. Over time, Arlo's breathing steadied, and his tremors ceased.

Eli stole a glance at Shira. He wondered how long it would take for those impenetrable walls of hers finally collapsed. And the thought stirred an excitement deep in his soul.

"You all right?" Eli whispered.

"I'm half-frozen," she said, "but otherwise, yes. You?"

Eli nodded. "I'm all right."

Another ear-splitting scream echoed among the storm, but this one sounded deeper—and less human.

"What in the rotting Hells is that?" Shira asked.

"I don't know," Eli said, "but something is mimicking human screams."

Arlo looked at him as though his head popped off. "What? What can do that?"

"My dad used to read me books about folklore," Eli explained. "He tried to bring me home a new book each time he left on a trip, and I've read all of them more than a dozen times. One mentioned something called Mirthren, but they change names depending on where you're from. Their call sounded so similar to human screams that people would wander into the woods thinking someone needed help. But I thought they were nothing more than myths."

"Whatever is screaming outside isn't a myth," Shira added.

Eli sighed, thankful for the brief respite from the challenge. As he sat, cold hands slipped around his left arm, Shira's fingers gently lacing together. Her touch sent a quiet jolt through him. He didn't move, afraid even a breath might break the moment.

He caught Shira's glance at Arlo, whose eyes remained closed. A slow, involuntary smile curved on Eli's lips. Shira hadn't said anything, but she didn't need to. The moment was enough.

"I don't care, Fenner!" Lara shouted, her unease having morphed into unshakable determination.

*I'm leaving this rotting prison*

"Did you not hear that thing outside?" Fenner shouted.

Lara and Fenner faced each other in the middle of the stone room. Most of the recruits were awake, muttering whispered concerns at the scene before them, no doubt as confused as Lara was when she woke.

"We need to leave!" Lara protested. "We'll face that thing together!"

"Why?" Jezza asked, butting into the conversation. "Why can't we stay here and wait for our squad?"

"Because it doesn't make sense!" Lara urged. "Remember what Renard said, we get rescued *only if* we're worthy. How does hunkering down like cowards make us worthy?"

"I don't know," Fenner said. "But walking out into the jaws of whatever the Nines is out there, doesn't sound any better!"

The creature outside gave another guttural roar.

"What about the note?" she asked, pulling it back out, the warning message only igniting her sense to flee.

"Where did you get that?" Jezza asked.

"It was on me when I woke up," Lara said.

"How do we know you didn't bring it with you?" Jezza asked.

"What? Why would I do that?"

"What if you're the challenge?" Fenner asked. Lara looked at him like he'd gone crazy. "What if Renard put you up to this? What if you're supposed to convince us to open the door, and we're supposed to say no?"

"Fenner that doesn't make any sense!"

"I don't know. I think we should put it to a vote!" Fenner announced, motioning to the entire room. "Who votes to keep the door shut, *by any means necessary*?"

Fenner raised his hand. The majority of recruits did as well—including Jezza. Lara glanced around the room, heart racing.

"Looks like you're outvoted," Fenner said. "Sit down, Lara."

Lara shook her head, stepping back toward the door. "No."

Fenner lunged forward, grabbing for her. Lara punched him square in the nose, frantically checking to see if the other recruits would attack her.

"Do not touch me!" she shouted. "I am leaving, Fenner! Stay if you want!" Rushing to the door, she used her inner panic to bring strength to her muscles, throwing her shoulder against the door.

She was running out of time.

"Stop!" Fenner yelled, standing up and wiping the blood from his nose.

Pain shot through Lara's arm as she slammed into the stone again—but it budged. Other recruits began gathering around Fenner. Another bellow sounded outside, with a scraping coming from the narrow slit at the back wall. The creature was trying to claw its way inside.

Fenner and two other recruits grabbed Lara and yanked her back.

"You're going to kill us!" Fenner yelled.

Lara spun around, kicking Fenner square in the chest and disabled the other two recruits. Three more rushed her, and her senses spiked. With rapid, intentional attacks Lara took down her still groggy comrades. One fell unconscious from the blow to her head.

Lara spun and rushed the door again, this time with a kick, grunting as she threw all of her strength and bodyweight into the motion. Her right arm was going numb, but she wouldn't stop, throwing her shoulder against the stone again.

She couldn't stop—something in her screamed to flee.

"You're going to die for nothing!" Fenner mocked. "Our blood is on your hands!"

Lara felt his hands grasp at her armor as she ran for the door again.

"Stop her!"

With one final shove, the stone door flung open. Lara fell forward, crashing onto the frozen stone floor at the base of a narrow staircase carved into the mountain. The cold air bit her face as she stood, sprinting up the short staircase and onto the snow-covered mountainside.

Terror gripped her chest as she sucked in the frigid air, snowflakes melting on her skin. Her heart pounded in her ears as a murderous roar sounded behind her. A chill ran down her spine—she didn't dare look back.

Forcing her way through the knee-deep snow, Lara sprinted into the cover of the evergreen canopy, which blocked most of the snowfall. She weaved between the trunks, panic clawing at her mind as she heard the footsteps of a creature's pursuit.

A stone clipped her boot. She fell face first into the unforgiving mountain-side, the sharp rocks and pine needles clawing at her hands and face. With the cold beginning to drain her body heat, Lara scrambled to her feet. A snarling growl came from behind her—much closer than before.

The dread rising in her chest was overwhelming, her lungs burned as they cried for more air. Tears welled in her eyes as she stumbled again. Terror threatened to steal her focus, her movements were becoming sloppy and awkward. Her body was refusing her commands, weakness creeping in like an unwanted fog.

Everything in her told her to run and flee for her life. But as an unrelenting and foreign panic gripped her, she clenched her eyes shut.

*This isn't you*

She was a warrior—a Guardian. And Guardians didn't quit. They didn't back down, and they didn't give in to fear.

*If you are worthy*

Lara stopped, bracing against a narrow trunk to dampen her trembling. The creature's footsteps grew closer—its breathing paired with a deep growl. She wouldn't outrun it, but she didn't have to. She would face it, here and now. Casting aside her fear, she commanded her mind to settle.

Lara spun around, with fists clenched and teeth bared, ready to face death with honor.

But met only empty forest.

She waited, heart beating out of her chest for the creature to emerge and attack. But nothing came. She stared at the scattered trees, the cold white powder covering the forest floor.

Her jaw slackened.

*What in the Nine is happening*

She waited, listening for any indication of the beast. But there was nothing behind her, except her own footprints in the snow.

"Lara!" a voice sounded from down the mountain, inside the forest. It was faint and distant.

"Arlo?" she shouted, turning toward the voice. No response came. Glancing behind her once more, confident nothing was pursuing her, a newfound bravery filled her blood. Perhaps it was nothing more than a test of her will.

With the darkness of dread falling off, Lara resumed her descent and ran deeper into the forest.

Eli marched through the snow, which only worsened the now unbearable aching in his legs. The storm had finally broken, and the gentle warmth of the sun shone down once again. Yet the temperature remained crisp.

His lungs grasped at the thinner air, demanding more oxygen. They all expressed a growing dizziness the further they ascended, which slowed their progress. Arlo had turned their blanket into a makeshift cloak and was tolerating the cold far better. Eli checked the map, tracing his finger along the path they'd come.

"Guys!" he shouted. "It should be just over this rise." Eli pointed to the ridge ahead and to the left.

Spurred forward with new momentum, the three climbed the ever-increasing incline. The screams had ceased near two hours earlier, shortly after leaving their snowy fort. Eli was grateful, but it only made him question why the silence stretched as evening drew closer.

Regardless, they couldn't afford any more delays. Their descent needed to begin by morning, or Eli was positive they wouldn't make it back in time.

*Heavens let Lara be okay*

As they crested the rise, Eli saw what looked like a stone hut buried partially under the ground. Arlo broke into a sprint and ran up to the structure.

"Lara!" Arlo shouted.

The building was a square structure, its walls etched with strange markings and symbols. Snow melted the moment it touched the roof, and a narrow stairway on one side led down to a door—left ajar.

Arlo ran inside. "Lara!"

"Arlo wait!" Eli yelled, following right on his heels. Shira stepped in behind them.

The stench of dead flesh filled Eli's nose the moment he crossed the threshold. The air was thick, turning his stomach into knots with each breath. The same carvings from the outside were etched into the inside walls and ceiling.

But otherwise, it was a plain, stone room with only a narrow slit for a window—and the bones that littered the floor.

"What in the living Hells is this place?" Arlo asked, glancing around.

Eli crouched next to some of the remains. The bones appeared to be at different levels of decay, but all had clearly been dead for some time.

"Some kind of burial?" Eli mused. "A tomb?"

"What kind of tomb holds multiple people in the same space?" Shira asked, remaining by the door. "Are you sure this is the location on the map?"

"I think so," Eli said, standing and pulling the map from his pocket.

Shira strode over, reading the map alongside him. Arlo stared at the ceiling, entranced by the markings.

"Look," Eli said, pointing at the circle marking their goal. "This is the right structure. That cliffside is East of us, and this is where we stopped. It's almost a straight line from the base."

Shira silently double checked the map, tracing their route.

"So, where's Lara?" Arlo asked, restless. His cheerful demeanor had yet to return, having left the moment the challenge began.

"I don't know," Eli said, "but we should search the area. She's got to be around here somewhere. Maybe she left a sign."

"None of these look fresh," Arlo said, gesturing to the bones.

"No," Eli agreed.

He glanced to Shira, a silent question of whether she agreed he'd led them to the right location.

She nodded. "Let's check the area. Either she's somewhere close by—"

"Or she left." Eli finished.

He and Shira turned to leave, Shira stepping outside. But Eli paused, glancing to Arlo who was staring at the pattern on the ceiling again.

"Arlo, let's go."

"Archancy," Arlo whispered.

"What?" Eli asked, stepping to the door.

Arlo shook his head, as if shoving aside an invasive thought. "Where would Lara go?" Arlo asked, striding from the room behind Eli.

But Eli didn't hear his question, having frozen on the spot. Kairah Richter held a blade to Shira's neck, keeping her hostage with an arm wrapped around her stomach. A sickening smile came over Kairah's face as her eyes met Arlo's.

Eli raised his hands in surrender. "What do you want?" he asked, refusing to panic. Shira could eat Kairah alive but seeing the steel against Shira's skin—it was everything he could do to remain where he was.

"Kairah?" Arlo asked.

"I told you regret would find you," Kairah said, spite dripping from every syllable.

"What are you talking about?" Arlo said.

"Shut up!" Kairah shouted. "Where's the medallion?"

Shira remained very still, but her nostrils flared. Eli knew she was already scolding herself for being taken prisoner.

"Why am I not surprised Sol's team is stealing medallions?" Arlo asked, anger building behind his tone. "This program is hard enough, just finish the challenge for rot's sake!"

"Because the strong conquer the weak!" Kairah argued. "Not everyone is worthy to be a Guardian. We found our comrade first, and we deserve to be the best. Each of us took another team to steal from. Besides, the Captains wanted this. They said we would be rewarded handsomely."

"If you think we'll just hand over—" Arlo began.

"Wait," Eli said. "If we give you the medallion, will you tell us what happened to Lara?"

Kairah's smile grew. "Deal," she hissed.

Eli's eyes locked with Shira's. He knew what she was thinking. She would rather fight—rather risk death—than surrender. And he would agree, if it were him with a blade to his neck. But he'd rather guarantee Shira's safety and try to retrieve the medallion from Kairah after the fact. Besides, they hadn't found Lara.

"Shira, give her the medallion," Eli said calmly.

Kairah turned her face toward Shira.

"No," Shira said through clenched teeth.

"Do it," Eli said sternly. "That's an order."

"*Slowly* now," Kairah hissed as Shira moved her hand to a pocket near her right thigh.

Pulling the gold medallion out, Shira lifted it over her shoulder. As Kairah touched the shining metal, Shira threw her body backwards, pushing them both to the ground. Shira yanked Kairah's arm, forcing the blade away from her throat. Kairah screamed as Shira pried herself from her grip, the blade slicing along Shira's right cheek. Blood poured down Shira's face, a piece of her dark hair falling onto the snow.

Shira spun around and engaged Kairah. The narrow entryway provided no room for more than one person to fight at a time. Eli drew his practice sword and tried to find an opening, but the two women were on each other, vying for more blood to be spilled.

Kairah jabbed at Shira's chest with her dagger, but Shira caught her arm and brought it down onto a knee. Kairah cried out in pain as her blade dropped to the ground. She punched Shira in the face, in the exact spot as her laceration.

Shira screamed, letting go of Kairah's arm. The sound of Shira in pain filled Eli's blood with fury, and his vision blurred at the edges. That now familiar rage bellowed within.

Kairah fled, turning and retreating up the stairs, the medallion clutched in her hand. Shira clambered after her on the stone steps, chasing her adversary, but froze as she reached the top, a sharp gasp leaving her lips.

Eli's heart stopped when he saw the knife fly into Shira's back. He spun around to see Rowan standing on top of the stone structure.

# Chapter Thirty-Two

Bearing Lucas's sword over her back once again filled Eva with a sense of calm, dampening her situation as her weapons were returned to her. She carried her travel satchel while Beacon was led to the General's stable. An older male servant approached her as she stood awkwardly in the lobby, awaiting orders. All Malachi told her was to make herself comfortable—an impossible task in this den of snakes.

"Lady Katz," the man said, bowing. He was thin, with sharp and bony joints, which poked at the edges of his decorated light blue tunic—the uniform of all the King's servants. "My name is Sir Lora. I am here to assist you. May I show you to your quarters?"

"Yes, please. I thank you," she responded, her ingrained formality reflexively coming out. Eva followed Lora up the nearby staircase to the second level, lined with various quarters and storage rooms, the doors blended meticulously into the designs. It was difficult to keep note of each one, unless you knew where to look. The golden floral designs were nauseating. Never had she understood her father's design tastes.

The Capitol had changed drastically since she'd seen it last. The layout felt familiar, but many of the interior landmarks from her youth were gone. With each step, the walls closed in as memories surfaced—dark and terrible sensations locked away in the back of her mind crept in.

Sir Lora turned another corner, before arriving at a door carved flush with the wall. The floral pattern surrounded it in such a way that the center of the blooming rose covered the middle of the door. Eva could have appreciated its beauty and design, were she ignorant this place was no more than a prison.

"Here we are, Lady Katz." Lora opened the door gracefully and stepped through. Eva followed him, a breath of relief escaping when she realized it was not her old bedroom. It was surprising how much more luxurious the chambers in The Capitol had become. She grew up around some of the best amenities money could buy, but this was a completely new level of pretentiousness.

Natural light poured from a skylight onto the bed, dressed with a dozen pillows and covered with a purple quilt, accented by golden laces sewn into the edges. Two exceptionally crafted wooden nightstands sat beside the bed, complementing the vibrant painting hanging on the back wall. A quaint, personal washroom was tucked in the corner, along with a modest cooking space, complete with a stove, ice box, and table.

The grandeur of the room turned Eva's stomach and worsened the anxiety itching under her skin. She was a smear of dirt on a fine pair of shoes standing in the beautiful room with her worn military leathers. Throwing her travel bag on the bed, she sat down with a huff on one of the chairs at the table.

"A servant will be in twice daily to change the water in your washroom and refresh your ice box. If you require anything, please do not hesitate to ask any staff members, my Lady. It is so good to have you grace us with your presence once again."

"I thank you, sir Lora, but I do have a question," Eva said politely.

"Of course, my lady," he said, standing stiffly—properly.

"Where is Chosen Lieutenant Cooper?"

"I believe he is arriving here later this evening for the weekly briefing with the War Council. Do you require an audience with him?"

"Yes, actually. General Malachi granted me permission to speak with him regarding a particular matter. However, given how busy they both are, I wanted to ensure that Chosen Lieutenant Cooper was approached directly."

*Because I know father will take his rotting time before making it happen*

"Of course, my lady. I will send word immediately, rest assured. Is there anything else?"

Eva thought for a moment. There was. She had to escape. But that could only happen *after* she spoke with Cooper about the plan. Add to that, if there was even a hint of her planning to flee, she was sure to be placed under guard or house arrest. Everything needed to be very carefully handled—what she said and who she said it to.

"No. I thank you kindly, sir Lora," Eva said with a curt bow.

Lora's steps clicked against the polished floors until he paused, hand on the doorknob. "Apologies, my Lady, I almost forgot. You are encouraged to attend your father's dinner party this evening. He will send a female servant to meet you here and help you prepare."

"Of course," Eva said, dreading the prospect.

At that, Lora left, shutting the door with a light click. Eva's posture immediately relaxed, wiping her face. She always hated the prim and proper nonsense they called etiquette. If they were all liars and cheaters, why pretend to be anything but the dregs of society?

Her boots squeaked on the slippery flooring as she explored the living space, leaving fragments of dirt and dust with each step. She removed Lucas's sword and unbuckled her cloak, tossing both on the bed.

A sigh passed her lips. It was late afternoon at this point. She was sure the servant would be around soon to help her prepare, recalling full well how long her father's 'parties' could last. And if memory served, it took over an hour to dress appropriately for them.

The thought made her sick—like this entire place. With a slump, Eva laid down. Her tired muscles filled with a rush of euphoria at the welcoming sensation of actual cotton fabric and downy feather pillows.

Paralyzed by the plush mattress, Eva's gaze traced the paintings on the ceiling as she contemplated her plan. Perhaps there was some way to notify Jafeth she was safe, and likely wouldn't be coming back. Somewhere along the train of thought, she slipped into a deep slumber.

The chamber's dark and stifling presence was tolerable only from the gentle light emanating from the small glowing stone in the center, resting atop an intricately decorated pedestal. The light warmed Eva's skin, carrying a strange energy within. The walls were constructed entirely of black stone, jagged and shimmering, as if carved from the earth itself. A wide window at the far end opened to a high viewpoint, revealing only darkness beyond, as night had already fallen.

Eva stepped hesitantly toward the pedestal, the stone's presence drawing her forward—pulling at her mind. It was calling her, offering to be the answer to all their questions, their dire problems. Her boots clicked against the stony floor as she reached for the glowing object.

But a hand grasped her wrist, skin pale white with long sharp nails. Eva spun to the unseen figure—a tall menacing form bearing a thick violet robe. And under the shade of their hood—

Eva's eyes snapped open at the knocking on her door.

"Lady Katz?" a female voice called.

Eva sat up, wiping the sleep from her eyes, wondering how long she had been out. Either way, thanks to the luxurious accommodations, she felt quite rested.

"Yes, come in!" she said, loud enough to overcome the thickness of the oak door.

A moment later, a young woman wearing the designated sky-blue dress walked in. Honey-colored hair was kept perfectly retained in a tight ponytail, with a matching blue headband. She was young, by Eva's perception, given her fair skin and the wide-eyed eagerness at which she set about her duties. As she closed the door, and bowed, Eva's attention fell to the white dress in her arms.

*My dress*

"Good evening, Lady Katz. My name is Cass," she said softly. "I am here to help you get dressed, if that is all right."

"Yes, of course," Eva said, rubbing her eyes again as she stood from the bed. A brown and dusty blemish now adorned the otherwise pristine comforter. Eva blushed, glancing at Cass.

"Oh, think nothing of it, Lady Katz. We will have it cleaned before you return." Cass smiled, striding over to the ridiculously spacious dresser in the corner.

"Please, call me Eva," she said, out of habit, before remembering her father's conditions. "At least, when I'm in my quarters."

Cass turned over her shoulder as she brought out undergarments for her. "Of course, as you wish my Lady."

Eva stood next to the bed, waiting for Cass to unpack everything she needed to get dressed.

*Nine Hells, I forgot how many bloody things I have to wear*

"Are you aware of your waist size, Lady Eva?" Cass asked in all seriousness.

Eva smirked. "I *was* at fourteen." Cass looked up, brow wrinkled. "I haven't been here in a while."

Cass gathered Eva's meaning and smiled gently. "That is all right, Lady Eva. I can measure as we go. We have all sizes available."

Eva breathed out, releasing the pressure building in her chest. Cass finished setting out all the clothes and stood before her.

"All right," Cass said. "First, a bath. Please undress."

It had been quite some time since Eva was forced to dress with a dozen different articles of clothing, and in her distracted state getting undressed didn't register as the logical next step.

Her mouth opened. "Um . . ." she stammered.

Cass's eyes grew wide, realizing Eva's discomfort. "Oh, of course, Lady Eva. Please. Here," she said quickly, handing Eva one of the clean undergarments. "Once you're finished bathing, put this on."

Eva grabbed the clothing and entered the washroom, unsure of why she felt so embarrassed. Slamming the door, she leaned against it, staring into the massive mirror across from her—another luxury provided to the wealthy and powerful.

Rebellious strands of white hair lingered over her face, framing her blue eyes which yet held their fierceness, but were shaded by the dark circles underneath. The black leather of her armor was worn and dusty, revealing the evidence of her recent endeavors. The reality of her situation settled over her in the hushed silence. But she wasn't suffocated, nor did she feel claustrophobic as the prison cell latched shut.

She was numb.

If she truly was to remain here forever, then nothing mattered anymore. Losing her own life would be a small price to pay to not rot in this dungeon. Despair wrapped its arms around her, and she didn't have the strength to fight it.

After undressing, Eva watched the clean and warm water fade to a faint brown as she bathed. It felt euphoric to finally be clean, the soft cotton rag brushing across her skin.

In the quiet of the washroom, beneath the dim flickering light, Eva could not quiet her thoughts—fragments of choices made, lines crossed, and the road which led her to this moment.

She abandoned her post. Disobeyed orders. Lied to one of the few souls who trusted her and nearly cost her friend their life. Lucas was gone, and though she refused to acknowledge the truth, he was likely already dead.

Yet, she was dressing for a dinner party.

And as if her dishonor meant nothing, vanished in the steam and silence, she prepared to betray the King—her own father—and unravel the last shred of honor that tethered her to a crumbling ideal of duty.

Her word meant nothing. More fleeting than ashes in the wind.

She now stood between two choices, two ruinous fates, of which neither promised a return. Either she stayed, becoming a vessel emptied of will—an ornament beside the throne, lonely and lifeless. Or she ran. Pursued the last piece of her own heart and forever wore the names she earned like scars: traitor, deserter, liar, and exile.

But this choice—this she understood.

She would not abandon Lucas to the abyss, to a fate worse than death. It was inconceivable for her to remain idle while her people turned their backs on the one person she could not lose. Giving her own life for his was a trade she would make a thousand times over.

Eva understood the betrayal of her father and accepted it. He had never been a father in the first place, more concerned with uplifting his ideals and interests than his own daughter's well-being. She could turn her back on him without a second thought and be all right—live the rest of her life in prison knowing she chose to break her word—to him.

Even exile was familiar, and she understood the price of its presence. Loneliness had long been her only companion. An only child raised in silence, cloistered and strange—a misfit of blood and face. What punishment could the world inflict that she had not already endured?

All of this, these weights—these truths—Eva could carry.

But what she could not understand, as she dressed and stared into her own lifeless eyes, was why she no longer cared. Why beneath it all, after being crushed between duty and doubt, she felt nothing at all.

# Chapter Thirty-Three

Lara whirled around, now lost within the pine woods, gasping for breath as she fought against her returning panic. Something in the back of her mind ignited in horror—something outside herself. Her vision blurred against the cold wind, heart thumping in her chest. The ground was sparse with snow, dried branches and pine needles crunching under her boots as she spun in circles.

"Lara!"

"Over here!"

"Run!"

The voices sounded all around, eradicating her sense of direction. As terror tried to grip her completely, she closed her eyes and covered her ears, screaming for the voices to stop. Fighting against the dread, she tried to breathe, to focus, to gather her bravery, but it was as if it had a mind of its own.

Lara clenched her jaw. She was stronger than this—braver than this. Laranna Nightingale would never cower in horror, and she would not betray her promise by giving up now. She faced that creature. Whatever this was could also be felled. Fate cursed her to be a street urchin, but she claimed her own destiny as a Guardian. She would not die in these woods. She would fight with fists and teeth.

As she opened her eyes, ready to continue forward, the forest went silent. The voices stopped. Lara gazed at a woman in a scarlet dress, standing next to a broad tree, not twenty paces away. The woman stood six feet tall, with pale and perfect skin. The dress rippled along her feminine frame in silky waves, matching her crimson-painted nails. Her face was something from a dream—her beauty beyond measure with soft, inviting eyes.

"Come, my dear," the woman whispered, a gentle smile on her rosy lips. But the voice was close—inches away—as if the woman spoke directly into Lara's mind. "I will save you."

Lara couldn't avert her eyes as she took a step forward. Someone was calling her name in the distance, and it sounded familiar, but Lara ignored it. She didn't need help any longer.

Eli's world ground to a halt as his senses tried to process what happened. A blade protruded from Shira's back, her body rigid from the pain as she fell to the ground atop the stairs. His mind raced, every instinct commanding him to sprint to Shira's side. But he kept his focus and turned around.

Atop the stone structure, Rowan stood with a menacing glare. He held another dagger, having thrown the first at Shira, primed to jump onto Arlo's back. Eli acted before his mind could argue self-preservation, and shoved Arlo back into the structure. Arlo's face filled with shock, entirely unaware of the threat above him.

As his friend stumbled backwards, Eli watched Rowan fall toward him, knife aimed at his throat. Eli's training kicked in, his muscles recalling every minute of practice, his new reflexes and strength coming forth.

He grabbed Rowan's hand that held the blade and allowed himself to fall backwards, following Rowan's momentum. All of Eli's focus narrowed on keeping the dagger away from his throat, knowing Arlo was only moments from aiding him.

Rowan strained to press the blade further with his body weight, face burning red as it contorted in anger. Eli held his breath, veins building in his neck as he fought against Rowan's strength. The knife gently glided toward Eli's throat, the tip piercing his skin.

The pain registered moments before Arlo's face appeared over Rowan's shoulder. Arlo grabbed Rowan's collar, spinning him around, and delivered a decisive blow to Rowan's chin. Arlo drew Shira's long knives, no longer holding back against their comrade.

Arlo sliced at Rowan, who ducked underneath the attack. The long knife sparked as it grated against the stone. Rowan, now outmatched, leaped toward the stairs and swung wide for Arlo's midsection. Arlo jumped back, the blade grazing his chest. Eli clambered to his feet as Rowan sprinted up the stairs after Kairah.

Everything faded away as Eli ran to Shira's side. She was on her knees, rigid and gasping from the pain.

Arlo sprinted past them. "Rotting coward!" Arlo shouted. "Where is Lara?"

"Arlo, wait!" Eli yelled.

He stopped, gripping the long knives as Rowan and Kairah disappeared into the snowy mountainside. He cursed, but strode back and knelt beside Eli, who held Shira in his lap face down.

Eli swallowed, examining Shira's wound. The dagger was buried deep, near her right shoulder blade. It most certainly punctured her lung, judging by her labored breathing.

"I need to pull the knife out," Eli said, "but I can't without the medical supplies."

Arlo took the travel bag off, throwing the contents aside and dug for the medical kit. He pulled out a small cloth bag, colored gray and red, and unclasped the front buckle, setting it next to Eli.

"Wait!" Shira gasped, taking a deep ragged breath. Eli froze, her pained voice cracking his composure. That fury inside growled, wanting to tear Rowan's face off—hear him plead for his life.

Eli held her shoulders as Shira tried to sit up. "Stop! Stop! Don't move!"

"Lara went that way, into the woods," Shira said, her voice cracking. She grimaced with every breath.

They both scanned the pine trees and brush, which stretched beyond their sight.

"How do you know?" Arlo asked.

"Footprints. I saw them . . . before Kairah . . ." Her erratic breathing stole her voice.

Eli turned to Arlo. "I've got her. Go find Lara. When you do, head back to the Citadel. Do *not* come back here and risk finding Sol's squad."

"No, I'm not leaving you alone! We stand a better chance together."

"No! If Kairah returns with Rowan, or Soren wants a second chance we're both dead and it doesn't matter."

"What about the medallion?" Arlo asked.

"It means nothing now. Just get to Lara and to safety, that's an order!"

Arlo shook his head. "You've been squad leader one day and I'm already sick of hearing you bark orders."

"Arlo." Eli's voice changed, losing its urgency, but gaining a calm authority. "I'm serious."

Arlo drew a breath, glancing around, torn between two impossible choices. "If I don't see you guys at the bottom I'll hunt you down myself."

He stood and sprinted into the forest, roughly following the footprints. Still bent forward, Shira's chest heaved with each breath. Eli noted her pallor already changing. He couldn't focus on the blood dripping down her armor, or the agony in her face.

"Shira, I'm going to pull out the—"

"Just shut up and do it," she said, fear in her voice.

Eli swallowed, demanding the shaking in his hands to cease. Shira needed him, and he would not abandon her. He grabbed the clean cloth, ensuring the cleansing tonic was available. He laid Shira down in front of him and wrapped his hand around the knife.

"One. Two!" He yanked the blade from her back, immediately pressing the gauze into the open wound as Shira's scream filled his ears. Commanding his emotion to recede, he lifted the cloth to expose the bleeding wound long enough to pour the antiseptic solution over the open flesh.

Shira's hands clawed at the earth, and Eli's muscles trembled. The solution bubbled as it made contact with the contaminated wound. Eli used the hunting knife to tear open her armor around the injury, exposing the area. He grabbed the bandages and shoved them into the wound, one after the other.

Shira's whimpers ceased as she held her breath, baring her teeth. Once the bleeding was stopped, Eli carefully wrapped the remaining cloth around her chest, holding the bandages inside the wound. He laid her down and frantically packed up the needed supplies, leaving anything that would not help Shira. He sheathed his broadsword and buckled the travel bag shut.

Eli gently turned her head, inspecting the laceration to her face. It was relatively shallow but would likely leave a scar. It had trimmed a section of her hair, the cut running along her cheek all the way to her ear. A new swell of dread rose in his chest as he inspected the side of Shira's head.

"Eli," she whispered, her breaths becoming wet as her face grew more pale. "Yes?"

"How bad?" she asked, eyes closed as she spoke.

"It's okay. It could be worse," he said dryly, adjusting the hair around her right ear as he cleaned the wound.

"You're a terrible liar, remember? Just tell me, please."

He paused. The words felt like acid on his tongue. "The blade slipped between your ribs. It may have punctured your right lung. If we don't get you back to the Citadel in the next few hours, you'll drown in your own blood."

She took a moment to process the situation, opening her eyes to slits. "Pathetic way to go out."

"Well, fortunately for you, I'm your squad leader and I'm not going to let that happen. I'm giving you an order to stay alive," he said, in all seriousness, biting down on his fear.

She gave a pained laugh. Her chest hitched unevenly, one side rising, the other barely moving. Blood bubbled at the corner of her mouth before she sat forward to cough.

"Arlo was right, you do like giving orders."

"I expect a proper answer, recruit," he teased, despite everything in him screaming to move.

"Yes, sir Danon," she said, some strength returning to her voice.

At once, he threw the travel bag over his shoulder and pulled Shira to her feet, bearing her weight as much as possible. She clutched the right side of her chest, clawing at her armor as if she could tear the pain out with every sharp and shallow breath.

Eli ignored the burning of his own throat—the straining of his muscles. Nothing of his own discomfort mattered. He prayed that his strength would not fail him, desperation fueling his movements as they started down the mountain.

Arlo sprinted as fast as his legs could carry him, darting through the forest as he dodged the tree trunks. Fire burned in his chest, both in fear for Lara's safety, and from the cold, thin air. This pace was unsustainable, but he fought through the lightheaded sensation, refusing to slow down. Following the footsteps was easy at first, but now the snow became extremely thin and sparse beneath the forest canopy.

He stopped, not for his own ragged breathing, but to find the tracks again. Scanning the ground, all he saw was pine needles and dirt. He grunted and cursed. He wasn't a tracker. And had never been hunting a day in his life—a born and raised city kid.

"Lara!" he shouted.

Holding his breath, he waited for a response. None came. He yelled again but got the same result. Needing to keep moving, he jogged forward, desperately searching the ground to find some sign of Lara's path. He caught sight of a footprint in the mud, and another a few feet ahead of a broken branch.

*Rotting Hells, I don't know what I'm doing*

"Lara!" he shouted again, following the trail but glancing in all directions.

He heard a scream, to his left. Unlike what they were hearing earlier.

*Lara*

It was her, he was sure of it. Summoning all his might, he sprinted toward her voice, repeating her name—the desperate cry.

"Lara!"

Dizziness surged again in unison with the lethargy gripping his legs. Numbness crept through his limbs, and the burning in his chest intensified. Fingers white, Arlo pushed past his limits, driven forward by sheer will alone.

Not knowing if he was still heading in the right direction, he stopped again, searching the ground. A feeling of hopelessness began to enshroud him, panic clouding his thoughts. Whispers blended with a creeping sense of danger lifting the hairs on his neck.

"Over here!"

"Arlo help!"

"Where are you going?"

"Wrong way!"

The whispers became louder, turning into distant shouting. Arlo spun around, trying to find the source of the voices. None of them sounded like Lara.

"Hey!"

"You!"

"Over here!"

"Run away!"

Arlo turned to the direction of one of the voices. His eyes caught the shadow of a figure retreating behind a thick bush. He drew Shira's long knives as more figures danced behind every tree—surrounding him.

He burned his panic into rage. "Come on!" he shouted, sprinting to one of the figures as it disappeared behind a—

Nothing.

*What in the Hells*

"Hey!"

"Over here!"

"You missed!"

Frustration built in his chest.

*What is happening*

"Lara!" he shouted again but received no response.

Arlo shook his head, ignoring the voices as they clamored for his attention. Retreating to his previous spot, he found Lara's footprints again. Against every instinct in his own mind, Arlo sprinted into the woods, following her trail.

A hot stabbing pain ignited in Eli's neck as he refused to let go of Shira's arm, draped over his shoulders. Her pallor worsened each moment, and she was bearing less weight.

"Hey! Shira!" he said, squeezing her arm, shaking her with his other hand, soaked with her blood.

"What?" she whispered.

"Talk to me! Stay awake!"

It was all he could do to speak rather than simply gasp for air. The oxygen thickened as they descended the mountain, but he was at his limit.

"I can't."

"Yes, you can! Come on! Yell at me! Call me an idiot!"

"You're not an idiot."

"Yes, I am! I still can't beat you at sparring! What am I doing wrong?"

Eli bellowed at the rising panic, the doubts which crept at the edges of his thoughts. Losing her now—he couldn't think on it. Not while he drew breath.

*We will make it*

"Nothing," Shira breathed.

"Come on, Shira!" he yelled, stumbling across a loose patch of gravel. "We had a deal! You promised!"

"You think too much," she mumbled.

"When?"

"You overthink it." Shira's strong and determined voice was gone. She tried to speak, her lips moving, but nothing came out—only a wheeze and a thread of blood.

Eli strained to listen over his own breathing, the pounding in his head, the rocks crunching under his feet. At this point on the mountain, the snow was only a thin layer of white but proved to only slicken their steps.

*We need to move faster*

"Overthink what?" he said, cursing his own inability to move the mountain out of his way, because screaming at something was easier than listening to her fade.

Shira didn't answer.

"Shira!"

"Eli."

*Don't you dare*

"Keep talking!" he demanded.

"I can't."

"Yes, you can! What are we looking for? What is the Council hiding?"

". . . Guardians . . . help . . ."

Shira's voice trailed as her feet gave out. They stumbled, falling to the ground as her full body weight now rested upon him. The rocks bit into Eli's back as he wrapped himself around her—protection from the shards of stone. Shira tumbled limply in his grasp before they slid to a stop against the slope.

He turned her in his arms, pressing his fingers to her neck. Eyes closed, Shira's heartbeat thumped in response—only just.

"Shira!" he said, shaking her body, cradling her head in his lap. "Shira!"

"Eli," she breathed.

"Hey!" he said, glancing down the mountain. They had hours to go.

*Bleeding Hells*

*This will not happen*

"Shira! Stay with me! Stay awake!"

Eli fumbled with the traveling bag, tipping it upside down and dumping the contents onto the hillside. Finding the tiny bottle with the blue liquid, he bit off the cork. He wasn't sure if the tonic was for pain or not, but he was desperate to do something—anything.

"Eli," Shira breathed.

"I'm here."

"I'm sorry."

Eli's heart skipped, paralyzed at the words slipping past her pale lips. Everything was different, and he felt the earth tilt beneath him at the spoken truth. But he refused to think about it, to dwell on the realities beyond this moment, as her life hung in the balance.

He held the bottle to her mouth. Most of the liquid poured down her face, and she swallowed once before coughing. He cursed. It wasn't working.

*We won't make it*

He scoured the contents of the bag, willing a solution to be present. Throwing the flint, the torch, the rope, everything that could do nothing for Shira, he searched for an answer. He would do anything to save this woman's life.

When he had given up hope, he saw the one item he almost didn't bring: a vial of Leer Fly venom. A toxin from a local insect commonly used to keep someone awake. It gives them energy, making their mind sharper and their heartbeat faster.

*Please shining Heavens*

The bottle was no larger than his pinky finger, melted shut. Eli broke the tip of the vial—the sharp glass cutting his hand. He leaned Shira's head back and poured the green liquid into her mouth.

Without waiting for her to respond, he threw the empty vial and picked her up. Abandoning everything and calling upon whatever strength he had left, Eli ran down the mountain.

# Chapter Thirty-Four

E va's white dress flowed elegantly down her exposed shoulders, hugging her hips and waist as it kissed the floor. Her white hair nearly shined, brushed and decorated with jewels glistening in the firelight of the lanterns now lit on the walls. Cass applied facial powder to hide the dark circles under her eyes, and any unsightly blemishes on her otherwise pristine skin.

She was beautiful—more so than she ever dared to believe. The white dress shimmered like moonlight, turning her into something ethereal, almost bridal. It was ironic, when nothing about her felt like a bride. She was a wolf, about to dance among the unsuspecting sheep.

"Thank you, Cass," Eva said, turning toward her maidservant. Cass was tidying the room and putting away the unneeded garments. When she started unpacking the travel bag, Eva didn't argue. It couldn't appear as though she expected to leave.

"You look beautiful, Lady Eva," Cass said politely. "The event starts in just a few minutes. If you need anything further, please let me know."

Eva smiled as Cass bowed and left. The glow from the skylight was fading. She moved to her armor and unbuckled one of her blades. She lifted her dress and strapped it to the inside of her thigh—just in case.

With a deep breath, she exited her quarters. Lanterns adorned the hallway in equal intervals, warming the otherwise empty space. Eva turned left, strolling a bit awkwardly in her heeled shoes. They were terribly uncomfortable and the worst thing to wear if you wished to do anything other than sit down. She pleaded with Cass about wearing anything else, even going barefoot, but Cass *strongly* insisted.

As she rounded the corner, a soft roar of conversation reached her ears. Stepping up to the otherwise restricted landing which overlooked the war room, Eva saw the war room had been refitted to contain multiple round tables, as well as an open area for dancing. Each table was covered with a white silk cloth, accompanied by enormous bouquets of blue and yellow flowers in the center.

The shimmering glass chandelier held numerous candles, casting a gentle orange light throughout the room. A few musicians sat in the corner, quietly playing the native songs of Aniyan culture. Guests were still pouring in the front, despite the room being quite crowded already.

Eva turned toward the stairs to her right, scanning the crowd as she descended each step. It was assumed she wouldn't know any of the guests. Her father rarely invited the same people twice, unless they required an extra level of bribery and mingling to align their interests.

Malachi of course possessed his own private circle who visited more often, but those instances were never an open gathering. Typically, it involved them retreating to Malachi's private study and diving into bottles of firewater and tobacco.

She paused on the bottom step for a moment, standing a head taller than the crowd, searching the faces for her target.

"You look beautiful, Moonbeam."

Eva spun toward the feminine voice, her heart soaring in surprise. That same loving and soft smile filled her vision, with a few additional wrinkles on the familiar face. Grayed hair was held tightly in a well-decorated bun, adorned with two silver rods.

She ran over and embraced Glorana Vanwick—her guardian angel. "Nana!"

Glorana laughed, holding Eva gently. "Oh, my dear, sweet Evalynn."

Glorana smelled of lavender soap, her dress the same light blue color of the servants. Despite Malachi commonly using her to carry out many of his punishments, Glorana became Eva's saving grace. From slipping her favorite snacks through the door, to setting up a private dance for her and Lucas for her tenth birthday, Glorana had carefully watched over Eva in her childhood. She was the closest thing to a mother, or now a grandmother, she had ever known.

Eva stepped back, holding Nana's hands, a wide smile on her face. Her eyes burned, praying she wouldn't cry for fear of messing up Cass's hard work.

"I'm so glad to see you!" she said, taking in Glorana's appearance, memories flooding back.

"Oh, when I heard you had come back to The Capitol, I knew I needed to make sure to find you," Glorana said with excitement.

"Aren't you serving?"

"Oh no. My duties have dwindled to minor things, mostly overseeing the newer servants," Glorana explained. "Now, tell me everything!"

Eva's face fell, unable to speak all she wished. So much had happened since she left eight years before, she barely knew where to start. And if she could possibly prevent it, she wanted to keep Glorana out of her plans. If an escape plan was to be attempted, no suspicion could be aimed at her oldest friend.

"Well, there's a lot to tell," Eva said, letting two guests slip by her and ascend the stairs.

Glorana paused, glancing into the thick crowd among the open room, before guiding Eva to an empty table. The air held a constant roar of conversation, but not overbearing. It was considered inappropriate for guests of nobility to speak loudly—enthusiastically for that matter.

Glorana pulled a chair out for her, an old habit no doubt. It should be Eva performing the act of respect. Nevertheless, she sat down across from her Nana, who held her hand gently on the table.

"All right, Evalynn," Glorana said, a gleam in her eyes. "Tell me of your adventures."

She didn't know where to start. "Well, I was recently stationed at Manoach on patrol duty. It's a wonderful little town. I can really see myself enjoying it there."

"Oh, yes! I've been there once, years ago when I worked for a traveling healer. Such nice people. Is there still that inn on the main road? Oh, what was it called . . ." She touched her chin. "The White Horse?"

Eva smiled. "The Stallion Inn."

"Oh, right! Good! That place was so lovely, and they made the best roasted pig I've ever tasted!"

"Nana," she muttered, swallowing the knot in her throat, "I have to tell you something."

Glorana's brow wrinkled, her silver eyes holding no judgment.

"Lucas is missing," she said.

Shock engulfed Glorana's face. "What happened, dear?" she asked, sitting closer.

Glorana knew better than anyone the bond that Eva and Lucas shared. She had smuggled him into the mansion on multiple occasions, all to Eva's great delight. And they had spent countless hours talking about plans for the future with Lucas, which Glorana had said was her favorite part.

"He was leading a raid on Heika," she said in hushed tones. "It went badly, and now he's missing. Maybe dead. We don't know where they took him, if they took him at all."

Eva's posture fell alongside her gaze, unable to hide the weight on her heart.

Glorana studied her. "That's why you're here," she whispered, never missing a thing. "I wondered. You came to ask your father for help."

Eva nodded.

"And he's making you stay here as payment."

She nodded again.

"Evalynn, you cannot. Your leaving was the single greatest act of bravery, and I firmly believe it saved your future. Surely there are other ways to find Lucas."

It was only by Glorana's help that she was able to escape and join the military before her father could forbid it. They spent nights planning it, weeks before Eva's fourteenth birthday. While the rest of the servants were decorating and preparing for guests, Glorana sat with her and drew up plans to escape.

Despite her father's position and influence, he could not overrule her taking the oaths to serve the Legion. And Eva knew Malachi would never ask that she return, nor formally give the order for her to be stationed at The Capitol. That would be a show of weakness on his part—unacceptable.

"I didn't have a choice then. And I don't now," Eva whispered, a single tear falling. "I'm sorry I left you."

"Oh, Moonbeam, stop!" Glorana said, squeezing her hand. "I never, *for one moment*, felt abandoned by you. I was overjoyed that my little white bird finally flew into the sky. I always wondered what adventures you were on, but I never doubted that you would thrive. You were always filled with such grit and joy."

Eva smiled, before her gaze fell. "Not everything worked out, Nana. And I've earned myself a poor reputation for some of the things I've done."

"I'm sure you had every reason to do what you did," she said, shuffling her chair closer. "Now, tell me more of your adventures."

Eva straightened but grinned at the mischievous gleam in Glorana's eyes. Their conversation never slowed for the duration of the evening. Eva always wondered what happened after she left. Apparently, Malachi threw quite the temper tantrum, carrying a sour mood for weeks afterwards. But, as she predicted, he never pursued her. Besides, it was *his* edict that the Legion could accept recruits as young as fourteen.

Glorana's stories were so colorful, Eva's laughter bounced above the noise of the room. A few guests threw sour glances in her direction, but she couldn't care less. In her mind there was no one else in the room but her and her Nana.

The crowd lessened after supper was served but otherwise remained steady, with newcomers filtering in the door as the night drew on. Eva regaled Glorana with recent events, excluding her more serious acts of treason and desertion. There was so much to tell, not having seen her for so long. Eva's spirit was floating. She was a child again, dressed like a noble with the heart of a warrior, sitting with the only woman in the world that truly knew her.

As they spoke, Eva searched the sea of faces every few minutes, eventually spotting her target speaking with a foreign guest. Standing at a modest height, his sandy hair was tied in a bun and blended smoothly with his full beard. His smile was warm, and he carried himself with all the practiced discipline of a nobleman with a career in the military. Eva knew his identity by his formal military armor, and the yellow fabric tied to his sword's pommel.

She apologized to Glorana and excused herself to meet Chosen Lieutenant Cooper, but Glorana grabbed her arm.

"Now wait just a minute, young lady," she said. Eva sat back down. "Where exactly are you scurrying off to?"

"Nana." Eva started. "I can't say."

Glorana's eyes narrowed. "Boar spit."

"I'm serious."

"And so am I, young lady. You've never slipped anything by me, and I'm not about to tarnish a perfect record."

Eva bit her lip. She would never forgive herself for dragging Glorana down with her. "What do you know about the Citadel?"

"Very little," Glorana said in all seriousness. "Only rumors and likely what you already know."

"What about"—Eva glanced around, leaning closer—"these stones the Zentari are looking for? Obelisks they're called. They contain magic and can grant Guardians power."

Images of Heika flashed in her mind.

"Obelisks," Glorana mused, tasting the word. "I've read that before, somewhere."

"Where?" Eva asked quickly.

"I don't remember."

Eva breathed out her nose.

"Besides," Glorana continued. "I would never betray the King's confidence by saying I've seen references to such things while cleaning his bedchamber."

Eva's eyes widened, making a mental note. "Why does he care?"

"I don't know. But he seems convinced it's worth his attention. He has hundreds of letters and papers about those things, and something called Archancy."

"Lucas mentioned the same thing, but he thought it was hearsay. What is it?"

"I don't know, dear," Glorana admitted, "but whatever it is, tread *very* cautiously. Your father is chasing after it with more zeal than I've ever seen. And you know as well as I how ruthless he can be in his obsessive pursuits."

Eva's mind turned, but she set aside the restless thoughts.

*One thing at a time*

"Thank you, Nana." She squeezed Glorana's hand and stood, striding slowly toward Chosen Lieutenant Cooper. Summoning all her charm, she stood next to the two men, waiting for their attention to break to her.

Cooper was speaking with the same foreign dignitary from earlier, still dressed in his bright yellow and blue robes. His dark skin accented the color handsomely and his wide smile was nothing less than infectious and inviting. After a moment, Cooper noticed Eva waiting. He turned his attention to her as the foreign nobleman bid goodbye with a bow.

"Good evening," Cooper said with a grin. "You must be Lady Katz."

He reached for Eva's hand, which she offered in return. They intertwined their fingers in the traditional Aniyan welcome—the custom when greeting a woman of nobility.

"Good evening, Chosen Lieutenant Cooper. It is an honor."

"Oh, please, call me Leo. I know you hate formalities," Leo said, snagging a glass from the tray of a passing servant.

"I'm afraid you have me at a disadvantage then," she said, her smile genuine.

"Well, I've read enough reports about you from Lieutenant Drax to get a good idea." Eva's lips pursed. "Oh, don't worry, I don't believe a word of it. Drax can be more than over-the-top."

She smirked. "Well thank you for coming to my aid."

"Of course. I saw you speaking to that woman, the servant. Do you know her?"

"Yes," Eva said. "She practically raised me."

"Really?" he said, glancing at Glorana. "It must be nice to finally catch up after being away for so long."

"Indeed."

Cooper's eyes narrowed. "You're not one for parties, are you?"

She shifted. "How could you tell?"

"Well, I saw you descend the stairs with a glare that could kill a dire boar, only to sit in one place and speak with a single person for the past few hours."

Eva's gaze locked to his. "You're either very perceptive, Leo, or I was being watched."

Leo shrugged with a smirk, stepping aside as a guest squeezed through the crowd. "A bit of both, I suppose. When I was told you'd be here I wanted to see if you were everything Drax made you out to be."

Eva rolled her eyes. "I suppose my return has already spread throughout the entire Capitol."

"Well, most things never change," he mused. "Besides, you don't give yourself enough credit. The princess finally returning after eight years away? It's quite the event."

Eva took a breath, shunning the swirling thoughts in her head.

"So yes," Cooper continued, "I was watching you. But it's also hard to miss a beautiful woman."

Cooper took a drink. Eva blushed, oddly taken aback by the casual compliment.

"And how do you feel I stand up to your expectations?" she asked, eyebrow raised.

"Thus far? Exceedingly." He smiled, pausing for a moment. "Now, given we have both agreed that I am perceptive, why don't we get to the part where you ask what it is you approached me for."

"Who's to say I didn't simply come to pay my respects?"

Cooper gave a breathy laugh. "I think you and I both know you are not a woman caring for a political crowd."

She glanced around.

*Not here*

"Perhaps we can speak more privately?" she asked.

Cooper's gaze danced behind her. "How about up there?" he asked, jutting his chin to the upstairs balcony overlooking the room—sparse with guests.

Eva nodded and stepped aside, waiting for him to lead. He walked forward and offered his arm. Cheeks burning at the uncomfortable gesture, she took it, knowing refusal would be wildly inappropriate. If nothing else, it may help to stroke his ego, if his flattery was indeed nothing but ego.

As Cooper led the way through the crowd, Eva caught Glorana's subtle wink. She shot back a pointed look, hoping to make it clear this wasn't a romantic pursuit. They ascended the stairs and strolled to the secluded edge of the balcony.

Leo leaned on the banister, cradling his drink. "All right, I'm all ears."

Eva waited, weighing the Chosen Lieutenant's sincerity. She needed to be very cautious of her words, but this was also likely a one-time opportunity.

"Have you spoken to General Malachi about my request?" she asked.

"Your request?" he asked, brow knitted. "No. And why do you call your father by his title?"

"He is the General and you are in the Legion. I am required to speak about superior officers by their title."

Leo rolled his eyes. "An answer I'd figure would come from the daughter of the King and General. But not entirely the truth, is it?"

She waited, unsure of how much to tell. This was Malachi's right hand. If Cooper—for one moment—thought anything unusual was happening, he could report her immediately.

"It's a long story, Leo."

"How long? We've got time."

Eva clenched her jaw. "My father and I have rarely seen eye to eye."

"Ha," Cooper said. "My dear Lady Katz, you insult me. You forget I've been working alongside your father for the past six years."

"Then why ask if you already know?"

He shrugged. "I wanted to know your side of things."

Eva kept her guard up, possessing no trust for the man before her. And yet, he carried an aura of honesty—a humble man not easily swayed by the politics around him.

"My childhood was not pleasant," she said curtly. "I see Malachi as far more of a general than a father."

Cooper's expression softened. "I can't imagine."

"It's fine," Eva said, lifting her chin.

The corners of Cooper's mouth turned down. "Fair enough."

"What about you?" she asked. "How did you climb to the coveted rank of Chosen Lieutenant at such a young age?"

Cooper smiled. "Flattery will get you nowhere, my dear lady. But the truth is, I know enough people. I was a good little warrior, but at this rank, it's more about who you know than anything else."

Eva sighed, hating how much the politics of her kingdom revolved around individuals concerned with their own interests when so many of her people were suffering.

"All right," he said, catching her growing indifference. "What's your request?"

"It's the reason I'm here," she said, her formality dropping. "My friend Lucas was leading a raid on Heika, the one you and Malachi approved a few weeks ago."

Leo's brow ruffled. "I don't recall that."

"Lucas told me Drax had presented the plan to attack Heika because of the recent withdrawing of troops from the area. He said Drax had the plan approved by you or Malachi."

□"Hmm. It must have been your father, because I don't recall this at all. The withdrawal of warriors, sure, but nothing about Heika. But that's not out of the ordinary, mind you. The General and I approve so many different orders, it's not unusual for he or I to approve some without consulting each other."

Eva shoved down the anxiety which tried to gain purchase.

*Drax better pray to the Nine Hells if he lied*

"I came here and made a deal with General Malachi," she said, lowering her voice. "If I agreed to remain here, he would send someone to find Lucas."

□Leo paused, piecing together the unspoken facts. "Okay."

□"I asked him to allow me to go on the mission."

□"But he said no, because he knows you'd never return, and he wants you here."

She answered his question with silence. "Please, Leo," she said. "I need to get into the Citadel. Help me save my best friend."

Cooper straightened, taking another drink. Eva's heart thundered.

□"Well, Lady—" He caught himself. "Can I call you Evalynn?"

She shifted but nodded.

"Well, Evalynn, as a matter of fact, we have recent intelligence that may be just what you need."

# Chapter Thirty-Five

With each step Lara took toward the scarlet woman, longing and desire overflowed from within, the fear and panic of the Crucible melting underneath the torrent of emotion. Nothing else mattered. Everything gave way to quiet peace, as if this strange woman was truly able to save her, to carry her away from here and all of Adiel.

Lara took another step, and the woman held her hands outstretched, a softness beckoning her closer.

"That's right," the voice whispered in her mind. "Come, my dear. Rest."

Fenner was wrong. *This* was the challenge—finding her. To have the courage to break out of the structure, overcome her fear of whatever was outside, and fall into the arms of saving grace.

Lara reached out her hand. Fear was now completely gone, giving way to joy, a contentment as vast as the sky and as beautiful as the first bloom of spring. Lara would have everything she wanted, everything she needed. Discomfort would be relegated to memory, denial would cease to exist. With but a whisper of a request, the entire world would be hers.

Lara's fingertip touched the woman's hand, her skin warm and soft as it enveloped her own.

"Your worries are over," the woman said in a sweet, sultry tone. She slowly clasped her hand around Lara's, beckoning her closer. Lara closed her eyes as she stepped into the warm embrace, falling into the tide of euphoria.

"Lara!" A voice called.

She didn't care. It was probably a trick from that creature. She'd won—beaten the challenge and found the answer to all things.

Fatigue enveloped her, exhaustion seeping into her bones. With shaking muscles, and waning strength, Lara felt grateful to rest within the arms of peace.

Arlo slammed into the creature with his right shoulder, throwing it sideways as it screeched with an inhuman shriek. Lara fell to the ground and Arlo prayed she was all right.

The creature righted itself on its short hind legs, its long arms giving it balance as it stood on all fours. Gray, hairless skin covered its near skeletal form, bearing eyes of complete blackness. With a guttural growl it opened its maw, revealing rows of ebony teeth, as black saliva dripped down its chin. A hairless tail flicked behind it, dragging on the ground.

It stood up on its legs, spreading its arms wide, howling at Arlo. His ears rang, vision blurring at the edges, and a haunting whisper sounded in his own thoughts.

*"Flee."*

Everything in Arlo screamed to run—to save himself. Yet he stayed, standing between that thing and Lara. Shira's long knives weren't very sharp, but they'd have to do. He spared a glance to Lara's unconscious form and readied himself.

The creature charged, galloping on the rocky ground using its long arms as another pair of legs. It raised its right claw, swiping at him with frightening speed. Arlo skillfully lunged toward the creature, stepping in close. The claws missed their mark, but his blade found the creature's arm. It yelped as black ooze spilled from the wound.

The creature grabbed the back of Arlo's armor and tossed him near effortlessly. He landed fifteen feet away on his back, the wind knocked from his lungs.

*Bleeding Hells*

*What is that thing*

Before Arlo recovered, the creature was on top of him. A scream escaped its mouth, reminiscent of a human—like the ones they'd been hearing. Arlo screamed as its claws plunged into his left shoulder. The creature's vile black spit dripped onto his face as it leaned closer to him.

Tiny slits for a nose flexed as it sniffed him. The voice in his head spoke again, hissing like water sizzling in a pan.

*"Your skin will nourish me."*

Arlo clenched his jaw and stabbed the creature's belly with his blade, unable to move his left arm. The beast roared and leaped off him, the pain in his shoulder burning like an acid. He shifted Shira's other long knife from his now injured left arm to his right.

The creature yanked the blade from its belly with a shriek, before tossing it far into the woods—lost. It stood facing him, and Arlo swore the creature grinned.

Lara floated in pure darkness, despite everything feeling weighted and slow. All she wanted was to rest. The joy and euphoria had left, and she now felt alone—isolated.

A voice sounded.

*Someone screamed*

The hard, uneven ground pressed against her side as the sensation of gravity returned, the veil of unconsciousness easing. Lara opened her eyes to slits, trying to focus on the blurred image before her. The white sky peeked through the overhead canopy, and something flashed to her left.

Movement.

*Someone's here. Was that them shouting*

*Maybe it's Arlo*

She couldn't deny her attraction for him anymore, if she was being honest. But it didn't matter. They were friends, and it could never be anything more. Though his kindness was refreshing. And having someone near—someone consistent—filled a hole in her heart she'd forgotten was even there.

The same voice.

*Someone is screaming. Someone is hurt.*

Lara pulled herself from her stupor, slowly sitting up at the protest of her blazing joints. Blurred vision and grogginess prevented her from focusing on whoever was—

Another scream.

No, a roar. Some*thing* was here.

Her heart rate rose, the tendrils of sleep slipping away. Lara stumbled forward as she stood, grabbing the nearby tree for a brace. Standing on aching muscles, she shook her head, her vision finally clearing.

*Arlo*

A tall gray creature held him by the neck with a single arm. Arlo thrashed, trying to break its grip, blood dripping down his left shoulder and forehead. Lara, summoning her strength, ran awkwardly toward the creature. Its head slowly turned to her, and a voice entered her mind again. But this was different than before—indifferent. Nothing but death.

*"Lay down and die."*

Lara pressed forward, the steadiness of her gait improving. As she neared, it dropped Arlo, who landed with a harsh thud. He grunted, pulling himself back to his feet with a protective fierceness as the creature turned toward her. Lara saw Arlo pick up a blade from the ground. Keeping the creature's attention on her, Arlo lunged at it, slicing its right shoulder.

The beast roared and swiped at Arlo who jumped back, its claws tearing across his chest. It turned toward him, slowly stalking its prey once again.

"Lara!" Arlo shouted, tossing the long knife to her. The creature paid no mind as she caught the blade and came at it from behind. It bellowed a sickening screech as she plunged the blade into its back.

The beast reared back, swiping at Lara. Searing pain rushed through her side as its claws found their mark. She tossed the long knife back to Arlo. He wasted no time, lunging for the knife as it tumbled on the forest floor, and plunged it into the creature's neck. A muted screech escaped its jaws as it reached for the blade. Its other arm grabbed Lara by the stomach and tossed her from the ground. She landed with a thud, her head spinning.

The creature pulled the blade from its throat, streams of black fluid coating its skin. It spun around, galloping into the forest, leaving a trail of ebony liquid in its wake.

Lara grabbed her throbbing head, willing the world to stop spinning. As the creature fled, she heard its screams in her mind—the pain in its flesh. It was alone. *So terribly alone*. Ever since the gate closed, an unbearable pain and longing was its only existence.

Lara gritted her teeth, overcome with the agony pouring into her mind from the creature. Among the anguish, a hand touched her face.

"Lara," Arlo gasped, kneeling by her side.

As the creature ran further away, the screaming in her thoughts lessened to a whisper—the pain molding into sadness—then silence. She opened her eyes, finding Arlo holding her face, worry etched into his expression. At once, she embraced him, wrapping her arms around his neck.

He grunted in pain, and she pulled away. "I'm sorry," she said. "Are you all right?"

Arlo sat back with a sigh, still catching his breath. "That's *my* question," he said with his smirk.

Lara checked his shoulder. Four puncture wounds pierced straight through his leather armor. It didn't seem severe, but she couldn't assess the damage appropriately with his armor on.

"Hey," he said, touching her shoulder, "are you all right?"

Her attention shifted to him, mind reeling from the event. "Yeah, I'm okay. What in the Bleeding Nine was that thing?"

"Hells if I know, but you were walking right toward it when I came upon you."

Her brow furrowed. There was no way she would—

*The woman*

"It was a woman," she said with surprise.

Arlo gave a puzzled expression. "What?"

"That's who I saw. It wasn't that thing, it was a beautiful woman in a red dress."

"Look, I know women, *that* wasn't one."

Lara rolled her eyes. "Yeah, I know. I'm saying that's what I saw."

He paused. "You're saying you saw a woman, but really it was that thing? Like it tricked you?"

"I don't know," she said, now beginning to question her sanity altogether. "I've never seen a creature like that before."

"Eli said he read about creatures mimicking human screams, luring them to their deaths. But it was from a book of myths."

"I've heard rumors of creatures in the Ha'Negev mountains, but I never imagined—" She paused, glancing around. "Wait, where's Eli and Shira?"

"Shira was injured. Eli's bringing her back to the Citadel. We need to go." Arlo winced as he moved his shoulder. Lara gently touched the wound on his forehead.

"What did the others say?" she asked.

Arlo frowned. "What others?"

"The rest of the trapped recruits in the shelter. We were all in there together. Everyone else wanted to stay, but I ran out. Fenner tried to stop me."

Arlo's forehead wrinkled in concern, grabbing her hand that touched his face.

"Lara, there was nothing but bones in there."

Her face paled. "What?"

"Yeah. No one was in the shelter when we got there."

Lara leaned backwards, face filled with horror. "I killed them," she whispered.

"Killed who?"

Her breath hitched. "I opened the door. I killed them."

"Lara, no one died!" Arlo said with concern. "The bones were old."

"Old?"

"Yeah, the bones were ancient, dusty things. They'd been there a long time. Eli thought some were even dead at different points, like people were killed at different times."

Lara held her hands over her face, breathing deeply.

"Hey hey hey," Arlo said, reaching out and gently pulling her hands down. Her eyes uncovered, filled with tears.

"I don't understand," she breathed, tears wetting her cheeks. "They were all there!"

"What did you see in the shelter?"

"Everyone! Fenner and Jezza, and about twenty others."

"There's no way we missed a dozen people coming out of that place. Lara, you didn't kill anyone."

Arlo waited for her to accept the truth—but she still could not comprehend her experience.

Arlo said, "Could that creature have had anything to do with it?"

Lara's eyes widened a touch. "There was a creature. It was outside. It was why Fenner and the others wanted to stay."

"Okay. Maybe it was whatever that thing was."

"I don't know," she replied, rubbing her forehead.

"Wait, if that thing was outside, why did you want to leave?"

"I can't explain it, Arlo. I just had this feeling. Renard told us we would survive and escape only if we were worthy." Arlo's jaw clenched. "I couldn't understand how I would be found worthy by sitting in that room. Just waiting for someone else to save us. And the note."

"Someone left you a note?"

"Yeah," she replied, feeling her pockets, "stuffed in my armor. All it said was 'leave.'"

Arlo's eyebrows lifted briefly. "Cryptic."

Lara kept searching but found nothing. "It must have fallen out."

"Who wrote the note?"

"I don't know. But whoever it was, I owe them."

It was a moment before she caught Arlo staring at her.

"What?" she asked.

"I'm glad you're okay," he said, his voice barely a breath from his lips, softer than she had ever heard him speak. He must have been worried, and his concern warmed her heart—and burned a terrible fear in her bones.

"I'm all right," she said, squeezing his hand. After a moment, a thought entered her mind. "Why was I chosen? Why did I get picked out of the squad?"

Arlo shifted uncomfortably, rubbing his wounded shoulder.

"Arlo, what did the Captains say?"

He sighed. "That you were chosen because you were the weakest of the group."

She scoffed, "What?"

He shrugged. "That's just what they said."

"But I could kick Eli's—"

"Look, I agree," he said with a grin. "I don't know how they made the decision, but it doesn't matter. It's over."

She dropped it, despite the distaste of the insult. Regardless, they needed to ensure the others were all right. After she inspected Arlo's injuries once more, she helped him to his feet.

"Okay," she said. "Where's Eli and Shira?"

"I don't know. He ordered us to go back without them."

"That's stupid! We can't leave them!"

"I know, I agree, but he's probably halfway back by now. Shira took a blade to her back."

Lara gasped. "Let's go, you idiot! Why didn't you say that sooner! He's probably back to the Citadel by now!"

Eli couldn't feel his arms. The weight of Shira's unconscious form was no longer pain, it was a torment which gnawed at his very bones—tore at his inner being. Each step was made through sheer will, a grit-laced refusal to hand this woman over to death. He wouldn't stop—he couldn't. Giving up would mean Shira died here, and he would sooner crawl until his fingers bled than let that happen.

The air was considerably warmer at the bottom of the mountain, and now running across the flat plain, his pace quickened once again. Iron coated his tongue against his rasping breaths, each one staving off the clutches of dizziness a moment longer. Shira hadn't woken or moved since she passed out. Eli stopped three times to check her pulse, but couldn't bear to again, in case the worst had happened.

Empowered by some force beyond himself, his legs continued to move. Every part of him was screaming to stop, begging for a reprieve—but his soul was screaming louder. Spurred forward by a desperate determination he had never known, he pressed on.

He imagined it was Harper in his grasp, that his little sister was the one bleeding in his arms, and it granted his muscles strength for a second longer. If this was what it took to become a Guardian, his training was for this moment, when the life of a friend was his to reclaim—he would not fail.

Among the quiet of the night, and the insects chirping hidden in the plains, voices sounded ahead, alongside rushing water. Eli caught the faint glimmer of lantern light.

*The river*

His eyes, having adjusted to the dark, gathered the dark outline of his comrades.

"Help!" Eli shouted, his raspy voice a combination of despair and dehydration. It was a risk, he knew, unaware of who waited at the river side. He prayed with every ounce of his soul that Sol's team was long gone.

Murmurs stirred ahead. Eli didn't stop. He wouldn't until Shira was safe inside the Citadel.

"Eli?" A familiar voice called from the crowd.

*Thank the Heavens*

"Maelyn! Shira's hurt!"

At the agony in his voice, footsteps rushed toward him. Maelyn's face emerged as Esme came up beside her holding a lantern, followed closely by Fenner. Concern engulfed Maelyn's face as she saw Shira's pale complexion—and Eli's bloodied arms.

"Bloody Nines," Fenner muttered.

Esme immediately checked Shira's pulse. Eli's heart stopped, until she nodded at him.

"Please," he said, "we need to get her to the Citadel."

Esme handed the lantern to Maelyn and took Shira from Eli. Relief flooded him at the loss of weight. Esme turned and ran with Shira in her arms. Eli started behind her, but Maelyn put a hand on his chest.

"Stop," she said. "You need to rest, or you'll be no better off!"

"I'm not leaving her," Eli argued, pulling out of her grip, and jogging after Esme.

Maelyn cursed but ran alongside him. The four of them moved together, taking turns carrying Shira to keep up a brisk pace. Eli demanded he be allowed to help, though his turns were much shorter once his legs started to give out. Fenner couldn't carry her and run, so Maelyn and Esme bore most of the task.

There was no triumphant chant, nor welcoming parade as they crossed the finish line. Approaching the border of the practice field, Captain Evergreen stood guard with two Operatives. Four nearby healers rushed to their side.

"What happened?" a female healer asked, assessing Shira's cold pale skin.

"Stab wound to the back." Eli gasped. "I think it punctured her right lung. She was having trouble breathing and passed out hours ago."

"Give her to us," a male healer said, grabbing Shira's body from Esme. "We'll take her from here."

Two of the healers left, running toward the Citadel. Eli started after them.

"Recruit Danon!" Evergreen shouted. "As squad leader you are to report to me immediately for a debrief."

Eli froze, glancing to the healers, but stepped toward Evergreen. "Captain, please."

Evergreen waited, watching the healers carry his comrade.

"Captain."

"Your report, recruit."

Eli took a deep breath, clenching his fists. "My team and I ascended the mountain as ordered and found the predetermined location unguarded and open. While searching for our comrade, we were ambushed by two others, and Shira received a life-threatening injury. After fighting off the attackers, our kidnapped squadmate was still lost, but we found her trail, and I assigned a squadmate to pursue her."

"Your medallion, recruit," Evergreen said, holding out her hand.

Eli held her stern gaze. "It was taken, Captain. I traded it for my comrade's life."

Evergreen lowered her arm. "So, help me understand. You arrive here with a near dead comrade, no medallion, having not found your captured squadmate, and abandoned one of your own to finish the mission on his own?"

Eli's shoulders sank. "Yes, Captain Evergreen."

She took a deep breath. "I'm afraid you are the first to return without a medallion, recruit Danon. You will be informed of the assigned punishment when all remaining squads have returned. Go see to your wounded comrade, and report back here by sunset tomorrow."

"Captain," Eli said, "what is the punishment?"

"It has not been decided yet," she said coldly. "The squad leader who returns with the most medallions chooses the form of punishment for those that fail."

Eli swallowed the dread lodged in his throat. There was little doubt who would be deciding his fate tomorrow. As he turned toward the Citadel, Maelyn grabbed his shoulder.

"Eli, what happened?" she asked, Esme standing beside her. "Who attacked you?"

"Rowan," he said, death in his voice. "He and Soren attacked us at the base, and then he and Kairah again at the shelter."

Esme cursed.

Fenner's eyes widened. "What? Why would he do that?"

"*That's* where he went," Maelyn spat. "Rotting pig slipped away before the start. Esme and I had to find Fenner on our own."

"Let me know when you find him." Eli growled, taking a step.

"No," Esme said. "Leave that to me, Danon."

# Chapter Thirty-Six

Two days after her talk with Cooper, Eva was scheduled to meet him tonight to discuss the plans. With her borrowed time, she volunteered to help patrol The Capitol grounds, allowing her some much-needed sunshine. It also provided a perfect opportunity for her to examine the area, finding any and all escape routes past the King's personal guards. She'd formed a plan, but leaving wouldn't be easy. And before all that—

"Thank you again so much!" Eva said, with as much innocence as she could muster, buttering up the assistant to the Master Servant.

"What were you leaving for him again?" Sir Grior asked as they strode to Malachi's quarters. A stout man, dressed as well as a servant could hope.

"A letter," she said, pulling out the fake envelope she had wax sealed. It looked authentic—because it was. It just didn't say anything. "It's an apology letter, for all my mistakes. I've treated him so horribly over the years, and he's so generous to let me back into The Capitol. I want him to be proud of his only child."

"Oh, I see. That's so humble of you, Lady Katz, and quite mature. I have a few siblings myself, though I wasn't particularly close with my father."

"That's sad to hear," Eva said, giving Grior her undivided attention. Feigning interest in dull topics of conversation was a needed skill in noble households. Yet guilt clung to the heels of her words. Grior seemed very kind, but obtaining his keys was the only way she could think of to get into Malachi's office—and personal quarters.

Everything else was set. Her travel bag, packed and ready for the two-week ride to the Citadel, was stashed in the narrow ditch she spotted while on her patrols around The Capitol. It was hidden by tall grass for the moment, but it wouldn't stay that way forever. The problem was getting Beacon out of the stables without a fuss, but she already thought of a plan for that.

She took a deep breath as they approached Malachi's private quarters. This was when her plan became suicidal.

"Here we are," Grior said, standing in front of beautifully adorned double doors at the end of one of the hallways to the rear of The Capitol. He fumbled for the correct key.

"I suppose someone as important as you has a key to every room in The Capitol," she said with a smile.

"Oh, certainly. The master servant and I both—" The key clicked in the lock. "Perfect. We must hurry before someone sees. It is a kind gesture, but I want to ensure there is no concern of invasion of the master's suite."

"Oh, of course!" she said innocently.

While Grior held the door, Eva slipped past him and into Malachi's bedchamber. The bed was disgustingly spacious—thrice the size of any mattress she had ever seen, with invaluable silk sheets stretched across it. The cabinetry and décor was all ornate cherry colored wood and polished to a mirror shine.

Eva glanced at Grior, whose focus remained on the empty hallway. Despite Glorana's hint, there was no desk or pile of papers to investigate. Cursing under her breath, she moved briskly to the bedside table and dropped the letter on top, pretending to position it perfectly. With childlike excitement, she returned to Grior.

As she approached, he scanned the hallway once more, still holding the doorknob. Without notice, Eva placed her foot on his and stepped down hard. Grior grunted at the pain, and she stumbled into him, forcing them both down with a thud.

"Oh, my goodness!" Grior said, fumbling on the ground under his girthy weight.

"Sir Grior, I'm so sorry," she said, helping him from the floor.

"No, no," he said, brushing his formal attire. "My mistake, Lady Katz. I apologize."

"Oh, I'm so pathetic," Eva muttered. "Please don't say anything to my father."

Grior smiled. "My dear, think nothing of it," he said, beet red, before bowing. "I must be going."

"Of course." Eva stepped aside as Grior closed Malachi's door, ensuring the handle was locked. He lifted his chin and strolled down the hallway.

She waited, ensuring he wasn't returning, before pulling out the master key ring she'd snagged from his pocket. In less than a second, she was back in Malachi's quarters.

*I need to hurry—Cooper will be here soon*

This was only a detour. Once Cooper gave her the needed information, about how to infiltrate the Citadel with the lowest probability of death, she could leave The Capitol before anyone was wise to her deceit. At least, that was the plan. Despite her volunteering for patrol, there were no escape routes she could find, and no way past the city guards.

For a moment, Eva questioned whether escaping was the right play. It was possible Malachi would be true to his word and help get Lucas rescued, assuming he was still alive. But she shook her head, banishing the thought. Lucas *was* alive. She knew it in her heart, and the decision was already made. Malachi would never honor his promise, and she refused to stay here and trust him.

*I will not wither here as his trophy*

Turning to the matters at hand, Eva scoured Malachi's bedroom for the supposed trove of papers, checking every drawer, every nightstand. Glorana never gave any further information regarding the whereabouts of important papers, and Eva hadn't pressed the issue, not wanting any trouble for Glorana.

The bedroom was spotless, as if Malachi hadn't set foot in the place for months. Every shelf, every table, was free of dust, the sheets absent of wrinkles. This was indeed the quarters of a King, polished and prepared numerous times each day.

Eva strode toward the two doors at the back of the room. One opened into a personal washroom, the other was locked. Her heart rate jumped. Fumbling for the master keys, she tried the lock. Nothing. Sweat cooled her forehead as she tried all six of the keys on the ring. None of them worked.

She cursed, pressing hard against the door, assessing the security—how many locks kept it closed. The wood flexed at the edges, indicating only one latch. Despite her ability to pick a lock, she didn't have the right tools, nor the time.

Stepping back, she glanced towards the entrance before planting her foot against the door with a kick. The wood groaned and splintered but didn't open. The noise sent her heart racing, but she kicked again, and the frame split. One final push, and the door flew open, revealing a private study riddled with books, papers, and a broad desk sitting against the back wall.

Holding her breath, Eva listened for any commotion outside. Malachi was sure to realize once he returned tonight, but if all went well, she'd be long gone by that point.

Various parchment and letters were strewn about the desk, mixed among a sea of books and journals. It was overwhelming at first, but she shuffled through the information as quickly as she could read. There was no point in hiding her tracks, not with the door broken down.

All of the letters appeared hastily opened, some torn at the edges. Most of them were signed by foreign dignitaries, from Nations she'd never heard of before. She skimmed one, received from the ambassador of a Nation called Borllo. Most was political smoke, carefully worded speech geared to say very little without being insulting.

But something caught her attention.

*I regret to inform you, King and General, our people have no record of that which you seek. Yet, the objects you describe are intriguing, and I wish to know more about them if possible.*

Eva's curiosity piqued. Numerous other letters reported the same answer, apologizing for the disappointing news. Others mentioned building frustration, nobles and emperors wondering when the agreed upon aide would arrive. Apparently, Malachi handed out a few empty promises.

Among the chaos, she spotted a journal buried at the bottom of a pile. The leather was creased with time, the pages swollen from use. Grabbing it, she sifted through, landing on a page which gave her pause. An endless list of names, each one assigned under a different Nation—and each one crossed out.

*Is he looking for more Obelisks*

In the pages that followed, another list of names was seen, similar to the first—but these she recognized. They were all towns, villages, throughout Adiel.

Lost in her thoughts, Eva's mind churned with ideas. Evidently, Malachi was so convinced of the Obelisks' power, he was using all his political influence to find them.

Voices sounded outside in the hallway. Her heart jumped and she held breath before the voices faded.

*Hurry*

She scoured the journal, which contained years' worth of notes. There was a monumental amount of information, but most of it was indecipherable scientific jargon she didn't understand. It would take far too long to sift through and dissect. But as she was about to toss the journal and search elsewhere, something stole her attention.

Written on a page, at the start of the journal, was a word she'd never seen. Her brow wrinkled as her eyes traced the letters.

*Everstone*

It was circled multiple times, surrounded by comments which all ended in questions. There were two things Eva could decipher quickly: Malachi did not have one and he couldn't find one. The following page was dominated by three letters, surrounded by different glyphs and symbols drawn into circles.

*How*

Eva knew she'd found the answers to her questions but was helplessly lost to understand them. She skipped forward a few pages, coming to a journal entry dated eighteen years prior.

*Thirteenth Era, Year eleven, Day seventeen, Autumn's Touch*

*Trial seventy-two. Still no viable breach. The modified glyph sequence—replacing the third base glyph with an inverted perigruul sigil—produced a brief oscillation in the outer ring, but the reaction collapsed before full alignment. I suspect the problem lies more in power than purity. Her configuration was strange and anomalous. And despite my best efforts: unrepeatable.*

*But that implies intention or design where there was none. Unless she knew. Unless she hid something from me, some missing piece of the final solution.*

*I've begun substituting traditional binding glyphs with what I'm calling "latent anchors"—fragments of more complex sequences I have yet to decipher. They don't correspond to any known lexicon, but their presence is quite prominent in the eighth era scrolls. And the solution to their control over the reaction still eludes me, yet the ambient field bends around them like light through water.*

*Promising. And dangerous. I've adjusted the Sha'ar, wondering if there's too much focus on the earthly connection. I'm also running out of living fuel. Tomorrow, I'll increase the strain and consider other options.*

More voices sounded outside, snapping her from her thoughts. She slammed the journal shut, questioning whether to bring it with her. It was far too late to hide her tracks. Either she escaped tonight, or the remainder of her years would be spent in a damp dungeon.

Cooper would be arriving any minute, and each second she spent in this office was another moment with a noose around her neck. She rearranged the papers into some semblance of what it looked like before and closed the office as best she could. Waiting at the entrance of Malachi's quarters, Eva listened for voices. She opened the door to a slit and peered through, finally leaving before her overzealousness ruined her well-laid plans.

She rushed back to her quarters, hiding the journal underneath her pillow. Easy enough to grab before leaving. But now the clock was ticking.

Taking a deep breath, she gave herself a moment. Two moments, allowing her heart rate to drop. She strode for her door and pulled it open. A female servant stood in the doorway, shocked at her sudden presence.

"Lady Katz," she said, bowing. "I'm sorry. Chosen Lieutenant Cooper is here to see you."

*Bleeding Hells that was close*

"Thank you," Eva said, glancing at Cooper who stood nearby. He turned and gave a strained smile.

The maid walked away, and Cooper stepped up to the doorway. "May I come in?"

She swallowed, still rattled. "Yes." She stepped aside, and he strolled in. Despite his casual gait, Cooper's expression tightened.

Something was wrong.

"Look, Evalynn." He started. Eva braced herself. "General Malachi changed his mind."

She breathed in, sweat forming on her palms.

"He wants the mission to be kept an utmost secret—top ranks only. When I told him about your interest in the details, he wasn't shy about speaking to your recent questionable behavior."

The walls closed in. Panic rose in her chest, telling her to flee out the front doors before they locked forever. She stifled her breathing, demanding it remain steady.

*Day thirty, Winter's Touch*

"Is it true?" Cooper asked, brow knitted.

She hesitated. "Which part?"

"Any of it. All of it," he said. "Did you abandon your post to come here?"

"No," Eva said sternly. "The Lieutenant gave me permission."

*The rest is probably true*

Cooper's gaze drifted, no doubt weighing the truth of Malachi's words. "Listen," he said, "I understand your emotional investment in this. I promise that I will ensure the plan works out. And if Lucas is still alive, we'll get him out."

Eva bit her lip, now crawling out of her skin. Cooper's shoulders fell, his face painted with pity. It was comforting, for what it was worth, to know he was sympathetic.

"Is there *anything* I can do?" she pleaded.

"No. The General closed the matter."

"When are you planning to draw up preparations?"

"They're already drawn up. We were supposed to meet today and finalize everything, but the General felt the need to expedite the process. We organized the entire thing last night. I came early to speak with you. After this, we're meeting with the warrior chosen for the mission."

"Now?"

Cooper nodded. "The mission starts tonight."

"What's the plan?"

"Evalynn, I like you, but you are asking for privileged—"

"Leo, I've heard that so many times I should have it tattooed on my forehead," she argued. "You know as well as I do what he's doing. I understand I'm being sent to the block, but for Nine's sake at least tell me how you'll save my greatest friend."

He sighed, pursing his lips. "Evalynn, he's not the only reason we're going. And we don't even know if he's—"

"He is." She bit, swallowing the lump in her throat.

*He has to be*

"It's a scouting mission," Cooper said quietly. "We know captives are being held at the Citadel, or at least we suspect. But at this point we feel a seek and report is our best option for success."

"Who was chosen?"

Cooper sighed again, twitching his fingers. "Swordsman Aria Phoenix."

Eva blinked. The name didn't register. "Who is she?"

"She's a first choice. Top of her unit and up for a promotion already."

She rubbed her face, trying to salvage the situation. "Leo, can you at least tell me how you plan to get in?"

"I'm sorry Evalynn, but the answer is no." He placed a hand on her shoulder. "For what it's worth, I'm sorry it worked out this way."

He stepped around her, and she spun around. "Wait, Leo," she said, desperate for help.

He waited, hand on the doorknob.

"Never mind," she breathed. "Thank you."

"Sure," he said, closing the door behind him.

Eva's mouth went dry, but her mind turned. She would not accept defeat so easily.

*The snake would realize it had slithered into the jaws of a wolf*

# Chapter Thirty-Seven

E li sat motionless next to Shira's medical bed, bathed in the cold blue light of the mage stones, his attention fixed on her still face. A pressure remained inside him, hours after she was treated, counting each rise and fall of her chest, as if her life yet walked a razor's edge. The healers assured him she was stable, that he could leave and recover himself, but he refused. He couldn't, not while she lay so pale and motionless, fear twisting in his gut.

But as evening drew near, the opportunity to say goodbye was fading. Nazzat, with endless mercy, remained in the medical ward past her allotted time, watching over them. It was a blessing—for Shira's sake more than his.

Eli sat up straight, mouth parting as Shira's eyes fluttered open. Her hand was cold in his.

"Hey," he whispered.

Shira turned her bandaged head, the fabric starkly white against her black hair. Given how many tonics Nazzat administered, Eli wasn't sure how drowsy she would be.

"Hey," she rasped.

Something in Eli finally relaxed. "How do you feel?"

"Like death."

"Well, considering, that makes sense," he said plainly, shifting in his seat. He wasn't sure what else to say.

It was too close. If Maelyn and Esme weren't at the river, or if he hadn't found that vial of Leerfly venom, Shira wouldn't be here. Too many things had to go correctly. Luck and coincidence were not tools a leader could trust on every mission. Whatever needed to be done as a squad leader to step up and ensure her safety, as well as that of Arlo and Lara, he needed to figure it out.

That is, *if* he was given the chance.

Shira's eyes closed and didn't reopen. But it didn't matter. She was alive, and he needed to leave. He squeezed her hand gently before he stood.

*How the Hells did this happen*

He nearly lost his mind on that mountain, oblivious to how deep his affection for her truly ran. That's not how a leader, or a Guardian, should fight. It's not how a warrior enters the battlefield. Comrades die all the time. It was why the Leadership organized the program to include death. But he was helpless. The feelings poured out of him like a river finally breaking free from a dam, and it swept him away without mercy.

Eli stepped to the curtain, glancing back at Shira, her face partially obscured from the bandages. She was still the most beautiful woman he'd ever seen, the most cunning, and the most capable. He hoped to see her again after tonight.

Pushing aside the drapes, he walked to the medical station.

"Nazzat," Eli said. She turned from her notes with a polite smile. "She's awake."

"Oh, excellent," Nazzat said, standing. "She's talking?"

"Barely," he said, glancing back at the curtain around her bed. "She still seems out of it."

"That's likely the tonics. Some can be very sedating."

"Yeah," he muttered. "Listen, I need to go. Make sure she's kept safe?"

"I promise. But—" Nazzat paused, wringing her hands. "Please, have you reconsidered my offer?" she whispered.

"No, I don't want you to get into trouble. Thank you, Nazzat."

"Of course, sir Danon," she said, a grim smile on her face.

"Please, call me Eli."

"Sir Eli is the best I can do," she said with a wink. He smiled and turned to leave. "Oh! I have that book you requested."

She strode to and from her desk, grabbing the modest sized, blue leather-bound book. It was heavy in his hands, and he stared as if it was a snake about to bite him. A rock formed in his stomach as his fingers traced the title.

"Thanks," he said, leaving.

He returned to the barracks and stashed the book under his blankets. He wouldn't be able to read it tonight anyway. Or for a while, most likely. Only a few other recruits were present in the barracks, exhausted from the Crucible. Eli wasn't sure if all the squads had returned yet, but tonight was the deadline.

As he descended the stairs, starting for the practice field to meet the Captains, he noted two Operatives near the watch station speaking in hushed tones and wide gestures. Arlo rounded the corner and stormed up to meet him at the bottom. His left arm was in a sling, his shoulder bandaged with white cloth.

"Hey!" Arlo shouted. "What's the punishment? No one will tell me!"

Eli stood before his friend and placed a hand on his shoulder. "Go rest, Arlo. I'll see you tomorrow," he said, pushing past him.

Arlo followed. "Boar spit! Tell me now!"

"Arlo, it doesn't matter."

"It does because it involves my squad leader!" Arlo grabbed Eli's shoulder and spun him around.

"You're out of line!"

"Like Hells!"

"Hey!" The night watch Operative stood from his desk, pausing his conversation with a female Captain. "Is there a problem?"

"No, sir," Eli said, holding his hands up.

He sat down, and the Captain resumed speaking. "No, I'm serious, the whole outpost was *slaughtered,* Tak. No one knows what happened."

Eli turned to his friend. "Look, Arlo, they gave the squad leaders the call of how to take the punishment for returning without a medallion. I made the decision."

Arlo pursed his lips. "How bad is it?"

Eli's face fell. "I'll be fine. And all three of you go unpunished, which is the whole point. None of you did anything wrong."

"Why do I get the feeling you're lying to me?"

"If you're not sure, it means I'm getting better at it."

"So what, you get promoted and now you shut the rest of us out? Look I owe you all right, so let me help!"

"That has nothing to do with it. I'm sparing you the guilt—"

"No, to Hells with that, I didn't ask you to spare me rot!"

"Shira won't survive it," Eli said firmly, trying to keep his voice down. He saw the realization come over Arlo.

"We were given a choice," Eli continued. "The squad could get punished as a whole, but Shira would never survive it. The only other option is for me to take it all as the leader."

Arlo shifted uncomfortably. "Tell them to let me split it with you. Fifty-fifty. I volunteer."

"They won't. And besides, you did nothing wrong."

"Neither did you!"

Eli paused. He disagreed. He had failed, in more ways than one.

"Goodnight, Arlo," he said solemnly, before turning to leave.

Arlo didn't pursue this time. Eli heard a huff as he walked away.

Grateful for some headspace before tonight, Eli took his time walking to the practice field. He was utterly exhausted. His limbs were heavy, his muscles still screaming after carrying Shira for miles.

Though it was a debt he could never repay, Eli would have to find some way to thank Esme and Maelyn for their aid, even Fenner. Despite him pushing his body far beyond its limits, Eli was certain Shira wouldn't have survived without their help.

After his debrief with Evergreen, Eli tailed the healers as they brought Shira to the medical ward, demanding Nazzat be the one to treat her. Arlo and Lara came in a few hours later, having returned safely. Eli only left Shira's side once, leaving Lara with her, to speak with Evergreen about the punishment. The decision to take it upon himself meant nothing, knowing his friends would be all right.

Not telling any of them the punishment was something he'd promised himself he'd do. If they knew, they'd never let him go through with it, demanding they share it together. But he refused to let them be harmed for his mistakes. He was the one who ordered Shira to give away the medallion and allowed an ambush to slip past him. He should have set up a perimeter, kept someone on watch, done *anything* other than blindly walk into that building.

Exiting the Citadel, Eli marched across the practice field toward Evergreen and Renard, standing near the cliff's edge. Four other recruits waited before the captains—and Sol. The air grew brisk as the sun's rays faded from the orange sky. Eli stepped up to the silent group, glancing at the four other squad leaders.

Abott, Eli recognized, by his shaved head and soft face. A gentle man, as far as Eli could tell, always walking alongside his wounded comrades to the medical ward. The other three were strangers.

Eli stared at the recruit next to him. She bore severe injuries, with lacerations to her face and arms, holding her side. He wondered how badly her squadmates were hurt for her to take the punishment in her current state. She was most certainly giving her life for them.

Their eyes met, and Eli's stomach turned at her solemn gleam of acceptance. He nodded, nothing more than a pathetic attempt to honor her sacrifice before the end.

"Squad leaders." Renard started. "You are here because you failed. You were each given a command position and a single objective to keep a medallion safe, by any means necessary. None of you were able to accomplish this task."

"In war, Guardians are commonly given precious items to protect from the enemy. Intelligence, weapons, even dignitaries are placed under our care. If you are unable to protect a simple piece of metal, then you need to learn the price of failure."

As Renard spoke, Eli saw stakes in the ground near the cliffside. Attached to each was a short length of chain, which ended in thick rope.

"Sol Richter!" Evergreen said. "You have performed exceptionally in accordance with the challenge rules. Not only did you succeed at your mission, returning with your medallion and all of your squadmates alive and well, you obtained additional medallions. Your reward, per the rules, was to choose the punishment for the other squad leaders, within reason."

"Sol has made his choice," Renard said. "He is to deliver forty lashes to each of you. You will be left chained to these stakes overnight, giving you time to think upon your failure. Per our discretion, we gave each of you the choice to divide the lashings equally among your squad. I will say proudly, none of you chose that option. You have all decided to bear the burden of failure yourselves, as the leaders. If you survive the night, it is my hope that you continue that level of accountability in the future."

Eli's attention drifted to Sol, who stood with a prideful smirk, gripping a menacing whip. The leather was masterfully wrapped, its brown leather braided down to a fine point. A wave of fear rose in Eli's chest. He turned away, stealing his courage.

Harper's young face entered his thoughts, like sunlight breaking through the clouds. Her laughter played in his mind like a melody, her soft hair a whisper beneath his fingers. Shame clung to the thought, but it was Harper who nearly stayed his hand—nearly swayed him to let Shira die, so he might live on and make it home. But what kind of man would he be? How could he stand before his sister with pride, knowing he traded honor for blood—traded someone's life for his own?

He gripped his left wrist, vowing to survive tonight. The punishment was meaningless, the pain was hollow, and Sol could burn in all Nine Hells. Nothing would keep Eli from graduating and seeing his family again. He would return home a changed man, having never sacrificed his morals—his honor—to achieve this goal.

That was the entire point of his leaving, the truth beneath each step which brought him here. If this was the price the fates demanded, if blood and sacrifice were the toll for his own character, then so be it. He would pay it without flinching.

The naive country boy grieving his mother and dreaming of grandeur would not be tainted by these trials. He would conquer them, crush them underfoot, and bellow in the face of the adversities which fate had thrust upon him. Harper was the very reason Eli was here and would be the reason he survived. Shira would never live through ten lashings, let alone a night outside. He was saving her life, and that was enough.

The four squad leaders were led to a stake each and stripped of their upper armor and clothing. The rope constricted his wrists so tightly his hands went numb within minutes. The abrasive material bit into his skin as he shifted his weight, the chain only long enough to allow him to kneel.

Goosebumps erupted as the ocean breeze drifted past. Eli stared into the horizon, the night sky growing darker as the red and orange colors faded. His heart thundered with each passing moment, and he took a deep breath to steady himself.

His face was set.

He was ready.

Without warning, Eli felt a searing pain on his back. Agony radiated through his body as the whip made contact, ripping through his skin. Sol was giving each strike every ounce of his strength, and there was no doubt he started with Eli intentionally, not wanting to waste it on the other recruits.

"One!" Renard shouted.

Another strike sliced Eli's ribs on his right side. His breath caught as he felt warmth dripping down his skin. He willed his mind to drift, to flee the present. Eli tried to find something to think about, anything to grab his attention and hold himself steady. Yet each time, he was brought back to the cold unforgiving ground as the next lashing made contact.

"Three!"

He told himself to breathe, gritted his teeth so hard his head thundered. He would not give Sol the satisfaction of hearing him scream. Another crack of the whip sounded, biting his shoulder and wrapping around the collar bone. The next one found the side of his neck, scourging his throat. Eli bent forward, coughing and gagging at the burning pain. With the next strike, as the skin on his back went numb, Eli's mind forcefully fled reality.

"Six!"

Drifting further from the present, his mind flew through memories and into his dreams. He let go and allowed himself to wander into the place he felt most at peace.

"Nine!"

The sun's warmth kissed his face as it gracefully touched the horizon, casting the fiery glow across the sky like a painter's canvas. The breeze carried the scent of sand and oceans, mixing the warmth of the sky and the cool of the water. Eli felt light and strong. There was no pain—only stillness. The sand caved beneath his feet, the brisk water reaching him with each wave, caressing his skin.

"Eleven!"

*"You don't understand the horrors of war, what the Military actually is! Becoming a Guardian will not bring your mother back!"*

*"Stop telling me that! I know that! It's you who keeps reminding me it's my fault!"*

*"How can you say that?"*

*"Admit it, dad! You've blamed me every second of the last twelve years!"*

*"I have done no such thing! I only ever—"*

*"Yes, you have! I see it in your face! I hear it in your voice! You stopped loving us after she died! You abandoned us!"*

*"I'm right here! I've built a life for you and Harper!"*

*"That's not the same thing!"*

"Fifteen!"

A hand rested on his shoulder, as warm as the sunlight around him, throwing a tingling sensation through him as euphoria spread. He turned, gazing into those eyes he had seen a hundred times, but was lost again in their ocean depths. Shira stared with a softness—a longing—that set his heart ablaze.

"Nineteen!"

Eli barely heard the voices over the gentle sound of the water as it danced with the shoreline. He looked back at the sunset, grasping her hand in his, intertwining their fingers. Ecstasy filled his heart as he took a deep breath.

"Twenty-four!"

*"Promise you'll come back?"*

*"Yeah, I promise, Harp. Nothing will keep me from coming home."*

*"Dad will be mad for a while."*

*"Don't worry about him."*

*"Will you teach me what you learned when you come back?"*

*"Sure. All the fancy tricks."*

*"Eli?"*

*"Yeah?"*

*"What do you think mom would say?"*

*"That she loves you. That she's proud of us. And that nothing in this world will keep us apart."*

*"Can you tell me what she was like?"*

"Twenty-nine!"

Eli breathed in the open air, peace filling his lungs. He wanted to stay here, stand on this beach for the rest of eternity, gazing at the beauty of creation, resting far from the evils of Adiel.

"Thirty-two!"

*"Look mom! I did it! I did it!"*

*"Good job, my handsome boy."*

*"It wasn't even that hard!"*

*"Only because you're so talented, Elijah."*

*"Will I be strong like you someday?"*

*"Only if you wish, my son. But remember you don't have to be. Being strong is needed at times, but love is what really matters."*

*"Is that why you married dad?"*

*"Yes. It is. He taught me love. Forgiveness. And that true strength is knowing when to be gentle."*

*"Then I'll do both! I'm going to be the strongest there is just like you and love more than anyone! I'll even win the heart of a beautiful lady like dad did!"*

*"I have no doubt about that, Elijah."*

"Thirty-six!"

In his heart, Eli knew he couldn't stay. Something in his soul whispered it wasn't time yet. Harper needed him, and there was so much to be done. Glancing down at his empty hand, he turned, seeing Shira was gone. The sun fell below the horizon, the warmth of its rays lost, as Eli let himself go to the growing darkness.

Shira opened her eyes to the dim blue light, wincing at the aching in her back. Her right arm tingled as she touched her face, tracing the bandages over her wound. Every movement sent a shock through her.

The curtain opened abruptly. Shira didn't recognize the female healer who approached.

"You're awake," the healer said, coming to her bedside. "I'm Nazzat. I took care of you after Sir Eli brought you here."

Nazzat listened to her heart and lungs, pressing her ear to her chest.

"Take a deep breath," Nazzat instructed.

Shira obeyed, wincing at the shooting pain through her back. Nazzat inspected Shira's fingers, pinching them a few times, and watched as she wiggled her toes. After a time, she seemed satisfied.

"How are you feeling?" Nazzat asked.

"I'm all right," Shira rasped, her tongue sticking to the roof of her mouth.

Nazzat attentively brought a cup to her lips. She drank, the cool liquid running down her throat. It was refreshing, but her stomach now ached.

"You're lucky," Nazzat said. "In more ways than one."

"Yeah."

The healer paused, glancing over her shoulder. "Please, whatever you do, be kind to him."

Shira's brows furrowed. "Who?"

"The man you owe your life to. He's outside receiving your team's punishment."

*Punishment*

*The medallion*

Nazzat took a step to leave, but Shira grabbed her hand, biting the pain from the sudden movement.

"Wait. Tell me what's happening." Her voice had no force behind it, unable to convey the urgency she felt in her chest. Nazzat looked around nervously, but she leaned toward Shira.

"Do you care for him?" she whispered. Shira hesitated but nodded. "Then do not worry. I will ensure he survives the night."

She stepped away from the bed and left without another word.

*No Eli*

*Not for me*

# Chapter Thirty-Eight

E va paced in the hallway outside Malachi's study, restless as she waited for the right moment. The next step of the plan—the final step—had changed. Grior's key ring rattled in her pocket as she wandered up and down the hall, feigning nonchalance. Thankfully he somehow hadn't found it missing yet.

Despite what Cooper said, Swordsman Phoenix hadn't arrived, and Malachi was still in his private office. Leo left her quarters more than an hour ago, and their meeting hadn't yet started. Pacing the hall was the only way to keep an eye on both the front door and her father's office.

Eva checked the main lobby but saw no one, no Swordsman. She moved back to the door leading to her father's study and paused. Malachi didn't speak much, unless someone entered his room to ask a question. She couldn't understand what they said, no doubt by design, but she heard movement and noises indicating his presence.

A servant rounded the corner. Eva whipped out the parchment containing utter gibberish and pretended to be reading an emotional letter. The servant glanced at her as he passed, concerned, but noted the letter in her hands and continued without question. She didn't know what their assumptions were about the daughter of the General acting frantic over some unknown letter, but she didn't care. Their gossip was the point of the poor disguise.

Rustling sounded from Malachi's office and Eva decided to check the front door again. Striding down the hallway, she peered around the corner. A Swordsman was checking in with the servant managing guests. It was a woman, though Eva had no idea whether it was Aria.

The woman had beautifully thick, fair hair. Her black armor was well kept and fitted, supportive of Cooper's mention of her excelling among the ranks.

Standing at Eva's height, the woman was fit and muscular, with a determined look in her eyes. She smiled at the servant and walked past her toward the war room. Eva quickly turned around, only to come face to face with Glorana.

She gasped in surprise, holding her chest as she breathed away the adrenaline rush.

"What is it you're doing, Evalynn?" Glorana asked with a raised eyebrow.

"Nothing. I'm just wasting time," she lied, glancing back toward the front, knowing if the meeting was starting, her window of opportunity was now.

"Very well," Glorana said with a shrug. "I have some business to attend to, but I'll swing by your quarters later tonight. I'll bring some Burberry wine and sweet rolls."

Glorana smiled and walked past her before Eva could give a rebuttal. She would never live down standing her up, but she had no choice. Whether Malachi found his study invaded, or Grior noticed his lost keys, nothing waited for her beyond tonight.

Eva raced down the hallway and put an ear to Malachi's private study. Nothing. This was it. Either she lived to see tomorrow, or she would rot in a jail cell. She pulled the key ring from her pocket, glancing frantically up and down the hallway. Throwing the first key inside, she tried to turn the lock.

It wouldn't budge. She tried the next key, with the same results. Heartbeat drumming in her ears, sweat cooled on her forehead. Footsteps approached from the front room, accompanied by voices. Eva shoved the next key in the lock and turned it. It clicked open, and she rushed inside, shutting it as quietly as possible.

The study was empty. Malachi was gone. This was the second time she was tempting fate, and she didn't have much time. She rushed over to his desk, looking for any information regarding the new mission. The recon reports, ideas of slipping past security, anything to help her once she was on her own.

Sifting through the papers, she skimmed reports from each outpost, letters from Lieutenants, consultation reports, updates, as well as a few papers speaking about dignitaries she didn't recognize. There were a few letters still sealed with wax, which she didn't dare open.

This time, she was taking great care to ensure nothing appeared disturbed. She may have left a mess in his private study, but if he noticed anything amiss now, her chances of escape would evaporate.

Swallowing with a dry mouth, she frantically searched his desk. Each drawer, each pile, reading as fast as her frayed mind could handle. Murmurs sounded outside—the meeting was taking place. There was no way to know how long it would last, but she assumed her time was fleeting.

She pulled open the drawers on the sides of the desk. Each one carried more papers of varying importance. One contained the fanciest glass decanter of fire-water she had ever seen, alongside some pipe tobacco.

The voices in the war room grew louder, and a key clanked in the handle as the door to the war room burst open. Eva ducked, squatting below the far side of the desk, opposite to where Malachi entered.

". . . absolutely. I think it's a dastardly plan, but very ingenious," the General said.

"Thank you, sir." It was Cooper. "I appreciate the compliment."

"Swordsman Pheonix is a perfect choice, although if I'm being honest this mission holds little hope of success," Malachi said. "Regardless, it will be quite an interesting trial of infiltrating the Citadel."

"I agree, sir. I believe Swordsman Pheonix is capable of seeing the mission through, and I would hate to lose such a valuable warrior."

Malachi hummed. "This is war, Chosen Lieutenant. Warriors die all the time. Listen, by the way, I hope my daughter didn't give you too much trouble."

"Oh, not at all, sir. I took care of it."

Eva's blood boiled.

"I appreciate that. I'm sure that over time we'll be able to mold her into some semblance of a model warrior, but I'll see the Hells frozen over before I know how it'll happen. Fourteen years at home and nothing to show for it."

"I agree sir, but rest assured we can do it together."

A loud thunk sounded as something hollow and metal landed on the desk.

"Well, that's something we can take in stride. Oh, has Chief Arron given his report on the mess over in Terakh? It may prove problematic for this mission."

"No sir, but I will speak with him first . . ."

The voices faded as the door was closed again. Eva peered over the edge of the desk.

Time to leave

But her eyes jumped to the object thrown onto the desk. It was a small metal container, with no identifiable markings. Underneath it was an open letter and a map. Eva recognized the Citadel's architecture from Jafeth's description and spotted the word captives.

At once, she jumped up and grabbed the letter. This was it. It was the plan and the scouting report about the Aniyan captives. The map detailed Citadel security, boundaries of Eldan City and the known sentry points, options for retreat—everything she needed to get in.

She folded the papers and tucked them inside her tunic. As she grabbed the box, her eyes caught more letters about the Obelisks. Overcome with curiosity, Eva grabbed the letters and shifted around the desk to leave, tucking them away.

As she neared the adjacent door, leading back to the hallway, she pried open the box, her brow furrowing at the contents. As she reached for the doorknob, the door to the war room opened again. Eva spun around in horror as Cooper entered the study. He didn't see her, and she stole the opportunity.

Her thoughts came at lightning speed as she tossed the container on the chair in front of Malachi's desk. She lunged forward, spanning the room in moments. Before Cooper noticed her, Eva closed the door behind him and held a blade to his neck.

His stunned appearance slowly turned to disappointment—and anger. Eva didn't speak. Her face was stern, but her eyes betrayed her fear.

"So, what's the plan, Evalynn? Kill me and steal the mission?"

"I'm sorry, Leo. But I refuse to stay here with that monster."

"And how far will you get? Your face will be recognized by every scout and outpost across Adiel. The moment you leave, every Legion will be watching for you. You *will* be arrested and imprisoned."

He was right. This was insanity.

"You can just let me go."

"I already helped you. Twice."

"Come on, Leo. There's more to this war than rules and duty. If we don't help our own—"

"Evalynn, the moment you broke into this office you forfeited your place in the Legion and Aniyan society. You know I can't ignore that."

"Do not tell me you cannot see him for the monster he is! That he is using this war for his own personal gain!"

"That monster is the General of the Legion and my King! There is nothing you can say that will disregard that."

"I'm not a criminal." She pleaded, trying desperately to stifle the tremor in her hands. "I am trying to save our comrade, my best friend!"

"And that is not your job nor your obligation as a member of the Legion. You knew when you joined you gave up the ability to decide what you do and where you go."

Eva's breathing quickened. This wasn't working. She could likely incapacitate Cooper, or at least escape him, but running out of The Capitol with the alarms buzzing was impossible.

"Please Leo. Don't condemn me to this prison," she whispered, praying that his earlier kindness was not just flattery. "Let me chance fate at the Citadel. Because I promise, I'm dead even if I stay here."

He paused for a moment, searching her face.

"You would do that?" he asked with sincerity. "Rather than be here with him?"

Eva remained silent, unsure of her own conviction. It was a truth she never spoke to anyone, yet she'd considered it many times in her youth. It takes a great horror to convince a child that death is sweeter than hoping in the future.

"You don't understand what he is."

Cooper held her gaze for a long moment. She waited for him to attack, to engage and defend his King. Yet he remained still, with kindness behind his eyes.

"I'll give you five minutes before I sound the alarm," he said finally.

Eva backed away slowly, holding her dagger aloft. She picked up the metal tin off the chair, retreating until her back was against the opposite door. Cooper, to his credit, did not move an inch. She lowered her blade and sheathed it.

"Thank you."

"Don't thank me. Run."

The seriousness in his face spurred her forward. Throwing open the door, she sprinted down the hallway toward the front of The Capitol. The tin box clutched in her arm, she slowed to a casual walk before rounding the corner to the front of the building. She froze. Malachi was speaking with one of the guards at the door. There was no getting past him, and she couldn't wait for him to move.

Before being seen, she spun around, going back the way she came, only to be met face to face with Glorana again. Panic rose like a tsunami. She didn't have time for this.

"Hello, Moonbeam," Glorana said with a smile.

Frantic, Eva watched for running guards, strained her ears for the sound of a warning bell.

"Nana, I have to go. I'm sorry," she said, rushing around Glorana.

Before she made it a few steps, Glorana grabbed her arm. Eva spun around and saw the serious look on her face. Glorana's eyes drifted to the metal box and then back up to Eva's. A gentle, yet devious, smile Eva had seen a hundred times formed on Glorana's mouth.

"Follow me," her Nana said, leading Eva by the hand down the hallway.

Eva frantically scanned for guards. She estimated another three minutes before Cooper raised the alarm. Once they were halfway down the hallway, adjacent to her father's study, Glorana stopped at a door, unassuming in its appearance. She pulled out a golden key and turned the lock with a loud thud. As the door swung open, Eva's breath caught. It was a staircase descending into near blackness, the dim light of a lantern hanging on the wall of what looked like a mineshaft.

One of the escape routes

She spun to Glorana, who still bore the devious grin.

"I knew your plan the second I heard you came back. I've spent all day searching for Grior's lost keys, who was terribly embarrassed to have misplaced them." Glorana winked. "I snagged the spare key from the master's office and tied up your horse by the exit to the tunnel. There's a travel bag packed with enough provisions for a four-day ride."

Eva's eyes burned. Eight years, and this woman was still her guardian angel.

"How did you—"

"Oh, don't think for one second this old lady doesn't know all the tricks. Don't forget who taught you."

"Thank you, Nana." Eva embraced the woman who by all rights was her grandmother.

"Go now, Evalynn, before anyone sees. I'll throw them off course if I can."

Eva started down the stairs, stopping once to look back one last time. Glorana smiled as she closed the door, the lock turning again. Darkness engulfed the staircase. Eyes adjusting, she descended as quickly as she dared and grabbed the lantern hanging on the hook.

The escape tunnel was just that—a tunnel. It was essentially a glorified mineshaft, with wooden rafters holding up the five-foot ceiling. Eva hunched over as she raced through the passage, the air musty and stale against her heavy breathing.

At the end of the corridor was a makeshift wooden door, held closed by a latch with no lock. It was heavy and swung open into the cool evening air—outside The Capitol walls.

Eva exited the burrow, spotting Beacon tied to a nearby tree. The escape door was well camouflaged into the hillside, impossible to spot.

She sprinted to Beacon. "Hey, buddy," she said, leaping atop his saddle. "Let's go."

Galloping down the side roads, Eva made for the front gate. She wasn't a criminal yet, so the guards in the area paid no mind to a Swordsman leaving. The sound of alarm bells never came as Eva passed through the city gate and eventually through the Duran wall.

# Chapter Thirty-Nine

Shira forced down her lunch among the clamor of the mess hall, knowing her lack of appetite would eventually catch up to her. Maelyn, Esme, and Fenner all shared their table now, ever since the Crucible. Shira didn't recall what happened after she passed out, but Fenner spilled that Maelyn and Esme helped carry her back to the Citadel, a fact they neglected to mention.

"You going to see him before practice?" Lara asked, still finishing her roasted pig.

Shira turned to her, unashamed at this point. Her affection for him was no longer a secret.

"Yeah," she said, knowing all three of them felt the weight of what happened, sharing the guilt.

"How is he doing?" Maelyn asked, taking a large gulp of water.

"The healers said he's stable and slowly recovering. He's still pretty out of it though."

"I'm not surprised," Fenner added. "Out of the five leaders punished, only two survived, including him. Sol didn't hold back."

Arlo cursed. "I'll kill him."

"No," Shira said firmly. "If we do anything to him, it may come back on Eli. It would only make it worse."

Arlo said, "Don't tell me you don't want a piece of him."

Shira's silence was answer enough. She'd thought about it every moment since she was released from the medical ward.

"I found out what he did," Maelyn said. "If you truly want to know."

The table quieted.

"How?" Lara asked.

"Abott," Maelyn answered. "Or at least, one of his squadmates."

Shira clenched her jaw, wondering if ignorance was better. Eli never told them what happened, despite their repetitive requests for him to explain why he was in the medical ward for so long, three days of which he spent in critical condition.

When Shira demanded to know why the healers weren't doing more for him, they said they were not permitted certain treatments for injuries sustained by disciplinary measures. She knew they were holding back because her injury was nearly healed already.

Shira felt the program was completely opposite of what a training camp should be. The same number of recruits were killed while being punished as had died during the Crucible itself.

"No," Shira said. "If Eli doesn't want us to know, then we should respect that."

"She's right," Lara added. "Besides, it doesn't change anything."

Maelyn nodded.

"Hey," Shira addressed Maelyn, "what happened to Rowan?"

Maelyn glanced over her shoulder. Their fourth teammate sat by himself across the mess hall, which he had been doing all week. The left side of his face bore intensely dark purple bruises, and he chewed with a grimace. Shira couldn't remember seeing him at the stone structure on the mountain, and Arlo said they barely touched him. It was as if Maelyn's squad was hanging by them as bodyguards.

"After we heard what happened we waited for him to return," Maelyn said. "I addressed him directly, as the squad leader, demanding he answer for his actions."

"She let him have it!" Fenner commented.

"Esme was the one that gave him the bruises." Maelyn finished.

Esme said nothing, keeping her eyes on her food.

"Thank you, for what it's worth," Shira said.

"Don't worry," Arlo said. "If he does that again, I'll kill him myself."

"You'd have to beat me to it," Esme muttered.

Shira grinned, grateful for her friends. She said, "Speaking of the Crucible, did you ever find out what the Hells happened in that room?"

Everyone turned to Lara and Fenner.

"I told you I heard a creature, right?" Lara asked.

Shira nodded. "Yeah, and that gray creature that hypnotized you."

"What?" Fenner asked, brow knitted. "I never saw a creature."

"You didn't?" Lara asked, astonished.

"All I heard was roaring and screaming outside," Fenner said. "It sounded so real, I thought my squad needed help, so I opened the door. Barely. But when I got outside, no one was there. Maelyn and Esme found me a few hours later."

"I had a similar experience," Lara said. "There was a creature outside, but everyone wanted to stay except me."

"Everyone?" Fenner asked.

"Yeah," Lara said. "You and about two dozen other recruits were there."

Fenner shrugged. "I was by myself."

"Either way," Lara continued, "I don't think that gray thing was the creature outside the structure. I don't know if there was something in that tonic they gave us, or if it was some form of magic, but I'm not convinced any of it was real."

"That gray creature was as real as the Hells," Arlo said, rolling his left shoulder.

"It makes sense if you think about it," Maelyn said. "From what I've heard, it sounds like our challenge was physical and yours was mental. You both had experiences of the mind that demanded you stay in the room. From what Renard told me, the only way to open those structures is from the inside. Even if we reached you, opening the door was entirely on you."

"I asked Evergreen yesterday about it," Arlo added. "She wouldn't say as to what they gave Lara, in fact she never admitted they gave you guys anything. But she told me that 'the battlefield of the mind is as crucial as the one we face out here.'"

"Poetic," Shira snarked.

"I can go the rest of my life without hearing that thing again," Lara mused.

Shira finished her plate and returned her tray to the kitchen counter, as well as Maelyn and Esme's. Skirting out of the mess hall, she briskly strode to the medical ward before afternoon practice. Pulling back the curtain carefully, in case Eli was asleep, she stepped into the space. It was silent, and his eyes were closed. She shuffled over and pulled the nearby chair to his bedside.

His hand was warm underneath her own, a welcomed grace, considering how cold and pale he was only days earlier. The open wound on his throat poured lead into her stomach.

*What in the rotting Hells did Sol do*

It was for Eli's own protection—his safety—that stayed her hand from seeking retribution. The guilt she bore, knowing it was *she* who placed the medallion in Kairah's hands, was overwhelming, pressing down on her like a storm cloud, heavy and relentless.

She dreamed of vengeance, because it was her fault. She allowed herself to be ambushed, taken prisoner. Eli tasked *her* with protecting the medallion, and she willingly handed it over. And knowing that single act carved the path of Eli's suffering—that *her* mistake summoned his torment—filled her heart with iron.

For days she'd carried it, warring with her feelings for him, caught between longing and loathing, tenderness and regret. But the choice had already been made before the mountain. She chose to step over that invisible line and follow her heart. She knew the cost of watching him flirt with death would be one of the consequences, but she accepted that when she let go.

Either way, it was too late to change her mind. Somehow, somewhere along the way, this orange-eyed idiot had stolen her heart. With his naive virtue, and his reckless courage, Eli claimed her affection for his own. If she was being honest with herself, crossing that line changed nothing. It was simply an acknowledgement of what had already transpired—what had already taken root.

Eli's eyes opened to slits as he shifted in bed. Shira remained silent, holding his hand, giving him time to wake. He rubbed his eyes before turning to her.

"Morning," he mumbled.

"Afternoon," she corrected, with a smirk. "How are you feeling?"

"Fine," he said, sleep evident in his voice.

"How's the pain?"

"Tolerable. They gave me a tonic earlier."

"Okay." Shira couldn't shake the feeling that something changed. He was distant—different than she knew him to be. Although he was also in critical condition just yesterday, which may be the simple explanation.

"Lecture was boring, as usual," she said. "Darby went on about the advantages of offensive measures that simultaneously provide a defensive result."

Eli grunted in response, his eyelids heavy.

"Lara has completely recovered now. I feel like she's gotten her confidence back, and Arlo's shoulder healed in no time. It's almost like he was never injured."

He held her gaze for a long moment. "I know you want to ask."

Her cheeks burned, but he was right. "You don't have to tell me. Maelyn offered, but I think I know why you won't."

"It doesn't matter now. It's done."

"I know, I'm sorry, I just—"

"Shira, stop apologizing," he said, no strength behind his voice.

"Don't tell me what to do."

A faint smile touched his lips, the first Shira had seen since he woke nearly two days ago. She didn't bother denying the satisfaction she felt, knowing she was the one who had brought it out of him. Yet, as if he had just realized she was holding his hand, he moved it and cradled both across his stomach. She didn't protest, drawing her hand off the bed, but the action stung.

"I need sleep," he said.

The uneasy feeling worsened in her stomach. "Okay. I'll stop by tonight."

"You don't have to."

"Stop telling me what to do," she teased.

No smile this time. She stood, returning the chair to its proper place, and left without another word.

Eli was released from the medical ward that evening, after a full week, but he felt as brittle as frozen glass. Among the physical toll of the Crucible, the hypothermia, and the blood loss from the lashings, his body nearly ceased to function, demanding rest.

The healer who treated him was far harsher than Nazzat, scolding him for being so foolish to think he could withstand forty lashes. He said thirty was enough to kill a man, let alone being left outside to bleed. Eli already knew this. Three of the other squad leaders didn't make it. He had a sneaking suspicion there was a guardian angel to thank for his own survival. It seemed Nazzat had still gone ahead with her offer to help him, despite it being starkly against the rules.

Eli wore only his brown tunic, his leather armor being far too abrasive. The skin on his back was so raw it was agony to get dressed, as if he wore jagged rocks instead of wool. He wondered how this would affect the program for him. The Rune Blade Ceremony was only a few weeks away, and then the Reaping. Not even the Heavens could save him if it were truly the worst of this program.

Class continued, no doubt, despite his absence. But it would be a few days before he was even capable of sparring, let alone anything close to their previous challenges. Maybe he wasn't cut out to be a Guardian after all.

He cast the thought from his mind and slowly walked to the barracks. The walkway was busy, despite the day winding down. Keepers, Healers, Operatives, some dignitaries, and scattered Captains, all walked with intent through the massive hallway.

He wasn't sure how the program handled severely injured recruits, other than patching them up enough to be thrown back into the fray. It made little sense to test someone unlikely to survive, but the program also wouldn't let anyone coast through on a medical bed. Either way, he didn't plan to be out for long. His body felt like it was healing faster than usual, relative to the minor injuries at the beginning. Maybe he was imagining it, but that's how it seemed.

Entering his bunkroom, he noted each bed was unkempt except his. Eli wondered if Arlo had made it for him. He pulled back the bed sheets, revealing the blue book Nazzat found for him—right where he left it.

The air thickened. He didn't know if he wanted to know the truth. After all this time, asking all these questions, he never thought it would be like this. But he had to know, at least before his mind crumbled from the stress, or his body finally gave out.

Eli sat on the bunk and skimmed the pages, not intending to read the entire thing—only confirm something. The memory of the first time Shira brought him down to the library surfaced, when they spoke about inner magic. She was asking the perfect questions.

Frantic to slow his thoughts, he scanned the pages carefully. He had to be sure. *Absolutely sure.* This would unravel everything, and there was no room for doubt.

After a brief search, Eli found his answer. His thoughts scattered like dry leaves as he stared at the words on the page. He slammed the book closed. No one could know this—not even Arlo. Sweat formed on his palms as he took a breath, reeling from the newfound revelation.

Eli tucked the book under his arm and strode for the door. As he reached for the handle, it turned on its own. The door opened, revealing Captain Renard standing before him.

"Oh, good to see you up and about, Recruit Danon," he said, stepping into the bunkroom.

Eli's heart stuttered. It was too late to hide the book, so he did his best to make it disappear.

"Absolutely, Captain Renard, sir. Thank you." He smiled politely. "I was just coming back to the bunkroom before heading to supper. I want to see how the others are doing."

"Oh, of course. I'm glad you're feeling better." Renard's eyes danced to the book.

*Rotting Hells*

"Doing some research?" the Captain asked.

Eli swallowed. "Yes, sir. I've been trying to expand my knowledge base."

"Excellent." Renard held his hand out, and Eli handed him the book.

Swallowing the lump in his throat, Eli watched Renard flip through the pages. A bead of sweat formed on his forehead as the Captain's eyes jumped to him.

"I'm glad you're keeping your mind sharp, son. Just remember to keep your nose clean." Renard handed the book back to him.

"Yes sir!" Eli said, standing at attention. His back ached from the stiff position.

"Ven'so, Danon. You head to the mess hall. I just saw the recruits moving that way."

"Yes sir, thank you sir," Eli said, relaxing his posture.

Renard reached for the door before turning toward him. "Remember, recruit, I'm always watching."

Eli let out a breath as Renard strolled away. He waited until the nausea settled before heading down to the mess hall. The roar of conversation met him as he entered, spotting his squad at their table, accompanied by Maelyn, Esme, and Fenner. He still needed to thank them.

Scanning the room, Eli caught Sol throwing a snide grin his direction. Rowan was eating by himself, his face evident of a recent beating. Something cold and cruel in Eli took satisfaction in it. He shuffled up to his squad, muscles already tiring from being out of bed. The group saw him coming and Arlo approached him.

"You're up!" Arlo said. He put a hand on Eli's shoulder instead of hugging him, which Eli appreciated.

"Yeah," Eli said. "They released me an hour ago. How has practice been?"

"You didn't miss anything," Lara said from the table as Arlo sat back down.

The food appeared delicious, but Eli had no appetite.

"Good to know," Eli said, "but you'll have to fill me in on anything I missed."

"Catching up on some reading?" Arlo asked playfully.

"Yeah," Eli responded, casually holding the book behind his back. "By the way, Esme, Maelyn, I—"

"You're welcome," Esme said.

"Don't mention it," Maelyn said, taking a bite of her sandwich.

"I know, but I just wanted—"

"Hey." Arlo stopped him, holding a hand up. "Shira's been disgustingly nice all week on your behalf. Don't worry about it."

Eli turned to Shira. They shared a glance, before Eli quickly turned away, motioning to Rowan across the room.

"Who do I have to thank for that?" Eli asked with a dark satisfaction.

"You're welcome," Esme answered.

"Don't worry," Maelyn said. "He won't touch you again."

"Any of us," Arlo added.

"Well, thank you," Eli said, shifting his weight. "I'm tired though. I'm going to turn in. I'll see you guys tomorrow."

Eli gave Shira a knowing look as the group waved goodbye. He hoped she picked up on his intent as he turned and left. It was a short walk to the library from the mess hall, but each step was heavier than the last. And despite his haggard body, his mind was no better. He grabbed one of the lanterns on the desk by the door and lit it.

Distracted by his wandering thoughts, Eli had to double back a few times, not quite remembering the path to their meeting place. He set the lantern on the table at the end of the alcove, along with the blue book, next to the stack left over from the last time they were here.

Sitting in the chair, he leaned forward. It was too painful to rest against the hard wood. He rubbed his face, fiddled with his hands, before standing and glancing at a few titles, pulling one off the shelf before immediately returning it.

Footsteps echoed in the quiet space. His heart quickened.

*This is it*

Shira rounded the corner, slowly approaching. Eli was lost again in her eyes, as vast as the sky, and sharp as any steel. Every step closer, the world faded further. Her fingers brushed the scabbed wound across this throat.

"Will you tell me?" she whispered.

Eli carefully pulled his tunic off and turned around. Shira's breath caught at the marred and mutilated sight of his back. Each lashing had found its mark, something Sol ensured Eli experienced. The lacerations were already beginning to scar over, extending from his neck down to the small of his back.

Shira's warm fingers explored the wounds, and he flinched subtly in response, taking a deep breath.

"Why?" she breathed.

"Because we failed to return with our medallion."

"That's not what I meant. Why did you take it yourself?"

He turned around and put his tunic back on. Shira remained close. She didn't apologize, which he expected. She knew he'd immediately dismiss it as unneeded.

"You would have died," he said, feeling the weight of that decision—even more. "I couldn't let that happen."

"How are you feeling?" she asked. "Actually?"

"Fine. In pain, but—" He paused for a moment, summoning his courage. "When we were on the mountain, you apologized for something. What was it?"

Her brow knitted, and she shook her head. "I don't remember that."

He searched her face, as if the answer to all their questions would be found there.

She asked, "When did I say it?"

"When I was helping you down the mountain. Arlo had already left to find Lara. You were growing weaker, and I was yelling at you to keep talking."

"*That* I remember," she teased.

"I was panicking. I emptied the travel bag looking for something, *anything*, to save you. While I was searching you said that, and it left me frozen."

"I'm sorry Eli, I don't know."

His heart fell. But he pressed harder. "Can you try? Is there anything you can think of that you'd have to apologize to me for? Anything at all?"

He swallowed, overcome by her silence. Her gaze fell, but she shook her head.

"*Anything*?" he breathed.

Shira reached for his arm. "What are you getting at?"

Eli ripped his gaze away as his emotions roiled, a raging sea in his chest.

"When I thought you were going to die on that mountain, I didn't know what to do. I couldn't breathe. I couldn't think. I would have given you my own blood to save you if I had the ability. I don't think I can ever go through that again."

She stepped closer to him. "You won't have to."

"I found something," he said, stepping back. "I haven't told anyone."

Shira gave a puzzled look. "About the Citadel?"

"No. It's in the book on the table."

She waited for more explanation but eventually stepped around him. He turned, watching her read the title in bold black letters.

"I don't understand," Shira said, freezing as she turned around, seeing the deadly look in Eli's eyes.

His hand shook as he held the dagger toward her.

"I trusted you," he whispered.

# Chapter Forty

Eva sat atop Beacon in the midday sun, staring at the looming tower on the horizon. The peaks of the highest buildings in Eldan City barely touched the foundation of the Zentari's mighty Citadel. A knot formed in her stomach as she gazed into the heart of the enemy stronghold, wondering if she was truly prepared for this. Every moment of the past twelve days riding here, she'd asked herself that question—without an answer.

But this was for Lucas. Whether or not she was ready, whether or not she would survive, didn't matter. Lucas was being held prisoner in that tower—she knew it in her soul. And also, she was granted an opportunity for her kin.

She touched the paper in her pocket, thinking back on the words she'd read in her father's office.

*Everstone*

She'd read the letters a hundred times, pulling every piece of usable information from them. It was infuriating to have forgotten his journal in her quarters, but even without it one thing was certain: *nothing made sense.*

The Legion was pursuing the Obelisks because of the power they contained, but it seemed no one knew how the black stones were created. If she understood her father's claims, and if her guesses were even close to correct, an Everstone was far more powerful. And dangerous. Lucas was right. Whatever was going on, her father was at the center of it.

Despite Malachi's wretched sins, he was the most cunning person she'd ever known. If he was convinced of the Everstone's power, that their people's victory in this war lay with Obelisks and Archancy, then it would become her secondary target, next to finding Lucas.

Beacon stirred, and she patted his neck. "Easy, buddy," she whispered, "I won't leave you in there. You'll make your way back from a safe distance, I promise."

Eva thought through the Legion's plan again, reciting each step, each contingency. It was ingenious—and suicidal. The Legion had been in contact with a Zentari informant—someone stationed at the Citadel, sympathetic to the Aniyan cause. Immediately Eva would be suspicious, if it wasn't Cooper who had been in direct contact with the informant. The information Eva stole from Malachi's office provided little reassurance to trusting someone she'd never met. But she had no choice. It was the only way inside.

Eva glanced down at the tin box, stained fingers tucking away a rebellious strand of her newly dyed black hair. A deep unease settled as she stared at the four well-crafted, eerily realistic, prosthetic pointed ears. There was also a leather pouch containing some sort of sticky material, which she assumed was an adhesive. The ears weren't quite identical to her natural skin tone, but she could use watered down leather dye to adjust it, and keep her ears covered at all times.

Posing as a Guardian recruit was bold—hiding in plain sight. The informant agreed the only way past the guards was to be welcomed by them. She took a deep breath in, spurring Beacon forward for the last leg of this journey. She would find Lucas, uncover the secrets of the Obelisks and Everstones, the Hells as her witness.

And as the tower neared, she set aside her identity. Evalynn was gone. She was no longer the daughter of the King, traitor and defector to her people. She was Shira Weiss, Citadel recruit, longing to become a Guardian.

# Chapter Forty-One

Eli's hand ached from gripping his dagger, the tip trembling as he held it out—toward Shira.

*No*

*Not Shira*

She remained still, her face unreadable. It wasn't aggressive, but it wasn't surprised either. The air in the library was heavy and thick, the walls closed in.

He needed answers.

"Who are you?" he asked quietly, despite the panic building in his chest.

Shira sighed, raising her eyebrows. "What are you doing?" she asked, with a nonchalance that mocked the situation. It threw fuel onto his frustration.

"Stop playing games. It all makes sense now. Your suspicions, your curiosity, even dragging me along with you. You're just gathering information."

"Yes, *we* are trying to figure out what *they* are hiding," she pressed, moving her hands between them.

"No, not them. *You.*" Eli held tightly to his emotions. He would not allow this woman to manipulate him any longer. "What's your real name?"

"Eli, stop," she said, taking a step closer.

"*Do not* move!"

She stilled against his rising voice—and icy glare.

"On the mountain," he said, "you got that cut to your face."

As he spoke, Shira gently touched the now scarring laceration to her right cheek.

"You didn't know the cut made it all the way back to your ear. Only, your ear wasn't bleeding. Your ear tips are fake."

Shira's eyes darkened.

"I moved your hair to cover it up. When we got you back to the Citadel I made sure it was Nazzat that treated you. Once I got the chance, I told her about what happened. She assured me that some Zentari are born differently, *Az'an syndrome* she called it. But I didn't believe her. That's when I asked her to get me that book on Aniyan Physiology."

Shira's expression remained blank. She didn't acknowledge anything he was saying, but she didn't deny it either. Those indigo eyes only shifted between his.

"Only Aniyan blood gives blue eyes," he said, with as much intimidation as he could muster.

It wasn't foolproof, but if he was right, everything made sense. Eli gripped his dagger harder, quelling the tremor in his hands. He watched her for answers, any sign of hostility. While his heart hoped he was wrong, his mind demanded the truth.

Shira's features softened as her gaze drifted to the ground, before returning to him, filled with the same resolve that had become so familiar.

"My name is Evalynn," she said plainly. "I'm a Swordsman in the Legion and heir to the throne of the Aniyan kingdom. I'm General Malachi's daughter."

She gently moved her hair aside and carefully peeled away what looked like skin glued to her ears. Before his very eyes, his friend removed her pointed ears, revealing very real, rounded ones underneath.

"You said your father was dead," Eli muttered, desperately trying to organize his thoughts.

"He's been dead to me for a long time."

Eli bit down on his grief—his anger—seeing how she knowingly misled him.

*No*

*Lied*

"What about your hair?" Eli pressed, a shudder in his voice. "According to that book, every Aniyan, for *generations,* has had straw colored hair."

"Leather dye," she answered softly. "Arrowberries mixed with squid's ink. We use it to dye our armor black."

*We*

*It's true*

The reality settled on his shoulders like a ten-ton weight. With his free hand he rubbed his face, still holding the blade upright. The wounds on his back burned from the rigid posture, but the pain was lost among the sea of uncertainty.

Shira took a step toward him. "Eli, listen to me."

"When were you going to tell me?"

"Before the Rune Blade Ceremony."

Whether or not it was true, he couldn't believe her anymore.

"Why then?"

"Because Aniyans don't have magic. I won't pass the ceremony. I'll be put in the Reaping with no chance of success. I'm going to need your help to escape."

"Why should I help you? I don't know who you are!" he shouted.

Shira held her hands up in a motion to keep his voice down. "Yes, you do," she argued. "I haven't lied about that."

Anger rose in his chest, the slumbering fury waking. After all this time thinking he was going crazy, thinking she was helping him, that she needed him, it turns out he was right about this—and wrong about her.

She used him.

"Eli, you don't understand."

"What? Don't understand that you invaded our city? Masqueraded as one of us for the past two months? Lied to me? Lied to Arlo? To your friends?"

"It's not that simple!"

"Then tell me the truth! That you pretended to care! Asking me about my mother, pretending to know what that's like. That you played with my emotions! Took advantage of my memory! Tell me that it was all fake!"

"It wasn't! I promise you!"

"Then what part of it was true?"

"Eli, I saved you. I've been helping you. I've confided in you. Why would I do that if I was nothing more than your enemy?" Her voice calmed, trying to settle him down.

But she was trapped in a corner. He started to wonder if she'd let him leave, or if she would attack him. He knew he wasn't strong enough to fend her off, especially under the circumstances.

"Of course you would do those things," he said. "That's how you fit in, how you infiltrate. You blend in and pretend to be like everyone else."

"Come on, Eli, *think about it.*"

"*Stop* saying that!"

"Eli, you told me that you joined to save Harper, to find yourself, to save lives and end the war. That's all I'm trying to do."

"Save it for *your* people! How many of us need to die for that to happen?"

"The war is not what we were told! That's why I'm here. I'm not here to infiltrate the Citadel program, I'm here for—"

"Our magic," he said, realization hitting him. "You're trying to figure out how to undo our magic."

"No, Eli, you don't get it."

"*Then explain it!*"

"Yes, all right, I have been searching for information on the source of Zentari magic. But not because I'm trying to undo it, only to understand it. There are these stones, called Obelisks, that contain a source of power that Guardians can use. I came here to find my friend Lucas, and figure out how those stones can help us, but along the way I discovered the Obelisks are only the beginning."

"Who is Lucas?"

"He's my best friend I've known since childhood. He was taken after a raid on Heika. He's probably dead, but based on the information I was told, he may have been taken here."

Eli didn't respond. His mind couldn't process everything at once. Maybe it was the WAVEs, maybe his emotions, but his mind was desperately fighting with his heart.

"Eli," she said softly, taking another step. "I am your friend."

"No, you're not." He scoffed, stepping back.

Tears welled in her eyes. But Eli couldn't trust them.

"Eli, I care about you," she whispered.

He drew a sharp breath, clenching his jaw. "No, you don't."

"Yes, I do!" she pressed, stepping closer.

"I don't believe you!"

"Then what can I do?"

"Stop—"

Before Eli could react, Shira pushed his arm to the side, moving the blade as she rushed forward. He braced himself, expecting an attack, but froze—as her lips pressed into his.

Shocked, his body turned to stone, eyes glazed like morning frost. Then, softly, Shira's hand came to rest at the back of his head, and the world faded. Euphoria unfurled within him like a slow-burning flame, and his eyelids drifted shut as his hands found her waist—and he kissed her in return.

He was weightless as their lips met. The room dissolved around them, leaving only the hush of their breath. Her lips were softer than air—sweeter than honey. He sank into her presence, intoxicated by her scent, her warmth, her rhythm. Every part of her echoed through his senses like the gentle rumbling of a storm.

When she finally pulled away, she lingered close, her body pressed against his. Her ragged breath was warm on his face, tethering him to this moment of trembling stillness. And again—just as it had been from the start, from that first fleeting glance in the Sparring Hall—he was undone by those ocean blue eyes. Her heart, alongside his own, thundered in the quiet between them.

"I am your friend, Eli. If you trust nothing else, trust this." She placed a hand gently on his chest.

"How do I know you're not lying?" he whispered. "How do I know what to believe?"

She stepped back and gently grabbed his arm which held the dagger, bringing it to her own throat.

"You have to decide."

He held the blade where it was, despite his instinct to immediately remove it. "Why?" he asked, torn between deceit and desire. "I'm your enemy."

"You saved my life twice. You took a punishment for me *after* you suspected the truth. I've watched you since the beginning. Eli, you are anything but my enemy."

He couldn't move. Even the trembling of his hands ceased, not for any other reason but to keep the steel from cutting her skin. If she truly was a traitor, he should report it, scream it aloud and drag her to the Leadership. If she was Aniyan, *the enemy,* a killer of his kin, then she deserved no mercy.

But could he do that to his friend? To Shira?

*No, not Shira*

*Evalynn*

But what if she was telling the truth? She was just given the perfect chance—to disarm him, flee, strike him down, silence him forever.

Yet she didn't. She even put the blade to her neck.

Either this was a reckless game of manipulation, or the conviction in her voice was no act. If there truly was more going on than they'd been told, if secrets ran deeper than orders, then this wasn't just about her. He didn't know if their end goals would align, but they could work together to bring darkness to light.

And whether by fate or his own foolishness, none of it mattered. Because somewhere between denial and destiny, Shira had claimed him—heart and soul. And as he fell into her stare, he couldn't fathom a world where he let harm touch even a single strand of her hair. Utterly helpless, Eli would rather die believing in her than live any other way.

With a low breath, he lowered the knife from her throat and let it fall from his grasp. It hit the rug with a muffled thud.

Shira exhaled—waiting. He straightened filled with a new determination. Resolve. And surrender.

"Everything changed on that mountain, Shira," he whispered. "Either you're lying, in which case I'd rather just be done with it all. Or you're still . . ."

She froze as his voice trailed. A vulnerable longing lingered in her expression, one she refused to speak aloud, but couldn't quite hide.

"Still what?" she breathed.

Eli remained silent, drinking in her presence. The ebony hair, the moonlit eyes, the pinkish hue of her soft lips, *all of it*, as if he could memorize it in the moment, as if he never expected to see it again.

He choked down the swell of emotion, buried it under guise of indifference, as he turned and slowly walked away. A heaviness settled over him, pressing his shoulders to the ground as it seeped into his very bones.

"Eli, wait."

He paused at the tone of her voice.

*But you can't trust her anymore*

"Please."

He turned around, seeing her tears glisten in the faint light.

"You didn't tell me," he said. "I would've given anything, Shira. I would have—" He stopped himself, desperately holding back the dam of emotions clawing to escape. "But I asked you, and you didn't tell me."

Before she could respond, spew lies to confuse him, he walked away, leaving Shira standing alone in the dim light of the lantern.

# Part Three: The Escape

CnC Publishing

# Chapter Forty-Two

E li's sword bit into his hands as his blade met Arlo's, the steel ringing out into the surrounding chaos of the Sparring Hall. Practice was indoors for the afternoon, given the torrential downpour outside. Eli didn't care, as long as he was allowed to hit something.

He spun and kicked Arlo in the stomach. Arlo took the brunt of the blow to his armor but staggered backward.

"Take it easy, man!" Arlo said, his face glistening with sweat. Per Eli's request, Arlo was acting only defensively, blocking his attacks. Eli wanted to practice aggressive maneuvers, since he usually was on the defensive as the weaker party. And it kept him distracted.

Shira's identity remained secret. It'd been a week since he confronted her in the library and he could barely stand to look at her, let alone speak with her. She lied to him—*had been* lying to him. It was all he could do to bury his feelings and focus on training.

Turning her in crossed his mind, wondering if keeping her secret was a betrayal of his people. He even went as far as approaching Captain Renard, but the words wouldn't leave his mouth. Despite the truth, the thought of her imprisonment—interrogation and torture—was too much.

Either way, everything was different. He stopped meeting with her at night, and she stopped training him. But the Rune Blade ceremony was approaching—only a week left. And the Reaping was scheduled immediately after that.

Despite his jump in progress after the second WAVE, Eli was still so far behind everyone else, the unbearable pressure crushed him underfoot. If he failed to manifest a Rune Blade and was forced into the Reaping, there was little doubt his journey to becoming a Guardian would meet a swift end. Shira would have to figure out how to escape before then, but Eli didn't have the luxury of avoiding the looming challenges ahead.

Either he became a Guardian, or he would die in this program.

Arlo held his hands up, needing a moment. Eli caught his breath and waited, his attention drifting to Shira and Lara's bout.

Shira grunted as her long knives clashed against Lara's staff. Lara shoved her back and spun, striking Shira in the chest. Shira countered with a spinning kick, but Lara dodged and landed another hit to her leg. Shira's knee gave out, and she collapsed. Lara stepped in, pressing the end of her staff to Shira's head.

*She lost*

*Again*

It was satisfying, for what it was worth, to see Shira so distracted. Granted, it could be her own anxiety, panic over him discovering her secret, but a part of him hoped she was struggling as much as he was. Everything had fallen apart. But they were enemies, no matter how much he desired for that to be change. The sooner she left, the better.

"Again," Shira said.

Eli caught sight of Soren in the corner of the room, speaking with one of the proctors. There were more matches called today than usual, and he wondered if Soren had something to do with it, or if it was the encroaching Rune Blade ceremony.

Once Arlo was ready, Eli threw a series of quick blows, one after the other. Arlo was barely keeping up, his heavy claymore far more unruly on the defensive. But Eli was unrelenting, pushing Arlo backward, forcing a retreat.

Finally, face red with exertion, Eli placed a strike right at Arlo's neck, stopping before the steel broke the skin. He'd finally won a match, in a weak sense of the word. And with heavy breaths, Eli held his blade still as his thoughts drifted.

"Feel better?" Arlo asked with eyebrows raised.

Eli was grateful Arlo was helping him, but he was pushing too hard. He needed to be careful before he hurt one of his own comrades. It was more dangerous for him to be letting his anger out with his sword, but he wanted to focus on his swordsmanship.

A powerful sensation was growing in his chest. He was getting stronger and faster, but he was behind, since he assumed everyone else was also getting stronger after the WAVEs. And there was that inner wrath, which hadn't emerged since the mountain.

Eli kept trying to find his niche, a hidden talent that would grant him an edge, but came up empty-handed. Each day it became more difficult to remain calm and level as an inner anger brewed.

He lowered his blade. "Yeah," he said, stepping backwards to catch his breath. "Sorry."

Arlo leaned on his sword. "Don't be, you're getting better! Just take it down a notch. Your aggression was good, but you left yourself open a few times."

Eli nodded, wiping the sweat from his brow.

"You ready to talk about it?" Arlo asked pointedly.

Eli couldn't. Both Arlo and Lara quickly noticed something was different between him and Shira after the library. Eli was able to keep them at bay by using the Crucible and his punishment as an excuse, but that wouldn't work for very long.

The guilt keeping Arlo in the dark grew, but this wasn't the first time. And there was no way of explaining what happened without compromising Shira's identity. Despite the turmoil churning inside, Eli still felt a deep need to keep her safe.

Eli sighed, shaking his head. He stepped off the mat and pulled a long drink from his waterskin. Sheathing his broadsword, he glanced at Lara, who was besting Shira fair and square. Again.

"Arlo Miller and Sol Richter!" a proctor shouted from across the room.

All four of them froze. Arlo appeared momentarily panicked, glancing at Eli who was immediately by his side.

"You can beat him," Eli said, mind racing.

"Yeah, sure," Arlo mocked. "I'll just take down the overgrown mountain man." He walked off the mat and set his claymore aside, grabbing a drink.

"Use his weight against him," Eli said. "Find easy opportunities to deliver damage, and don't be afraid to step off the mat."

"You want me to quit?" Arlo asked quietly, disgust twisting his face. "So, I can end up like Orion?"

"This isn't about pride, this is about survival," Eli rebutted.

Sol had already killed four other recruits himself. Kairah and Soren weren't far behind.

"He favors his right side," Shira said, approaching them. "Focus on his left and keep your distance."

"It's rigged!" Lara spat. "I saw Soren talking to the proctor!"

"Me too," Eli said. "Can recruits ask for match ups?"

"I don't know," Shira said.

"You step off the mat if it gets too much," Lara said, pinning Arlo with a stare.

"Guys, I got this!" Arlo said, holding his hands up, the confidence in his voice sorely lacking.

*To Hells with practice*

The three of them followed Arlo to the proctor's mat, finding they weren't the only ones waiting to watch a clash of the titans. At least a third of the room had gathered.

Sol stood waiting, a devilish grin on his face. The female proctor stood at the side with a blank expression.

"I hope you enjoyed your time here, pretty boy," Sol taunted.

"Flattery will get you nowhere, though I appreciate the compliment." Arlo raised his fists, eyes locked on his opponent. Eli had never seen him so serious or focused on a fight, and it brought dread climbing up his throat.

Sol stood casually with his arms at his sides, his red leader band mockingly bright against his armor.

"Begin!"

Arlo bounced on the balls of his feet, ready to dodge at any moment. Sol grinned, before throwing a wide arching punch. Arlo dodged the blow and delivered a solid jab to Sol's abdomen. Sol was unfazed, spinning around for another attack. Arlo successfully blocked the blow, but it knocked him sideways.

Eli watched Arlo move with a feral energy, delivering a devastating kick to Sol's left leg. The giant grunted, before Arlo threw a powerful strike to Sol's face.

Eli shifted, clenching his fists. His blood turned to ice, praying for Arlo's safety.

Sol swung his left arm back in a rising arc, shouting with the effort. Arlo leaped back, then lunged forward with a punch that caught Sol on the chin. Arlo pressed harder, bringing his knee into Sol's nose, blood coating the giant's teeth.

Sol stepped back, making no retaliation this time. He stood with his brawny arms raised—waiting. Arlo threw a kick at Sol's side, but it was blocked with his massive forearm. Arlo threw another punch at Sol's face but was deflected expertly. Sol continued carefully defending against Arlo's attacks, having stopped any aggressive actions.

"Sol's wearing him down," Shira whispered, stepping next to Eli.

"Waiting for an opening." Eli finished.

*Take your time, Arlo*

Arlo kept pushing Sol harder, delivering a flurry of attacks. Blood splattered on the mat. Eli was amazed at the physical prowess of his friend, and was thankful Arlo never attacked him with that same ferocity.

As a kick found purchase to Sol's stomach, Arlo's eyes went wide—the giant seizing his leg with an iron grip. Sol gave a bloody smile and Eli's stomach lurched.

Sol brought his elbow down on the side of Arlo's left knee, a sickening crack shooting through the room, drowned out by Arlo's scream. Eli tasted bile in his throat as Sol pulled Arlo to him, bringing his fist squarely to Arlo's face.

Arlo's head snapped back, a spray of blood arcing from his mouth. Sol released his leg, and Arlo collapsed onto the mat, gasping for breath. Without hesitation, Sol drove a boot into Arlo's stomach with a sickening thud, folding Arlo in half.

Sol dropped to one knee beside him, his shadow swallowing Arlo's curled form. The giant grabbed a fistful of Arlo's hair, yanking him upward and slamming a fist into his skull.

Again.

And again.

And again.

Each punch came down like a hammer. Flesh split. Knuckles cracked against bone. Blood smeared across Arlo's face, now a mask of red. His eyes fluttered, unfocused, barely clinging to the edge of awareness as Sol's attacks continued.

Eli took a step forward, unwilling to hold himself back any longer. The program be damned—he would face the consequences. And watching his friend

beaten, that now familiar inner wrath growled in response. But as he reached for
his sword, Shira grasped his wrist, keeping his blade sheathed, and yanking him
back.

Eli whirled.

"Don't be an idiot," she whispered.

"You're pathetic!" Sol mocked, still pummeling Arlo. "You call yourself a
warrior!"

Eli ground his teeth.

"Come on pretty boy!" Sol yelled. "Get up and challenge me!"

Eli thought for a moment, shoving aside his panic. "Sol!" he shouted. "What
kind of insecure weakling needs to keep beating a defeated comrade? If you need
to feel tough that badly, maybe you should challenge a child next!"

Sol threw Arlo down, spinning around. Death lingered in his gaze as he held
his arms out.

"The hero speaks," Sol muttered with pink teeth.

Eli's fists ached as he clenched them at his sides. He knew Sol would kill him,
but he wanted the fight. And he would challenge Sol now, if it saved Arlo.

"You're a sadist," Eli growled. "If you want blood so badly, why don't you let
me spill yours?"

"Oh?" Sol mocked, standing at the edge of the mat, bending over. "Strong
words for a worm. How's your back, Danon? Still sting when you lie down at
night?"

Shira stepped closer, brushing Eli's shoulder. Sol's eyes danced to her.

"Come on, Danon. Stop hiding behind your squad. What say you and I settle
this? Leader to leader, eh?"

"I promise you, Sol, I will be the one to kill you."

"Oh, will you? Because I believe I just took down your best. Maybe I should
have a go at her next." He pointed to Shira. "Slowly kill your entire team and leave
you for last."

Eli held his stare, fury in his veins, the beast within bellowing for blood.

"Match is over," the proctor announced. "Recruit Richter is the victor."

Sol spun around. Arlo was still on the ground, grimacing as he held his stomach. But had crawled off the mat.

Sol stomped over to the proctor. "That doesn't count!"

"Recruit Miller is clearly defeated," she replied.

"No, he quit! Punish him!"

"The opponent ceased aggressive action and removed his focus from the fight."

"I did not! I never left the mat!"

"It is the sole call of the proctor to determine when and if a match ends! Remember your place, recruit!" she shouted, drawing her long knives as she stared down the giant.

Sol turned back to Eli, who held a mocking grin.

"Oh, you are a smart one," Sol muttered, his voice filled with a quiet malice. "That little distraction was cute, Danon. I'd be counting my days if I was you."

As Sol turned and left, healers ran over. Lara's eyes remained on Arlo as three of them carried him to the door.

"Lara. Go," Eli said, jutting his chin. Fear molded her face. "We'll cover for you if anyone asks."

Lara jogged after them without a word. Eli turned and strode back to their mat, Shira following closely. There was still just under two hours of practice. He took a drink from his waterskin, before drawing his sword and standing ready on the mat.

Shira stepped opposite him, long-knives in her hands. It was difficult to meet her gaze, but Eli would have to if they were to spar together.

"When are you going to talk to me?" she asked.

"There's nothing to talk about." Eli lunged at her with a strike to the left. She deflected it with practiced ease but didn't retaliate.

"Eli, I still have to leave," she said, speaking between movements, keeping her voice as quiet as possible. "The Rune Blade Ceremony is just around the corner."

"I know," he said, landing a kick to her hip. "That's what I'm still training for. I don't have the luxury of running away."

She finally fought back with a jab to his shoulder, but it was minor. She was holding back.

"Is that what you think I'm doing?"

Eli feigned an overhead strike. Shira held her blades up to block, but he shifted at the last moment, planting himself on one leg and kicking her square in the chest. She flew backwards and landed in a huff.

Eli took a deep breath. "Come on, Shira, you're not even trying."

She sat up. "Oh? I thought I wasn't your teacher anymore?"

Eli turned and squared up. "Again," he said plainly.

Shira rolled her eyes and stood. He waited, refusing to make the first move. Shira struck, not with her blades, but with a spinning kick, the same move that had once knocked him unconscious. This time, he was ready. He ducked low beneath the arc of her leg and lunged forward with his sword. Shira reacted a beat too late. She blocked with her knives, but not fast enough. His blade grazed her left arm, slicing a shallow cut near her shoulder.

She winced, and Eli immediately stopped. "Are you—"

Shira deflected his sword, before delivering a punch to his right hand, throwing his weapon to the floor. She threw her blades aside and spun a kick to his side. Eli grunted but remained upright. He blocked her jab and grabbed her right arm, tossing her over his shoulder.

Landing with a grunt, she spun on the ground, kicking his feet from under him. Eli fell on the mat, and before he could recover, Shira jumped on him, pinning his hands above his head.

He struggled to free himself, but she had the advantage—which was all she needed. He flailed his feet but made no progress in freeing himself. Eli scoffed, unable to tell if Shira was frustrated or amused.

"Congratulations, you won. *Again*," he said, grunting as he tried to free his arms.

Shira leaned down, and he turned away as he felt himself blush, strands of her hair touching his face.

"Eli, I still need your help."

"I am helping you. By not turning you in."

"You can escape with me."

Eli's attention shot to her. Her face betrayed her longing.

*She was serious*

In a burst of energy, catching her off guard, Eli rolled all his body weight to the left. As Shira fell, he used the sudden shift to free his hands, now pinning her down.

"I'm not about to abandon my nation because you placed yourself in a dangerous position."

"Then at least help me. I need someone to cover for me to give me time to escape."

"And when is that supposed to happen? We have drills and lectures every single day. The only openings are during meals and after hours, but all the doors are guarded day and night. You can't just slip out while everyone is sleeping. And even if you wait until everything is over, there's another six months of training after this."

"I hadn't figured that part out yet," she admitted. "That's where you come in."

"Shira—"

"It's still me, Eli," she bit out, holding his gaze with her piercing eyes. "I am the same woman you saved on that mountain."

Eli took a breath, glancing around. No one paid them any mind.

"Shira, I will honor our friendship by not handing you over to be tortured for information. But I will not betray my people by helping you escape."

He saw the disappointment ripple through her face. "There are other ways to help me."

He sighed, letting her arms go and helping her up. The thought had already crossed his mind, but giving her more information was tantamount to treason—handing secrets to the enemy. Yet he still could not reconcile that his heart told him to follow her.

"What is it?" she asked, eyeing him.

He grabbed her by the arm and pulled her aside, away from itching ears.

"Those stones you mentioned."

Shira's brow wrinkled. "The Obelisks?"

He nodded, nervously glancing around. "What are they?"

"Sources of magic. I think. No one knows."

"For who?"

She shrugged. "The Guardians I assume. I don't know much about them, other than what we've discovered."

Eli took a breath. "The healers use them on critical patients. They used one on you after I brought you back."

Shira's eyes widened. "That's how the recruits heal so quickly?"

He nodded. "But it begs the question—"

"How can they use them if they aren't Guardians?" Shira finished.

# Chapter Forty-Three

S hira stared at the bottom bunk, the minutes crawling by as she waited before meeting Eli in the library. Though she was able to convince him to help her once more, everything was still so broken. The reality settled on her chest, a painful reminder that Eli was now so important to her that even his indifference left a deep wound, and the careful façade she had built around herself was beginning to crumble.

He barely looked in her direction anymore, and she loathed how much it hurt. In the beginning, she tried desperately to keep him at arm's length, pushing him away at every chance, even as her heart reached for him in the quiet moments. Falling for the enemy was never part of the mission, but now—entangled in a danger of her own making—she wished she'd stayed away.

Everything had fallen apart. Over the past week, Shira swung between chastising herself for not telling Eli, ruining what they had built, and allowing herself to become indifferent, knowing she had to leave anyway. The truth of who she was tore a gaping chasm between them, one that grew wider each day. And now it was far too late. He had fallen for a lie, one she let him believe because she longed to forget the past and live in the comfort of a borrowed name.

But Eli deserved the truth, deserved more than her selfish silence. And there was still more to confess.

Shira marched out of the bunkroom, she and Eli's last conversation repeating in her mind. She was close, *so close*, to finding the truth of the Obelisks and saving her people.

Yet, the woman that walked into this spire, the woman she was, determined to do anything to find Lucas and bring home the secrets of her enemy, had withered inside. Where she expected to find callous indifference and bloodlust among the Zentari, she instead found determination and kindness—camaraderie and compassion.

And what surprised her most was how much she grew to cherish the weightless freedom of a new identity. She arrived with a single mission, yet found herself swept into a life she'd never imagined. No longer Evalynn, daughter of the General, branded traitor, and defiant rebel of the Legion—she was respected, honored among her peers, and rising among the best.

More than that, she had *friends*. Here, no one whispered about her lineage or hair color, no one questioned her aptitude for accomplishment or the ease of her upbringing. For the first time in her life she felt seen, as if she finally belonged.

Shira entered the empty walkway, heading for the medical ward before meeting Eli. She reached inward and called upon the unwavering determination which came so easily from the depths of her soul. Her heart was torn, but it was too late. Eli had discovered the truth while she refused to let go of the identity she adopted. It had become her fantasy. She knew she should have told him sooner, trusted him to not turn her in, but the idea had terrified her.

She considered leaving without saying anything, taking the coward's way out and escaping the trap she willingly approached. But the thought of leaving Eli without answers hollowed her insides. And though it was never her intention, at some point, she stayed not to continue chasing after Lucas's ghost, but to linger in the realm of her new person.

When Eli began to pursue her, drawn not to a title or the shadow of her father, but chosen among a sea of identical warriors, she couldn't help but feel flattered. Her own logic scoffed at the idea, but she recognized Eli from her dreams. He was the man standing beside her—sword raised.

And because she now wriggled in the web of her own making, she needed his help to escape, or at least, the help of the informant. She still didn't know who that was, but would leave another coded message tonight.

"Excuse me," Shira said softly. "Nazzat?"

The healer spun around, setting aside her medical text. "Yes, recruit Weiss?"

"I have a question," Shira said, swallowing as the healer approached quizzically.

"Of course," Nazzat said, standing with hands clasped. "Are you feeling all right?"

"Yes. Thank you."

"And sir Eli?"

"He's recovered well. Thanks to you."

Shira bit her lip. She came to ask about the stones, but now wondered if telling her would be a betrayal of Eli's trust. It was clearly not common knowledge, otherwise the truth of the Obelisks wouldn't be buried.

Nazzat caught her hesitation and whispered, "I haven't said anything."

Shira's heart skipped. "About?"

Nazzat glanced around them, before her eyes flickered to Shira's ears. Eli told her he demanded it was Nazzat that treated her.

*For this reason*

He was protecting her—even then.

"Why?" Shira whispered, surprised again to find kindness where her instinct expected wrath.

"I have taken vows to never harm. And I have spent enough time in the company of death. I wish not to become its forebear."

A knot formed in Shira's throat. "Thank you."

Nazzat gave a solemn smile.

"You saved him that night," Shira said.

Nazzat nodded. "Yes."

"I'm assuming that was strictly against the rules?"

Nazzat laced her fingers before her, squeezing until they blanched, the formality of the gesture unraveling in her grip. "Just because our peoples are at war does not mean we have the liberty of forsaking our humanity. Though I would never abandon my people to fight and die alone, I find myself longing desperately for the bloodshed to end. Showing kindness where I can is a simple way to step toward that dream."

"We need more people like you."

Nazzat paused. "I have no skill to fight or protect. And my people would be long gone, were it not for our warriors."

Shira's gaze fell. "I never felt like I was making a difference."

"It is a tragedy that our generation is forced to continue a violence we were never guilty of starting."

Shira glanced around.

"Recruit Weiss. What is it you came to ask?" Nazzat said, touching Shira's arm.

"How did I recover so quickly? So many recruits receive what would be life threatening injuries for my own—" Shira caught herself. Nazzat's gaze danced around. "How is it possible?"

"Magic is a powerful thing."

"But is there more? Anything that might help me save . . . others?"

Concern pressed Nazzat's brow together. "I cannot speak of my people's secrets, you understand. Just believe me when I tell you, our tools would not help your people in such a manner."

Shira nodded, turning to leave. Nazzat grasped her arm.

"Recruit. You should leave. I know too well the price of crossing the Citadel's Leadership."

For a fleeting moment, Shira wondered if Nazzat was the informant. But if she were, surely she would have said so. And as Shira met the healer's gentle yellow eyes, the suspicion slipped away, leaving only a quiet, uneasy truth: there were more kind hearts among her enemies than she was ever willing to believe.

"I know," Shira said, "but there's something I need to do first."

# Chapter Forty-Four

E li grabbed the next book off the shelf labeled *Herbal Potions of the Fore-bears,* while Shira read one titled *Spells and Secrets of the Elders.* Though he agreed to meet once more in the library, it had only been ten minutes, and the discomfort was already unbearable. Telling her about the healers using the stones weighed on his conscience, and helping her escape was certainly crossing a line. But his curiosity about the secrets of the Citadel hadn't lessened in the least.

They continued, in silence, searching titles along the section dedicated to folklore and ancient history. It was nearly impossible to determine at face value which books were historical record and which were works of fiction. It wasn't terribly late, but time was running short.

Shira slammed her book closed, the thud stretching in the silence. She rough-ly placed the book back, and began searching for another, scanning across the shelves. Eli turned to a random page, his mind fighting his demand to focus.

*Take ye the root of mandragore, pulled at the darke of moone, and steep it in the elixir of springe water for seven nyghts. Mix therein the powdered tusk of a Dire Boar, and stirre thrice widdershins. This potion, when quaffed by the ailing, shall restore strength and vigour, and guard 'gainst the malady of the wynd.*

He sighed, replacing the book. This entire process felt hopeless. There were hundreds of thousands of books in this library. Finding one among them that contained the answers they needed was hilariously impossible.

Eli assessed the shelves amidst the quiet of the library, and his mind drifted to the night everything changed. But as regret formed like swirling clouds overhead, he shook off the feeling, grabbed his lantern, and walked back toward the front of the entrance.

"Hey, we just started," Shira said. "Where are you going?"

"To check upstairs," Eli answered over his shoulder. Being in her presence was too distracting.

Navigating through the rows of bookshelves, Eli read the cryptic headings, guessing at their general contents. He saw labels pertaining to the art of war, herbal medicine, meditation, and lost wonders of the world, but nothing of note. Reaching the staircase at the far right of the library, Eli began his ascent to the second level, each step stirring a puff of dust from the long-neglected runner, a clear sign that no one had been up there in quite some time.

As he reached the top of the stairs, he was met with more bookshelves—an endless sea of literature. With a sigh, he meandered through the forest of tomes, praying for answers. A wave of curiosity rose, as Eli noted these books were more obscure topics, speaking to fantasies and ancient myths. His interest spiked when his eyes found the gold lettering along the spine of an old green tome, the text barely visible through the white film of dust.

*The Inner Power of Adiel*

The spine creaked with protest after such a long slumber. Eli scoured the contents, skimming through the pages that seemed to speak only of unknown mysteries behind creation itself. He paused, as he turned to a new chapter—staring at its heading.

*Harnessing the Veil*

His brow stitched. Something in his gut said this may be what they were looking for. He stopped at a sentence, written in an outdated dialect.

*In the venerable praxis of the field of Archancy, the sagacious adept attune to the inert resonance of natura, availing the telluric essence, the zephyrs' vitality, the igneous fervency, and the aqueous purity. Through arcane rites and esoteric formularies, this subtle dynamis draws from upon the liminal veil, transmuted and imbued into lithic vessels. Now suffused with the quintessence of the unseen currents, the aforementioned become prodigious and potent reliquaries, to be wielded by those versed in the ancient arcana and the equilibrium of the primordial forces.*

Eli's thoughts clambered as he tried to understand the old text, but something very clear and intriguing stuck out. Something Arlo mentioned. His attention drifted to the opposite shelf—a dust shadow left from a book that was recently taken but not returned.

"Find anything?"

Eli jumped at Shira's voice. He closed the book and let out a breath.

"Sorry," she said, taking the tome from his hands.

"No, it's fine. I think I found something," he said, helping her flip back to the page he just read.

Shira scanned the text, her expression mirroring his own, trying to understand the outdated writing.

"This might be talking about the Obelisks," she said, turning the page.

"You think this is the solution the Council found?" he asked.

"I don't know, but Eli, this is huge. Last I spoke with Lucas, he said the Zentari don't know how the stones are made."

*Lucas*

"How could they know about them, and how to use them, but not know how they're made?"

"That's the burning question. But this book is a first step. Nice job."

Eli couldn't help but feel guilty with her attempt at kindness. She was trying, but the chasm between them was also her fault.

"That's not the only thing," he said, feeling her eyes on him. "Look at this word, here."

*Archancy*

"I've heard it before," she said. "What about it?"

"Arlo mentioned it in the stone prison Lara was kept in," he said, taking a step away. Just standing near her overwhelmed him, threatened to dissolve his very will.

"On the mountain?"

"Yeah. He said it when he was looking at those weird markings on the walls."

"That's what it means by 'esoteric formularies,'" she muttered.

"Hells if I know, but he said it while looking at the symbols."

Shira bit her lip in thought. Eli wondered what she was thinking. Or what she was keeping from him.

"You said you've heard of Archancy before?" he asked.

"Yes," she answered. "Lucas mentioned it when I first learned about the stones. And in my father's study before I left. He had dozens of letters, and a journal, talking about finding something called an Everstone."

Eli's brow wrinkled. "Everstone?" he said, tasting the word. "Is it just another Obelisk?"

Shira shook her head. "I don't think so. Based on what I could understand of my father's notes, an Everstone is something from legend. All knowledge of it is lost, but anyone who has one could single-handedly win the war. Rule the country."

"Which means nothing without any context," Eli said.

"Like whether someone could actually use one." Shira finished. "Or if one can even be found."

Eli nodded, organizing his thoughts. "Hang on. If Archancy is related to the Obelisks, and the Zentari are searching for more stones, then we can assume they don't understand Archancy at all."

"But that assumes Archancy is the key to creating Obelisks."

"True, but let's assume it is for a minute. If Archancy is an ancient science of the Zentari and lost to time, then how does your father know about it?"

"That's easy," Shira said.

Eli caught her sheepish glance. "Spies. Right."

"But I don't think it is lost to time," Shira muttered.

Eli's eyes narrowed. "How so?"

Shira's attention flickered to him—apprehensive. "If I tell you, I betray my King."

Eli huffed.

"No, Eli," she said quickly, "I'm saying you're not the only one willing to share with the enemy."

He waited, seeing the truth in her softened expression. And he found himself longing—for a moment—to bridge the chasm between them.

"My father knows the science," Shira said. "At least, I'm fairly certain."

"From his journal?"

"Yes."

"You said he was looking for an Everstone."

"Yes, but there was more," Shira said, a warning in her tone. "I think he's trying to *make* an Everstone. The journal was filled with archaic terms and symbols. It sounded like he was working through a puzzle or formula. If we assume Everstones and Obelisks are created in a similar fashion, then I am certain my father is at least adept in the science."

"That would explain how the stones exist when Archancy seems forgotten," Eli mused, "but that begs the question, how does General Malachi know about it when the Council doesn't?"

"How do you know they don't?"

"Because they wouldn't be searching otherwise."

"Maybe," Shira said. "A better question is, how does Arlo know what Archancy is?"

"I don't know," Eli said, pausing as a cautious idea presented itself. "We could ask him."

Shira's eyes darkened as she closed the book. "No. We can't."

"Shira, I don't think he'll turn you in."

She set the book on the shelf, wringing her hands through her hair. Eli knew she was desperate for answers, and every moment she spent here was a risk. He wondered why she hadn't left yet.

"Have you found your friend?" Eli asked softly.

Shira's stilled, her gaze dropping. "No," she breathed.

"Where have you looked?"

"Everywhere I'm allowed."

"Is he why you haven't left?" Eli asked pointedly.

Shira's attention moved to him, and he saw the truth she carried, even before she spoke. "He's not the only reason anymore."

Eli held her stare, restraining his desire to comfort, feel her hair run through his fingers. "How do you know he's still alive?"

Shira shook her head, her bottom lip quivering for the briefest moment. "I don't. He's probably gone. But I can't live without knowing for certain."

Eli took a breath. "Look, I can't help you find Lucas. But I don't have to tell Arlo about you. Maybe I can talk to him and see if he remembers anything about Archancy without bringing you up."

A heavy silence settled between them. Eli was dancing on a razor's edge, pretending semantics was an argument for treason.

"I thought you weren't helping me," she said, taking a step toward him.

He shifted his weight, wanting to step away, if only to control himself. In truth, he didn't know what he was doing, or how much honor he had left.

"Eli, I don't know what I can do to—"

"You can't, so don't try." Regret clung to his words as they were spoken, but he couldn't deny his anger. She'd hurt him—deeply.

"I'll talk to Arlo when I can and let you know what he says," he muttered.

"Fine," she replied, brushing the dust off a shelf with her thumb.

Eli stepped around her and left the library.

"Eyes up, recruits!"

Eli's eyes snapped open. His limbs thrummed with energy, but his mind was hollow. Shira's betrayal festered like rot in his stomach, and he couldn't stop wondering who else in his life was lying. Thanks to the WAVEs influence, and what he hoped was his inner magic awakening, his body felt invincible—powerful and boundless. But his thoughts dragged like chains, twisting and heavy with doubt.

Hopping out of bed, he glanced at Arlo's empty bunk. The healers were confident Arlo would be released today, despite having to keep him overnight. Eli swallowed his anxiety, knowing Sol would have killed Arlo if given the chance.

He dressed himself and strapped on his practice sword. As he was leaving the bunkroom, Eli spotted Fenner mixed with the crowd of recruits heading for breakfast and moved to his side.

"Hey, how're you feeling?" Eli asked. He hadn't spoken much with Fenner, despite him being Maelyn's squadmate.

"Good," Fenner said. "Think I've finally recovered from the Proving."

Eli recalled hearing of Fenner's back injury from his fall as they descended the barracks steps, crammed between the recruits.

"Good to hear. How's sparring going?"

"Better. Esme and Maelyn are helping me a lot. Is Shira still helping you?"

"Yeah, but not as much. Arlo and I have been practicing more." Eli attempted to shake the heaviness draped over his shoulders.

Fenner said, "Hey, can I ask you something?"

"Of course."

"Is Shira okay?"

Eli's heart skipped a beat. "Yeah, why?"

"Hells Elijah, it was my squadmate that caused her injury."

"Right." He bit down on the fury rising in his chest, thinking back to the mountain.

"Yeah, I just wanted you to realize how ruthless the lecture from Maelyn was. And Esme nearly didn't stop beating his face in. I thought she might kill him honestly."

A smile crept on Eli's face. "Good to know."

They reached the mess hall and sat at their table. Eli intentionally sat next to Lara, with Shira across from him. All were present, apart from Arlo, which made the table feel entirely empty. Esme, Maelyn, and Fenner fit in well, and Eli was forever in their debt. Rowan, to no surprise, still ate by himself at another table.

"Think he wants to sit with Kairah and Soren?" Fenner asked, sipping his porridge.

Esme and Maelyn glanced to their solitary squadmate.

"He can do as he wishes," Maelyn said, biting her bread. "But he'll face the consequences."

"How's he doing?" Eli asked Lara.

"He's fine," she said—too quickly. "He's already making jokes again."

Lara had been quiet ever since the match and still appeared unsettled. It was close. Too close.

Shira said, "Only Arlo can get his Nines handed to him and make a joke about it."

"I'm glad he's okay," Maelyn added.

Lara gave an appreciative smile. After a quiet breakfast, the recruits gathered in the Lecture Hall.

"Class, today is a day no doubt many of you have been eagerly awaiting." Darby began. "Today, we delve into the art of magic."

*Finally*

The room leaned forward in anticipation.

"As you are aware, the magic within all Zentari can be harnessed and used combatively. History is unclear when the use of Spirit Steel was founded, but the oldest texts speak that the Primarchs were able to manifest the most powerful forms of magic. We presume this to be in part due to this lost science. Spirit Steel is a combination of metallurgy and alchemy, creating a weapon that can draw out and focus a Guardian's inner magic.

"The weapon created with Spirit Steel is known as a Rune Blade. Each one is unique, bonded to its Guardian. It is through the use of our Rune Forge that this process is accomplished, and though it greatly pains me as a Keeper to admit, the truth behind this science has been lost. We do not know how they are constructed. It is some combination of inner magic and the science of the Rune Forge that we no longer understand."

A female recruit raised her hand from the front row. Darby nodded, unfazed there was already a question.

"Can a Guardian release their inner magic without a Rune Blade?"

"Yes, though it is exceedingly difficult and dangerous. The reason we utilize these magical weapons is to not only allow our warriors to be more efficient on the battlefield, but to ensure the safety of their comrades. A Guardian who is unwieldy with his magic, can not only cause serious damage to others, but themselves as well."

Another hand raised. Darby sighed but nodded at the male recruit in the center of the room.

"How does one know the limit of their inner magic?"

"If you would allow me to continue the lecture, many of your questions would already have answers." Darby threw a look at the recruit. "Nevertheless, the answer to your question is simple: you cannot. The depth and width of the pool of magic within each Guardian is different, and the type of magic utilized can also drain the pool at differing rates. It is another reason Rune Blades are utilized. With a more focused effort of expending inner magic, Guardians can become attuned to their own auras, sensing when their bodies are pushed to their limit. With unwieldy, explosive uses of magic, you may inadvertently cause your own destruction."

No other hands raised, but murmurs persisted throughout the crowd.

"For recruits such as yourselves, those of you who are able to obtain a Rune Blade and begin practicing, your limits will be short indeed. Taking heed of the warning signs is paramount to survival. I need not explain the danger in depleting your very life force. Weakness, lethargy, chest pain, and dizziness are the most common symptoms that you are nearing your limit."

Eli raised his hand. Darby gave a reluctant glare, before nodding.

"What can you tell us about the Reaping?"

The room filled with chatter. Some were upset by the change of subject, while others were glad the question was finally brought up. Darby waited for everyone to quiet before answering.

"I am glad to hear you finally ask a question that does not push the boundaries of the program, recruit Danon. There is a reason the Leadership waits to explain the Reaping. It is the final stage of the program, and many consider it to be your third and most deadly challenge."

Eli swallowed.

"If any among you are unable to summon a Rune Blade at the Rune Forge, you are immediately a participant in the Reaping. Recruits are chosen in pairs, at random, to battle to the death. There are only two ways to survive the Reaping. You either successfully manifest magic during combat or you kill your opponent."

Murmurs spread like a rustling wind. Eli and Shira shared a concerned glance. He had all confidence she could survive against anyone in the room, unless they discovered their magic first. But if he failed to obtain a Rune Blade—

A hand raised to the back of the room.

"Keeper Darby, sir," a female recruit asked. "So, it is possible for someone to survive the Guardian program without ever manifesting magic?"

"Technically yes, recruit Nuvo. Very astute. By the methods utilized in this program, there is a possibility that one, and only one, recruit can survive the Reaping and graduate without ever finding inner magic. They are not granted the title of Guardian but are promoted to the rank of Operative and begin the next phase of military training."

Another hand raised. "How often has that happened, sir?"

"There has been only a single occurrence."

# Chapter Forty-Five

S hira pulled her boot laces taut, leaving her leather armor on the bed as she strolled out of the bunkroom before morning light. Jogging before dawn had become a habit, a way to clear her mind, ever since the Crucible. Not only was she forcing her body to recover but could sense herself falling behind.

She was so used to being the best, easily rising above her peers, it was a foreign thing to rank in the middle of the pack—to feel average. Lara and Arlo were so challenging on the mats now, she was exhausted by the end of practice. Even Eli was getting annoyingly good. She could still best him in a fair fight, but she wondered if it was only because he was distracted by her presence.

Shunning him from her mind, she stepped into the silent walkway.

"Mind if I join you?"

Shira spun around at Lara's voice, holding a hand to her chest.

"What?" Shira gasped.

"Sorry, didn't mean to scare you," Lara said with a smile. "I noticed you've been jogging in the mornings, and I thought it'd be nice to have some girl time."

"Oh, sure, yeah, that's fine," Shira stammered, continuing toward the practice field.

"You don't sound very convincing," Lara teased, having also left her armor behind, wearing a black, slimming outfit.

"Where did you get those clothes?" Shira asked with a grin.

"Oh, I've had them. You just haven't seen them."

"Has Arlo seen them?" Shira pried.

Lara's jaw dropped, yet her grin persisted. She slapped Shira's shoulder as they walked out into the fresh morning air of the practice field. The dew wet their boots as they started out in a slow jog, making a wide circle around the open plain.

"How's your back?" Lara asked.

"Fine. Doing a lot better actually. It's why I started running," Shira responded, unable to remember a time when she felt physically inferior to those around her.

"Good, I'm glad."

"Arlo's supposed to be released today, right?" Shira asked, her breathing labored compared to Lara's.

"Yeah." Lara's demeanor darkened. "I can't stop thinking about it. It was so close. I was afraid he wouldn't tap out."

"Everyone's afraid to tap out after what happened with Orion. They made it pretty clear it was unacceptable."

"Better than to die at the hands of Sol Richter."

Shira sadly agreed. If you were doomed to die, it's good to recognize there are fates worse than death.

"I think you're why he did it," she said.

"What do you mean?"

"You gave him quite the death glare before the match. I think Arlo hoped he could beat Sol, but decided to chance the proctor instead of waiting for Sol to kill him slowly. In front of you, no less."

Lara was silent, the fear from that match still clinging to her like a second skin. They had all felt it—the lingering terror, like being trapped in a pond with a hungry shark.

"Hey," Lara said. "Remember when you made a deal to ask me a question?"

"Oh no," Shira responded, her shirt darkening with sweat.

"What in the Nine Hells happened with you and Eli?"

Shira huffed. "Come on, nothing happened!"

"Boar spit! It's obvious."

"Nothing. Happened."

"Did he come on to you too strong?"

"What?" Shira turned to Lara, stopping for a rest. "No!"

"Did he steal a kiss?"

"I wouldn't let him."

"Confess his love?"

"For Rot's sake, stop, or I'm leaving!"

"Was it your fake ears?"

Shira's heart skipped a beat. She tried to think of a response, but the moment passed.

"I don't know what—"

"Oh, stop, I can spot those things from across the room."

Shira stammered, playing on her heavy breathing to buy herself time to think.

"Why haven't you said anything?" she asked, watching Lara carefully.

"It's not my place to point out someone's birth defect."

Shira forced her breathing slow, sweat glistening on her forehead.

"It's *Abz'ane* syndrome, or something, right? You probably know it better than I do."

Lara appeared sincere. A pang of guilt tugged at Shira as they resumed running.

"I don't like to talk about it."

"Hey, I get it, but you didn't answer my question. Was that it?"

"No, it wasn't that," she said quickly. The pit in her stomach grew. Perhaps all she was good at was lying to those closest to her. "We just got in a fight. That's it."

"Oh, just a good ol' lover's spat, huh?"

"Stop, Lara, please," Shira said. "I hurt him. And I really don't want to talk about it."

Her friend gave a solemn nod. "Okay. But if you change your mind, I'm here."

The heat of the afternoon sun warmed the practice field, banishing the recent rainfall from the ground, markedly increasing the humidity. The recruits were scattered about the open plain, shouts of effort and clanging metal sounding near the coastline.

Shira was bathed in sweat as she sparred with Lara. Lightheadedness suppressed her focus as she strained to keep up with her opponent. Everyone in the program had improved so significantly, Shira felt like she was stagnant by comparison, as if suddenly a novice among seasoned warriors.

She assumed that as everyone's inner magic grew, it directly enhanced their physical skills. It surprised her at first, knowing she was always able to best the Zentari she faced on the battlefield. But then again, those weren't Guardians in training.

She switched to a defensive stance as Lara threw another strike with her staff. The wood collided with Shira's knives before she ducked under Lara's second attack. Shira countered with a kick to Lara's side, but it left her open. Lara feigned a jab to Shira's left, but brought the strike from the right, which found purchase on Shira's back.

The blow hit near her previous injury, and she cried out in pain, falling to one knee.

"Oh, Shira, I'm sorry!" Lara said, touching her shoulder with concern.

Shira held her hand up. "It's all right," she said with a grimace. "I'm fine."

As the pain lessened, Shira sat and squinted in the sunlight, watching Eli and Arlo spar. Eli was far less aggressive than he'd been over the past week, no doubt in light of Arlo's recovery. It was admirable that although Arlo's body was bruised, his confidence appeared unshaken.

The two had removed their shirts, and Shira noticed the wide birthmark on the left side of Eli's chest. Arlo was sweating so much he appeared to have jumped in a lake. The four scars on his shoulder were notably pink against the rest of his skin, similar in appearance to the scars on Eli's back. The sight chewed at her insides.

Arlo swung his sword wide to Eli's left. Eli deflected it upward and countered, striking at Arlo's chest. Arlo lifted his blade, blocking with the hilt and shoving Eli back. Eli stumbled but kept his eyes fixed on his opponent.

"Don't think you can beat me just yet," Arlo mocked.

"You're favoring your left knee pretty hard," Eli retorted with a grin. "I could do more if I wanted."

Shira's breathing calmed as the pain subsided. Sheathing her blades, she reached for her waterskin. Fed up with the heat, she wished she could jump over the cliff and bathe in the cool ocean for an hour—without the risk of drowning, of course.

"You all right?" Lara asked.

Shira nodded, taking another gulp.

"Doesn't hurt to watch the boys for a minute." Lara teased with a smile, which Shira mirrored.

"I think Rowan tried to get moved to Sol's squad," Shira said, praying for a cloud to provide some much-needed shade.

Lara's eyes widened. "Seriously? Is that what Maelyn said? I knew a handful of squads were getting new members, but I didn't know a recruit could request it."

"I heard some of the other recruits snickering about the change in ranks. Someone mentioned a few directly requested changes, including Rowan. I assume he wanted to be on Sol's squad after the mountain."

Lara thought for a moment. "What a rotting coward."

In light of the deaths after the Crucible, a few squads were permanently short members and were dissolved, merging to other squad openings. Captain Renard and Evergreen made the needed decisions and informed the squads of their new members, which didn't go over well.

Arlo and Eli stopped sparring. Shira could tell Arlo needed rest, though he never would admit it. His heavy breathing made the sweat on his muscular chest glimmer in the sunlight.

"Lara!" Eli shouted, not looking at Shira. "Swap with Arlo?"

"Sure!" Lara said, grabbing her staff.

Arlo shuffled over, dragging his sword with the slightest limp. Shira caught it, despite his subtle—yet very conscious—effort to hide it.

"Mind taking a break?" Arlo asked, sitting next to her.

Shira shook her head, coming to enjoy his calm demeanor. It reminded her of Lucas.

"How's the knee?" she teased.

Arlo gave a breathy laugh. "Doing fine. I'm sure it'll heal okay."

"If I get paired with Sol I'll return the favor," she said, not bothering to hide the anger in her voice.

Arlo huffed. "Sure."

"What? Don't think I can?" Shira smiled. She couldn't believe she was trying to cheer *him* up. "I'm serious. I'll rip out his Nines and feed 'em to him."

Arlo laughed. "I would pay to see that, actually."

"That can be arranged." Shira chuckled. There was something about Arlo that lifted her spirits, something deeply familiar.

As their banter faded, Arlo's demeanor darkened. "Shira," he said softly. "Did he ever tell you what happened?"

"Didn't Maelyn tell you?"

"No. I agreed with you. If he chose not to tell us, we should leave it. But—" Arlo said. "Since you're closer to him, I thought maybe he said something."

Shira paused, the memory of the library returning, guilt and sorrow following on its heels.

"Yes. He did." She breathed. "Sol decided to punish the squad leaders by lashings."

"How many were there?" Arlo asked, watching Eli and Lara battle.

"Forty," she said grimly, averting her eyes to hide the swell of emotion.

"He told you that?" Arlo's eyebrows stitched as he turned in surprise.

"I counted them."

"Ten for each of us," he mused. "That's what he meant. Bleeding Hells, he should have died."

"He almost did, Arlo," Shira said. "One of the healers saved him overnight."

"Who?"

Shira paused. "They could get in serious trouble if—"

"You think I'd turn in someone who saved his life?" Arlo asked, astonished—offended.

"It was Nazzat. Eli told her not to, but she did it anyway."

The heaviness of the topic faded as their conversation died. Both rested in the humid afternoon heat, watching the other recruits, many of whom also took frequent breaks. Shira heard an official match called in the distance, thankful it wasn't anyone she recognized.

"Hey, we're friends, right?" Shira asked pointedly.

Arlo laughed. "Why do I get the feeling I'm not going to like what comes next?"

"What are you running from?" she asked, giving him a serious look.

"Holy Hells woman, go for the throat, why don't you?" Arlo smirked, and Shira couldn't help but smile.

"I'm serious! Answer the question. You said I wasn't observant, and now I'm proving you wrong. You walk with unwavering confidence and a cheerful attitude that no one else even attempts. Either you're something inhuman, or there's a truth you refuse to acknowledge."

"Look, I'm not running from anything. Your observations are off." He winked with his crooked grin.

"Oh, fine," she spat. "Then what is it?"

"Oh, that my dear, is a story for another time. In the meantime, you should hone your skill of miscalculation."

Shira turned to hit him but stopped. "You're lucky you hurt your shoulder."

Arlo huffed. "Hey, I'm used to getting beaten up."

"You said you had a lot of siblings, didn't you?"

"Yep. Eleven total."

Shira's mouth fell open, her muscles turning rigid. "Where are you in the lineup?" she asked carefully, hiding her shock.

"Second to oldest. Why? You have siblings?"

She willed her heart to settle and commanded her mouth to speak.

"What's your middle name?"

Arlo gave a questioning look. "Matthias."

Shira was silent, ears ringing—mind racing.

Arlo said, "Hey, you didn't answer my question."

"No, I'm an only child," Shira said curtly.

Arlo's brow furrowed. "Oh, that makes the whole demanding, abrasive personality thing make sense."

The joke was lost, as her mind drifted miles away.

Shira hurled the book down the aisle, barely containing the anger swirling within. Everything was unraveling, spiraling straight into the Hells. She was suffocating. Her instincts screamed for her to run—to survive. But something deeper, heavier, chained her in place. Trapped between two worlds, she desperately held to both, even as it tore her soul apart.

It was the fragile experience of her identity as Shira which granted her the strength and comfort to begin facing the truth that by all rights Lucas was gone. And Eli had become her saving grace, impressing the idea that even if her childhood friend were lost, there were yet some things worth living for.

That truth was now her reality. Everything that made her life worth fighting for was trapped inside this spire. But if she stayed, it was only a matter of time before she was found—and the price would be her death.

She had to leave. Every instinct, every shred of reason demanded it. But after today, and given everything else, there was no way in the rotting Hells she could simply leave. But the Rune Blade Ceremony was only a few days away. Her deadline to leave was nearly here, and there was so much left to be done.

Shira had skipped supper and spent the entire evening in the library, knowing the answer was somewhere among the shelves. But without Eli's help, she felt adrift in a vast ocean. She collapsed on the ground, leaning against a bookshelf lining a narrow alcove. The aisle ended against a stone wall, with a round table and two wooden chairs. The air remained musty and stale, grating her throat as she took a deep breath.

A noise cut through the silence, and her eyes shot open.

"Eli?" she asked, standing and checking the aisle next to hers.

There, on the rug, lay a folded piece of parchment. The informant responded to her message already.

Grabbing the note, footsteps sounded nearby, growing faint as the informant left. Shira retreated to her alcove, unfolding the note and reading the contents. Her eyes narrowed at the scribbled message, recognizing the familiar handwriting. The message was exactly what she needed but still left too many unanswered questions. And was a bit late.

Tossing the letter on the table, Shira sat in a huff. As her weight shifted on the old wood, it creaked, one of the legs breaking. She gasped as it threw her onto the floor near the wall. Anger boiled in her chest as she stood, touching the cold stone wall with her hand. Yet her frustration evaporated as she glanced at the previously unnoticed markings etched into the rock.

They were glowing faintly.

# Chapter Forty-Six

E li guided the ax down on the piece of firewood, splitting it down the middle, two pieces clunking onto the pile created after a long afternoon. The sun settled on the horizon, and Eli's energy followed suit. He wiped the sweat from his brow, taking a moment. Harper should be done with her schoolwork soon. He'd have to check it before the inn became busy with the evening customers.

Eli picked up an armful of the freshly chopped logs, stacking his day's work at the back of the house. Winter wasn't far away, and his father's bad back meant Eli was tasked with most of the work preparing for the colder months.

After setting the firewood aside, Eli walked around to the front. The siding on their inn needed replacing at the corners, and he wasn't sure if they were doing well enough financially to pay for it. His father kept everything so close to the chest these past few years, it was unclear where they stood with their debts.

Whenever Harper needed something, their father would make it happen. But Eli typically was met with some excuse about how *it could wait.* Yet as frustrating as that was, Eli couldn't resent his father for it. He had provided a home and living for them, away from the war and in a safe place for Harper to grow up. Eli knew his father was trying to make ends meet in an impossible time.

He stepped onto the front porch and opened the door. The inn flashed with orange light as a toppled lantern sparked the corner of the room ablaze. The sound of screaming and fighting erupted in his ears. Among the chaos, Eli's attention snapped to the imposing figure standing at the center of the room, his back turned. Time ground to a halt as the man lifted Harper by her neck, her body thrashing helplessly in his grasp.

"Harper!" Eli shouted, waking to a figure standing over his bed.

He leaped up, grabbing the front of the intruder's armor, raising his right fist to strike. It took a moment, as gentle hands touched his arm, before he realized it was Shira.

He was in the bunkroom. In the Citadel.

The other recruits stirred.

"Keep it down!" one grumbled from the corner.

Shira waited until he let go, his hand aching from clenching her armor.

"Hey," Arlo whispered from his bed. "You all right, man?"

Eli spoke over his shoulder. "Yeah. I'm fine. Go back to bed, Arlo."

"Nightmares again?"

"I said I'm fine," Eli bit, striding out of the bunkroom around Shira, who followed closely behind. The air in the common room was cool on his exposed chest, sweat stealing his body heat. He wrung his hands through his hair with a sharp breath.

*Why won't these rotting nightmares stop*

Shira waited, closing the door and giving him a moment. He felt better as he paced.

"I didn't know you were having nightmares," she said softly.

"Yeah, well, I have. Ever since the beginning of this rotting program." Eli walked over to the vacant common area and sat on one of the chairs, placing his face in his hands. He was shaking. The image of Harper in distress coiled around his mind like a venomous snake.

"Are you all right?"

Eli flinched as Shira's hand gently touched his shoulder. He shifted uncomfortably at her affection.

"Yeah, I'm fine. What do you need?" he asked quietly, hoping his outburst hadn't drawn attention. But guilt softened his frustration, seeing genuine concern written on Shira's face.

"I need to talk to you."

He exhaled as he stood. "Shira, not tonight."

"No, you don't understand," she said, holding her hands up. "I found something *below* the library."

Eli's brow wrinkled. She knew how to play off his curiosity.

"Like what, there's a cellar?" he asked.

"No, I asked someone weeks ago in passing whether there were more levels to the library than the two we know. Whatever this place is, it isn't common knowledge."

"Then how did you find it?"

She paused before answering. "I have to show you."

Eli sighed. "Shira—"

"Eli," she pressed. "Trust me."

He didn't think she realized how badly he wanted to do just that.

"Fine," he muttered, sneaking back into the bunkroom for his shirt, before following her down the stairs. "You're still in your armor."

Shira's hair drifted behind her as they stepped into the walkway, catching Eli's attention despite himself.

"You're observant," she snarked. "I haven't been to bed yet."

"What time is it?"

"Hells if I know, but I don't have the luxury of sitting around."

He rolled his eyes but made no reply. They arrived at the library and each grabbed a lantern from the supply table near the door. Shira led him through the aisles until she stopped at a narrow alcove, different from their usual spot.

She set her lantern on the table and turned to him. "You want me to be completely honest? This is me being honest," she said plainly.

Eli's eyes narrowed, unsure of her intention.

"I wasn't sent here. Not officially. I took this mission from someone else. I asked my father to send me on a mission to rescue Lucas and he refused, saying he would send another Swordsman."

Eli remained silent, somehow not surprised she stole the mission from a comrade.

"On my way here, I read the report explaining the mission details. I was to go undercover as a Citadel recruit to infiltrate the ranks and find if and where the Aniyan prisoners of war were being held. If I found them, I was to try and see if there was any way to rescue them, Lucas included."

He crossed his arms. As much as he still harbored an anger born from the betrayal, he was glad she was trusting him with this information—even if it was too late.

"The only way to infiltrate the Citadel safely was to have someone on the inside looking out for the spy." She took a breath. "Eli, there's a Zentari warrior stationed here at the Citadel that's been helping me."

Eli's mouth fell open.

*What in the Hells*

"Wait," he said. "How is that—"

"I told you before that you don't understand everything. Let me explain."

His lips pursed, but he stopped talking.

"This informant, who apparently reached out to the Legion of their own volition, has been helping me. It's why I haven't undergone the WAVEs and why I haven't been discovered yet."

"Wait, you haven't had any WAVEs?"

"Eli, come on, where's that brain of yours?"

His jaw clenched, but she was right. Of course she wouldn't get a Thought Wave Analysis done. The recruits weren't told much of anything about it, and there was no reason for her to have it done. She didn't possess magic. It would only serve to increase her chances of exposure.

It also explained why she questioned him about his responses to the procedure. Though it pained him to admit, she was likely more curious about the WAVEs effects on Zentari, rather than how he personally felt.

"Okay, go on."

"The informant and I have been exchanging messages periodically here in the library. We've been helping each other, but there's very little we can discuss on paper, since it could be intercepted. Tonight, I came here because of something Arlo said."

"Wait, you already talked to Arlo?"

"Shut up and let me finish," she said. "Eli, what I'm about to tell you will sound insane, but I need you to trust me."

Eli took a deep breath. He didn't know if he could at this point. Everything was growing more complicated, pulling him deeper into a mire pit.

"I think Arlo is Lucas's brother," Shira said.

"Lucas, the guy you came here to find?"

Shira nodded.

"But that would mean—" His eyes widened at the realization. "You think he's Aniyan?"

"This afternoon on the practice field—"

"Shira, that doesn't make any sense!" he whispered harshly, looking around them for prying ears.

"I know it doesn't but listen to me! There's been something familiar about Arlo this entire time, and this afternoon he told me he grew up with eleven siblings and is second in the line, which is identical to Lucas's family. Lucas is the eldest, *and* they have the same last name!"

"Miller is an extremely common name! Besides, why didn't you recognize his name sooner?"

"Because I've only known him by Matthias, which is apparently his middle name!"

"And your *best friend* never mentioned his brother's middle name?"

"He probably did, but Lucas has eleven siblings I've never met. My father barely tolerated Lucas being around."

"It's a coincidence Shira, nothing more!"

"Eli, just think about it for a second!"

He rubbed his face. This was ridiculous. He knew she was desperate but never thought she would try something like this.

"He has pointed ears, brown hair, and brown eyes." Eli started. "He remembers volunteering and remembers his previous life perfectly, living around *Eldan City*. He hasn't had a feeling of uneasiness or spoken about any troubled feelings, otherwise he'd be asking questions with us. He hasn't mentioned being kidnapped recently. Stop me when I've made my point."

Shira was silent, her expression soft with expectation. He knew that look. She was waiting for him to catch up to her thoughts. And the idea hit him like a brick to the skull.

Shira whispered, "What color is Harper's hair?"

Eli scoffed at the absurdity of the question. Harper's hair. It was—

*What is happening*

"That doesn't mean anything," he spat, his mind beginning to race. It was blonde, the color of sunshine and dry sand. He could picture it—clear as day. But in his mind, she had pointed ears. He couldn't remember her eye color. He rubbed his face, straining to remember the details, but something pressed against his mind's pursuit.

And a thunderous aversion ignited his emotions.

"I still can't remember my father's name!" he argued. "There's dozens of holes in my memory, I could easily be remembering Harper wrong, it's not that far-fetched!"

"What if that was by design?"

"Whose design? Why would the Citadel be brainwashing Aniyans, they have actual volunteers!"

"I don't know!"

"How would they even—" He stopped. It was infuriating how she slowly led him along, waiting for him to figure it out. "You think the WAVEs are capable of physically *and* mentally changing someone?"

"All I'm saying is it's possible."

"How do you explain the magic then? If there are Aniyans in the program, how do they manifest magic?"

"I don't know! I'm just trying to explain everything and be honest."

"You're reaching Shira, and you know it," he said, stifling the anger building in his chest.

But a deep, unknown terror stirred within, slithering between his thoughts like a snake. He felt like she was trying to pull the wool over his eyes, preying on his own amnesia to get him so confused he would agree to anything. She did it once.

*Why wouldn't she do it again*

"Eli, I'm not lying to you."

"You said you found something," he bit. "That you had proof of your claims."

She made no further arguments, only pulled a note from her pocket and handed it to him. Eli took the crumpled letter. The words were written hastily, but the message was clear.

*No messages safe. Here. After Ceremony.*

"What does it mean?" he asked.

"It means the informant and I are meeting in four days after the Rune Blade Ceremony here in the library. We're meeting to help me escape and exchange information. I asked them two days ago if they had a way for me to leave, and this was their response."

"Wait—"

"*Please*, stop saying that."

"Okay fine. *Hold on a second*. You're certain this came from the informant?"

"Why would anyone in this rotting spire drop this note right in front of my face in the middle of the night?"

"Maybe someone who knows you've been involved in suspicious activity. Maybe someone who caught the informant and has been feeding you false information, someone who wants to catch you as well."

Shira gave no reaction. No doubt she had thought about this already.

"I have no choice," she muttered.

Eli sighed and started pacing, rubbing his eyes. Things kept getting more complicated. His loyalty to his own people was stretching, growing frailer the longer he followed Shira. He didn't believe her lofty claims, but the reality of an informant was real enough. And now he had to contend with the fact that Shira would be gone in a matter of days, which was a heavier burden than he cared to admit.

"Eli, I'm going to need your help to escape." She stepped closer to him, a pleading look in her eyes.

"No, you don't," he said. "You want me to come with you."

Shira's gaze softened. "Is that so hard to understand?" she whispered.

It had crossed his mind, since she said it in the Sparring Hall. And he assumed her telling him everything now was simply a plan to sway his loyalty.

"You said you had two things to tell me."

"Show you, actually."

She stepped up to him and grabbed his hand, his heart skipping at her touch. She led him into the back of the alcove where a chair lay broken on the ground. A table and short bookshelf had been moved aside, exposing more of the stone wall. Everything else seemed like a normal, forgotten part of an old library.

Shira said, "I found proof that there is more going on than you think."

"We've already—"

"Just," she interrupted, "wait."

Shira reached out, touching the cold stone wall. Eli noticed the subtle markings carved into its surface, identical to those scattered around the Citadel. He stepped next to her and traced along the patterns of an ornate circle. After a moment, the markings on the wall began glowing, white light filling the etched cavities.

Eli tensed. "Shira?"

"Just wait."

He stared as the circular symbol glowed brighter—and began to move. The wall itself remained still, and he could feel no vibrations under his feet. And yet, he was watching the intricate markings revolve around themselves inside the circle.

After a moment, the light flashed. Eli squinted, stepping back and guarding his face. But before the light was too much to bear, darkness returned. The markings on the wall had disappeared. Nothing remained but a round opening to an ancient staircase, leading down into darkness.

# Chapter Forty-Seven

S hira stood mesmerized by the doorway once again, witnessing a magic long forgotten. The first time the stone vanished with ethereal light, she thought perhaps stress finally cracked her mind. The fact that Eli displayed a similar reaction put her at ease.

The ominous stairwell stretched before them, but neither moved. It was clear the library was rarely accessed, neglected to all but the lowest levels of care, but this stairwell appeared to not have been touched in centuries.

Stale dusty air wafted from the opening, beckoning them downward. Shira wanted to step forward but couldn't find her bravery in the moment. There was a strange presence from the darkness—something calling to her in the deep unknown.

"Are we going down?" Eli asked quietly, a question to himself as well as to her.

"We have to," she replied.

He turned and grabbed the lantern from the table. Doubt lurked in her mind, whether Eli would continue helping her or decide to finally turn her in. If he was smart, he would run away, sparing himself the punishment of aiding the enemy. The thought of him being punished on her behalf—again—turned her stomach.

The pain of her deceit was evident in his voice, the aversion of his gaze, his downcast demeanor. But she doubted greatly that he understood what he had become to her, how he saved her from the despair of losing Lucas, of facing the darkness of her own identity. Whatever trust they built had crumbled, yes, but he still listened when she spoke, lingered in her presence. And despite his words, despite his scoffing, he followed her here. She hoped in the end he might change his mind and come with her. But even if he didn't, she wouldn't stop rebuilding what was lost.

Eli stepped around her, through the threshold of the gaping doorway. Shira followed closely, examining the decrepit state of the stony tunnel. Thick sheets of spider webs coated the walls and hung from the ceiling, crackling as Eli broke the tiny white threads. The stagnant air dried Shira's throat and mouth. The stairwell descended in a spiral to the left, their footsteps quietly rustling the dust.

Eli held the lantern out, lighting the way with a faint orange glow, which proved more than enough to illuminate the narrow space. The stairs continued their descent longer than Shira expected. They had looped around at least three times, though it was difficult to tell inside the tunnel. The walls seemed to grow warmer—not colder—as they continued forward.

*Odd*

Finally, the stairwell opened into a vast hallway, the ceiling dozens of feet above their heads, dwarfing even the library itself. The walls were lined with tomes, ancient books, and scrolls, for the first eight feet. Above the shelves, the room was covered with ornate symbols and markings—circles with intricate designs inside, surrounded by indecipherable glyphs. A quiet hum sang as they stepped across the threshold, the hallway stretched beyond the lantern's reach, fading into darkness.

Shira and Eli stood, mouths agape, at a loss for what they found.

"What is this place?" Shira asked, astonished at the vastness of the architecture.

"It's another part of the library," he replied, head cocked backwards as he stared at the high ceiling.

"Not any part I've heard about."

"Forgotten, probably. Based on the magic doorway, this place was clearly designed to be hidden and secured." Eli shuffled to one of the shelves.

"Hidden but not forgotten."

"You'd be surprised at the things that can be lost to time."

"Like dark secrets of the nation you serve," she said pointedly.

Eli gave a knowing look. "Archives."

"What?" she asked, standing at the opposite wall, transfixed by the books and scrolls. Her fingers moved gently over a few, brushing the thick layer of dust from their spines.

"Archives. This is a vault. A security measure. It's where priceless items, things that can never be replaced, are kept."

"You have experience?"

"Just observant. And I read about something similar."

Shira pulled a scroll off one of the shelves and opened it carefully. The faded letters on the page were difficult to read in the dim light.

"Eli, bring the lantern over here."

He stepped behind her, his chest gently touching her shoulder. She loved and hated that his proximity was so distracting. As the firelight danced across the page, Shira tried to interpret the text.

*Shal'tor NVek, zultar Gaithi Ven'kath. Ser'an Kul'eth rungar Tivar, mek'tor Zankith Lurvan. Hram'ut Rov-an tarnek Yz'ul, veklor Qanthar zulkor. Nel-var Kray'eth Zonkir, Val'ath Uthan zulgar. Vor'Irath melkor Zan'gar Tivar, Bruktar Kry'eth Zulkith.*

"It's all Primarch script," Eli said, reading over her shoulder.

"Great. Any idea what it says?"

"None. If I could read Primarch before, I can't remember how to now."

Shira sighed, praying they hadn't hit another dead end.

"Wait," he said, pointing to a word on the page. "That, right there."

"*Rov-an?*"

"Yeah."

"What does it mean?"

"Hells if I know, but Soren called me that when he and I collided in the mess hall."

"What is a derogatory slur doing in an old Primarch scroll in the basement of the Citadel?"

"I don't know. A better question is how does Soren know that word, and why did I fit the definition of it?"

Unsure of the answer, Shira opened the scroll further but was met with more obscure verbiage. Eli stepped away as Shira returned the scroll and grabbed a journal. Skimming the pages, a word instantly caught her eye.

"Wait, Eli," Shira said. "Look at this."

*In the seventy-seventh year of the Eighth Era, beneath Luna's fullest gaze, was wrought the genesis of Archancy's dread craft. Two hundred souls, bold in their folly and blind in their fervor, did march upon the sundered veil, naming themselves The Quadmai. Yet, in their grasping for dominion o'er the unseen, they did unshackle forces beyond foreknowledge, rending the firmament of Adiel and ushering forth the transmutation of the aetheric veil.*

"That's when Archancy started," Eli said. "But that's nearly five hundred years ago."

"Yeah," Shira mumbled, reading through the barely decipherable notes. "It keeps mentioning a group called the Quadmai and the dangers of Archancy."

"Then it makes sense why Archancy is a lost science," Eli mused.

"Especially if it was considered dangerous," Shira said, scouring the journal. "This says it's taken tens of thousands of lives."

"Hang on. The Primarchs first arrived here hundreds of years ago, right?"

"You should know. If the history books are to be believed, it was around the same time the war started."

Eli's gaze bounced around, and Shira watched him chase the racing thoughts through his keen mind. "What are you thinking?"

"We were wrong."

"About which part?"

"Archancy can't be the solution to our fading magic. They've known about it for hundreds of years."

"Unless that knowledge was buried," Shira countered.

"The text upstairs was written in the tenth era. This predates it."

"But what if the science was lost, and now they're trying to reclaim it?"

Eli sighed. "Either way, we need more information."

He moved along the bookcase, whispering the titles. Shira set the journal back, feeling a sense they were finally getting answers.

"Hey," Eli said over his shoulder, holding a book with a strange symbol on the cover. Shira stepped behind him, greeted by more Primarch script as Eli opened the book.

"We still don't know what it means," she said in frustration.

"Yes, but the state of this place proves that even the Council doesn't know about it."

"Possibly. Or they do, and they decided there's nothing worth protecting down here."

Eli turned the page, revealing more indecipherable words near a well-drawn picture. Shira's hand shot out, holding the page open. It was another ornate circle, with obscure symbols. Next to it, however, was a drawing of a dark stone.

*We were right*

"Eli, that's an Obelisk," Shira whispered.

"So, they *are* connected," he said. "Which means—"

"My father is right and may be the only one capable of making them." Shira finished. "And the Council really doesn't know about Archancy."

"We need to figure out what these symbols mean and what they're for," Eli said, his voice carrying a newfound determination. "If it made no difference, there wouldn't be two nations digging up the past."

"Maybe the past was buried for a reason," Shira said, strolling past him, moving further down the hallway. Eli remained behind her, holding the lantern aloft, attention hovering on the shelves and etched patterns. Only a short ways forward, the hallway opened into an intersection. To their left was another hallway ending with what appeared to be a massive stone door. Shira turned to their right and her eyes widened in shock.

On a wooden table, thin and elongated as it sat along the wall in a recess, lay numerous gold pedestals. And atop each one were shimmering, entirely black rocks.

Shira rushed to the table, staring in disbelief at their discovery. *Dozens* of Obelisks.

Eli strolled to the table—unfazed. "Are these them?"

"Yes," she said, slack-jawed. This could be her answer to everything. To saving Lucas, to her people winning the war. But as triumph claimed victory in the moment, it was struck down by a darkness which pressed on her chest. This was also exactly what the enemy needed to overthrow the Legion once and for all—give the answers the Zentari were seeking. And Eli was right. If these stones were here, untouched, this place was unknown to even the Council.

The realization sent thoughts flying through her mind. She glanced over at Eli, who had picked up one of the Obelisks.

She lunged at him, grabbing his arm. "Don't touch them!" she shouted.

Eli remained calm, gently rolling the Obelisk in his bare hand.

She stared, wide-eyed. "I don't understand," she whispered.

"What?"

"It didn't burn you," she said, staring at the ebony rock. Flashes of her first experience—the agony and sense of power—melded with images of Heika.

"No," Eli said. "It feels warm though, which I think is unusual."

It was a beat before Eli registered her reaction.

"Why did you think it would burn me?" he asked, their eyes locking.

This didn't feel like the defining moment between them, when everything would either shatter or mend—but they were dangerously close. To speak of the stones now, her experience with the power she wielded at Heika, could mean the end of her people.

If Eli chose the path of the Guardian, and if his loyalty to his kin ran as deep as she feared, he would seize them for his nation. His conviction would become the instrument of destruction for the Legion.

She stepped back, stealing her nerves, hoping her fear didn't register on her face.

But it was too late. Eli immediately caught her change in demeanor.

"Shira," he said sternly, "tell me the truth."

"That depends on which side you choose."

"Are you serious? You just told me you were being completely honest!"

"These stones could turn the tide of the war! In the hands of the Guardians it could change the fighting overnight! Why else do you think the Council is so desperate to find them?"

His eyes narrowed, and she could see his mind working.

"Shira, what do the Obelisks actually do?"

She said nothing.

"How powerful are they?"

Turning away at his question, she ran her hands through her hair.

"Shira!"

She couldn't look at him, unsure of what to do in the face of an impossible decision. Regardless of how she felt about Eli, the life of one man could never be worth jeopardizing her entire nation. She pulled a blade from her side as she turned around—but her resolve was brittle.

"What are you doing?" he asked, glancing down at the knife.

Conviction kept her lips shut. Eli's posture stiffened, arms at his side.

"So that's it then?" he asked, his voice turning deathly calm as he tossed the stone onto the table and set down his lantern. "This is when your true colors show?"

Still, Shira remained silent against the torrent of raging thoughts.

"You use me until you find what you've been looking for. Then once you have it, you kill me and what—leave me down here to rot?"

Her gaze was steady, despite the trembling in her soul—fixed on Eli. The man who'd slipped past every carefully built wall, drew her to him like the mighty and steady pull of a river joining the vast ocean, the one she'd been unknowingly waiting for her entire life. It was unthinkable. But the cold steel in her hand reminded her of the truth, of what was really at stake. His life, or thousands more.

Eli scoffed, laughing as he rubbed his face. "Bleeding Hells, I really am pathetic."

"I can't let you leave with the Obelisks. If the Council learns they're here, it would be the end of the Legion," she said, pressing against her growing panic.

"Yeah, and what about *my* people? Arlo and Lara, Maelyn, Esme, Fenner, how much greater are their odds of surviving this war if they have these stones to help them?"

She slowly walked toward him. Eli stood very still, his posture unchanged. He didn't appear defensive, nor did he take a step back.

"Shira, are you saying we mean nothing to you?"

"No," she breathed. "I'm not."

The air thickened, the world held its breath in the darkness.

"So now it's your turn to make the same decision I did?" Eli asked.

She couldn't read his face as she stopped in front of him, palms sweating.

"I'm sorry, Eli," she whispered.

The muscles in his jaw flexed. In a flash, he seized Shira's wrist and struck her forearm, releasing her grip. Her blade hit the floor with a sharp clank. Instinct kicked in, and she countered with a jab to his throat. He doubled over with a cough, and Shira threw her knee to his stomach.

But Eli, who seemed faster each day, caught her leg mid-strike and yanked her off balance. He pulled, lifting and hurling her into the stone wall behind him. Shira slammed into the unforgiving surface with a grunt, the breath knocked from her lungs. Eli was on her instantly, his fist flying toward her head. She deflected the blow and drove her knuckles into his stomach. He grimaced but came back with a brutal elbow to her temple.

Shira staggered, vision sparking. On muscle memory, she palmed and flung her second blade. It flew toward his chest, but Eli dodged—the edge grazing his tunic. He lunged forward with a spin, kicking for her head. Shira bent backwards, the wind from his boot brushing her face. She righted herself in time to find Eli's backhand careening toward her. She caught his wrist, twisting it behind him and bracing against his shoulder.

Eli grunted at the torsion. Memories flashed through her mind of their first confrontation. But Eli didn't give her the privilege of pinning him the same way twice. With renewed strength, he tore free, spun, and swung at her chin.

Shira shoved his arm aside and placed her leg behind his as she pressed against his chest. He toppled backwards, head cracking against the stone. In the moment it took him to refocus, Shira was on him—blade in hand, pressed to his throat.

Their heavy breaths mixed as she pressed against his chest. Eli stilled, his left arm limp above his head, his right pinned under her knee.

It was over. Her gaze danced to the scar on his throat, where her steel begged to cut his skin.

"Go ahead," he said, eyes flickering between hers. "Finish it."

"Idiot," Shira mocked. "I wasn't going to."

His brow furrowed. "You're still holding a blade to my neck!"

"You held a blade to mine," she quipped.

"That *you* put there, as I remember."

"Can't you see I'm trying?"

"You lied!"

"I told you the truth!"

"After I caught you!"

"I was scared!"

Shira scoffed, smiling as she straddled his waist. She tossed the blade aside and released his arm. Leaning forward, both her hands rested on either side of his head.

His face consumed her vision as her hair hung down in sheets of rich black. He moved his hand to rest against hers, and a shiver ran through her. She couldn't pull her gaze from his fiery eyes, glimmering in the darkness like the embers of a warm fire. Her body reacted to his intoxicating proximity, tearing down any feeble attempt to deny it.

Whether by fate or chance, her feelings for him had come when she least expected them. There was nothing logical about what she felt, only that her very soul begged to be near him. And if she was to be a traitor, she would rather be a traitor by his side.

"Please just come with me," she whispered.

It was a moment before he spoke, and she caught a flash of longing. "You know I can't."

"Eli, I can't stay. The Rune Blade Ceremony is coming. I won't remain hidden forever."

"Shira, we're on opposite sides of this war whether we like it or not."

"Why? Why can't we be on *our* side?"

"That's not how the world works," he said softly, brushing his thumb against her hand.

"What if the side we're fighting for isn't the right one?" she asked, not bothering to hide her desperation.

"It's not up to us to decide which nation we serve. It's our job to protect our people."

"Right and wrong is written on our hearts, Eli, it's not a subjective truth."

"Shira, you're talking about treason. A betrayal of everyone we know."

"I'm already a deserter for coming here. And I'm already a traitor for keeping you alive. So are you."

Pain clung to the heels of her words, a truth she already knew. Eli said nothing, his silence speaking its own agreement.

"Eli, what if, just *what if*, I'm right about this? What if the people you serve aren't who you think they are, that they are holding hundreds of Aniyans for torture and slavery?"

"And the Aniyans are completely innocent, is that it?" he quipped.

"No, that's not what I'm saying."

"Then what? You could take your argument and turn it right around. Just list some sins of the Legion, I'm sure there are plenty!"

"I did!" She paused, allowing the frustration to pass. "That's why I'm here. My father, the *leader* of the Legion, is in the wrong. I held a Zentari warrior's hand as he died telling me the Legion is known for their torture."

Eli pursed his lips. She was finally getting through.

He said, "There is still no proof that the Citadel has done anything to that level of evil."

"But I know how we can find out."

"These Archives don't prove anything."

"The informant," she corrected.

His brow knitted. "The traitor, you mean."

"No! The one who looked at which nation they were serving and decided to choose a side, rather than blindly obey orders."

"You don't know that."

"Then we'll just have to ask."

# Chapter Forty-Eight

Morning crawled closer, the minutes passing steadily as Eli stared at the bottom of Arlo's bunk. Today was the Rune Blade Ceremony, and Eli had been awake all night.

Over the past four days, he and Shira had spent each night orchestrating a plan of escape for her, unsure of what the informant was planning. He shared Shira's belief that right and wrong weren't subjective, that their leaders could be in the wrong. And it was this conviction which kept his guilt at bay—clinging to the hope that sparing her wasn't a betrayal of his people—but standing for truth in an impossible situation.

His mind said to follow the rules, uphold justice. But his heart told him to follow Shira and question what he was being told. It was the only reason he continued helping her—and why he secretly grabbed an Obelisk before leaving the Archives.

By the time the night watch Operative entered the bunkroom to announce wake-up, Eli was already dressed and ready.

"Eyes up, recruits!" the man shouted, before seeing Eli. "Never mind."

Eli strapped his practice sword to his waist and headed for the door. As Arlo stirred in his bunk, Eli spoke over his shoulder.

"I'll meet you down there!"

Arlo made no response as he squinted in Eli's direction, raising his hand as confirmation. He met Shira waiting outside the bunkroom and followed her down the steps at a brisk pace.

"How'd you sleep?" he asked quietly.

"I didn't."

"Me either. What did you find out about the guard change?"

They strode through the already busy walkway toward the mess hall, glancing around for itching ears.

"They exchange near midnight, or at least two hours after everyone is in bed."

"Okay. What's the window?"

"I say just before change, when the guards are the least rested," she responded, acting casual as a Captain walked by them.

"Okay. We'll have to figure out a distraction," Eli said.

"What did Darby say about the Reaping?"

"We've got less time than we thought. The ceremony is this afternoon, and the Reaping starts immediately tomorrow morning, before afternoon practice with the Rune Blades."

"Okay, so we have less than a day. More if needed. I'm sure I can survive a battle or two."

"Maybe Shira, but there's a problem."

"On top of everything else?"

"The Reaping occurs every day afterward, until each recruit is either dead or a Guardian."

Shira gave a breathy laugh. "Bleeding Hells, this just keeps getting better."

The mess hall was mostly unoccupied, save a few Operatives scattered about. Eli and Shira were served breakfast and sat at a table in the corner, across the room from their squad. Eli felt guilty for distancing himself from his friends, but this took precedence for the moment. And it was for their protection, should he and Shira be caught.

"You need to get out before the Reaping starts," Eli said, biting into his food.

"I can handle a few fights."

"I'm not doubting that, but every match runs the risk of your opponent discovering their magic."

"I've killed a Guardian before."

Eli shifted uncomfortably. Shira paused, acknowledging his point.

She said, "But that means we have to convince the informant to help me escape *tonight*."

He nodded grimly. "Hopefully they already have a plan. What have they said?" Eli whispered. "Have you told them about the time crunch?"

"No. It's impossible to speak with them when you don't know who they are. They've refused to reveal their identity in case I'm caught. I can leave another note, but based on our previous communication, it'd take at least two days to get a reply."

Shira took a bite of her bread before washing it down with a swig of water.

"Speaking of which," Eli said, "do you think it was the informant that gave that note to Lara?"

Shira's brow furrowed. "What note?"

"Arlo said during the mountain challenge there was a note on Lara which told her to leave. It was part of the reason she ran away and left the structure."

"I don't know. Why would they do that?"

Eli shrugged, finishing the last of his meal. "It just seems like such an odd thing for Lara to find, knowing now their challenge was to escape. Someone helped her."

A group of recruits entered the mess hall, filling the room with chatter. Based upon the glances during mealtime, their squad was wondering why they were suddenly eating alone. It didn't matter. By tomorrow, or the next day, Shira would be gone. And things would be back to whatever semblance of normal there was.

*Assuming I don't end up dead in the Reaping*

"Tell me about the guard exchange again," Eli said.

Eli sat next to Arlo for lecture, distracted by the scattered empty seats, the impending ceremony hauntingly close, like a roiling storm on the horizon. The open chairs left by the fallen remained unoccupied, almost as if it'd be disrespectful to claim them. And Eli couldn't but wonder if his own seat would be empty soon.

"Okay, spill it," Arlo whispered, turning to him. "Why are you and Shira eating alone all of a sudden?"

"It's nothing, seriously."

"Come on, I'm not stupid. And don't you dare shut me out for a girl. You guys were at each other's throats not two weeks ago. Now you're having a date every morning. What changed?"

Arlo had no way of knowing how accurate his metaphor really was.

"Nothing, Arlo, I swear. We're just trying to figure out a problem."

Arlo's eyebrows raised. "Like a *personal* problem?"

Eli rolled his eyes. "No. I'll explain later."

"I'm going to hold you to that," Arlo said, as Darby entered the Lecture Hall and the room quieted.

"Recruits, welcome to your final lecture. This afternoon, you will all be brought to one of the most sacred places in the Citadel and undergo the Rune Blade Ceremony. This honor is granted to only a select few, those whose determination and skill reach far beyond that of their kin. Everything you have endured here culminates to your success today. I want to say I am proud of each of you for reaching this point in the program, a feat that only a small percentage of Zentari can say they've accomplished. Congratulations to all of you."

Darby paused, allowing his words to hang in the air. No one made a sound. It didn't feel like a victory. Not with so many lost, and some still awaiting a death sentence in the Reaping.

"Your final lecture is entirely up to you all. I will speak briefly about the Rune Blade Ceremony itself, and continue our lecture about Spirit Steel, but otherwise, you may ask any questions plaguing your minds."

No one raised a hand.

"Very well. The use of the Rune Blades is paramount to a Guardian's ability to effectively and efficiently utilize their inner magic. As we've discussed, the source of our magic comes from the very life force within us. Overuse causes the warrior to collapse or become unconscious, and in dire cases, they can perish outright from exertion. There have been some records proposing that Guardians seem to have shorter life spans than other native Zentari, though this is not confirmed.

"How precisely the Spirit Steel draws out the inner magic is still a mystery to us Keepers. Despite our best efforts, we have not discovered the secret to these magical artifacts, though we are highly suspicious of the distinct Runes etched into their surface, the symbols and glyphs of which they get their name. As previously discussed, it is the combination of your inner magic and the alchemic science of the Primarchs which allow us utilization of these weapons today. Our forebears laid the foundation for our success."

*Alchemic science*

*Archancy*

As Darby continued, Eli leaned over to Arlo.

"Hey, I need to ask you something," he whispered.

"Only if you give me answers," Arlo responded.

"Arlo, it's not my business to tell."

"Boar spit. I was here first," Arlo said, turning to him. "You owe me this much."

Eli sighed. In truth, he owed Arlo far more than this. But sharing Shira's wild claims was out of the question, and he'd promised to keep her secret. Still, he could offer a few of their thoughts and see how receptive Arlo might be.

"Fine," Eli whispered. "What's your question?"

"Where do you guys go at night?"

"What?" Eli asked, mouth open. "How do you—"

"Come on, man, now you're just being insulting. You guys have been having late night meetups since the first week. Not to mention your freak out recently. I thought you two were just really into each other at first, but then your behavior over time made no sense."

Guilt washed over Eli like a rising tide. All this time, thinking he was keeping Arlo in the dark—and he knew all along. The memory of their earlier conversation resurfaced, when Arlo asked why Eli wasn't getting sleep. He knew then, and therefore knew Eli lied.

"Look I'm sorry," Eli said, glancing around. "Fine, I'll tell you, but not here. Suffice it to say she and I are investigating something going on at the Citadel. Something that, if found out, could get us in serious trouble."

Arlo searched his face, before giving a curt nod, turning back to Darby.

"What's your question?" Arlo asked quietly.

"On the mountain, inside the building where Lara was kept, you said something about *Archancy*. What is it?"

Arlo's brow stitched. "There's not much to tell."

"Tell it anyway."

"I just recognized those markings on the wall. Don't ask me what the Hells Archancy is, but that's what popped into my head when I saw them."

"What do you mean it just popped into your head?"

"I don't know. I can't remember what they mean, but I felt like I'd seen them before, and that's the name that came to mind."

"You don't remember anything at all? Nothing other than the name?"

"Nope."

Eli sighed, disappointed at the dead end. But the answer wasn't entirely fruitless.

A hand raised in the front row.

"Sir, what happens if a Rune Blade is destroyed or irreversibly damaged?"

"A very astute question, recruit. The answer to your inquiry is complex to say the least. While these weapons are indeed nothing more than tools to be utilized, there seems to be a connection between the Guardian and the weapon they bear. It has not been fully tested, but there are two anomalies that raise suspicion.

"The first, is that each Rune Blade is unique to its bearer. No two are alike. You will witness firsthand this process today. Second, the longer a Guardian uses their inner magic, their ability to manifest it in larger and more skilled amounts grows easier. Either this is simply the Guardian growing in his craft, or there is some misunderstood bond between them and their weapon.

"Given this, the loss of a Rune Blade has been detrimental in the past. Guardians whose weapons are destroyed, suffer wretched, yet unseen, injuries themselves. If it is simply lost, it can still feel as though part of your own body has been left behind. And similarly, each time a Guardian perishes, their Rune Blade subsequently shatters."

Once the lecture was completed, Eli and Arlo waited until most recruits shuffled out for lunch. They walked silently at the back of the crowd. Eli caught Shira's glance but gave her a nod to continue without him.

"Hey guys!" Lara said excitedly. "Are you ready? I can't believe it's already here!"

"Nervous, actually," Eli responded.

"I'll probably get the biggest one," Arlo teased.

"Whatever!" Lara argued. "You say that, and you'll end up with the tiniest dagger!"

Arlo laughed. "You wish."

"Hey, Eli!" Lara whispered. "What's with you and Shira having breakfast dates?" Judging by the smile on Lara's face, her interest was far different than Arlo's, and more about the gossip.

"He won't say," Arlo blurted, saving Eli. "I already asked him. Which means it's something serious." Arlo's eyes widened in jest, and Lara raised her eyebrows.

"Hey Lara," Eli said, "we'll meet you at lunch. Arlo and I are running back to the barracks."

Her eyes narrowed. "Very well. Keep your secrets," she said snidely.

Arlo smirked, giving Eli a knowing look. "She's fine."

As the crowd filtered into the walkway, Eli spotted a vacant hallway and nudged Arlo to break away from the group. They slipped into the dim light, and Eli rubbed his forehead. He had no idea how to explain without compromising everything.

Silence spread between them. No one paid them any mind.

*Here we go*

"If you start kissing me, I'm out," Arlo teased, crossing his arms and leaning against the wall.

Eli grinned. "You're not *that* handsome," he said, before pausing to gather his thoughts. "Arlo, have you, at *any* point being here, gotten the sense that we aren't being told the whole story?"

Arlo tilted his head. "What do you mean?"

Eli exhaled. "What if the Citadel was hiding something? What if they had this massive secret that completely changed the viewpoint of the war and our place in the military?"

"Of course they have secrets. That's why there are different ranks and restricted information. If everyone knew everything then it'd take only one captured recruit, and the enemy would have our vital secrets."

"I understand that, but what if they were actually in the wrong? What if they stood for something that we couldn't?"

"There's no right and wrong in war, man. Besides we're grunts, we march into battle, we don't ask questions. That's not for us to say."

"Arlo it's not that simple!"

"Only because you're trying to overcomplicate things. Look, there are some severely questionable things that happen in war and impossible decisions that must be made. Making a choice between two bad options doesn't mean our leaders are evil, it just means they're doing what they have to."

Eli clenched his fists, willing his nerves to calm. This wasn't going well, but he needed Arlo on his side.

"Okay, fine," Arlo said. "If this is all you guys have been discussing, why all the secrecy?"

Eli remained silent, debating what he could and could not reveal. Arlo watched closely, and Eli saw him piecing the puzzle together. He *was* smarter than Eli gave him credit for.

Arlo pressed harder. "What did you guys find out?"

"I can't tell you." Eli spoke sternly.

"No no no, don't give me that boar spit!" Arlo argued, stepping off the wall. "We have been through hell and back together. I have stuck by your side, and we have stayed together as a team. I deserve to know."

"There's a spy in the Citadel."

The two spun at the sound of Shira's voice as she rounded the corner and stalked down the hallway.

# Chapter Forty-Nine

Shira's ears rang, wiping her palms on her pants.

*Please, shining Heavens, let this not have been a mistake*

"What?" Arlo whispered, mouth agape.

"It's true," Eli said. "She is." Arlo fidgeted, and Eli held his hands up. "Arlo, just hear us—"

"Shut up!" Arlo shouted, pointing a finger at Eli, a dark look in his eyes. "You lied to me. Again."

Shira's heart thundered, but they were still alone in the hallway. "Arlo, you don't—" Shira began.

"And you!" he said, now pointing at Shira. "You're a rotting spy."

Eli and Shira's faces became panicked, glancing down the hallway for anyone within earshot.

"For Hell's sake, keep your voice down!" Eli whispered harshly. "I didn't even know she was Aniyan until a few weeks ago."

"Then you should've told me weeks ago!" Arlo scolded, though he matched Eli's volume.

"How could I? One wrong move, one wrong conversation, and she gets tortured by Azazel for rot knows how long. She's our friend Arlo, whether we like it or not. She's saved both our lives. What if she were Lara?"

"But she's not! She's the bleeding enemy! Hell's man, you're thinking with the wrong head!"

"Can you not talk about me like I'm not here!" Shira added, panic turning to frustration. The threat of taking action—against Arlo—came to mind. But Eli would never forgive her. Anxiety rose in her gut as she didn't know whether Eli would choose her over Arlo if the issue were forced.

Arlo huffed, hands on his hips. "When did you find out?"

"On the mountain," Eli said plainly. "I asked her after I recovered."

Shira felt the emotions of that confrontation prompting a return, but she shoved them back down.

"You didn't tell him outright?" Arlo asked, addressing Shira.

"He found out before I planned to tell him."

Arlo scoffed. "If you were ever going to."

"Arlo, I asked her the same questions," Eli said. "If you don't trust her, then trust me. I was suspicious beyond Shira's involvement. Something is going on that they aren't telling us."

"And that warrants corroborating with the enemy?"

"For now," Eli said with a level conviction that brought Shira both comfort and concern.

She waited, still clinging to a fool's hope she wouldn't leave here alone—if she left at all.

"I'm assuming you're trying to escape?" Arlo asked her.

"Yes."

"That's what you two have been discussing?"

Eli nodded.

"When?" Arlo bit. "And with what sensitive information?"

"Likely tonight, before the Reaping starts," she said. "And nothing definitive, so far."

"Right, you don't have magic," Arlo mused. "You'd never graduate anyway or survive the Reaping."

Arlo paced, arms crossed. Eli and Shira stood silently, letting him process the situation. Eli seemed relieved Arlo now knew, but she was sick to her stomach. Telling Arlo herself was only a way to let Eli off the hook.

"I'm telling Lara," Arlo said finally.

"You can't," Eli blurted.

"Why not? She deserves to know who her squad mate really is."

"Arlo, if—"

"It's fine, Eli," Shira said, acceptance of her likely fate suffocating her fear of death.

"Shira, if they find out—"

"Don't you think I know that? I've known that since I came here. Eli this isn't just about me anymore. Even if I'm captured, you need to find out the answers to the questions. And please, *promise me*, you'll find Lucas."

She held his fiery gaze, now her only hope as the circumstances continued to worsen. If the Heavens would permit it, she prayed that whatever was left of their bond was enough to see this through, even if she wouldn't be there. Enemies or not, she cared for her friends, Eli most of all. And if Arlo really was Lucas's brother, then she needed him safe as well.

"No. I won't promise that," Eli said. Shira's lips parted. "Because you're going to escape. I don't know Lucas, and as far as I'm concerned, he's the enemy and subject to whatever role he's played in this war. But you are not something I'm willing to give up. Even if that makes me a traitor."

Eli glanced at Arlo as he spoke. He was making his choice.

"Eli, saving Lucas is saving me," Shira urged. "I don't think I can exist without him."

Eli's gaze dropped. She hoped her words hadn't hurt as much as they sounded, but it was the only way she could express how much Lucas meant to her in the moment. Even if it was only a half-truth.

"Fine," Eli said. "We'll do what we can."

"Arlo." Shira started. "I'd like to think that you and I are friends, and more than just what our circumstances make us. I don't expect you to help, but please give me the chance to rescue and help my loved ones."

Arlo's face was stoic. "Only as long as that endeavor doesn't come at the price of *my* loved ones," he said, nodding to Eli. "Which includes him."

"Recruits!" an Operative shouted from the hallway entrance. "You get lost on the way to the mess hall? Break it up!"

Shira didn't push the issue as they headed to the mess hall in silence, hoping for a bite of food before lunch ended. Lara, Fenner, Esme, and Maelyn were sitting at their table, surprised by their late entry.

"Where the Nine have you three been?" Maelyn asked as they sat down, Arlo already biting into his food.

"They were having a lovers quarrel," Lara teased.

"Eli and Shira?" Fenner asked innocently.

"No, Eli and Arlo!" Maelyn teased.

Shira rolled her eyes but said nothing.

Arlo spun to Eli, food half chewed in his mouth. "That's why you had the attitude a few weeks ago!"

Eli blushed. "Yes. And thank you for announcing it to everyone," he quipped, taking a hard drink from his cup.

"Wait!" Lara said. "You know what happened?"

"Can't tell you, sorry. Trade secret," Arlo said with a wink.

"I'm so lost," Maelyn commented.

"You'd be surprised how much drama men can be." Lara added with a grin.

Before Shira, Eli, and Arlo could eat half their meals, Renard strolled into the mess hall. Everyone quieted in his presence, anticipation hanging in the air like a fog. This was the moment they had been waiting for, and the moment Shira had been dreading.

The Captain walked to the center of the room, scanning the crowd, but remained silent. After a moment, Captain Evergreen entered as well, stepping up beside Renard with a gentle smile. The two whispered to each other. Murmurs rippled as recruits stirred. Everyone's attention was on the Captains, their food entirely forgotten. Shira felt a stone slide into her stomach.

For everyone else, this was a triumph—the last step to becoming a Guardian. To her, it was a sentence. Leave everything or die.

The room held its breath, and the hair on Shira's neck raised as Commander Voss entered the mess hall with two Operatives flanking either side. Everyone stood at attention. Voss marched in, her commanding presence drowning each of them in silence. Her steel plated armor clanked quietly as she moved, her white cape trailing behind her.

She paused by the two Captains, before turning to address the room.

"Recruits!" Voss shouted. "Are you all ready to become Guardians?"

"Yes! Commander Voss, ma'am!" The room bellowed in response.

"Are you ready to become the best? To stand out among our people as warriors of the ethereal?"

"Yes! Commander Voss, ma'am!"

"You have prevailed this far. Endured and overcome each challenge demanded of you. Do not be fooled, those sacrifices will yield results today. And now is your opportunity to grasp the reward for your efforts."

The air was electric, buzzing with expectation. Shira only felt heavy, and surprisingly, left out.

"Congratulations to each of you. You are all about to be part of a ceremony honoring only a select few. I know you will not disappoint. Follow me!"

"Yes! Commander Voss, ma'am!"

Voss walked briskly out of the mess hall, followed by Renard and Evergreen, trailed by the sea of recruits.

"This is it!" Lara said ecstatically with a wide smile, turning to Maelyn. "You think you'll get a Warhammer like your father?"

Maelyn gave a solemn grin. "I don't know. But for sure it'll be a bigger weapon than Arlo's."

"Ha!" Arlo teased. "Not on your life."

"Shira!" Lara said. "What weapon do you hope to get?"

Shira swallowed, trudging through the slew of emotions within. While most recruits were excited, many wore sullen faces, knowing not everyone would succeed at the ceremony. It was why the Reaping existed. You were either marching to a future filled with glory or condemned to a deathmatch.

"I would take any, really," Shira said, forcing a smile for her friend.

Shira positioned herself to walk next to Eli, hoping his presence would calm her pounding heart. All she had to do was survive today and she would be gone by tomorrow. It was life-giving, watching Eli protect her and stand his ground in front of Arlo, but everything was still so broken.

She wished she could rewind time—not to change it, but to relive this experience. The quiet moments, the camaraderie, the sense of belonging. Never in her wildest dreams did she think she would stand behind enemy lines, longing to stay. It startled her, how deeply she'd come to care for them, and how hard it was to say goodbye. She wasn't ready to be Evalynn again. Not ready to leave

Eli—to abandon the fragile rhythm she'd found among enemies who had become something more.

Walking beside Eli, Shira watched him. His expression gave nothing away, eyes fixed forward, shoulders squared. Despite his mask, she knew he sensed the weight of what was coming. Everything hinged on today. Surviving the Reaping meant one final chance to find Lucas, whether or not he was alive. The informant might have answers she couldn't reach alone, access the prison, and the idea fostered a sliver of hope.

And despite her harsh words, it was possible now to imagine living on without Lucas—what before seemed insurmountable. Because of Eli.

Never in her life had she needed a crutch, a strong arm to keep her upright. But Eli was something more, a presence akin to comfort. He was the promise after what she'd lost, the thread she clung to when grief threatened to take over. And in his own silent way, with words spoken not from his mouth, Eli convinced her of the same truth Lucas had: that her life was worth living.

Commander Voss led them past some guards and up the staircase near the Sparring Hall, and Shira recalled the first time she saw Eli. Astonished he had called her name as a squadmate, she became infuriated, thinking him a leech, another recruit searching for an edge. Who could have guessed what was next to come?

As they reached the second level, they passed the outer walls of the Lecture Hall. Questions swirled in her mind, unanswered and mocking. Whatever information the informant discovered, Shira hoped it was worth it. And selfishly, she prayed it would be enough for Eli to come with her.

Finally reaching the third level, Shira heard gasps from the recruits ahead. Setting foot on the final step, she witnessed the cause of the astonished reactions. The third level of the Citadel was one vast open space. The rounded exterior walls wrapped around them in a giant cylinder, windows scattered about casting natural light against the gray stone. An ominous pillar jutted from the center, touching the ceiling at least two hundred feet above their heads.

The room felt sterile, lifeless, apart from the etchings carved into each warm stony surface. Shira noticed the floor boasted one massive Archanic circle, the same design they had been trying desperately to decipher.

None of this was what stole the breath of the recruits. In the center of the room, joined to the pillar, was a wall of stone, reaching half the height of the ceiling. Primarch script and more Archancy symbols adorned its surface. At the base of the wall was an area stained red, near a short table holding nothing more than an old dagger.

Shira froze, taking in the enormity of the room, a perfect physical representation of the overwhelming dread threatening to consume her. She pursed her lips, breathing out slowly.

*Day thirty, Winter's Touch*

*Day eleven, Harvest's Moon*

As she grounded herself, vowing to survive beyond this day, a hand grabbed hers. Eli's face molded with concern as he interlaced their fingers.

"You all right?" he whispered.

She nodded, staring into the fiery eyes that communicated a silent promise. Warmth spread through her, strength rising from the depths of her soul. With a deep breath, she and Eli moved toward the center of the room, where the anxious recruits gathered.

Voss waited near the center of the wall, Renard and Evergreen beside her. Keeper Darby was standing off to the side, accompanied by two other Keepers, judging by their clothing.

"Recruits!" Voss shouted, her voice echoing relentlessly through the open room.

Everyone remained at attention.

"Ven'So! Welcome to the Rune Forge. This sacred tradition has been the Zentari's highest honor for generations. And now, each of you is extended the privilege to participate. To summon your very own Rune Blade will officially grant you the title of Guardian."

With her words hanging in the air, Voss nodded at Renard, who stepped forward.

"It is my honor, recruits, to give you one final instruction in this program." Renard said. "The ceremony is simple, but difficult. You are to approach the *Kir Kadosh*, the sacred wall, at the base. Using the ceremonial knife, you must create a cut on your palm, then place your hand on the wall. To summon your Rune

Blade, you must activate the Rune Forge. Reach within yourselves and bring forth your inner magic, and the sacred wall will answer. How to precisely do that is different for each Guardian."

Renard stepped back, and Evergreen took his place. Shira was annoyed at the formality of the process, wishing they would hurry and get her humiliation over.

"Recruits," Evergreen said, "everything you experienced in this program has led you to this moment. Your will to live, your honed physical abilities, your defiance of death, your teamwork, your sacrifices, each experience has moved you that much closer to finding the magic deep within your soul. And now, you must claim it. As you touch the *Kir Kadosh*, reach within yourselves for the reason you fight, for the reason you are here, and lay it bare. If you are worthy, the sacred wall will acknowledge you. But there is no way to explain exactly how to perform this final task. We can only open the door. *You* must walk through it."

Evergreen stepped back into line next to Renard. Murmurs echoed as recruits nervously shifted, the air electric with anticipation. Keeper Darby pulled out a scroll and read the first name.

"Esme Vogel!"

The name rang in Shira's ears as Esme strode through the crowd. It was a perfect first choice. Esme moved with such confidence, her quiet nature suited her well. Because her strength was so evident, there was no need for boasting. She carried the same energy as Evergreen.

Maelyn gave a smile of encouragement to her squadmate. Esme approached the wall, grabbing the dagger off the table. Shira stared at the looming structure, feeling its ominous presence like the heat of a roaring fire.

Esme carved a shallow cut to her left palm, set down the blade, and firmly planted her hand on the crimson stained stone. Her head fell forward, eyes closed.

Nothing happened. The room became so still and silent, Shira was afraid to breathe. Eli gently squeezed her hand, and warmth rushed through her again.

Esme slowly pulled her hand from the wall. A bright purple glow erupted from where she'd touched the stone. The handle of a sword followed her palm as she pulled away, her fingers grasping around the end. She took a step as the weapon fully emerged in the void of purple light.

Esme stared at her two-handed claymore, holding it aloft. Its blade was double edged and long, jutting out from the twisted metal which formed its guard. The steel was silver, adorned with unique markings carved into metal. The hilt was shaped like a lion's head, its eyes the color of amethyst.

"Congratulations, Guardian Vogel!" Voss announced, and the room erupted in chants and applause. Each recruit shouted and cheered at the success of one of their own. Maelyn raised her arms in triumph. Esme smiled proudly, before being ushered to stand behind the keepers, cradling her new weapon.

Voss raised her hand to silence the cheering, and Darby announced the next name. Shira didn't recognize the recruit. She started fidgeting nervously again, the amazement already wearing thin. She leaned into Eli, relishing his proximity.

"Don't be nervous," he said quietly.

"Easy for you to say," she said. "You can actually get a Rune Blade."

He huffed softly. "We'll see."

She glanced at him. "Don't want one? Isn't this what you've dreamed of?"

"I do. More than anything," he said, now meeting her gaze. His expression softened. "Well. Almost anything."

She gripped his hand tighter. His orange eyes seemed brighter somehow.

"Thank you," she whispered.

"For what?"

Before she could respond, cheers sounded again at the recruit who pulled an exquisite spear from the *Kir Kadosh*. Darby announced the next name on the heels of the cheering.

"Soren Mitchell!"

Eli's focus darted to Soren. While Shira despised Sol with a burning passion, her instincts demanded more caution of Soren Mitchell, who carried a deep amorphous malice. Something about him made her skin crawl—like a snake hiding in shadow.

Soren approached the stone, yanking the knife from the pedestal. The laceration he created was far longer than needed, blood pouring from the wound. He held his arm up, crimson dripping onto the floor. Shira saw his mouth move in silent words, as his eyelids fluttered.

He slapped his hand on the sacred wall, and a red aura glowed from where his palm made contact. A pulse of crimson flowed up the *Kir kadosh*, and Shira felt a gentle thrum beneath her feet. A thick heavy fog emanated around his arm, falling to the ground and lingering at his feet.

A fiendish grin formed as he pulled his hand out. The hilt of a one-handed sword followed—a curved, jagged, and wicked blade. It looked apt to cut the bearer as much as its opponent.

"Congratulations, Guardian Mitchell!"

Soren held his blade, touching the Spirit Steel, before raising it high and shouting in triumph. Roars and shouts erupted, though Shira could tell a fair number of the crowd chose not to partake. Her brow wrinkled, seeing the wound Soren had created was already healed.

"Of course he gets a Rune Blade," Eli murmured.

"It looks as wicked as his soul," she added.

"Actually, I think that's expected."

"What do you mean?"

"Remember what Darby said. That each blade is unique to its bearer. I don't think it's far-fetched these Rune Blades are like an extension of your soul, a physical manifestation of your inner self."

"How is that possible?"

Eli shrugged. "I don't know."

"Arlo Miller!" Darby announced.

"Go get 'em!" Lara whispered with a wide smile.

Eli slapped Arlo's shoulder as he made his way to the front, his crooked smirk on his face. Lara fidgeted next to them, wringing her hands. Shira swallowed, thinking back to what Arlo said on the practice field. If she was right about him and Lucas, then he wouldn't receive a Rune Blade.

Arlo approached the wall, gingerly grabbing the knife. He made a short cut, setting the knife down gently, and held his hand against the stone. As his head bowed, his muscles tensed. They waited, and Shira prayed for his success, despite her suspicions.

In a flash of yellow light, Arlo pulled his Rune Blade out in one swift motion. An explosion of golden magic occurred from where the weapon emerged. Arlo held his new war hammer, the silver metal accented with gold on the edges with beautifully ornate floral designs throughout. By the way he turned the hammer in his hands, it appeared to be significantly lighter than it looked.

He spun and raised his Rune Blade as his comrades cheered, Shira joining along with them. Her disappointment in the outcome was overshadowed by joy for her friend. Eli shouted from her side, never letting her hand go.

Darby announced the next name, and she pressed into Eli more, not holding back her desire to be closer. As odd as it seemed, she wished this moment would last as long as possible.

"What did you thank me for?" he asked.

His ember eyes caught her breath. "For standing beside me, despite everything."

Eli didn't respond, glancing at the fading scar on her cheek. He opened his mouth to speak, but his attention was stolen by Darby's shout.

"Sol Richter!"

A heaviness settled in the room. Shira glared in his direction as the giant approached the stone. Sol grabbed the knife, cutting his palm, and tossing the ceremonial dagger onto the table. He pressed his thick hand against the stone wall, before yanking it away.

Nothing happened.

A few snickers sounded, but Sol ignored them. He replaced his hand on the stone, waiting another moment. His muscles tensed, his face turning red. He slowly pulled his hand away.

Again—nothing. With a loud grunt, Sol slapped his hand back onto the *Kir Kadosh*. Shaking, he clenched with effort, his face turning purple. He pulled his hand away once more, but only silence lingered. Sol shouted, smashing his hand on the stone repeatedly, before holding it there. Bracing himself with his other arm, he pushed against the sacred wall, pulling his hand back.

Nothing. Only blood trickling to the floor.

Sol shouted, punching the wall.

"Recruit Richter," Voss said calmly, "step away from the sacred wall and resume your place among the recruits."

Sol spun to her, face twisted with fury. Keeping silent, the giant strode back angrily into the crowd. Shira assumed many were glad at the failure, but wished to avoid his wrath, were their mocking heard.

"Shira Weiss!" Darby announced.

Shira's heart skipped, and Eli squeezed her hand. Sweat formed on her brow as she turned to leave.

"Just give them a show and come right back," Eli whispered.

She nodded, letting go of his hand, the cold air now over her palm.

"You got this!" Lara whispered.

Shira shuffled to the front, feeling exposed and vulnerable. Eyes glued to the patterns on the floor, she approached the pedestal. The ceremonial dagger was a simple, single edged knife with a wooden handle. No theatrics or symbols, no real markings of any kind. The blade bore aged blood stains, with parts now wet from the recent use. Fighting the desire to wipe the blade clean, she reached for the dagger.

The handle was warm. Applying gentle pressure, Shira made a shallow cut to her left palm, just enough for a drop of blood. A wave of dizziness hit her, staring up at the intimidating wall. The words were all Primarch script, their meaning still illusive. She stepped up to the spot tarnished with previous attempts, now noticing it centered around another smaller Archanic circle.

Bloody handprints and a growing pool of crimson at her feet caused a rush of adrenaline and fear.

*Just get this over with*

The wall was surprisingly warm under her palm, its surface smooth. Her wound throbbed with her heartbeat, pulsing against the stone. Unsure of how long to stay to seem believable, she bowed her head, her thoughts drifting to Eli and Lucas. She would survive this and escape. There was more for her to do—so much more.

After what she assumed was long enough, she pulled her hand away. A white light filled her vision, exploding out from the wall. The pain in her hand vanished as hot wind blew past her, throwing her hair in its wake. A tingling sensation of power rose up her arm, radiating into her chest, exploding within. The *Kir Kadosh* lit up with white light, filling with an arching pattern like lightning flowing from her touch. The Primarch words glowed brightly, blending with the streaks of light. A thunderous crackling bellowed around the room, as if the sky itself were responding to her presence.

She pulled further, a handle emerging from the storm of light. Staring in amazement, she drew a short dagger from the sacred wall. Instinctively, her free hand reached toward the shimmering black steel and found another hilt waiting. An identical blade now rested in her grip, which wasn't present a moment before.

Now bearing two identical daggers in each hand, Shira turned them and marveled. They were compact but heavy, the handles molding to her palms perfectly, conforming to each curve. The blades bore two edges, starkly black, with white markings etched into the steel.

Shira balked, mouth agape, astonished to be holding a Rune Blade. *Her* Rune Blades. She flinched as the recruits cheered. Spinning around, she found Eli's gaze. His expression held the same level of disbelief.

She was a Guardian.

*What in the Nine Realms*

Though most were cheering, clearly her display was unusual. The Primarch words on the *Kir Kadosh* faded once more. Shira was frozen for a moment, before moving rigidly toward the crowd of growing Guardians. Panic ignited. This made absolutely no sense. Sure, there was that event at Heika, but that was because of the Obelisk she touched. Or perhaps her mind cracked, like a blackout.

*She isn't Zentari. Not even a little. And her father doesn't have magic.*

"Stop!"

# Chapter Fifty

The ground tilted beneath Eli.

*What in the Hells is going on*

His heart drummed, muscles rigid. This made absolutely no sense.

*Did she steal an obelisk*

*Could you use one of those for this*

Shira's gaze locked with his, and in one glance he asked the questions buzzing in his mind. Eli blinked, watching Shira walk to the crowd of those who claimed their Rune Blades. He waited for any sign of communication, but she appeared as shocked as he was.

*This changes everything*

Eli flexed his hands, unsure of what to do. Arlo was across the room with the Guardians, and Lara didn't know yet. He took a deep breath.

*This could be a good thing. Now she isn't suspicious*

*But what in the cursed Hells was that lightning*

"Stop!" Voss shouted.

The world froze, and vile dread bore under his skin as the Commander approached Shira.

*No no no no*

Voss clamped a hand on Shira's shoulder, turning her around with a menacing stare. The Commander said something to Shira, and fear coiled in Eli's stomach as Voss took one of her Rune Blades.

The Commander examined the blade closely. "This is an incredible Rune Blade, recruit Weiss," Voss said. "Guards! Arrest her!"

Gasps sounded. Eli reflexively took a step but stopped himself. He couldn't. It was suicide and would only incriminate himself and his squad mates. His mind buzzed, thoughts racing for a solution. Faintness threatened to pull him down, but he locked his knees.

As Shira's hands were bound, she asked Voss something. The Commander responded, equally as quiet.

She knew.

*How the Hells did Voss know*

"Take her to High Captain Azazel!" Voss shouted. "I have questions I need answered."

*Shining Heavens, no*

Voss handed Shira's Rune Blades to one of the Operatives before turning and resuming her place next to the *Kir kadosh*. Murmurs and whispers spread, like wind blowing through a forest. Watching the Operatives escort her past, Shira's gaze locked to his. It was only a moment, but Eli caught it, unable to tear his attention from her.

The connection stretched outward. In a single glance, Eli saw the fear, the longing, and the acceptance all melded together. She could have left, *should have left,* but she stayed.

For him.

He should have gotten her out sooner. But it was too late now. Convincing himself to keep her secret was one thing, and helping her leave spared the needless shedding of blood. But breaking a prisoner out of the Citadel was insanity and the epitome of treason. To rescue her now would be to turn his back on his comrades—his friends. As much as he cared for Shira, he couldn't do that.

Yet the image of her screaming in agony under Azazel's torture flashed in his thoughts, rattling his resolve. But before he spiraled, Eli was shocked back to reality as Lara pulled on his shoulder.

". . . is going on?" she whispered harshly.

Eli turned around, ears ringing above the muffled voices. Darby called the next name, and Lara grabbed his face.

"Eli! What is going on?" she asked again.

Unable to speak through his shock, Eli managed a single word.

"Arlo," he said. Lara's brow knitted before understanding.

*Wait to talk to Arlo*

Pretending to pay attention, Eli faced the front. The next dozen recruits passed in a blur, including Lara, who obtained an immaculate, shining metal staff. Green floral patterns covered the shaft, with both ends rounded with gold. Maelyn received a beautiful longsword, boasting a timeless composition and purple etchings on the blade.

Eli was alone now. Standing by himself, he fought the urge to fidget, feeling his skin crawl. Renard threw a glare in his direction, a dark look in his eyes. Maybe he had something to do with this. Either way, Eli remembered to feign surprise if approached.

"Elijah Danon!" Darby announced.

The sound of his name broke through the silence, pulling him from his thoughts. Eli flexed his hands and stepped forward, shoulders stiff as he approached the pedestal. This was supposed to be his moment. His dream. The culmination of everything he'd fought for. Here, he would finally become the man he'd long imagined.

Yet it felt hollow as his fingers closed around the ritual knife. He drew the blade across his palm, sharp pain biting deep. Blood welled quickly, warm against his skin, and he used it to anchor himself. Bleeding onto the floor, he pressed his palm to the stone. Symbols flickered faintly at his touch, the Rune Forge *almost* acknowledging his presence. Yet it was not triumph or ceremony which called his attention—it was Shira.

Jaw clenched, he bowed his head and squeezed his eyes shut.

*Focus*

This was his chance to escape the Reaping, to return home a Guardian. To see Harper again. To tell dad it was all worth it. But as he reached for that purpose—the fire that had driven him here—it faltered and slipped through his grasp. He searched for it. For Harper's laugh. For his father's tired but steady voice. For the need to protect what little remained.

But the edges of those memories were frayed, the shape of them half lost. The reasons that had once burned like stars now flickered behind a veil he couldn't pierce. The faces of his friends surfaced instead. To Arlo, unwavering and true.

Shira, merciful and determined. Lara's gentle heart. Maelyn's grit. Fenner's gentleness. Esme's grace.

They knew who they were. And he didn't.

All that he claimed was a trail of borrowed convictions. Devotion stretched thin over broken ground. A husk of a boy still waiting to become something more.

His blood dripped on the stone.

*Please*

After all the effort, all he suffered, he still didn't know what it was he wanted. But he knew he needed strength—needed power. And more than the very air in his lungs, he needed to know it was all worth it.

*Let something be there*

Eli reached into his soul, willing his magic to come out. He asked for it—pleaded that it rise. Pulling his hand away slowly, he opened his eyes.

Nothing.

Desperation surged. Eli slammed his hand back onto the wall. With an inner bellow, he demanded his power come forth.

*I have nothing without this*

He reached deeper, grasping for the core of who he was. But the further he searched, the more he realized he didn't know what that even meant. His entire life had been spent pushing others forward, standing in the wings, carrying weight that was never meant to be his. Every step was for someone else. And now it was finally *his* turn. This was his moment, to step up and no longer trail behind.

Drawing away from the slab, Eli opened his eyes to an empty hand. The cut wept blood, but nothing more. No spark. No trace of magic.

He closed his fingers into a fist, each heartbeat pulsing with a deeper burn.

*You're pathetic*

Turning sharply, Eli marched behind the now scarce crowd of recruits—failures. The pain in his hand throbbed, and he welcomed it. It was the only thing that felt honest—a fitting punishment.

*For weakness*

Eli stared blankly at the slats above him, the underside of Arlo's bunk a fixed, colorless blur. He was the only one in his squad without a Rune Blade. The only one condemned to die in the Reaping. Shira was gone. His friends were off celebrating, basking in their victory, while his world quietly collapsed.

The recruits who passed the Rune Forge had been granted an audience with Voss and a special dinner with the Captains. Praised. Honored. Meanwhile, those left behind drifted into the lower levels, silent and scattered, each one branded a failure.

*Get up and do something*

The mission wasn't over. He and Shira were supposed to meet the informant tonight. But without Shira, it was a lost cause. If he showed up alone, the contact might never reveal themselves, and he'd lose the only thread connecting him to the truth. And more importantly, to Shira.

Arlo couldn't be involved. Not after that handsome idiot aced the program so effortlessly.

*'Come on, Eli. Think about it.'*

Shira's voice echoed in his thoughts, clear and cutting. Nothing made sense anymore. Shira called herself the daughter of the Aniyan King. That meant she shouldn't have magic. By her lineage alone, it was impossible. So, either she lied—unlikely—or the Citadel deceived them.

*Zentari aren't the only ones with magic*

But if that were true, then why hadn't the Legion produced Guardians of their own? Surely, someone among them would've awakened magic in battle. Yet history remained unshaken. The Zentari always held the edge. As far as Eli knew, no Aniyan had ever displayed inner magic.

Until her.

Which made Arlo's story plausible. If Shira could access magic, then so could Arlo—Lucas's brother or no.

*And if I can't . . . does that mean she was right about me*

*Am I*

No. Not all Zentari manifested their magic. And Eli felt something with each WAVE, a growing sensation humming beneath his skin. If he were Aniyan, it would have been silent.

Right?

"Ah." Eli grunted, pushing to his feet.

Everything was unraveling. He raked his fingers through his hair, trying to untangle his thoughts. Nothing made sense—and maybe that was the only truth worth trusting. Pacing helped. Moving helped. Anything to keep from drowning in questions. He needed to find the informant, if not for answers, then at least for Shira's sake.

*Shira*

Her face surged to the front of his mind, twisted in agony, screaming in pain, and an invisible knife pierced his chest. He tried to shake the image, but it wouldn't leave.

*She's the enemy*

Yes. But she was more than that now. *Much more.* And despite every reason to fall back in line with his comrades, the thought of leaving her behind—to be tortured, to be killed—left him hollow. Wasn't this what he believed in? Loyalty? Courage? Standing by the people who mattered?

The dissonance inside him cracked louder than before, and that inner fury growled. If Shira was telling the truth, then the Citadel wasn't a sanctuary. It was a prison. A machine that fed on obedience and demanded silence. And if they were willing to let him die in the Reaping without hesitation, then maybe they never saw him as one of their own.

He felt discarded. Like a tool worn down with use, only to be thrown away and labeled as worthless.

*Shira*

The image of her returned, clearer this time, and his resolve hardened. Every instinct screamed at him to stay alive—for Harper, for himself—but his hand was already forced. He made this decision once before, when he saved Shira from the punishment. If he left Shira to die now, would he still be able to return home with honor, having stood by a corrupt Leadership—having left Shira to a fate worse than death?

After hours of circling the same thoughts and realizing there was only one path ahead, the decision became simple. Eli strode to the door, face set. If death awaited either way, better it come while doing something that mattered—something he believed in. He would try. For Shira. For the woman who showed him that courage isn't born from loyalty to a cause, but from the willingness to stand for truth. Even when it means standing alone. He would not abandon the woman he'd come to—

Eli stopped short. Fenner stood just outside the bunkroom, hand reaching for the doorknob.

"Oh, sorry," Fenner said. "I didn't know if you were in here. You didn't come down for supper."

Eli snapped his thoughts back to the present. Fenner didn't make it either. There was no way in the living Hells he would survive the Reaping. Eli's heart grew heavy, staring at the recruit who was nothing more than a teenager.

"Yeah," Eli said. "I wasn't hungry."

Fenner scuffed his boot on the floor. "I'm sorry, Eli. I can't believe you didn't get one either. You of all people."

Eli scoffed. "Somehow I'm not surprised."

Fenner's shoulders slumped. "Yeah. Everyone else did. Even Rowan, Hells knows why."

It was hard not to feel left behind—a dim failure among the best and brightest.

"How many of us are there?" Eli asked. With the distraction of Shira's arrest, he never caught how many returned in shame to the lower levels.

"Twenty," Fenner said solemnly. "Sol included."

Eli rubbed his face. Nearly a third of the remaining recruits would have to participate in the Reaping. Which meant the chances of graduating as a Guardian were as little as one in four.

"Listen, I came to see if you'd help me tonight," Fenner said. "I still need to work on my sparring. Esme has been helping me, but my squad is at the celebration. And it sounds like we go directly to the Reaping tomorrow morning, and they practice with their Rune Blades after that. So, there won't be any extra time."

Eli fidgeted. "Look, I can't right now, there's something I need to do. And besides, I'm not much of a teacher. Shira was helping me, same as you."

Fenner's eyes widened at her name. "That's right! What the Hells happened? Why was she arrested?"

Eli did his best to appear casual and equally surprised. Praying, ironically, to have become a better liar.

"I don't know. We were all shocked."

"Of course, that's where you're going tonight, isn't it? To the prison?"

Eli's brow furrowed. He didn't know they could go there. "Yeah," he said, "to try at least."

"Okay, I won't get in your way. But I'll be in the Sparring Hall until I collapse. If you get a minute, I'd appreciate any help."

Eli bit his lip. He hoped Esme was an amazing teacher. "Hey Fenner." The kid turned back around. "Why did you join the program so young?"

Fenner hesitated. "It wasn't really my choice," he said with a breathy laugh.

"Long story?"

Fenner nodded. "Yeah."

"I'll make time, Fenner," he said earnestly. "I promise."

Fenner smiled and nodded. "Thanks man," he said, descending the stairs.

Eli remained in the doorway, thoughts racing again. He shook his head, willing them to calm, and strode for the library. Lantern in hand, he shoved down the longing that rose as he reached the alcove he and Shira had been using. Memories flashed in his mind, the sense of urgency growing uncontrollably.

*One step at a time*

Eli waited, glancing around, but saw nothing and heard no one. Unsure of what to do, he stood in the aisle awkwardly, wondering if he should sit in the open or hide. Given the circumstances, the informant likely wouldn't even know he was a friend.

He sat on the available chair, deciding it would be better to remain in the open. If the informant saw him lying in wait, it would only raise suspicion.

*Bleeding Hells, I'm not cut out for this espionage boar spit*

Mind wandering in the silence, Eli glanced at the etchings on the wall. He stood, moving the table aside. Perhaps grabbing some additional Obelisks would prove useful, since he was set on a suicide mission. The stone was warm under his fingers as he traced the grooves. He waited for the light, but none came.

His brow wrinkled, and he pressed both hands on the stone, willing the door to open.

Nothing.

*Right. I don't have magic, but Shira did. She opened the door*

With a huff he slumped back into the chair, defeated once again.

*Why didn't my magic manifest*

There was something present after each WAVE. He was stronger, faster—Eli *knew* he'd changed. He thought back to his first encounter with Shira during the squad selection. She only toyed with him then. Their clash in the Archives had been different. And now, Evergreen's words at the ceremony echoed like a warning. Whatever he'd done wrong, his chances of becoming a Guardian had dropped to near zero.

Anger simmered. The fury within growled. He wanted more. *So much more.* He'd done everything right—pushed harder, carried heavier burdens, held to every ideal preached. He'd come here to find himself, to gain strength to face the darkness which claimed his mother and threatened Harper every day.

But that wasn't enough.

And after his defeat at the Rune Forge, something stirred within—a hidden truth at the furthest recesses of his mind. Gaining strength to shield others was noble, but not the answer lingering under the simmering shadowed depths.

"Who are you?" A female voice cut through the silence.

Eli jumped up, a silhouette standing before him. "Elijah Danon. I—"

The woman raised her hand, stepping forward. Her black hair blended into the darkness of the library, but her emerald eyes reflected the light of his lantern. She wore the armor of an Operative.

"Who are you?" she asked again, her voice low and raspy.

He swallowed. "A friend of Shira Weiss."

The woman narrowed her eyes, giving no reply. She turned to leave. Eli reached out a hand, taking a step.

"Wait! Are you the informant?" he asked, not bothering to hide his desperation.

The woman froze, eyes drifting to him. A shiver ran through him. Her stare gave the same energy as a venomous snake. She slowly approached, and Eli caught a glimpse of polished metal before the blade reached his throat. He didn't move.

The woman's skin was fair, gentle freckles adorning her nose. She searched his face for what felt like hours. "What is her name?" she asked softly.

Eli gathered the threat. She was confirming he would know Shira's true identity, something only shared with those aware she was Aniyan.

"Evalynn Katz. Daughter of General Malachi."

It was a moment before the woman removed the blade from his neck, sheathing it at her side. "She has been captured then?"

Eli nodded. "What's your name?"

After a long pause, the informant spoke, staring with those serpentine eyes. "Names are a precious commodity around here, recruit."

Something about her made him nervous. "Why didn't you meet with Shira sooner?"

Again, another pause. The woman chose her words very carefully. No doubt a habit that kept her alive.

"For this very reason," she said, "were she captured, Azazel could see my face or name. An unacceptable risk."

"Does that mean he'll know I'm involved?"

"Perhaps. If you trust your comrade to resist his invasion, then your involvement may yet remain secret."

"Fine." He paused, still grappling with the dissonance in his mind. "How do we get Shira out?"

"We don't."

Despair grasped at his chest. The more he thought about it, the less he could stomach leaving her to her fate.

"Is there any possible way? I'm willing to do it myself, but I'm asking for your help."

"You don't understand. There is far more going on than you realize. The life of one woman means nothing."

"I know that. And I have questions that need answering, but I cannot leave her down there."

"Then you will die, recruit. I am no fool. I would not willingly march over a cliff expecting to fly."

Eli pursed his lips. "Where is she being held?"

"In the *Kifsho*. The prison, below the Citadel."

"Is there a prisoner named Lucas Miller there?"

"You are referring to the woman's friend?"

"Yes. She already mentioned him?"

"Indeed. And I already sought him out but was unable to verify his presence or his death. It does not matter. Not a single Aniyan has ever left that prison alive. If the friend is there, he is likely long dead."

Eli sighed at the absurdity of the situation. He would have to do this on his own, but at least this woman could give him information. He knew the burning question in his mind but didn't want the answer that it came with.

"Is the Citadel using Aniyans in the program?"

The woman's eyes narrowed. "I did not come here to answer your questions," she spat.

He scoffed. "So, what do you want then? Why meet tonight?"

"Listen, *recruit*, I've been hiding among the ranks ever since I returned from the field and have been investigating the Citadel for *months*. You two have just barely scratched the surface. You have no idea how far you are into the snake pit."

"Well, I'm apparently dead anyway, so why don't you just explain it?"

"Yes, please!" Renard said loudly as he rounded the corner, sword drawn. "Explain it for us both."

The woman spun around, long knives in her hands. Eli froze, the color drained from his face. He reached slowly for his practice sword, knowing he didn't stand a chance against the Captain.

Renard stepped forward. "Operative Nyx, a pleasure to officially make your acquaintance."

Nyx gave no response, but her jaw clenched. Renard glanced at Eli, his eyes dancing to his practice sword.

"Put the weapon down son, before someone gets hurt."

Eli's blade slickened beneath his palms, but he drew the broadsword. "With all due respect, sir, I refuse."

A smile tugged at Renard's mouth. "I knew there was a reason I liked you." He returned his attention to Nyx. "Do you know how long I've been trying to hunt you down? I am extremely impressed by your cunning mind. Were it anyone else but me, you would've never been found tonight."

Nyx lunged at Renard, blades in hand. In a flash, Renard reached his hand out, blue magic shooting from his fingertips. The stream of flowing indigo paralyzed Nyx on the spot.

She stood frozen, a grimace on her face.

Renard turned to Eli. "You've officially crossed the line, Danon."

# Chapter Fifty-One

Abrasive ropes bit into Eva's wrists, each tug of the Operatives jolting her forward as they led her down the narrow stairwell. Every pull wrenched her shoulders, threatened to steal her resolve under the control of her captors. The dungeon had been so close, so near to her grasp, but even escape was now no more than a whimsical idea lost on the wind.

The air thickened as they descended, clinging damply to her skin, carrying the stagnant rot of dust and decay. The stone walls sweated, their cold slick surfaces swallowing the meager light of the torches and mage stones mounted to the walls. Eva forced herself to take in everything—every turn, every guard position, every door—etching the details into memory.

At the base of the stairs, they emerged into the dungeon, a cavernous chamber shaped with merciless precision. One corridor stretched ahead, another veering sharply left. Rows of heavy cell doors flanked both halls, iron bars mottled with rust, streaked with the remnants of older cruelties. Cries of anguish and gentle groaning echoed, choked whispers of men and women who no longer remembered the feeling of hope.

Eva stole her courage. One of the Operatives yanked her arm, leading her down the hallway to the left. Judging by what she could see, there were at least fifty prison cells lining the walls. If there were four identical hallways, that made for up to two hundred cells.

Emaciated Aniyan prisoners occupied each one, judging by their sandy hair. Sullen faces greeted her behind each barred door, and Eva's heart wrenched from the suffering of her kin. Despite her stubborn refusal to believe Lucas was gone, as she laid eyes on the current state of the Citadel prisoners, she knew in her heart he would have never survived this long.

As they followed the hallway to the right, Eva caught sight of a broad metal door on the back wall. It didn't look like a prison cell, but they were leading her directly to it. With a loud *clunk*, one of the Operatives opened the door and Eva's heart stuttered at what she saw inside.

Dried blood caked the floor, with bits of flesh surrounding a narrow drain in the center. The walls told past stories of torment, crimson splatters stained on the stone from years of unspoken horrors. Two chains hung from the rear wall, with handcuffs at their ends.

Eva struggled, unable to withstand the panic exploding at the sight of her own death. The Operatives dragged her forward. Her boots scraped on the floor, grunting as she pulled against their iron grip. She thrashed and screamed, kicking one in the foot, but there was nothing she could do.

Thrown against the back wall, one Operative grabbed the chain on her left. The other slammed his hand to her throat. Her bonds were released, and her left wrist was secured tightly with the chain. Eva couldn't breathe but still struggled—fought with everything inside. Pressure built unbearably in her head as her right arm was bound.

With a gasp, the hand on her throat was removed. As they gathered the rope off the ground, one ripped her prosthetic ears off. The other threw his fist into her right cheek.

"Rotting Cretin."

The door slammed shut, and Eva listened to the fading footsteps against the gentle clanking of her chains. Her bonds forced her upright, arms spread wide.

*Day thirty, Winter's Touch. Day eleven, Harvest's Moon. Day four, Midsummer's Eve*

With deep breaths, her panic settled, replaced by dread. She knew—all too well—what came next. Biting down on her fear, Eva readied her mind, stealing her nerves. She would not betray Eli, nor their secrets.

*Day nineteen, Autumn's Sigh*

Footsteps sounded outside. The door wrenched opened, and Voss stepped in. The woman's fury was evident as she left her guards outside and approached Eva.

"Did you think I would not recognize the daughter of my mortal enemy?" Voss asked.

Eva said nothing, stifling her sarcasm. She would not willingly give away any details, nor make this process any easier for them.

*Day twenty-two, Spring's Promise*

"I am not a monster, my dear," Voss said. "If you provide the answers I seek, I can see to it you are released. If the information you offer is useful, perhaps your freedom is not out of the question."

Eva studied the Commander. Whether it was her eye patch, or years of training, Voss's face was entirely unreadable—the truth of her words hidden. Eva doubted very much they would willingly let her leave, especially if they knew what she and Eli discovered.

"You made quite a spectacle at the Rune Forge," Voss continued. "In all my years I have never seen a reaction like that from the sacred stone. How were you able to do that?"

Eva waited a moment, choosing her words carefully. "I don't know. I didn't expect to get anything."

"Is there anyone else who knows your true identity?"

Voss's black eye bored into Eva with a stifling, calculated malice, but was met with equal stubbornness.

"No."

"Who else knows you're here?"

"Well, if I know my father, very few. I wasn't exactly ordered to come here."

Voss's eye narrowed. "Do not play games with me, Cretin. Do you really expect me to believe the daughter of General Malachi came here of her own volition? Willingly leaped into the snake pit? What were your orders?"

"I wasn't given any. I came here looking for our prisoners of war that you Shells keep capturing. Thanks for showing me where the dungeon is."

Voss waited. Eva swallowed, nervous she said too much.

"I do not believe you," Voss said finally, turning to leave. "She's all yours."

As Voss left, High Captain Azazel entered the room. His black armor and cloak were more intimidating than before, but it was the dark look of satisfaction in his eyes that sent a shiver down her spine.

Azazel said nothing. Other than closing the door, he didn't move an inch—only watched her closely. Eva wondered if this was one of his interrogation tactics. Waiting for fear and dread to weaken the will, before having to do anything at all.

"Why don't we get this over with?" Eva said after minutes of silence, her nerves beginning to fray.

A smile tugged at his lips. "Oh, my Cretin princess, you do not get to rush this."

Eva blinked and shook her head. Her vision blurred, ears ringing. An insatiable discomfort came over her, as if insects crawled beneath her skin, worms burrowed through her joints. Her attention shot to Azazel. He hadn't moved. *At all.* She didn't know how his abilities worked, but he hadn't done anything yet.

*It's your nerves. Calm down*

The door opened behind the High Captain. Tearing her gaze from Azazel, Eva's world stopped. Her breath hitched as she stared in disbelief. Shiny black armor creaked as he strolled in, standing next to Azazel, whose stare never faltered from Eva.

She stared in horror, mouth agape.

"Father?" she breathed.

Malachi gave his political smile, placing a hand on Azazel's shoulder. "Well done, High Captain. I'm glad the traitor is finally caught. Congratulations."

"What are you doing here?" Eva said through gritted teeth, fury rising in her throat. Tears crept into her eyes as her emotions boiled over.

"I would start with breaking her fingers," Malachi said. Eva gasped. "She's always been proud of her physical superiority, it might do her some good to maim her temporarily."

Azazel said nothing. Malachi stepped forward, and Eva couldn't tear her eyes from her father. Her cheek burned as he slapped her, but it was nothing compared to the pain of his presence.

"What a disappointment you are," he muttered, before turning to leave, slamming the door behind him, as if sealing her fate himself.

Eva's breathing worsened as grief twisted its claws in her gut, sorrow blooming in the edges of the wound. She hung her head—weeping—ashamed she couldn't help herself. Her chains pulled taut as her knees caved. Inside, she could feel herself stepping to the edge of that precipice once again.

Lucas had been her anchor, keeping her from falling into the darkness of her father's wrath. And Eli single-handedly yanked her away from the edge, promising more beyond her next breath. Now there was nothing and no one. Her fingernails bit into her hands until she felt warm liquid drip from her palms.

The door to the room opened, and chains rattled as an Operative dragged in another prisoner. His blonde hair and pale blue eyes instantly registered. Lucas was thrown down, blood dripping from his face and hands, splattering on the floor. His breathing was erratic, his eyes fluttering to stay open.

"Lucas!" Eva shouted, yanking against her chains, desperately trying to reach him.

The Operative addressed Azazel. "Sir, this one isn't giving us anything any longer. Should we proceed with the execution?"

Eva's eyes widened. Azazel turned his head, nodding at the Operative.

"No!" Eva cried, her voice breaking at the force. "Lucas!"

The Operative dragged Lucas's broken body out, smearing his blood on the stone as they left. Eva continued shouting, thrashing against the chains, the torrent of sorrow and rage feeding her desperation. Her eyes bore into Azazel's, willing her stare to strike him dead. But his face betrayed no emotion.

He simply stood—unmoving. Her attention remained on Azazel, until she heard his voice.

"I'm glad you got my message. Waiting until the Rune Blade Ceremony was a smart move, High Captain."

*Eli*

He stood with arms crossed, his red squad leader band bright against his armor. It was the same face she had come to know—the same fiery eyes—but they held no warmth.

"It's amusing how gullible she is though," Eli said. "I knew Cretins were stupid, but rotting Hells. She didn't tell me much, but I don't think you'll have any problems getting everything from her."

Eva's brow stitched. Something was wrong. She studied Eli as he approached.

"I have a secret for you," he said, leaning in close, inches from her face. "I lied."

Eva felt an overwhelming wave of emotion, more explosive and volatile than anything in her life. Anger, grief, hatred, fury, despair, all flowing through her at his words—a torrent of a heart's tide erupting without cause, without question, and without permission.

"Goodbye, Evalynn," Eli said over his shoulder as he left, no lament in his words.

The storm within calmed. And a smile tugged at Eva's mouth. She was right.

*Azazel is already in your head*

But he hadn't touched her, hadn't taken a single step.

*Kick him out*

That's right. She was a Guardian. A warrior of the ethereal.

*With magic*

Eva shut her eyes, fists clenched tight, reaching inward—back to Heika, to the moment the Rune Forge burned in her veins. But there was nothing. No spark.

Only weakness.

*Don't stop*

She pictured Eli's determined gaze, Lucas's easy smile, Arlo's maddening laugh, Maya's sisterly embrace. Each memory anchored her, and she dug her heels in. She would not break, would not betray them, would not be easily overcome. Whatever this monster wanted, he would never get it.

A cry tore from her lungs. Light exploded from her limbs in a surge of pale blue. Chains screamed in protest as Eva yanked hard against them, and Azazel was blasted backward, slamming into the wall beside the door. Her knees shook as she stood, heart pounding, breath raw. The light dimmed, her magic fading into flickering echoes across the stone.

Azazel stirred, unsteady. Sweat clung to his brow. His gloves and cloak lay in a heap near the door. Eva scanned the floor where Lucas was dragged in—nothing.

No blood.

A strained, bitter laugh left her lips. "Nice try."

She stared down the High Captain, chest heaving. For the first time, he looked shaken. Azazel crossed the room in a rush, and his fist caught her jaw in a flash of white pain.

# Chapter Fifty-Two

E li stepped forward, ready to attack the Captain but stopped as Renard released his magic. Nyx fell to one knee with a gasp.

"Put the sword away, son," Renard said. "I'm not here to arrest you."

His brow stitched. "Sir?"

Renard sheathed his sword before leaning forward, extending a hand to Nyx. She took it hesitantly, standing and sheathing her blades as well.

Nyx scoffed. "*Cho-luk.* You're the *Shad'har.*"

Renard smiled, bowing. "At your service."

"You're another informant," Eli said, trying to keep up.

"No," Nyx corrected. "He is the *Shad'har*, the infamous oath breaker who forced the entire Citadel under lock and key for the past year."

"I never liked that term," Renard mused. "It's misleading, though not from the Council's point of view."

Eli had no words. He put away his own blade, feeling entirely over his head.

Renard said, "Son, you have achieved in a few weeks what I have not been able to in months. I was aware of another informant within the Citadel, though I didn't know who. Turns out keeping an eye on you was the right decision."

Nyx said, "And it is unfortunate that the *Shad'har* is nothing more than a Captain in charge of the training program."

"Actually, quite the contrary. As a program Captain I can keep a close eye on the recruits, doing what I can to protect the Aniyans. As well as sniff out any possible candidates for future endeavors. Like this one," he said, nodding at Eli.

Eli felt lightheaded and swayed. "What did you say?" he whispered.

"I am surprised the Aniyan spy spoke so highly of this one," Nyx said. "There's too much to explain and not enough time, recruit."

Renard held his hand up. "He deserves to know, Operative."

"And risk his mind collapsing on the eve of the Reaping? Are you also signing his death warrant?"

"This one is different."

"Than all the others? You give him too much credit."

Renard sighed. "Elijah, sit down."

Eli's heart raced, his vision blurred. But he stood his ground. Renard reached into a breast pocket and retrieved a letter. Unfolding it, Eli took it with sweaty, shaking hands. The official wax seal of the Commander was only recently broken.

*To Commander Talia Voss,*

*The most recent group of Aniyan prisoners are enroute, per standing orders. Minimal physical trauma induced. Twelve prisoners in total, taken from the latest confrontation near Tekhpal.*

*Eight males, four females in total. Seven are Legion members, five are citizens.*

*Each prisoner is a prime candidate for the Guardian program.*

*Prisoners sent directly to the Citadel for Thought Wave Analysis.*

*Vor'Irath*

Eli read the letter over. And over. And over. It felt impossible to even understand, let alone process all the new information. And the more his thoughts dwelled on this truth, the more he felt himself collapse. His eyes skimmed the page, desperately trying to connect the dots.

"It's true?" He breathed.

The Captain nodded. "Yes."

*Shira was right*

Eli's numb hands dropped the letter. The room spun, and he stumbled backwards into a bookshelf, grabbing his head. Everything was a lie. Everything he thought he knew, everything he held as important was a well fabricated deception. If he was Aniyan—not Zentari—then nothing was real. If he never volunteered, if he never came here seeking to be a Guardian, then nothing he'd felt this entire time was true.

"Who am I?" he whispered.

Something slithered into his stomach, burrowing inside like an invasive darkness. His face flushed, and he grasped the shelf for balance. The entirety of his being was shattering. Nothing was real. Nothing he knew was real.

"*Rhu'Da!*" Nyx whispered harshly. "Now you get to pick up the pieces, Captain!"

Renard strode to him, gripping his shoulders to keep him steady. "Elijah, look at me," Renard demanded. Eli's attention shifted restlessly, desperate for something solid, before finding the steadiness in the Captain's gaze. "For your sake, you need to take a deep breath. Your mind can shatter from this."

Renard's hold was the only thing keeping Eli on his feet.

*This is all wrong*

*Everything is wrong*

"I do not know if you are Aniyan or not," Renard said. "There is no way to know for certain, without the transport records."

"What about the others?" he asked, eyes burning as emotion welled.

"There's no way to know." Renard let go as Eli steadied, digesting the truth.

"I've been having nightmares," Eli whispered. "Ever since the beginning. I've had a gnawing sensation in my gut, like I don't belong here. Is this why?"

Each word was sharp steel biting through his chest, tearing and slicing his inner being until even his own internal screams ceased to register.

"Yes," Renard answered. "And you've also had a severe reaction to the WAVEs, both indications that you're fighting its influence."

"Which means I really am . . ." his voice trailed, swaying once again.

"Hey, hey, stay with me," Renard said, gripping his shoulders again.

"I need you to—" Eli couldn't finish his thought before his vision turned black.

"Kael!" Eli shouted, tackling the warrior about to gut his friend. The hard ground rattled his skull as they fell, and the warrior threw his fist into Eli's temple. Stars flashed in his vision as he held the warrior down, bearing the pain.

"Kael! Get to Harper! Now!" he shouted.

Pain seared in his side as the warrior sliced his abdomen. Amid the struggle, a hand grabbed the back of Eli's tunic, ripping him to his feet. He spun around, punching whoever had—

*Dad*

"Harper is upstairs!" his father shouted. "Grab her and run into the forest!"

Eli sprinted for the house as his father lunged at the warrior behind him. Before he reached the front door, his gaze found Kael, lifeless in the dirt with a blade in his chest. He kicked open the door of the burning inn, sprinting upstairs as fast as his feet could carry him.

"Harper!" he shouted, sitting up in Renard's bed. Eli frantically searched the room, the flames now absent from his vision, heat of the fire gone. He trembled, drenched in sweat.

Renard was at his side in an instant. "Hey, hey, Elijah, calm down. You're safe!" Renard assured. "And keep your voice down. My protection only goes so far."

Eli took a deep breath, willing his body to relax. He nodded, closing his eyes for a moment. That was the worst nightmare yet—by far. Renard's quarters weren't spacious, but far more luxurious than the recruits' barracks. The bed was wider, and the room was modestly decorated with various portraits and mementos from any number of adventures.

Renard ushered Eli to sit with him at the table in the corner. Nyx leaned against the door across the room. She acted impatient, annoyed even, which grated his frayed nerves. He didn't remember passing out, or how they got to Renard's quarters.

The Captain grabbed a glass bottle of orange firewater and two small cups from a wardrobe near the table. He sat and poured a helping into each glass.

"Captain," Eli said, desperately needing answers.

Renard nodded before pushing one of the glasses across the table. Eli sat.

"About a year ago." Renard started. "We discovered that at our current rate of population decline, we'd lose the war in about five years. The Legion outnumbers us ten to one. We need soldiers. Guardians are even better. So, the Council ordered us to begin capturing Aniyan warriors, saying it was to gather information through torture. In truth, we were instructed to coerce them into fighting for us. That's when the WAVEs came."

Eli's blood turned cold.

"At first," Renard continued. "They only wiped memories. Whatever it is the Council does is even beyond High Captain Azazel. It made compliance easier. But over time, they discovered the WAVEs could do more—awaken dormant Zentari blood, alter physical appearance, even manipulate loyalty."

"Are you saying my memories are fake?"

Renard took a sip of his firewater. "No. Only distorted—twisted. The WAVEs don't implant memories, they muddy them. If you wanted to fight for the Legion, they convinced you it was the Guardians. They prey on your convictions. Rewire your compass. How they change your appearance, I think is the Ev—"

"Captain," Nyx growled.

"What?" Eli asked.

Renard shook his head. "Just a weightless theory."

Eli downed his firewater in one gulp. "I don't understand," he said. "Why not just use the WAVEs on native Zentari? Surely pure blooded Zentari in Eldan City are more apt to have magic."

Nyx said, "A novel idea. And also naive. You forget the Captain's earlier point. Our population cannot support the war any longer."

"Elijah, nothing about this war makes sense." Renard began. "The deeper I investigate the more questions I'm left with, and the more I wonder what the Council is truly after. The Council has been *knowingly* foregoing strategic advantages, like this recent retreat from the front. There was no need for it. It left the Legion panicked about a sneak attack, but in truth the Council simply ordered a stop. And *just* when our people were getting the upper hand in the North."

"Why?" Eli asked. "Don't they want to win the war?"

"No," Nyx said. "As I said, there is more going on than you realize."

Eli rubbed his face, clinging to his last shred of sanity. "Are you sure they don't grant memories?" he pressed.

Renard shrugged. "From what I've gathered, it's the melding of the Council's own intentions with the candidates that help convince them to serve the Zentari. Some memories—ideals—slip through from the Council's mind to the recruits. It's why we execute those who fail the first WAVE treatment. It's a contingency."

"But Arlo—" Eli said. "Arlo mentioned something called Archancy. But he didn't know how he knew it."

Renard stiffened, glancing at Nyx again. Eli got the distinct impression he wasn't getting the whole truth, only what he could safely comprehend.

When neither answered, Eli clarified. "Shira and I have been trying to investigate what's been going on, and that word keeps coming up in the old documents. It's connected to the Obelisks, but we don't know much beyond that. She said her father knows about it too and has been studying it. What is Archancy?"

Renard opened his mouth, but Nyx spoke for him. "It is a science lost to time. Do not waste your efforts."

"But Shira said it could win the war!" Eli argued. "We think Archancy is how the Obelisks are created, and that the stones are the tool to victory. Otherwise, the Council—"

"They are not!" Nyx scolded. "Your friend is mistaken."

"But we found the Archives!"

Renard's brow furrowed. "The what?"

"Below the library. A hidden chamber that contains books about Archancy and dozens of Obelisks. Untouched."

Renard stiffened.

Nyx asked, "Where, *precisely*, is this located?"

"Just what I said. *Below* the library. There's a magical door sealing it shut, and only someone with inner magic can open it. It seemed long forgotten."

Nyx mumbled a curse before Renard spoke. "I'll check it out, *if* we have time. But Elijah, be extremely cautious about who you mention Archancy to."

"Why?" Eli argued, frustrated at being kept in the dark. "Why is it so secret?"

"For reasons you do not need to know," Nyx said.

"Then tell me about Everstones! Give me some rotting answers!"

"Enough!" Nyx spat. "You would be wise to heed the warning, *recruit*. You are a child meddling in affairs that can crumble nations. We are not—"

She stopped as Renard held up a hand. "Son, just trust us. Drop it."

The inner wrath shifted, and Eli cursed. A nebulous sense of helplessness settled over him.

*All that work for nothing*

Silence stretched, and he stared at the glass in his hand. "Why me?" he breathed.

"Either your appearance changed after the first WAVE, or the Council sensed a well of inner magic within you. I chose you because your mind refused to listen, despite it being flayed alive."

Nyx's voice cut like a blade. "Most Aniyans do not survive the transition. As few as one in ten contain enough Zentari blood to manifest inner magic. The rest are . . . disposed of."

Eli's brow wrinkled. "So Zentari and Aniyans *have* been intermarrying?"

"For centuries," Renard said. "The bloodlines are so entangled, it's impossible to separate them anymore. The fact that the Leadership says otherwise is nothing more than propaganda. It keeps the war alive."

Eli leaned forward, shaking his head. "You told me—"

"To be cautious, and to not believe everything you thought. You were the first recruit I've seen to ask questions after being subjected to the WAVEs."

"And no one else reacted like I did?"

Renard shook his head. "Not one. Most break. Others go quiet. Some are . . . handled."

Nyx shifted her weight on the door. "Your reaction would be considered mild, recruit."

Eli stood and paced, raking a hand through his hair. "We have to tell the others."

Renard raised a calming hand. "Hold on, son."

"No, we have to escape!"

"You are assuming your friends want the truth," Nyx said. "They do not."

"Elijah, we don't know who is and isn't Aniyan. And if we go around shouting the truth, not only would we be executed, but the other recruits won't believe it."

"You don't know them. Arlo and Lara—they would believe me."

Renard's expression darkened. "Do you remember that crazed recruit in your bunkroom?"

Eli nodded.

"When the mind is subjected to world ending dissonance, it can cease to function. The mind, when enough pressure is placed upon it, will willingly accept what it knows to be false to eliminate that dissonance. Your friends won't *want* to know the truth."

Eli sank back into the chair, chest hollowing. "I can't leave them."

"You can," Nyx said, "and you must. No one has ever escaped the program after uncovering the truth."

Eli's gaze lifted, a thought sparking. "Is anyone else aware?"

Renard and Nyx shared a glance.

"Soren Mitchell," Nyx said. "We do not know how he discovered the truth, but he was given an ultimatum: silence or death."

"He's been reprimanded more times than I can count," Renard added. "But always slithers his way out of the consequences. From what I can gather, he has contacts within the Zentari military, protection beyond even the highest levels of influence. Which is no doubt how he found out the truth."

Eli's brow furrowed. "That's why he called me Rov-An?"

"It means 'enemy' in Primarch script," Nyx said. "He is fluent in the old language as well. His subtle way of telling you, without actually telling you."

"I saw him speaking to others in the middle of the night, back when we first arrived."

Renard nodded. "Go on."

"That's why Sol's squad was so aggressive." Eli realized. "They were killing the Aniyan recruits."

"No," Renard said, eyes downcast as he took another drink. "They were guessing."

Nyx added, "But neither Richter nor Mitchell needed reasons. They wanted excuses."

Eli pressed his fingers to his temples. "How much of the Leadership knows?"

Renard hesitated. "Few. Enough to keep it quiet, not enough to stop it."

The Captain poured another drink, slow and heavy. "When I discovered the truth, I almost left the Citadel. I nearly relinquished my position and joined the resistance in Sheket. But I realized I could do more good from the inside."

Eli stood, pacing. He remembered what Shira said in the Archives.

*'The one who looked at which nation they were serving and decided to choose a side, rather than blindly obey orders.'*

"Why did you become an informant?" Eli asked Nyx.

Her ears twitched at the question. "I am not a traitor," she said, jaw tight.

Eli met her glare. "I didn't say you were. And that wasn't an answer."

A long breath escaped her nose, something between annoyance and resignation. She shifted her weight on the door.

"Your friend—the princess—challenged everything I believed about my enemy. She showed mercy to me and honor to my comrades, which at the time only left me with questions. And despite my efforts, those questions grew."

Eli didn't interrupt, watching the guarded emotion flicker across her face. There was pain, and something buried—long wrestled with.

"When I returned from my mission, I began digging. Searching for answers. What exactly sparked the war, and why it has continued for so long. In that process I found nothing but corruption and selfish allegiances. Secrets buried beneath time and ignorance. I came to realize my goals, and your friend's, were not very different."

"What did she do?" he asked, desperate to know who Shira was before the Citadel.

Nyx's throat bobbed. "She spared my life. After I attempted to kill her. She left food and supplies for my journey home and gave my comrades an honorable burial."

A stillness settled. Eli blinked as Shira's face surfaced unbidden in his thoughts. It brought a tide of longing and regret, sudden and overwhelming.

He drew a sharp breath. "Do we know if there is a prisoner named Lucas here?"

"Hard to say," Renard said. "Depends on when he was captured."

"A few months ago, before the program started."

The Captain sighed. "Then I doubt he's alive. If he was suitable, they would've put him through the program. If not . . ."

Eli clenched his jaw, face set. "I'm going to save her from the prison." If this truly wasn't his home, or his people, then he had nothing left to lose.

"Then you will die, recruit," Nyx said.

"I don't care. That woman, who showed you honor and mercy, saved my life a dozen times over. I won't leave her to die below my feet."

Renard leaned forward. "Son, I promise you Azazel has already invaded her mind. Every minute she spends down there, the less attached to reality she becomes."

Eli's hands clenched. "Then we don't waste time."

Renard held his hand up again. "Elijah, Azazel's methods are brutal. She may not be the same person she was when she was taken."

"I don't care," Eli said, voice steady. "I won't leave without her."

Renard studied his face. "Is she really that important to you?"

Without hesitation, Eli nodded. "She's also Malachi's daughter."

Renard's eyes narrowed before he gave a breathy laugh, taking another hard drink. "I knew she was Aniyan, but I didn't know she was *that* Aniyan."

Eli's mouth fell open. "How long have you known?"

"From the beginning," Renard said with a grin. "I was expecting her. It's why I made sure to be the one jotting names that first day. I was the one who put her on the list."

Eli scoffed at the absurdity—and enormity—of the circumstance. "How am I the only one who noticed her blue eyes?"

"You're not. But anyone suspicious knows well enough to keep quiet. That book you found is outdated, son. Intermarrying alone has sprinkled icy eyes throughout the country. Uncommon, but not impossible. Besides, Grisham was known for his politically harsh separation of Zentari and Aniyan lineage."

The Captain finished the last of his drink, setting the glass down with a loud *thunk*. "I need a day."

"A day?" Eli argued.

"Yes," Renard said grimly. "Son, you are asking me to arrange an escape from the most safeguarded prison in Adiel. We need diversions, to reroute guards, clear a path west, forge paperwork. I think it's possible, at least to create a short window, but it will cost everything. One misstep and none of us make it out alive. Nyx and I will do what we can and get you when the time comes."

"Thank you," Eli said, looking between them. "Thank you for helping us."

"I cannot speak for the Captain," Nyx said, "but I am ready to leave this place."

"I don't need a reason to help those in need, Elijah," Renard said, walking to his closet. "And I have a lifetime of sins to make up for."

Eli turned in a circle, growing more restless by the minute. "What can I do?" he asked.

Renard was strapping his Rune Blade across his waist while Nyx pushed off the wall.

"Go back to the barracks and pretend nothing happened," Renard answered. "Stay alive in the Reaping tomorrow morning, and if you can, unlock your magic. We'll need every edge we can get."

He sighed. "Okay. But I have someone to visit first."

# Chapter Fifty-Three

As consciousness threatened to slip from her grasp, the stifling confines of the dungeon warping her sense of reality, Evalynn drew each breath with quiet defiance. Refusing to give in to the growing despair, every gasp demanded what little strength she had left. Her chains bit into her wrists as she hung with arms raised, shoulders aching while fresh blood trailed from the raw wounds.

Another blow to the stomach. Eva gagged, iron coating her tongue.

"Your boldness must know no bounds for you to think you could invade the Citadel and leave unscathed," Azazel mocked.

"Save the speech," Eva grunted. "I just walked right in. Turns out the great spire has lax security."

Eva's vision blurred as another punch found its mark, her head recoiling at the force. The chains bit her wrists, punishing the movement. A new layer of crimson dripped to the stony floor.

*Breathe*

Stubborn strength rose within, willing herself to endure—refusing to betray her secrets. She focused her mind beyond her cell, outside the cold stone walls, away from the prison's suffocating darkness. She thought of Eli's hand in hers, and Lucas's laughter in her ears.

A face appeared beside hers. "I can't believe you failed," Arlo mocked. "Here you were trying so hard to save Lucas, but you can't even save yourself. Pathetic little princess, aren't you?"

Eva clamped her eyes shut, willing the illusions to flee.

*They're not real*

"You know it was all a joke, right?" Eli's voice came from her other side. Hallucination or not, his presence tore her heart from her chest. "I only wanted to see how gullible you were. It was too easy. You're a bloody traitor. A liar. You actually thought someone could care about you? After everything you've done?"

A hand grabbed her jaw, wrenching her head upwards, Azazel now inches from her face.

"Tell me why you're here," he drawled, a promise of pain.

Eva breathed in and spit in his face.

"Oh," Eli mused. "Bad move."

Azazel closed his eyes, wiping the blood and saliva away with his free hand. He shifted his grip on her left arm, driving his elbow down onto it and unleashing a sickening crack. Pain tore through her chest, her vision filling with stars at the fresh fracture.

A gut-wrenching cry drowned out her scream.

"Help!" Lucas cried from the corner, laying in a bloodied heap. Eva squeezed her eyes shut again, clenching her jaw as tears formed at the sound of his voice.

*It's not real*

*It's not real*

"He's going to die because of you," Eli said, his breath hot in her ear. "It's your fault."

"Evalynn! Help me!" Lucas screamed.

*Day thirty, Winter's Touch*

*Day eleven, Harvest's Moon*

"I can't believe you still don't get it!" Arlo sneered. "You really are the most pathetic person I've ever met. Hells, you couldn't even figure out what Archancy is!"

The images vanished. The screaming stopped. Eva heard nothing but her own heaving breaths and quiet whimpers.

"Archancy?" Azazel mused. Her eyes shot open. "What is Archancy?"

"I don't know," she whispered.

Dread came over her as she felt hands grab her little finger. A quick motion, a loud snap, and pain erupted through her arm. Eva screamed. She couldn't move her left hand.

"Tell me," Azazel ordered, another dreaded promise in his voice.

"I'm telling the truth!" she cried, her voice hoarse and cracking. "I don't know!"

Pain exploded in her scalp as Azazel grabbed her by the hair and lifted her head.

"Then show me," he growled, grasping the sides of her head.

Fire erupted in her skull as Azazel invaded her mind again, the burning—

Little Evalynn lay on the marble floor in front of her locked bedroom door, listening. Watching the pair of feet outside, she prayed silently to whatever force dwelt within the Heavens.

"My Lord, she keeps pleading to be let out," Nana's voice was muffled from behind the solid oak wood. "Sneaking outside is forbidden, yes, but she is only six. Would you consider mercy?"

"I don't recall asking your advice on how to raise my child, Glorana," Malachi said.

"My Lord, if I may be so bold, I still remember what happened. Her life is a miracle. A blessing. It should not be squandered."

"You have made your opinions clear," Malachi said, biting off the words.

"It has been *five days*—"

A loud smack silenced Glorana's beseeching.

"My daughter is learning a valuable life lesson. She will be released when I say, and not a moment sooner. Unless of course you'd like to leave her under the care of another."

Footsteps faded as her father marched down the hallway, before silence fell. Evalynn didn't move as Glorana unlocked her door and slipped back inside.

"Oh, my dear!" Nana said, kneeling and gently touching her back. "Why are you on the ground?"

Eva was numb, no longer having the capacity to cry. "Why doesn't daddy love me?" she whispered.

She hoped Nana would be able to explain it, to tell her what she was doing wrong—how to change. Surely there was an answer. Something that made sense. Something she could become.

Glorana stroked her back in silence.

"Is there something wrong with me?" Evalynn whispered, wracking her youthful mind to decipher the truth that made entirely no sense in her heart.

Quiet whimpers sounded, and Evalynn looked up.

"Oh, Nana, don't cry!" she said, sitting up and hugging Glorana's neck. "I'm all right, truly! It's okay! I'll be good and won't get in trouble ever again! Don't be sad!"

It was hours before her personal maid—her only friend in the world—stopped weeping.

# Chapter Fifty-Four

Eli kicked at Fenner's ribs, who leaped back with a swift dodge. They had sparred for hours, and with every bout Eli felt his dread over the Reaping lessen. Whether through determination—or resignation—he was ready to face the challenge that awaited in the coming morning. But his heart sank for Fenner. The kid was worse than he thought. Despite their continued bout, Eli was barely challenged.

With heavy breaths, they stood on the practice mat, torchlight flickering on the walls of the dim Sparring Hall. The entire space was theirs to claim. It was late enough, most others were resting before tomorrow. Eli and Fenner were likely the only ones that needed more practice. Besides, he knew he wouldn't find any rest tonight—not with Shira being tortured under his feet. Though it was likely foolish to exhaust yourself before a death match.

"You're doing well, Fenner. Remember to keep your balance though. Stay on the balls of your feet so you can change direction with each attack."

Fenner nodded, bending over his knees. By the time Eli arrived to help, Fenner was already winded and sweating. The best thing for the kid at this point would be a few hours of sleep.

"Hey, you should go to bed," Eli said. "You'll need rest, and a fresh mind is your greatest weapon."

Fenner exhaled and nodded. "Okay. Thank you, Elijah."

Guilt clutched his heart as Fenner shuffled away. He should tell him the truth, ask him for help, let him escape to safety with them. But Renard and Nyx's warning played back in his mind. They were right. It could destroy their entire plan if anyone blew the whistle early.

As Fenner left the Sparring Hall, Arlo barged past him. With his new war hammer slung over his back, Arlo strode with intention, something akin to anger on his face. He marched up to Eli, having returned from the private party upstairs.

"What in the *rotting Hells* was that?" Arlo shouted, clearly a bit inebriated.

Eli held his hands up. He peered over Arlo's shoulder, making sure Fenner was gone. "Keep your *bloody* voice down!" he scolded in a harsh whisper. "What?"

"Shira is a Guardian!" Arlo responded, not having lowered his voice even a bit.

Eli bit down on his anger. His control was slipping. It surprised him, the fury welling inside. Over the past day he had been humiliated, thrown into despair, had his entire identity turned upside down, and was scheduled for his own execution in the morning. Even if he did survive, he would likely die attempting an escape—all while Arlo was drinking and celebrating.

"I said, 'Shut up!'" he snapped.

Arlo's mouth parted as realization came over him, grasping the enormity of the situation—as well as the glare in Eli's eyes.

"Bloody Nines man, this doesn't make any sense," Arlo said quietly. "What is going on?"

Eli flexed his hands, allowing his anger to pass. "It means what we were trying to tell you is true."

He glanced around them. This wasn't a safe place, but he didn't know if they'd have another chance. Arlo ran his hands through his hair.

"Arlo." Eli started. "I'm escaping tomorrow, along with Shira, Captain Renard and another Operative."

Arlo stilled. "*What*? Why them? Why would you do that? They'll kill you!"

"No, Arlo, you don't understand."

"*Then tell me*! Stop lying for rot's sake!"

"Some of the recruits are Aniyan!" Eli said, panic rising at his raised voice.

Arlo paused. Disbelief widened his eyes. "What?" he whispered.

Eli exhaled sharply. There wasn't any other way to say it. Whether or not Shira was right about Arlo didn't matter. He only needed help saving Shira.

"Captain Renard told me today that the Citadel has been kidnapping Aniyans and using the WAVEs to manipulate their memories. He doesn't know who is and isn't Aniyan, but Shira is and they will *kill her* if we don't escape."

Arlo stepped back, his gaze distant. He held his head and slowly paced. Eli could do nothing as he watched his friend's world collapse, knowing full well the turmoil running through him.

"Arlo."

His friend turned to him, reading his thoughts, as his eyebrows came together. "You?"

Eli nodded, a tear falling down his cheek, formed and gone before he felt the wave of amorphous sorrow.

"But you have pointed ears!" Arlo shouted.

"I don't have magic!"

"How? *How do you know*?"

"I don't! But I haven't felt normal this entire time! I can't remember things that I should!"

Eli caught himself, reining in his anger. Renard warned him of the turmoil his mind was undergoing, deconstructing the WAVEs influence. Keeping himself together took every ounce of his self-control.

"I lied to you," Eli admitted. "My nightmares have been getting worse. And I've been losing my mind. I can't remember my father's name or where I grew up. I'm imagining things, like Soren disappearing for days on end. There are dozens of holes in my memory and Captain Renard said the more your mind fights the Thought Wave Analysis, the more you end up forgetting."

Arlo paused in thought, wrinkling his brow. "Am I?"

"I don't know, and it doesn't matter," he said abruptly, heeding the warning of crazed recruits. "What matters is I can't stay here, and Shira will die if we don't save her."

Arlo scoffed. "We? She's the bleeding enemy, man. I don't understand why you would throw your life away for them."

Eli grappled with the remark, surprised at the distaste of it, knowing Shira's identity. Every line he had drawn in the sand meant nothing.

"So am I, Arlo."

"No, no you're not! You're making assumptions!"

"It doesn't matter!" Eli shouted, throat bobbing. "I feel it in my soul. Arlo my bones have been rotting ever since I came here. Nothing about this experience feels right."

Arlo rubbed his face, pressing his knuckles into the dark circles under his eyes. "So when you pulled me aside and asked me what if the Citadel had a secret, did you know then?"

"No. I just found out a few hours ago. You were already gone upstairs."

Arlo shifted his weight, cursing softly. Eli said nothing, giving him all the time he needed, praying his friend would remain beside him.

"How is Captain Renard tied up in this?" Arlo asked.

"He knows what they're doing, and he's been trying to help the Aniyan captives. He said this started a year ago, and that's when he defected. I'm the first one to figure it out without going insane."

Arlo gave a quizzical look. "The crazy guy in the bunkroom?"

Eli nodded. "Probably Aniyan."

Arlo huffed. Eli waited, wondering the best words to speak to convince his friend that—

"When do we leave?" Arlo asked, face set.

Eli's brow furrowed. "Arlo—"

"Don't. I know," Arlo said, holding up a hand. "Look, man, I don't know what in the dark Hells is happening, but I know that I trust you. If Shira was arrested, then she really was a spy, and if she really was a spy, then she shouldn't have activated the Rune Forge. Which means they aren't telling us the truth, and something *seriously* doesn't add up. And if Captain Renard is involved, Hells knows how deep this goes. I don't care that you lied for Shira, I know your character, man. You saved my life, more than once, so I owe you that much. If you're convinced of this . . . then I'll follow your lead."

"There's no coming back," Eli said. "If you do this, then it's us versus them. We don't get another chance."

Arlo nodded, staring at the floor.

"Arlo, you can ask her but wait to tell Lara until the last moment. If what Captain Renard and Nyx said is true, even if she is Aniyan, she'll likely want to stay."

Eli's heart ached as he watched sorrow fall over his friend's stoic face.

"So, when do we leave?" Arlo asked.

"Tomorrow. Heavens willing."

Neither of them slept after they returned to the bunkroom. Once hours of tossing and turning forced them from bed, both Eli and Arlo dressed, gathering a few items they refused to leave behind. Together they sat in the common area in the silence of the morning, waiting for sunrise.

And for everything to change.

Eli poured them each another glass of the firewater Arlo was given at the celebration. A narrow glass, adorned with a sword crest and *Vor'Irath* molded into the crimson bottle.

"Arlo, are you sure you want to do this?" he asked, hearing distant voices downstairs.

It was time.

"I don't have a choice," Arlo said, his gaze a thousand miles away. "With everything going on I can't just pretend it's all fine. Now that I know, there's no going back to what it was. And I won't stand by and leave you and Shira to fend for yourselves. Besides you'd be helpless without me."

Eli grinned. "Thank you," he said, watching the Operative climb the stairs to announce wake up.

"You can thank me by surviving the Reaping."

Eli reached into his pocket and touched the Obelisk. With the Archives now unable to be accessed, he was glad he grabbed one when he did.

After the first of the recruits funneled out of the barracks and into the walkway, Eli and Arlo stood, corked the bottle and left it on the table. In silence, they walked behind the sea of recruits to the mess hall. Eli sat down at their table, while Arlo remained in line. He wasn't hungry and still felt the calming effects of the firewater.

He stared at each glazed eye, each sullen face. Some were regretting their indulgences last night yet proudly carrying their Rune Blades. Others bore signs of no rest, fearing their looming death match. Fenner sat across from him, and both remained silent. Dark wrinkled circles adorned Fenner's eyes, and Eli prayed silently for them both.

Arlo and Lara sat down with their breakfast, Arlo smashing his food as usual.

"You're not eating?" Lara asked with concern.

Eli turned to her. "Would you?"

She bit her lip. "You need your strength. You too, Fenner."

Eli sighed grimly, wishing he could convey all that was on his mind in the moment. Neither she nor Fenner had any way of knowing everything that was about to transpire. Of course, if he didn't survive, then nothing would change from their perspective.

Arlo gave him a knowing look.

"I'll be fine," Eli said, but turned to Fenner. "Go get some food, man."

Fenner said nothing as he slowly stood, shuffling to the back of the line. Once Fenner left, with Maelyn and Esme awaiting their food as well, Lara leaned over to Eli.

"Will you please tell me now what happened with Shira?" she whispered.

Eli looked at Arlo. "Everything's changed. Ask Arlo."

It may have been a way to offload the responsibility, but he felt the news would be better received coming from him. If either of them possessed a chance at convincing her, it was Arlo.

Eli nodded his head toward the door in a silent command.

*Don't you dare tell her in here*

Arlo stood, leaving his breakfast, motioning for Lara to follow. They didn't return before Captain Evergreen strode into the mess hall.

Silence fell, the air growing thick as each recruit turned to the Captain.

"Recruits, today begins the Reaping. You are all aware of what it entails. Everyone follow me," Evergreen said, though her voice was plain, her face was downcast.

Eli stood as the recruits shuffled out. Fenner was walking back to the table with his food but set it down and stepped alongside him. They were led through the walkway to an unremarkable door, nearly hidden against the surrounding stone. It opened to an ominous stairwell, which descended to a lower level of the Citadel.

After the long flight of stairs, Eli stepped into a round room, barely more than a cave. Entirely bare, apart from torches lining the walls.

And a massive pit in the center.

Everyone shuffled forward, an oily sense of unease slipping into Eli's gut. He glanced behind him. Arlo and Lara continued their private discussion near the door. Judging by their body language, Arlo wasn't having much luck. Eli wondered if his friend would still come with or decide to stay for Lara.

Bile reached his throat as he laid eyes on the pit. A chain ladder was anchored to the side nearest the door. It sat roughly thirty feet deep, and three times as wide, with perfectly smooth walls. There would be no way to climb out without the ladder being lowered.

Its presence was ominous, but what caught Eli's attention, and caused his hands to shake again, were the blood stains inside. Spots, smears, gashes, and other unidentifiable marks of battle lay scattered about, littering every part of the chasm. He noted the floor bore a circular etching in the stone, yet another Archanic symbol. Primarch words were carved on the walls, though many were damaged from previous battles.

Eli played with the Obelisk in his pocket, praying it would be his saving grace. Fenner stood rigid beside him. The kid was petrified.

"All right!" Evergreen shouted. "The Reaping begins now! Those of you who failed at the Rune Forge will have a chance to redeem yourselves, to prove your right to bear the title of Guardian once again. I will call your names two at a time, and you both will enter the pit. The only way out is to manifest your magic or survive. If you survive without magic, you duel again tomorrow."

Eli swallowed, placing a hand on Fenner's shoulder. He glanced behind him, watching Arlo and Lara bicker in the corner.

"Finn Adler and Torin Hart!" Evergreen announced. "Enter the pit!"

Eli recognized Finn from the first day in the Sparring Hall, the memories flashing back to what felt like lifetimes ago. Tension built in the air, and the recruits stirred—even the Guardians among them who were safe. This was a death match. By all rights, they were about to witness ten of their own perish in battle, killed by their comrades.

"Begin!"

Finn and Torin wasted no time, each bearing their own desperation. With blood and fists, they fought evenly matched, though neither of them were physically exceptional. Finn was too skinny, lacking muscle, and Torin was short, his punches lacking reach. They traded blows for roughly an hour, before Torin threw a knuckle into Finn's stomach, causing a bright flash of light.

The room gasped, and Eli covered his face. Stars danced in his vision.

*What in the rotting Hells*

Squinting into the pit, Finn and Torin stood apart, ceasing their bout. It was Torin who had unlocked his magic. Finn yelled in effort—and dire need—coming at Torin with animalistic aggression. Torin blocked the blows, their combat identical to what they had been doing, but the moment Torin threw a counterattack, another bright flash shone.

Finn covered his face, completely blinded. And wide open. He attacked again, throwing wild punches with his eyes closed, clinging to the hope the match wouldn't be over. Torin grimaced—hesitant. Everyone knew he'd won, but it wasn't enough. Torin held back, allowing Finn to continue fighting, waiting for something else to happen. But Finn was only sparring. No magical essence could be seen, despite the additional time.

"Recruit Hart!" Evergreen shouted. The two froze, turning to the Captain. "This is a battle to the death. Refusal to follow the commands of your leaders is treason. Finish this, *now*."

Eli swallowed the lump in his throat.

Finn lunged at Torin. "No! I'm not ready!"

Torin didn't attack, his face still pained. This wasn't combat—it was a test. Eli wondered if this was the third challenge. Could they kill a comrade in cold blood, simply because they were ordered to do so. If he was right, the Reaping was one final effort to place the recruits in a state of self-preservation—force the emergence of life-saving magic. And unless there was a real threat of death, that couldn't happen.

He closed his eyes as Torin's attack flashed brightly once more. Finn stumbled back, and Torin used his opening, snapping Finn's neck. Torin stood, swaying with heavy breaths. Clearly even a subtle use of his new magic was taxing.

"Congratulations, Guardian Hart!"

A few scattered claps were offered, but this wasn't a celebration. Eli was fairly certain only Sol would receive cheers upon his death. The ladder was lowered, and Torin moved toward it. As two healers descended into the pit and retrieved Finn's body, quiet whimpers surfaced from the crowd.

Once the pit was cleared, Evergreen called the next match: Calista Bringer and Darian Lake. Eli didn't recognize the names, which wasn't surprising. No one really knew each other outside their immediate squad. The program deterred it by design, keeping everyone isolated. No attachments. No grief.

Darian never found his magic, but brute strength carried him through. Calista took a hard blow to the hip early and crumpled, screaming underneath Darian's boot as it crushed her throat. Unlike Torin, Darian didn't hesitate, no pity on his face.

"Recruit Lake!" Evergreen said. "You survive another day."

Next came Lorine Walker and Thane Black. Their fight was longer, more violent. Neither one wanted to die. Lorine was the first to draw out her magic, bursts of green smoke trailing from her fists. Thane didn't flinch. He came at her like a hammer, raw and fast, and somewhere in the chaos, his own magic surfaced. Flashes of yellow cut Lorine's chest, throwing blood onto the stone floor.

"Stop!" Evergreen announced. "Congratulations, Guardians Walker and Black!"

Eli watched in silence, a knot tightening in his chest. He already knew who his opponent would be. It didn't matter. He wasn't getting out of this.

"Fenner Hayes and Sol Richter!"

The world ground to a halt. Fenner didn't move, eyes staring into the pit.

*No*

Eli squeezed the obelisk in his hand, the sharp edges biting his palm. He would not let Sol play with Fenner, standing idly while Sol broke his body.

He placed a hand on Fenner's shoulder. "Don't go in."

Eli moved past him, toward Evergreen. Sol drifted through the crowd toward the chain ladder, smiling leisurely. Evergreen stood at the far end on the Reaping pit, arms crossed.

"Captain Evergreen, ma'am," Eli said.

She glanced at him, before returning her attention to the pit. "Speak, recruit."

"I formally request to be paired with recruit Richter. I ask that you exchange my place with recruit Hayes."

He clenched his fists to stop shaking, listening to himself sign his own death warrant.

"I'm not in the habit of changing my mind, recruit."

"I understand that, Captain. But with all due respect, Fenner doesn't stand a chance."

"That's unfortunate for him," she retorted, face blank.

"Captain, I also have a score to settle."

Evergreen's brow lifted. "Oh?"

"Yes, ma'am. Recruit Richter and his squadmates have harmed those under my command more than once. I request the opportunity to repay him in kind."

He held Evergreen's brazen stare. His mind was made up. If he didn't do this, Fenner would die. And in truth, something deep in his soul stirred.

*He wanted this.* Wanted to watch the giant bleed and be the one to do it.

"Granted, recruit. May the Heavens bless you."

Eli turned around and headed back toward Fenner, and his own demise. His heart thundered, the reality of the situation bearing down on his shoulders. But the quiet wrath within stirred in excitement, rose from its slumber, ready to be unleashed. He would survive. He must. For Shira. For Harper. For his father. And he would show everyone that the hulking giant was nothing more than a man.

As he passed Fenner, who was anxiously searching his face, Evergreen's voice cut through the silence.

"Recruit Hayes will be replaced by Recruit Danon, at personal request!"

Fenner shook his head, eyes wide. "You can't."

"I did," Eli said with a solemn grin. "Just promise me you'll fight like the Hells when the time comes."

Fenner made no reply—astonished. Before Eli could step toward the ladder, Arlo and Maelyn emerged from the crowd.

"Why, Eli?" Maelyn asked.

He couldn't tell if her tone was worried, or accusing, but his eyes darkened. "I'm getting even."

"What are you doing, man?" Arlo said, panicked.

"I'll be fine."

"Like the dark Hells! He's going to—"

"Elijah Danon, enter the pit!"

Eli turned abruptly, shutting everything out. Sweat formed on his forehead, but his breathing remained steady. The enemy was known to him. He had watched Sol fight, could read his movements, knew his weaknesses. He could beat him.

In theory.

He descended the ladder and strode to the center of the circle, focus narrowing to one goal. The ladder was raised, and he gripped the Obelisk harder in his right hand. No escape.

"I'm so glad you were able to arrange this dance of ours, Danon," Sol mocked with a snide grin. "Though I doubt it will last long. Just try to make it entertaining for me."

"Not today, Sol."

"Begin!"

The moment the order was given, Eli lunged. There was no point waiting. This wasn't a duel—it was survival. Either he left a Guardian, or he would die here under the ground.

Sol braced as Eli opened with a spinning kick, one Shira had used so many times. Sol blocked it, but Eli was already inside, landing a punch to his chin.

*Living Hells, it's like hitting stone*

"Ha!" Sol barked, throwing a wide hook. "Is that the best you've got?"

Eli ducked, adrenaline flooding his body. The edges of his vision blurred, the world faded away. All his attention remained on Sol's movements—hands, feet, and eyes. His senses flared, screaming his enemy's intentions. And the beast within bellowed in expectation.

Eli dodged Sol's wide arching attacks, keeping himself nimble, but one of Sol's punches grazed his shoulder. No harm, but the force rattled his bones. Eli kicked low, striking Sol's favored thigh—the same one Arlo had injured. Sol's knee buckled, and Eli drove an elbow to his temple. A knee to his face.

Sol staggered, swinging wildly and slamming Eli in the chest, throwing him back.

The giant stood, blinking and shaking his head. "That tickled." Sol laughed, blood streaking his nose. "Come on, Danon. I'm not even sweating."

Sol lunged, this time with a kick. Eli ducked low, wind kissing his skin. But as he righted himself, Sol spun, landing the back of his fist square across Eli's face. Stars exploded behind his eyes. Blood filled his mouth. Eli fought to stay upright, keeping his eyes open. Sol reached for his neck, but Eli leaped back, shoving the hand away.

He blinked rapidly, willing his head to clear. His vision wavered as he spit blood onto the floor. Sol threw a punch, and Eli twisted into it. Using the momentum, Eli drove his knee into Sol's ribs. A satisfying *crack* followed. Sol roared, swinging back and catching Eli's shoulder. Eli remained on his feet, but his body screamed in protest. Both men paused to rest.

Sweat soaked Eli's clothing. This wasn't working. It would take hours to best Sol. And though he was proud of the damage dealt, every time Sol made contact Eli's body was worn down.

*Let's try something else*

Eli clutched the Obelisk in his right hand, willing himself to steady. He reached inward as dread seeped in, searching for his inner magic—seeking the power he felt before. Funneling his desperation, he dove into his soul.

But found nothing.

Only exhaustion.

*And rage.*

He refused to panic and turned his thoughts to strategy. If he couldn't overpower Sol, he'd outlast him.

"Come on, Sol! Where's all that brawn?" he taunted. "I've known children who hit harder."

Sol snarled. "Ha! Says the weakest of the lot!"

"This weakling is in the same pit as you, Richter. Too bad you don't have your sister to bail you out."

Sol growled. "I'm going to enjoy breaking you."

The giant charged with a shout, throwing reckless blows. Eli ducked and weaved, calling on every ounce of his training, spending energy only when necessary. No counters. No risks. He kept moving, forcing Sol to burn himself out. One wrong move, one broken limb, and it was all over.

"You're pathetic!" Eli mocked. "After all this time, all that arrogant boar spit, I thought you'd be a harder opponent!"

Sol screamed and grunted. The giant threw punch after punch, desperate to make contact. But Eli remained just out of reach.

"Come on, Richter! I'm right here!"

Eli landed a quick punch, just enough to poke the bear. Sol shouted in frustration, but his movements slowed.

Finally, Sol paused with a grin.

"You think this is clever?" he rasped, chest heaving. "That fear in your chest? Let it grow, Danon. When I get my hands on you—"

"Then shut up and do it!" Eli snapped, holding back the flood of panic pressing at the edges.

Sol rushed in—faster than before. Eli dodged the first swing but missed the second. Sol's knee slammed into his ribs. Air vanished. Eli hit the ground, scraping against the stone. Choking, his mouth opened in a silent scream. Sol was on him in seconds, throwing his foot down. It missed by inches as Eli rolled away.

He leaped up and struck fast—fist to jaw, elbow to mouth. Blood flew from Sol's face, Eli's fists now painted red. He let his anger and fear fuel his muscles, gave in to the wretched cry within. He spun, landing a kick to the side of Sol's head. Eli spared no quarter, spinning around for another strike. But his breath caught—the ground falling from under him.

Sol gripped Eli's right hand. The giant grinned, lips smeared red.

"Now you're mine."

Sol wrenched Eli's arm upward, and a sickening crack split through his wrist, white-hot pain tearing down his arm as a scream escaped his lips. The giant reeled him in without pause and drove a brutal fist into Eli's face. Darkness flared across his vision. The world spun.

Still gripping Eli's hand, Sol delivered blow after blow, until Eli's senses blurred, the pain no longer sharp but pulsing, like lightning in his veins. Then, with a snarl, Sol gripped the front of Eli's armor in both hands and hurled him across the pit with a shout. Eli grated against the stone floor, colliding with the wall in a crunch of bone and leather.

For a moment, he lay still. His vision spun, his chest tightened, each gasp sharp with pain—his rib fractures cracking. Blood filled his mouth, and he coughed—gagging on the iron. His wrist was screaming, and he couldn't feel anything but the echo of suffering.

*Get up*

The thought was quiet, but insistent. Trembling, he pushed himself onto his elbows, pain gripping the heels of the motion. But Eli clenched his jaw, closing his eyes.

*Remember why you're here*

*You can't die*

*Not yet*

He pictured Harper, her golden hair catching the firelight at the inn, their father's laughter rising as they sat together after closing. He thought of Shira—fierce and brilliant—the way her voice steadied when everything else fell apart, the way her indigo eyes saw directly to his being. She was everything he wanted to be—determined and steadfast, worthy and true.

And it was here, in the darkness and blood of the Reaping, that Eli finally stopped fighting the truth—finally acknowledged what she had become to him—why he stood by her side despite everything.

Enemy or not, he loved her.

Not in passing, not out of loneliness or desperation. It happened slowly, against his better judgment, but settled incessantly like the sun. She had become the center of his gravity, the one thing that still made any sense. And his safety in leaving the Citadel no longer mattered, accepting now he would rather die than leave her in chains.

And within that conviction, laid the truth he was seeking. To leave her now would be to abandon the only part of himself worth saving—the part Shira unearthed, drawn from the wreckage he didn't know still remained. Shira hadn't made him someone new, only revealed who he had always been inside. The need to become a better man, to find himself, was never the quest. And if he walked away, he wouldn't only be losing her, he would surrender the very thing he sought to become—to preserve.

But there was more.

The rage within grew, and the drive to protect changed. This was never solely about protecting what he loved, it was about destroying what tried to take it from him. Sol was cruel for cruelty's sake, the same evil which claimed his mother and threatened his sister each day. The same cruelty which destroyed his father, and tortured Shira this moment.

As Sol's foot slammed into his ribs, Eli gritted his teeth, remaining on his elbows. Breath torn from his lungs, Sol kicked him onto his side. Stars flashed in his vision, and fire shot through his side.

"Come on, Danon!" Sol bellowed, looming over him. "Where's all your talk? You said to bring it! So here I am!"

Sol grabbed Eli by the back of his armor and belt, spinning him with inhuman strength, and hurled him across the arena once more. He hit the wall with a sickening crack, pain erupting from his left hip—sharp and deep. When he opened his mouth to scream, nothing came out.

He lay still, vision swimming, unable to move. His body refused to obey him. All he could feel was anguish. All he could hear was his own heartbeat, pounding in recognition of the end.

Sol's footsteps grew louder.

*You're pathetic*

The words slithered through his mind. He wasn't strong enough. He needed more. More than hope. More than faith. He needed *power*. Not to protect. That wasn't enough. To punish. It was why he was here, to bring—

Flashes of images and memories ripped through Eli's mind. Something deep within him cracked open, morphing from despair—to clarity. The truth flooded back, uncoiling from the fog the WAVEs buried it beneath.

*He remembered.*

Eli's mind was breaking, but with every fracture, truth spilled through. And in that brokenness, something ancient stirred, erupted like a volcano within, burning and furious. His memories returned—not just of home, but of the ire that led him to enlist, the grief which swallowed him long before the Citadel touched him. He never came to protect. That was an illusion. He didn't come to save anyone, he came to unleash his wrath, seeking something to take the brunt of his restless indignation.

That's why his father was against him joining, and why they had drifted apart. The young, gentle kid Eli once was died years ago.

And he hated them. Hated them all.

Because he was a tempest—furious at the world, at those who murdered his mother, who burned his home under ash and hatred, destroyed his childhood, twisted his father into a hollow shell and left Harper terrified of every shadow. Renard was wrong. Eli wasn't Aniyan. But he *was* their reckoning.

They weren't forging him into a Guardian, they only sharpened the blade he already was. A cold, hardened steel which cried out for their blood and roared from within. The anger inside him finally bellowed in recognition—and Eli embraced it. They were coming for Shira, and he wouldn't allow it. Shira didn't need his protection. Her enemies needed death.

Eli was no longer the noble soldier inside. That version of himself was the story his mind believed to keep from drowning in rage. It was the part of him—the youthful idealistic boy he was—which was the only thing left after the WAVEs. And beneath it, burning like coal amongst ruin, was the truth. The military wasn't his chance to serve—it was to strike. And now he would take the power they promised and use it against them.

They had taken everything. And now he would take everything back.

Eli forced his body onto its hands and knees, pain swallowing every part of him. He reached inward, past the anguish, past the broken ribs and splintered wrist—and found it.

Fury.

*Vengeance*

He would become the demon that made them shudder, fight until this world burned to ashes, until they cowered and bled like his family had for years.

The Obelisk burned in his palm. Eli barely registered the blood trailing down his arm onto the stony floor. His right hand trembled, but he was still holding it.

Still fighting.

Sol strode forward with loud steps and a mocking laugh. "Come on, Danon! Fight me!"

His words rang hollow, drowned out by the force which ebbed within. A burning sensation formed over his chest, and his limbs tingled with electricity. Power surged through him, answering the call of his wrath. Eli welcomed it, gave himself to it, and brought it all forth.

Sol stepped up to him as Eli planted onto one aching knee, bracing himself with his broken wrist. He didn't fight the pain. He used it—let it feed the blaze within.

Sol was shouting, but his voice was distant, like thunder over the horizon. Eli opened his eyes and watched red droplets hit the floor with hazy vision. Right arm covered in crimson, still clutching the Obelisk.

*Make him burn*

Eli looked up at Sol, who reared his fist back, beckoning Eli's death. With strength that exploded from the core of his being, Eli screamed with all his might and brought his right fist to match. He poured every ounce of his ferocity—every drop of his hatred—into the effort.

As their fists collided, the Obelisk in Eli's hand shattered. An explosion of orange magic erupted from the fragments with a guttural roar. The shockwave hurled Sol across the pit like a rag doll. Eli remained down on one knee, but his pain vanished. His wrist and hip felt perfect—his body healed. And in his right hand, he gripped a flaming sword.

Power flowed through him like a river, steady and unrelenting. Magic burst from his very core, strength rose like a tide. Eli stood as Sol climbed to his feet, skin charred and blistering, eyes wide.

"No!" he roared, charging.

As both hands gripped his sword, the flames grew taller—hotter—and Eli pressed into the power. As Sol neared, he raised his Rune Blade over his head. With a cry that echoed from the walls, he brought it down, an explosion of flames engulfing the entire pit. The fire kissed the ceiling, erupting from his weapon like waves pressed by a storm.

Eli stood within, feeling the heat, but untouched. And in that moment, as Sol's scream was drowned beneath the firestorm, he felt something break loose inside—the last chain binding him. He was no longer their recruit, no longer their weapon. He was their reckoning.

*Their Reaper*

At long last, in a rush of euphoria, Eli broke open the dam of his vengeance and unleashed the first of his judgements.

Sol's scream faded as his body melted, burning into a pile of ash.

# Chapter Fifty-Five

Eva shuffled across the polished wooden floors of the throne room, pulling at the edges of her blue dress Glorana had gifted her for her ninth birthday last year. It already fit snugly after her recent growth spurt, but she refused to be rid of her favorite possession.

She slowly approached Malachi, who sat at the front of his enormous table, surrounded by a group of foreigners she didn't recognize. Her father always had company, which was why using them as an excuse to lock her up was unfair. But she summoned the courage to ask him. It was the only way to see Lucas.

A few of the foreigners nodded with welcoming smiles. She returned the gestures with a tight grin of her own but didn't think for one moment any of them were genuine in their kindness.

Eva stepped up to Malachi, a few feet off to his right, reminding herself to be respectful and proper. She waited for him to acknowledge her, to grant her permission to speak.

She waited.

And waited.

And waited.

It wasn't until supper had been served and eaten that her legs started to go numb. She felt dizzy, her small knees beckoning to give out after standing in her uncomfortable—but socially appropriate—footwear. Her bladder became a burning source of pain in her abdomen.

Still, he did not address her, nor inquire what she needed. But Eva would not yield. This was to see Lucas.

A few of the foreigners gave concerned glances, no doubt wondering what it was she needed. The foreigner directly sitting to Malachi's left, even touched his arm to signal her presence. Her father dismissed him, saying it was all right, without looking in her direction.

Finally, as the sun fully retreated hours later, and as most of the foreigners left for the night, she could not hold her tongue any longer.

"Father," she said, her voice cracking from lack of use.

He instantly stopped, turning to her. "Evalynn. I didn't see you there."

She swallowed her response, stifling her impatience. Yelling would only make it worse. Her ribs still ached from her punishment last week, though the bruises had faded.

"I was hoping I could spend my tenth birthday with Lucas."

Malachi hummed, watching her closely, his face a mask.

"I can plan everything and be home by nightfall. No tricks this time. I promise."

His gaze drifted around the table as he sucked on his teeth. A few scattered dignitaries were still present, each speaking in their own quiet conversations.

"Three times," he muttered.

Eva swallowed. "Three wha—"

"Four," he quipped, turning to her again. An ache in her chest budded. "I don't recall giving you permission to speak."

Her lower lip quivered, but she bit her tongue until it bled. Crying in front of him meant nothing—only made him angry.

"I know, father, but—"

"Five," he said casually, as if it were a correction of her grammar and not a list of charges. "How many times do you need to learn this lesson?"

He sighed, muted disappointment on his face. Eva stood frozen, eyes burning, unable to plead her case—unable to stop standing straight and proper, speaking with the enunciation and poise of royalty, still yet trying to be the daughter she thought he desired.

"I think it's a wonderful idea," Malachi said finally. Her heart skipped. "You and that boy get along so well, I don't see any reason you couldn't have the party."

Her mouth gaped, eyes widening. "Thank y—"

"Of course, that would require me to disregard your behavior tonight. Standing like an invalid in front of my guests, without so much as giving them a polite hello or a bow. And then, as usual, there's the problem of your mouth. I refuse to reward such behavior."

She collapsed inside herself, having come here thinking the worst he could say is no. Yet, as he had done so many times before, he somehow found a way to sneak around the wall guarding her heart. The crushing indifference of his watchful gaze seared the last piece of hope in her heart. She clenched her jaw as a seed planted within, the first sewing of an incurable, insatiable malice for the man that called himself her father.

"I hate you," she whispered, a tear falling down her cheek.

Malachi stared for a long moment, watching her suffering like a man studying a curious insect. A gentle smile tugged at the corner of his mouth.

"Good," he muttered, turning back to the table. "Then we're making progress."

Eva was ripped from the memory, the darkness and pain of the dungeon returning in a flash. Azazel stepped away, face sweating.

"Stop fighting!" he shouted, slapping her. "I don't care about your childhood!"

The memories Eva relived over and over tore open old wounds, long ago scarred—buried under a lifetime of tears and questions. The chains rattled against the shuddering of her cries as she wept.

Azazel sighed. "Perhaps it is time to switch tactics."

He clasped the side of her head with both hands again. Fervid anguish returned, and she opened her mouth in a silent scream, her muscles going rigid as he invaded her consciousness again.

*"Show me who you've told."*

Azazel's voice bellowed in her mind. Light flashed in Eva's vision as her memories were brought forward, filling her mind's eye, her body's sensations linking with her experience. His magic struggled against her defiant will, searching for her recent experiences. Eva reached for anything to hide the truth. Casting her mind to the distant past, another moment lost to time was forcibly brought to the surface.

"Thank you, Lucas. For being my friend," Eva said quietly as they sat on the balcony railing, overlooking the Southern portion of Ashdod against the setting sun.

This was the last day she would sleep in this dreaded castle—this prison. Everything was set, and Malachi knew nothing about her leaving. She and Glorana planned everything perfectly.

Lucas blushed. "Well, you're not hard to like," he teased with a laugh, rubbing the back of his head. "Besides, the only reason we're best friends is because you don't really have any other friends!"

Lucas paused when she didn't respond to his joke. "Hey, Marie, I didn't mean—"

"Promise me you'll never leave," she whispered, still staring at the city. "No matter what happens."

He was taken aback by the seriousness in her voice. "Of course." He encouraged. "I'd never leave. Why do you say that?"

It was a moment before she turned to him and spoke, the idea now fully settled in her mind. "Have you ever thought about joining the Legion?"

His brow wrinkled. "The military? No, why?"

Eva returned to the cold dungeon, writing against Azazel's influence.

*"We've been here already!"* His voice bellowed in her skull. *"Take us forward!"*

Shira woke long before the call sounded, unable to rest any longer. The Crucible was tomorrow. And Eli's words the night before wouldn't leave her alone. She had to know more about the WAVEs, about what the program was doing to him. If he truly was losing his memories, how long until he forgot everything? Until he forgot her?

*He's the enemy*

She repeated the words like a warning. But they'd lost their edge. There was something about him, something which cut through the noise of her mind. Eli had been scarred, abandoned, pushed to the edge, and yet he stood tall. He believed in something, carried the weight of his convictions when others would have abandoned them.

Her own mind was a battlefield—torn between bitterness and mercy, vengeance and grace. But Eli remained still in the storm.

And Lucas.

Her breath caught, a tear slipping down before she could stop it. She clutched the edge of her blanket in the stillness of the night. It was impossible to accept he was gone, and the loss hollowed her out—every day. But Eli's persistence, his faith, *that* gave her something she hadn't felt in a long time.

Hope.

Not the soft, fleeting illusion people told themselves to avoid grief. This was different. It was forged. Eli could never replace Lucas, and she wasn't searching for someone to carry her. But Eli was proof that a soul could be thrown in the fire and still choose the light. That you could survive the unthinkable and still scream at the heavens—not in surrender, but defiance.

And maybe, so could she.

She slipped from her bed and dressed in silence. Dawn was near. She would go to the library before breakfast, dig into everything she could find about the Thought Wave Analysis, and find a way to protect him. The line between them was one she had drawn with her own trembling hand. And stepping over it meant letting go—not just of the past, but of the safety that came with remaining angry.

She never meant to fall for the enemy. But maybe it was time to stop pretending she hadn't already crossed her own line. She would face the consequences later.

Only if she had to.

The world morphed back into darkness and pain. Dizziness and fatigue washed over Eva with the recoil.

*"We're getting closer."*

Pain shot through her as Azazel punished her resistance. Her emotions frayed, her will crumbled, and her strength failed under his iron grip. The memory of the library flashed in her mind, but Eva willed it to lapse, banishing it from her consciousness.

*"What is that? What do you hide, Cretin?"*

Eva strained with all her might to bury the truth, to cast her thoughts to something—anything but the library. But Azazel's magic overtook her, and he reached for the truth, crushing her weakened mind.

Eva's breath came ragged as she pulled away from Eli's lips. Everything truly was on the line now. She had never felt this drawn to anyone, not even Lucas. She needed him, in a way she had never needed anyone else. And she prayed, with everything, that he needed her.

"I am your friend, Eli. If you trust nothing else, trust this." She placed a hand gently over his chest.

"How do I know you're not lying? How do I know what to believe?"

She stepped back and gently grabbed his arm which held the dagger. She slowly brought it up to her throat. This was it. Either he accepted the woman she truly was, or he would walk away as the fantasy died.

"You have to decide."

He held the blade motionless. A million thoughts cascaded, roiling into a storm of uncertainty, but she kept still. She would not affect his decision any longer. If he was to choose her, she needed to know it was of his own volition.

"Why? Aren't I your enemy?" he whispered.

"You saved my life twice and took a punishment for me *after* you suspected the truth. I've watched you since the beginning. Eli, you are anything but my enemy."

She waited with bated breath, praying her deceit would not be the tool which separated them. With a low breath, Eli lowered the knife from her throat and let it fall from his grasp. It hit the rug with a muffled thud.

Eva breathed out, anticipation rising in her chest.

*He didn't—*

Eva snapped back to the present as Azazel released his grip. The burning in her head was gone, her senses screaming in alarm.

The door to the cell opened.

"Bring me Elijah Danon!"

# Chapter Fifty-Six

Flames licked the edges of the Reaping pit, scattering the crowd of recruits. Guarding their faces against the infernal tempest, the recruits gasped. One cried out at the burn on his left arm. The torches in the room flashed before settling alongside Eli's magic.

As the fire dissipated, Eli stood catching his breath. Like a flood, exhaustion rushed back. He took a knee, bracing his weight on his Rune Blade as he plunged it into the stone. It was incredible. Eli stared in amazement, watching the flames from the Spirit Steel lick his hand without pain.

The sword bore a single edge, curved slightly at the tip. Crimson symbols were etched along the blade, evident despite the orange fire. The handle ended in a round pommel with a ruby in the center. Longer than his practice sword, it was surprisingly half the weight.

"Congratulations, Guardian Danon!"

The cheers of the crowd barely registered through the ringing in his ears. Eli waited for his breathing to calm, staring at the ashes that were once his adversary. The flames on his sword faded. He glanced to the edge of the pit, watching the ladder be thrown over. He stood but was dragged back to his knees with a wave of dizziness. The room spun, and he clamped his eyes shut.

He did it. He had beaten Sol Richter. The victory, though triumphant, felt a bit hollow, knowing he used the Obelisk. But Eli shook away the misguided sense of fairness. Sol deserved death a hundred times over.

A hand grasped his shoulder, and Eli's eyes shot open. It was Arlo, but there was an urgency in his face.

"That was amazing, you crazy idiot," Arlo whispered, helping Eli to the ladder, "but an Operative came and spoke to Captain Evergreen. They're waiting for you."

Eli felt the anger in his chest melt into concern. They discovered his involvement with Shira, which meant—

"It's time to leave," Eli said, as Arlo helped him onto the ladder.

Each movement was a conscious effort, forcing his muscles to comply despite the exhaustion overcoming him. He never doubted Darby was telling the truth about their limitations as new Guardians, but Eli underestimated the weight of using your life force.

Standing at the edge of the pit, the nearby recruits smiled and nodded. Some were slack-jawed, surprised at the display. None of them knew about the stone Eli used. And he didn't realize it was a one-use item. The taste of euphoria lingered, subtle as it faded from his system. He definitely wanted to find more.

Arlo climbed over the lip of the pit and stepped beside him. Eli searched for Renard or Nyx, hoping now was the time. When he couldn't see either of them, he leaned toward Arlo, casually navigating toward the staircase.

"What did Lara say?" Eli whispered.

The corners of Arlo's mouth sank. "She didn't believe me."

Eli stopped and turned to his friend. Arlo made no attempt to hide his quiet distress. There was no choice for Eli or Shira. If they stayed, only death awaited them. But Arlo was in a different position.

"Arlo, do you want to stay?"

"What?" Arlo gave a quizzical look, though Eli could tell he had already thought about the possibility.

"Elijah Danon!" Two male Operatives stepped off the staircase, swords drawn. "Come with us!"

*Time is up*

"What's the meaning of this?" Evergreen asked, pushing through the crowd and approaching the Operatives.

"Elijah Danon is to be brought to High Captain Azazel immediately for questioning."

"On whose authority?"

"The High Captain's, ma'am."

"We are in the middle of an exercise. Guardian Danon is—"

"With all due respect, Captain," one of them interrupted, "please step aside."

To Eli's surprise, Evergreen clenched her jaw. She turned to the crowd. "Everyone remain where you are!" she said, turning to the stairs. "I'm going to have a word with our High Captain."

Evergreen disappeared up the stairs, and Eli gripped his Rune Blade harder. He and Arlo faced the Operatives—waiting.

"Elijah Danon," one Operative said. "Drop the weapon and come with us."

Murmurs spread through the crowd, and Eli used the gentle noise.

"Arlo," Eli said quietly. "You can stay and keep Lara safe. Find us when you graduate."

"No," Arlo said firmly. "I go where you go."

The two Operatives stepped toward them, cautiously.

"There's no going back. You don't owe me anything."

"I'm not abandoning you." Arlo pulled his hammer from his back, a gentle yellow glow around the weapon.

Eli smirked, feeling some strength return as his friend stayed by his side. The Operatives shifted to defensive stances.

"Then shall we dance?" Eli asked, lunging at the Operative on the left.

"Stand down!" one shouted.

The Operative on the left deflected Eli's advance, meeting his blade. Arlo followed suit, striking at the other warrior, preventing him from helping his comrade.

Eli resisted reaching for the power that now lingered within his grasp. He needed to save his strength until the final moment. Thankfully, his training was more focused on swordplay as of late. His Rune Blade boasted a longer reach, and was much lighter, allowing him faster, more devastating attacks.

The Operative swiped at Eli's left. He parried the blow, spinning around and planting an elbow to the man's temple. Dazed, Eli used the chance to bring his razor-sharp sword across the Operative's throat. The man collapsed, holding his neck.

Without missing a beat, Eli engaged the other Operative who poised an over-head strike at Arlo. Eli blocked the attack, and Arlo used the opening to bring his hammer into the man's chest. A thunderous crack sounded, a gust of air rushed past Eli, as the Operative was violently thrown into the wall. His body fell limp, and Eli noted a faint crack in the stone wall.

Ears ringing, he glanced at Arlo with eyebrows raised. Arlo shrugged. Clearly it was unintentional, yet highly impressive.

"Eli, what the Hells are you doing?" Maelyn shouted, standing at the front of the restless recruits.

Urgency threatened his focus. They needed to find Renard. Or Nyx.

"Maelyn, the Council lied! The program is not what we think it is! Some of us are Aniyan captives! The WAVEs made us think we volunteered!"

Maelyn stepped back with a look of shock. "That's complete nonsense, Eli listen to yourself!"

"I was told so by Captain Renard!" Eli argued. "That's why Shira was arrested, she's Aniyan!"

His heart thundered. They didn't have time for this.

"Eli, you sound crazy!" Maelyn shouted. "That doesn't make any sense!"

Eli flexed his jaw. This wasn't going to work. Renard was right. None of them wanted to believe. Eli caught sight of Lara, who held Arlo's gaze. Her auburn hair drifted as she shook her head, still refusing to come along.

"Fenner!" Eli shouted. The kid meekly pressed to the front of the crowd, next to Maelyn. "Fenner come with us. Don't throw your life away for them!"

Fenner glanced down at the floor, before taking a step toward Eli.

Maelyn grabbed his shoulder. "Absolutely not, Fenner!"

He spun to her. "I don't belong here, Maelyn. I don't know if Eli is right, but I know I won't survive if I stay here. Thank you for helping me."

Maelyn's mouth opened in disbelief as Fenner ran to where Eli stood. "I won't let you!" Maelyn shouted, drawing her sword.

But as she took a step forward, Lara placed a hand on her chest, holding her back. Eli was grateful, for what it was worth.

The three of them turned and bolted up the stairwell. Eli prayed to not run into Evergreen on their way out, as he heard distant shouting from the recruits.

Pushing through the exhaustion, Eli could feel the last effects of the Obelisk leave his veins. Though the stone healed his injuries, he assumed it would take a while to recover from using his magic.

Shira was right.

*Those things are dangerous*

Sprinting down a hallway, they arrived at the door leading into the walkway. Bustling with morning activity, Eli took this as a good sign.

"Just act normal," Eli whispered. "Make for the Practice Field."

Eli opened the door casually, striding to his left toward the rear of the Citadel, Arlo and Fenner flanking him. It was a guess, but he assumed it was the safest way to exit the Citadel and make a run for it.

*Where in the Hells are Renard and Nyx*

They cautiously moved around the Keepers, Operatives, Captains, dignitaries, and Healers littering the walkway, some stopped in conversation. As the door to the practice field came into view, Eli heard commotion behind them. He glanced back, to find Soren and Rowan in the walkway speaking with a nearby Captain.

*You're next Soren*

Eli flinched as a hand clasped the back of his neck, ushering him to look forward.

"Easy now, Danon," Renard muttered. "This is just a bump in the path. Keep walking to the Practice Field."

Renard nodded and smiled at the passing comrades.

"How did you know?" Eli asked.

"You and I think alike, it seems. Nyx is waiting for you, with five horses. And before you ask, yes, I assumed you'd drag a comrade or two with you despite my warnings."

"Is Shira still captive?"

"Son, there is nothing we can do at this point. She's being personally guarded by the High Captain, and before you ask, yes, I checked myself. But Elijah, if you do not leave, they *will* kill you."

Eli bit his lip. This was his chance—he could escape and run to safety with Arlo and Fenner. But the decision was already made.

"Captain, get Arlo and Fenner to the horses. Make sure they escape. I'm going back for Shira. Wait for me if you can, otherwise, I'll assume we're on our own."

"That overconfidence of yours is going to get you killed."

"Maybe," Eli said, a weight of finality draping over him. "It's also what's saved my life a few times."

Renard gave a breathy laugh. "That door that we just passed on the left, near the squad barracks, leads to the dungeon. It's not locked but the doors are guarded, typically five to eight, but I ensured it's only three."

"Thank you," Eli said. He turned to leave, but Renard grabbed his arm, placing a small object in his hand.

"Use this if you need to. Apparently, you already know how."

Eli was amazed, the black stone warm against his palm. Renard ushered Arlo and Fenner to keep walking. Arlo gave Eli a look as he passed, tantamount to some combination of panic and thoughts of homicide. Eli nodded his head to follow Renard. He tried his best to move with the crowd and remain unremarkable. Though immaculate in every way, his new Rune Blade was exposed, awkwardly slung through his belt.

Navigating to the door Renard mentioned, he glanced behind. Soren and Rowan had disappeared. The door to the dungeons was unremarkable, camouflaged and unassuming. Hiding in plain sight. It opened into a dim hallway, lined with mage stones and torches.

A female Operative stood guard next to a stairwell. Eli remained casual, trying his best to approach slowly, despite the shaking in his hands.

The woman held out a hand. "State your business, rec—"

Eli didn't bother incapacitating her. With lightning speed, he grabbed her throat and pulled one of her own daggers from her side, plunging it into her temple. She went limp and dropped to the ground. Despite his exhaustion, he felt infinitely more capable. Unlocking his magic granted his physical skills a massive improvement, and his only regret was not finding it sooner.

The woman bled onto the floor, and Eli crushed the guilt which formed in his stomach. This woman would have killed him without a second thought. Stepping around the corpse, Eli took the stairs two at a time, drawing his Rune Blade. He would have to attack on sight. There was no reason for a lowly recruit to be in the dungeon unescorted.

The stairs, as dimly lit as the hallway, spiraled down to the left. His boots beat the stone in rhythm with his pounding heart. Though his muscles cried for rest, he carried a newfound confidence with another stone in his pocket.

As Eli reached the bottom of the steps, he spotted two guards at the door, a male on the right and a female on the left. Spirit Steel igniting with fire, he cut a sweeping arc toward the guard on his right. The man screamed as his flesh seared and blistered.

Eli paid no mind. He swung hard at the second guard, who barely drew her blade in time to block the strike. She countered low, forcing him back, his heel catching the edge of the step. The space was too tight—every movement mattered. His flames flickered out, and a wave of exhaustion slammed into him. Muscles trembling, he feigned left, then slashed right, catching her arm. She cried out, stumbling back. His steel remained hot, even without the fire.

Eli pressed in, running his blade across her throat. Blood sprayed as she crumpled. He spun—ready—but the other guard was no longer a threat. The Operative slumped in the corner, gasping, skin blistered and twitching in silence.

Eli burst through the door into the dungeons, met with the rank odor of decay, groans of agony, and two hallways lined with cells. One ahead and one to his left.

*Where are you Shira*

In a guess, Eli cut left, sprinting through the dungeon, scanning each cell. Dozens of prisoners, all Aniyan. Each one lay beaten and bruised, emaciated from maltreatment. Shira was right, and Eli's heart wrenched, refilling with the hatred he uncovered while fighting Sol. He would burn this spire to ashes, sending everyone here to the Hells.

It took less than a second, glancing at each prisoner, to know Shira wasn't there. The hallway turned right, and he followed. To his right lined more prison cells, but his left was mostly vacant—leaving room for one metal door.

Quickly studying the cells in the adjacent wall, he turned for the metal door. As much as it pained his heart to leave them, he couldn't save them all. Shira told him that once. But his focus wasn't to save them, it was to end their captors.

Yanking the metal door open, Eli gasped. Blood pooled on the floor, coagulating as it reached the drain in the center. The room was dim, but his eyes caught everything.

Iron and vomit filled his nose, mixed with stale uncirculated air. The walls held the testimony of more prisoners, blood splattered from more violent methods of interrogation. And there, sitting head down against the back wall was Shira. The chains binding her arms hung broken against her still form, her chest moving steadily.

Her eyes opened to slits as he rushed to her side, his blade clanging on the floor as he threw it down. Nausea rushed through him at the state of her. Bruises. Torn flesh. Her left eye was swollen shut, and her skin was ghostly pale.

Eli's heart shattered. He was too late. He should have come sooner, when she was first taken. Now he was going to lose her. Holding against the overflow of sorrow and guilt, he cradled her face in his hands, blood smearing his skin.

"Shira, it's me," Eli whispered.

She groaned quietly, barely conscious. "Eli?"

Her voice was raspy and wet. Bloody drool spilled from her mouth as she spoke.

"I'm here. I'm getting you out. Can you move?" he asked.

He would save her, if he had to burn everything around him to ashes.

"No," she whispered. "I can't feel my legs."

"It's okay. I can carry you," he said, grasping her back and legs. But as he lifted her, she cried out in pain. The sound of her scream rattled his very being. He was suffocating—drained of blood but forced to remain alive.

"Eli," she whispered.

He set her down, holding her face again.

"Shira, we need to go. I need you to come with me."

"Leave and save yourself. I won't make it."

"No, you can. We do this together."

"No, I won't," Shira rasped. "You made sure of that."

Time stopped. Eli's breathing halted.

"What?" he whispered.

"You . . . you waited too long."

The room spun. Eli's vision doubled.

"Why, Eli? Why didn't you come sooner? We could have . . ." her voice trailed as she went limp.

Eli's mind shattered as he stared at her lifeless body, the weight of it sinking through his bones like lead. A sudden rush of weakness overtook him. He clutched his head, fingernails digging into his scalp, squeezing his eyes shut as if he could cage the scream building in his chest.

But it was too late.

Images struck like lightning, fast and merciless. Shira's corpse, eyes glazed and still. His father's charred remains, twisted and blackened, mouth frozen mid-scream. Harper—sweet Harper—her face torn open, her tiny frame unrecognizable, arms reaching for him, begging for help that never came. And Arlo—his body crushed, throat sliced agape, lifeless eyes staring upward in betrayal.

The floodgates burst. Memory merged with nightmare, tearing Eli open from the inside with violent force. Everything the WAVEs had buried rose among the chaos—unfiltered, unsoftened, and raw. And Eli saw it. Relived it. Every scream, every broken body, every fear, every moment he couldn't save them.

Again.

And again.

And again.

A scream tore through the chamber, piercing and inhuman. It was agony given voice, a howl of such grief and fury it curdled the blood.

It took Eli a moment to realize, it was his own.

# Chapter Fifty-Seven

Dread of an unknown kind, darker and more urgent than Eva had ever experienced, arose the moment she heard Azazel speak Eli's name.

*He knows*

Eli would be captured—dragged into this pit of torment, his mind laid bare and forced to relive his grief until the agony broke him. All for protecting her, for showing her mercy, for choosing to believe in someone he had every right to condemn.

She wouldn't let that happen.

A piece of her refused to give up the hope that Lucas might yet be here. But even if the worst were true, Eli *was* here. He was *real.* Above ground, living, breathing, fighting. And that was all she needed.

A rush of strength filled her weakened limbs, the power awakened at the Rune Forge now surged like a tidal wave, rising at her call. The magic she tasted felt limitless, floodgates bursting open to a river that would never run dry. Darby's warning echoed in her memory, but she didn't care. She would burn every last shred of her life force to ash if it meant Eli was safe from Azazel.

Call it fate. Call it destiny. Call it the will of the Heavens. Whatever force led her here—led her to *him*—she would not curse it. Eva never expected to find anything other than hatred and bitterness in the Citadel. But she found laughter in the barracks, found courage and kindness in the heat of fire. She found humanity—real and flawed—in her enemies, identical to that of her kin.

And what surprised her most, was she found love.

Eli knew who she was, what she was, and still chose her. Saved her life not once, but twice, and had taken the lashes meant for her and never once asked for anything in return. Harboring her secret, he kept her safe, when all it would have taken was a word to see her destroyed. He remained silent, choosing to believe in her, even after learning the truth. She didn't know if he still cared. Maybe she didn't need to.

Because she knew she loved him.

After a lifetime of feeling inadequate—never strong enough, never obedient enough, never what her people wanted—Eli showed her that love didn't have to be earned. It could be given. Freely and undeserved. And Eli became her lifeline in the dark, the hand that caught her as she staggered over the edge. Because of him, she finally believed she could be more than what the world made her, and demand the world be greater than it was. Because of him, she witnessed the light which burned in a place as dark as this, scattering the shadows that held her down.

And now it was her turn.

She would not let this filth-stained evil extinguish the very thing that had guided her to safety. Azazel would never lay a finger on the one person who had shown her the truth. Eli needed her. He would never survive against so many. Not down here. And she knew, without a doubt, he would come—would walk straight into the maw of the Hells.

*For me*

And she refused to be the reason he died, to be his downfall. Evalynn Katz would never be the helpless prisoner waiting to be rescued. She would pull herself from this nightmare and become the strength Eli needed.

In that moment, in the lingering darkness, something inside her shattered, replaced by radiance. The tethers of shame and fear slipped from her shoulders, and for the first time the voice in her head—which always spoke to her weakness—became silent. Echoes of the past no longer weighed her identity, and sins of others bore no right to define her. The shame of her person evaporated in the warm presence of truth, the expectations of others now a whisper on the wind. Witnessed by Eli's hand, she saw the true shape of love—not as a transaction, but as a grace undeserved. He gave it freely, opposite to her father. And from this day forward, she would walk in the truth he had lit within her.

Eva clenched her fists, grinding her teeth as she commanded her legs to bear her weight again. Her left arm screamed as she pulled against the fracture, iron rattling, beating the stone wall. The door closed.

Azazel turned, holding a patronizing smile. "Oh, did that upset you, girl?" he mocked. "Don't bother with theatrics, I know what he means to you."

She used his words to build her rage. She reached down for that well of power within and ripped it out. A tingling formed in her limbs. Her senses heightened, even as the cry of her injuries quieted, as if her wounds were healing themselves.

"Worry not, girl. I won't kill him. I'll toy with his mind, find all his dark secrets, torment him for days. And only when he begs for death will I execute him for his treason." Azazel stepped forward, meeting her icy gaze. "And I'll make you watch."

The dim room flashed with white light, streaks of electric magic leaping from her limbs, arcing into the air with a hiss. Power exploded within, replacing her weakness with strength. Eva took a step, pulling against her chains, the metal biting her wrists. Pain was now a distant memory, and fury was her weapon.

Azazel's attention drifted to the streaks of blue, grinning. "Be careful, I wouldn't want this to be over so—"

The cuffs binding her wrists broke open. Azazel's eyes widened as she grabbed the front of his armor and threw him against the wall. A sickening crack sounded as his body slammed against the stone. Falling into a slump, Azazel sat against the wall, raising his arms in defense.

As Eva turned to face him, time slowed—same as in Heika. Each second stretched, each breath drawn long and deep. Azazel barely moved as she reached his throat. Indigo sparks surged from her limbs into his flesh as her hand connected. Time snapped back to speed as her magic crackled, paralyzing his muscles. Pain erupted from her left arm, but she bellowed for it to be silent.

Azazel grunted, teeth clenched. Eva pulled back and slammed her knuckles into his face. He barely moved, but the damage showed—blood dripping from his nose. She hit him again. And again. Her whole body ached, but she refused to stop.

The door burst open. Eva spun around. Two Operatives stood framed in the entry, blades drawn. The pain in her left arm remained silent.

*No time*

As if responding to an unspoken command, Eva's magic returned, flooding her veins, and time slowed again. She lunged forward, catching the first Operative's chin mid-sprint as they entered the torture chamber. Her momentum carried the motion as she leaped between them, her hands twisting sharply. The Operative's neck snapped clean, and he crumpled to the floor.

The second was already moving, blade slicing outward. She dodged low, watching it all happen moment by moment. She scooped the fallen Operative's sword as she rose. The Operative countered, and time shifted again. Eva's blade caught his, everything returning to normal speed. But now the weapon felt hollow in her hands, as if the Operative were barely pressing against her. Her limbs were feathers, and her opponent's strength vanished.

She shoved his weapon aside and drove her fist into his gut. It didn't stop. Her arm burrowed through armor and flesh alike—punched clean through. Shocked, she pulled back, and her enemy crumpled to the ground.

As Eva's magic relaxed, she dropped to a knee, lethargy engulfing her. Hand braced against the wall, a tremor emerged in her muscles. The time in the cell, and her new power, both took their due toll.

Azazel stood, sword in hand. Eva staggered, limbs shaking, left arm going numb. A pressure in her skull formed, and her vision blurred at the edges. He was trying to break inside her head.

*Never again*

She reached for her power once more—consequences be damned. Time slowed, and she quickly found a dagger off the Operative at her feet. With the last surge of speed she could summon, Eva flung the blade at Azazel. The steel whistled as she turned and slammed the door shut behind her. There was no handle on the inside. He was sealed.

She leaned hard against the frame, chest heaving as her magic dissipated. Her strength was nearly spent, the price of the ethereal draining her like an open wound. But her resolve held. She wouldn't die in chains. And if death came, it would find her on her feet—fighting for those she loved.

Stumbling forward across the hallway, Eva took one last chance to check the prison cells. Cradling her left arm, she scanned the sullen faces, all bearing blue eyes and sandy hair. None of them noticed her, most seemed half alive. With each new prisoner she witnessed, her heart ached, all of them long having welcomed death. She ran weakly down the next hallway, searching for a hope which had already faded in her heart. She needed to find Eli, but maybe—just maybe.

As she rounded the next corner, everything went silent. She froze, then stepped back, breath caught in her throat. Peering into the cell she'd passed, her gaze latched onto the figure slumped against the back wall. His sandy hair struck a familiar chord.

Eva's fingers curled around the iron bars. "Lucas?" she whispered, voice barely audible, trembling on the edge of hope.

The man stirred but didn't lift his head.

"Lucas," she tried again, louder this time, desperation rising in her chest. "Is that you?"

He shifted, groaning faintly, and slowly raised his head. His face was thinner—pale and gaunt—but she would know him anywhere. Even blind and deaf, she'd recognize him by scent and touch alone.

"Lucas, it's me!" she cried, reaching through the bars, vision blurred from tears wetting her face.

He blinked, eyes bloodshot and unfocused. He was silent as his gaze drifted to her, but remained distant, as though she were only a ghost.

"No! No, it's me! Eva!" she pleaded. "My hair, it's black now! I dyed it!"

Still no reply. Only a faint furrow of his brow.

"I came here to find you. I *am* Evalynn. Lucas, it's me!"

His eyes remained glazed, but his head raised again.

"Marie," she said suddenly, her voice breaking. "It's *Marie.*"

At the sound of her name, his eyes lit up. "Marie?" he rasped, voice hoarse and broken.

"Yes! Yes!" she choked out, reaching further through the bars. "I'm here!"

Lucas tried to rise but collapsed. Crawling forward on trembling arms, he dragged himself to her. When he reached the bars, she touched his face, her fingers brushing over bruises and dried blood. His skin was fevered and fragile, but it was him.

He leaned against the iron grate, focus now fully on her. "Marie. . ." he whispered again in disbelief.

A breathy laugh escaped her mouth as Eva smiled, brushing his hair. She nodded through the flood of tears as his hand touched hers.

"You came," he breathed.

"I'm here. And I'm going to get you out!" she said. Scanning the cell door, her mind snapped back to the present.

"There's a key ring at the end of the hall," he said weakly, pointing to her right, back the way she came. "On the wall."

She didn't bother asking how he knew—he'd been here for months. She stood and sprinted down the hallway, adrenaline fueling her tired form. Rounding the corner, it took only a moment to spot the silver ring on a hook. She missed it the first time, designed to camouflaged into its environment. Yanking the keys from the hook, she ran back to his cell. Lucas had crawled away from the door, allowing it to swing inward as Eva shoved it open. She threw herself into his embrace.

Joy and relief overflowed like sunlight breaking through a storm. She had done it—she found him. He was different, thinner and frail, but her soul recognized his. Gently holding her in return, they stilled for a moment.

Only a moment.

"I found you," she whispered into his shirt, uncaring of the stench he bore.

"Evalynn Marie," he whispered. "I remember you."

She pulled away, searching his face at the odd statement, but saw no emotion there. His face was glazed and distant, lacking the emotion she expected. A dread crept into her mind.

"Lucas, what did they do?" she asked, hand on his cheek.

"I can't remember," he rasped, brow wrinkled.

A rock settled in her stomach, but she refused to dwell on the unknown. Footsteps outside snapped her from her thoughts. They had to escape.

"We need to leave. Can you walk?"

He bobbed his head weakly. Reaching under his arm, Eva helped him stand on shaking legs. They took one step toward the cell door when a wretched scream bounced around the dungeon.

She froze—heart crashing out of her chest.

*That was Eli*

Panic threatened to steal her focus as she set Lucas back down.

"Stay here. I'll be right back," she said sternly.

Eva raced out of the cell, noticing the bodies lying in the doorway of the stairwell to her right. She ran down the hallway, searching for Eli. A violent current pulsed in her veins, senses heightening with urgency. She willed herself to heal, to endure past her exhaustion. And to her surprise, her left arm no longer ached.

She rounded the corner but saw nothing. Fearing the worst, she returned to the interrogation chamber.

The door was open.

Another scream escaped the small room. Eva jumped, but this voice was different. She sprinted to the doorway, and saw Eli standing before Azazel, who sat on the floor against the wall. Blood poured from the High Captain's mouth, which was thrown open in an anguished cry. Eli gritted his teeth, tears streaming down his face, as he plunged a sword deeper into Azazel's stomach.

Eva stepped forward, reaching out when Eli's sword burst into flames. She flinched, watching Azazel's body ignite. Eli didn't see her, knuckles white as he gripped his weapon. Azazel writhed in pain, screaming as his skin blistered.

*Is this Eli's magic*

"Eli!" she shouted.

He didn't flinch—didn't move. His face deformed with rage and sorrow. Azazel's flesh melted, filling the room with a foul stench, turning Eva's stomach.

*What is happening*

"Eli!" she shouted again, stepping closer. The heat of the fire bit her skin. Eli's breathing remained heavy, the pain in his face unlike anything she'd ever seen. At the sound of her voice, Eli shook his head—as if pulling himself from a trance.

He let go of the sword, and the flames immediately dispersed. Turning his head, his mouth fell open, and his features slackened. Eva waited a moment, allowing him to comprehend whatever nightmare Azazel showed him. He studied her face, before embracing her in one lengthy stride.

She wrapped her arms around him, finding him shaking as he buried his face in her neck.

*What in the Nine Hells did Azazel do*

Wishing the closeness to never end, she held him. He was safe, and she was his.

But they needed to leave. Eva pushed him away gently, studying his face which remained stricken with sorrow so heavy it gripped her throat. Her fingers brushed his cheek.

"I thought you were dead," he whispered, staring at her with an intensity she'd never seen—as if she were an oasis in a desert.

"I'm okay, Eli. I'm all right," she whispered with a smile. "I knew you'd come for me."

Eli said nothing as he cupped her face and kissed her. A rush of warmth surged through Eva, her breath caught between heartbeats as she pulled him closer. It was desperate and aching, a promise made in silence. The drumming of his heart set her own ablaze, the passion of his movements ignited a fire within, catching the fortress of her control, sending it into a flaming torrent of longing. The world fell away—nothing remained but him and the way their souls met in the quiet fleeting moment. Eva kissed him in return with everything she had, daring the world to tear them apart.

# Chapter Fifty-Eight

E li couldn't tear his eyes from Shira's. Hands trembling, he cradled her jaw, the entirety of his love for her communicated with that kiss. Everything he was belonged to her now. The wounds she bore were nothing compared to what Azazel showed him, but carved his chest hollow all the same.

"Are you all right?" he asked again.

"Stop it. I'm okay," she whispered, touching his cheek.

Some weight lifted from his shoulders as he waded in her presence, soaking up her affection in a fleeting and desperate attempt to calm his own fear of her safety. He loved Shira and prayed they could stand together after this. It didn't mask what Azazel wrought from his memories, but it was more than enough for this moment. He would deal with what Azazel showed him after they were free—assuming he lived to see it.

"We need to leave," Eli said, glancing at High Captain's lifeless corpse.

"I know. But Eli, I found Lucas!" she said, pulling his hand toward the door.

"You what?" he gasped. "He's alive?"

"Yes! Help me!"

Eli yanked his Rune Blade from Azazel's stomach, wishing he could kill the High Captain twice. Shira led him back to a cell, where a blonde-haired prisoner lay slumped on the floor. Shira knelt beside him before helping him to his feet.

Eli gripped his sword tighter and pulled the Obelisk from his pocket. "Bring him, I'll carve a way out of here."

Shira spotted the stone in his hand. "Where did you find that?"

"A gift from Captain Renard."

Her brow wrinkled. "How do you have a Rune Blade?"

"It came during the Reaping."

"Those flames were your magic?"

Eli nodded.

She bit her lip. "Tell me later. Let's go."

Slow-moving, they ascended the staircase. Eli strained his ears for new guards, alarms or shouting, waiting for more Operatives to come after them. Surely their actions—

Voices sounded outside the door leading to the walkway. Eli pressed his ear to the wood.

"Oversee the evacuation! The Council ordered a full retreat. The traitors are not to be harmed."

Eli's instincts screamed on high alert.

*Not harmed*

"Sir! Captain Renard sent orders to reinforce Captain Blan at the front gate!"

"You lot! Back them up! We'll wait for the girl."

*Renard*

Shira and Lucas stumbled up to him, and Eli's stomach lurched. Something inside spoke to his coming death—the price of their escape. He opened the door a sliver, spotting a room full of Operatives, Captains, and two Guardians. All waiting. Another two dozen ran toward the front entrance.

Lucas was already out of breath, and Shira had spent the last day being tortured. Gripping the stone in his hand, he knew there was only one way out for them.

"What's wrong?" Shira asked.

"They're waiting for us."

She cursed. "How many?"

"I don't know. Too many."

Shira breathed out. "We take them together. Leave Lucas here—"

"No, Shira. You take him and run. Our only option is chaos. I can do that. Make for the Practice Field and don't stop for anything."

She straightened. "Don't you dare."

Lost for only a second more in the infinite depths of ocean blue, Eli threw open the dungeon door. He felt his panic give way to that well of inner rage, the beast bellowing from within. They would regret standing between him and Shira's safety.

"Go Shira!" he shouted, crushing the Obelisk in his hand. Fire exploded across his blade, the flames roaring upward—finally unleashed. The surge of power struck instantly, euphoria wrapped in a burning heat, fueled by his wrath. This was it. He wasn't leaving alive. And in a twisted, poetic way, that was fine. As long as this cursed spire burned with him.

The slew of Operatives acted on instinct, four dozen rushing toward them as one united front. The Captains remained to the rear, screaming orders. The two Guardians, clad in steel-plated armor, readied their Rune Blades.

The path to Eli's left was closed off—Shira's escape—the guards holding a semicircle around the dungeon door. Eli reached deep into his soul and tore free every ounce of magic he had left, every drop of his life force, pouring it into the weapon in his hand.

And swung wide.

Flames danced in a sweeping arc, scorching the ground, sending his enemies staggering backward. Eli focused his will, commanding the fire to spare Shira and Lucas. The ethereal storm emerged before him, carving a path through his enemies. Shira flinched, but the inferno curled around them—untouched. Reeling from the heat, the Operatives were pushed back, but the Captains shouted commands to pursue Shira.

*Not while I'm breathing*

Shira raced toward the Practice Field, striding through the orange blaze without harm, dragging Lucas with her. Eli met his enemies with another flare, sweeping his Rune Blade across their ranks. Screams filled the air as bodies hit the ground, thrashing against the heat. Flesh blistered, smoke billowed, and some hesitated.

Eli leaped to the side, standing between the army of warriors and Shira. He raised his Rune Blade overhead, just as one of the Guardians lunged forward, Rune Blade glowing green.

*Too late*

Eli brought his weapon down with everything inside him. With a shout, he unleashed the fury in his soul which called for vengeance. An explosion of orange light burst outward—an infernal tidal wave blasting through the hall, searing stone, shattering banners, reducing anything in its path to cinders. The ethereal flames roared, tearing through the stone structure with the might of a chosen bloodline. The fire stretched to the rear wall, climbing the tower, setting the great tapestries ablaze.

The Citadel, at last, was burning. And Eli had placed an infernal wall between everyone and Shira, burning every Operative between them and the Practice Field to ash. The charging Guardian laid in a heap, steel armor red hot and melting into his dead flesh. The first rush of exhaustion pressed against Eli, as the other Guardian raced forward with a shout.

Light blue magic surrounded her form as she charged, raising her Rune Blade in attack. Eli stepped forward, meeting her advance with his own. Flaming sword clashed against polished steel as their weapons met. But despite the tempest of power within, Eli didn't predict the Guardian's magic.

Like an echo, a hazed image of the Guardian formed, bringing an ethereal sword down to his right side, a mirror opposite image to her first attack. The magic steel sliced his right arm, even though the Guardian's Rune Blade remained caught against his own. He leaped back, and she struck again. Eli deflected the blow, but another strike appeared from a hazed image to his left.

A few Operatives seized the opening, chancing the fire and charging forward. He cursed, pulling back, closer to the flames which fed on the fuel around him. The Guardian pressed forward, and Eli was being overrun.

He focused his mind, the Obelisk's gift offering destruction at his fingertips. Every moment he purchased gave Shira another step to safety, until the stone's power was gone. He charged forward into the group of six Operatives flanking the Guardian. Chaos ensued as the flames spread higher, feeding on the tapestries and wooden structures inside. Some cowered. One Captain ordered a retreat, while others pressed forward.

Before the Guardian could unleash her magic again, Eli threw an arc of flames at them. Staggering from the overwhelming heat, he brought his infernal sword down on the Guardian. She held her blade up, stopping his Rune Blade—but not his fire.

Mixing with his own shout, Eli's flames screamed as they unleashed from his weapon, cascading over the Guardian like a waterfall until only her smoldering bones and simmering steel remained. He turned and charged into a group of six Operatives, now in chaos as flames spread around them. Some stumbled back in fear, others pressed forward.

He met them with flame, steel, and fury—fighting with everything he had learned, every hour he had bled, every scar claimed. And each strike landed. His Rune Blade cried out for their blood and was granted it. Two Operatives rushed him, and another four circled. Eli drew more magic from within, flames spiraling outward. One fell screaming, his armor seared through. Another took the fire across his legs and collapsed.

Eli drove his sword into the gut of one, yanked it free, and parried a second strike just in time. He chanced a glance. Shira and Lucas were almost out.

*Bring it down*

Eli tore more magic from within, the limits of his power lingering like a shadow, claiming rights to the life inside him. He raised his sword, bringing down another strike, flames climbing the walls of the walkway once more. The firestorm around him responded to his will and he could feel its presence. He commanded the fire to feed—reduce everything to ashes. With the inferno out of control, the remaining Captains ordered a retreat, and only four Operatives remained. They hesitated, wary now, and Eli felt the stone's power beginning to slip.

*Not yet*

He launched himself at the two on his right. The first parried. Eli struck him with a solid kick to the gut, then slashed across his chest before turning and deflecting a blow from behind. He spun, reigniting his Spirit Steel. With a cry, he sent a wall of fire bursting outward in a wide circle. The heat pushed back the last three warriors, and Eli surged forward, piercing his blade into the nearest one's chest.

With a shock—without warning—the surge ended. A wave of crippling weakness claimed Eli's bones, and the fire over his sword snuffed.

*Bleeding Hells*

His body screamed, his knees buckled. Eli stumbled to the ground, bracing against his sword. Every muscle trembled, every joint was filled with sand. He could feel life leaving him. There was nothing left.

*Yes there is*

He looked up. The final two Operatives came at him, seeing his vulnerable state. Eli flexed his jaw, the wrath within him still alive. Amid the anguish, he deflected one strike, twisted away from another, and managed to land a knee to the gut of one. But the other's blade sliced into his shoulder, and white-hot pain followed.

Eli screamed, ducking under a follow-up strike. He retaliated with a thrust that tore through the Operative's side. But his comrade drew his blade across Eli's ribs. Eli parried the steel at the last moment, sparing the mortal injury. He fell back to his knee, shaking his head to be free of the dizziness. Blood ran down his arm, slicking his grip. His vision blurred, and every breath brought coals to his flesh.

He had seconds left.

Eli forced one last surge of magic into his blade, feeling death's call with the last of his life force. The fire returned, alive for only moments. He swept it forward, and the flames consumed the last two warriors. They dropped, writhing with their crackling armor.

Eli braced against his Rune Blade, scanning around. All of them fleeing—or dead.

He glanced to the practice field. The door was open. Shira made it.

*Thank the Heavens*

The fire dimmed at his will, opening a path of escape, but his body seized, every muscle clenching at the same moment. Eli collapsed, an unbearable tearing sensation burrowing through his chest. Paralyzed on the floor, he gasped for air as his vision darkened.

Tapestries and woodwork crackled. Even the stone groaned against the heat. It was all burning. And it was beautiful.

Eli let go. The heat warmed his face, and he closed his eyes, letting the sound of crackling flames drown the chaos within. He had nothing left. And somehow, it was enough. If this was the end—so be it. Shira was safe. Even Lucas was free. Fenner would live, and Arlo would look after them all.

Harper's laughter entered his thoughts, and Shira's indigo eyes flashed in his mind before he was lost to darkness.

Eva squinted at the bright morning light over the empty Practice Field. She didn't know what Eli's plan was other than running North into the plains. But that idiot must not know her very well, if he thought she would abandon him.

Guiding Lucas to the left, she sat him against the tower. His face was drenched in sweat. She glanced around but still heard no one.

*Please Shining Heavens, let us make it*

"Lucas, rest for a minute. I'm going back for Eli," she said, brushing his thinned hair.

Lucas nodded weakly, catching his breath. Searing heat met her as she ran back into the walkway. A blaze of orange coated the walls and licked the high ceiling. A path absent of flame led to where Eli fought, and she saw no one standing among the fire. Bodies lay everywhere—some seared to their bones, others bloodied and lifeless. A figure moved behind the fire, before vanishing amid the smoke.

"Eli!"

Pulse fluttering, she reached for her inner magic to grant her speed. Blue sparks danced across her limbs, and strength filled her muscles once again. The pain of Azazel's torture had vanished.

Eva raced to the piles of bodies, panic rising as she searched for Eli. Shouting sounded from the distance, and she guarded her face from the heat. He had laid waste to so many and somehow, he'd learned how to use the Obelisks. If this was the level of destruction wrought from the hands of a novice, Eva couldn't fathom what a seasoned Guardian could do.

She frantically searched for him, pulling more magic to buy as much time as she could. The tendrils of fire slowed as her magic heightened, the heat on her skin lessened. And there. On the ground among the Operatives, lay Eli—unmoving. She prayed a desperate plea as she rushed to his side.

As death's embrace took hold, a warmth sparked in Eli's back. The cold black arms of passing retreated as strength filled him again. Life poured into the empty chasm of his soul. He felt the cold leave, the numbness receding.

Eyes opening to slits, flickering orange met his vision, covering the walls and ceiling. Though completely drained of energy, he no longer felt lifeless. Something pulled him from the jaws of death.

A hand reached under his arm and pulled him up. He blinked and found Shira's determined gaze.

"It's my turn to save you," she whispered.

A smile pulled at his lips. Eli stood, with her help, but dizziness yet stole his balance. With brittle strength, he picked up his sword and stumbled toward the rear exit. The heat was growing unbearable, but the fire bent around them in his presence. Sweat fell from his brow, and blood slid down his Rune Blade as he braced against it.

"Eli, what did you do?"

"You were right," he said with heavy breaths.

When they reached the door, more yelling sounded from behind them. Operatives poured into the walkway, running to the wounded and extinguishing the flames. He and Shira crossed the threshold, closing the door, praying no one saw their retreat.

Eli didn't see Renard or Nyx in the field, though he wasn't sure if they were able to wait.

"Help Lucas. I'll be all right," Eli said, leaning against his sword.

With Shira bracing Lucas, they took a step toward freedom—

"A very valiant effort, I will say," Commander Voss said. "Especially you, Madam Weiss. You're someone I intend to keep my eye on."

They all froze. Her voice sent shivers down Eli's spine.

He stepped toward Voss, raising his sword. Shira cried out, before Voss vanished. Eli straightened, sensing her presence behind him.

"Oh please, child, don't bother with theatrics," Voss said.

Eli reflexively swung with his sword, but his blade met nothing but air. Voss vanished again, before a pain seared his left side. His Rune Blade clanged to the ground as he dropped to his knees facing Shira and Lucas. Cold steel touched his neck. Voss moved with such blinding speed he never even saw her shift her weight.

"No!" Shira screamed, gently kneeling with Lucas. "Please! We surrender!"

"Oh, my dear, don't worry. You don't have to surrender," Voss mocked. "The Council has great plans for each of you. Though Lord Gevir has concerns about keeping *this one* alive."

Voss pressed her blade into Eli's neck.

"Eli, move away from Voss!"

Renard's voice cut through the silence of the open field. Voss's blade nicked Eli's neck as he turned his head. Renard held Voss frozen in his magic. Eli wriggled free from her rigid grip. The Captain approached slowly. Two horses followed Renard, and Voss was frozen—for the moment.

Eli picked up his blade and swung, the Spirit Steel crying out as it met the side of Voss's neck. But the weapon bounced off, the vibrations biting into his hands.

"It won't work," Renard said. "My magic will hold her, but it also protects from any damage. I can buy you time to escape. Take the horses, *now!*"

Eli didn't hesitate, unable to register the situation. Freedom was only a stone's throw away. Moving as quickly as his injuries allowed, he aided Shira in getting Lucas on a horse.

Voss's eyes met Renard's, fury incarnate, as the Captain strolled toward her.

"I've got a few things to say, *Commander.*"

Eli and Shira spurred the horses into a gallop, rounding the Northern edge of the Citadel into the safety of the Teimana plains. Eli barely claimed the strength to stay atop the stallion, but Shira held Lucas steady. As they moved around the spire, Eli lost sight of Renard. He prayed silently for the Captain's safety—or a quick death for his new friend.

# Chapter Fifty-Nine

With the sun high in the sky, the six fugitives sat upon their horses. Evalynn, Elijah, Arlo, Fenner, Nyx, and Lucas stared at the billowing plume of smoke rising above the Citadel. Now a few hours' ride from the great spire, they still saw no pursuers.

They seized the moment to rest the horses and regroup. Arlo was kind enough to take Lucas on his horse instead, having the largest horse of the group, more apt to bear the extra weight. Eva's heart was heavy knowing the cost of their freedom. Yet it was tempered with relief, having both Lucas and Eli safe. She was surprised Fenner decided to join them and wondered about his reasons.

Arlo coming along made sense, seeing his loyalty to Eli firsthand. She didn't know what happened with Lara and knew better than to ask outright. It was clear now, the resemblance between him and Lucas. It could yet be a falsehood, but they would know soon enough.

The last member of the party was the real surprise. Eva didn't recall Nyx at first, but the woman's black hair and emerald eyes stirred a recent memory. Either way, Eva was forever grateful for the assistance in their escape.

"We need to keep moving," Nyx said.

No one moved.

"Where?" Arlo asked. "We're enemies of both the North and the South now."

"We make for Sheket," Nyx said. "Captain Renard advised as such, were he unable to make it."

As the group turned their horses to leave, Eli was the only one who remained—standing alone, staring at the distant spire. He'd been quiet since they left, and she remembered the agony in his face when he killed Azazel. She didn't know what it was he had seen, or what had happened after her capture, but they had time to work through it together.

"We'll catch up," Eva said, dismounting and stepping next to Eli.

Arlo nodded and turned his horse, Fenner following suit. Nyx gave her a snide look but ushered her mount behind the others. Eva reached for Eli's hand, grasping it gently. As she did, his attention drifted to their interlocked fingers before returning to the city.

"We should go," she said softly.

He didn't speak, his gaze a thousand miles away. There were so many unanswered questions—about the Obelisks, the war, the Council—she felt the unease of buried truths. Despite everything they'd learned, there were far more secrets hidden in the shadows of this war. And whatever it was that weighed on Eli, she would help him bear it. He had been her light burning in the window, guiding her home, and she would be the same for him.

"Eli?"

His attention never wavered, locked to the rising smoke on the horizon. Eva waited, unwilling to break the silence that pressed around them. She hadn't been surprised to learn he possessed magic. But the *magnitude* of it—what he unleashed—was terrifying.

"Harper is dead," he breathed.

The words pierced like a dagger. Grief swelled instantly, not just her own, but his—heavy and cold and lifeless.

"How do you know?" she asked, barely above a whisper.

"I remember, Shira," he said. "I remember what happened. Before I was brought here."

*Brought*

There were no tears, no emotion in his face as he turned to her. He looked the same, his tousled black hair and orange eyes identical to what she fell in love with, his voice and touch so familiar.

But those fiery eyes held something previously absent—a hollowness. As if the light she loved, that had beckoned her home, had gone out.

# Epilogue

The shining stone sat upon its pedestal, casting its faint white light against the ebony walls. Stale and musty air met Voss as she crested the top of the staircase and strolled into the Council chamber. Her metallic armor clanked subtly with each footstep, the only sound among the stillness. She knelt before the pedestal which held *The Light*, facing the two robed and hooded figures standing at the far end, staring out the wide window.

Voss waited in trepidation and fear, sweat beading on her forehead. Their presence always made her nervous, sent a shiver down her spine. Countless battles she had fought, and countless lives she had taken in the name of her people and country—yet nothing rattled her stoicism as the two that now shared this space with her.

"*Kor'ith Irata,*" the male figure spoke.

*She has escaped*

"Yes, Lord Gevir. She is safe," Voss answered, commanding the tremor in her voice to flee.

"*Hatukhal le'asher ki kesem lah?*"

*Can you confirm she possesses the ethereal*

"Yes, Lord Gevir. The Aniyan demonstrated magic of her own, wielded without a Rune Blade."

"*Bru'geir Hui'vet pyruvate?*"

*The flame wielder*

"He lives, Lord Gevir."

Voss kept her eye on the floor, muscles tense.

"*Ha-ya'ad shelahem?*"

*Their destination*

"We have begun interrogating the traitorous Captain that aided their escape. From what we have gathered, they are heading west. We believe they may be seeking refuge in the town of Sheket or planning passage through the Farron Gap."

It wasn't the answer they wanted. They wanted assuredness—absolutes—and she could not provide any. The color drained from her face as Lady Mar turned around and addressed her directly.

"And what do you have to say for your failure?" Mar questioned with a piercing voice.

"The recruits were aided by Captain Drake Renard and others. The circumstances of their escape did not permit the capture of either the pyruvate or the girl without harming them. My best efforts were not enough, given your instructions to not intervene before the Rune Forge. I have no excuse, my Sovereigns."

Voss swallowed at the lingering silence. It was a dreadful burden being the Council's primary contact within the Zentari military. Each time a mission failed, or one of their specific instructions were unmet, Voss would ready herself before entering their presence, knowing it could be her final moments. She felt more fear for the Sovereigns than actual reverence, but she wouldn't dream of ever voicing that inner weakness.

"*Ma'tza Otam.*" Gevir seethed, disdain evident in his deep guttural voice. *Find them*

Voss said nothing as she stood, keeping her gaze to the floor, not daring a glance at either of the two Sovereigns.

Mar turned back around and stepped beside Gevir as Voss's footsteps faded, staring through the clear glass out into the high viewpoint of the Southern coast. This portal to the outside world was nothing more than a source of mocking—a reminder of their continued imprisonment.

Mar said, "It is a great frustration to be so close to our goal, yet unable to see it through ourselves."

She gazed at the beauty of the ocean on the horizon, where she had watched countless cycles of the sun, trying desperately to remember the feeling of water on her skin, or the smell of the grassy fields.

"We have set the pieces into place. The river is diverted, the flame unleashed. We must simply be patient," Gevir responded, never taking his eyes from the window.

Mar hated that phrase, more than this prison, more than anything in all creation that her unstimulated mind could think of, because she had spent the last four centuries waiting. She wanted nothing more than to take action, to pillage this country, eradicate and enslave the infestation that had gained rule over the land only because of the absence of a greater power.

"I grow tired of waiting," she mused.

"I would think it a skill to be mastered, given our current fate."

"What does it matter? None now live who remember our sacrifice. There is no one who recalls what we witnessed, what we tried to stop! We deserve glory, not suffering!"

The agony of watching from the cold stone tower as their kin were hunted, slaughtered, was a wound Mar felt even after four centuries. And now, resentment was firmly rooted in her heart. Too many had forgotten what occurred, too many had allowed themselves to slip into a false sense of security, believing themselves to be the dominant beings on the planet.

Gevir said, "They will remember one day. Our rule will be restored in time."

"And how much more shall we endure? We are not preserving our power over these insects. You do not even keep the language of our kin sacred."

"Speaking our tongue preserves reverence. It reminds them we are different—not of the same destiny."

Mar huffed. She disagreed. She and Gevir were gods compared to the beings that now claimed Adiel—infested this spire. To share the language created by her kin was nothing short of climbing into a mud pit with pigs.

But they would know someday. They would all bow before them once again. Mar could feel their freedom coming closer. She dared not allow herself to fantasize about being outside, feeling the warmth of the sun on her face, the touch of the long grass at her feet, or the taste of food in her mouth.

And ever since she felt the girl's presence in the tower, elated after learning about her from Azazel's interrogation of the nameless Aniyan Chief, Mar vowed that nothing would stand between her and freedom—even the withered immortal which stood beside her.

"You are confident we will be able to draw them back here?" she asked. "I need not remind you of the fallibility of their kind."

Mar was tired of playing the skeptic in their little schemes, but was forced to be, given Gevir's overconfidence.

"They have no choice. Regardless of what happens, there is no escape for them."

"They are children. Infants, both erratic and unpredictable. We should find other solutions, plan for their failure."

She was growing more easily flustered by his pompous attitude. The pyruvate was a known risk, one Mar had already accounted for. But this girl. She was a blessing that Gevir allowed to escape. To think she once harbored feelings for this man sent a wave of nausea through her stomach.

Her kin remained silent.

Mar growled. "If you are wrong, we have lost everything. Archancy is forgotten—out of our grasp. And the stones only buy us time. None have summoned magic from the blood of the Aniyan kingdom, but you've allowed the only chance—"

"Be silent!" Gevir spat. "You know as well as I there has not been a flame wielder since Sylvara. If by his hand the door opens—"

"You are a coward!"

Gevir spun to her, eyes white with magic under his purple hood. Mar could feel the touch of his power on her mind.

"Speak again, *Ov'i*, and I will bind your tongue for *another* decade."

Mar clenched her jaw but remained silent. Gevir may be more powerful, but she wasn't so foolish to assume fate would set them free. Which was why she took advantage of Gevir's hubris—took matters into her own hands without his knowledge. She was wise to keep her ethereal prowess hidden from him as she silently mastered void walking.

Gevir cowered at the memory of Sylvara, the wretched witch gifted with the power of the sun. Arrogance incarnate—and the strongest of all the Primarchs.

The pyruvate child was not the question. Mar, *not Gevir*, had been watching Elijah since before he ever set foot in the Citadel. And thus far, her plan was working perfectly, though Gevir's knowledge of the boy was an unfortunate set back.

Her problem was the girl—Evalynn. Even if she could be convinced, Gevir allowed her to escape. From Azazel's own interrogation, Evalynn and the pyruvate were bonded, which threatened Mar's plans. If there was anything more unpredictable than mortals, it was the fleeting emotion of infatuation.

Yet Mar still possessed tools to lure them back. And if she was cunning, if she shifted the very stars to align, either the girl would return to the tower and become the key to their freedom, or the boy would fulfill his destiny and destroy their prison.

Gevir would never allow the latter.

Which was why Mar worked toward one final solution—one that would summon death upon all of Adiel.

*A small price to pay*

# Pronunciation Glossary

**Ala** – *AY-lah*

**Aniyan** – *ah-NYE-ahn*

**Aria** — *ah-RYE-ah*

**Azazel** – *ah-ZAY-zell*

**Danon** – *DAH-nun*

**Gevir** – *GHEH-vee-ar*

**Kairah** – *KYE-rah*

**Katz** – *KAHTZ*

**Manoach** – *MAN-oh-ack*

**Mar** – *MAHR*

**Obelisk** – *OBB-uh-lisk*

**Primarch** – *PRY-mark*

**Rollo** – *ROH-yoh*

**Sheket** – *SHEH-ket*

**Xerza** – *ZER-zah*

**Yaqar** – *yah-KAHR*

**Zentari** – *zen-TAH-ree*

# Acknowledgements

Before I attempt a thorough and respectful acknowledgment of those whose contributions to this project were invaluable, I want it to be known that it is not possible for me to overstate the gratitude in my heart. I have been blessed with the privilege and honor of standing alongside some of the most incredible and loving people who helped make this dream a reality.

First and foremost, it is by the blessing of God and His infinite grace that I was able to undertake this dream and see it to completion. I am nothing without my friend and Savior Jesus, and all glory and credit goes to Him in every aspect and every way. I claim no credit for effort or creativity as these are simply tools I was given and allowed to relish and enjoy.

Second, my dear wife Taborah. Your support and love from the very beginning humbled and inspired me in such a way that, were it possible, I would have conquered the world by the power of your unconditional support alone. Time and time again you prove your love for me and remind me the power of a spouse. I would not be half the man I am without you, and certainly not a published author. Words like *Thank You* fall entirely short, and at worst are nothing more than an insult to the insurmountable effort and aid you provided in this project. It is my greatest blessing from Heaven that I am privileged to stand by you as your husband, and there is no human being on this planet I would rather walk through this life with. I'm sorry for the late nights, the distractions, and the time I've spent in my own head during this project. I won't pretend it'll be the last, but I want to acknowledge the sacrifices you've made on my part. I love you dearly and wholly.

Third, to my immediate and extended family, a most sincere thanks is given. My mother, and my dear friend Brian, spurred me forward in the trenches. Thank you both for being cheerleaders from start to finish. A special thank you to my sisters for being my first editors and dealing with the steaming pile of grammar that was my initial attempt at a novel. Thank you to my brother for your inspiration with the cover art, and my mother-in-law for reading the series in record time.

Fourth, a most sincere and honorary thank you to Ellie and Maelin, whose inspiration and influence were the very spark which started this undertaking. Your names will forever be etched into Adiel's legacy, as you were both present at its inception.

Fifth, there exists an entire crowd of dear friends who've supported me along this journey. Steve, Wendy, Robbie, Kelsey, and Alex are only a few of the many. A special thank you to Brennan, whose involvement was less than we planned, yet I cannot overstate the importance of your unflinching and vivacious support.

Sixth, to my editor Caitlyn, who took a chance on an enthusiastic and inexperienced author. The opportunity you gave me to have my rather lengthy manuscript edited amidst the chaos that is my current life, was one whose value I can never overstate.

Lastly, to my dear friend reading this, unable to find their name in the list. Please accept my sincerest and heartfelt apology. Were it possible to name everyone who lent a helpful hand, a creative idea, or an encouraging word, I would have done so. Rest assured, every kind word and encouraging smile was seen, felt, received, and deeply appreciated. Thank you, in every sense of the expression.

AJ Chase is a self-published fantasy author and practicing Family Medicine PA-C in Minnesota. Active in his local church and community, AJ considers his faith in Jesus to be the cornerstone of his life and the heart behind his writing. A husband and father of three, AJ is also a cancer survivor and lifelong storyteller who finds joy in both real and imagined adventures. When he's not writing, he can be found reading, playing board games, out on the frisbee golf course, or practicing his hide-and-seek skills with his boys.